P9-DMX-212

AUTO-DA-FÉ

By Elias Canetti

THE TORCH IN MY EAR

AUTO-DA-FÉ

THE CONSCIENCE OF WORDS

CROWDS AND POWER

EARWITNESS: FIFTY CHARACTERS

ESSAYS IN HONOR OF ELIAS CANETTI

THE HUMAN PROVINCE

THE PLAYS OF ELIAS CANETTI

THE PLAYS OF THE EYES

THE TONGUE SET FREE: REMEMBRANCE
OF A EUROPEAN CHILDHOOD

THE VOICES OF MARRAKESH:
A RECORD OF A VISIT

THE SECRET HEART OF THE CLOCK

THE AGONY OF FLIES

NOTES FROM HAMPSTEAD

AUTO-DA-FÉ

ELIAS CANETTI

*Translated from the German under the
personal supervision of the author by*

C. V. WEDGWOOD

Farrar, Straus and Giroux

New York

To Veza

Farrar, Straus and Giroux
18 West 18th Street, New York 10011

Copyright © 1935 by Herbert Reichner Verlag
Copyright renewed 1963 by Elias Canetti
English translation copyright © 1947 by Elias Canetti
Copyright renewed 1963, 1974 by Elias Canetti
All rights reserved
Distributed in Canada by Douglas & McIntyre Ltd.
Printed in the United States of America
Originally published in 1935 by Herbert Reichner Verlag, Germany, as *Die Blendung*
First English edition published under the title *Auto-da-Fé*
First American edition published under the title *The Tower of Babel*
First Farrar, Straus and Giroux paperback edition, 1984

Library of Congress Cataloging-in-Publication Data
Canetti, Elias.
    Auto-da-fé.
        p.   cm.
    Translation of: Die Blendung.
    First American ed. published under title: The Tower of Babel.
    Reprint. Originally published: New York : Continuum, 1947.
    Paperback ISBN-13: 978-0-374-51879-0
    Paperback ISBN-10: 0-374-51879-3
    I. Title.   II. Title: Tower of Babel.

PT2605.A58 B553   1984
833'.912—dc19

                                        84-10164

www.fsgbooks.com

20   22   23   21

CONTENTS

CONTENTS

PART THREE

THE WORLD IN THE HEAD

AUTO-DA-FÉ

PART ONE

A HEAD WITHOUT A WORLD

———

CHAPTER I

THE MORNING WALK

'WHAT are you doing here, my little man?'
'Nothing.'
'Then why are you standing here?'
'Just because.'
'Can you read?'
'Oh, yes.'
'How old are you?'
'Nine and a bit.'
'Which would you prefer, a piece of chocolate or a book?'
'A book.'
'Indeed? Splendid! So that's your reason for standing here?'
'Yes.'
'Why didn't you say so before?'
'Father scolds me.'
'Oh. And who is your father?'
'Franz Metzger.'
'Would you like to travel to a foreign country?'
'Yes. To India. They have tigers there.'
'And where else?'
'To China. They've got a huge wall there.'
'You'd like to scramble over it, wouldn't you?'
'It's much too thick and too high. Nobody can get over it. That's why they built it.'
'What a lot you know! You must have read a great deal already?'
'Yes. I read all the time. Father takes my books away. I'd like to go to a Chinese school. They have forty thousand letters in their alphabet. You couldn't get them all into one book.'
'That's only what you think.'
'I've worked it out.'

9

'All the same it isn't true. Never mind the books in the window. They're of no value. I've got something much better here. Wait. I'll show you. Do you know what kind of writing that is?'

'Chinese! Chinese!'

'Well, you're a clever little fellow. Had you seen a Chinese book before?'

'No, I guessed it.'

'These two characters stand for Meng Tse, the philosopher Mencius. He was a great man in China. He lived 2250 years ago and his works are still being read. Will you remember that?'

'Yes. I must go to school now.'

'Aha, so you look into the bookshop windows on your way to school? What is your name?'

'Franz Metzger, like my father.'

'And where do you live?'

'Twenty-four Ehrlich Strasse.'

'I live there too. I don't remember you.'

'You always look the other way when anyone passes you on the stairs. I've known you for ages. You're Professor Kien, but you haven't a school. Mother says you aren't a real Professor. But I think you are — you've got a library. Our Marie says, you wouldn't believe your eyes. She's our maid. When I'm grown up I'm going to have a library. With all the books there are, in every language. A Chinese one too, like yours. Now I must run.'

'Who wrote this book? Can you remember?'

'Meng Tse, the philosopher Mencius. Exactly 2250 years ago.'

'Excellent. You shall come and see my library one day. Tell my housekeeper I've given you permission. I can show you pictures from India and China.'

'Oh good! I'll come! Of course I'll come! This afternoon?'

'No, no, little man. I must work this afternoon. In a week at the earliest.'

Professor Peter Kien, a tall, emaciated figure, man of learning and specialist in sinology, replaced the Chinese book in the tightly packed brief case which he carried under his arm, carefully closed it and watched the clever little boy out of sight. By nature morose and sparing of his words, he was already reproaching himself for a conversation into which he had entered for no compelling reason.

It was his custom on his morning walk, between seven and eight o'clock, to look into the windows of every book shop which he passed.

He was thus able to assure himself, with a kind of pleasure, that smut and trash were daily gaining ground. He himself was the owner of the most important private library in the whole of this great city. He carried a minute portion of it with him wherever he went. His passion for it, the only one which he had permitted himself during a life of austere and exacting study, moved him to take special precautions. Books, even bad ones, tempted him easily into making a purchase. Fortunately the greater number of the book shops did not open until after eight o'clock. Sometimes an apprentice, anxious to earn his chief's approbation, would come earlier and wait on the doorstep for the first employee whom he would ceremoniously relieve of the latch key. 'I've been waiting since seven o'clock,' he would exclaim, or 'I can't get in!' So much zeal communicated itself all too easily to Kien; with an effort he would master the impulse to follow the apprentice immediately into the shop. Among the proprietors of smaller shops there were one or two early risers, who might be seen busying themselves behind their open doors from half past seven onwards. Defying these temptations, Kien tapped his own well-filled brief-case. He clasped it tightly to him, in a very particular manner which he had himself thought out, so that the greatest possible area of his body was always in contact with it. Even his ribs could feel its presence through his cheap, thin suit. His upper arm covered the whole side elevation; it fitted exactly. The lower portion of his arm supported the case from below. His outstretched fingers splayed out over every part of the flat surface to which they yearned. He privately excused himself for this exaggerated care because of the value of the contents. Should the brief case by any mischance fall to the ground, or should the lock, which he tested every morning before setting out, spring open at precisely that perilous moment, ruin would come to his priceless volumes. There was nothing he loathed more intensely than battered books.

To-day, when he was standing in front of a bookshop on his way home, a little boy had stepped suddenly between him and the window. Kien felt affronted by the impertinence. True, there was room enough between him and the window. He always stood about three feet away from the glass; but he could easily read every letter behind it. His eyes functioned to his entire satisfaction: a fact notable enough in a man of forty who sat, day in day out, over books and manuscripts. Morning after morning his eyes informed him how well they did. By keeping his distance from these venal and common books, he showed his contempt for them, contempt which, when he compared them with the dry and ponderous tomes of his library, they richly deserved. The boy was quite small, Kien exceptionally tall. He could easily see over his head. All the same he felt he had a right to greater respect. Before administering a reprimand, however, he drew to one side in order to observe him further. The child stared hard at the titles of the books and moved his lips slowly and in silence. Without a stop his eyes slipped from one volume to the next. Every minute or two he looked back over his shoulder. On the opposite side of the street, over a watchmaker's shop, hung a gigantic clock. It was twenty minutes to eight. Evidently the little fellow was afraid of missing something important. He took no notice whatever of the gentleman standing behind him. Perhaps he was practising his reading. Perhaps he was learning the names of the books by heart. He devoted equal attention to each in turn. You could see at once when anything held up his reading for a second.

Kien felt sorry for him. Here was he, spoiling with this depraved fare an eager spiritual appetite, perhaps already hungry for the written word. How many a worthless book might he not come to read in later life for no better reason than an early familiarity with its title? By what means is the suggestibility of these early years to be reduced? No sooner can a child walk and make out his letters than he is surrendered at mercy to the hard pavement of any ill-built street, and to the wares of any wretched tradesman who, the devil knows why, has set himself up as a dealer in books. Young children ought to be brought up in some important private library. Daily conversation with none but serious minds, an atmosphere at once dim, hushed and intellectual, a relentless training in the most careful ordering both of time and of space, — what surroundings could be more suitable to assist these delicate creatures through the years of childhood? But the only person in this town who possessed a library which could be taken at all seriously was he, Kien, himself. He could not admit children. His work allowed him no such diversions. Children make a noise. They have to be constantly looked after. Their welfare demands the services of a woman. For cooking, an ordinary housekeeper is good enough. For children, it would be necessary to engage a mother. If a mother could be content to be nothing but a mother: but where would you find one who would be satisfied with that particular part alone? Each is a specialist first and foremost as a woman, and would make demands which an honest man of learning would not even dream of fulfilling. Kien repudiated the idea of a wife. Women had been a matter of indifference to him until this moment; a matter of indifference they would remain. The boy with the fixed eyes and the moving head would be the loser.

Pity had moved him to break his usual custom and speak to him. He would gladly have bought himself free of the prickings of his pedagogic conscience with the gift of a piece of chocolate. Then it appeared that there are nine-year-old children who prefer a book to a piece of chocolate. What followed surprised him even more. The child was interested in China. He read against his father's will. The stories of the difficulties of the Chinese alphabet fascinated instead of frightening him. He recognized the language at first sight, without having seen it before. He had passed an intelligence test with distinction. When shown the book, he had not tried to touch it. Perhaps he was ashamed of his dirty hands. Kien had looked at them: they were clean. Another boy would have snatched the book, even with dirty ones. He was in a hurry — school began at eight — yet he had stayed until the last possible minute. He had fallen upon that invitation like one starving; his father must be a great torment to him. He would have liked best to come on that very afternoon, in the middle of the working day. After all, he lived in the same house.

Kien forgave himself for the conversation. The exception which he had permitted seemed worth while. In his thoughts he saluted the child — now already out of sight — as a rising sinologist. Who indeed took an interest in these remote branches of knowledge? Boys played football, adults went to work; they wasted their leisure hours in love. So as to sleep for eight hours and waste eight hours, they were willing to devote themselves for the rest of their time to hateful work. Not only their bellies, their whole bodies had become their gods. The sky God of the Chinese was sterner and more dignified. Even if the little fellow did not come next week, unlikely though that was, he would have a name in his head which he would not easily forget: the philosopher Mong. Occasional collisions unexpectedly encountered determine the direction of a lifetime.

Smiling, Kien continued on his way home. He smiled rarely. Rarely, after all, is it the dearest wish of a man to be the owner of a library. As a child of nine he had longed for a book shop. Yet the idea that he would walk up and down in it as its proprietor had seemed to him even then blasphemous. A bookseller is a king, and a king cannot be a bookseller. But he was still too little to be a salesman. As for an errand boy — errand boys were always being sent out of the shop. What pleasure would he have of the books, if he was only allowed to carry them as parcels under his arm? For a long while he sought for some way out of the difficulty. One day he did not come home after school. He went into the biggest bookstore in the town, six great show windows all full of books, and began to howl at the top of his voice. 'I want to leave the room, quick, I'm going to have an accident!' he blubbered. They showed him the way at once. He took careful note of it. When he came out again he thanked them and asked if he could not do something to help. His beaming face made them laugh. Only a few moments before it had been screwed up into such comic anguish. They drew him out in conversation; he knew a great deal about books. They thought him sharp for his age. Towards the evening they sent him away with a heavy parcel. He travelled there and back on the tram. He had saved enough pocket money to afford it. Just as the shop was closing — it was already growing dark — he announced that he had completed his errand and put down the receipt on the counter. Someone gave him an acid drop for a reward. While the staff were pulling on their coats he glided noiselessly into the back regions to his lavatory hide-out and bolted himself in. Nobody noticed it; they were all thinking of the free evening before them. He waited a long time. Only after many hours, late at night, did he dare to come out. It was dark in the shop. He felt about for a switch. He had not thought of that by daylight. But when he found it and his hand had already closed over it, he was afraid to turn on the light. Perhaps someone would see him from the street and haul him off home.

His eyes grew accustomed to the darkness. But he could not read; that was a great pity. He pulled down one volume after another, turned over the pages, contrived to make out many of the names. Later on he scrambled up on to the ladder. He wanted to know if the upper shelves had any secrets to hide. He tumbled off it and said: I haven't hurt myself! The floor is hard. The books are soft. In a book shop one falls on books. He could have made a castle of books, but he regarded disorder as vulgar and, as he took out each new volume, he replaced the one before. His back hurt. Perhaps he was only tired. At home he would have been asleep long ago. Not here, excitement kept him awake. But his eyes could not even make out the largest titles any more and that annoyed him. He worked out how many years he would be able to spend reading in this shop without ever going out into the street or to that silly school. Why could he not stay here always? He could easily save up to buy himself a small bed. His mother would be afraid. So was he, but only a little, because it was so very quiet. The gas lamps in the street went out. Shadows crept along the walls. So there *were* ghosts. During the night they came flying here and crouched over the books. Then they read. They needed no light, they had such big eyes. Now he would not touch a single book on the upper shelves, nor on the lower ones either. He crept under the counter and his teeth chattered. Ten thousand books and a ghost crouching over each one. That was why it was so quiet. Sometimes he heard them turn over a page. They read as fast as he did himself. He might have grown used to them, but there were ten thousand of them and perhaps one of them would bite. Ghosts get cross if you brush against them, they think you are making fun of them. He made himself as small as possible; they flew over him without touching him. Morning came only after many long nights. Then he fell asleep. He did not hear the assistants opening up the shop. They found him under the counter and shook him awake. First he pretended that he was still asleep, then he suddenly burst out howling. They had locked him in last night, he was afraid of his mother, she must have been looking for him everywhere. The proprietor cross-questioned him and as soon as he had found out his name, sent him off home with one of the shopwalkers. He sent his sincerest apologies to the lady. The little boy had been locked in by mistake, but he seemed to be safe and sound. He assured her of his respectful attention. His mother believed it all and was delighted to have him safely home again. To-day the little liar of yesterday was the owner of a famous library and a name no less famous.

Kien abhorred falsehood; from his earliest childhood he had held fast to the truth. He could remember no other falsehood except this. And even this one was hateful to him. Only the conversation with the schoolboy, who had seemed to him the image of his own childhood, had recalled it to him. Forget it, he thought, it is nearly eight o'clock. Punctually at eight his work began, his service for truth. Knowledge and truth were for him identical terms. You draw closer to truth by shutting yourself off from mankind. Daily life was a superficial clatter of lies. Every passer-by was a liar. For that reason he never looked at them. Who among all these bad actors, who made up the mob, had a face to arrest his attention. They changed their faces with every moment; not for one single day did they stick to the same part. He had always known this, experience was superfluous. *His* ambition was to persist stubbornly in the same manner of existence. Not for a mere month, not for a year, but for the whole of his life, he would be true to himself. Character, if you had a character, determined your outward appearance. Ever since he had been able to think, he had been tall and too thin. He knew his face only casually, from its reflection in book-shop windows. He had no mirror in his house, there was no room for it among the books. But he knew that his face was narrow, stern and bony; that was enough.

Since he felt not the slightest desire to notice anyone, he kept his eyes lowered or raised above their heads. He sensed where the book shops were without looking. He simply relied on instinct. The same force which guides a horse home to the stable, served as well for him. He went out walking to breathe the air of alien books, they aroused his antagonism, they stimulated him. In his library everything went by clockwork. But between seven and eight he allowed himself a few of those liberties which constitute the entire life of other beings.

Although he savoured this hour to the full, he did all by rote. Before crossing a busy street, he hesitated a little. He preferred to walk at a regular pace; so as not to hasten his steps, he waited for a favourable moment to cross. Suddenly he heard someone shouting loudly at someone else: 'Can you tell me where Mut Strasse is?' There was no reply. Kien was surprised: so there were other silent people besides himself to be found in the busy streets. Without looking up he listened for more. How would the questioner behave in the face of this silence? 'Excuse me please, could you perhaps tell me where Mut Strasse is?' So; he grew more polite; he had no better luck. The other man still made no reply. 'I don't think you heard me. I'm asking you the way. Will you be so kind as to tell me how I get to Mut Strasse?' Kien's appetite for knowledge was whetted; idle curiosity he did not know. He decided to observe this silent man, on condition of course that he still remained silent. Not a doubt of it, the man was deep in thought and determined to avoid any interruption. Still he said nothing. Kien applauded him. Here was one among thousands, a man whose character was proof against all chances. 'Here, are you deaf?' shouted the first man. Now he will have to answer back, thought Kien, and began to lose his pleasure in his protégé. Who can control his tongue when he is insulted? He turned towards the street; the favourable moment for crossing it had come. Astonished at the continued silence, he hesitated. Still the second man said nothing. All the more violent would be the outburst of anger to come. Kien hoped for a fight. If the second man appeared after all to be a mere vulgarian, Kien would be confirmed in his own estimation of himself as the sole and only person of character walking in this street. He was already considering whether he should look round. The incident was taking place on his right hand. The first man was now yelling: 'You've no manners! I spoke to you civil. Who do you think you are? You lout. Are you dumb?' The second man was still silent. 'I demand an apology! Do you hear?' The other did not hear. He rose even higher in the estimation of the listener. 'I'll fetch the police! What do you take me for! You rag and bone man! Call yourself a gentleman! Where did you get those clothes? Out of the rag bag? That's what they look like! What have you got under your arm! I'll show you! Go and boil your head! Who do you think you are?'

Then Kien felt a nasty jolt. Someone had grabbed his brief-case and was pulling at it. With a movement far exceeding his usual effort, he liberated the books from the alien clutch and turned sharply to the right. His glance was directed to his brief-case, but it fell instead on a small fat man who was bawling up at him. 'You lout! You lout! You lout!' The other man, the silent one, the man of character, who controlled his tongue even in anger, was Kien himself. Calmly he turned his back on the gesticulating illiterate. With this small knife, he sliced his clamour in two. A loutish creature whose courtesy changed in so many seconds to insolence had no power to hurt him. Nevertheless he walked along the streets a little faster than was his usual custom. A man who carries books with him must seek to avoid physical violence. He always had books with him.

There is after all no obligation to answer every passing fool according to his folly. The greatest danger which threatens a man of learning, is to lose himself in talk. Kien preferred to express himself in the written rather than the spoken word. He knew more than a dozen oriental languages. A few of the western ones did not even need to be learnt. No branch of human literature was unfamiliar to him. He thought in quotations and wrote in carefully considered sentences. Countless texts owed their restoration to him. When he came to misreadings or imperfections in ancient Chinese, Indian or Japanese manuscripts, as many alternative readings suggested themselves for his selection as he could wish. Other textual critics envied him; he for his part had to guard against a superfluity of ideas. Meticulously cautious, he weighed up the alternatives month after month, was slow to the point of exasperation; applying his severest standards to his own conclusions, he took no decision, on a single letter, a word or an entire sentence, until he was convinced that it was unassailable. The papers which he had hitherto published, few in number, yet each one the starting point for a hundred others, had gained for him the reputation of being the greatest living authority on sinology. They were known in every detail to his colleagues, indeed almost word for word. A sentence once set down by him was decisive and binding. In controversial questions he was the ultimate appeal, the leading authority even in related branches of knowledge. A few only he honoured with his letters. That man, however, whom he chose so to honour would receive in a single letter enough stimuli to set him off on years of study, the results of which — in the view of the mind whence they had sprung — were foregone conclusions. Personally he had no dealings with anyone. He refused all invitations. Whenever any chair of oriental philology fell vacant, it was offered first to him. Polite but contemptuous, he invariably declined.

He had not, he averred, been born to be an orator. Payment for his work would give him a distaste for it. In his own humble opinion, those unproductive popularizers to whom instruction in the grammar schools was entrusted, should occupy the university chairs also; then genuine, creative research workers would be able to devote themselves exclusively to their own work. As it was there was no shortage of mediocre intelligences. Should he give lectures, the high demands which he would necessarily make upon an audience would naturally very much reduce its numbers. As for examinations, not a single candidate, as far as he could see, would be able to pass them. He would make it a point of honour to fail these young immature students at least until their thirtieth year, by which time, either through very boredom or through a dawning of real seriousness, they must have learnt something, if only a very little. He regarded the acceptance of candidates whose memories had not been most carefully tested in the lecture halls of the faculty as a totally useless, if not indeed a questionable, practice. Ten students, selected by the most strenuous preliminary tests, would, provided they remained together, achieve far more than they could do when permitted to mingle with a hundred beer-swilling dullards, the general run of university students. His doubts were therefore of the most serious and fundamental nature. He could only request the faculty to withdraw an offer which, although intended no doubt to show the high esteem in which they held him, was not one which he could accept in that spirit.

At scholastic conferences, where there is usually a great deal of talk,

Kien was a much-discussed personality. The learned gentlemen, who for the greater part of their lives were silent, timid and myopic mice, on these occasions, every two years or so, came right out of themselves; they welcomed each other, stuck the most inapposite heads together, whispered nonsense in corners and toasted each other clumsily at the dinner table. Deeply moved and profoundly gratified, they raised aloft the banner of learning and upheld the integrity of their aims. Over and over again in all languages they repeated their vows. They would have kept them even without taking them. In the intervals they made bets. Would Kien really come this time? He was more spoken of than a merely famous colleague; his behaviour excited curiosity. But he would not trade on his fame; for the last ten years he had stubbornly refused invitations to banquets and congresses where, in spite of his youth, he would have been warmly acclaimed; he announced for every conference an important paper, which was then read for him from his own manuscript by another scholar: all this his colleagues regarded as mere postponement. The time would come — perhaps this was the time — when he would suddenly make his appearance, would graciously accept the applause which his long retirement had made only the more vociferous, and would permit himself to be acclaimed president of the assembly, an office which was only his due, and which indeed he arrogated to himself after his own fashion even by his absence. But his learned colleagues were mistaken. Kien did not appear. The more credulous of them lost their bets.

At the last minute he refused. Sending the paper he had written to a privileged person, he would add some ironical expressions of regret. In the event of his colleagues finding time for serious study in the intervals of a programme so rich in entertainment — an eventuality which in the interests of their general satisfaction he could hardly desire — he asked leave to lay before the conference this small contribution to knowledge, the result of two years' work. He would carefully save up any new and surprising conclusions to which his researches might have brought him for moments such as these. Their effects and the discussions to which they gave rise, he would follow from a distance, suspiciously and in detail, as though probing their textual accuracy. The gatherings were ready enough to accept his contempt. Eighty out of every hundred present relied entirely on his judgment. His services to science were inestimable. Long might he live. To most of them indeed his death would have been a severe shock.

Those few who had known him in his earlier years had forgotten what his face was like. Repeatedly he received letters asking for his photograph. He had none, he would answer, nor did he intend to have one taken. Both statements were true. But he had willingly agreed to a different sort of concession. As a young man of thirty he had, without however making any other testamentary dispositions, bequeathed his skull with all its contents to an institute for cranial research. He justified this step by considering the advantage to be gained if it could be scientifically proved that his truly phenomenal memory was the result of a particular structure, or perhaps even a heavier weight, of brain. Not indeed that he considered — so he wrote to the head of the institute — that memory and genius were the same thing, a theory all too widely accepted of recent years. He himself was no genius. Yet it would be unscholarly to deny that the almost terrifying memory at his disposal had been remarkably useful in his learned researches. He did indeed carry in his head a library as well-provided and as reliable as his actual library, which he understood was so much discussed. He could sit at his writing desk and sketch out a treatise down to the minutest detail without turning over a single page, except in his head. Naturally he would check quotations and sources later out of the books themselves; but only because he was a man of conscience. He could not remember any single occasion on which his memory had been found at fault. His very dreams were more precisely defined than those of most people. Blurred images without form or colour were unknown in any of the dreams which he had hitherto recollected. In his case night had no power to turn things topsy turvy; the noises he heard could be exactly referred to their cause of origin; conversations into which he entered were entirely reasonable; everything retained its normal meaning. It was outside his sphere to examine the probable connection between the accuracy of his memory and the lucidity of his dreams. In all humility he drew attention to the facts alone, and hoped that the personal data which he had taken the liberty of recording would be regarded as a sign neither of pretentiousness nor garrulity.

Kien called to mind one or two more facts from his daily life, which showed his retiring, untalkative and wholly unpresumptuous nature in its true light. But his irritation at the insolent and insufferable fellow who had first asked him the way and then abused him, grew greater with every step. There is nothing else I can do, he said at last; he stepped aside into the porch of a house, looked round — nobody was watching him — and drew a long narrow notebook from his pocket.

On the title page, in tall, angular letters was written the word: STUPIDITIES. His eyes rested at first on this. Then he turned over the pages; more than half the note-book was full. Everything he would have preferred to forget he put down in this book. Date, time and place came first. Then followed the incident which was supposed to illustrate the stupidity of mankind. An apt quotation, a new one for each occasion, formed the conclusion. He never read these collected examples of stupidity; a glance at the title page sufficed. Later on he thought of publishing them under the title 'Morning Walks of a Sinologist'.

He drew out a sharply pointed pencil and wrote down on the first empty page: 'September 23rd, 7.45 a.m. In Mut Strasse a person crossed my path and asked me the way to Mut Strasse. In order not to put him to shame, I made no answer. He was not to be put off and asked again, several times; his bearing was courteous. Suddenly his eye fell upon the street sign. He became aware of his stupidity. Instead of withdrawing as fast as he could — as I should have done in his place — he gave way to the most unmeasured rage and abused me in the vulgarest fashion. Had I not spared him in the first place, I would have spared myself this painful scene. Which of us was the stupider?'

With that last sentence he proved that he did not draw the line even at his *own* failings. He was pitiless towards everyone. Gratified, he put away his notebook and forgot the man in the Mut Strasse. While he was writing, his books had slipped into an uncomfortable position. He shifted them into their right place. At the next street corner he was startled by an Alsatian. Swift and sure-footed the dog cleared itself a path through the crowd. At the extremity of a tautened lead it tugged a blind man. His infirmity — for anyone who failed to notice the dog — was further emphasized by the white stick which he carried in his right hand. Even those passers-by who were in too much of a hurry to stare at the blind man, cast an admiring glance at the dog. He pushed them gently to one side with his patient muzzle. As he was a fine, handsome dog they bore with him gladly. Suddenly the blind man pulled his cap off his head and, clutching it in the same hand as his white stick, held it out towards the crowd. 'To buy my dog bones!' he begged. Coins showered into it. In the middle of the street a crowd gathered round the two of them. The traffic was held up: luckily there was no policeman at this corner to direct it. Kien observed the beggar from close at hand. He was dressed with studied poverty and his face seemed educated. The muscles round his eyes twitched continually — he winked, raised his eyebrows and wrinkled his forehead — so that Kien mistrusted him and decided to regard him as a fraud. At that moment a boy of about twelve came up, hurriedly pushed the dog to one side and threw into the cap a large heavy button. The blind man stared in front of him and thanked him, perhaps in the slightest degree more warmly than before. The clink of the button as it fell into the cap had sounded like the ring of gold. Kien felt a pang in his heart. He caught the boy by the scruff of the neck and cuffed him over the head with his brief-case. 'For shame,' he said, 'deceiving a blind man!' Only after he had done it did he recollect what was in the brief-case: books. He was horrified. Never before had he taken so great a risk. The boy ran off howling. To restore his normal and far less exalted level of compassion, Kien emptied his entire stock of small change into the blind man's cap. The bystanders approved aloud; to himself the action seemed more petty and cautious than the preceding one. The dog set off again. Immediately after, just as a policeman appeared on the scene, both leader and led had resumed their brisk progress.

Kien took a private vow that if he should ever be threatened by blindness, he would die of his own free will. Whenever he met a blind man this same cruel fear clutched at him. Mutes he loved: the deaf, the lame and other kinds of cripples meant nothing to him; the blind disturbed him. He could not understand why they did not make an end of themselves. Even if they could read braille, their opportunities for reading were limited. Eratosthenes, the great librarian of Alexandria, a scholar of universal significance who flourished in the third century of the pre-Christian era and held sway over more than half a million manuscript scrolls, made in his eightieth year a terrible discovery. His eyes began to refuse their office. He could still see but he could not read. Another man might have waited until he was completely blind. He felt that to take leave of his books was blindness enough. Friends and pupils implored him to stay with them. He smiled wisely, thanked them, and in a few days starved himself to death.

Should the time come this great example could easily be followed even by the lesser Kien, whose library comprised a mere twenty-five thousand volumes.

The remaining distance to his own house he completed at a quickened pace. It must be past eight o'clock. At eight o'clock his work began; unpunctuality caused him acute irritation. Now and again, surreptitiously he felt his eyes. They focused correctly; they felt comfortable and unthreatened.

His library was situated on the fourth and topmost floor of No. 24 Ehrlich Strasse. The door of the flat was secured by three highly complicated locks. He unlocked them, strode across the hall, which contained nothing except an umbrella and coat-stand, and entered his study. Carefully he set down the brief-case on an armchair. Then once and again he paced the entire length of the four lofty, spacious communicating rooms which formed his library. The entire wall-space up to the ceiling was clothed with books. Slowly he lifted his eyes towards them. Skylights had been let into the ceiling. He was proud of his roof-lighting. The windows had been walled up several years before after a determined struggle with his landlord. In this way he had gained in every room a fourth wall-space: accommodation for more books. Moreover illumination from above, which lit up all the shelves equally, seemed to him more just and more suited to his relations with his books. The temptation to watch what went on in the street — an immoral and time-wasting habit — disappeared with the side windows. Daily, before he sat down to his writing desk, he blessed both the idea and its results, since he owed to them the fulfilment of his dearest wish: the possession of a well-stocked library, in perfect order and enclosed on all sides, in which no single superfluous article of furniture, no single superfluous person could lure him from his serious thoughts.

The first of the four rooms served for his study. A huge old writing desk, an armchair in front of it, a second armchair in the opposite corner were its only furniture. There crouched besides an unobtrusive divan, willingly overlooked by its master: he only slept on it. A movable pair of steps was propped against the wall. It was more important than the divan, and travelled in the course of a day from room to room. The emptiness of the three remaining rooms was not disturbed by so much as a chair. Nowhere did a table, a cupboard, a fireplace interrupt the multi-coloured monotony of the bookshelves. Handsome deep-pile carpets, the uniform covering of the floor, softened the harsh twilight which, mingling through wide-open communicating doors, made of the four separate rooms one single lofty hall.

Kien walked with a stiff and deliberate step. He set his feet down with particular firmness on the carpets; it pleased him that even a footfall such as his waked not the faintest echo. In his library it would have been beyond the power even of an elephant to pound the slightest noise out of that floor. For this reason he set great store by his carpets. He satisfied himself that the books were still in the order in which he had been forced to leave them an hour before. Then he began to relieve his brief-case of its contents. When he came in, it was his habit to lay it down on the chair in front of the writing desk. Otherwise he might perhaps have forgotten it and have sat down to his work before he had tidied away its contents; for at eight o'clock he felt a very strong compulsion to begin his work. With the help of the ladder he distributed the volumes to their appointed places. In spite of all his care — since it was already late, he was hurrying rather more than usual — the last of the books fell from the third bookshelf, a shelf for which he did not even have to use the ladder. It was no other than Mencius beloved above all the rest. 'Idiot!' he shrieked at himself. 'Barbarian! Illiterate!' tenderly lifted the book and went quickly to the door. Before he had reached it an important thought struck him. He turned back and pushed the ladder as softly as he could to the site of the accident. Mencius he laid gently down with both hands on the carpet at the foot of the ladder. Now he could go to the door. He opened it and called into the hall:

'Your best duster, please!'

Almost at once the housekeeper knocked at the door which he had lightly pushed to. He made no answer. She inserted her head modestly through the crack and asked:

'Has something happened?'

'No, give it to me.'

She thought she could detect a complaint in this answer. He had not intended her to. She was too curious to leave the matter where it was. 'Excuse me, Professor!' she said reproachfully, stepped into the room and saw at once what had happened. She glided over to the book. Below her blue starched skirt, which reached to the floor, her feet were invisible. Her head was askew. Her ears were large, flabby and prominent. Since her right ear touched her shoulder and was partly concealed by it, the left looked all the bigger. When she talked or walked her head waggled to and fro. Her shoulders waggled too, in accompaniment. She stooped, lifted up the book and passed the duster over it carefully at least a dozen times. Kien did not attempt to forestall her. Courtesy was abhorrent to him. He stood by and observed whether she performed her work seriously.

'Excuse me, a thing like that can happen, standing up on a ladder.'

24

Then she handed the book to him, like a plate newly polished. She would very gladly have begun a conversation with him. But she did not succeed. He said briefly, 'Thank you' and turned his back on her. She understood and went. She had already placed her hand on the door knob when he turned round suddenly and asked with simulated friendliness:

'Then this has often happened to you?'

She saw through him and was genuinely indignant: 'Excuse me, Professor.' Her 'Excuse me' struck through her unctuous tones, sharp as a thorn. She will give notice, he thought; and to appease her explained himself:

'I only meant to impress on you what these books represent in terms of money.'

She had not been prepared for so affable a speech. She did not know how to reply and left the room pacified. As soon as she had gone, he reproached himself. He had spoken about books like the vilest tradesman. Yet in what other way could he enforce the respectful handling of books on a person of her kind? Their real value would have no meaning for her. She must believe that the library was a speculation of his. What people! What people!

He bowed involuntarily in the direction of the Japanese manuscripts, and, at last, sat down at his writing desk.

CHAPTER II

THE SECRET

EIGHT years earlier Kien had put the following advertisement in the paper:

> A man of learning who owns an exceptionally large library wants a responsibly-minded housekeeper. Only applicants of the highest character need apply. Unsuitable persons will be shown the door. Money no object.

Therese Krumbholz was at that time in a good position in which she had hitherto been satisfied. She read exhaustively every morning, before getting breakfast for her employers, the advertisement columns of the daily paper, to know what went on in the world. She had no intention of ending her life in the service of a vulgar family. She was still a young person, the right side of fifty, and hoped for a place with a single gentleman. Then she could have things just so; with women in the house it's not the same. But you couldn't expect her to give up her good place for nothing. She'd know who she had to do with before she gave in her notice. You didn't catch her with putting things in the papers, promising the earth to respectable women. You hardly get inside the door and they start taking liberties. Alone in the world now for thirty-three years and such a thing had never happened to her yet. She'd take care it never did, what's more.

This time the advertisement hit her right in the eye. The phrase 'Money no object' made her pause; then she read the sentences, all of which stood out in heavy type, several times backwards and forwards. The tone impressed her: here was a man. It flattered her to think of herself as an applicant of the highest character. She saw the unsuitable persons being shown the door and took a righteous pleasure in their fate. Not for one second did it occur to her that she herself might be treated as an unsuitable person.

On the following morning she presented herself before Kien at the earliest possible moment, seven o'clock. He let her into the hall and immediately declared: 'I must emphatically forbid any stranger whatsoever to enter my house. Are you in a position to take over the custody of the books?'

He observed her narrowly and with suspicion. Before she gave her answer to his question, he would not make up his mind about her. 'Excuse me please,' she said, 'what do you take me for?'

Her stupefaction at his rudeness made her give an answer in which he could find no fault.

'You have a right to know,' he said, 'the reason why I gave notice to my last housekeeper. A book out of my library was missing. I had the whole house searched. It did not come to light. I was thus compelled to give her notice on the spot.' Choked with indignation, he was silent. 'You will understand the necessity,' he added as an afterthought, as though he had made too heavy a demand on her intelligence.

'Everything in its right place,' she answered promptly. He was disarmed. With an ample gesture he invited her into the library. She stepped delicately into the first of the rooms and stood waiting.

'This is the sphere of your duties,' he said in a dry, serious tone of voice. 'Every day one of these rooms must be dusted from floor to ceiling. On the fourth day your work is completed. On the fifth you start again with the first room. Can you undertake this?'

'I make so bold.'

He went out again, opened the door of the flat and said: 'Good morning. You will take up your duties to-day.'

She was already on the stairs and still hesitating. Of her wages, he had said nothing. Before she gave up her present place she must ask him. No, better not. One false step. If she said nothing, perhaps he would give more of his own accord. Over the two conflicting forces, caution and greed, a third prevailed: curiosity.

'Yes, and about my wages?' Embarrassed by the mistake which she was perhaps making, she forgot to add her 'excuse me'.

'Whatever you like,' he said indifferently and closed the door.

She informed her horrified employers — they relied entirely on her, an old piece of furniture in the house for twelve years — that she wouldn't put up with such goings on any more, she'd rather beg her bread in the street. No arguments could move her from her purpose. She was going at once; when you have been in the same position for twelve years, you can make an exception of the usual month's notice. The worthy family seized the opportunity of saving her wages up to the 20th. They refused to pay them since the creature would not stay her month out. Therese thought to herself: I shall get it out of him, and went.

She fulfilled her duty towards the books to Kien's satisfaction. He

27

expressed his recognition of the fact by silence. To praise her openly in her presence seemed to him unnecessary. His meals were always punctual. Whether she cooked well or badly he did not know; it was a matter of total indifference to him. During his meals, which he ate at his writing desk, he was busy with important considerations. As a rule he would not have been able to say what precisely he had in his mouth. He reserved consciousness for real thoughts; they depend upon it; without consciousness, thoughts are unthinkable. Chewing and digesting happen of themselves.

Therese had a certain respect for his work, for he paid her a high salary regularly and was friendly to no one; he never even spoke to her. Sociable people, from a child up, she had always despised; her mother had been one of that kind. She performed her own tasks meticulously. She earned her money. Besides, from the very beginning she had a riddle to solve. She enjoyed that.

Punctually at six the Professor got out of his divan bed. Washing and dressing were soon done. In the evening, before going to bed, she turned down his divan and pushed the wash-stand, which was on wheels, into the middle of the study. It was allowed to stand there for the night. A screen of four sections in Spanish leather painted with letters in a foreign language was so arranged as to spare him the disturbing sight. He could not abide articles of furniture. The wash-trolley, as he called it, was an invention of his own, so constructed that the loathsome object could be disposed of as soon as it had performed its office. At a quarter past six he would open his door and violently expel it; it would trundle all the way down the long passage. Close to the kitchen door it would crash into the wall. Therese would wait in the kitchen; her own little room was immediately adjoining. She would open the door and call: 'Up already?' He made no answer and bolted himself in again. Then he stayed at home until seven o'clock. Not a soul knew what he did in the long interval until seven o'clock. At other times he always sat at his writing desk and wrote.

The sombre, weighty colossus of a desk was filled to bursting with manuscripts and heavy laden with books. The most cautious stirring of any drawer elicited a shrill squeak. Although the noise was repulsive to him, Kien left the heirloom desk in this state so that the housekeeper, in the event of his absence from home, would know at once if a burglar had got in. Strange species, they usually look for money before they start on the books. He had explained the mechanism of his invaluable desk to Therese, briefly yet exhaustively, in three sentences. He had added, in a meaning tone, that there was no possibility of silencing the squeak; even he was unable to do so. During the day she could hear every time Kien looked out a manuscript. She wondered how he could put up with the noise. At night he shut all his papers away. Until eight in the morning the writing desk remained mute. When she was tidying up she never found anything on it but books and a few yellow papers. She looked in vain for clean paper covered with his own handwriting. It was clear that from a quarter past six until seven in the morning, three whole quarters of an hour, he did no work whatever.

Was he saying his prayers? No, she couldn't believe that. Nobody says their prayers. She had no use for praying. You didn't catch her going to church. Look at the sort of people who go to church. A fine crowd they are, cluttered up together. She didn't hold with all that begging either. You have to give them something because everyone is watching you. What they do with it, heaven knows. Say one's prayers at home — why? A waste of beautiful time. A respectable person doesn't need that sort of thing. She'd always kept herself respectable. Other people could pray for all she cared. But she'd like to know what went on in that room between a quarter past six and seven o'clock. She was not curious, no one could call her that. She didn't poke her nose into other people's business. Women were all alike nowadays. Poking their noses into everything. She got on with her own work. Prices going up something shocking. Potatoes cost double already. How to make the money go round. He locked all four doors. Or else you could have seen something from the next room. So particular as he was too, never wasting a minute!

During his morning walk Therese examined the rooms entrusted to her care. She suspected a secret vice; its nature remained vague. First of all she decided for a woman's body in a trunk. But there wasn't room for that under the carpets and she renounced a horribly mutilated corpse. There was no cupboard to help her speculations; how gladly she would have welcomed one; one against each wall preferably. Then the hideous crime must be concealed somehow behind one of the books. Where else? She might have satisfied her sense of duty by dusting over their spines only; the immoral secret she was tracking down compelled her to look behind each one. She took each out separately, knocked at it — it might be hollow — inserted her coarse, calloused fingers as far back as the wooden panelling, probed about, and at length withdrew them, dissatisfied, shaking her head.

29

Her interest never misled her into overstepping the exact time laid down for her work. Five minutes before Kien unlocked the door, she was already in the kitchen. Calmly and without haste she searched one section of the shelves after another, never missing anything and never quite giving up hope.

During these months of indefatigable research, she couldn't think of taking her money to the post-office. She wouldn't lay a finger on it; who knew what sort of money it might be? She placed the notes, in the order in which he gave them to her, in a large clean envelope, which contained, still in its entirety, the stock of notepaper she had bought twenty years before. Overcoming serious scruples she put the whole into her trunk, with the trousseau, specially selected and beautifully worked, which had taken her many years and hard-earned money to accumulate.

Little by little she realized that she would not get to the bottom of the mystery as easily as all that. She knew how to wait. She was very well as she was. If something were to come to light one day – no one could blame her. She had been over every corner of that library with a fine-tooth comb. Of course if you had a friend in the police, solid and respectable, who wouldn't forget you were in a good job, you might say something to him. Excuse me, she could put up with a lot, but she'd no one to rely on. The things people do these days. Dancing, bathing, fooling around, nothing sensible, not a stroke of work. Her own gentleman, though he was sensible enough, had his goings on like anyone else. Never went to bed before midnight. The best sleep is the sleep before midnight. Respectable people go to bed at nine. Very likely it wasn't anything to write home about.

Gradually the horrible crime dwindled into a mere secret. Thick, tough layers of contempt covered it up. But her curiosity remained; between a quarter past six and seven o'clock she was always on the alert. She counted on rare, but not impossible contingencies. A sudden pain in the stomach might bring him out of his room. Then she would hurry in and ask if he wanted anything. Pains do not go away all in a minute. A few seconds, and she would know all she wanted to know. But the temperate and reasonable life which Kien led suited him too well. For the whole eight long years during which he had employed Therese he had never yet had a pain in the stomach.

The very morning on which he had met the blind man and his dog, it happened that Kien urgently wanted to consult certain old treatises. He pulled out all the drawers of the writing desk violently one after

30

the other. A vast accumulation of papers had piled up in them over the years. Rough drafts, corrected scripts, fair copies, anything and everything which had to do with his work, he carefully preserved them all. He found wretched scraps whose contents he had himself long since surpassed and contradicted. The archives went right back to his student days. Merely in order to find a minute detail, which he knew by heart anyway, merely to check a reference, he wasted hours of time. He read over thirty pages and more; one line was all he wanted. Worthless stuff, which had long since served its purpose, came into his hands. He cursed it, why was it there? But once his eye fell upon anything written or printed he could not pass it over. Any other man would have refused to be held up by these digressions. He read every word, from first to last. The ink had faded. He had difficulty in making out the pale outlines. The blind man in the street came into his mind. There was he, playing tricks with his eyes, as if they would last for all eternity. Instead of restricting their hours of service, he increased them wantonly from month to month. Each single paper which he replaced in the drawer cost his eyes a part of their strength. Dogs have short lives and dogs do not read; thus they are able to help out blind men with their eyes. The man who has frittered away the strength of his eyes is a worthy companion of the beast that leads him.

Kien decided to empty his writing desk of rubbish on the following day immediately he got up; at present he was working.

On the following day, at six o'clock precisely, in the very middle of a dream, he started up from his divan bed, flung himself on the crammed giant and pulled out every one of its drawers. Screeching filled the air; it shrilled through the entire library, swelling to a heartrending climax. It was as if each drawer had its own voice and each was vying with its neighbour in a piercing scream for help. They were being robbed, tortured, murdered. They could not know who it was who dared to touch them. They had no eyes; their only organ was a shrill voice. Kien sorted the papers. It took him a long time. He disregarded the noise; what he had begun, he would finish. With a pyramid of waste paper in his lean arms, he stalked across into the fourth room. Here, some distance from the screeching, he tore them, cursing, into small pieces. Someone knocked; he ground his teeth. Again that knock; he stamped his feet. The knocking changed to hammering. 'Quiet!' he ordered and swore. He would willingly have dispensed with the unseemly row. But he was sorry on account of the manuscripts. Rage alone had given him strength to destroy them. At last he stood, a huge lonely stork on guard over a mountain of scraps of paper. Embarrassed and timid, he stroked them with his fingers, softly mourning over them. So as not to injure them unnecessarily, he lifted a cautious leg and cleared them. The graveyard behind him, he breathed again. Outside the door he found the housekeeper. With a weary gesture, he indicated the pyre and said: 'Clear it away!' The screeching had died down; he went back to the writing desk and closed the drawers. They were silent. He had wrenched them open too violently. The mechanism had been broken.

Therese was in the very act of finding her way into the starched skirt which completed her attire, when the screeching had broken loose. Terrified out of her wits, she fastened her skirt provisionally and glided fast to the door of the study. 'For Heaven's sake,' she wailed, flute-like, 'What has happened?' She knocked, discreetly at first, then louder. Receiving no answer, she tried the door, in vain. She glided from door to door. In the last room she heard him, shouting angrily. Here she hammered on the door with all her strength. 'Quiet!' he shouted in a rage, in such a rage as she had never heard him. Half indignant, half resigned, she let her hard hands drop against her hard skirt, and stood stiff as a wooden doll. 'What a calamity!' she murmured, 'what a calamity!' and was still standing there, out of mere habit, when he opened the door.

Slow by nature, this time she grasped in a flash the opportunity which was being offered to her. With difficulty she said 'At once', and glided away to the kitchen. On the threshold she had an idea: 'Gracious Heaven, he's bolting himself in, just out of habit! Something will happen, at the last minute, that's life! I've no luck, I've no luck!' It was the first time she had said this, for as a rule she regarded herself as a meritorious and therefore as a lucky person. Anxiety made her head jerk to and fro. She sneaked out into the corridor again. She was stooping far forward. Her legs hesitated before she took a step. Her stiff skirt billowed. She would have reached her goal far more quietly by gliding as usual, but that was too ordinary a process. The solemnity of the occasion demanded its own solemnities. The room was open to her: In the middle of the floor the paper was still lying. She pushed a great fold of the carpet between the door and its frame so that it should not be blown to. Then she went back to the kitchen and waited, dustpan and brush in hand, for the familiar rattle of the wash-trolley. She would have preferred to come and fetch it herself, for she had a long time to wait. When at last she heard it crash against the wall, she forgot herself and called, out of habit, 'Up already?' She pushed it into the kitchen and, stooping even lower than before, crept into the library. She set down dustpan and brush on the floor. Slowly she picked her way across the intervening rooms to the threshold of his bedroom. After every step she stood still, and turned her head the other way about so as to listen with her right ear, the ear which was the less worn-out of the two. The thirty yards which she traversed took her ten minutes; she thought herself foolhardy. Her terror and her curiosity grew at the same rate. A thousand times she had thought out how to behave when she reached her goal. She squeezed herself tightly against the door frame. She remembered the crackling of her newly starched skirt too late. With one eye she tried to survey the situation. As long as the other one was in reserve she felt safe. She must not be seen, and she must see everything. Her right arm, which she liked to hold akimbo and which was constantly doubling itself up, she forced into stillness.

Kien was pacing calmly up and down in front of his books, making incomprehensible noises. Under his arm he carried the empty brief-case. He came to a halt, thought for a moment, then fetched the ladder and climbed up it. From the topmost shelf he extracted a book, turned over the pages and placed it in the brief-case. On the ground again, he continued his pacing up and down, stopped, pulled at a book, which was recalcitrant, wrinkled his forehead, and when he had it at last in his hands, gave it a sharp slap. Then it too disappeared into the brief-case. He selected five volumes. Four small ones and one large one. Suddenly he was in a hurry. Carrying the heavy brief-case he clambered up to the highest rung of the ladder and pushed the first volume back into its place. His long legs encumbered him; he had all but fallen down.

If he fell and hurt himself, there'd be an end of this wickedness. Therese's arm could be controlled no longer; it reached for her ear and tugged vigorously. at it. Both eyes were fixed, gloating, on her imperilled employer. When his feet at length reached the thick carpet, she could breathe again. So the books were a fraud. Now for the truth. She knew every inch of the library, but secret vices are crafty. There's opium, there's morphia, there's cocaine — who could remember them all? You couldn't fool her. Behind the books, that's it. Why for instance did he never walk straight across the room? He stood by the ladder and what he wanted was on the shelf exactly opposite. He could fetch it as easy as anything, but no, he must always go creeping round by the wall. Carrying that great heavy thing under his arm, he goes all the way round by the wall. Behind the books, that's it. Murderers are drawn to the scene of the crime. Now the brief-case is full. He can't get anything more into it; she knows the brief-case, she dusts it out every day. Now something must happen. It can't be seven yet. If it's seven he'll go out. Where is it seven? It shan't be seven.

Shameless and sure of herself, she stooped forward, pressed her arm to her side, pricked her two large ears and opened her little eyes greedily. He took the brief-case by both ends and laid it firmly on the carpet. His face looked proud. He stooped down and remained stooping. She was running with sweat and trembling in every limb. Tears came into her eyes, under the carpet then, that's it. She'd always said, under the carpet. What a fool! He straightened himself, cracked his joints and spat. Or did he only say 'There!' He took up the brief-case, extracted a volume and slowly replaced it on the shelves. He did the same with all the others.

Therese came over faint. No thank you, indeed! There's nothing more worth looking at. So that's your sensible man, with never a smile or a word! She's sensible herself, and hard-working, but would she demean herself? You could cut her hand off, you don't find her mixed up in such things. He acts stupid in front of his own house-keeper. A creature like that to have money! And so much money, heaps and heaps of money! Ought to be put away. The way he wastes his money! Anyone else in her position now, any of that rag-tag and bobtail there is these days, they'd have had the last stitch of clothing off his back long ago. Doesn't even sleep in a decent bed. What does he want with all these books and books? He can't be read-ing all of them at once. If you ask her, he's nothing but a loony, ought to have his money taken away before he wastes it all, and then let him go his own way. She'll teach him! Enticing a respectable woman into his house, indeed. Thinks he can make a fool of anyone, does he? Nobody can make a fool of her. For eight years perhaps, but not a moment longer!

By the time Kien had made his second selection of books for his morning walk, Therese's first anger had evaporated. She saw that he was ready to go out, glided in her normal, self-possessed manner back to the heap of paper and inserted the dustpan underneath it with dignity. She seemed to herself a more interesting and distinguished person than before.

No, she decided, she would not give up her post. But she's found him out now. Well, that's something to know. If she sees anything, she knows how to make use of it. She doesn't see many things. She hasn't ever been outside the town. She's not one for excursions, a waste of good money. You don't catch her going bathing, it's not respectable. She doesn't care for travelling, you never know where you are. If she didn't have to go shopping, she'd prefer to stay in all day. They all try to do you down. Prices going up all the time, things aren't the same any more.

CHAPTER III

CONFUCIUS THE MATCHMAKER

ON the following Sunday Kien came back elated from his morning walk. The streets were empty on Sundays at this early hour. Humankind began each holiday by lying late. Then they fell upon their best clothes. They spent their first wakeful hours in devotions before the looking glass. During the remainder they recovered from their own grimaces by looking at other people's. Each thought himself the finest. To prove it he must go among his fellows. On weekdays: sweat and babble to earn a living. On Sundays: sweat and babble for nothing. The day of rest had been first intended as a day of silence. Kien noted with scorn that this institution, like all others, had degenerated into its exact opposite. He himself had no use for a day of rest. Always he worked and always in silence.

Outside the door of his flat he found the housekeeper. She had evidently been waiting for him some time.

'The Metzger child from the second floor was here. You promised him he could come. He would have it, you were in. The maid saw someone tall coming upstairs. He'll be back in half an hour. He won't disturb you, he's coming for the book.'

Kien had not been listening. Only at the word 'book' did he become attentive and understood in retrospect what the matter was. 'He is lying. I promised nothing. I told him I would show him some pictures from India and China if I ever had time. I have no time. Send him away.'

'Some people have a cheek. Excuse me, such ragtag and bobtail. The father was a common working man. Where they get the money from, I'd like to know. But there you are. Everything for the children, these days. Nobody is strict any more. Cheeky they are; you wouldn't credit it. Playing at their lessons and going for walks with teacher. Excuse me, in my time it was very different. If a child didn't want to learn its parents took it away from school and put it to a trade. With a hard master, so it had to learn. Nothing like that these days. You don't catch people wanting to work now. Don't know their places any more, that's what it is. Look at young people these days, when they go out on Sundays. Every factory girl has to have a new blouse. I ask you, and what do they do with all their fancy stuff?

36

Go off bathing and take it all off again. With boys, too. Whoever heard of such a thing in my time? Let 'em do a job of work, that'd be more like it. I always say, where does the money come from? Prices going up all the time. Potatoes cost double already. It's not surprising, children have a check. Parents don't check them at all. In my days, it was a couple of good smacks, left and right, and the child had to do as it was told. There's nothing good left in the world. When they're little they don't learn, when they grow up they don't do a hand's turn.

Kien had been irritated at first because she was holding him up with a long discourse, but soon he found himself yielding to a kind of astonished interest in her words. So this uneducated creature set great value on learning. She must have a sound core. Perhaps the result of her daily contact with his books. Other women in her position might not have taken colour from their surroundings. She was more receptive, perhaps she yearned for education.

'You are quite right,' he said, 'I am happy to find you so sensible. Learning is everything.'

They had entered the flat while they were talking. 'Wait a minute!' he commanded and disappeared into the library. He came back with a small book in his left hand. As he turned over the pages, he thrust his thin, hard lips outwards. 'Listen!' he said and signalled her to stand a little further from him. What he was about to utter called for space. With an abundance of feeling, grotesquely unsuited to the simplicity of the text, he read:

'My master commanded me to learn three thousand characters every day and to write down another thousand each evening. In the short winter days the sun went down early and I had not finished my task. I carried my little tablet on to the veranda which faced the west and finished my writing there. Late in the evening, when I was going through what I had written, I could no longer overcome my weariness. So I placed two buckets of water behind me. When I grew too sleepy, I took off my gown and emptied the first bucket over myself. Naked, I sat down to my work again. Gradually I would grow warmer and sleepy again. Then I would use the second bucket. With the help of two shower baths I was nearly always able to complete my task. In that winter I entered my ninth year.'

Moved and ablaze with admiration, he clapped the book to. 'That was the way they used to learn! A fragment from the childhood recollections of the Japanese scholar Arai Hakuseki.'

37

During the reading, Therese had drawn closer. Her head waggled in time to his sentences. Her large left ear seemed to reach out of itself towards the words, as he translated freely from the Japanese original. Unintentionally, he was holding the book a little crooked; doubtless she could see the foreign characters and was astonished at the fluency of his rendering. He was reading as if he had a German book in his hands. 'Well I never!' she said. He had finished; she took a deep breath. Her amazement amused him. Was it too late, he thought, how old can she be? It is never too late to learn. But she would have to begin with simple novels.

The bell rang violently. Therese opened the door. The little Metzger boy pushed his head through the crack. 'I may come in!' he shouted, 'the Professor said I could!' 'No books for you!' screamed Therese, and slammed the door. Outside the little boy raged up and down. He yelled threats at the door; he was so angry that they could not understand a word he said. 'Excuse me, he takes a whole fistful in one. They'd be dirty in no time. I've seen him eat his piece of bread and butter on the stairs.'

Kien was on the threshold of the library: the boy had not seen him. He nodded approvingly to his housekeeper. He was happy to find the interests of his books so well defended. She deserved thanks: 'Should you ever wish to read anything, you may always apply to me.'

'I make so bold, I often thought of asking.'

How she jumped on her opportunity, when books were in question! She was not usually like this. Until this moment she had behaved herself very modestly. He had no intention of starting a lending library. To gain time he answered: 'Good. I shall look something out for you to-morrow.'

Then he sat down to his work. His promise made him feel uneasy. It was true that she dusted the books every day and had not yet injured one of them. But dusting and reading are different. Her fingers were coarse and rough. Delicate paper must be delicately handled. A hard binding can naturally stand rougher handling than sensitive pages. And how did he know that she *could* read? She must be more than fifty, she had not made much use of her time. 'An old man who learnt late', Plato called his opponent, the cynic philosopher Antisthenes. To-day we have old women who learn late. She wanted to quench her thirst at the fountain head. Or was she only ashamed of admitting in my presence that she knew nothing? Charity is all very well, but not at other people's expense. Why should the books have to foot the bill? I pay her high wages. I have a right to, it is my own money. But to hand over books to her would be cowardly. They are defenceless against the uneducated. I cannot sit by her all the time she is reading.

That night he saw a man standing, fast bound, on the terrace of a temple, defending himself with wooden clubs from the savage attacks of two upright jaguars on his left and right. Both animals were decked with strange streamers in all colours. They gnashed their teeth, roared and rolled their eyes so wildly that it made the blood run cold. The sky was black and narrow, and had hidden his stars in his pocket. Tears of glass trickled out of the eyes of the prisoner and splintered into a thousand pieces as they reached the pavement. But as nothing further happened, the savage combat grew boring and made the spectator yawn. Then by chance his eye fell on the feet of the jaguars. They had human feet. Aha, thought the spectator — a lanky, learned man — these are sacrificial priests of ancient Mexico. They are performing a sacred comedy. The victim knows well that he must die in the end. The priests are disguised as jaguars but I see through them at once.

The jaguar on the right seized a heavy stone wedge and drove it into the victim's heart. One edge of it clove sharp through the breast bone. Kien closed his eyes, dazzled. He thought, the blood must spirt up to the very sky; he sternly disapproved of this medieval barbarism. He waited until he thought the blood must have ceased to flow, then opened his eyes. Oh horrible: from the cleft victim's wounded breast a book appeared, another, a third, many. There was no end to it, they fell to the ground, they were clutched at by viscous flames. The blood had set fire to the wood, the books were burning. 'Shut your breast!' shouted Kien to the prisoner, 'Shut your breast!' He gesticulated with his hands; 'you must do it like this, quickly, quickly!' The prisoner understood; with a terrific jerk he freed himself of his bonds and clutched both his hands over his heart; Kien breathed again.

Then suddenly the victim tore his bosom wide open. Books poured forth in torrents. Scores, hundreds, they were beyond counting; the flames licked up towards the paper; each one wailed for help; a fearful shrieking rose on all sides. Kien stretched out his arms to the books, now blazing to heaven. The altar was much further off than he had thought. He took a couple of strides and was no nearer. He must run if he was to save them alive. He ran and fell; this cursed shortness of breath; it came of neglecting his physical health; he could tear himself into pieces with rage. A useless creature, when there was need of him he was no use. Those miserable wretches! Human sacrifices he had heard of — but books, books! Now at last he was at the altar. The fire singed his hair and eyebrows. The wood pyre was enormous; from the distance he had thought it quite small. They must be in the very centre of the fire. Into it then, you coward, you swaggerer, you miserable sinner!

But why blame himself? He was in the middle of it. *Where are you? Where are you?* The flames dazzled him. And what the devil was this, wherever he reached out, he could get hold of nothing but shrieking human beings. They clutched hold of him with all their strength. He hurled them from him, they came back to him. They crept to him from below and entwined his knees; from above his head burning torches rained down on him. He was not looking up yet he saw them clearly. They seized on his ears, his hair, his shoulders. They enchained him with their bodies. Bedlam broke loose. 'Let me go,' he shouted, 'I don't know you. What do you want with me! How can I rescue the books!'

But one of them had thrown himself against his mouth, and clung fast to his tightly closed lips. He wanted to speak again, but he could not open his mouth. He implored them in his mind: *I can't save them! I can't save them!* He wanted to cry, but where were his tears? His eyes too were fast closed; human beings were pressing against them too. He tried to step free of them, he lifted his right leg high in the air; in vain, it was dragged back again, dragged down by a burden of burning human kind, dragged down by a leaden weight. He abhorred them, these greedy creatures; could they not be satisfied with the life they had had? He loathed them. He would have liked to hurt them, torment them, reproach them; he could do nothing, nothing! Not for one moment did he forget why he was there. They might hold his eyes forcibly shut, but in his spirit he could see mightily. He saw a book growing in every direction at once until it filled the sky and the earth and the whole of space to the very horizon. At its edges a reddish glow, slowly, quietly, devoured it. Proud, silent, uncomplaining, it endured a martyr's death. Men screamed and shrieked, the book burnt without a word. Martyrs do not cry out, saints do not cry out.

Then a voice spoke; in it was all knowledge, for it was the voice of God: 'There are no books here. All is vanity.' And at once Kien knew that the voice spoke truth. Lightly, he threw off the burning mob and jumped out of the fire. He was saved. Did it hurt then?

Terribly, he answered himself, but not so much as people usually think. He was extraordinarily happy about the voice. He could see himself, dancing away from the altar. At a little distance, he turned round. He was tempted to laugh at the empty fire.

Then he stood still, lost in contemplation of Rome. He saw the mass of struggling limbs; the air was thick with the smell of burning flesh. How stupid men are! He forgot his anger. A single step, and they could save themselves.

Suddenly, he did not know how it could have happened, the men were changed into books. He gave a great cry and rushed, beside himself, in the direction of the fire. He ran, panted, scolded himself, leaped into the flames and was again surrounded by those imploring human bodies. Again the terror seized him, again God's voice set him free, again he escaped and watched again from the same place the same scene. Four times he let himself be fooled. The speed with which events succeeded each other increased each time. He knew that he was bathed in sweat. Secretly he began to long for the breathing space allowed him between one excitement and the next. In the fourth pause, he was overtaken by the Last Judgment. Gigantic wagons, high as houses, as mountains, high as the heavens, closed in from two, ten, twenty, from all sides upon the devouring altar. The voice, harsh and destructive, mocked him: 'Now come the books!' Kien cried out and woke.

This dream, the worst dream he could remember, weighed upon his spirit for half an hour afterwards. An ill-extinguished match dropped while he was enjoying himself in the street — and his library would be lost! He had insured it more than once. But he doubted if he would have the strength to go on living after the destruction of twenty-five thousand books, let alone see about the payment of the insurance. He had taken out the policies in a contemptible frame of mind; later he was ashamed of them. He would have liked to cancel them. Indeed he only paid the necessary fees so as not to have to re-enter the office in which books and cattle were subject to the same laws, and to be spared the visits of the companies' representatives who would doubtless be sent to call on him at home.

Divided into its elements a dream loses its terrors. He had been looking at Mexican pictorial writings only yesterday. One of them represented the sacrifice of a prisoner by two priests disguised as jaguars. His chance meeting with a blind man a few days before had made him think of Eratosthenes the aged librarian of Alexandria.

The name of Alexandria would naturally provoke the recollection of the burning of the famous library. A certain medieval woodcut, whose ingenuousness always made him smile, depicted about thirty Jews on a burning pyre flaming to heaven yet obstinately screeching their prayers. He was a great admirer of Michelangelo; above all he admired his Last Judgment. In that picture sinners are being dragged to Hell by pitiless devils. One of the damned, the picture of terror and anguish, covers his cowardly flaccid face with his hands; devils are clutching at his legs but he has never seen the woes of other people and dare not look at his own now. On the height stands Christ, very un-Christlike, condemning the damned with muscular and mighty arm. From all these recollections sleep had concocted a dream.

When Kien pushed the wash-trolley out of his bedroom he heard on an unexpectedly high note the exclamation: 'Up already!' Why did the creature speak so loud early in the morning when he was still almost asleep? Very true he had promised to lend her a book. A novel was the only thing worth considering for her. But no mind ever grew fat on a diet of novels. The pleasure which they occasionally offer is far too heavily paid for: they undermine the finest characters. They teach us to think ourselves into other men's places. Thus we acquire a taste for change. The personality becomes dissolved in pleasing figments of imagination. The reader learns to understand every point of view. Willingly he yields himself to the pursuit of other people's goals and loses sight of his own. Novels are so many wedges which the novelist, an actor with his pen, inserts into the closed personality of the reader. The better he calculates the size of the wedge and the strength of the resistance, so much the more completely does he crack open the personality of his victim. Novels should be prohibited by the State.

At seven o'clock Kien once again opened his door. Therese was standing in front of it, as trusting and modest as always, her prominent left ear perhaps a trifle more crooked.

'I make so bold,' she reminded him impertinently.

What little blood Kien had rushed to his head. So she would stick to it, this cursed creature in her starched skirt, and exact what had once been thoughtlessly promised. 'You want that book,' he cried and his voice cracked. 'You shall have it.'

He slammed the door in her face, strode with quivering steps into the third room, inserted one finger into the shelves and extracted *The Trousers of Herr von Bredow*. He had possessed this book from his earliest schooldays, had then lent it to all his classmates, and on account of the deplorable condition in which it had been ever since could not bear the sight of it. He looked with malice at its grease-spotted binding and sticky pages. Calm now, he went back to Therese and held the book close to her eyes.

'That was unnecessary,' she said and pulled out from under her arm a thick bundle of paper, packing paper, as he now noticed for the first time. With some ceremony she selected a suitable piece and wrapped it round the book like a shawl round a baby. Then she selected a second piece of paper and said, 'A stitch in time saves nine'. When the second piece of paper did not lie smoothly enough, she tore it off and tried a third one.

Kien followed her movements as though he were seeing her for the first time. He had underestimated her. She knew how to handle a book better than he did. This old thing was loathsome to him, but she wrapped it carefully up in two layers of paper. She kept the palms of her hands clear of the binding. She worked with her finger tips alone. Her fingers were not so coarse after all. He felt ashamed of himself and pleased with her. Should he fetch her something else? She deserved something less shabby. Still, for a beginning she could make do with this one. Even without encouragement she would soon be asking for another. For eight long years his library had been safe in her care; he had not known it.

'I have to leave to-morrow,' he said suddenly, as she was smoothing down the paper cover with her knuckles. 'For some months.'

'Then I shall be able to dust properly for once. Is an hour long enough?'

'What would you do if a fire broke out?'

She was horrified. She dropped the paper to the ground. The book remained in her hand. 'Gracious Heavens, save the books!'

'But I am not really going away: I was only joking,' Kien smiled. Carried away by this picture of extreme devotion — himself absent and the books alone — he came closer to her and patted her on the shoulder with his bony fingers, saying in a tone almost friendly, 'You're a good creature.'

'I must have a look what you've chosen for me,' she said, and the corners of her mouth seemed to reach out almost to her ears. She opened the book and read aloud, '*The Trousers*' — she interrupted herself but did not blush. Her face was bedewed with a light sweat.

'Excuse me, Professor,' she exclaimed, and glided away, swiftly triumphant, towards her kitchen.

During the ensuing days Kien exerted himself to recover his old power of concentration. He too knew moments when he was tired of his services to the written word and felt a secret desire for more of the company of human kind than his strength of character normally permitted. When he entered into open conflict with such temptations he wasted much time; they tended to grow stronger if he fought them. He had contrived a more ingenious method: he out-manœuvred them. He did not pillow his head on the writing desk and lose himself in idle desires. He did not walk up and down the streets and enter into trivial conversations with fools. On the contrary he filled the library with the distinguished friends he had read. Mostly he inclined to the ancient Chinese. He commanded them to step out of the volume and the shelf to which they belonged, beckoned to them, offered them chairs, greeted them, threatened them, and according to his taste put their own words into their mouths and defended his own opinions against them until at length he had silenced them. When he entered into written controversy he found his words acquired from this practice an un-expected force. In this way he practiced speaking Chinese and took pride in the clever phrases which flowed from his lips so easily and so emphatically. If I go to the theatre (he thought) I hear a conversation in double-Dutch which is entertaining but not instructive, and in the end not even entertaining, only boring. Two or even three whole valuable hours must I sacrifice only to go to bed feeling irritated. My own dialogues do not go on so long and have meaning and balance. In this way he justified to himself the harmless game which might have seemed odd to a spectator.

Sometimes Kien would meet, either in the street or in a bookshop, a barbarous fellow who amazed him by uttering a reasonable sentiment. In order to obliterate any impression which contradicted his contempt for the mass of mankind he would in such cases perform a small arith-metical calculation. How many words does this fellow speak in a single day? At a conservative reckoning ten thousand. Three of them are not without sense. By chance I overheard those three. The other words which whirl through his head at a rate of several hundred thousand per day, which he thinks but does not even speak — one imbecility after another — are to be guessed merely by looking at his features; fortunately one does not have to listen to them.

His housekeeper, however, spoke little, since she was always alone. At a flash, they seemed to have something in common; his thoughts recurred to it hourly. Whenever he saw her, he remembered at once

44

how carefully she had wrapped up *The Trousers of Herr von Bredow*. The book had been in his library for years. Every time he passed it the sight of its back alone smote his heart. Yet he had left it, just as it was. Why had it not occurred to him to care for its improvement by providing it with a handsome wrapper? He had lamentably failed in his duty. And now came a simple housekeeper and taught him what was right and seemly.

Or was she play-acting for his benefit? Perhaps she was merely flattering him into a sense of false security. His library was famous. Dealers had often besieged him for unique editions. Perhaps she was planning some vast robbery. He must find out how she acted when she was alone with the book.

One day he surprised her in the kitchen. His doubts tormented him; he longed for certainty. Once unmasked, he would throw her out. He wanted a glass of water; she had evidently not heard him calling. While she made haste to satisfy his wishes, he examined the table at which she had been sitting. On a small embroidered velvet cushion lay his book. Open at page 20. She had not yet read very far. She offered him the glass on a plate. It was then he saw that she had white kid gloves on her hands. He forgot to close his fingers round the glass; it fell to the floor, the plate after it. Noise and diversion were welcome to him. He could not have brought a word to his lips. Ever since he was five years old, for thirty-five years, he had been reading. And the thought had never once crossed his mind, to put on gloves for the purpose. His embarrassment seemed ridiculous, even to himself. He pulled himself together and asked casually: 'You have not got very far yet?'

'I read every page a dozen times, otherwise you can't get the best out of it.'

'Do you like it?' He had to force himself to go on speaking, or he would have fallen to the ground as easily as the glass of water.

'A book is always beautiful. You need to understand it. There were grease spots on it, I've tried everything but I can't get them out. What shall I do now?'

'They were there before.'

'All the same, it's a pity. Excuse me, a book like this is a treasure.'

She did not say 'must cost a lot', she said 'is a treasure'. She meant its intrinsic value, not its price. And he had babbled to her of the capital which was locked up in his library! This woman must despise him. Hers was a generous spirit. She sat up night after night trying to remove old grease spots from a book, instead of sleeping. He gave her his shabbiest, most dog-eared and worn-out book out of sheer distaste, and she took it into loving care. She had compassion, not for men (there was nothing in that) but for books. The weary and heavy-laden could come to her. The meanest, the most forsaken and forgotten creature on the face of God's earth, she would take to her heart.

Kien left the kitchen in the deepest perturbation. Not one word more did he say to the saint.

In the lofty halls of his library he paced up and down and called on Confucius. He came towards him from the opposite wall, calm and self-possessed — it is easy to be self-possessed when you have been dead for centuries. With long strides Kien went to meet him. He forgot to make any obeisance. His excitement contrasted strangely with the bearing of the Chinese sage.

'I think that I am not wholly without education!' he shouted from a distance of five paces, 'I think I am not wholly without tact. People have tried to persuade me that education and tact are the same thing, that one is impossible without the other. Who tried to persuade me of this? You!' He was not shy of Confucius; he called him 'you' straight out. 'Here comes a person without a spark of education and she has more sensibility, more heart, more dignity, more humanity than I or you and all your learned disciples put together!'

Confucius was not to be put out of countenance. He did not even forget to make his bow before he was spoken to. In spite of these incredible accusations, he did not even raise his eyebrows. Beneath them, his eyes, very ancient and black, were wise as those of an ape. Deliberately he opened his mouth and uttered the following saying:

'At fifteen my inclination was to learning, at thirty I was fixed in that path, at forty I had no more doubts — but only when I was sixty were my ears opened.'

Kien had this sentence firmly fixed in his head. But as an answer to his violent attack, it disturbed him greatly. Quickly he compared the dates to see if they fitted. When he was fifteen he had been secretly devouring book after book, much against his mother's will, by day at school, and by night under the bedclothes, with a tiny pocket torch for sole wretched illumination. When his younger brother George, set to watch by his mother, woke up by chance during the night, he never failed to pull the bedclothes off him, experimentally. The fate of his reading programme for the ensuing nights depended on the speed with which he could conceal torch and book underneath his body. At thirty he was fixed in the path of knowledge. Professorial chairs he rejected with contempt. He might have lived comfortably on the income from his paternal inheritance. He preferred to spend the capital on books. In a few more years, three perhaps, it would all be spent. He never even dreamed of the threatening future, he did not fear it. He was forty. Until this day he had never known a doubt. But he could not get over *The Trousers of Herr von Bredow*. He was not yet sixty, otherwise his ears would have been opened. But to whom should he open them?

Confucius came a step closer to him, as if he had guessed the question, bowed, although Kien was at least two heads taller, and gave him the following confidential advice:

'Observe the manner of men's behaviour, observe the motives of their actions, examine those things in which they find pleasure. How can anyone conceal himself! How can anyone conceal himself!'

Then Kien grew very sad. What had it availed him to know these words by heart? They should be applied, proved, confirmed. For eight long years he had had a human being in the closest proximity, and all for nothing. I knew how she behaved, he thought, I never thought of her motives. I knew what she did for my books. I had the evidence of it daily before my eyes. I thought, she did it for money. Now that I know what she takes pleasure in, I know her motives better. She takes the grease spots off wretched and rejected books for which no one else has a good word to say. That is her recreation, that is her rest. Had I not surprised her in the kitchen, out of shameful mistrust, her deeds would never have come to light. In her solitude she had embroidered a pillow for her foster-child and laid it softly to rest. For eight long years she never wore gloves. Before she could bring herself to open a book, and *this* book, she went out and bought with her hard-earned money a pair of gloves. She is not a fool, in other things she is a practical woman, she knows that for the price of the gloves she could have bought the book, new, three times over. I have committed a great sin, I was blind for eight years.

Confucius gave him no time to think again. 'To err without making amendment is to err indeed. If you have erred, be not ashamed to make the fault good.'

It shall be made good, cried Kien. I will give her back her eight lost years! I will marry her! She is the heaven-sent instrument for preserving my library. If there is a fire I can trust in her. Had I constructed a human being according to my own designs, the result could not have been more apt for the purpose. She has all the elements necessary. She is a born foster-mother. Her heart is in the right place. There is room for no illiterate fools in her heart. She could have had a lover, a baker, a butcher, a tailor, some kind of barbarian, some kind of an ape. But she cannot bring herself to it. Her heart belongs to the books. What is simpler than to marry her?

He took no more notice of Confucius. When he chanced to look in his direction, he had dissolved into air. Only his voice could still be heard, saying faintly but clearly: 'To see the right and not to do it is to lack courage.'

Kien had no time to thank him for this last encouragement. He flung himself towards the kitchen, and seized violently upon the door. The handle came off in his hand. Therese was seated in front of the cushion and made as if she were reading. When she sensed that he was already behind her, she got up, so that he could see what she had been reading. The impression of his last conversation had not been lost on her. She had gone back to page 3. He hesitated a moment, did not know what to say, and looked down at his hands. Then he saw the broken door handle; in a rage he threw it to the ground. He took his place stiffly in front of her and said: 'Give me your hand!' 'Excuse me,' breathed Therese and stretched it out to him. Now for the seduction, she thought and began to sweat all over. 'No,' said Kien; he had not meant her hand in that sense. 'I want to marry you!' So sudden a decision had been beyond Therese's expectations. She twisted her astonished head round in the opposite direction and replied proudly, though with an effort not to stammer: 'I make so bold!'

CHAPTER IV

THE MUSSEL SHELL

THE wedding took place quietly. The witnesses were an oddman who could still strike a few last sparks from his tottering frame, and a worthy cobbler who, having cunningly evaded marriage himself, for the drink-sodden life of him, enjoyed watching other people's. Superior clients he would urgently press to have sons and daughters who would marry soon. He had convincing arguments in favour of early marriage. 'Settle your children properly, you'll have grandchildren in no time. Look sharp and get your grandchildren settled, and you'll have great-grandchildren!' In conclusion he would point to his good suit which could mix with anybody. Before grand weddings he had it pressed at the cleaners, for ordinary ones he ironed it himself at home. Only one thing he begged leave to ask, and that was reasonable notice. When his services had not been in request for some time, he would offer — slow worker though he was by temperament — repairs while-you-wait for nothing. Usually unreliable, in this sphere he was a man of his word, did the shoes on the spot and charged really very little. Children — mostly young girls — so lost to their duty as to marry without their parents' knowledge, but not so lost as to dispense with marriage altogether, sometimes made use of him. Indiscretion incarnate, he was in these matters silent as the grave. Not by a flicker did he betray his clients, even though he recounted in pompous detail the tale of her daughter's wedding to her own unsuspecting mother. Before setting off for his 'little bit of heaven' — as he called it — he would fix to the door of his workshop an enormous notice. On it could be read in writhing, soot-black letters the message: 'Out on my business. Back sooner or later. The undersigned: Hubert Beredinger.'

He was the first to learn Therese's luck and doubted the truth of her story until, offended, she invited him to the registry office. When all was over, the witnesses followed the happy pair into the street. The oddman received his tip bowed down with gratitude. Muttering his congratulations he made his way off. ' . . . at your service any other time . . .', echoed in the ears of Mr. and Mrs. Kien. Ten paces off, his empty mouth was still mumbling with zeal. But Hubert Beredinger was bitterly disappointed. He did not hold with this sort of wedding.

He had sent his suit out to be pressed; the bridegroom was in his working clothes, his shoes trodden over, his suit threadbare; without love or joy, instead of looking at the bride, he had been reading the words in the book. He said 'I will' no different from 'thank you'; then never even gave his arm to the old stick, and as for the kiss, the kiss on which the cobbler lived for weeks — a kiss by proxy was worth twenty of his own — the kiss which he'd have paid good money for, the kiss which was the 'business' hung up on his workshop door; the public kiss under official eyes; the bridal kiss; the kiss for all eternity; that kiss, that kiss had never happened at all. When they parted the cobbler refused his hand. He disguised his resentment under a hideous grin. 'Just a moment please,' he giggled, like a photographer, while the Kiens hesitated. Suddenly he bent down towards a woman, chucked her under the chin, smacked his lips loudly and with eager gestures outlined her opulent figure. His round face grew rounder and rounder, his cheeks blew out to bursting, his double chin splayed out far and wide, the lines round his eyes twitched, tiny nimble snakes; his tensed hands drew ever broader curves. From second to second the woman grew fatter. Twice he looked at her, the third time, encouragingly, at the bridegroom. Then he gathered her into his arms and felt with his left hand shamelessly for her bosom.

True, the woman with whom the cobbler was fooling was not there, but Kien understood the shameless dumb show and drew the watching Therese quickly away.

'Drunk even before lunch!' said Therese, and clamped herself to her husband's arm; she too was indignant.

At the next stop, they waited for the tram. To make it clear that one day — even a wedding day — was no different from any other Kien took no taxi. The tram came up; he mounted the step before her. One foot on the platform, he recollected that his wife ought to go first. His back to the street, he stepped off again and collided violently with Therese. Exasperated, the conductor rang the bell. The tram went on without them. 'What's the matter?' Therese asked reproachfully. He had certainly hurt her a good deal. 'I wanted to help you up — that is, to help you, my dear.' 'Oh,' she said, 'that would be a nice thing.'

When they were at last seated, he paid for both of them. He hoped this would make amends for his clumsiness. The conductor gave the tickets to her. Instead of thanking him, she grinned broadly and nudged her husband with her shoulder. 'What?' he asked. 'The things people think of!' she giggled and flourished the tickets at the stout back of the conductor. She was making fun of him, thought Kien, and he said nothing.

He began to feel uncomfortable. The tram filled up. A woman sat down opposite him. She had, in all, four children with her, each smaller than the next. Two of them she clutched tightly on her lap, two of them remained standing. A gentleman, sitting on Therese's right, got out. 'Over there!' cried the mother, pushing her little brood across the gangway. The children made a rush for it, a little boy and a little girl, well under school age, the two of them. From the opposite direction an elderly gentleman was approaching. Therese put out her hands to protect the free seat. The children crept underneath it. They were in haste to show they could manage by themselves. Close by the seat, their little heads popped up. Therese flicked them away like specks of dust. 'My children!' screamed their mother, 'what are you thinking of?'

'I ask you,' countered Therese and gave a meaning look at her husband. 'Children last.' By this time the elderly gentleman had reached the goal, thanked her, and sat down.

Kien understood the look in his wife's eyes. He wished his brother George were here. He had set up as a gynaecologist in Paris. Not yet thirty-five years old, he enjoyed a suspiciously high reputation. He knew far more about women than about books. A bare two years after he had completed his studies, society had placed itself in his hands in so far as it was ill, and it was always ill, all those sickly women anyway. This outward sign of success had earned him Peter's well-deserved contempt. He might perhaps have forgiven George his good looks, they were congenital, he was not to blame. He could never have forced himself to undergo a plastic operation in order to escape the injurious results of so much beauty; his was unhappily a weak character. How weak was clear from the fact that he had abandoned the special branch of medicine which he himself had first chosen in order to pass with flying colours into the realms of psychiatry. It was alleged that he had done some good work in this field. In his heart he had remained a gynaecologist. Loose living was in his blood. Eight years before, indignant at George's vacillation, Peter had abruptly broken off all correspondence with him and had subsequently torn up a whole series of anxious letters. He was not in the habit of answering letters which he had torn up.

His marriage would make the best possible occasion for resuming relations with him. Peter's suggestions had first awakened in George his taste for a career of learning. It would be no disgrace to ask for his advice on a subject which lay within the domain of his real and natural branch of medicine. What was the right way to treat this timid, reserved creature? She was no longer young and took life very seriously. The woman who sat opposite was certainly a great deal younger, but she already had four children; Therese had none. 'Children last.' That sounded straightforward enough, but what did she really mean by it? She probably wanted no children; neither did he. He had never thought about children. For what purpose had she said that? Perhaps she took him for a person of no morals. But she knew his life. For eight years she had been aware of all his habits. She knew that he was a man of character. Did he ever go out at night? Had a woman ever called on him, even for a quarter of an hour? When she had first taken up her post with him, he had most emphatically explained to her that he received no visitors on principle, male or female, of whatever age, from infants in arms to octogenarians. She was to send everyone away. 'I have no time!' Those had been his very words. What devil had got into her? That shameless cobbler, perhaps? She was an innocent ingenuous creature; how otherwise, uneducated as she was, could she have acquired so great a love for books? But that dirty fellow's pantomime had been all too obvious. His gestures were self-explanatory; a child, without even knowing the reasons for his movements, would have understood that he had a woman in his arms. People of that kind, capable of losing control of themselves in the open street, ought to be segregated in asylums. They induce ugly thoughts in hard-working people. She was a hard-working woman. The cobbler had insinuated ideas into her head. Why else should children have occurred to her? It was not impossible that she might have heard something about such things. Women talk among themselves. She had perhaps been present at a birth, when she was in some other service. What did it signify if she did indeed know all there was to know? Better perhaps than if he had to explain it to her himself. There was a certain bashfulness in her expression; at her age it was faintly comic.

I never thought of asking anything so vulgar of her; it did not cross my mind. I have no time. I need six hours sleep. I work until twelve, at six o'clock I get up. Dogs and other animals may do such things by day. Perhaps she expects something of the kind from marriage. Hardly. Children last. Fool. All she meant was that she knew what was necessary. She knew the chain of circumstances whose conclusion is the perfected child. She was trying to explain herself gracefully. She took the occasion of this little incident, the children were importunate, the words were apt, but her eyes were fixed on me alone; it did for a confession. Most understandable. Such admissions are naturally painful. I married because of the books; children last. That means nothing at all. I remember her saying that children learnt too little. I read out to her a paragraph of Arai Hakuseki. She was quite carried away. That was how she first betrayed herself. Who knows how otherwise I could have guessed her feeling for books. At that moment we were drawn together. Probably she only meant to remind me of that. She is still the same. Her views on children have not altered since then. My friends are her friends. My enemies will be her enemies. The brief speech of an innocent mind. She had no conception of any other relationship. I must be careful. She might be frightened. I shall act very cautiously. How shall I open the subject to her? It is difficult to speak of it. I have no books on it. Buy one? What would the bookseller think? I am not that kind of man. Send someone for it? But who? She herself — for shame — my own wife! How can I be so cowardly. I must try myself. I, myself. But suppose she is unwilling. Suppose she screams. The people in the other flats — the caretaker — the police — the mob. But they can do nothing to me. I am married to her. I have a right. How disgusting! How came I to think of it? I am the one whom that cobbler has infected. Shame on you. After forty years. And now to behave in this way. I shall spare her. Children last. If I only knew what she meant. Sphinx.

The mother of the four children stood up. 'Look out!' she urged them, and shepherded them forward on her left. On the right, on Therese's side, she exposed herself only, a valiant commander. Contrary to Kien's expectation, she bobbed her head at her enemy, greeted her affably and said: 'You're the lucky one, still single,' and laughed, her gold teeth glittering a parting signal. Only when she had gone did Therese explode, screaming in a voice of fury, 'I ask you, my husband, I ask you, my husband! No children for us! I ask you, my husband!' She pointed at him, she pulled at his arm. I must calm her, he thought. The scene was painful to him, she needed his protection, she screamed and screamed. At last he drew himself to his full height and spoke out before their fellow-travellers: 'Yes,' he said. She had been insulted, she had to defend herself. Her counter-attack was as coarse as the attack had been. She was not to blame. Therese relaxed in her seat. No one, not even the gentleman next to her for whom she had saved the seat, took her part. The world was corrupt with kindness to children. Two stops further the Kiens got out. Therese went first. Suddenly he heard someone saying just behind him: 'Her skirt is the best thing about her.' 'What a bulwark!' 'Poor fellow!' 'What can you expect, the old starch box.' They were all laughing. The conductor and Therese, already peacefully on the outer platform, had heard nothing. But the conductor was laughing. In the street Therese received her husband joyfully: 'A jolly fellow!' she observed. The jolly fellow leaned out of the moving tram, put his hand to his mouth and bellowed two incomprehensible syllables. He was shaking all over, doubtless with laughter. Therese waved and excused herself, seeing his astonished look, with the words: 'He'll be falling out in a minute.'

But Kien was surreptitiously contemplating the skirt. It was even bluer than usual and had been more stiffly starched. Her skirt was a part of her, as the mussel shell is a part of the mussel. Let no one try to force open the closed shell of a mussel. A gigantic mussel as huge as this dress. They have to be trodden on, to be trampled into slime and splinters, as he had once done when he was a child at the seaside. The mussel yielded not a chink. He had never seen one naked. What kind of an animal did the shell enclose with such impenetrable strength? He wanted to know, at once: he had the hard, stiff-necked thing between his hands, he tortured it with fingers and finger-nails; the mussel tortured him back. He vowed not to stir a step from the place until he had broken it open. The mussel took a different vow. She would not allow herself to be seen. Why should she be so modest, he thought, I shall let her go afterwards, as far as I'm concerned I shall shut her up again, I shan't hurt her, I promise I shan't, if she's deaf then God can surely explain to her what I'm promising. He argued with her for several hours. But his words were as impotent as his fingers. He hated roundabout methods, he liked to reach his goal the direct way. Towards evening a great ship passed by, far out at sea. His eyes devoured the huge black letters on its side and read the name *Alexander*. Then he laughed in the midst of his rage, pulled on his shoes in a twinkling, hurled the mussel with all his strength to the ground and performed a Gordian dance of victory. Now her shell was utterly useless to her. His shoes crushed it to pieces. Soon he had the creature stark naked on the ground, a miserable fleck of fraudulent slime, not an animal at all.

Therese without her shell — without her dress — did not exist. It was always immaculately ironed. It was her binding, blue cloth.

She set great store by a good binding. Why did the folds not crumple up after a time? It was evident that she ironed it very often. Perhaps she had two. There was no visible difference. A clever woman. I must not crush her skirt. She would faint with grief. What shall I do if she suddenly faints? I shall ask her to excuse me beforehand. She can iron her skirt again immediately afterwards. While she is doing it I shall go into another room. Why does she not simply put on the other one though? She puts too many difficulties in my way. She was my housekeeper, I have married her. She can buy herself a dozen skirts and change more often. Then it will be quite sufficient to starch them less stiffly. Exaggerated hardness is absurd. The people in the tram were right.

It was not easy going up the stairs. Without noticing it, he slackened his pace. On the second floor he thought he was already at his own door at the top, and started back. The little Metzger boy came running down the stairs singing. Hardly had he seen Kien, when he pointed to Therese and complained: 'She won't let me in! She always shuts the door in my face. Scold her, Professor!'

'What is the meaning of this?' asked Kien threateningly, grateful for a scapegoat in the hour of need.

'You said I could come. I told her you said so.'

' "Her". Who is that?'

'Her.'

'Her?'

'Yes, my mother said, she's no right to be rude, she's only a servant.'

'Miserable brat!' shouted Kien and reached out to box his ears. The child ducked, tripped, fell forwards and to save himself from shooting down the stairs clutched at Therese's skirt. There was the sound of starched linen cracking.

'What!' cried Kien, 'more impertinence!' The brat was making fun of him. Beside himself with rage, he gave him a couple of kicks, dragged him panting to his feet by the hair, boxed his ears once or twice with his bony hands and pushed him out of the way. The child ran up the stairs whimpering. 'I'll tell mother! I'll tell mother!' A door on the floor above was opened and closed again. A woman's voice was heard raised in protest.

'It's a shame for the beautiful skirt,' Therese excused the violence of the blows, stood still and looked in a special way at her protector. It was high time to prepare her for what was to come. Something must be said. He too stood still.

'Yes, indeed, the beautiful skirt. "Youth's a stuff will not endure,"'
he quoted, happy for the chance of indicating in the words of a beautiful ancient poem what must later come to pass. A poem was always
the best way of saying something. Poems can be found for every
occasion. They call things by the most formal of names and yet they
are perfectly comprehensible. As he walked on up the stairs, he turned
back towards her and said:

'A beautiful poem, don't you think?'

'Oh yes, poems are always beautiful. You've got to understand
them, though.'

'Many things need understanding,' he said slowly, and blushed.

Therese jogged him in the ribs with her elbow, shrugged up her
right shoulder, twisted her head round the opposite way and said
pointedly and with a challenge in her voice: 'We shall see what we
shall see. Still waters run deep.'

He had the feeling that she meant him. He took her remarks for a
sign of disapproval. He regretted his immodest hints. The mocking
tone of her answer robbed him of the rest of his courage.

'I — er, I didn't mean it quite like that,' he faltered.

The door of his own flat saved him from further embarrassment.
He was relieved to be able to dive into his pocket for the keys. It gave
him at least a reasonable excuse for lowering his eyes. He could not
find the keys.

'I have forgotten the keys,' he said. Now he would have to break
open his own flat, as he had once broken open the mussel. One
difficulty after another; he could do nothing right. With a sinking
heart he dived into the other trouser pocket. No, the keys were
nowhere to be found. He was still searching, when he heard a sound
from the lock of the door. Burglars! The idea flashed through his
mind. At the same moment he saw her hand on the lock.

'That's why I brought mine with me,' she said, puffing herself out
with satisfaction.

How fortunate he had not shouted for help. The cry had been on
the tip of his tongue. He would never have been able to look her in
the face again. He was behaving like a small boy. Not to have his
keys with him, such a thing had never happened before.

At last they were inside the flat. Therese opened the door to the
room in which he slept and signed him to go in. 'I shall be back at
once,' she said, and left him there alone.

He looked round and breathed deeply, a man set free.

Yes, this was his home. Here no harm could come to him. He smiled at the mere idea that any harm could come to him here. He avoided looking at the divan on which he slept. Every human creature needed a home, not a home of the kind understood by crude knock-you-down patriots, not a religion either, a mere insipid foretaste of a heavenly home: no, a real home, in which space, work, friends, recreation, and the scope of a man's ideas came together into an orderly whole, into — so to speak — a personal cosmos. The best definition of a home was a library. It was wisest to keep women out of the home. Should the decision however be made to take in a woman, it was essential to assimilate her first fully into the home, as he had done. For eight long, quiet, patient years the books had seen to the subjugation of this woman for him. He himself had not so much as lifted a finger. His friends had conquered the woman in his name. Certainly there is much to be said against women, only a fool would marry without a certain testing time. *He* had been clever enough to put off the event until his fortieth year. Let others seek to emulate his eight years of testing! Gradually the inevitable had borne fruit. Man alone was master of his fate. When he came to think it over carefully, he saw that a wife was the only thing he had lacked. He was not a man of the world — at the word 'man of the world' he saw his brother George the gynaecologist before his eyes — he was everything else, but not a man of the world. Yet the bad dreams of these last days were doubtless connected with the exaggerated austerity of his life. Everything would be different now.

It was ridiculous to feel any more depression at the task before him. He was a man, what was to happen next? Happen? No, that was going too far. First he must decide when it was to happen. Now. She would put up a desperate defence. No matter. It was understandable, when a woman was fighting to save her last secret. As soon as it was over, she would fall in admiration before him, because he was a man. All women are said to be like that. The hour had struck. Resolved. He gave himself his word upon it.

Next: where was it to happen? An ugly question. True, all this time he had been staring straight at a divan bed. His eyes had been gliding over the bookshelves, and the divan bed with them. The mussel from the seashore lay on it, gigantic and blue. Wherever his eyes rested, the divan bed rested too, oppressed and clumsy. It looked as if it had to bear the whole burden of the bookshelves. When Kien found himself in the neighbourhood of the real divan bed, he would

twist his head round and the bed would come gliding all the way back
to its right place. Now that he had made a resolution on his word of
honour, he examined it more accurately and at greater length. His
eyes indeed, out of habit no doubt, still wandered from time to time.
But in the end they came to rest. The divan bed, the real live divan
bed was empty and had neither mussels nor burdens upon it. But
suppose it were made to carry a burden? Suppose it were covered
with a layer of beautiful books? Suppose it were covered all over
with books, so that it could not be seen at all?

Kien obeyed his inspired impulse. He collected a mass of books
together and carefully piled them up on the divan. He would have
preferred to select some from the top shelves but time was short; she
had said she would be back directly. He renounced the idea, left the
step-ladder as it was and made do with selected works from the lower
shelves. He laid four or five heavy volumes one on top of another,
fondled them briefly and hurried off in search of others. Inferior
works he rejected, so as not to hurt the woman's feelings. True she
knew nothing about them, but he selected carefully on her behalf all
the same, for she had insight and sensibility where books were concerned. She would be coming directly. As soon as she saw the divan
bed covered with books, orderly woman that she was, she would go
up to it and ask where the volumes belonged. In this way he would
lure the unsuspecting creature into the trap. A conversation would
easily arise on the titles of the books. Step by step he would go on
ahead, guiding her gradually on the way. The shock which lay before
her was the crowning event in a woman's life. He would not frighten
her, he would help her. There was only one way of acting, boldly and
with determination. Precipitancy was hateful to him. He blessed the
books in silence. If only she didn't scream.

A little while before he had heard a faint sound as though the door
in the fourth room had been opened. He took no notice, he had more
important things to do. He contemplated the armoured divan from
his writing desk, to see the effect, and his heart overflowed with love
and gratitude towards the books. Then he heard her voice:

'Here I am.'

He turned round. She was standing on the threshold of the neighbouring room, in a dazzling white petticoat with wide lace insertions.
He had looked first for the blue, the danger. Horrified, his eyes
travelled up her figure; she had kept on her blouse.

Thank God. No skirt. Now there would be no need to crush

anything. Was this respectable? But how fortunate. I would have been ashamed. How could she bring herself to do it? I should have said: Take it off. I couldn't have done it. So naturally she stood there. As though we had known each other for a long time. Naturally, my wife. In every marriage. How did she know? She was in service. With a married couple. She must have seen things. Like animals. They know what to do by nature. She had no books in her head.

Therese approached swinging her hips. She did not glide, she waddled. The gliding was simply the effect of the starched skirt. She said gaily: 'So thoughtful? Ah, men!' She held up her little finger, crooked it menacingly and pointed down at the divan. I must go to her, he thought, and did not know how but found himself standing at her side. What was he to do now — lie down on the books? He was shaking with fear, he prayed to the books, the last stockade. Therese caught his eye, she bent down and, with one all-embracing stroke of her left arm, swept the books on to the floor. He made a helpless gesture towards them, he longed to cry out, but horror choked him, he swallowed and could not utter a sound. A terrible hatred swelled up slowly within him. This she had dared. The books!

Therese took off her petticoat, folded it up carefully and laid it on the floor on top of the books. Then she made herself comfortable on the divan, crooked her little finger, grinned and said 'There!'

Kien plunged out of the room in long strides, bolted himself into the lavatory, the only room in the whole house where there were no books, automatically let his trousers down, took his place on the seat and cried like a child.

CHAPTER V

DAZZLING FURNITURE

'I'm not going to eat in the kitchen like a servant. The mistress eats at table.'

'The table does not exist.'

'I always say, there ought to be a table. Who ever heard of such a thing in a respectable house, eating off a writing desk? Eight years that's what I've been thinking. Now, it's come out.'

The table was bought together with a dining-room suite in walnut. The vanmen set it up in the fourth room, the one furthest away from the writing desk. Every day, usually in silence, they ate their lunch and their dinner at the new dining table. Hardly a week later Therese said:

'To-day I've a request. There are four rooms. Husband and wife are equal. That's the law these days. Two rooms each. The rights of one are the privilege of the other. I take the dining-room and the one next it. The master keeps the beautiful study and the large one next door. That will be simplest. The furniture stays where it is. No need to work it all out. It's a pity wasting all that time. Things must be settled. Then both parties can get on with it. The master settles down at his writing desk, the mistress gets on with her work.'

'Indeed, and the books?'

Kien considered her plan. He was not a man to be deceived. Even if it cost him two sentences, he would discover what she was after.

'They take up nearly all of my two rooms.'

'I will take them into my part!'

His voice was angry. Gracious, you couldn't get him to give up a thing. He was even upset about two or three sticks of furniture.

'And why, please? Gadding round and about never did books any good. I tell you what. Leave the books where they are. I won't touch anything. I'll take the third room instead. Fair's fair. There's nothing in the room, anyway. The master shall have the beautiful study all to himself.'

'Will you undertake to remain silent during meals?'

The furniture meant nothing to him. He would sell at a price. She often began to talk at meals.

'Yes indeed, I shall be glad not to speak.'

'I should prefer to have that in writing.'

Following in his footsteps, she glided at top speed to the writing desk. The contract, which he hastily drew up, was not yet dry when she set her name to it.

'You are aware of the contents of what you have signed!' he said, lifted up the paper, and to make doubly sure, read the sentences out loud to her.

'I hereby declare that all the books in the three rooms which have been ceded to me, are the true and lawful property of my husband, and that I shall in no circumstances whatever alter any particular relating to his property. In return for the cession of three rooms, I hereby undertake to remain silent during meals.'

Both were satisfied. For the first time since the wedding ceremony, they shook hands.

In this way Therese, who had before been silent out of habit, learnt how highly he prized her silence. Yet she kept meticulously to the terms of the agreement by which she held her concession. At table she passed the dishes to him in silence. She had voluntarily to forego an age-old, long cherished wish to explain to her husband everything that went on in a kitchen when a meal was being prepared. But she had the terms of the contract firmly in her head. The compulsion to silence was harder for her to bear than silence itself.

One morning as he was leaving his room, ready for his morning walk, she intercepted him with the words:

'Now I may speak. This isn't a meal. I couldn't sleep on that divan bed! It doesn't go with the writing desk. Such an expensive old piece, and that shabby divan. In a decent house there's a decent bed. It's a shame before visitors. I've had that divan on my chest a long time. I meant to say so only yesterday. But I kept it back. The mistress can't take no for an answer. The divan is much too hard! Who ever heard of such a hard divan. Hard isn't beautiful. I'm not one of your fly-by-nights. But a person has to sleep. Early to bed, and a real good mattress, that's how it should be, not a hard thing like that!'

Kien let her talk. Sure of her silence at other times of day he had drawn up the contract wrongly and made a condition only of her silence at meals. Technically she had not broken her contract. But morally she had laid herself open. Not that that would trouble a person of her kind. Next time he would be cleverer. If he spoke, he would give her an opportunity of speaking further. As if she were dumb, as if he were deaf, he stepped aside and went on his own way.

But she came again. Morning after morning she took up her place at the door and each time the divan became a little harder. Her monologue grew longer, his temper worse. Although he did not flicker an eyelid, he listened to her, carefully, to the end. She was as well informed about the divan as if she had slept on it herself for years. The insolence of her opinion impressed him. The divan was soft rather than hard. He was tempted to close her foolish mouth with a single sentence. He asked himself how far her impertinence would go, and in order to discover, he risked a small, malicious experiment.

One day while she was decrying the hard, hard, hardness of the divan, he scornfully approached his face to hers — two bloated cheeks and a black mouth — and said:

'You can know nothing about it. *I* sleep on it!'

'I know it all the same, the divan is hard.'

'Indeed! And how?'

She leered. 'I say nothing. I have my memories.'

Suddenly her leer recalled something. A piercing white petticoat machicolated with lace, a gross arm smiting books. They lay all about on the carpet, like corpses. A monstrosity, half naked, half a woman's blouse, briskly folded up the petticoat and laid it upon them, their shroud.

Kien's work this day was clouded. He could get on with nothing; before his meal he felt a sensation of nausea. Once he had managed to forget. For that reason he now remembered all the more clearly. At night he could not close an eye. The divan was contaminated. Had it but been hard indeed! A vile memory clung to it. Several times he got up and swept the burden off it. But the woman weighed heavy and stayed where she would. He thrust her emphatically off the divan on to the floor. No sooner did he lie down again, than he felt her presence near him. He could not sleep for loathing. He needed six hours sleep. His work to-morrow was doomed, like his work of yesterday. All evil thoughts, he noticed, centred on the divan alone. Towards four in the morning a happy idea saved him.

He ran to his wife's door, next the kitchen, as fast as he could and hammered on it until she recovered from her shock. She had not been asleep. She did not sleep much since her marriage. Still every night she secretly expected the great event. Now it had come. It took her several minutes to believe it. Softly she got out of bed, took off her

62

nightdress and slipped on the petticoat with the lace insertions. Night after night she had taken it out of her trunk and laid it over the chair at the foot of the bed; you never could tell. Round her shoulders she threw a large open-work shawl, the other and outstanding treasure of her trousseau. His first rejection of her she ascribed to the blouse. She pushed her huge, flat feet into crimson slippers. At the door she whispered hoarsely:

'For Heaven's sake, shall I open the door?' What she had really intended to say was, 'What has happened?'

'For the Devil's sake,' screamed Kien, 'no!' He was beside himself to find she could sleep so sound.

She saw her mistake. The masterful ring of his voice kept hope alive for a moment longer.

'To-morrow you will go out and buy a bed!' he shouted. She made no answer.

'Is that clear?'

She summoned all her art, and breathed softly through the door: 'As you please.'

Kien turned about, in confirmation of his act, slammed the door of his room so that the house shook, and at once fell asleep.

Therese pulled off her shawl, laid it tenderly on the chair and flung her massive bust across the bed.

Manners, indeed! What next! As though I cared. The conceit of the man! Is that a man? Here am I in my beautiful knickers with the expensive lace, and he doesn't bother. It can't be a man. I could have had a very different kind! What a lovely man that was who used to call at my other place! When I opened the door he tickled me under the chin and said, 'Younger every day!' That *was* a man, big and strong, he *did* look like something, none of your skin and bones. The way he stared at me! I'd only to say the word ... When he was there I went into the sitting-room and asked:

'What would madam prefer to-morrow? Roast beef with greens and roast potatoes, or boiled bacon with sauerkraut and dumplings?'

The two old people never could agree. He wanted dumplings, she wanted greens. So I walked up to the visitor and said:

'Mr. John shall choose!' He was their nephew.

I can see myself still, how I used to stand in front of him, and he — the cheek of him — he used to jump up and slap me on the shoulders, both hands at once — strong he was! — and say:

'Roast beef with greens and dumplings!'

63

I had to laugh. Beef with dumplings! Who ever heard of such a thing? You never saw such a thing in your life.

'Always bright and cheery, Mr. John,' I used to say.

A retired bank clerk he was, without a job, but a handsome bonus, all very well, but what do you do when you've eaten the bonus up. No, I'm for someone solid with a pension, or else a gentleman with something of his own. Well, I've managed it. Silly to throw it away for a lovely man, I must be careful. In my family we live to be old. Respectable people do. It makes a difference, early to bed and no gadding around. Even my old ma, the dirty old hag, was past seventy-four when she died. Not a natural death, hers. Starved she was, hadn't a bite of bread to put in her mouth in her old age. Wasted everything, she did. Every winter a new blouse. My old dad wasn't cold in his grave six years, and she took up with a fellow. He was a one, a butcher he was, knocked her about, and always after the girls. I scratched his face for him. He wanted me, too, but I didn't fancy him. I only humoured him to annoy the old woman. Everything for my children, she used to say. She looked a picture that time she came home from work and found her man with her daughter! Nothing had happened yet. The butcher tried to jump out of bed. I grabbed tight hold of him, so he couldn't get away until the old woman came right in and up to the bed. She did take on! Hunted him out of the room with her bare hands. She hugged hold of me, howled and tried to kiss me. But I didn't care for that and scratched her.

'No better than a step-mother, that's what you are!' I screamed. To her dying day she thought he'd done me wrong. He never did. I'm a respectable woman and never had anything to do with men. If a girl doesn't look out for herself, she'd have ten at every finger's end. And what would you do then? Prices going up every day. Potatoes cost double already. Where'll it end? You don't catch me that way. I'm a married woman with nothing to look forward to but a lonely old age. . . .

From the personal columns of the newspapers, her only reading, Therese knew certain delightful phrases which, in moments of great excitement or after coming to some weighty decision, would inter-weave themselves in her thoughts. Such phrases exercised a sedative influence upon her. She repeated to herself: nothing but a lonely old age, and fell asleep.

On the following day Kien was comfortably at work when two men brought the new bed. The divan disappeared and its horrid freight. The bed occupied the same position. On leaving, the removal men forgot to shut the door. Suddenly they reappeared carrying a wash-stand. 'Where do we put this?' One of them asked the other.

'Nowhere!' Kien protested. 'I ordered no wash-stand.'

'It's been paid for,' said the shorter of the two men. 'And the commode too,' added the other, hastily fetching it from outside, a wooden witness.

Therese appeared on the threshold. She had come in from shopping. Before entering the room she knocked at the open door. 'May I come in?'

'Yes!' shouted the removal men without waiting for Kien, and laughed.

'Already here, gentlemen?' She glided with dignity over to her husband, nodded to him familiarly with head and shoulder, as though they had been the closest friends for years, and said:

'You see how well I lay out your money. Everything inclusive. The master expects one piece, the mistress brings home three.'

'I don't want them. I only want the bed.'

'But why not; good gracious me, a person must wash.'

The removal men nudged each other. They probably believed that he had never washed. Therese was forcing him into a private conversation. He had no desire to make himself a laughing stock. If he were to start explaining about the wash-trolley they would think him a fool. He preferred to leave the new wash-stand where it was, in spite of its cold marble top. It could be at least half concealed behind the bed. In order to finish quickly with the inconvenient piece of furniture he helped to move it.

'The commode is superfluous,' he said (it was still where they had put it down) and pointed to the narrow, squat object which looked ridiculous in the middle of the lofty room.

'And the chamber?'

'The chamber?' The idea of a chamber pot in his library struck him dumb.

'Do you want to keep it here, under the bed?'

'What's the meaning of this?'

'Don't take up your wife before strangers.'

All this was simply an excuse for her to talk. She wanted to talk, and to talk and to do nothing else. For this purpose she was taking advantage of the removal men. But she could not impose her chatter on him. In comparison to her chatter, a chamber pot could be classed as a book.

'Put it here, by the bed!' he said briefly to the men. 'There, now you can go.'

Therese accompanied them to the door. She treated them with exquisite affability, and gave them, breaking her usual custom, a gratuity out of her husband's money. When she returned, he showed her the back of his chair, on which he was again seated. He wished to have no more exchanges with her, not so much as a look. As he had the writing desk in front of him she could not pass round him to look in his face and had to make do with an angry profile. She perceived how necessary justification was, and began to complain of the old wash-trolley.

'Twice every day the same job. Once in the morning, once in the evening. Is it reasonable? A wife wants a little consideration too. A servant does at least get ...'

Kien jumped up and, without turning round, gave his orders:

'Silence! Not another word! The arrangements will stay as they are. Further discussion is superfluous. From now on I shall keep the door into your rooms locked. I forbid you to step over my threshold as long as I am here. If I want books from your rooms I shall fetch them myself. At one o'clock and at seven o'clock precisely I shall come to meals. I request you not to call me; I can tell the time myself. I shall take steps to prevent further interruption. My time is valuable. Kindly go!'

He struck the tips of his fingers together. He had found the right words: clear, practical and superior. She would not with her clumsy vocabulary dare to answer him. She went, closing the communicating door behind her. At last he had found means to stop her chattering plans. Instead of making contracts with her, whose true meaning she failed to understand, he must show her who was master. He sacrificed something: the clear vista of those dim, book-filled rooms, the inviolate emptiness of his study. But he had in exchange something he valued more; the possibility of continuing his work, for which the first and most important condition was quiet. He panted for silence as others do for air.

All the same the first necessity was to accustom himself to the oppressive change in his surroundings. For some weeks he was irritated by the narrowness of his new quarters. Confined to a fourth part of his original living space, he began to understand the wretchedness of prisoners, whom he had earlier been inclined — for what exceptional opportunities for learning they have, men learn nothing in freedom — to regard as fortunate. It was all over now with his pacing up and down when a significant idea visited him. In days of old, when every door stood open, a healing wind coursed through the library. Through the lofty skylights poured illumination and inspiration. In moments of excitement he had only to rise and stride fifty yards in one direction, fifty yards back again. The unbroken view of the sky was as uplifting as the invigorating distance. Through the glass above him he could see the condition of the heavens, more tranquil, more attenuated than the reality. A soft blue: the sun shines, but not on me. A grey no less soft: it will rain, but not on me. A gentle murmur announced the falling drops. He was aware of them at a distance, they did not touch him. He knew only: the sun shines, the clouds gather, the rain falls. It was as if he had barricaded himself against the world: against all material relations, against all terrestrial needs, had builded himself an hermitage, a vast hermitage, so vast that it would hold those few things on this earth which are more than this earth itself, more than the dust to which our life at last returns; as if he had closely sealed it and filled it with those things alone. His journey through the unknown was like no journey. Enough for him to watch from the windows of his observation car the continued validity of certain natural laws; the change from night to day, the capricious incessant working of the climate, the flow of time — and the journey was as nothing.

But now the hermitage had dwindled. When Kien looked up from the writing desk, which was placed across one corner of the room, his view was cut off by a meaningless door. Three quarters of his library lay behind it; he could sense his books, he would have sensed them through a hundred doors; but to sense where once he had seen was bitterness indeed. Many times he reproached himself for thus of his own free will mutilating a living organism, his own creation. Books have no life; they lack feeling maybe, and perhaps cannot feel pain, as animals and even plants feel pain. But what proof have we that inorganic objects can feel no pain? Who knows if a book may not yearn for other books, its companions of many years, in some way strange to us and therefore never yet perceived? Every thinking being knows those moments in which the traditional frontier set by science between the organic and the inorganic, seems artificial and outdated, like every frontier drawn by men. Is not a secret antagonism to this division revealed in the very phrase 'dead matter'? For the dead must once have been the living. Let us admit then of a substance that it is *dead*, have we not in so doing endowed it with an erstwhile *life*. Strangest of all did it appear to Kien that men thought less highly of books than of animals. To these, the mightiest of all, these which determine our goals and therefore our very being, is commonly attributed a smaller share of life than to mere animals, our impotent victims. He doubted, but he submitted to the current opinion, for a scholar's strength consists in concentrating all doubt on to his special subject. Here he must let doubt surge over him in a ceaseless and unrelenting tide; in all other spheres and in life as a whole he must accept current ideas. He may question with full justification the exist-ence of the philosopher Lieh Tse. But he must take on trust the earth's circuit round the sun and the moon's round us.

Kien had graver things to consider and to overcome. The bedroom suite filled him with aversion. It disturbed him by constantly standing there, it wormed its way into his treatises. The amount of space it usurped contrasted with the pettiness of its meaning. He was delivered over to it, to these blockish lumps, what did he care where he washed or where he slept? Soon he would find himself discussing his meals, like nine-tenths of human kind; and the more plentiful they are the more they talk about them.

He had become absorbed in the reconstruction of a damaged text; the words rustled in the undergrowth. Keen as a hunter, his eye alert, eager yet cool, he picked his way from phrase to phrase. He needed a book and got up to fetch it. Even before he had it, that damnable bed crossed his mind. It broke the taut connections, it put miles between him and his quarry. Wash-stands confused the fairest trails. By broad daylight he saw himself asleep. Resuming his seat, he had to start again from the beginning, to find his way once more into the preserve, to recapture the mood. Why this waste of time? Why this despoiling of his energy and concentration?

Little by little he conceived loathing for the hulking bed. He could not change it for the divan; the divan was worse. He could not put it in another room; the other rooms belonged to that woman. She would never have agreed to give up what she had once got into her possession. He felt this, without discussing it with her. He would not even open negotiations with her. For he had gained one priceless advantage over her. For weeks not a word had passed between them. He took care not to break that silence. He would not rashly give her courage for more chattering; rather he would endure bed-table, wash-stand and bed. To give full sanction to the existing situation, he avoided her rooms. Such books as he needed thence, he would gather up at midday or in the evenings, after his meals, since, as he assured himself, he had legitimate business in the dining-room. During meals he looked past her. He was never wholly free of a lurking fear that she might suddenly say something. But distasteful as she was to him, he had to give her her due: she kept to the letter of the contract.

When washing, Kien closed his eyes at the touch of water. This was an old custom of his. He pressed his lids together more tightly than was necessary, to prevent the infiltration of the water. He could not safeguard his eyes too thoroughly. His old custom stood him in good stead with the new wash-stand. On waking in the morning, he rejoiced at the thought of washing. For at what other time was he released from the oppression of the furniture? Bending over the basin, he was blind to every one of these traitor objects. (Whatever diverted his attention from his work was fundamentally traitorous.) Plunging into the basin, his head under water, he liked to dream of earlier years. Then a still and secret emptiness had reigned. Happy conjectures fluttered about his rooms, colliding with no projecting surfaces. A divan, by itself, created little disturbance; it might hardly be there at all, a mirage on a far horizon, appearing only to vanish again.

Naturally enough Kien developed a taste for keeping his eyes shut. His washing concluded, still he did not open them. For a little longer he continued his blissful fantasy of the vanished furniture. Before he reached the wash-stand, as soon as he got out of bed, he closed his eyes, savouring in advance the relief so soon to be his. Like those people who determine to overcome a weakness, who keep careful tally of their doings and are at pains to improve themselves, he told himself that this was no weakness, rather a strength. It must be developed, even to the point of eccentricity. Who would know of it? He lived alone; the service of knowledge was more important than the opinion of the mob. Therese was not likely to discover, for how would she dare, contrary to his express prohibition, to surprise him when he was alone?

First of all he prolonged his blindness beyond his getting up. Next he made his way, blind, to his writing desk. When he was at work he could forget the objects standing behind him, all the more quickly if he had not seen them at all. In front of the desk he could give his eyes the run of all there was to see. They rejoiced in being open; their

69

agility increased. Perhaps they gathered strength in the periods of rest
he so generously allowed them. He protected them against sudden
shocks. He used them only where they could be fruitful: for reading
and writing. Books, when he wanted them, he now fetched blind.
At first he laughed to himself at these extraordinary tricks. Often
he selected the wrong place and came back to his writing desk all
unknowing, his eyes still closed. Then he noticed that he had been
three volumes too far to the right, one too far to the left, or on occasion
had even reached too low, missing his aim by an entire shelf. It
worried him not at all — he had patience — and a second time he set
out. Often enough he was overcome by the desire to peep at the title,
to spy out the back of the book, before he actually reached the shelves.
Then he blinked: in certain conditions he might give a quick look and
then turn away. More often he was master of himself and waited
until he was back at his writing desk, and there was no more danger in
opening his eyes.

Practice in walking blind soon made him a master of this art. In
three or four weeks he could find, in the shortest possible time, and
without any cheating or self-deception, any book he wanted, with his
eyes really and truly shut; a bandage would not more effectually have
blinded him. Even mounted on the steps, he retained his instinct. He
set them up exactly where he needed them. With long, eager fingers
he grasped hold of each side and clambered, blind, up the rungs. Even
at the top or climbing down, he easily kept his balance. Difficulties
which, in the days of unrestricted sight, he had never fully overcome,
because they were a matter of indifference to him, were swept aside
by the new process. He learnt even to manage his legs like a blind
man. Earlier they had hindered his every movement; they were far
too thin for their length. Now they moved firmly, with calculated
steps. They seemed to have acquired muscles and flesh; he trusted
himself to them and they supported him. They saw for the blind; and
he, the blind, had given the halt strong new legs.

While he was still uncertain of the new weapon, which his eyes were
forging for him, he abandoned some of his peculiarities. He no longer
took the brief-case full of books with him on his morning walk. If he
stood an hour irresolute before the shelves, how easily might his glance
fall on that evil trinity — as he called the three pieces of furniture —
which vanished but slowly, alas, from his conscious mind. Later
success made him audacious. Bold and blind, he would fill his brief-
case. Should its contents suddenly displease him, he would empty it

and make a new selection, as if all was as before: himself, his library, his future, and the punctilious, practical subdivision of his hours.

His room at least was in his power. Learning flourished. Theses sprouted from the writing desk like mushrooms. True, in earlier times, he had scorned and despised the blind for positively enjoying life despite this, of all, afflictions. But no sooner had he transformed his prejudice into an advantage, than the necessary philosophy came of itself.

Blindness is a weapon against time and space; our being is one vast blindness, save only for that little circle which our mean intelligence — mean in its nature as in its scope — can illumine. The dominating principle of the universe is blindness. It makes possible juxtapositions which would be impossible if the objects could see each other. It permits the truncation of time when time is unendurable. Time is a continuum whence there is one escape only. By closing the eyes to it from time to time, it is possible to splinter it into those fragments with which alone we are familiar.

Kien had not discovered blindness, he only made use of it: a natural possibility by which the seeing live. Do we not to-day make use of every source of power of which we become possessed? On what means and possibilities has mankind not already laid hands? Any blockhead ⸺ ⸺ ⸺ can handle electricity and complicated atoms.

⸺ ⸺ ⸺ ⸺ e man as well as another may well be blind, fill ⸺ ⸺ ⸺ ⸺ ngers, his books. This printed page, clear and ⸺ ⸺ ⸺ ⸺ other, is in reality an inferno of furious electrons. ⸺ ⸺ ⸺ conscious of this, the letters would dance before ⸺ ⸺ ould feel the pressure of their evil motion like so ⸺ ⸺ n a single day he might manage to achieve one ⸺ ⸺ It is his right to apply that blindness, which ⸺ ⸺ excesses of the senses, to every disturbing ⸺ ⸺ furniture exists as little for him as the army ⸺ ut him. *Esse percipi*, to be is to be perceived. ⸺ does not exist. Woe to the feeble wretches ⸺ own way, whate'er betide.

⸺ logic, it was proved that Kien was in no

Transit to: PTREE
Transit library: ALPH
Title: Auto-da-fé
Item ID: R0119796431
Transit reason: LIBRARY
Transit date: 4/13/2019,16:09

CHAPTER VI

MY DEAR LADY

THERESE's confidence, too, increased with the weeks. Of her three rooms only one, the dining-room, was furnished. The two others were unfortunately still empty. But it was in these two that she passed her time so as to spare the dining-room furniture. Usually she stood behind the door which led to his writing desk, and listened. For hours at a time, for whole mornings and afternoons, she stayed there, her head against a crack through which she could see nothing at all; arms akimbo and elbows pointing sharply in his direction, without even a chair to lean on, propped up on herself and the starched skirt, she waited, and knew exactly why she was waiting. She never tired. She caught him at it, when he suddenly began talking although he was alone. His wife wasn't good enough for him, there he was talking to thin air, a judgment on him. Before lunch and dinner she withdrew to the kitchen.

He felt contented and happy, at his work, far, far away from her. During almost all this time she was not two paces off.

True the thought sometimes occurred to him, that she might be planning a speech against him. But she said nothing and still nothing. He resolved, once a month, to check the contents of the shelves in her rooms. No one was safe from book thefts.

One day at ten o'clock, when she had just comfortably installed herself at her post, he flung open the door, aflame with inspectional zeal. She bounded backwards; she had all but fallen over.

'A nice sort of manners!' she cried, emboldened by the shock. 'Come into a room without knocking. You'd think I'd been listening at doors, and in *my* rooms. Why should I listen? A husband thinks he can take any liberty simply because he's married. Shame, that's what I say, shame! Manners indeed!'

What did she say? He was to knock before he could go to his books? Insolence! Ridiculous! Grotesque! She must be out of her mind. He would as soon slap her face. That might bring her to her senses.

He imagined the marks of his fingers on her gross, overfed, shiny cheeks. It would be unjust to give one cheek preference over the other. He would have to slap both at once. If he aimed badly, the red finger-marks on one side would be higher up than those on the other. That would be unpleasing. His preoccupation with Chinese art had bred in him a passionate feeling for symmetry.

Therese noticed that he was examining her cheeks. She forgot about the knocking, turned away and said enticingly: 'Don't.' So he had conquered without slapping her face. His interest in her cheeks was extinguished. With deep satisfaction he turned towards the shelves. She lingered, expectant. Why didn't he say something? Squinting cautiously, she discovered the changed expression of his features. Better go straight to her kitchen. She was in the habit of solving all her problems there.

Why did she have to say that? Now again he wouldn't want to. She was too respectable. Another woman would have thrown herself straight at him. You couldn't do anything with him. That was the way she was. If she were a bit older, she would have jumped at him. What sort of a man was that? Maybe he wasn't a man after all. Trousers have nothing to do with it, they wear them just the same. They aren't women either. There are such things. Who could tell when he'd want to again? It might take years with people like that. Not that she was old, but no chicken either. She knew that herself without being told. She looked thirty, but not twenty. All the men stared at her in the street. What was it the young man in the furniture shop said: 'Yes, around thirty, that's when the best people get married, whether ladies or gentlemen.' As a matter of fact, she'd always thought she looked forty; could you wonder, at fifty-six? But when a young man like that says a thing like that, all of his own, he must know what he's talking about. 'Well I ask you, the things you don't know!' she had answered him. Such a superior young man! He had guessed she was married too, not only her age. And there she was tied to an old man. Anyone would think, he didn't love her.

'Love' in all its parts of speech was a heavy-type word in Therese's vocabulary. In her youth she had grown accustomed to terser expressions. Later, when in her various places she had learnt this word along with many other things, 'love' still remained for her a foreign sound of wondrous import. She rarely took the blessed consolation between her lips. But she lost no other opportunity: wherever she read the word 'love' she would linger, and carefully sift all the surrounding matter. At times the most tempting 'situations vacant' were overshadowed by offers of marriage and love. She read 'good wages' and held out her hand; joyfully her fingers curled up under the weight of the expected money. Then her eye fell on 'love' a few columns further on; here it paused to rest, here it clung for broad moments. She did not of course forget her other plans, she did not open her hand to return the money. She merely covered it over for a brief, tremulous space with love.

Therese repeated aloud: 'He doesn't love me.' She drew out the pivotal word, pursing her mouth, and already she felt a kiss on her lips. This comforted her. She closed her eyes. She put the peeled potatoes on one side, wiped her hands on her apron and opened the door into her little room. Sparks made her close her eyes. Suddenly it was hot. Little globes danced through the air, glow-worms, red ones; it was narrow, the floor gaped in front of her, her feet fell into it; fog, fog, a strange fog, or was it smoke; wherever she turned her eyes, all was empty, cleared out, so much room; she clutched for support, anywhere; deadly sick she was; her trunk, her trousseau, who had taken them away; help!

When she came to herself, she was lying across the bed. Clean and orderly, the room reappeared to view, everything in its right place. Then she was afraid. First the room was empty, then full again. What was she to make of that? She wasn't staying here. The heat had made her come over queer. It was too small in that room, too shabby. All of a sudden she might die a lonely death.

She straightened the folds of her crushed skirt, and glided across to the library.

'I've just nearly died,' she said simply. 'It all went black. My heart stopped. Too much work and a bad bedroom. No wonder.'

'What, as soon as you left me, you felt sick?'

'Not sick, it all went black.'

'That's a long time. I have been standing at least an hour by the bookshelves.'

'What, so long?' Therese swallowed. She had never been ill since she could remember.

'I shall fetch the doctor.'

'I don't need the doctor. I'd rather move. Why shouldn't I sleep? I need a good night's sleep. The room next to the kitchen is the worst in the house. It's a servant's room. If I had a servant, she'd sleep there. You can't sleep there. You've got the best room yourself. I've a right to the second best, the next one. A man really thinks only he needs to sleep. If things go on like this, I'll be laid up, and where'll you be then? You've forgotten what a servant costs!'

What did she want of him? She was at liberty to move her rooms round as she liked. He didn't care where she slept. Owing to her fainting fit he did not interrupt her. Luckily fainting fits were not a common occurrence. Out of pity — false pity, as he told himself — he made himself listen.

'Who'd think of pestering? One room each. Then nothing can happen. I'm not one of those. Disgusting the way other women go on. Fit to make you blush. I don't need to. I want some new furniture! That large room holds a lot. I'm not a beggar, am I?'

Now he knew what she wanted: furniture again. He had slammed the door open in her face. He, then, was responsible for her fainting fit. Doors should not be flung open so roughly. The shock had affected her. He had been startled himself. She spared him her reproaches; he would allow her the furniture as a compensation. 'You are right,' he said, 'buy yourself a new bedroom suite.'

Immediately after lunch Therese glided from street to street, until she had found the best possible furniture shop. Here she listened to the prices of bedroom suites. Not one of them seemed outrageously expensive enough. When the proprietors, two fat brothers, each overreaching the other, at length named a price which would surely be too high for any honest person, she twisted her head round, jerked it towards the door and announced defiantly:

'You gentlemen seem to think my money's not honestly come by.'

She left the shop without further greeting and went straight home, to her husband's study.

'What do you want?' He was furious: at four o'clock in the afternoon she was in his room.

'I have to warn my husband of the price of things. If not, he'll be upset when his wife asks for so much money all of a sudden. The prices of bedroom suites these days! If I hadn't seen it with my own eyes, I wouldn't credit it. I've looked out a good one, nothing special. Everywhere the same prices.'

Reverentially, she uttered the figure. He felt not the least desire to chew over things which had been decided long ago, that morning even. Hurriedly he wrote out a cheque for the sum she had stated, pointed with his finger to the name of the bank where she was to cash it and then to the door.

Only when she was outside did Therese convince herself that the crazy price she had named was really written down on the paper. Then her heart bled for the beautiful money. She didn't need the most expensive bedroom suite. She'd always kept herself respectable and decent. Now that she was a married woman, was that a reason for breaking out? She needed no luxuries. Better buy one for half the price and put the balance in the post-office. Then she'd have something to fall back on. The years she'd have had to work to earn all that money! It's not to be reckoned in years. She'd slave for him plenty more years yet. What would she get out of it? Not a brass farthing! A servant gets more than the mistress. A mistress indeed, she'd have to look out for herself or nothing would ever come of it. Why was she such a fool? She ought to have made an agreement with him at the registry office. She ought to have her wages back again. She'd got the same amount of work to do. She'd got more work than before, there was the dining-room suite and the furniture in his room. It all had to be dusted. That wasn't nothing. She ought to have higher wages. There was no justice anywhere.

The cheque in her hand quivered with indignation.

At supper she put on her most evil smile. The corners of her eyes and mouth met close to her ears. Her eyes in their narrow slits glinted green.

'There'll be no cooking in this house to-morrow. I've no time. I can't be in two places at once.' Curious as to the effect of her words she paused. She was revenging herself on him for his wickedness. She was breaking her contract and talking at table. 'Am I to take the first thing I see because of getting your lunch? Lunch happens every day. A bedroom suite is only bought once. More haste less speed. No cooking to-morrow. No!'

'Really not?' A colossal idea had flamed up in his mind, devouring the needs and rights of everyday. 'Really not?' his voice sounded as if he were laughing.

'It's no laughing matter!' she replied, annoyed. 'Work, work, work, morning, noon and night. Am I a servant, then?'

In the highest good humour he interrupted her:

'I ask you only to proceed with caution! Go to as many shops as you can! Compare the prices with each other before making any decision. Shopkeepers are swindlers by nature. They always think they can make a woman pay double. In the lunch-hour you ought to have a long rest in a café and a good lunch, because you were unwell to-day. Don't come home! The weather is very hot, you will overtire yourself. After lunch you can take your time and look at some more shops. Don't hurry on any account! As for supper, you need have no anxiety.

I most strongly advise you to stay out the whole day until the shops close.'

He had forcibly expelled from his memory the fact that she had already found the bedroom suite, and demanded of him the exact sum for it.

'We can always have a bit of cold meat for supper,' said Therese, and thought: now he's after me again. It's easy to see when a person's ashamed of himself. Manners indeed, to make a convenience of your wife! You can do as you like with a servant. Excuse me, but you pay for that. Not with the mistress, though. That's why you make yourself mistress!

When she left the house next morning, Therese had already firmly decided only to buy her furniture from that superior young man who had known, as soon as he looked at her, both her age and about her marriage.

She cashed the cheque at the bank and immediately took half the money to the post-office. To inform herself more thoroughly about prices, she visited several furniture stores. She spent most of the morning obstinately haggling. She saw that her calculations about savings were quite right. She would be able to add still more money to them. Her ninth call was to the shop where she had protested at the prices on the previous day. They recognized her at once. The way she held her head and her manner of speaking in jerks impressed everyone who had seen her, once and for all. After their yesterday's experience they showed her the cheaper things. She examined the beds from top to bottom, tapped the wood and put her ear to the bedsteads to find out if they sounded hollow. Things are worm eaten these days even before you buy them. She opened every commode and stuck her nose in to find out whether it had not already been used. She breathed on the mirrors and then polished them over two or three times with a cloth which she had extracted from the two unwilling 'gentlemen'. All the wardrobes aroused her disapproval.

'Nothing would go into these. I ask you what sort of boxes do they make to-day! These may do for poor people. They haven't anything to put away. For our sort of things, we need space.'

They behaved obligingly in spite of her unassuming appearance. They took her for a fool. Fools are embarrassed at leaving without buying something. The brothers' psychology of clients was not exhaustive. It was confined to young couples, whose happiness they successfully kindled with ambiguous advice, to be understood cynically or cosily, according to taste. For the excitement of this elderly person, the pair of them, *bon vivants* and themselves elderly, had no interest left. After half an hour of offering personal guarantees, their zeal declined. Therese had been waiting for just this insult. She opened the enormous handbag which she carried under her arm, felt for the stout packet of notes and said pointedly:

'I must just see if I have enough money with me.'

Before the eyes of the two swarthy, tubby brothers, who had not reckoned on any such contents to her bag, she slowly counted over the notes. 'Merciful heavens, she *has* got money!' Delighted, they thought as one. As soon as she had done, she tucked the notes tenderly away in her bag, snapped it to, and went. On the threshold she turned round and exclaimed: 'You two gentlemen don't seem to value respectable customers!'

She directed her steps towards the superior salesman. As it was already one o'clock she hurried so as to get there before they closed for lunch. She created quite a sensation; among all the men in trousers and the women in short skirts, she was the only one whose legs, concealed under the starched blue skirt which reached to her feet, functioned in secret. It was clear to every passer-by that gliding was as good as walking. It was even better, for she overtook them all. Therese felt all eyes upon her. Like thirty, she thought and began to perspire with haste and pleasure. It gave her some difficulty to keep her head still. She put on an adored smile. Uplifted by her ears, broad wings, her eyes flew up to heaven and settled in a cheap bedroom suite. Therese, a lace-trimmed angel, made herself comfortable in it. Yet she did not seem to have fallen from the clouds when all of a sudden she fetched up in front of the shop she knew. Her proud smile was transformed into a joyful grin. She stepped inside and glided over towards the superior young man, swinging her hips with such vigour that her wide skirt billowed about her.

'Here I am again!' she said coyly.

'At your service, dear lady, what an unexpected honour! What brings you back to us, dear lady, if I may ask?'

'A bedroom suite. You know how it is.'

'I thought it must be that, dear lady. A double-bed, naturally, if I am permitted to use the expression.'

'Excuse me, everything is permitted you.' He shook his head, sadly.

'Oh no, not to me, dear lady. Am I the happy man? You would never have married me, dear lady. A poor shop assistant.'

'Why not? You never can tell. Poor people are human too. I don't hold with pride.'

'That's because you have a heart of gold, dear lady. I hope the gentleman you've made happy knows how fortunate he is.'

'I ask you, what are men like these days?'

'You surely don't mean, dear lady . . .'. The superior young man raised his eyebrows in astonishment. His two eyes were the moist adoring nose of a dog; he nuzzled her gently.

'They take you for a servant. But they pay you nothing at all. A servant gets wages.'

'So you are going to choose yourself a handsome bedroom suite instead, dear lady. This way please! Excellent, first class quality, I knew that you'd be coming again, dear lady, and I specially kept this on one side for you. We could have sold it six times over, honour bright! Your husband will be delighted with it. When you get home, dear lady, welcome home, darling, he'll say. Good afternoon, darling, you'll say, dear lady. I've got a bedroom suite for us both, darling — you follow me, dear lady, that is what *you* will say, and perch yourself on the gentleman's knee. Excuse me, dear lady, I say what is in my mind, no man could resist that, not a single man in the world, not even a husband. If I were married, I won't say if I were married to you, dear lady, a poor shop assistant like me, how could I dream of such a thing, but if I were married, even to an elderly lady, say to a lady of forty — but there, you couldn't even imagine that, dear lady!'

'Excuse me please, I'm no chicken.'

'I can't agree with you at all, dear lady, with your permission. I dare say you may be a shade over thirty, dear lady, but that's of no consequence. I always say: the important thing about a woman is her hips. Hips a woman must have, hips that can be seen. What's the point of having them at all if they can't be seen? Now here you can see for yourself, here you have the most magnificent . . .' Therese was on the point of crying out; enraptured, she could not find words. He hesitated an instant and completed the sentence: 'mattresses!'

She had not even glanced at the furniture. He talked her into suitable excitement, he approached his hand within an inch of her quivering hips and at the last minute replaced them by the well-designed, the magnificent mattresses. The gesture of resignation with which — poor shop assistant as he was — he bade farewell to her unattainable hips, moved Therese, if anything, even more profoundly. What a day! Here she was running with sweat again. Bewitched, she followed the movements of his lips, of his hand. Her eyes, usually aglint with every malicious light, were peaceful, watery, almost blue, as they obediently appraised the furniture. Of course it was magnificent. The superior young man knew everything. What a lot he knew about furniture! She felt almost ashamed in front of him. A bit of luck, she didn't have to say anything. What might he think of her! She knew nothing about furniture. None of the others had noticed. Why, because the others were stupid. The superior young man noticed everything at once. A good thing she didn't have to say anything. He had a voice like melted butter.

'I implore you, dear lady, don't forget the most important thing of all! As madam's husband's bed is made, so madam's husband does. Give him a good bed, you can do what you like with him. Believe me, dear lady. Married bliss doesn't only flow from the stomach, married bliss flows just as much from furniture, pre-eminently from bedroom furniture, and I should like to say, most pre-eminently from beds; the marriage bed if I may use the phrase. You follow me, dear lady, husbands are human beings. A husband may have the most charming lady wife, a lady wife in the bloom of her years; what use is she to him if he sleeps badly? If he sleeps badly, he'll be bad tempered; if he sleeps properly, well, he'll come a bit closer. I can tell you something, dear lady, you can rely on what I say, dear lady, I know something about business, I've been in the trade twelve years, eight in the same shop, what good are hips when a bed is bad? A man will disregard even the loveliest hips. Even madam's husband. You can tempt him with oriental stomach-dancing, you can display your beauty in all its charm, unveil it in front of him, nude as it were — but, I take my oath on it, nothing will help, if the gentleman is in a bad mood, not even if it were you, my dear lady, and that's saying something! Do you know what gentlemen have been known to do, supposing, dear lady, a worn-out old thing — the bed I mean — gentlemen have been know to fly out and find more comfortable beds. And what sort of beds, do you think? Beds made by this firm. I could show you testimonials, dear lady, written by ladies like yourself. You would be astonished if you knew how many happy marriages we carry with pride on our clear conscience. No divorces with us. We know nothing about divorces. We do our part, and our customers are satisfied. This is the one I particularly recommend, dear lady. All are of the best quality, guaranteed, dear lady, but this one I do most particularly recommend to your heart of gold, my dear lady!'

Therese drew nearer, if only to please him. She agreed with every word he said. She was afraid she might lose him. She gazed at the suite which he was recommending to her. But she could not have said what it was like. An anguished search took place in her for some excuse to prolong the pleasure of his butter voice. If she said 'Yes', and paid the money down, she would have to leave and that would be good-bye to the superior young man. She might as well have something for all that beautiful money. These people were making a profit out of her. There was no shame in making him talk a bit longer. Other people walk out of the shop without buying anything. They don't worry themselves. She was a respectable woman and never did such things. She could take her time.

She found no way out; to say something, she said: 'Excuse me please, that's easy said!'

'Permit me, dear lady, or if I may say so, my very charming lady, I would never deceive you. When I specially recommend something to you, then I specially recommend it. You can have implicit faith in me, dear lady, everyone trusts me. I owe you no proof of that, dear lady. Will you step this way a minute, sir?'

The chief, Mr. Gross, a diminutive mannikin with squashed features and hunted little eyes, appeared on the threshold of his separate office, and, small though he was, immediately folded himself into two even smaller halves.

'What can I do?' he asked and sidled, embarrassed, like a frightened small boy, into the orbit of Therese's wide-spreading skirt.

'Tell the lady yourself, sir, has any customer ever failed to trust my word?'

The chief said nothing. He was afraid of telling a lie before mother; she might box his ears. The conflict between his business sense and his reverence for mother betrayed itself in his expression. Therese saw the conflict and misinterpreted it. She compared the assistant to the chief. He wanted to chip in but didn't dare. To enhance the victory of the superior young man, she came to his help with a flourish of trumpets.

'I ask you, what do we want him for? Anyone would believe you from your voice alone. I believe every word. What's the good of lying? Who wants him? I wouldn't believe a word he said.'

The little man retreated with all speed into his private office. It was always the same. He had not so much as opened his mouth, before mother told him he was lying. With every woman, it was the same story. When he was a child, it was his mother, later it was his wife, an ex-employee. His marriage even had begun in the same way, with his having to soothe his typist whenever she complained of anything by calling her 'mother'. Since his marriage he was allowed no more girl clerks. But mothers kept coming into the shop all the time. That was certainly one of them. So he had had his private office built at the back. He was only to be called out of it when it was essential. He would take it out of Brute for doing this. The man knew perfectly well he couldn't play his part as chief in front of mother. That Brute wanted to be taken into partnership, so to make him look small he was showing him up in front of the customers. But Mr. Gross himself was head of the firm of Gross & Mother. His real mother was still alive and a partner in the business. Twice a week, Tuesdays and Fridays, she came to go through the books and shout at the assistants. She checked over the figures exactly; that was why it was so very difficult to cheat her of anything. He managed it all the same. If it were not for this cheating he couldn't have gone on living. For this reason he regarded himself, justly, as the real head of the firm; all the more so as her shouting stood him in good stead with his employees. On the days before her visits he could order them about as he liked. They tumbled over each other to obey him, because he might very possibly tell her on the following day if anyone had been impertinent. Tuesdays and Fridays she stayed all day in the shop, anyway. It was mousy quiet then, not a soul dared whisper; not even he; but it was beautiful. Wednesdays and Saturdays were the only days when they were impertinent. To-day was a Wednesday.

Mr. Gross sat on his high stool and listened to what was going on outside. That Brute talked like a waterfall. The fellow was worth his weight in gold, but a partnership he would not get. What's that, the lady's asking him to go out to lunch with her?

'The chief wouldn't hear of it, dear lady; it would be my dearest wish, dear lady.'

'Excuse me please, you can make an exception. I shall pay for you.'

'You have a heart of gold, dear lady, I am deeply touched, but it is out of the question, quite out of the question. The chief won't have liberties.'

'Well, he can't be such a brute.'

'If you knew my name, dear lady, you would laugh. Brute is my name.'

'I don't see anything funny in that, Brute is as good a name as another. You aren't a brute.'

'Warmest thanks for the compliment; I kiss your hand, dear lady. If I go much further I shall kiss that sweet hand in earnest.'

'Excuse me please, if anyone were to hear us, what would they think?'

'It wouldn't worry me, dear lady. I've nothing to be ashamed of. As I said, when one has such magnificent hips, excuse me — hands was what I meant, of course. Which have you decided on, dear lady? You have settled on this one?'

'But first I'm taking you out to lunch.'

'You would make me the happiest man in the world, dear lady, a poor salesman, I must ask you to excuse me. The chief . . . '

'He has nothing to say.'

'You are mistaken, dear lady. His mother is as good as ten chiefs. He's no worm, either.'

'What sort of a man is that? That's not a man. My husband's a man compared to him. Well then, are you coming? You go on as if you didn't like the look of me.'

'What are you saying, dear lady? Show me the man who doesn't like the look of you! You can lay me any odds you like, you'll never find him. He doesn't exist, dear lady. I curse my cruel fate dear lady. The chief would never allow us this glory. What, he'll say, there's a customer going out with a mere assistant, suppose the customer should suddenly run into her husband. Madam's husband, if I may say so, would be beside himself with rage. That would make a sensational scandal. The assistant'll come back to the shop, but the customer, never. Who will foot the bill? I shall! An expensive outing, that's what the chief will say. It's a point of view, dear lady. Do you know the little song, dear lady, about the poor gigolo, the pretty gigolo? "No matter though your heart should break . . ." well, let's leave it there! You'll be satisfied with the beds, dear lady.'

'But I ask you, you don't really want to. I'll pay for you.'

'Ah, if you were free this evening, dear lady, but what a question. Madam's husband is inexorable on that point. I must say, I understand him. If I were lucky enough to be married to a beautiful lady — well my dear young lady, I can't begin to tell you what care I should take of her. "No matter though her heart should break, I would not let her leave my side." The second line is my own. I've an idea, dear lady. I'll write a dance tune about you, dear lady, about you lying in the new bed, wearing nothing but pjyamas so to speak, with your magnificent . . . excuse me, we'd better leave it there. May I trouble you, dear lady, to step over to the cash desk?'

'But I wouldn't dream of it! First we'll go and eat.'

Mr. Gross had listened with mounting indignation. Why had that fellow Brute always to be running him down? Instead of being pleased to be taken out to lunch by mother. All these assistants got above themselves. Every single evening a different girl met him outside the shop, radiant young things, young enough to be his daughters. That mother might go away without buying the suite. Mothers didn't like having their invitations rejected. That fellow Brute took too much on himself. That fellow Brute was getting too big for his boots. Today was Wednesday. Why shouldn't Gross be master in his own shop on Wednesdays?

Listening with all ears, he felt his hackles rise. He felt that mother out there, who was so stubbornly arguing with his assistant, was seconding him for the fight. She spoke of him, Gross, in the same tone of voice as all mothers always did. How was he to speak to Brute? If he said too much, he would be certain to give him a back answer, being Wednesday, and he would lose a good customer. If he said too little, perhaps he wouldn't understand him. It might be best to issue a brief command. Should he look mother in the face as he gave it? No. Better place himself in front of her with his back to her; confronted by them both Brute would be more likely to be respectful.

He waited a short time until it was clear that a peaceful agreement was out of the question. Softly he jumped off his office stool and in two tiny strides was at the glass door. With a sudden movement, he flung it open, shot out his head — the largest thing about him — and cried in a shrill falsetto:

'Go with the lady, Brute!'

'The chief', dished up as his excuse for the hundredth time, stuck in his throat.

Therese twisted her head round, and snorted triumphantly: 'Excuse me, what did I tell you?' Before they went out to lunch she would have liked to reward the chief with a grateful glance, but he had long since vanished into his office.

Brute's eyes had an evil gleam. Scornfully he fixed them on the starched skirt. He took good care not to look into hers. His melted butter voice would have tasted rancid. He knew it and was silent. Only when they reached the door and he stood back for her, did his arm and lips move, out of habit, and he said: 'By your leave, dear lady!'

CHAPTER VII

MOBILIZATION

FROM beggars and hawkers No. 24 Ehrlich Strasse had for many years been free. The caretaker, in his little box adjoining the entrance hall lay in wait day after day, ready to spring upon any passing derelict. People who counted on alms from this house held in mortal terror the oval peep-hole at the usual height, under which was written PORTER. Passing it, they stooped low, as if bowing down in gratitude, for some particularly charitable gift. Their caution was vain. The caretaker troubled himself not at all about the ordinary peep-hole. He had seen them long before they crouched past it. He had his own tried and tested method. A retired policeman, he was sly and indispensable. He did indeed see them through a peep-hole but not the one against which they were on their guard.

Two feet from the floor he had bored in the wall of his little box a second peep-hole. Here, where no one suspected him, he kept watch, kneeling. The world for him consisted of trousers and skirts. He was well acquainted with all those worn in the house itself; aliens he graded according to their cut, value or distinction. He had grown as expert in this as he had been in former times over arrests. He seldom erred. When a suspect came in view, he reached out, still kneeling, with his short, stout arm for the door latch; another idea of his — it was fixed on upside down. The fury with which he leapt to his feet opened it. Then he rushed bellowing at the suspect and beat him within an inch of his life. On the first of every month, when his pension came, he allowed everyone free passage. Interested persons were well aware of this, and descended in swarms on the inmates of No. 24 Ehrlich Strasse, starved of beggars for a full month. Stragglers on the second and third days occasionally slipped through, or were at least not so painfully dealt with. From the fourth onwards only the very green tried their luck.

Kien had made friends with the caretaker after a slight incident. He had been coming back one evening from an unusual walk and it was already dark in the entrance hall. Suddenly someone bellowed at him:

'You sh—house you, off to the police with you!' The caretaker hurled himself out of his room and sprang at Kien's throat. It was very high up and difficult to reach. The man became aware of his clumsy misapprehension. He was ashamed; his trouser-prestige was at stake. With fawning friendliness he drew Kien into his room, revealed his secret patent to him and commanded his four canaries to sing. They were, however, unwilling. Kien began to understand to whom he owed his peace. (Some years ago now, all beggars had stopped ringing at his door bell.) The fellow, stocky and strong as a bear, stood there in the narrow space, close against him. He promised the man, who was after all efficient in his own line, a monthly gratuity. The sum which he named was larger than the tips of all the other tenants put together. In the first flood of delight the caretaker would gladly have battered the walls of his little room to pulp with his red-haired fists. In this way he would have shown his patron how much he deserved his thanks, but he managed to hold his muscles in check, only bellowed: 'You can count on me, Professor!' and hurled open the door into the hall.

From this time forward no one in the house dared to speak of Kien by any other title than 'Professor', although in fact he was no such thing. New tenants were immediately informed of this prime condition on which alone the caretaker would tolerate their staying in the building.

Scarcely had Therese left the house for the whole day than Kien put the chain up on the door and asked himself what day of the month it was. It was the eighth, the first was well past, no beggars were to be feared. He needed more quiet to-day than usual. A ceremony was in prospect. For this reason he had sent Therese out of the house. Time was short; at six o'clock, when the shops closed, she would come back. His preparations alone needed hours. Much manual labour had to be done. During its performance he could write his address in his head. It was to be a miracle of learning, not too dry, not too popular, interwoven with topical allusions, summing up the experiences of a well-filled life, the sort of speech to which a man of about forty would listen gladly. To-day Kien was abandoning his silence.

He hung his coat and waistcoat over a chair and hurriedly rolled up his shirt sleeves. He despised clothes, but he was willing to defend even them against furniture. Then he threw himself towards the bed, laughed and showed it his teeth. It seemed foreign to him although he slept in it every night. In his imagination it had grown more squat and more vulgar, so long was it since he had last looked at it.

'How goes it, my friend?' he cried. 'You've recovered yourself I see!' He had been in high good humour since the previous day. 'But now, out with you! And quickly too!' He seized it with both hands

by the top and pushed. The monstrosity did not budge. He pressed
his shoulders to it; he hoped for more from a second attack. The bed
merely creaked, evidently it was making fun of him. He panted and
gasped, he shoved it with his knees. The exertion was too much for
his feeble powers. He was overcome with trembling. He felt a great
rage swell up in him, but he tried speaking it fair.

'Be a good boy!' he flattered, 'you shall come back again. It's only
for to-day. I have to-day free. She's away from home. What are you
afraid of? You're not going to be stolen!'

The words which he thus lavished on a piece of furniture cost him
so much self-control that in the interim he forgot altogether about
pushing. For a long time he tried to talk the bed into obedience, his
arms wearily drooping at his sides; they ached cruelly. He assured the
bed that he meant it no harm, it was only that he had no use for it at
present. Could it not understand that? Who then had originally
bought it? He had. Who had laid out money on it? He had, and with
pleasure. Had he not until this very day always treated it with the
greatest respect? Only out of respect had he deliberately disregarded
it. A person is not always in the mood to show respect. But bygones
are bygones and time heals all wounds. Could it reproach him with a
single expression of dislike? Thoughts are free. He promised it a safe
return to the site which it had already conquered for itself; he pledged
his word to that; he took his oath on it!

In the end the bed might have given in. But Kien put into his words
all the force of which he was capable. None was left over for his arms,
none whatever. The bed stayed where it was, unmoved and mute.
Kien broke into anger. 'Shameless block of wood!' he cried. 'To whom
then do you belong?' He thirsted to administer a reprimand to this
insolent piece of furniture.

Then he remembered his powerful friend, the caretaker. On winged
stilts he left the flat, devoured the stairs at a flight, as though there were
a dozen or two instead of a hundred, and fetched from the little cell off
the hall the biceps he did not himself possess.

'I need you!' His sound and shape reminded the caretaker of a trom-
bone. He preferred a trumpet, he had one himself. But he liked per-
cussion instruments best of all. He bellowed only: 'Ah, womenfolk!'
and followed him. He was convinced the onslaught was to be on
Kien's wife. In order to feel this more certainly he told himself she had
already come home. He had seen her go out, through his spy-hole.
He hated her because she had been a common housekeeper and now

she was a professor's lady. In this matter of titles he was incorruptible, for he had once been a government servant; he stood by the consequences of having promoted Kien Professor. Since the death of his daughter, a consumptive, he had not thrashed a woman; he lived alone. His exacting profession left him no time over for women, and moreover unfitted him for conquests. He sometimes happened to make a grab under a servant girl's skirt and pinch her thigh. But he performed this operation with such vigour as to destroy altogether his always rather ill-founded hopes. The beating stage never came. For years he had longed in vain for an opportunity to smash up a nice piece of woman's flesh. He went first, banging his fists alternately against the wall and the banisters. In this way he got a little practice. The noise made the other tenants open their doors to contemplate the ill-assorted yet united pair, Kien in his shirt sleeves, the caretaker in his fists. No one dared to utter a word. Glances were exchanged only when they were safely past. When the caretaker was on his day not a midge dared buzz in the staircase and the boldest pin would not have dropped.

'Where is she?' he bellowed helpfully, when he got to the top. 'Now we've got it.'

He was directed into the study. The Professor remained standing on the threshold, pointed with grim pleasure his long index finger at the bed, and commanded: 'Throw it out!' The caretaker thrust his shoulders once or twice against it to test its resistance. He found it slight. Contemptuously he spat in his hands and put them in his pockets — he would not need them — thrust his head against the bed and in the twinkling of an eye had it outside. 'Heading the ball!' he explained. Five minutes later all the furniture out of all the rooms was outside in the passage. 'You've got plenty of books, anyway,' stumbled the helpful blockhead. He wanted to pause for breath without being noticed. So he spoke up simply, no louder than a person of normal strength. Then he went; from the staircase, having regained his breath, he bellowed suddenly back towards the flat: 'When you want anything, Professor, rely on me!'

Kien was not in a hurry to answer. He even forgot to put the chain up on the door, and merely cast a glance at the enormous junk heap which lay higgledy-piggledy in the corridor, a pile of unconscious drunks. Not one of them could have said for certain whose legs were which. Had someone cracked a whip across their backs, they would have found themselves quickly enough. There lay his enemies, trampling on one another's toes and scratching their varnished heads bare.

Stealthily, so as not to profane his holy day with ugly noise, he drew the door of the room to behind him. Greatly daring, he glided along his shelves and softly felt the backs of his books. He forced his eyes wide and rigidly open, so that they did not close out of habit. Ecstasy seized him, the ecstasy of joy and long-awaited consummation. In his first confusion he spoke words which were neither well composed nor intelligent. He trusted in them. Now they were all at home together again. They were persons of character. He loved them. He asked them to take nothing amiss. They had a right to be offended; had he not tried to assure himself of them by brute force? But he could not trust his eyes any longer, since he had had to make use of them in certain ways. He would confess these things only to them, to them he would confess everything. They could keep council. He misdoubted his eyes. He misdoubted many things. Doubts of this kind would make his enemies rejoice. He had many enemies. He would name no names. For to-day was a great day in the Lord. He would pass over these things. Reinstated in his rights, he could once more forgive and love.

As he paced up and down them the shelves grew longer, the library rose up again as of old, more inviolate, more withdrawn, so that his enemies appeared all the more ridiculous. How could they have dared to quarter this living body, this whole, by closing the doors? No tortures had prevailed against it. With hands bound, tortured week after horrifying week, it had remained in very truth unconquered. A sweet air coursed once again through the reunited limbs of a single body. They rejoiced in belonging once again to each other. The body breathed, the master of the body breathed too, deeply.

Only the doors on their hinges swayed to and fro. His solemn mood was disturbed by them. Coarse and crude, they interrupted the vista. There must be a draught from somewhere. He looked up, the sky-lights were open. With both arms he seized the first communicating door, lifted it off its hinges — how his strength had grown! — carried it out into the hall and laid it across the bed. The same thing happened to the other doors. Hung over the back of a chair which the caretaker had thrown out mistakenly — as it belonged to the writing desk — Kien noticed his jacket and waistcoat. So he had opened the ceremony in shirt sleeves. He felt a trifle embarrassed, dressed himself respectably again and returned, somewhat more soberly, to the library.

89

Abashed, he excused himself for his earlier behaviour. Excess of happiness had made him interrupt the programme of events. Mean spirits alone care nothing for the way they approach the beloved. A noble soul has no need to play the great man before her. What need is there to convince her of a self-evident love? Let the beloved enjoy protection without display. In a solemn moment let him take her to his heart, not in the flush of wine. True love is spoken at the altar alone.

This avowal was now Kien's plan. He pushed the faithful old ladder to a suitable place and climbed up with his back against the shelves; his head touched the ceiling, his extended legs — the ladder — reached the ground, and his eyes embraced the whole united extent of the library; then he addressed his beloved:

'For some time, more precisely, since the invasion of an alien power into our life, I have been labouring with the idea of placing our relationship on a firm foundation. Your survival is guaranteed by treaty; but we are, I take it, sage enough not to deceive ourselves as to the danger by which, in defiance of a legal treaty, you are threatened.

'There is no need for me to call to mind the ancient and glorious story of your sufferings. I shall single out one incident alone, to display in all its nakedness before your eyes, how closely love and hatred are interwoven. In the history of a certain country, a country honoured in equal measure by all of us here, a country in which you have yourselves been the object of the greatest respect, the most profound love, nay even of that religious veneration which is your due, in the history of this country, I say, one fearful event took place, a crime of legendary proportions, a crime perpetrated by a fiendish tyrant at the instigation of an adviser more fiendish than himself against you, my friends. In the year 213 before Christ, went out word from the Emperor of China, Shi Hoang Ti, a brutal usurper who had even dared to arrogate to himself the titles 'the first, the auspicious, the godlike', that every book in China was to be burnt. This loutish and superstitious criminal was himself too ill-educated to understand at its true value the meaning of books, on the evidence of which his tyranny was opposed. But his first minister Li Si, though himself suckled on books, a contemptible traitor, led him by means of a subtle manifesto to undertake this unspeakable measure. Nay, for the mere crime of speaking of China's classical lyrics or works of history, the death penalty was to be inflicted. Oral tradition was to be rooted out with the written word. Only a wretched minority of books was excluded from the order of general confiscation; you yourselves will readily supply the names of the varieties: works on medicine, pharmacy, fortune-telling, agriculture and forestry — a vulgar mob of practical handbooks.

'To this very day, I tell you, the smell of that burning stings my nostrils. Of what avail the merited fate which within three years closed in upon this barbarous Emperor? He indeed died but the dead books did not live again. They were burnt for all time. Albeit, let me recall the fate which a few years after the Emperor's death overtook the traitor Li Si. He was deprived by the Emperor's successor, who had penetrated his fiendish nature, of the office of first minister which he had enjoyed for thirty years. He was loaded with chains, thrown into prison, and sentenced to a bastinado of a thousand strokes. Not one blow was forgiven him. By means of this torture they brought him to confess his appalling crimes. Not only had he his hundred thousand-fold massacre of books on his conscience but many other abominations. His later attempt to deny his confessions failed. In the market-place of the city of Hien Yang he was sawn in two, slowly, and by the longitudinal method which is of longer duration. The last thought of this bloodthirsty beast was of hunting. Nor was he ashamed to burst into tears. His entire progeny, from his sons to a seven-day-old great-grandchild, were wiped out, women as well as men, but instead of suffering a just death by burning they were allowed to die by the sword. And in China, the land where the family is held in highest esteem, the land of ancestor worship and of long personal remembrance, no family was left to preserve the memory of Li Si, the mass murderer; history was to be his only memorial, that very history whose existence the wretch, who had died under the saw, had himself tried to wipe out.

'Each time I come upon the story of this burning of the books in a Chinese historian I never fail to follow it by rereading in every available source the tale of the exemplary end of Li Si, the mass murderer. Fortunately it has been described over and over again. Until I have seen him sawn in half before my eyes ten times at least I can neither rest nor close my eyes in slumber.

'Often I have asked myself, in deep sorrow, why had this unutterable thing to take place in China, the Promised Land of all scholars? Our enemies, quick to take advantage, cite the catastrophe of the year 213 in opposition to us when ever we point to the great revelation of China. We can only answer that even in that country the number of the educated is, compared to the mass of the population, small almost to vanishing point. It often happens that slime from the bog of illiteracy overwhelms at one and the same time both books and the learned men who are a part of them. In the whole world no land is free from the operation of natural phenomena. Why should we ask the impossible of China?

'I know well that the horror of those days runs in your very bloodstream, like that of so many other persecutions. It is not coldness of heart or lack of better feelings which forces me thus to call to your minds the bloody witness testified by your illustrious forefathers. No, no, I speak only to rouse you, to gain your support for those measures by which we are to defend ourselves against the danger.

'Were I a traitor I could smooth over with fair words the catastrophe which threatens us. But it is I, I myself, who am responsible for that very situation in which we now find ourselves. I am a man of character enough to confess that to you. If you should ask me how I came so to forget myself — you have a right to ask this question — then I can only answer to my shame: I forgot myself because I forgot what our great teacher Mencius had said: They act, but know not what they do; they have their customs, but do not know how they came by them; they wander their whole life long, but still they cannot find their way: even so are the people of the masses.

'Always and without exception, the master tells us in these words, we must beware of these people of the masses. They are dangerous because they have no education, which is as much as to say no understanding. But the thing has happened; I preferred the care of your bodies, preferred your humane treatment to the advice of Meng, the great master. My short-sighted action has brought a heavy retribution. The character, not the duster, is the essential man.

'But let us beware of falling into the opposite extreme! Up to this moment not a hand has been laid on one letter of your pages. I could never forgive myself if anyone were to charge me with the least neglect of my obligation for your physical welfare. If any of you have any complaint to make, let him speak.'

Kien paused and stared around him half challenging, half threatening. The books were as silent as he; not one stepped forward. Kien went on with his well-prepared speech:

'I had counted on this response to my challenge. I see that you have absolute trust in me, and since you have deserved no less, I can now initiate you into the plans of our enemy. First of all I must surprise you with an interesting and important communication. At the general muster I became aware that in that part of the library which is in enemy occupation, unauthorized changes of alignment have been made. In order to avoid the creation of yet greater confusion in your ranks, I raised no alarm. I take this occasion immediately to contradict all rumours and herewith solemnly declare that we have yet no losses to mourn. I give my word of honour that the assembly gathered here to-day is in full force and competent therefore to take any decision. We are still in the position, as a complete and self-sufficient body, to arm ourselves in our own defence, one for all and all for one. What has not yet happened may yet happen. The morrow of this very day may find gashes in our ranks.

'I am well aware what the enemy intends by this policy of shifting your ranks; the enemy seeks to aggravate the difficulty of surveillance. The enemy believes we shall not dare to render void conquests in territory already occupied; trusting in our ignorance of these new conditions, the enemy seeks to initiate a policy of abduction, unnoticed by us, and without an open declaration of war. Have no doubts of this, the enemy will lay hands first of all upon the noblest among your ranks, upon those whose ransom will be highest. For at least the enemy has no thought of using these hostages to fight their own comrades. The enemy knows well how hopeless a prospect that would be. But the enemy needs for the prosecution of war money, money, and yet more money. What is a treaty to such a foe but a scrap of paper?

'Who among you would be reft from your native land, scattered through all the world, treated as slaves, to be priced, examined, bought, but never spoken to — slaves who are but half listened to when they speak in the performance of their duties, but in whose souls no man cares to read, who are possessed but not loved, left to rot or sold for profit, used but never understood? Who among you would choose this fate? Let him lay down his arms and surrender to the foe! Who among you feels a brave heart beating in his breast, a high soul, a great and noble spirit? Let him on with me to the Holy War.

'Do not overestimate the strength of the enemy, my people! Between the letters of your pages you will crush him to death; each line is a club to batter out his brains; each letter a leaden weight to burden his feet; each binding a suit of armour to defend you from him! A thousand decoys are yours to lead him astray, a thousand nets to entangle his feet, a thousand thunderbolts to burst him asunder, O you, my people, the strength, the grandeur, the wisdom of the centuries!'

Kien paused. Exhausted and uplifted, he collapsed on the top of the ladder. His legs trembled — or was it the ladder? The weapons of war which he had named were enacting a war-dance before his eyes. Blood was flowing; since it was the blood of books, he felt deadly sick. But he must not faint, he must not lose consciousness! Then gradually there rose a whirlwind of applause, it sounded like a storm rushing through a forest in leaf; from all sides came joyful acclamations. Here and there he recognized a single voice by the words it spoke. Their own words, their own voices, ah yes, these were his friends, his liege-men, they would follow him in the Holy War! Suddenly he straight-ened himself on the top of the ladder, bowed two or three times and — confused by his excitement — laid his left hand on his right breast, a place where he, like other men, had no heart. The applause showed no sign of abating. He felt as though he were drinking it in with eyes, ears, nose and tongue, with the whole of his moist, tingling skin. Never would he have thought himself capable of such words of fire. He remembered his stage fright before the speech — for what had his apologies been if not stage fright? —and he smiled.

In order to put a term to the ovation, he climbed down the ladder. On the carpet he noticed bloodstains and felt for his face. The pleasing moistness was blood, and now he did indeed remember that he had fallen on to the floor in the interval, but, prevented from losing con-sciousness by the outburst of applause, had then again climbed up the ladder. He ran into the kitchen quickly, quickly he must get out of the library — who could say if the blood had not already spurted on to the books — and carefully washed away all the red marks. It was better so, that *he* should be wounded and not one of his soldiers. Re-invigorated, filled with a new courage for combat, he hastened back to the scene of conflict. The tumultuous applause was silenced. Only the wind whistled mournfully through the skylight. We have no time now for songs of lamentation, he thought, or we shall be singing them next by the waters of Babylon. Afire with zeal he leapt upon the ladder, drew out his face to its sternest length and shouted in stentorian command, while the window panes above him rattled in terror.

'I am glad to see that you have come to your senses in time. But wars are not won by shouting. I assume from your approbation that you are willing to do battle under my command.

'I hereby declare:

'1. That a state of war is now in existence.

'2. That traitors will be shot out of hand.

'3. That all authority is united in one hand. That I am commander-in-chief, sole leader and officer in command.

'4. That any inequalities among those taking part in the war, be they of ancestry, reputation, importance or value, are for the time being abolished. The democratization of the army will be practically expressed in the following form: from to-day onwards each single volume will stand with its back to the wall. This measure will increase our sense of solidarity. It will deprive the piratical but uneducated enemy of the means to measure us one against the other.

'5. That the word is Kung.'

With this statement he ended his brief manifesto. He did not wait to see the effect of his words. The success of his earlier speech had swelled his sense of power. He knew himself to be borne up on the unanimous devotion of his entire army. He held the earlier expression of their approbation to suffice, and proceeded immediately to action.

Each single volume was taken out and placed with its back to the wall. As he held his old friends one by one in his hand — quickly and during the natural course of his work — it distressed him thus to reduce them to the namelessness of an army ready for war. In earlier years nothing could have persuaded him to such harshness. *A la guerre comme à la guerre*, he justified himself, and sighed.

The peace-loving works of Gautama Buddha, threatened with soft speeches to refuse military service. He laughed scornfully and cried: 'Try if you like!' Confidently as his words rang out, his confidence was nevertheless shaken. For the works of Buddha filled several dozen volumes. There they stood, shoulder to shoulder, in Pali, in Sanskrit, in Chinese and Japanese, Tibetan, English, German, French and Italian translations, an entire company, a force which commanded some respect. Their conduct seemed to him pure hypocrisy.

'Why did you not notify your decision earlier?'

'We did not join in the applause, O master.'

'You might at least have raised your voices in disagreement.'

'We were silent, O master.'

'How like you!' with these words he cut short any further discourse.

Yet the pinprick of their silence remained with him. For who, in the decades past, had elevated silence into the first principle of his existence? He had, he Kien. Whence had he learnt the value of silence, to whom did he owe this decisive turn in his own development? To Buddha, the Enlightened. Buddha was usually silent. Possibly he owed much of his fame to this fact — his frequent silence. He had few words left over for knowledge. He answered all possible questions either with silence, or by making it clear that an answer was not worth while. The suspicion that he could not give an answer was not far off. For what he did know, his famous Chain of Causation, a primitive form of logic, he would apply to every possible occasion. If he did not remain silent, he merely repeated over and over again, exactly the same things. Take away the parables from his works, and what was left? Nothing but a miserable Chain of Causation. A poor-spirited creature. A mind which had put on fat simply through inertia. Can anyone imagine a thin Buddha? There is silence and silence.

Buddha revenged himself for the unspeakable insult: he remained silent. Kien made haste to turn his sayings all with their backs to the wall, hurrying to be free of this defeatist, demoralizing group.

He had assumed a heavy task. Warlike resolutions are easily made. But it is essential afterwards to keep firm hold of each individual. Those who objected to war in principle were only a minority. It was the fourth point of his manifesto which met with the greatest opposition, the democratization of the army, the first really practical measure. What a multitude of vanities were here to be overcome! Rather than renounce each his individual reputation, these idiots preferred to be stolen! Schopenhauer announced his will to live. Posthumously he lusted for this worst of all worlds. In any case he positively refused to fight shoulder to shoulder with Hegel. Schelling raked up his old accusations and asserted the identity of Hegel's teachings with his own, which were the older. Fichte cried heroically, 'I am I!' Immanuel Kant stood forth, more categorically than in his lifetime, for Eternal Peace. Nietzsche declaimed all his many personalities, Dionysus, anti-Wagner, Antichrist and Saviour. Others hurried into the breach and made use of this moment, even of this critical moment, to proclaim how much they had been neglected. At long last Kien turned his back on the fantastic inferno of German philosophy.

He imagined that he would find compensation among the less grandiose and perhaps all too precise French, but he was received with a shower of raillery. They mocked at his absurd figure. He could not manage his body, so he went to war. He had always been a lowly creature, so now he was lowering the status of his books in order to appear the greater himself. This was the manner of all men in love: they invent opposition, to appear victorious. What lay behind this Holy War? Nothing but a woman, an uneducated housekeeper, old-fashioned, past use, and without savour. Kien became furious: 'You do not deserve my leadership!' he yelled, 'I shall abandon you all and sundry to your fate!'

'Go to the English!' they advised him. They were far too much interested in *esprit* to let matters come to a serious clash with him, and their advice was good.

Among the English he found what he needed at the present time: the solid ground of facts on which they throve so well. Their objections, in so far as their rigidity permitted them to utter any, were sober, practical, yet well thought out. All the same they could not let him go without one serious reproof. Why had he taken the word for the day from the speech of a coloured race? At that Kien was beside himself and shouted abuse even at the English.

He cursed his fate which showered upon him one disillusion after another. Better be a coolie than a commander-in-chief, he cried, and ordered the many-headed multitude to be silent. For hours he worked at turning them all round. How easily he might have flicked them on their covers, but he did not trust himself to enforce his new disciplinary order, and did no one any hurt. Weary, oppressed, tired to death, he dragged himself along the shelves. He completed his task out of firmness of character, no longer out of conviction. They had robbed him of his faith. For the upper shelves he fetched the ladder. This, too, met him without affection, even with hostility. Time and again the ladder jumped off its hooks and settled rebelliously, flat on the carpet. With thin, nerveless arms he lifted it up and each time it seemed to weigh more. He had not pride enough left to scold it as it merited. Climbing up again, he treated the rungs with deference, lest they too should play him tricks. So bad were things with him, he must even temporize with the steps, a mere auxiliary. When the books in the quondam dining-room had been turned, he stared at his handiwork. He ordered a rest of three minutes duration. He passed the time, horizontal, panting, on the carpet, watch in hand. Then he turned to the neighbouring room.

97

CHAPTER VIII

DEATH

On the way home Therese aired her indignation.

She had taken the fellow out to lunch and in return he had been impertinent. She didn't want anything of him, did she? She'd no need to run after every man she saw. A married woman like her. She wasn't a servant girl to pick up just anyone.

At the restaurant first of all he took the menu and asked, what should he order for us. Like a fool, she said: 'Oh, but I'm going to pay.' The things he ordered! Now, she'd have been ashamed before all the people. He swore he was a better-class gentleman. Never had he dreamed he'd have to be a poor employee. She comforted him. Then he said, yes, on the other hand he was always lucky with women, but what did he get out of that? He needed capital, not very much, but still capital, for every man likes to be his own master. But women have no capital, only savings, wretched little savings; you can't start a business with trifles like that, some people might try, but not him, he was after the lot, no chicken feed for him.

Before he begins on his second cutlet he's taking her hand and saying: 'This is the hand which will make my fortune.'

Then he tickles her. He could tickle beautifully. Nobody ever called her his little fortune before. And does she want to take shares in his business?

But where has the money come from all of a sudden?

Then he laughs and says: my sweetheart will give me the money.

She feels the blood rush to her head with rage. What does he want a sweetheart for when she's there, she's human too.

How old is your sweetheart? she asks.

Thirty, he says.

Is she pretty, she asks.

Pretty as a picture, says he.

Then she asks, couldn't she see a photo of her.

At your service, this very moment if you please. And all at once he sticks his finger into her mouth, such a handsome thick finger as he has too, and says: 'Here she is!'

When she doesn't answer, he chucks her under the chin, such a very

98

forward young man — what can he be up to under the table with his foot, squeezing close up to her, who ever heard of such a thing — stares hard at her mouth and says: he's all on fire with love, if he could only sample those magnificent hips? She can rely on him. He understands business inside out. She'll miss nothing with him.

Then she tells him straight, she puts truth above everything. She must frankly confess. She is a woman without any capital at all. Her husband married her for love. She was a simple employee like him. She doesn't mind admitting it to him. As for the sampling, well, she must see how she can fix things for him. She wouldn't mind trying. Women are like that. She's not like that as a rule, but she can make an exception. He needn't think she takes him because she must. In the street all the men stare at her. She's looking forward to it already. Her husband goes to bed on the stroke of twelve. He falls asleep at once, he's methodical like that. She has a room to herself, a room where the housekeeper used to sleep. There isn't a housekeeper any more. She can't bear her husband in the same room, she must have her night's rest. He's always taking liberties. And he isn't even a man. So she sleeps by herself where the housekeeper used to sleep. At twelve-fifteen she'll come downstairs with the front door key and open to him. He needn't worry. The caretaker sleeps heavily. He's so tired after his day's work. She sleeps all by herself. As for the bedroom suite, she was only buying that to make the flat look like something. She's plenty of time. She can arrange for him to come every night. A woman must get something out of life while she can. Before you know where you are you're forty and that's the end of the lovely time.

Good, he says, he'll dismiss his harem. When he's really in love, there's nothing he won't do for a woman. She ought to repay it as it's only right and fair, and ask her husband for the money. He'd take it from her — he wouldn't take it from any other woman — because to-night he's expecting the bliss of utter happiness, one night of love.

She puts truth above all, she'd like to remind him, and must inform him at once: her husband is stingy and grudges every penny. Never lets a thing out of his hands, not even a book. If she had money, now, she'd invest it at once in his business. Anyone would trust him on his word alone, anyone would have confidence in a man like him. Let him come along to-night. She's looking forward to it already. In her time there used to be a very good saying, it went: Time will tell. We all have to die some day. Such is life. Come round every night at twelve-fifteen and all of a sudden the money will be there. She didn't marry the old man for love. But a girl has got to think of her future.

Then under the table he moves away one of his feet and says: It's all very well, my good woman, but how old is your husband?

Past forty, she's sure of that.

Then he moves the second foot away under the table, gets up and says: 'Allow me, madam, this is beyond endurance.'

Please go on eating, she tells him. She can do nothing about it, but her husband looks like a skeleton and certainly isn't strong. Every morning when she gets up she thinks: To-day he'll be dead. But when she comes in with the breakfast, he's still alive. Her mother, God rest her, was just the same. Ill at thirty and not dead till she was seventy-four. And then she died of hunger. No one would have believed it, the dirty old hag.

At this the superior young man lays down his knife and fork for the second time and says: He can eat no more, he is afraid.

At first he wouldn't say why, then, when he did open his mouth he said: How easily a man can be poisoned! Here we two sit happily together savouring the sweetness of the coming night over our little dinner. The proprietor — or a waiter — out of sheer envy sprinkles a secret powder on our food and behold us both in the cold grave. There's an end of the love dream, before we've got into the very centre of bliss. But still he doesn't think they're going to do it; it's always found out in a public place. If he were a married man, he would live in terror. A woman stops at nothing. He knows women better than he knows himself, inside and outside, not only hips and legs, although those are the best in a woman if you understand a thing about it. Women are reliable. First they wait until the will is signed and sealed, then they make away with the husband and join hands in wedlock with the faithful lover across the fresh corpse. Naturally the lover keeps to his bargain and nothing ever comes out.

She had her answer ready at once. She wouldn't do it. A respectable woman like her. Sometimes things do come out, and then you go to gaol. A respectable woman doesn't go to gaol. Things would be much better, if you didn't have to go to gaol at once. The least little thing gets about and round come the police and you go to gaol in a minute. They don't care whether a woman can bear it. They poke their noses into every mortal thing. What business is it of theirs how a wife gets on with her husband? A wife has to put up with everything. A wife isn't human. And her man's no use for anything. Is it a man? It's no man at all. Nobody'll miss such a man. The best thing would be if her friend took an axe and hit him on the head in his sleep. But he locks his door every night because he's afraid. Her friend must think out how to do it himself. He says, nothing will come out. She won't do such a thing. A respectable woman like her.

At this the young man interrupts her. She mustn't shout so loud. He deeply regrets this unfortunate misunderstanding. Does she mean to say that he wants her to commit murder by poisoning? He's a kind-hearted soul and he wouldn't hurt a fly. That's why all the women want to eat him up.

'They know a good thing when they see it!' she says.

'So do I,' says he. All at once he gets up, takes her coat off the stand and pretends she's cold. Really he only does it to press a kiss on her neck. The man's got lips like his voice. And what does he say as he does it: 'I like kissing a beautiful neck — think the matter over.'

When he sits down again he starts laughing: 'That's the way to do it! How did it taste? We shall have to pay now!'

Then she pays for both. Why was she such a fool? Everything has been lovely. But out in the street the trouble begins. First of all he says nothing for a long time. She doesn't know what to answer to that. When they get to the furniture shop, he asks:

'Yes or no?'

'Yes, if you don't mind! On the stroke of 12.15.'

'I meant the capital!' he says.

Quite innocently she makes him a pretty answer: 'Time will tell!'

Then they both go into the shop. He disappears at the back. The chief suddenly pops out and says:

'I trust you enjoyed your lunch. The bedroom suite will be delivered to-morrow morning. Or have you any other directions?'

'No!' she says, 'I'd just as soon pay for it now.'

He takes the money and gives her the receipt. Then out comes the superior young man and says to her face, quite loud, in front of everyone:

'You'll have to choose another gentleman for the post of boy friend, dear lady. I have offers from younger ladies than you. And prettier, oh very much prettier too, dear lady!'

Then she ran out of the shop, banged the door and in the open street in front of all the people, began to cry.

She didn't want anything of him, did she? She paid for his lunch and then he was impertinent. A married woman like her. There was no need for her to run after every man she saw. She wasn't a servant girl to pick up just anyone. She could have ten at every finger end. In the streets all the men stared at her. Whose fault was it anyway? It was all her husband's fault! She had to go running around buying furniture for him. And what did she get in return? Nothing but insults. He might at least do his own dirty work. He was no use for anything. It was his flat after all. It couldn't be all the same to him what sort of furniture he'd got among his books. The patience of a saint, she had. That kind of man thinks he can simply trample on you. First you do every mortal thing for him, and then he leaves you to be insulted in front of all the people. Suppose it happened to the superior young man's wife! But then he hasn't a wife. Why hasn't he a wife? Because he's a real man. A real man has no wife. A real man doesn't marry until he has something to show for it. That old stick at home has nothing to show at all! What has he got to show for himself? Nothing but skin and bone! People would take him for dead already. What's a thing like that got to go on living for? But it does go on living. A creature like that is no good for anything. Simply taking other people's beautiful money.

She entered the house. The caretaker appeared on the threshold of his little room and bellowed:

'They're up to something to-day, Mrs. Professor.'

'We shall see!' she replied and contemptuously turned her back on him.

On the top floor she unlocked the door of the flat. Not a soul was moving. In the hall the furniture was all piled up anyhow. Noiselessly she opened the door to the dining-room. Then she started back in horror. The walls suddenly looked quite different. They used to be brown, now they are white. They'd been up to something. What had they been up to? In the next room the same change. In the third, the one she had planned to turn into a bedroom, a light dawned on her. Her husband had turned all the books round!

Books belong with their faces to the wall so you can get a hold on their spines. That's how it has to be for dusting. How are you to take them out if not? Well, he can have it his own way. She was sick and tired of all this dusting. For dusting, people keep a char. He's got money and to spare. On furniture he simply throws money away. He'd do far better to save a little. The lady of the house has a heart too.

She began to look for him, to hurl this heart at his head. She found him in his study. He lay, stretched out full length on the floor, the ladder on top of him, overlapping his head by a few inches. The beautiful carpet underneath him was soiled with bloodstains.

Bloodstains are very difficult to clean off. What would be the best thing to try? He never thinks for a moment of all the work he makes! He must have rushed up the ladder in too much of a hurry and fallen off the top. Just as she said, he's not at all strong. If the superior young man could see this now. Not that she was gloating over it at all, she wasn't like that. Is this a way to die, now? The creature almost makes her sorry for him. She wouldn't care at all to climb up a ladder and fall off it dead. Who ever heard of such a thing, not looking what you're doing? Everyone to his taste. Eight years and more she'd been up and down that ladder every day, flicking off the dust, and had anything like that happened to her? A respectable person holds on tight. Why was he such a fool? Now all the books belonged to her. In this room only half of them had been turned round. They were worth a fortune, so he always said. He ought to know what he was talking about, he bought them. She wouldn't lay a finger on the corpse. She might hurt herself struggling with that heavy ladder and the next thing you know you're in hot water with the police. She'd better leave it all just as it was. Not on account of the blood. She wasn't afraid of blood. It wasn't real blood, anyway. How would a man like that have real blood? Good enough to make stains with and that's about all. A pity about the carpet. All the same, it all belonged to her now; the beautiful flat was worth something too. She'd sell the books at once. Who'd have thought of such a thing yesterday? But that's the way things happen. First of all you take liberties with your wife and next thing you're dead. She always knew it would come to no good, but it wasn't for her to say so. A man like that thinks there's no one else in the world. Going to bed at midnight and never leaving his wife a moment's peace, who ever heard of such things? A respectable person goes to bed at nine and leaves his wife alone.

Taking pity on the disorder which reigned on the writing desk, Therese glided up to it. She switched on the table-lamp and searched about among the papers for a will. She took it for granted that before he fell down he would have put it out ready. She didn't doubt that she would be his only heir, for she had never heard of any other relations. But among all the scholarly notes which she read through from top to bottom, there was no mention of money. Sheets covered with writing in strange characters she laid conscientiously on one side. They must be specially valuable and could be sold. Once at table he had said to her that the things he wrote were worth their weight in gold, but he did not write for the sake of gold.

After an hour's careful tidying and reading, she was sure, to her indignation, that there was no will. He had made no preparations. Up to his very last minute he had been the same, a man without a care for anyone but himself and not a thought for his wife. Sighing, she decided to go through the interior of the desk as well, taking each drawer in turn, until she lighted on the will. But her first attempt brought bitter disappointment. The desk was locked. He carried his keys in his trouser pocket. A nice mess she'd got herself into now. She couldn't well take anything out of his pockets. If she were to get blood on her by accident, there was no saying what the police might think. She came close up to the body, bent down, and could make nothing of the geography of his pockets. She was afraid of simply kneeling down. At critical times such as these she was in the habit of taking off her skirt first. She faithfully folded it up and entrusted it to a remote corner of the carpet. Then she knelt down a step away from the corpse, pressed her head for better support on to the ladder and drilled the index finger of her left hand slowly into his right pocket. She could not make much headway. He lay so inconveniently. Deep in the recesses of his pocket she thought she could feel something hard. Then to her horror it occurred to her that there might be blood on the ladder. Quickly she stood up and put her hand to her forehead, where it had lain against the ladder. She found no blood. But the vain quest for the will and the key had disheartened her. 'Something's got to be done,' she said aloud, 'he can't be left lying about here!' She put on her skirt again and fetched the caretaker.

'What is it?' he asked threateningly. He did not lightly allow himself to be disturbed at his work by a common person. Moreover he had not rightly understood her, because she spoke very low, as was seemly with a corpse about.

'Excuse me, please, he's dead.'

Now he understood. Old memories stirred within him. He had been on the retired list too long to yield to them at once. Only by degrees did his doubts give place to belief in so wonderful a crime. In the same measure, his behaviour altered. He became innocuous and mild, as in his mighty days of action, when he had had a wily bird to ensnare. He seemed almost thin. His bellowing stuck in his throat. His eyes, usually fixed straight enough to outstare his opponent, seemed to withdraw timidly into the corner as if laying an ambush. His mouth attempted to smile. But his stiff, waxed, close-thatched moustache prevented him from completing this. Two faithful stumpy fingers came to his help, and pushed up the corners of his mouth into a smile.

The murderess has been knocked out and has no fight left; in full uniform he stands out before the judge and explains how such things can be done. He is the witness for the crown in a sensational trial. The public prosecutor would have been lost without him. As soon as the murderess falls into other hands she'll deny everything.

'Gentlemen!' he cries in a ringing voice, while reporters take down every word he says. 'People need handling. Criminals are only people. I have been a long time on the retired list. In my leisure I study the goings and comings, the soul, as one might say, of the suspect. Handle her properly, and a murderess will confess her guilt. But I warn you, gentlemen, mismanage a person of this class, and your murderess will impudently deny everything and the prosecution can whistle for its evidence. In this sensational murder trial you can rely on me. Gentlemen I am witness for the prosecution. I ask you, gentlemen, how many witnesses like me will you find? I'm the only one! Now take careful note. These things are not as easy as you imagine. First, you have your suspicions. Next you say nothing but closely observe the culprit. Only half way up the stairs you begin to talk:

'A brute of a man?'

Ever since the caretaker had begun to look at her with such kindliness, Therese felt an indescribable terror. She could not explain this change. She would have done anything to start him bellowing again. He did not pound up the stairs in front of her as usual, he walked up submissively by her side, and when he asked for a second time 'A brute of a man?' she had still not understood whom he meant. At other times he was easy to understand. In order to put him back in the humour which she trusted, she said: 'Yes.'

He nudged her and while he kept his eyes humbly and slyly fixed upon her, he challenged her with his whole body to defend herself against the brutality of her husband. 'You've got to defend yourself.'

'Yes.'

'Accidents may happen.'

'Yes.'

'A man can be done in in no time.'

'Done in, yes.'

'Some extenuating circumstances.'

'Circumstances.'

'The fault was on his side.'

'His.'

'He forgot to make a will. '

'Impossible.'

'One needs a little something to live on.'

'To live on.'

'Why poison him?'

Therese had thought the same thing at the same minute. Not another word would she say. She wanted to tell him that the superior young man had tried to talk her into it, but she had refused. That's the sort of thing that gets you into hot water with the police. But she suddenly remembered that the caretaker had once been a policeman. He would know everything. He would say at once: Poisoning is against the law. Why did you do it? She wasn't going to put up with that. The superior young man was to blame. His name was Mr. Brute and he was nothing but an employee at the firm of Gross and Mother. First of all he wanted to be let into the house on the stroke of 12.15 to disturb her night's rest. Then he said he would take an axe and hit him on the head while he was asleep. She didn't agree to any of it, not even to the poisoning, and now she was in hot water just the same. What had it got to do with her, if her husband went and died? She had a right to the will. Everything belonged to her. Day and night she kept house for him and worked her fingers to the bone like a servant. He couldn't be trusted alone for a minute. She went out just one day to choose him a bedroom suite — he knew nothing about furniture. He went climbing up his ladder and got his death of a fall. Excuse me please, it made you almost feel sorry for him, perhaps it wasn't moral for a wife to inherit anything?

Floor by floor, she began to regain her courage. She convinced herself that she was innocent. The police could come as often as they liked. As the mistress of all within, she unlocked the door of the flat. The caretaker closely observed the light-hearted manner which she had now assumed. As far as he was concerned it did her no good. She had already confessed. He rejoiced at the coming confrontation of murderess and victim. She made way for him to go first. He thanked her with a sly wink and did not let her out of his sight.

The situation was clear to him at the first glance, he was still standing on the threshold of the study. She had put the ladder on top of the body as an afterthought. You couldn't catch him with a trick like that. He knew his way about.

'Gentlemen, I go immediately to the site of the crime. I turn to the murderess and I say: "Help me to lift this ladder!" Don't imagine, gentlemen, that I can't lift a ladder by myself' — he shows his biceps — 'I wanted to take note of the defendant's face. The face is the key to everything. You can read it all there. Men make faces.'

In the very midst of his discourse he noticed that the ladder was moving. He started. For one moment he was sorry the Professor was still alive. His dying words threatened to deprive the witness for the prosecution of a great part of his glory. With official strides he gained the ladder and lifted it with one hand.

Kien was just coming to himself, writhing with pain. He tried to stand up but could not.

'He's nothing like dead!' bellowed the caretaker, quite himself again, and helped him to his feet.

Therese could not believe her eyes. Only when Kien, strangely shrunken but still overtopping his supporter, was actually standing in front of her, saying in a weak voice 'That wretched ladder!' did she grasp that he was alive.

'Now that's the limit!' she shrieked. 'Who ever heard of such goings on! A respectable man, indeed! I ask you! What will people think of us!'

'Shut up, sh—house!' the caretaker interrupted her frenzied lament. 'Fetch the doctor! I'll put him to bed!'

He slung the lean Professor over his shoulder and carried him into the hall, where, among all the other furniture, the bed was standing. While he was being undressed Kien was persistently asserting: 'I was never unconscious, I was never unconscious.' He would not accept the fact that he had lost his senses for a short time. 'Where are the muscles to this clothes prop?' the caretaker was asking himself and shaking his head. Pity for the miserable skeleton made him forget the glorious trial scene of his dream.

Therese meanwhile had gone for the doctor. In the street she gradually calmed down. Three rooms belonged to her, she had that in writing. Only now and again she sobbed softly to herself:

'What next, being alive when you're dead, whatever next?'

CHAPTER IX

THE BED OF SICKNESS

FOR a full six weeks after his serious fall Kien lay in bed. After one of his visits, the doctor drew his wife aside and explained:

'It all depends on your nursing, whether your husband lives or dies. I can say nothing definite yet. I am still in the dark as to the true constitution of this strange case. Why did you not send for me sooner? Health is not a joking matter!'

'My husband always looked like that,' countered Therese. 'Nothing's ever gone wrong with him. I've known him for more than eight years. Where would doctors be if nobody was ever ill!'

This statement satisfied the doctor. He knew his patient was in the best of hands.

Kien did not feel at all comfortable in bed. Contrary to his will, the doors had been closed again, and only the one into the neighbouring room, in which Therese now slept, remained open. He wanted to know what was going on in the rest of the library. At first he was too weak to lift himself up. Later, despite violent shooting pains, he managed to bend the upper part of his body so far forward that he could see a part of the opposite wall in the adjoining room. Not very much seemed to have altered in that direction. Once he dragged himself out of bed and tottered to the threshold. Full of joyful anticipation, he hit his head against the edge of the door frame even before he had looked through it. He collapsed and fainted away. Therese found him soon after and to punish him for his disobedience let him lie there for another two hours. Then she shoved him back towards the bed, lifted him on to it and tied his legs firmly together with a strong cord.

She was on the whole perfectly satisfied with the life she was now leading. The new bedroom suite looked well. In remembrance of the superior young man she had a certain tenderness for it and was happy to sit among it. She had locked up the two other rooms and carried the keys in a secret pocket which she had sewed into her skirt for this purpose. In this way she always had at least a part of her property with her. She went in to her husband whenever she wanted; she had to nurse him, it was her right. She did in fact nurse him, day in day out she nursed him, following the instructions of the intelligent and trustful doctor. In the meantime she had looked through the interior of the writing desk and found no will. From her husband's delirium she learnt of a brother. Since he had been concealed until this moment, she believed all the more readily in his fraudulent existence. This brother simply lived to do her down, when it was a matter of her own hard-earned inheritance. Her husband had betrayed himself in his fever. She would not forgive him for being alive when he was dead, but she was ready to overlook it, since he still had his will to make. Wherever she was, she always seemed to be with him. For she talked all day long so loudly that he could hear her everywhere. He was weak, and must, as the doctor had advised him, not open his mouth. He could not interrupt her when she had something to say. During a few weeks she perfected her method of speech; everything which came into her head she spoke out at once. She enriched her vocabulary with expressions which she had thought often enough in the past but which had never actually crossed her lips. She was only silent on subjects connected with his death. She hinted at his crime in general terms:

'A man doesn't deserve so many sacrifices from a woman. A woman does everything for her husband, what does her husband do for her? A man seems to think he's the only person in the world. A woman has to stand up for herself and show him his plain duty. A mistake can be put right. Where there's a will there's a way. It would be much better if each party had to make a will at the registry office, so that one party wouldn't starve if the other party were to die. We've all got to die some day, that's life. Everything in its right place, that's what I say. I don't hold with children, that's what I'm here for. I'm human too. Love doesn't pay the bills. When all's said and done man and wife belong together. Not that a wife bears a grudge. Work, work, work, morning, noon and night. I have to keep an eye on him all day long. He may have another of his attacks, and all the trouble falls on me.'

When she had reached the end, she began at the beginning. Several dozen times every day, she said the same thing. He knew her speech, word for word, by heart. At each pause between her sentences he knew which variant she was about to select. The litany drove all thoughts out of his head. His ears, which he had at first sought to accustom to some movement of defence, became inured to a series of useless convulsions in rhythm. Flaccid and inert as he lay there, his fingers could not find their way to the ears which they should have stopped. One night he grew lids to his ears, he opened and closed them as he pleased, just as with his eyes. He tried them out a hundred times and laughed. They fitted exactly, they were soundproof, they grew as if they had been ordered and were complete at once. Out of sheer joy he pinched them. Then he woke up, his earlids had become ordinary bedclothes and he had dreamed. How unfair, he thought; I can close my mouth whenever I like, as tight as I like, and what has a mouth to say? It is there for taking in nourishment, yet it is well defended, but ears — ears are a prey to every onslaught.

When Therese came over to his bed, he pretended to be asleep. If she was in a good temper she said, softly: 'He's asleep!' If she was in a bad temper, she shouted loudly: 'The cheek of it!' She herself had no control whatever over her moods. They depended on the place in the monologue at which she happened to stop. She lived now entirely in her words. She said: 'A mistake can always be put right, where there's a will there's a way,' and grinned. Even if he who was to put the mistake right was fast asleep — she must nurse him back to health, and then there'd be a will and a way. Afterwards he could die again. But if, just at that moment, a man was thinking he was the only person in the world, then his sleep infuriated her the more. She proved to him on these occasions that she too was human, and woke him up with her 'The cheek of it!' Hourly she inquired into the state of his bank balance and whether all his money was in one bank. Everything need not be left in a single bank. She quite agreed, some should be *here* and some *there*.

His suspicion that she had an eye on his books had considerably lessened since the unlucky day of which he thought most unwillingly. He understood exactly what it was that she wanted of him: a will, a will, in which he disposed of money only. For that very reason she remained a total mystery to him, well as he knew her from her first to her last word. She was sixteen years older than he; as far as anyone could tell she would die long before he did. What was the value of money of which one thing only was certain: she would never gain possession of it. If, equally unreasonably, she had been grasping for his books, she might have been sure of some sympathy, despite his natural hostility towards her. Her eternal drilling on the nerve of money was a riddle to him. Money was the most impersonal, most inarticulate, most characterless object which he could imagine. How easily, without merit or effort, he had inherited it.

Sometimes his curiosity got the better of him and made him open his eyes, when he had only just closed them at the approaching footstep of his wife. He hoped for some change in her, some unfamiliar gesture, some new look, some native sound, which would betray to him why she spoke so unceasingly of money and wills. He felt at his best when he could relegate her to the one category where there was room for everything which he was unable, for all his education and understanding, to explain. Of lunatics he had a crude and simple idea; he defined them as those who do the most contradictory things yet have the same word for all. According to this definition Therese was — in contra-distinction to himself — decidedly mad.

The caretaker, who came daily to visit the Professor, was of a different opinion. He had nothing whatever to expect from the woman. Fears for his little monthly something grew within him. He was sure of the juicy titbit so long as the Professor lived. But who could rely on a woman? He shattered the normal routine of his day and every morning, for a full hour sat at the Professor's bedside, personally inspecting the position.

Therese led him silently in and — she thought him common — left the room at once. Before he sat down he glared contemptuously at the chair. Then he said 'Me on that chair!' or he fondled its back pity-ingly. As long as he was sitting on it, the chair quaked and creaked like a sinking ship. The caretaker had forgotten how to sit. In front of his peep-hole, he knelt. For hitting, he stood up. For sleeping, he lay down. He had no time over for sitting. Should the chair fall silent for a moment, he became uneasy and cast an anxious glance at his thighs. No, they hadn't grown thinner. They would have done for a show. Only when he could hear them again at work would he go on with his interrupted discourse.

'Women ought to be beaten to death. The whole lot of them. I know them. I'm fifty-nine. Twenty-three years I was a married man. Almost half my life. Married to the same old woman. I know women. They're all criminals. You just add up the poisoners, Professor, you've got books, have a good look at them. Women haven't any guts. I know all about it. When a man tries anything on with me, I smash his face in so he has something to remember me by, you sh—, I say, you dirty little sh—, how dare you? Now you try that with a woman. They run, that's what they do, I'd back my punch against anyone's, look here now, you won't see a better pair of fists. I can say what I like to a woman, she won't move an inch. Why won't she? Because she's frightened. Why's she frightened? Because she's got no guts! I've beaten a woman up a treat, you ought to have seen it. My old woman now, she was black and blue to the end of her days. My poor daughter, God rest her, I was that fond of her, there was a woman for you now,

as the saying is, I started on her when she was that high. "Here," says I
to my old woman — set up a screeching she did if I laid a hand on the
kiddy — "if she marries, she'll go to a man. Now she's little, she'd
better learn something about it. If not, she'll be running off and leaving
him. I won't let her have a man who doesn't know how to use his
hands. Some miserable beggar. A man ought to know how to use
his hands. I'm all for fists, I am." Now d'you think it was any good,
talking to her like that? Not bloody likely! The old woman got in
front of the kid, and I had to give it to them both. Because womenfolk can't interfere with me. Not *me*. You must have heard what a
screeching those two set up. Everybody was up, we had the whole
house listening to us. They've all got respect for me in this house.
You stop, I said, and maybe I'll stop too. Then they'd be as quiet as
you like for a bit. Then I'd sample a bit to see if they'd start up again.
Mousy quiet, that's how it had to be. I'd just give 'em one or two right-
handers. I couldn't stop sudden. I'd got to keep me hand in, see? It's
an art, that's what I say. You have to study it. I've got a colleague
now, first thing, he hits below the belt. His man crumples up at once
and can't feel another thing. That's right says my colleague, now I
can beat him up till I'm sick of it. Well, I say, what do I get out of it
if he can't feel anything? I'm against hitting a man when he's down,
he can't appreciate it. That's my motto, all along. What I say is a man
must learn how to use his fists so that he never knocks the object out.
Unconsciousness must not supervene. That's what I call beating up.
Any fool can knock a man out. That's nothing. Now look, I do that,
and spatter your brains out. You don't believe me? I'm not conceited.
Any fool can do that. See here, Professor, you can do it as well as
anyone. Maybe to-day's not the best time to start, with you on your
death bed. . . .'

Kien saw the fists growing at the recapitulation of the heroic deeds
which they had achieved. They were larger than the man to whom
they belonged. Soon they filled the entire room. Their red hairs
grew with them. They dusted the books vigorously. The fists stormed
into the next room and suffocated Therese in bed, where she was
suddenly lying. At some point one of the fists encountered her skirt,
which broke into pieces with stupendous clatter. It's a pleasure to be
alive! cried Kien with flashing voice. He himself was too insignificant
and thin to have anything to fear. He took the precaution of making
himself even smaller. He was as thin as the sheet. Not a fist in the
world could have had anything against him.

The trusty, well-made creature fulfilled its duty with speed. It had not been there more than a quarter of an hour and already Therese had been annihilated. Nothing could stand up to this force. But then it would forget to go; for no apparent purpose it would stay three-quarters of an hour longer. It did no harm to the books, but all the same gradually it became annoying to Kien. A fist should not talk so much, otherwise you cannot fail to notice that it has nothing to say. Its purpose is to strike. Having struck it should go away, or at least be silent. But it didn't bother about the nerves or the desires of an invalid; it emphatically enlarged on the subject of its one and only quality. At first it paid a little consideration to Kien and dilated on the criminal class of womankind. But, alas, when it had exhausted womankind, all that was left was a fist, *in se*. It was as strong as in the flower of its youth, and yet had already reached an age much and gladly given to detailed recapitulation. And so Kien was to learn its entire glorious history. Had he closed his eyes, it would have pounded him to a pulp. Even earlids would have served him little; no stopper could avail him against such bellowing.

The visit was not half done and Kien ached with old and long forgotten pains. Even as a child he had not been steady on his legs. It was as if he had never rightly learnt to walk. In the gymnasium he regularly fell off the bars to the ground. Despite his long legs he was the worst runner in the class. The teachers considered his physical feebleness as unnatural. In all other subjects he was, thanks to his memory, first. But what good was that? Nobody really respected him because of his ridiculous appearance. Countless feet were stuck out in his path, and he tripped religiously over them all. In the winter he was used as a snow man. They threw him down in the snow and rolled him over until his body acquired almost normal thickness. These were his coldest but also his softest falls. He had very mixed memories of them. His whole life had been an unbroken chain of falls. He had recovered; he suffered from no personal wounds. But his heart grew heavy and despairing when there began to unroll in his brain a list which he usually kept wholly and strictly secret. It was the list of innocent books which he had caused to fall; this was the true record of his sins, a catalogue most carefully kept in which the day and hour of each occasion was exactly set down. Then he saw the angelic trumpeters of the Last Judgment, twelve caretakers like his own, with cheeks blown out, and sinewy arms. Out of their trumpets the text of the catalogue burst upon his ears. In the midst of his terror Kien had to smile at the poor trumpeters of Michelangelo. They were cowering piteously in a corner; their trumpets they had hidden away behind them. Faced with such fine fellows as these caretakers, they laid down their long weapons abashed.

In the catalogue of fallen books, there figured as No. 39 a stout antique volume on *Arms and Tactics of the Landsknechts*. Scarcely had it curvetted off the ladder, with fearful crash, than the trumpeting caretakers were transformed into *landsknechts*. A vast inspiration surged up in Kien. The caretaker was a *landsknecht*, what else? His stocky appearance, his deafening voice, his loyalty for pay, his foolhardy courage which shrank from nothing, not even from women, his brag and bluster which yet said nothing — a *landsknecht* in the flesh!

The fist had no more terrors for him. Before him sat a familiar historical figure. He knew what it would do and what it would not do. Its hair-raising stupidity went without saying. It behaved itself as was suitable for a *landsknecht*. Unhappy, late-born creature, who had come into the world a *landsknecht* in the twentieth century, and must crouch all day in its dark hole, without even a book, utterly alone, shut out from the epoch for which it had been created, stranded in another to which it would always remain a stranger! In the innocuous remoteness of the early sixteenth century the caretaker dwindled to nothing, let him brag as he would! To master a fellow-creature, it suffices to find his place in history.

Punctually at eleven o'clock the *landsknecht* got up. As far as punctuality was concerned he was heart and soul with the Professor. He repeated the ritual of his arrival and cast a pitying glance at the chair. 'What not broken?' he asserted, and proved it by taking it in his right hand and battering it on the floor, which sustained the assault with patience. 'Nothing to pay!' he completed his sentence, and bellowed with laughter at the idea of paying the Professor anything for a chair he had sat through.

'Keep your hand, Professor! I'd squash it to a pulp. Good-bye. Don't kill the old woman! I can't stand the old starch box.' He threw a bellicose glance into the neighbouring room although he knew she was not over there. 'I'm for the young ones. See here, my poor daughter, God rest her, she was the one for me! Why not? Because she was my daughter? Young she was, and a woman, and I could do what I liked with her, being her dad. Well, she's dead and gone. That tough old starch box keeps on living.'

Shaking his head he left the room. At no time and place was he so much affected by the injustice of the world as when he visited the Professor. At his post in his little room, he had no time for contemplation. But as soon as he stepped out of his coffin into Kien's lofty rooms, thoughts of death swelled up within him. He remembered his daughter, the dead Professor lay before him, his fists were out of work and he felt that he was insufficiently feared.

He seemed absurd to Kien as he took his leave. *Landsknecht's* costume suited him well, but times had changed. He regretted the fact that his historical method could not always be applied. As far as he was familiar with the history of all cultures and barbarisms, there was not one into which Therese would have fitted.

The routine of these visits continued day after day in exactly the same order. Kien was too clever to shorten it. Before Therese was struck down, while the fist still had a legitimate and useful purpose, he could have no fear of it. Before his terrors had grown so violent that the secret catalogue of his pains stirred, *landsknechts* did not enter his mind, and the caretaker had not yet become one. When the man crossed the threshold at ten o'clock Kien would say to himself, filled with joy: a dangerous man, he will smash her in pieces. Daily he rejoiced in Therese's destruction, and raised a silent hymn of praise to life; he had always known about life, but never before had he seen reason to praise it. He omitted neither the Last Judgment nor the incidental mockery of the Sistine trumpeters; every day, as an obligatory part of his curriculum he carefully registered their discomfiture and duly dealt with them. Perhaps he only managed to endure the bleakness, rigidity and pressure of these long weeks while his wife was in the ascendant, because a daily discovery gave him strength and courage. In his life as a scholar discoveries were numbered among the great, the central events of existence. Now he lay idle, he missed his work; so he forced himself daily to re-discover what the caretaker was: a *landsknecht*. He needed him more than a crust of bread — of which he ate little. He needed him as a crust of work.

Therese was busy during visiting hours. The caretaker, that common person (whose conversation she had overheard on the first occasion) she only allowed into her flat because she needed the time. She was making an inventory of the library. It had made her think, her husband's turning the books round like that. Besides she feared the arrival of the new brother, who might even take away the most valuable pieces with him. So as to know what was really there, so as to prevent anyone from doing her down, one fine day, while the caretaker was with the patient abusing womankind, she began her important job in the dining-room.

First she cut the narrow empty margins from old newspapers, and thus armed, took up her stand before the books. She grasped one in her hand, read the name, spoke it out loud and wrote it down on one of the long paper strips. At every letter she repeated the whole name, so as not to forget it. The more letters there were, the more often she said the whole word, and the more strangely did it become transformed in her mouth. Blunt consonants at the beginning of a name, B, D, or G became sharp and sharper. She had a preference for anything sharp, and it gave her great pains not to tear the newspaper strips with her sharp pencil. Her wooden fingers could produce only capital letters. She became indignant with long scientific titles, because there was no room for them from one end to the other of her strips. One book, one line: that was her rule, so that the strips could be the more easily counted and would look more beautiful. She would break off clean in the middle of a name if she reached the end of the paper, and send the rest, which she did not want, to the devil.

Her favourite letter was O. From her schooldays she had retained some practice in writing Os. (You must all close up your Os as nicely as Therese, teacher used to say. Therese makes the best Os. Three years she stuck in the same class, but that was no fault of hers. It was teacher's fault. She never could stand her, because in the end she made her Os better even than her. All the children had to copy her Os. Not one of them wanted to copy teacher's Os any more.) So she could make an O as small as she liked. The neat regular circles were dwarfed by their neighbours, three times their size. If a long title had a great number of Os she would count first, *how* many, then write them all down quickly at the end of the line and use what room there was left at the beginning of it for the title itself, duly deprived of its Os.

When she had completed a strip she drew a line, counted up the books, made a note of the sum in her head — she had a good memory for figures — and wrote it down as soon as she had added it up three times to the same figure.

Her letters grew smaller week by week, the circles along with them. When ten strips were completed they were neatly sewn together at the top and became another piece of her hard-earned possessions — an inventory of 603 books, hidden away in the pocket of her clean skirt together with her keys.

After about three weeks she fell upon the name of Buddha, which she had to write out countless times. Its gentle sound moved her. *This* was the name for the superior young man, not Brute. She closed her eyes, standing on the top of the ladder, and breathed as softly as she could, 'Mr. Puda'. Thus her original form of the word, Puta, became Mr. Puda. She felt herself to be known by him and was proud because there was no end to his books. How beautifully he talked, and now he had written all these books too. She would have liked to take a peep inside. But she simply hadn't time.

His presence spurred her to haste. She saw that she was progressing too slowly. An hour a day was too little. She decided to sacrifice her sleep. She passed sleepless nights on the library steps, read and copied. She forgot that respectable people go to bed at nine. In the fourth week she had done with the dining-room. Her success gave her a taste for night life and she now felt happy only when she was wasting electricity. Her behaviour towards Kien gained in assurance. The old phrases acquired new intonations. She spoke on the whole more slowly, but with emphasis and a certain dignity. He had handed over the three rooms to her voluntarily. She was earning the books in them herself.

When she resumed the job in her bedroom she had overcome the last vestiges of fear. In broad daylight — with her husband lying awake in the neighbouring room — she climbed the steps, drew out a strip of paper and fulfilled her duty towards the books. In order to be quiet, she ground her teeth together. She had no time to talk, she must keep her head, otherwise a title might go wrong and she'd have to start all over again. The will, the most important thing of all, she had not forgotten, and she continued to nurse her husband with care and devotion. When the caretaker came, she interrupted her task and went into the kitchen. Anyway, he'd only disturb her at her work, the rowdy fellow.

In the sixth and last week of his sickness, Kien began to breathe more freely. His precise premonitions no longer came true. In the midst of her speech she would break off suddenly and fall silent. At a careful reckoning she now only spoke for about half the day. She said, as always, the same things; but he was prepared for surprises, and waited with beating heart for the great event. As soon as she was silent, he closed his eyes and went to sleep in earnest.

CHAPTER X

YOUNG LOVE

THE moment the doctor had said: 'To-morrow you can get up!'
Kien felt well again. But he did not at once leap from his bed. It was
evening, he intended to begin life as a healthy man in orderly fashion
at six o'clock in the morning.

The following day he began it. For many years he had not felt so
young and strong. While he was washing it seemed to him suddenly
that he even had biceps. The enforced rest had suited him well. He
closed the doors into the adjoining room and sat down bolt upright
at the writing desk. His papers had been disarranged, cautiously, but
he did not fail to notice it. He rejoiced at putting them in order; the
touch of the manuscripts was pleasant to him. An endless perspective
of work stretched before him. The woman had searched here for his
will, immediately after his fall, when fever had robbed him of his
senses. Among the varying moods of his sick-bed, one principle had
remained constant: he would not make a will since she set so much
store upon it. He decided to attack her sharply as soon as he saw her;
to order her back, swiftly and effectually, within her ancient limits.

She brought him his breakfast and wanted to say: 'The door must
be kept open.' But she had planned a smiling campaign to win the
will from him, and since she did not know his temper now that he
was again on his feet, she mastered herself so as not to irritate him too
soon. She merely stooped and pushed a small wedge under the door so
that it could not simply be closed again. She was in a reconciling
mood and willing to go roundabout to get her own way. He shot
to his full height, looked her boldly in the face and declared with acid
emphasis:

'Among my manuscripts I find an unholy disorder reigning. I cannot forbear to ask: how came the key into hands which had no right to
it? I have found it again in my left trouser pocket. I am regretfully
compelled to assume that it has been illegally removed, misused and
subsequently replaced.'

'That would be a fine thing.'

'I demand for the first, and also for the last time; who has been
tampering with my writing desk?'

'Think of that!'

'I insist on knowing!'
'I ask you, I haven't stolen anything!'
'I demand enlightenment.'
'Enlightenment, that's easy.'
'What is the meaning of this?'
'The things people do.'
'What people?'
'Time will tell.'
'The writing desk . . .'
'I always say . . .'
'What?'
'You've made your own bed, now you must lie in it.'
'I am not interested.'
'He said they were good beds.'
'What beds?'
'The double beds are a picture.'
'Double beds?'
'That's what they say.'
'I am not interested in matrimony.'
'Maybe you think I married for love?'
'I need peace!'
'A respectable person goes to bed at nine . . .'
'In future this door remains closed.'
'Man proposes, God disposes.'
'I have lost six full weeks owing to my illness.'
'Work, work, work, morning, noon and night.'
'This shall go no further.'
'And what has a husband done for his wife?'
'My time is valuable.'
'At the registry office both parties ought . . .'
'I shall make no will.'
'Who would think of poisoning?'
'A man of forty . . .'
'A woman of thirty.'
'Fifty-seven.'
'Nobody ever called me that.'
'It can be plainly read on your birth certificate.'
'Reading! Anyone can read.'
'Well!'
'A woman must have it in writing. Where are the joys of life?

Three rooms belong to the wife, one belongs to the husband, I've got that in black and white. A woman gives a man her everything and there she is — landed. Why was she such a fool? In black and white, that's the only way. Words don't count. One fine day the husband drops down in a fit. I don't even know which bank. A wife ought to know the name of the bank. If she doesn't know which bank, "No", she says. I ask you, am I right or not? What's the use of a husband without a bank? Her husband won't tell her which bank. What a man, he won't even tell her the bank. That's not a man at all. A man ought to tell her which bank.'

'Get out!'

'Anyone can get out. What does a wife get out of that? A husband should make a will. A woman never knows. A man isn't the only person in the world. His wife's human too. In the street all the men stare at me. Wonderful hips make all the difference. Get out won't do at all. The room must be kept open. I have the keys. He's got to get the keys first of all, then he can lock up. He can whistle for the keys, the keys are here!' she tapped her skirt — 'You don't want to get there, do you? You do, but you daren't!'

'Get out!'

'First a wife saves her husband's life, then she's told to get out. The man was dead. Who fetched the caretaker? He did, didn't he? He was lying under the ladder. I ask you, why didn't he call the caretaker himself? He couldn't move a finger. First he was dead, and now he grudges his wife the least little bit. That new brother would never have known. The bank must tell me. A woman wants to marry again. What did I get out of my husband? All of a sudden I may be forty and the men won't stare at me any more. A woman's human too. I ask you, a woman has a heart!'

From nagging she had fallen to sobbing. The heart, the heart a woman has, sounded on her lips like a broken one. There she stood propped up against the door jamb, her body for once as crooked as her head, presenting a piteous spectacle. She was determined not to move from her place, and quite expected a physical attack. Her left hand she held protectively over her skirt, in the very place where, in spite of its stiffness, it bulged with the keys and the catalogue of the books. The moment she had made sure of her property, she repeated: 'A heart! A heart!' and, overwhelmed by the strangeness and beauty of this word, fell once more to sobbing.

The scales fell from Kien's eyes; the hated will was forgotten. He saw her, wretched, begging for love; she wanted to seduce him, he had not seen her like this before. *He* had married her for the books, *she* loved him. Her sobs filled him with a great fear. I will leave her alone, he thought, alone it will be easier for her to calm herself. Hurriedly he left the room, the flat and the house.

So her touching solicitude for *The Trousers of Herr von Bredow* had been addressed to him, not to the book. She lay down on the divan only for love of him. Women are sensitive to the mood of their beloved. She had understood his embarrassment. His thoughts, as he left the registry office with her, she had read from his forehead as from an open book. She had wanted to help him. Women who love become weak. She had wanted to say: Come! but she had been ashamed and instead had swept the books to the floor. Translated into words this meant: As little as I care for books, so much do I care for you. This was love. Since then she had wooed him ceaselessly. She had forced her company on him at meals, she had forced the new furniture on him. She stroked him, as often as she possibly could, with the stiff skirt. Because she wanted the opportunity to talk about a bed, he had been given a bed instead of the divan. She had changed her bedroom and bought a new suite of furniture for two. Her harping on the will during his illness, was but a pretext for speaking to him, What was it she always said: Where there's a will there's a way. Poor, blinded creature! Months have passed since the wedding, and still she hopes for his love! She is sixteen years older than he, she knows that she will die before him, yet she insists that both of them must make wills. Surely she must have some savings which she would like to give to him. So that he shouldn't refuse them, she demands a will from him. What advantage could she gain from it since she would die so much earlier than he? On the other hand he would benefit by hers. She proves her love with money. There are old maids who will part with the savings of a lifetime, the savings of long decades, the best fragments of those very days, which in order to save, they had never fully lived — they will part with it all, in one fell swoop, to a man. How could she rise above her domestic sphere? Among illiterates money is regarded as the measuring rod for all things: for friendship, goodness, education, power, love. With a woman this simple state of affairs is complicated by her weakness. Merely because she wanted to give him her savings, she had to torture him six long weeks with the same words. She could not tell him simply to his face: I love you, you can have my money. She hides the key of the communicating door. He cannot find it and she may breathe his air. More he cannot have to do with her, she must content herself with his breath alone. He might not have asked himself, whether the bank where he houses his money, is safe. She trembles fearing he may lose his money. Her own savings are too scanty to keep him above water for long. In a roundabout manner, as if she herself were anxious, she asks him ceaselessly the name of his bank. She longs to rescue him from a possible disaster. Women are anxious for the future of their beloved. She has only a few years left to her. Her last efforts are to ensure his safety after her death. In her despair during his illness she had searched through his writing desk hoping for more precise data. In order not to upset him, she had not left the key in the lock; she had put it back where she had found it. She had, uneducated as she was, no conception of his precision or his powers of memory. She was indeed so uneducated that at the mere recollection of her speech he felt a slight nausea. He could not however give her any help. A person was not born into the world for love. He had not married for love. He had wanted to safeguard the future of his books, and she had seemed a suitable person for this purpose.

For the first time in his life Kien felt as though he were in the open street. Among the people whom he met, he differentiated men and women. The book shops which he passed held him up it is true, but by the very windows he had once avoided. Mountains of unseemly books did not disturb him. He read their titles, and walked on without even shaking his head. Dogs trotted across the pavement, met their own kind and snuffed at each other joyfully. He slackened his pace and looked at them in surprise. Close against his feet, a little packet fell to the ground. A lad pounced upon it, picked it up, banged into him and made no apology. Kien followed the fingers which were unfastening the little packet; a key appeared, on the crumpled paper there was writing. The reader grinned and looked up at the house. At a window on the fourth floor a girl was leaning out across a couple of mattresses hung out to air, she waved vigorously and disappeared as quickly as the key into the lad's pocket. 'What can he want with the key, a burglar, the maid throws him the key, she is his sweetheart.' At the next turning stood an important booksellers; he passed by on the other side. At the opposite corner a policeman was talking passionately to a woman. Their words, which Kien saw from afar, attracted him; he wanted to hear them. When he was close enough they separated. 'Good-bye!' croaked the policeman. His red face shone even in the broad daylight. 'Au revoir! Au revoir! Inspector!' sputtered the woman. He was fat, she was plump; Kien could not forget the pair. As he was passing by the cathedral, warm, uncanny sounds reached his ears. He would have sung in the same key, had his voice, like his mood, been at his command. Suddenly a spot of dirt fell on him. Curious and startled, he looked up at the buttresses. Pigeons preened themselves and cooed, none was to blame for the dirt. For twenty years he had not heard these sounds; every day on his morning walk he passed this spot. Yet cooing was well known to him out of books. 'Quite so!' he said softly, and nodded as he always did when he found reality bearing out the printed original. To-day he did not enjoy sober verification. On the head of a Christ, who grew out of a column, sickly and thin, his face drawn with suffering, a pigeon had perched itself. She was not happy alone, this was noticed by a second pigeon who joined her. This Christ's suffering is too much for people; they think he has toothache. That is not the case; he can't bear life amongst these pigeons; they probably carry on like this the whole day. Then he thinks how lonely he is. He mustn't think of this, or he will never achieve anything. For whom would Christ have died, if he had thought of his loneliness on the cross? — Yes, he was indeed very lonely, his brother never wrote to him now. For some years he had answered no letter from Paris until his brother grew tired of it and stopped writing. *Quod licet Jovi, non licet bovi.* Since women had become George's main interest he took himself for Jove. George was a lady's man, never alone; he could not bear to be alone, so he surrounded himself with women. A woman loved *him* too. Instead of staying with her, he had run away and was now complaining of his loneliness. Immediately he turned on his heel, and with long, hopeful steps walked through the same streets back to his home.

Compassion drove him along more swiftly than was good for his temper. He was the master of her fate. He could embitter and shorten the last years of this poor creature who had eaten her heart out in love for him. A compromise must be found. Her hopes are vain, he would never become a man of the world. His brother had fathered enough children, anyway. The posterity of the Kien family was already assured. Women are said to be uncritical, they cannot discriminate between people. For more than eight years she has lived with him in one flat. Christ would have been more easily seduced than he. Pigeons may betray the object of their lives, for they have none. A woman as well as his work — a crime against the nature of learning. He knows how to cherish her loyalty, within her limited powers she is quite useful. He hates thievery and embezzlement. Property is a matter not of greed but of order. He would never cry down anything in her favour. A woman, she had loved him in astonishing silence for eight long years. He had never noticed it. Only since her marriage her lips had overflowed with words. To escape her love, he will submit to her demands for his own sake. She fears the collapse of his bank? Good, he will tell her which it is, she knows it anyway, she cashed a cheque there once. She can then make inquiries whether the bank is a safe one. She wishes to give him her savings? Good, he will not object to this innocent pleasure; he will make a will, so that she may have a pretext for making hers. How little a human being needs to be happy. With this decision, he will satisfy her noisy and exaggerated love.

Yet to-day was one of his bad days. Secretly he hoped for failure. True love is never at rest and creates new cares even before the old ones are fully dead. He had never yet loved; he felt like a boy who knows nothing, but is about to know everything, and feels the same dark fear both of knowing and of not knowing. His head began to spin, he was chattering in his thoughts like a woman. Whatever thought occurred to him, he seized upon, without testing it, and then let go again without following it to its logical conclusion, because another, and not necessarily a better, thought had occurred to him. Two ideas dominated him, that of the loving, devoted woman, and that of the books, impatient for work. The nearer he was to his home, the more divided he was in himself. In his mind he knew what it was all about, and he was ashamed. He took love by the forelock and spoke harsh words to it, he seized on the ugliest of weapons: he brought Therese's skirt into the conflict. Her ignorance, her voice, her age, her phrases, her ears, all were effective, but the skirt tipped the balance. When Kien stood again before his door, the skirt lay shattered under the weight of the imminent books.

'How was it?' he said to himself. 'Lonely? I, lonely? And the books?' Every floor he climbed brought them nearer. From the entrance hall he called into the study: 'The National Bank!' Therese was standing before the writing desk. 'I will draw up my will!' he commanded and pushed her, more violently than had been his intention, aside. During his absence she had covered three beautiful clean sheets of paper with the word 'Will'. She pointed to them and tried to grin; but only a weak smile came. She wanted to say: 'I always say!' but her voice failed her. She all but fainted. The superior young man caught her in his arms and she came to herself again.

CHAPTER XI

JUDAS AND THE SAVIOUR

THE will, as he had written it down, she first suspected to contain a slip of the pen, then a silly joke, and last of all a trap. The capital he still had in the bank might cover his housekeeping expenses for another two years.

When she first set eyes on the figure she remarked innocently that there was a nought missing. She was convinced he had made a slip in writing. While he made sure that it was the right figure, she was counting on ten times as much and was bitterly disappointed. Where had he hidden the fortune? She wanted to get the superior young man the most beautiful furniture shop in the whole town. The will would just buy one like that of *Gross and Mother*. That much she had already learnt about business; for weeks past while going to sleep, she had been reckoning up the price of furniture. She had foregone the idea of a factory of her own, because she knew nothing about those things and wanted to have a say in the shop. Now there she stood, stunned, because the firm of *Brute and Wife* — she insisted on this trade mark — would not have a bigger start than that of *Gross and Mother*. On the other hand the superior young man was the heart and soul of *Gross and Mother*; once this heart and soul was theirs, the business would thrive so that the greater part of the profits could be invested in it. They wouldn't need anything. That's what love does for you. In a couple of years *Gross and Mother* could pack up. At the very point when she imagined the little proprietor behind his glass door, sighing and scratching his bald head because the new, high class firm of *Brute and Wife* was taking away all his customers, Kien said:

'There's no nought missing. There was one twenty years ago.'

She didn't believe him and said half teasingly: 'Well, then what's become of all the beautiful money?'

He pointed mutely to the books. That part of the money which he had spent on his daily life, he suppressed; it was in fact very little; moreover he was ashamed of it.

Therese was tired of the joke and asserted with dignity: 'The rest you are sending to that new brother. Nine parts go to the brother before you die, one part to your wife, when you're dead.'

She had unmasked him. She expected him to be ashamed, to write down that disputed nought before it was too late. She wasn't to be put off with chicken feed. She wanted the lot. She felt herself to be the steward for the superior young man and secretly made use of his arguments.

Kien did not quite hear what she said, for he was still gazing at the books. At last out of a sense of duty, he ran his eyes over the document and with the words: 'To-morrow we will take it to my solicitor!' folded it up.

Therese withdrew so as not to lose her temper. She wanted to give him time to think it over. He must surely find out that such things aren't done. An old wife is a nearer relation than a new brother. She did not think about the capital invested in the books, because three-quarters of it already belonged to her. All that concerned her now was the fortune apart from the library. She must postpone the visit to the lawyer as long as she could. Once the will was there, it was all up with the capital. Respectable people don't make a new will every day. They'd be ashamed before the lawyer. Therefore it would be better to make the right will at once, then there'd be no need for a second.

Kien would willingly have gone through all the formalities at once. But to-day he had a certain respect for Therese, because she loved him. He knew that she, a poor illiterate, would take hours to draw up a legal document. He did not offer her help for that would have humiliated her. Her feelings deserved at least that respect. There was meaning only in his conciliatory gesture, if he didn't betray that he had seen through her. He was afraid she might begin to cry if he referred to her intended offering. So he sat down to work, put off all thoughts of the will and left the door into her bedroom open. With the greatest energy he threw himself into an old thesis: 'On the influence of the Pali Canon on the form of the Japanese Bussoku Sekitai.'

At lunch they watched each other openly and spoke not a word. She was estimating the prospects for the rectification of the will, he was examining her document for orthographical errors, which it would naturally contain. Should he rewrite it or only correct it? One or other of these measures would be essential. His delicacy had been not inconsiderably blunted by the few hours of work. Yet enough of it was left to make him postpone his decision on this point until the following day.

All night Therese lay awake with business worries. As long as her husband worked, until twelve o'clock, the waste of light was very bitter to her. Since she had come so near to the fulfilment of her wishes, each wasted halfpenny hurt her twice as much as before. She lay cautiously and lightly on the bed, for she had the intention of selling the beautiful bedroom suite for new in her own shop. Up to now not a scratch had been made on it; it upset her to think the things might have to be repolished. Her responsibility for the bed and fear lest she should harm it kept her awake even after Kien was asleep and all her sums had come out. She had nothing more to think of, she was bored, but to-morrow she would not be bored.

For the remaining hours of the night she was busy increasing the sums of money she would inherit, by her skilfulness in writing Os. Competing women were soon left behind. Several popped up where they had no business to. Not one had a starched skirt. Not one looked like thirty. The best of them was more than forty, but her Os were nothing to write home about and the superior young man kicked her out at once. Men didn't stare at her in the street. You've got enough money, you filthy slut, screamed Therese to the impudent baggage, why don't you starch your skirt? Too lazy to do a hand's turn, and stingy on top of it, anyone can do that. Then she turned to the superior young man and was grateful to him. She wanted to tell him his beautiful name — Brute did not suit him at all — but she had forgotten it. She got up softly, switched on the bedside lamp, fetched her inventory from the pocket of her skirt and looked until she found the name; it made all the electric light in the world seem cheap. In her excitement she nearly burst out aloud with 'Puda'. But a name like that ought to be whispered. She turned the light out again and lay down heavily on the bed. She forgot the forethought with which it had to be treated. Countless times she said to him 'Mr. Puda'. But he was clever as well as superior and would not allow himself to be interrupted at his work. He looked at the women one by one. Many of them pretended they were bent double under the weight of their noughts. 'Now mind,' said Therese, 'that's old age, not the noughts!' She always put truth above everything. Mr. Puda had a beautiful clean sheet of paper in front of him, where he wrote down all the noughts ever so neat. Everything about him was neat and clean. Then he would pass his loving eyes over the paper and say with that voice: 'Deeply regret, dear lady, quite out of the question, dear lady!' And there was the old thing, thrown out. The very idea, an old thing like her! But what are women coming to these days? A little money, and they think they can have the loveliest man.

Therese was most pleased when Mr. Puda discovered that one such fortune brought to him was bigger than all the others. Then he said: 'Well I never! Dear lady, pray be seated, dear lady.' Just think, what an old thing such a woman must be. But she sat down just the same. Soon he would say to her: 'My dear young lady!' Therese winced slightly. She waited until he opened his mouth, then stepped forward and came between them. In her right hand she held her sharpened pencil. She only said 'Excuse me, one moment.' And on the paper, at the end of her capital, she made a beautiful O. Hers was right at the very top; she was after all the first woman with capital whom he had met. She might have said something now; modestly she withdrew and was silent. Mr. Puda did the talking for her: 'Deeply regret, dear lady, quite out of the question, dear lady.' Many an old thing burst into tears. So near and yet so far, that's no fun. Mr. Puda was not affected by their tears. 'A woman should look like thirty,' he said, 'then she has a right to cry.' Therese understood whom he meant and was proud. Eight years people go to school nowadays and don't learn a thing. Why don't they learn to make Os?

Towards morning she was too much excited to bear another moment in bed. She had long since got up when Kien woke at six. She kept perfectly still and listened to his movements, washing, dressing, tapping his books. The retirement of her life and his noiseless step had heightened to an abnormal degree the sensitivity of her ear for certain sounds. She knew precisely which way he turned, in spite of the soft carpet and his scanty weight. He went in one useless direction after another, only for the writing desk he didn't care. Not until seven did he approach it, and remained there a short time. Therese thought she heard the scratching of his pen. The clumsy creature, she thought to herself, his pen scratches when he writes an O. She waited for a second sound of scratching. After the events of the night she counted on at least two noughts. Yet she still felt herself to be miserably poor and murmured, 'At night it was all more beautiful'.

Now he stood up and pushed the chair aside; he had finished; the second time he had not scratched. She made towards him impetuously. On the threshold they collided. He asked: 'Have you done it?' She: 'Finished already?' He had slept off the last vestiges of his delicacy. This silly woman's story interested him no more. He had only remembered the will when he had found it among his papers. He read it through, bored, and noticed that the penultimate numeral of the figure was incomprehensibly wrong: instead of a five there was a seven. Annoyed, he corrected it and asked himself how it was possible to confuse a five with a seven? Presumably because both are prime numbers? This intelligent explanation, the only possible one since five and seven otherwise have nothing in common, mollified him. 'A good day,' he murmured. 'I must work and make use of it!' But first of all he wanted to settle with her, so that he would not be interrupted later on at his work. The collision hurt her not at all, she was protected by her skirt. He, naturally, hurt himself.

He waited for her answer, she for his. Since he gave none, she pushed him aside and glided to the writing desk. Right, there was the will. She noticed that the penultimate figure was now five instead of seven; a new nought she couldn't see anywhere. So, he had quickly cut her down still more, the old miser. As the figure was written there it was only a matter of twenty schillings. But if the new nought were there it would be 200. And if both the noughts were there it would be 2,000. She was not going to be done out of 2,000 schillings. What would the superior young man say, if he were to find out? 'Excuse me, dear lady, that's at the expense of our new business?' She must look out, or he would throw her out like the others. He needed a decent woman. He couldn't be bothered with a slut.

She turned round and said to Kien — he was behind her: 'The five has no business to be there!'

He took no notice. 'Give me your will!' he ordered curtly.

She heard him very well. Since yesterday she had been on the watch and noted his slightest motion. In all the many years of their life together she had not brought so much presence of mind to bear as now in these few hours. She grasped that he was demanding a will from her. The theoretical part of the sermon she had preached week after week came to her mind at once — 'At the registry office both parties ought . . . .'. Not a second had passed since his command before she delivered her counterstroke:

'Excuse me, is this a registry office?'

Genuinely indignant at his suggestion, she left the room.

Kien wasted no conjectures on her sharp answer. He assumed that she did not yet want to hand over her document. The wearisome visit to the solicitor was thus spared for to-day; all the better; he accepted the arrangement with joy and gave himself up to his familiar thesis.

The dumb show between the two of them lasted a few days. While he became calmer and calmer in the face of her silence — he was almost his old self again — her agitation grew from hour to hour. At meals she had to do herself physical violence to say nothing. In his presence she put not a single morsel into her mouth, for fear lest a word should fall out of it. Her hunger grew with her apprehensions. Before she sat down to table with him, she ate her fill in the kitchen. She trembled at every movement of his features; who could tell whether such a movement might not suddenly transform itself into the word 'Lawyer'? Every now and then he did utter a sentence; they were rare. She feared each one like a death sentence. Had he spoken more, her fear would have been splintered into a thousand little fears. He spoke so little, it was a consolation to her. But her fear remained vast and overpowering. When he began with 'To-day . . .' she would say to herself swiftly and with determination: 'There are no lawyers to-day!' and repeat this sentence with a speed which was for her new and unheard of. Her body broke out in sweat, even her face; she noticed it; if only her face didn't betray her! She rushed out and fetched a plate. She read wishes from his face which he did not have. She would have done anything for him now, if only he would not speak. Her officiousness aimed at those noughts but he had the advantage of it. She apprehended some fearful disaster. At her cooking she took especial pains; if only he would like it, she thought, and wept. Perhaps she wanted to fatten him up; to infuse him with strength for those noughts. Perhaps she only wanted to prove to herself how dearly she had earned her noughts.

Her contrition went deep. On the fourth night it occurred to her what the superior young man was: a sin. She called no longer on his name; when he crossed her path she gave him an ugly look and said: 'Everything in its proper time!' and nudged him with her foot, so that he should understand. The business no longer went well. A business must be earned before it can go well. One refuge yet remained, the kitchen; there she still seemed to herself the simple modest creature she had been before. There she almost forgot that she was the lady of the house, for there was no expensive furniture round about. One thing disturbed her even here, the directory which lay there dead, her property. For safety's sake she cut out the names of all the lawyers and disposed of them out of the house with the rubbish.

Kien noticed nothing of all this. It was enough for him that she was silent. Poised between China and Japan, he paused to assure himself that this was the outcome of his clever diplomacy. He had taken from her every excuse for speech. He had plucked out the sting of her love. In these days he was fertile in happy conjectures. An unspeakably corrupt text he had rehabilitated within three hours. The right characters simply streamed from his pen. The old thesis was completed at the end of three days. Of new ones, two had been started. Word by word, older litanies came back to him and he forgot hers. Gradually he was steering back to the time before his marriage. Her skirt reminded him occasionally of her existence, for it had lost much of its symmetry and stiffness. It rustled more swiftly and was emphatically no longer so well ironed. He ascertained the fact but did not worry his head about the causes. Why shouldn't he leave the door into her bedroom open? She never took advantage of his condescension and was careful not to disturb him. His presence at meals soothed her. She feared that he might put into practice his threat of discontinuing their common meals, and behaved herself, for a woman, with tact. He would have preferred rather less officiousness. She would doubtless get out of the habit: too may plates were superfluous. Each time she merely interrupted him in an important train of thought.

When, on the fourth day at seven o'clock, he had left the house for his usual walk, Therese glided — to all appearances the image of discretion — to the writing desk. She did not trust herself to go to it at once. She circled round it once or twice and without having accomplished anything started to tidy up the room. She felt that she had not yet got as far as she hoped and postponed her disappointment as long as possible. Suddenly she remembered that criminals were known by their fingerprints. She fetched her beautiful gloves out of her trunk (those very ones which had procured her husband for her), pulled them on, and cautiously — so as not to soil her gloves — she searched for the will. The noughts were still not on it. She feared that perhaps they really were there, but drawn so thin that no one would be able to make them out. A more exhaustive examination set her at ease. Long before Kien's return both of them, herself and the room, looked as though nothing in the least unusual had happened. She disappeared into the kitchen and re-enveloped herself in the universal gloom which she had broken at seven o'clock.

On the fifth day the same thing happened. She spent a little longer with the will and spared neither time nor gloves.

The sixth day was Sunday. She got up without enthusiasm, waited for her husband to go out for his walk, and looked as she had done every preceding day at the malicious figure written in the will. Not only the number itself, 12,650, but the very outline of each figure seemed to be written into her own flesh. She went to fetch a strip of newspaper and wrote down the number exactly as it was written in the

will. The figures resembled Kien's to the last hair; not even a graph-
ologist could have told them apart. She made use of the strip of paper
lengthwise so that she could put on as many noughts as she liked, and
added a round dozen. Her eyes brightened at the colossal result. She
caressed the strip two or three times with her rough hand and said:
'Isn't it beautiful!'

Then she took Kien's pen, bent over the will and changed the figure
12,650 into 1,265,000.

Her handiwork with the pen was as clean and precise as that which
she had just performed with the pencil. When she had completed the
second nought she was unable to straighten herself. The pen clutched
at the paper and began to outline another nought. Owing to the lack
of space this one would have had to be smaller and more compressed.
Therese recognized the danger in which she was poised. Any further
penstroke would have implied an error in the size and formation of the
other letters and figures. It would draw attention to this very spot.
She had all but destroyed her own creation. The strip with the many
noughts lay close at hand. Her glance which, to gain time, she had
diverted from the will, now fell on it. Her desire to make herself at
one stroke wealthier than any furniture shop in the whole world,
became larger and larger. If only she had thought of this sooner she
could have made the first two noughts smaller and so have squeezed in
a third. Why was she such a fool, everything could have been in order
by now!

She struggled desperately with the pen which wanted to write. The
effort was beyond her strength. With greed, anger and exhaustion she
began to gasp. The jerkiness of her breathing communicated itself to
her arm: her pen threatened to splutter ink on to the paper. Terrified
at this, Therese drew hurriedly back. She noticed that she had now
straightened the upper half of her body and began to breathe again —
rather more regularly. 'One must be moderate,' she sighed, and thinking of her lost millions interrupted her task for perhaps three minutes.
Then she looked to see if the ink was dry, put away the beautiful strip
of paper, folded up the will and laid it back where she had found it.
She did not feel at all satisfied; her desires aimed yet higher. Since she
had achieved only part of what was possible, her mood changed; suddenly she saw herself as a swindler and decided to go to church. It was
Sunday after all. On the door of the flat she pinned a note: 'Am in
church, Therese,' just as if this had been her most usual and natural
port of call for years.

She sought out the largest church in the town, the cathedral. A smaller one would only have reminded her how much more was owing to her. On the steps it occurred to her that she was not dressed. She felt utterly depressed, but turned round all the same and changed her blue starched skirt for her other blue starched skirt, which looked exactly the same. In the street she forgot to notice that all the men stared at her. In the cathedral she felt ashamed of herself. People were laughing at her. Is that a thing now, to laugh in church? She took no notice for she was a respectable woman. A respectable woman, she said in her thoughts with great emphasis, repeated it, and took refuge in a quiet corner of the cathedral.

There hung a picture of the Last Supper, painted in expensive oil colours. The frame was gilded all over. The tablecloth did not satisfy her. People don't seem to know what's beautiful, besides it was dirty. The money-bag looked as though you could touch it, thirty beautiful pieces of silver were inside, you couldn't see them, but still the money-bag was large as life. Judas held it tight. He wouldn't let go, he was so greedy. He grudged every penny. Just like her old man. That was why he had betrayed the Lord. Her old man is thin, Judas is fat and has a red beard. In the middle of it all sits the superior young man. Such a beautiful face, all pale, and eyes just as they should be. He knows everything. He's superior, but he's clever too. He looks at that money-bag. He wants to know how much. Anyone else would have to count it schilling by schilling; he doesn't have to, he knows it just by looking. Her husband's a dirty miser. To do such a thing for twenty schillings. She won't be done; the figure there was a seven. Then he goes and quickly makes it into a five. Now that's two thousand schillings. The superior young man will tell her off. She can't help it. She is the white dove. She is flying just above his head. She shines white, because of her innocence. The painter would have it that way. He must know what he's after, it's his job. She is the white dove. Let Judas try any of his tricks. He won't catch hold of her. She will fly wherever she wants. She will fly to the superior young man, she knows what's beautiful. Judas can say what he likes. He can go and hang himself. The money-bag won't help him either. He'll have to leave it behind. The money belongs to her. She is the white dove. Judas doesn't understand that. He thinks of nothing but his money-bag. That's why he gives the dear Lord a kiss and does him down. Soon the soldiers will come. They will seize him. Let them try. She will step forward and say: 'This isn't Our Lord. This is Mr. Brute, a simple salesman in the shop of *Gross and Mother*. You mustn't lay a finger on him. I'm his wife. Judas is always trying to do him down. It's not his fault.' She must look out that nothing happens to him. Judas can go and hang himself. She is the white dove.

Therese had knelt down before the picture and was praying. Again and again she was the white dove. She said it from the depths of her heart and kept her eyes fixed on the dove. She fluttered down into the hands of the superior young man; he caressed her softly, for had she not often saved his life, besides that's how people do treat doves.

When she got up, she was amazed to find she had knees. For a moment she doubted their reality and felt for them. When she left the church, it was her turn to laugh at the others. She laughed, in her own fashion, without laughing. People looked at her gravely and dropped their eyes, ashamed. What faces! a lot of criminals! The people who go to church these days! She managed to avoid the verger with the bag. Before the doors innumerable doves fluttered to and fro; not one of them was white. Therese was sorry she had brought nothing for them. At home there was so much stale bread and crumbs. Behind the cathedral a genuine white dove was perched on a stone statue. Therese looked at it: it was the Christ with Toothache. She thought to herself, what a bit of luck that the superior young man doesn't look like that. He'd be ashamed.

On the way home suddenly she heard music. Here come soldiers playing the loveliest marches. That's jolly, that's what she likes. She turns round about and glides along in time with them. The bandmaster never takes his eyes off her. The soldiers too, there's nothing in it, she looks back at them, she must thank them for the music. Other women join the crowd — she is the most beautiful of all. The bandmaster looks like something. That's a fine figure of a man, and how well he understands the music! The band wait for his wand. Without a sign from him not one of them moves. Now and again the music stops. She throws back her head, the bandmaster laughs and at once starts something new. If only there weren't all these children about. They get in her way. You ought to listen to music like this every day. The trumpets are best of all. Since she's joined the band, everyone has noticed how beautiful it is. Soon there's a huge crowd. She doesn't care. They make way for her. Not one forgets to look at her. Softly she hums in time with the music: like thirty, like thirty, like thirty.

CHAPTER XII

THE MILLION

KIEN found the note on his door. He read it, because he read everything, and as soon as he sat down at his writing desk, forgot all about it. Suddenly somebody said: 'Here I am back again!' Behind him stood Therese and drenched him in a downpour of words.

'Yes indeed, such a huge legacy! Just three doors off there's a lawyer. You can't leave a legacy like that lying about. The will may get dirty. It's Sunday to-day. To-morrow's Monday. You'll have to give the lawyer something. Or he'll do it all wrong. It needn't be much. It would be a shame for the good money. All that stale bread and crumbs at home. Anybody may be a dove. Naturally they don't get a crumb to eat. The soldiers play the loveliest marches. Marching along and looking at everything at the same time, you've got to be superior to do that. And who did the bandmaster keep looking at? I wouldn't tell anybody. People don't understand a joke. 1,265,000. What big eyes Mr. Brute will make to be sure! He's got beautiful eyes. All the women are after him. Maybe I'm not a woman? Handsome is as handsome does. I'm the first woman with a fortune. . . .'

Certain of victory, still flushed with the military music and the gaze of the bandmaster, she had come into the room. Everything to-day was beautiful. Days like this ought to happen every day. She had to talk. She drew the figure — 1,265,000 — on the wall, and tapped with her hand on the library in her skirt pocket. Who knows what that may not be worth. Maybe twice as much again. Her keys rattled. She puffed out her cheeks to talk. She spoke without pause because she had been silent for a week. In her ecstasy she betrayed her secret and most secret thoughts. She did not doubt that she had attained everything which could be attained; a determined woman. For all of an hour she talked at the creature in front of her. She forgot who he was. She forgot the superstitious fear with which, during the last few days, she had hung on every quiver of his features. He was human, she could tell him everything, she needed someone like that just now. She poured out the least little thing which had crossed her path or come into her mind that day.

He felt he had been out-manœuvred, something exceptional had happened. For a week she had behaved in an exemplary manner.

That she should break in upon him in this uncouth fashion must obviously have a special reason. Her speech was confused, reckless and joyful. He tried to follow what she was saying; slowly he understood:

Some superior person had left her a million, apparently some sort of a relation, and in spite of his wealth a bandmaster, for that very reason, superior. A man who at any rate must have thought highly of her, or he would not have named her his heiress. With this million she wanted to start a furniture shop; she had learnt of her good fortune only to-day and had therefore hastened to church to give thanks, and had recognized in a painting of the Saviour the features of the dead benefactor. (Gratitude as a cause of hallucinations!) In the cathedral she had made a vow to feed the doves regularly. She objected to the practice of bringing them stale breadcrumbs from home. Doves have feelings like human beings (why not!); to-morrow she would like him to take the will to the lawyer with her, to have it proved. She was anxious lest the lawyer should ask too much, seeing that so huge a legacy was involved, and wished his fee to be settled before the consultation. Thrifty and a housekeeper to the million.

But was this legacy such a very big one? 1,265,000 — how much was that? Let us compare it with the value of the library? The entire library had cost him the absurdly small sum of not quite 600,000 gold kroner. His father had left him 600,000 gold kroner, and there was a small fragment left over. What was this she wanted to do with her legacy? Set up a furniture shop? Nonsense! The library could be enlarged. He would rent the neighbouring flat and have the partition wall removed. In this way he would gain four more large rooms for the library. He would have the windows walled up and skylights inserted as he had already done in his own flat. In eight rooms there would be space for a good sixty thousand volumes. Old Silzinger's library had recently been offered for sale, it would hardly have been sold already, it contained about twenty-two thousand books, not to be compared with his of course, but one or two important things in it. He would take a round million then for his library, and she could do just what she liked with the rest. Possibly the remainder would be enough for a furniture shop, but he knew nothing about that; in any case he didn't care, he would have nothing to do with money and commerce. He would have to inquire whether old Silzinger's library had gone yet. He had all but lost an important acquisition. He buried himself too much in his studies. In this way he deprived himself of the means which were essential to learned researches. A sharp eye for the book-market was as much a part of a scholar's equipment as knowledge of the current rates to a gambler on the stock exchange.

Extension of the library from four rooms to eight. That would be an improvement. You must develop yourself, you mustn't remain static. Forty is no age to speak of. How can a man retire at forty? It is two years since your last important purchase. This is how you grow rusty. There are other libraries too, not only yours. Poverty is disgusting. How fortunate that she loves me! She calls me Brute because I have been a brute to her. She thinks my eyes are beautiful. She thinks that all women run after me. I am indeed too brutish to her. If she did not love me she would keep her legacy to herself. There are men who let themselves be supported by their wives. How repulsive. I would sooner commit suicide. She may do whatever she likes for the library. Do books need to be fed? I think not. I pay the rent. Support means free food and lodging. I will pay the rent of the neighbouring flat too. She is stupid and uneducated but she has a dead relation. Callous? Why? I never knew the man. It would be pure hypocrisy to regret him. His death is no misfortune, his death has a deeper significance. Every human being fulfils some purpose, be it only for a moment. The purpose of this man was his death. Now he is dead. No pity will bring him back again. Strange coincidence! Into my very house comes this wealthy heiress as housekeeper. For eight years she quietly performs her duties, suddenly, just before she inherits a million, I marry her. Scarcely have I discovered how deeply she loves me, when her rich bandmaster dies! A fortunate chance, undeserved, breaking in like a thief in the night. Illness was the turning point of my life, the end of straitened circumstances, of the oppressive small library in which I have hitherto lived.

Is there then no difference between a man born in the moon and on the earth? Even if the moon were half as big as the earth — it is not merely a question of the gross sum of matter, the difference in size expresses itself in each single object. Thirty thousand new books! Each one a starting point for new thoughts and new work! What a revolution of present circumstances!

In this moment Kien abandoned the conservative interpretation offered by evolutionary theory, to which he had hitherto subscribed, and marched with pages flying in to the camp of revolution. All progress is conditioned by sudden changes. The necessary proofs, hitherto buried, as in every system of the evolutionists, hidden away beneath fig leaves, sprang into his consciousness immediately. An educated man has everything to hand, as soon as he needs it. The soul of an educated man is a superbly furnished armoury. This is rarely noticed because such people, on account of that very education, do not often possess the courage to use it.

One word, which Therese flung out with mingled joy and passion, wrenched Kien back to hard facts. 'Dowry' he heard and accepted the phrase with gratitude. Everything he needed for the historic moment seemed to fall into his lap. The legacy of capitalism, favoured and practised by his family for centuries, awoke in him with colossal strength, as though in a struggle of twenty-five years it had not been always the loser. Therese's love, the pillars of the approaching paradise, brought him a dowry. It was his right not to spurn it away. He had proved his honourable intentions by taking her to wife, without the slightest suspicion of this wealthy relative on the brink of the grave, when she was nothing but a poor girl. It would give her pleasure, now and again, but not too often, to take a brisk walk through the eight rooms of the newly arranged library. The feeling that a relation of hers had had his part in creating this magnificent institution would compensate her for the loss of her furniture shop.

Filled with joy at the natural course his revolution was taking, Kien rubbed his long fingers. Not one single theoretical wall built itself in his path. The actual one dividing his own from the neighbouring flat would be pulled down. Negotiations with the neighbours must be opened at once. Putz the builder must be informed. He would have to start work to-morrow. The will must be proved immediately. Surely the solicitor could be seen to-day. When was the auction at old Silzinger's? The caretaker must go on some errands at once.

Kien took one step forward and commanded: 'Fetch the caretaker!'

Therese had got round again to the hungry doves and the crumbled bread. She reaffirmed this example of wastefulness, which irritated her housekeeper's thrift, and further enhanced her indignation with the words: 'That would be a fine thing!'

But Kien would have no resistance. 'Fetch the caretaker! At once!'

Therese noticed that he had said something. What had he got to say? He should let her have her say out. 'That would be a fine thing!' she repeated.

'What would be a fine thing? Fetch the caretaker!'

She had a grudge against this man, anyway, because of the tip he got. 'What's he got to do with it? He's not going to have any of it!'

'I shall decide on that. I am the master in this house.' He said this, not because it was necessary, but because he thought it salutary to show her that his mind was made up.

'Excuse me, the money's mine.'

In his heart, he had expected this answer. She would always remain the same ill-bred, uneducated person. He would yield only so far as his dignity must concede to his projects.

'Nobody denies it. We need him. He must run some errands at once.'

'It's a shame for the good money. That man gets a fortune.'

'Keep calm. The million is assuredly ours.'

Therese's mistrust became acute. He was trying to do her out of a bit more. Two thousand schillings he had snitched already.

'And the 265,000?' said she, pausing at every figure with a meaning look.

Now she must be won over swiftly and finally. 'The two hundred and sixty-five thousand belong to you alone.' He masked his lean features in a benefactor's fat smile; he was giving her a present, he took his thanks in advance and with pleasure.

Therese began to sweat. 'It all belongs to me.'

Why did she insist so much? He disguised his impatience in an official statement: 'I have already made it clear that no one disputes your claim. The matter is not at present under discussion.'

'Excuse me, I know that myself. Black on white, that's what I say.'

'We must co-operate in the organization of responsibilities arising from your legacy.'

'Is that any business of yours?'

'I ask you formally to accept my assistance.'

'Ask, ask, ask. First bargaining, then begging, it's not right.'

'My only fear is that you may be outwitted.'

'People pretend they're saints.'

'With a legacy of a million, it is not unheard of for false relations to make an appearance.'

'But there's only the one.'

'No wife? No children?'

'I ask you, I'm not a fool!'

'An incredible stroke of luck!'

Luck? Therese was baffled. The creature gave his money away even before he was dead. What luck was there in that? Since he had been speaking she had a growing conviction that he was doing her. She watched his every word, a hundred headed Cerberus. She exerted herself to answer, sharp and crystal clear. A slip of the tongue and the rope was round your neck. The creature had read everything. He seemed to her at once the defendant and the counsel for the defence. Protecting her infant property, she developed forces which almost frightened her. All of a sudden she managed to put herself in someone else's position. She felt that his will, as far as he was concerned, was no stroke of luck. She suspected behind this word of his a brand new trap. He was hiding something from her. What do people hide? A property. The creature possessed more than he would admit. That third nought, the one she had missed, burnt the palm of her hand. She raised her arm as in sudden pain. She wanted to throw herself over the writing table, to pull out the will and with one forceful stroke clap that nought into its right place. But she knew how much was at stake and controlled herself. This was what she got for her modesty. Why was she such a fool? Modesty's stupid. Now she'd be clever again. She must get it out of him. Where has he hidden the rest? She'd ask him so that he wouldn't notice she was asking. Broad and vicious, the familiar smile reappeared on her face.

'And what is happening to the rest of it?' She had reached the peak of her cunning. She didn't ask where he'd hidden the rest. He wouldn't have answered that one. She wanted him first of all to admit the rest.

Kien gazed at her in gratitude and affection. Her resistance had been the merest pretence. He had suspected it all along. He found it almost noble of her to speak of the million, the greater portion, simply as the rest. Evidently such sudden changes from rudeness to affection were, for people of her kind, very typical. He put himself in her place, realized how this declaration of devotion had for a long time been on the tip of her tongue, and how she had only hesitated to come out with it in order to heighten its effect. She was crude, but loyal. He began to understand her even better than before. A pity she was so old; it was too late to try to make a human being of her. He wouldn't allow her to have moods of the kind he had experienced. Education must begin in this way. All the thanks he had intended for her and all the love directed to his new books, vanished from his face. He put on an expression of severity and growled, as if he was offended: 'The rest will be spent on enlarging my library.'

Therese drew herself up, horrified and triumphant. Two admissions at one blow. *His* library! And she had the inventory in her pocket! So there was more. He had said so himself. She did not know on which side to begin her counter-attack first. Her hand, which had strayed involuntarily to her pocket, decided.

'The books are mine!'

'What?'

'Three rooms belong to the wife, one belongs to the husband.'

'We are now speaking of eight rooms. Four additional ones — those in the next flat, I mean. I need room to house the Silzinger Library. That alone contains twenty-two thousand volumes.'

'And where's the money coming from?'

Again! He was tired of these hints. 'From your legacy. There is no more to be said on that score.'

'Not a penny.'

'What, not a penny?'

'The legacy belongs to me.'

'But I have the disposal of it.'

'A man's got to die first, he can dispose after.'

'What is the meaning of this?'

'I won't bargain!'

What was this, what was this? Must he strike sterner chords? The eight-roomed library, of which he did not lose sight for a moment, gave him a last small residue of patience.

'Our common interest is concerned in this matter.'

'I want the rest!'

'You cannot but appreciate . . .'

'Where is the rest?'

'A wife must respect her husband.'

'And her husband steals the rest from his wife.'

'I ask a million for the acquisition of the Silzinger Library.'

'Ask, ask, ask. I want the rest. I want all of it.'

'I am the master in this house.'

'I'm the mistress.'

'I present you with an ultimatum. I demand categorically a million for the acquisition . . .'

'I want the rest! I want the rest!'

'In three seconds. I shall count up to three . . .'

'Anyone can count. I shall count too!'

Both were almost crying with rage. With clenched teeth they both counted, screaming louder and louder: 'One! Two! Three!' The numbers burst out in small, double explosions, exactly together each time. Her numbers were big with the millions which the rest added to her fortune. His contained the new rooms. She would have gone on counting for ever, he counted up to three, and then four. Here he stopped. In rigid tension, stiffer than ever before, he walked up to her and bellowed — the caretaker's voice, his model, ringing in his ears: 'Your will at once.' The fingers of his right hand strove to form themselves into a fist and smote with all their force into the air. Therese paused in her counting; so — he had smashed her to pieces. She was indeed astonished. She had expected a life and death struggle. And now suddenly he gave in. Had she not been so taken up with the rest, she would hardly have known where she was. When people weren't robbing her any more, her anger evaporated. Her anger wasn't her everything. She sidled round her husband and approached the writing desk. He moved out of her way. Although he had smashed her to pieces, he was afraid she might return that blow, which had been meant for her, not the air. She had noticed no blow. She grabbed about among the papers, threw them shamelessly one on top of another and pulled one of them out.

'How does — a strange will — come to be — among my papers?' He attempted to bellow this rather longer sentence, and could not therefore hurl it at his wife in one. Three times he paused for breath. Before he had finished, she answered: 'Excuse me, what strange will?' She unfolded it hurriedly, spread it out fine and smooth on the table, put ink and pen ready and made room politely for the owner of the rest. As he approached, still not perfectly reassured, his first glance fell on the figure. It seemed familiar to him, but the important thing was: it was right. During their argument a slight anxiety as to the stupidity of this illiterate had disturbed him, lest she should have read it wrongly. Contented, he turned his eyes to the upper half of the document, sat down and began to examine the will more minutely.

Then he recognized his own will.

Therese said: 'The best thing is, write it out over again.' She forgot the danger to which she was exposing her noughts. Her faith in their authenticity was as firmly impressed on her heart, as his in her love for him. He said: 'But this is my ...' She smiled: 'Excuse me, what did I ...' He stood up, furious. She explained: 'One man, one word.' Before he made a clutch at her throat he had understood. She was urging him to write. She was going to pay for a clean sheet of paper herself. He slumped down into the chair, as if he were gross and heavy. She wanted to know at last just how she stood.

A few moments later they had understood each other for the first time.

CHAPTER XIII

BEATEN

THE malicious pleasure with which he proved to her, from the evidence, how little he still possessed, tided Therese over the worst moment. She would have distintegrated into her chief components — skirt, ears and sweat — had not her hatred for him, which he was now intensifying with pedantic zeal, become the surviving core of her being. He showed her how much he had inherited. He fetched all the bills for books out of the different drawers among which his varying moods had distributed them. His memory for the trivialities of everyday, usually such a nuisance to him, now had its uses. On the back of the spoilt will, he noted down the sums. Broken as she was, Therese counted them up in her head and rounded them up to a total. She wanted to know what was really left over. It became evident that the library had cost far more than a million. He was not in the least consoled by this surprising result; its unexpectedly high value did not compensate him for the collapse of the four new rooms. Revenge for the way in which she had cheated him was his only thought. During the whole of this tedious operation, he spoke not one syllable too many, and — for him a heavier task — not one too few. A misunderstanding was impossible. When the annihilating figure was calculated at last, he added in loud staccato tones, like a schoolboy repeating a lesson: 'I have spent the rest on single books and on daily expenses.'

At that Therese dissolved, flowing out of the door in a torrential stream, across the corridor into the kitchen. When it was time to go to bed she interrupted her crying, took off her starched skirt, laid it over a chair, sat down by the stove again and went on crying. The neighbouring bedroom, in which she had lived so happily for eight years as a housekeeper, invited her to sleep. But she did not think it respectable to end her mourning so soon, and did not move from her place.

On the following day early she began to put into practice the decisions she had taken during her period of mourning. She locked the three rooms of the flat which belonged to her. The beautiful dream was over. People are like that, but after all she had three rooms and the books in them. She wouldn't touch the furniture until Kien died. It must be spared.

Kien had passed the rest of Sunday at his writing desk. He worked as a pretence only, for his mission of enlightenment was completed. In fact he was fighting his greed for new books. It had awakened in him with so great a vehemence that his study, with all its shelves and all the volumes on them seemed to him worn out and stale. Time and again he had to force himself to reach for the Japanese manuscripts on his desk. When he got so far, he would touch them, and immediately, as if repelled, draw his hand back again. What was the meaning of them? They had been lying around his cell for fifteen years already. At midday and in the evening he forgot his hunger. Night found him still at his desk. On the half-written sheet before him he had drawn, quite contrary to his habit, characters which had no meaning whatever. Towards six in the morning he began to nod; at a time when he was usually getting up, he was dreaming of a gigantic library built, on the site of the Observatory, at the crater of Vesuvius. Trembling with fear he walked up and down in it and waited for the eruption of the volcano, due in eight minutes. His fear and his pacing up and down lasted an eternity, but the eight minutes to the catastrophe remained constant. When he woke up the door into the neighbouring room was already closed. He saw this, but felt no more shut in than before. Doors did not matter, for everything was equally wearisome, the rooms, the doors, the books, the manuscripts, he himself, learning, his life.

Swaying a little with hunger he got up and tried the other doors which led into the hall. He found that he was locked in. He became conscious that his intention had been to fetch himself something to eat, and was ashamed in spite of his hunger. In the hierarchy of man's activities, eating was the lowest. Eating had become the object of a cult, but in fact it was but the preliminary to other, utterly contemptible motions. It occurred to him that he wanted to perform one of these too. He felt therefore that he was justified in rattling the door. His physical exertions and his empty stomach exhausted him to such an extent that he almost began to cry again, as he had done yesterday over the counting. But to-day he had not even strength for that; he could only call in a plaintive voice: 'I don't want anything to eat, I don't want anything to eat.'

'Now you're talking,' said Therese who had been waiting outside for some little time and listening for his first movements. He needn't think he'd get anything to eat from her. A man who doesn't bring a penny into the house gets nothing to eat. That was what she had to say to him; she'd been afraid he might forget about the eating question. Now, as he renounced eating of his own free will, she opened the door and informed him of her views on the subject. Nor would she have her house turned into a pig-sty. The passage in front of her own rooms belonged to her. That was the law. That's why they put up: 'No right of way.' Opening and spreading out a piece of paper which she held crumpled up in her hand, she read out: 'No right of way. Temporary thoroughfare only.'

She had already been out and bought food for one person at the butcher's and the greengrocer's, where she was equally disliked. It came dearer that way, and she usually bought for several days together. To their questioning glances she answered aggressively: 'From to-day he won't get anything more to eat from me.' Proprietor, customers and staff in both shops wondered. Next she carefully copied the inscription from a neighbouring alley on to a piece of paper. All the time she was writing, her shopping bag with the beautiful food lay on the dirty pavement.

When she came back, he was still asleep. She bolted the door into the passage and stood on guard. Now she'd got to the point, she'd speak straight out to him. She withdrew her permission to use her passage. He was not to use her corridor to go to the kitchen or lavatory any more. He had no business there. In future every time he made her passage dirty he'd have to clean it up. She was not a servant, she'd have the law on him. He could go in and out, but only if he kept to his own path. She'd show him where it was.

Without waiting for his answer she sidled all the way along the wall to the front door. Her skirt brushed against the wall, it did not trespass an inch into the part of the corridor which was hers. Then she glided into the kitchen, fetched a piece of chalk, a relic of her school-days, and drew a thick line between her corridor and his. 'Excuse me, this will do for now,' she said, 'we'll have oil paint later.'

In hungry bewilderment, Kien had not fully understood what was happening. Her movements struck him as senseless. Am I still on Vesuvius? he asked himself. No, on Vesuvius there was that terror about the eight minutes, but not this woman. Perhaps it was not so bad on Vesuvius after all. Only the coming eruption would have caused discomfort. Meanwhile his own discomfort was growing. It drove him on to the forbidden corridor, just as if Therese had made no chalk line down it. In long strides, he reached his goal. Therese came after him. Her indignation was a match for his necessity. She would have overtaken him, had he not had a good start. He bolted himself in, in the customary way, an action which saved him from violence at her hands. She rattled at the closed door and spat out in repetitive jerks: 'I ask you, I'll have the law on you! I'll have the law on you!'

When she saw that it was all in vain, she withdrew to the kitchen. Over her stove, where all her best ideas came to her, she hit on what was justice. Very well, he should have the corridor. She could be considerate. He had to go to the lavatory. But what would she get in return? Nobody ever gave her anything for nothing. She'd had to earn every penny. She'd give him the corridor and he in return must give her part of his room. She must take care of her rooms, where should she sleep? She had locked up the three rooms full of new furniture. Now she would lock up her old bedroom too. No one should go in. I ask you, she'd have to sleep in his room. What else could she do? She'd sacrifice her beautiful corridor and he'd have to make room for her in his study. She'd bring the furniture out of that little room where the housekeeper used to sleep. In return he could go to the lavatory as often as he chose.

She went down at once into the street and fetched up a porter. She would have nothing to do with the caretaker, who had been bribed by that man.

As soon as her voice left him in peace, Kien had fallen asleep out of sheer exhaustion. When he awoke he felt refreshed and courageous. He went into the kitchen and, without the least prick of conscience, helped himself to several slices of bread and butter. When, suspecting nothing, he returned to his own room he found that it had been cut down by half. Right across the middle stood the Spanish screen. Behind it he came on Therese in the midst of her old bedroom furniture. She was just putting the finishing touches and admiring the beautiful effect. That shameless porter had gone off, thank the lord. He had demanded a whole fortune, but she'd only given him half, and thrown him out again, of which she was very proud. But the Spanish screen did not satisfy her, for it looked crazy. On one side it was empty and blank and on the other were nothing but a mass of crooked marks; she would have preferred a blood-red sunset. She pointed to the screen and said: 'I can't have that here. As far as I'm concerned it can go out.' Kien was silent. He dragged himself to his writing desk groaning softly and lowered himself into his chair.

After a minute or two he gathered himself to his feet. He wanted to see whether the books in the neighbouring room were still alive. His anxiety arose more from a rooted sense of duty than from any real love. Since the preceding day he felt tenderness only for books which he did not possess. Before he could reach the door, Therese was already there. How had she noticed his movement in spite of the Spanish screen? How was it that her skirt carried her forward at a quicker pace than his legs? For the moment he laid a hand neither on her nor on the door. Before he had assembled even the courage which words cost him, she was already nagging:

'You dare! Because I'm good enough to let him use the passage, he thinks the rooms are his too. I've got it in writing. Black on white. He mustn't even touch the door handle. He can't get in anyway, I've got the key. I'm not giving it up. The handle belongs to the door. The door belongs to the room. Handle and door belong to me. I won't have him touching my handle!'

He fended off her words with an awkward movement of his arm and unintentionally touched her skirt. She began to scream loud and desperately as if for help.

'I won't have him touching my skirt! The skirt's mine! He didn't buy it! I bought it! He didn't starch it and iron it! I starch it and iron it! Are the keys in my skirt? The very idea. I'm not giving up the keys. Not if you were to bite it. The keys aren't in it. A woman gives her everything to a man. Not my skirt! Not my skirt!'

Kien passed his hand over his forehead. 'I'm in a madhouse!' he said, so low that she couldn't hear him. One glance at the books convinced him that he was not. He remembered the purpose for which he had got up. He had not the courage to carry it out. How was he to get into the next room? Over her dead body? What was the use of her dead body if he had no keys? She was crafty enough to have hidden the keys. As soon as he had the keys he would unlock the doors. He was not in the least afraid of her. Let him but have the keys in his hand and he would strike her out of his path like a mere nothing.

A struggle at this moment would have served no purpose whatever, so he withdrew to the writing desk. Therese kept watch on her door for another quarter of an hour. She went on screaming undeterred. That he was sitting at his desk again, the hypocrite, didn't impress her at all. She only stopped when her voice began to give out; then she gradually subsided behind the Spanish screen.

Until the evening she was not again to be seen. Now and again he

147

heard broken sounds from her; they sounded like fragments of a dream. Then she became quiet, he breathed more freely, but only for a short time. Across the refreshing silence and space there suddenly rang out unmistakable sounds. 'Hanging's too good for that kind. First they promise to marry you, then they don't make a will. Excuse me, Mr. Puda, more haste, less speed. The very idea, not to have enough money to make a will.' She's not talking at all, he told himself, these are the after effects of my own overheated hearing, echoes one might call them. As she was now quiet again, he reassured himself with this explanation. He even managed to turn over the pages of the papers in front of him. As he was reading his first sentence, the echoes disturbed him once more, 'Am I a criminal? Judas is the one. Books are worth something too. Things aren't what they were. Always such a nice-tempered gentleman, Mr. John was. A dirty old dolly-mop my old mum. Wait and see. There's keys and keys. People aren't like that. Nobody made me a present of the keys. All that good money for nothing. Anyone can beg. Anyone can knock you about. Not my skirt.'

It was precisely this sentence, the first one which registered in his ears as an echo of her earlier screechings, which convinced him that she was really talking. Impressions which he thought forgotten re-emerged in all their strength, radiating even a glow of happiness. He was ill again and lay in bed six long weeks condemned to hear her litany. At that time she repeated herself over and over again; he learnt her words by heart and was thus, in the truest sense, her master. At that time he knew in advance what sentence, what word would come next. At that time the caretaker used to come and strike her dead every day. That was a wonderful time. How long ago that was. He calculated it out and arrived at a bewildering conclusion. He had only got up for the first time a week ago. He searched for some reason to explain the chasm which had opened between that golden time and these grey days. He might have discovered it, but Therese suddenly began to talk again. What she said was incomprehensible, and therefore held despotic sway over him. It could not be learnt by heart, and who could guess what would come next? He was chained down and could not tell by what.

In the evening hunger released him. He took good care not to ask Therese whether there was anything to eat. Secretly, as he thought, and noiselessly, he left the room. Not until he reached a restaurant did he look about him to see if she had followed him. No, she was not

148

standing on the threshold. Let her dare, he said and boldly took his seat in one of the inner rooms, among couples who were evidently none of them married. So I too, in my mature years, have sunk to the underworld, he sighed, and was astonished not to see champagne flowing over the tables and to notice that the people, instead of behaving outrageously, were consuming cutlets and steak with cold-blooded greed. He might have been sorry for the men since they had let themselves be caught by women. But he forbade himself any emotion of this kind on account of their greed, possibly because he was himself so hungry. He insisted that the waiter spare him the perusal of the menu and bring him whatever he — as an expert — should think good. The expert at once revised his opinion of this shabbily dressed person and, recognizing the secret connoisseur concealed within this long, lean gentleman, served him immediately with the most expensive dishes. Hardly was he served than the eyes of all the loving couples were drawn towards his plate. The recipient of these luxuries noticed their attraction, and, although the food tasted delicious, he consumed it with evident repulsion. 'To consume' seemed to him the most unimpassioned and therefore the most suitable expression for the process of taking in nourishment. He stubbornly pursued his thoughts about this matter, expounding it in length and breadth for the benefit of his slowly reviving spirit. Emphasis on this peculiarity gave him back something of his self-respect. With joy he recognized that he still had a substantial share of integrity, and told himself that Therese deserved only his pity.

On the homeward journey he dwelt on the thought of letting her feel his pity. Briskly he unlocked the door of the flat. He knew already in the corridor that there was no light in his bedroom. The idea that she was already asleep filled him with a wild joy. Stealthily and softly, afraid lest his bony fingers should strike a noise from the handle, he opened the door. His intention of showing her his pity he recalled at a most unfortunate moment. Yes, he said to himself, so be it. Out of my great pity for her, I will not wake her up. He managed to wear his strength of character yet a little longer. He did not turn on the light, but crept on tiptoe to his bed. Undressing, he was exasperated at having a waistcoat under his coat and a shirt under his waistcoat. Each one of these garments gave rise to its own rustling. The familiar chair was no longer next to the bed. He decided not to look for it but laid his clothes on the floor. To keep Therese asleep, he would almost have crawled under the bed. He considered what was the quietest way of getting into it. Since his head was the heaviest part of him, and his feet were the furthest from his head, he decided that these, being the lightest part, should be placed on the bed first. One foot was already on the edge of the bedstead, the second was to join it immediately in one skilful movement. His head and body swayed for a moment in mid air, and then precipitated themselves, against his will, catching for support at anything, in the direction of the pillows. Then Kien felt something unexpected and soft, thought 'A burglar!' and closed his eyes as quickly as he could.

Although he was now lying on top of the burglar, he did not dare to move. Despite his fear, he could feel that the burglar was of the female sex. A fugitive and remote satisfaction crossed his mind that this sex, and the times, had sunk to such depth. The suggestion that he should defend himself, made in a far and murderous corner of his heart, he immediately repudiated. If the she-burglar, as at first appeared, were really asleep, he would withdraw quietly after giving the thing a longish trial, taking his clothes in his hand; he would leave the flat door open and dress again in the neighbourhood of the caretaker's little room. He would not fetch him up at once; he would wait a long, a very long time. Only when he heard steps coming from above would he beat a tattoo on the caretaker's door. In the meantime the she-burglar would have murdered Therese. She would certainly murder her, for Therese would defend herself. Therese would not let herself be robbed without defending herself. She *is* already murdered. Behind the Spanish screen Therese lies in her blood. If only the she-burglar had struck home . . . Perhaps she will still be alive when the police come, and will put the blame on him. To make really sure perhaps another blow . . . No, not necessary. The she-burglar has fallen asleep out of sheer exhaustion. She-burglars are not easily exhausted. A fearful struggle must have taken place. A remarkably strong woman. A heroine. He took his hat off to her. He would never have succeeded so well. Therese would have enveloped him in her skirt and suffocated him. The mere thought of it made him choke. She must have had some intention of this kind, certainly she had meant to murder him. Every woman wants to murder her husband. She had been waiting for that will. Had he made one, he would be dead in her place. So much malice can lodge in the human soul, no he must be just, in the female soul. He hated her still. He would divorce her. He would divorce her even though she was dead. He would not have her buried under his name. Not in any circumstances. No one must know that he had been married to her. He would give hush-money to the caretaker whatever sum he should ask. A marriage of this kind might injure his reputation. A true scholar would not have allowed himself so false a step. Of course she had been unfaithful. All women are unfaithful. *De mortuis nil nisi bene.* Ah, but they must be dead first, they must be dead first! He must go and look. Perhaps she was only in a trance. The strongest murderer may make a mistake. History knows countless examples. History is a shabby story. History makes you afraid. If she's alive, he'll beat her to pulp He has a right to do so. She has cheated him of the new library. He would have his vengeance on her. Then in comes a stranger and murders her. He should have cast the first stone. He had been robbed of it. He will cast the last stone at her. He will strike her. Dead or alive. He will spit on her! He will stamp on her, he will strike her!

Kien rose up in flaming wrath. At the same moment he felt a terrific box on the ear. He had almost cried out 'Hush!' to the murderess on account of the corpse, which after all might not be a corpse yet. The she-burglar began to shout. She had Therese's voice. After three words he knew that murderess and corpse were one flesh. Conscious of his guilt he said not a word and let her beat him cruelly.

As soon as he was out of the house Therese had changed the beds, pushed away the Spanish screen, and set all the other furniture at sixes and sevens. During this work, which she performed in radiant mood, she said the same phrase over and over again: Let it kill him! Let it kill him! When he was not back at nine o'clock, she lay in her bed as all respectable people do, and waited for the moment when he switched on the light so as to ease herself of the store of abuse she had hoarded during his absence. If he should not put on the light but come straight to bed to her, she would put off her abuse until he had got it over. However, as a respectable woman, she reckoned more on the first probability. When he undressed himself with perfect self-possession next to her, her heart was in her mouth. So as not to forget her anger, she decided to repeat to herself, all the time their matrimonial bliss lasted, 'Is this a man? This isn't a man!' When he suddenly fell on top of her, she made not a sound, she was afraid he might go away again. He lay on top of her for only a few moments; to her they felt like days. He did not move and was as light as a feather; she scarcely drew breath. Little by little her expectation gave way to bitterness. When he got up, she knew that he was escaping her. Like a creature possessed, she hit out at him, while she poured down upon him the foulest abuse.

Blows are balm to a moral character which has been on the brink of committing a crime. As long as it did not hurt too much, Kien smote himself with Therese's hands and waited patiently for the ugly name which he had deserved. For what was he, when he thought the matter over carefully? A desecrater of the dead. He was astonished at the mildness of her reproaches; he would have expected very different words and, above all, the foul name which he had merited. Was she sparing him, or keeping it for the last? He had no particular objection to the more general terms which she used. As soon as she called him a desecrator of the dead, he would bow his head and fully confess his fault, an act which for a man of his distinction was of infinitely greater importance than a few blows.

But the few blows did not end; he began to find them superfluous. His bones ached and with so many commonplace dirty words she seemed to find no time for the right one. She was standing up now and belabouring him alternately with her fists and elbows. She was a tough creature; only after a few minutes did she notice a slight weariness in her arms, interrupted her screeching, which had hitherto consisted entirely of substantives, with a complete sentence — 'I won't have it!' — and pushed him off the bed, taking care however to grab hold of his hair so that he should not escape her. Sitting on the edge of the bed she continued to trample on him with her feet until her arms had a little recovered. Then she seated herself astride his body, interrupted herself again, this time with — 'There's more to come!' — and cuffed his head alternately left and right. Gradually Kien lost consciousness. Long before, he had forgotten the trespass which he had committed against her. He regretted his length. Thin and small, he murmured, thin and small. Then there would have been so much less to hit. He shrank together. She hit wide. Was she still cursing? She hit the floor, she hit the bed, he heard the hard blows. She could hardly find him any more, he had made himself so small; that was why she was cursing. 'Abortion!' she cried. What a good thing he was! He was visibly dwindling; uncanny how fast. Already he had to search for himself; she'd never find him; he had grown so small, he couldn't see himself any more.

She went on striking hard and accurately. Then, pausing for breath, she said: 'Excuse me, I must have a rest,' sat up on the bed again and left the job to her feet, which performed it with less conscientiousness. Gradually they slowed down and at last stopped of their own accord. As soon as all her limbs had come to rest, Therese could not think of another word to say. She was silent. He did not move. She felt utterly exhausted. Behind his silence she scented new tricks. To protect herself from his attack, she began to threaten him: 'I'll have the law on you. I won't have it. A man mustn't assault his wife. I'm respectable, I'm a woman. You'll get ten years. The papers call it rape. I've got my proofs. I read the papers. Don't you dare move. Anyone can tell lies. I ask you, what are you after here? Another word and I'll fetch the caretaker to you. He'll have to protect me. A poor lone woman. Violence isn't everything. I'll have a divorce. The flat belongs to me. Criminals get nothing. Excuse me, I won't have a scene. I'm not asking for anything, am I? Ache in every limb, I do. Ought to be ashamed of yourself. Frightening a woman like that. I might be dead. Then you'd be in a mess. He hasn't even a night-shirt. It's no affair of mine. He sleeps without a night-shirt. That's telling. I've only to open my mouth and every-one'll believe me. I'm not going to jail. I've got Mr. Puda. You can look out for yourself. You'll have Mr. Puda to reckon with. You won't get the better of him. I'll tell him straight. And this is what comes of love!'

Kien remained obstinately silent. Therese said: 'Now he's dead.' No sooner had she spoken the word than she knew how deeply she had loved him. She knelt down beside him and sought the marks made by her kicks and blows. Then she noticed that it was dark, got up and switched on the light. Three paces off she saw the fearful condition of his body. 'Poor fellow,' she said, 'what a shame!' Her voice betrayed compassion. She took the sheet off her own bed — she'd almost have given the linen off her back — and carefully wrapped him up. 'Nothing to be seen,' she said, and took him up in her arms as gently as a child. She carried him to his own bed and tucked him in warm and soothingly. She even let him keep her sheet, 'So that he shan't take cold'. She wanted to sit down by the bed and nurse him. But she refused herself this gratification as he was sleeping so quietly, switched out the light and went to bed again. She did not grudge her husband the missing sheet.

CHAPTER XIV

PETRIFACTION

Two days passed in silence, and half-consciousness. As soon as he had come to himself again, he dared in secret to think over the immensity of his misfortune. Many blows were necessary to force his mind into submission. But he had received even more. Ten minutes less beating and he would have been ready for any vengeance. Possibly Therese had suspected this danger and had for that reason gone on striking to the bitter end. In his weakness he wanted nothing and feared one thing only: more beating. When she came near to his bed, he cowered, a whipped dog.

She put down a plate of food on the chair by the bed and immediately turned away. He needn't think there'd be more food for him. As long as he was ill she would be fool enough to feed him. He dragged himself towards it and with difficulty began to lap up a part of the alms she had bestowed on him. She heard the smacking of his greedy lips and was tempted to ask: 'How do you like it?' But she renounced this pleasure and comforted herself by thinking of a beggar to whom she had once given something fourteen years ago. He had no arms and no legs, excuse me, it's not human. All the same, he had a look of Mr. John. She wouldn't have given him anything; those people are all crooks; first they're cripples; when they get home they're as well as you and me. But then the creature said: 'How's your husband to-day?' That was a clever thing to say! He got a beautiful penny. She threw it into his hat herself. He was such a poor thing. Not that she liked giving money away; she'd never done such a thing before. But she could make an exception. So her husband got his plate of food.

Kien, the beggar, was in great pain, but he took care not to groan. Instead of turning towards the wall, he kept Therese in view and followed her actions with dread and suspicion. She was quiet and, in spite of her bulk, flexible. Or was it something to do with the room, that she so suddenly appeared and vanished? Her eyes had an evil glitter; they were cat's eyes. When she wanted to say something, but interrupted herself before she could get it out, it sounded like a cat spitting.

A bloodthirsty tiger lusting for men once disguised itself in the skin and dress of a young maiden. Weeping, it stood at a street corner and was so beautiful that a learned man came along. She lied to him cunningly, and out of pity he took her to his house, as one of his many wives. He was a very brave man and loved to sleep with her. One night she threw off her maiden's skin and tore open his breast. She ate his heart and vanished through the window. She left her shining white skin on the floor behind her. Both were found by one of the other wives who screamed her throat sore asking for an elixir of life. She went down to the most powerful man of the country, a madman who lived in the filth of the market-place, and for long hours rolled about at his feet. He spat into her hand for all the world to see, and she had to drink it. She wept and sorrowed day after day, for she loved the dead man though he had no heart. From the shame she had drunk for him, there grew a new heart out of the warm soil of her bosom. She gave it to the man and he came back to her.

In China there are women who know how to love. In Kien's library there was only a tiger. It was not even young and beautiful, and, instead of a shining skin, it wore a starched skirt. It was less concerned with the heart of a Chinese scholar than with his bones. The foulest Chinese spirit had better manners than the corporeal Therese. Ah, if only she were a spirit she could not hit him! He would gladly have left his own skin behind for her to beat to her heart's content. His bones needed rest, his bones needed to recover themselves, without bones even learning comes to an end. Had she dealt with her own bed over there as she had dealt with him? The floor had not caved in under her fists. This house had experienced much. It was old, and like all old things, strong and well made. She herself was another example. He must look at her dispassionately. Being a tiger, her physical force was naturally greater than that of any ordinary woman. She could probably take on the caretaker.

Sometimes in his dreams he beat against her skirt until she fell down. He pulled it off over her feet. Suddenly he had a pair of scissors in his hand and cut it up into tiny pieces. It took him a long time to do it. When he had cut up the skirt, the pieces seemed too big to him; she might sew them all together again. Without lifting his eyes he started all over again: he cut each piece into four. Then he emptied out a whole sack of little blue rags over Therese. How had all these rags got into the sack? The wind blew them away from her and on to him; they settled on him, he felt them, blue bruises, all over his body, and moaned out loud.

Therese sneaked up to him and asked: 'I won't have this moaning; what's the matter?' She was blue again. Some of the bruises must have settled on her. Strange, it seemed to him that he was carrying them all. But he did not moan again. She was satisfied with this answer. Suddenly she remembered the dog in her last place. He shushed before ever you said a word to him. That's how it ought to be.

In the course of a few days Kien was as tired of her care, which consisted in a plate of food to last him from morning to night, as he was of the pains of his bruised body. He scented the distrust of the woman when she came near to him. Already on the fourth day she had no desire to feed him any more. Anyone can lie in bed. She examined his body, for simplicity's sake, through the bed-coverings, and decided that he would soon be well. He did not cringe. People who don't cringe don't feel anything. He could get up, she needn't cook for him any longer. She might simply have ordered 'Get up!' But a certain fear warned her that he might leap up suddenly, tear the coverings and sheets off his body and leave nothing on it but a mass of blue marks, as though it were her fault. To prevent this she was silent, and on the following day brought him his plate only half full. Moreover, she had cooked badly on purpose. Kien noticed, not the difference in the food, but in her. He misinterpreted her searching glances and feared more blows. In bed he was defenceless. Stretched out to his full length, there he lay at her mercy; wherever she struck, higher or lower, there would be something to hit. She might make a mistake breadthways, that was all; this gave him no sense of security.

Two full days and nights went by before his fear had strengthened his will to get up; at last he made an attempt to do so. His sense of time had never failed him; he still always knew how late it was, and to re-establish order once and for all at a single stroke, he rose from his bed one morning punctually at six o'clock. His head crackled like dried twigs. His frame seemed to be out of joint, and would not balance properly. By skilfully leaning first in one direction, then in the other, he succeeded in avoiding a fall. Little by little he juggled himself into his clothes, which he dragged out from under the bed. Every new encasement he greeted with joy, an additional armour, an important defence. His movements to preserve his balance were like a mysterious dance. Tormented by pains, small devils, he had yet escaped their chief, death, and he danced his way to the writing table. There, dazed a little by excitement, he took his place, his legs and arms wobbling until, returning to their old obedience, they came to rest.

Since she had no more work to do, Therese had taken to sleeping until nine. She was the lady of the house, such people lie even later. Servants have to be up by six. But sleep would not stay with her so long, and as soon as she woke, her yearning for her possessions left her no more peace. She had to get up and dress herself so as to feel the pressure of the hard keys against her flesh. But a happy solution occurred to her since her husband had been beaten and was in bed. She went to bed at nine with the keys between her breasts. Until two in the morning she took good care to remain wide awake. At two o'clock she got up and hid the keys again in her skirt. No one could find them there. Then she went to sleep. She was so tired with her long vigil that she didn't wake up again until nine o'clock, just like a lady. That's the way it should be, and servants can do the rest.

So it was that Kien carried out his plan unnoticed by her. From the writing desk he could see her bed. He watched over her sleep as if it had been his dearest possession, and in the course of three hours was frightened to death a hundred times. She had the fortunate gift of letting herself go when she slept. When she had eaten something good in her dreams, she belched and broke wind. At the same time she said: 'The very idea!' and meant something of which she alone was aware. Kien applied it to himself. Her adventures tossed her from side to side; the bed groaned aloud, Kien groaned with it. Often she grinned with her eyes closed; Kien was near to tears. When she grinned yet more widely, she looked as though she were crying; then Kien nearly laughed. Had he not learnt caution, he would have laughed out loud. With amazement, he heard her calling on Buddha. He doubted his ears, but she repeated it: 'Puda! Puda!' just as she burst into tears, and he understood what Puda meant in her language.

When she drew her hand from under the coverlet, he winced. But she did not hit out, only clenched her fist. Why, what have I done, he asked himself, and gave his own answer: *she* must know. He had respect for her fine judgment. His crime, for which she had so cruelly punished him, was atoned for, but not forgotten. Therese clutched at the place where the keys were usually hidden. She took the thick coverlet for her skirt and found the keys although they were not there. She let her hand fall heavily on them, tickled them, played with them, took them one by one in her fingers, and in the excess of her pleasure covered them with great, shining drops of sweat. Kien blushed, he did not know why. Her thick arm was stuck into a narrow, tightly-stretched sleeve. The lace with which it was trimmed in front was directed at her husband, who slept in the same room. It looked crushed to Kien. Very softly he said this word which lay heavy on his heart. He heard — 'Crushed'. Who had spoken? Quick as lightning he lifted his head and turned his eyes on Therese. Who else could know how crushed he was? She was asleep. He mistrusted her closed eyes and waited, holding his breath, for a second remark. 'How can I be so foolhardy?' he thought, 'she is awake and I am looking her boldly in the face.' He forbade himself the only means of discovering the proximity of his danger and, lowered his eyes, a shame-faced child. With ears wide open — so it seemed to him — he waited a fearful scolding. Instead, he heard only regular breathing. So she was asleep again. After a quarter of an hour he spied out the ground again all round her with his eyes, ready to take flight at any moment. He thought himself wily enough, and allowed himself one proud idea. He was David watching the sleeping Goliath; on the whole Goliath was a fool. In the first round David did not win: but he had escaped Goliath's deadly designs and who could tell what lay in the future?

The future, the future, how was he ever to get into the future? Let the present be past, then it could do no more harm to him. Ah, if only the present could be crossed out! The sorrows of the world are, because we live too little in the future. What would it matter in a hundred years if he were beaten to-day? Let the present be the past and we shall not notice the bruises. The present is alone responsible for all pain. He longed for the future, because then there would be more past in the world. The past is kind, it does no one any harm. For twenty years he had moved in it freely, he was happy. Who is happy in the present? If we had no senses, then we might find the present endurable. We could then live through our memories — that is, in the past. In the beginning was the Word, but it *was*, therefore the past existed before the Word. He bowed before the supremacy of the past. The Catholic Church would have much to be said for it, but it allowed too little past. Two thousand years, a part of it only recorded, what does that matter compared to traditions of double or treble that space of years? A Catholic priest is surpassed by any Egyptian mummy. Because the mummy is dead, he may think himself superior. But the pyramids are no more dead than St. Peter's, on the contrary they are much more alive, for they are older. These Romans think they have all time in their pockets. They refuse to revere their ancestors. That is blasphemy. God is the past. He *believes* in God. A time will come when men will beat their senses into recollections, and all time into the past. A time will come when a single past will embrace all men, when there will be nothing except the past, when everyone will have one faith — the past.

Kien knelt down in his thoughts and prayed in his distress to the God of the future — the Past. He had long forgotten how to pray, but before this God he found the way again. At the end he asked for forgiveness for not having really knelt down. But God must know — *à la guerre comme à la guerre* — he did not need to tell him twice. This was the ineffable and truly divine in Him, that he understood everything at once. The God of the Bible was fundamentally a miserable illiterate. Many of the minor Chinese gods were far better read. He could say things about the Ten Commandments which would make the Past's hair stand on end. But then the Past knew better, anyway. He would however permit himself to relieve the Past of the absurd feminine gender with which the Germans have credited it. That the Germans should provide their finest achievements, those abstract ideas, with feminine articles is one of those incomprehensible barbarisms by which they nullify their own merits. He would in future sanctify everything connected with God with a masculine affix. The neuter gender is too childish for God. As a philologist he was fully aware of the odium he might bring upon himself by the act. But when all was said, speech was made for man, not man for speech. He therefore asked the (masculine) Past, to approve of the alteration.

All the time he was negotiating with God he was gradually coming back to his observation post. Therese was unforgettable, not even while he was praying was he altogether free of her. She snored in spasms which regulated the rhythm of his prayer. Little by little her movements grew more violent; there was not a doubt of it, she would soon wake up. He compared her to God, and found her wanting. It was just precisely in the Past where she was wanting. She was descended from no one, nor did she know whence she came. Pitiful godless carcass! And Kien considered whether it might not be wisest to go to sleep again. She might then wait until he woke up, and her initial fury at his arbitrary reappearance at his writing desk would have evaporated in the meantime.

At that moment Therese with a powerful movement threw her whole body off the bed and on to the floor. There was a loud crash. Kien trembled in every bone. Whither now? She has seen him! She is coming for him! She will kill him! He searches all time for a hiding place. He tears through history, up and down the centuries. The strongest castles fall before gunpowder. Knights in armour? Absurd — Swiss morning-stars — English muskets — burst armour and skulls asunder. The Swiss are wiped out at Marignano. Not *Landsknechts* at any price — not mercenaries — the first army of fanatics — Gustavus Adolphus — Cromwell — will mow us all down. Back from the Renaissance, back from the Middle Ages — back to the Greek Phalanx — the Romans break it open — Indian elephants — fiery javelins — the chivalry panics — whither — on ship-board — Greek fire — to America — Mexico — human sacrifice — they will slaughter us — China, China — Mongols — pyramids of skulls: in half a second he has exhausted his entire treasury of history. Nothing is safe, everything collapses, wherever you creep to, the enemy will drag you out, houses of cards, beloved civilizations fall, prey to barbaric robbers, empty-headed, wooden-headed.

Petrifaction.

Kien pressed his sapless legs hard against each other. His right hand, rolled into a fist, he laid on his knee. His lower arm and his thigh thus steadied each other. With his left arm he reinforced his chest. His head was slightly raised. His eyes were fixed on the distance. He sought to close them. From their refusal to close he recognized that he was the granite image of an Egyptian priest. He had turned into a statue. History had not forsaken him. In ancient Egypt he had found a safe retreat. So long as history was faithful to him, he could come to no harm.

Therese treated him as if he was made of air — of stone, he corrected himself. Gradually his fear gave way to a deep feeling of peace. She would take care what she did to a statue. Who would be fool enough to hurt a hand on a stone? He thought of the sharp edges of his body. Stone is good, stone edges are even better. His eyes, apparently fixed on nothingness, were examining the details of his body. He regretted that he knew himself so little. The picture which he had of his body was scanty. He wished that he had a looking-glass on the writing desk. He would have liked to pry under the skin of his clothing. Had he acted according to his present thirst for knowledge, he would have undressed stark naked and reviewed his body in detail, inspecting and encouraging it bone by bone. Ah, he suspected a great number of secret corners, hard pointed angles and edges! His bruises were as good as a mirror. This woman felt no awe in the presence of a man of learning. She had dared to touch him as if he were common clay. Her chastisement was — his metamorphosis into stone. On this tremendous rock her plans were shipwrecked.

Daily the same pantomime was repeated. Kien's life, shattered under the fists of his wife, estranged by her greed and by his own, from all books, old and new, became a serious problem. In the morning he got up three hours before her. He might have used this, his quietest time, for work, and so he did, but what he had once considered work, seemed far away from him now, postponed until some happier future. He gathered the strength he needed for the practice of his new art. Without leisure no art can exist. Immediately after waking one rarely achieves perfection. It is necessary to flex the limbs: free and uninhibited the artist should approach his creation. Thus Kien spent nearly three hours at leisure before his writing desk. He allowed many things to pass through his head, but he kept vigilant watch on them all so that he should not be drawn too far away from the matter in hand. Then, when the timepiece in his head, last vestige of the learned net with which he had ensnared time, rang its alarm bell — for nine o'clock was approaching — he began very slowly to stiffen. He felt the coldness gradually extending through his body, and judged it according to the evenness with which it distributed itself. There were days when his left side grew cold and stiff faster than his right; this caused him the most serious anxiety. 'Over with you!' he commanded, and streams of warmth despatched from his right side made good the error of the left. His efficiency in stiffening grew greater from day to day. As soon as he had reached the consistency of stone, he tested the hardness of the material by lightly pressing his thighs against the seat of the chair. This test for hardness lasted only a few seconds, a longer pressure would have crushed the chair to powder. Later on when he began to fear for the fate of the chair, he turned it to stone as well. A fall during the day, in the woman's presence, would have turned his rigidity to ridicule, and hurt him a great deal, for granite is heavy. Gradually, by developing a reliable sense for his degree of hardness, the test became superfluous.

From nine in the morning until seven in the evening Kien retained his incomparable pose. On the writing desk lay an open book, always the same one. He vouchsafed it not a glance. His eyes were occupied entirely in the distance. The woman was at least clever enough not to disturb him during these sessions. She busied herself zealously in the room. He understood how deeply housekeeping had become ingrained into her body and suppressed an unseemly smile. She described a wide curve round the monumental figure from ancient Egypt. She made it no offerings, neither of food nor of reproaches. Kien forbade himself hunger and all other bodily vexations. At seven o'clock he infused warmth and breath into the stone which speedily came back to life. He waited until Therese was in the furthest corner of the room. He had a sense of her whereabouts which never betrayed him. Then he leapt up and hurriedly left the house. While he was eating his only meal in the restaurant, he would all but fall asleep out of exhaustion. He enlarged on the difficulties of the past day and when a good idea for the morrow came into his head he nodded his agreement. Anyone else who tried to turn himself into a statue, he would immediately challenge. No one took up the challenge. At nine o'clock he went to bed and slept.

Therese too gradually settled down in these restricted surroundings. She moved freely about in her new room without anyone to disturb her. In the morning, before putting on her shoes and stockings, she would creep delicately here and there over the carpet. It was the most beautiful in the whole flat. The bloodstains could no longer be seen. It did her ancient horny skin good to be caressed by the carpet. As long as she was in contact with it, nothing but beautiful images flitted through her head. But always she would be disturbed by him; grudging her every penny.

In the stony silence of his new occupation, Kien had brought things to such a pitch of virtuosity that even the chair on which he sat, an old, obstinate piece of furniture, rarely creaked. The three or four times in the day when his chair made itself all the more noticeable were extremely painful to him. He regarded them as the first signs of weariness and deliberately overlooked them.

At the slightest creaking Therese scented danger, her happiness was shattered, she glided hastily to her stockings and shoes, pulled them on and continued yesterday's train of thought. She recalled the terrible worries which unceasingly tormented her. Out of pity she let her husband stay in the house. His bed didn't take up much room. She needed the key of the writing desk. His little bankbook was certainly inside it. Since she hadn't got hold of the bankbook with the rest in it, she'd let him have a roof for a few days. One day perhaps he'd remember it and be ashamed because he'd always treated her so meanly. If anything stirred in his neighbourhood, she despaired of ever getting the bankbook; at other times she was certain of it. She wasn't afraid of resistance from a piece of wood, which was all he was most of the time. But alive the man might do anything, even steal her bankbook.

Towards evening tension on both sides rose by several degrees. He gathered the scanty remains of his strength; he didn't want to warm up too soon. She was furious at the idea of his going off to the restaurant yet again to gorge and swill away her hard-earned money; as it was, there was hardly any of it left. How long had that creature been wasting her capital without bringing a penny into the house? She too had a heart. She wasn't a stone. She must rescue that poor fortune. Everyone was after it. Criminals are wild beasts. They all want to get something out of you. Not a scrap of decency. A poor, lone woman. Instead of helping her, the man drank like a fish and never stood up for her. He was no good for anything any more. He used to scribble whole pages full; they were worth money to her. Now he was too lazy even for that. She wasn't running a charity, was she? He ought to be in the workhouse. She couldn't have useless mouths round here. He'd have her begging in the gutter yet. He'd better try that himself. Thank you for nothing. He'd never get a penny out of anybody. He might look poor, but did he know how to ask nicely? He wouldn't dream of it. Excuse me, he'll have to starve. Just let him wait and see what'd happen to him when her pity came to an end. As if her old mother, God rest her, hadn't starved to death and now her husband was going to starve to death too!

Day by day her anger rose a degree higher. She weighed it up to see if it would suffice for the decisive act, and found it too light. The caution with which she went to work was only equalled by her persistence. She said to herself: to-day he's too wretched (to-day I'm no match for him) and immediately snapped off her anger so that she would have a piece left to start with to-morrow.

One evening Therese had just put her iron in the fire and heated it to a medium temperature, when Kien's chair creaked three times in succession. The cheek of it was just what she had been wanting. She hurled him, the great stick of wood, together with the chair to which he was fixed into the fire; it crackled furiously; a savage heat glowed on the iron. One after another, and with her bare hands — she had no fear of the red-hot glow, it was the red-hot glow she had been waiting for — she snatched out all the names he was: beggar, drunkard, criminal, and bore down with them on to the writing desk. Yet even now she would have done a deal. If he handed over the bankbook of his own free will, she would not throw him into the street until afterwards. If he said nothing she would say nothing. She would allow him to stay until she had found it. He must let her look for it; she had had enough of it.

With the sensitivity of a statue, Kien knew, as soon as his chair had creaked three times, how much was at stake for his art. He heard Therese coming. He suppressed a joyful impulse, it would have spoilt his icy temperature. He had practised for three weeks. The day of revelation had come. Now she would have to recognize the perfection of his achievement. He was more certain of it than any artist had ever been. Quickly, before the storm, he dispatched some superfluous cold through his body. He pressed the soles of his feet on to the ground: they were as hard as stone; degree of hardness: ten at least, diamond, the sharpest edges, penetrating. On his tongue — remote from the clash — he savoured a little of the stony pain which he had ready to inflict on the woman.

Therese grabbed him by the legs of his chair and shoved him heavily to one side. She let go of the chair, went over to the writing desk and pulled out a drawer. She searched through the drawer, found nothing, and made for the next one. In the third, fourth and fifth she still could not find what she wanted. He understood: a ruse of war. She was not looking for anything; what could she be looking for? The manuscripts would be all alike to her, she had found papers in the very first drawer. She was working on his curiosity. He was to ask, what was she doing there. If he spoke he would be stone no longer, and she would strike him dead. She was tempting him out of his stone. She tore and wrenched at the desk. But he kept his blood cold and uttered not a breath.

She hurled the papers wildly about. Most of them instead of putting back in their places she left lying about on top of the desk. Many sheets fell to the ground. He knew what was in each of them. Others she flung together in the wrong order. She treated his manuscripts like waste paper. Her fingers were coarse and good enough for the thumbscrew. In that writing desk were hidden the industry and patience of decades.

Her insolent activity exasperated him. She was not to treat his papers like that. What did her ruse of war matter to him? He might need those notes later. There was work waiting for him. If only he could begin on it now! He was not born to be an acrobat. Acquiring the technique had cost him too much time. He was a man of learning. When would the good times come again? His new art was a mere interim. He had been losing weeks and weeks of work. How long had he been at it now? Twenty, no ten, no five weeks, he couldn't tell for sure. Time had become confused. She was defiling his last thesis. He would exact a terrible vengeance. He was afraid of forgetting himself. Now she was waggling her head. She was darting glances full of hatred at him. She hated his rigid stillness. But there was no stillness; he could bear this no longer; he had to have peace; he would make her an offer; an armistice; she must take her fingers away; her fingers were shredding his papers, his eyes, his brain; she must close the drawers; away from the writing desk, away from the writing desk, that was his place; he would not tolerate her there; he would crush her to pulp; if only he could speak; stone is dumb.

With her skirt she shoved the empty drawers back into the desk. She stamped on the manuscripts on the floor. She spat on those which were on top of the desk. In blazing rage she tore up everything in the last drawer. The helpless cries of the paper burnt to the marrow of his bones. He forced down the rising heat, he would get up, a cold stone, he would crush her to fragments against himself. He would gather up the pieces and pound them into dust. He would break over her, break into her, a gigantic Egyptian plague. He grasped himself, the Tables of the Law, and stoned his people with them. His people had forgotten the commandment of their God. Their God is a great God and Moses has lifted up his arms to strike. Who is as hard as God? Who is as cold as God?

Suddenly Kien rose and hurled himself in fury on Therese. He was mute, he clipped his lips together with his teeth for pincers; if he spoke, he was no longer stone; his teeth bit deeply into his tongue. 'Where is the bankbook?' yelled Therese shrilly, before she broke in pieces. 'Where is the bankbook, drunkard, jail-bird, thief!' She was looking for the bankbook then. He smiled at her last words.

They were not her last words. She grabbed at his head and battered it on the writing desk. She hit him between the ribs with her elbows. She screeched: 'Out of my house!' She spat, she spat in his face. He felt it all. It hurt him. He was not a stone. Since she did not break in pieces, his art did. All was false, there was no faith in anything. There was no God. He evaded her. He defended himself. He struck back. He hit her, he had sharp bones. 'I'll have the law on you. Thieves get locked up! The police'll find it out! Thieves get locked up! Out of my house!' She clutched at his legs to pull him down. On the floor she could let herself go like that other time. She did not succeed, he was strong. So she seized him by the collar and dragged him out of the flat. She slammed the door thunderously behind him. In the corridor he slumped down on to the ground. How tired he was. The door came open again. Therese flung his coat, hat and brief-case after him. 'Don't you dare come asking for anything here!' she screamed and vanished. She had thrown out the brief-case because there was nothing in it; all the books she kept in the flat.

The bankbook was in his pocket. He hugged it happily though it was only a bankbook. She had no idea what had escaped her together with the beggar. I ask you, can you imagine a thief who always carries his crime around with him?

PART TWO

HEADLESS WORLD

CHAPTER I

THE STARS OF HEAVEN

SINCE Kien had been thrown out of his flat, he had been overwhelmed with work. From morning to night with a measured and persistent tread he walked through the town. Already at dawn his long legs were in motion. At midday he didn't permit himself either rest or food. So as to husband his strength, he divided the scene of his activities into sections to which he kept rigorously. In his brief-case he carried a vast plan of the town, scale 1:5,000, on which the book stores were designated by cheerful red circles.

He entered a book shop and demanded the proprietor himself. If he was away or out at lunch he contented himself with the head assistant. 'I urgently require, for a work of scholarship, the following books,' he said, and from a non-existent paper read out a long catalogue. To avoid repeating himself he pronounced the authors' names with perhaps exaggerated distinctness and deliberation. For he was concerned with rare works and the ignorance of such people is hardly to be conceived. Despite reading he could spare a watchful side-glance for the listening faces. Between one title and the next he introduced brief pauses. He delighted in hurling the next title rapidly at the listener, who had as yet not fully recovered from the preceding one. The bewildered expressions amused him. Some asked for 'One moment, please!' Others clutched at their forehead or temples, but he continued to read unperturbed. His paper included between two and three dozen volumes. At home he had them all. But here he acquired each afresh. These duplicates, at present oppressive to him, he planned to exchange or sell later on. For the rest, his new activity cost him not a penny. In the street he prepared his lists. In each new book shop he read out a new one. When he had finished he folded up his piece of paper with a few assured movements, replaced it with the others in his note case, bowed contemptuously low and left the shop. He waited for no answer. What could these numbskulls have answered? If he involved himself in discussions about the required books it would only be a waste of time. Already he had lost three whole weeks in the strangest circumstances, stiff and stark at his writing desk. To make up for the loss he walked all day, so cleverly, persistently, industriously that, without a suspicion of self-complacency, he could feel pleased with himself, as he was.

The people with whom his profession brought him into contact behaved, according to their mood and temperament, in different ways. A few felt affronted at not being given time to answer, the majority were glad enough to listen. His gigantic learning could be both seen and heard. One of his sentences outweighed the contents of a well-filled shop. His full importance was rarely recognized. Else the poor fools would have left their work, crowded about him, pricked up their ears and harkened until their eardrums split. Would they ever again encounter such a prodigy of learning? But mostly a lone assistant took advantage of the opportunity of hearing him. He was shunned, as all great men are, he was too strange and remote, and their embarrassment, which he had determined not to notice, smote him to his inmost core. As soon as he turned his back on them, for the rest of the day, they would talk of nothing but him and his lists. Strictly speaking, proprietors and staff functioned as his own private servants. He would not grudge them the honour of a collective mention in his biography. After all, they did not behave themselves ill, admired him and provided him with everything of which he had need. They divined who he was, and at least had the strength to be silent in his presence. For he never entered a book store twice. When he did so once in error, they threw him out. He was too much for them, his appearance oppressed them and they freed themselves of it. He sympathized with their humiliation and on that occasion bought the plan of the town with the red circles. In the circles denoting book shops he had already dealt with, he made a small cross; for him they were dead.

Besides, his activity had a pressing purpose. From the first moment when he found himself in the street his sole interest was for his theses at home. He was determined to complete them: without a library this was impossible. He therefore considered and compiled lists of the specialized books he needed. These lists came into being by necessity; caprice and desire were excluded, he only permitted himself to buy books indispensable to his work. Circumstances forced him to shut up his library at home for the time being. He apparently submitted to his fate, but in fact he outwitted it. He would not yield an inch of ground in this matter of learning. He bought what he needed and in a few weeks would resume his work; his plan of campaign was largely conceived and well-adapted to the peculiar circumstances, he was not to be subdued; in freedom he spread his wise wings; with each glorious day of independence he grew in stature, and this interim collection of a small new library comprising a few thousand volumes was reward enough for his pains. He was even afraid that the collection might grow too big. Every night he slept in a different hotel. How was he to carry away the increasing burden? But he had an indestructible memory and could carry the entire new library in his head. The brief-case remained empty.

In the evenings after closing time he became aware of his fatigue, and sought, the moment he had left the last book shop, the nearest hotel. Without luggage as he was, and in his shabby suit, he aroused the porters' suspicions. Pleased in advance at the way in which they would send him packing, they allowed him to speak his three or four sentences. He required a large, quiet room for the night. If none was to be had except in the vicinity of women, children or common people, he requested them to tell him so at once, since in that case he would be compelled to refuse it. At the phrase 'common people' every porter was disarmed. Before his room was allotted to him, he pulled out his wallet and declared his intention of paying in advance. He had drawn his remaining capital out of the bank; the wallet was crammed with highly respectable banknotes. For love of these the porters laid bare regions of their eyeballs which no one, not even titled travellers or Americans, had ever seen before. In his precise, tall, angular writing Kien filled in the usual form. His profession he declared to be: 'Owner of a library.' He would not state whether married or single; he was neither married nor single nor divorced and he indicated this by a crooked penstroke. He gave the porters fantastic tips, about 50 per cent on the price of the room. Every time he paid he rejoiced that his bank-book had escaped Therese. Their enthusiastic bows placed a coronet on his head; he remained unmoved, an English lord. Contrary to his custom — technical simplifications were odious to him — he made use of the lift, for in the evening, tired as he was, the library in his head weighed heavy. He had his dinner brought up to his room: it was the only meal in the day. Relaxing for a short while he set down his library, and then looking round decided whether there was enough room for it.

At first, when his liberty was yet young, he was not concerned with the kind of room he had taken; it was after all only a matter of sleeping and the sofa could hold his books. Later he used the wardrobe as well. Soon the library had outgrown both. The dirty carpet had to be used so he rang for the maid and asked for ten clean sheets of brown paper. He spread them out on the carpet and over the whole floor; if any were left over he covered the sofa with them and lined the wardrobe. Thus for a time it became his habit to order paper every evening as well as food; he left it behind every morning. The books built themselves up higher and higher, but even if they fell they would not be soiled for everything was covered with paper. Sometimes at night when he awoke, filled with anxiety, it was because he had most certainly heard a noise as of falling books.

One evening the piles of books were too high even for him; he had already acquired an amazing number of new ones. He asked for a pair of steps. Questioned why he wanted it, he replied, cuttingly, 'That is not your business!' The maid was of a rather timid nature. A burglary, which had recently occurred, had all but cost her her place. She ran to the porter and told him, excitedly, what the gentleman in No. 39 wanted. The porter, a character and man of the world, knew what he owed to his tip, although it was safe in his pocket.

'Go and get some sleep, sweetie,' he grinned at her, 'I'll deal with the murderer!'

She didn't move. 'Strange, isn't he,' she said shyly. 'Looks like a flagpole. First he asked for paper and now he wants a pair of steps. The floor's covered with paper.'

'Paper?' he asked; this information made an excellent impression on him. Only the most remarkable people carry precautions to that length.

'Yes, what do you think?' she said proudly; he had listened to her.

'Do you know who the gentleman is?' he asked. Even talking to the maid he didn't say he; he said 'the gentleman'. 'Proprietor of the Royal Library, that's what he is!' Each syllable of this glorious profession he launched into the air like an article of faith. To shut the girl up he added 'Royal' on his own account. And he realized how very refined the gentleman upstairs was since he had omitted 'Royal' when filling in the form.

'There aren't any Royal now, anyway.'

'But there's a Royal Library! Clever, aren't you? What do you think they did with the books, swallowed them?'

The girl was silent. She loved to make him angry because he was so strong. He only noticed her when he was furious. She came running to him with every little thing. For a couple of minutes he bore with her. Once he was enraged, you had to look out for yourself. His fury gave her strength. She gladly carried the steps to Kien. She could have asked the boots to do it, but she did it herself; she wanted to obey the porter. She asked the gentleman proprietor of the Royal library if she could help him.

He said: 'Yes, by leaving this room at once!' Then he locked the door — for he mistrusted the officious creature — stopped up the key-hole with paper, placed the steps cautiously between the piles of books and climbed up. One parcel after another, arranged according to the lists, he lifted out of his head, filling the entire room with them up to the ceiling. Despite the heavy weight he managed to keep his balance on the steps; he felt like an acrobat. Now, his own master again, he overcame difficulties easily. He had just finished when there was an obsequious knock at the door. He was annoyed at being disturbed. Since his experiences with Therese he was in mortal terror of any uninitiate looking at his books. It was the maid (who out of devotion to the porter) timidly asked him for the steps back again.

'Please sir, excuse me, sir, you won't want to be sleeping with the steps in the room!' Her zeal was genuine; she stared at the strange flagpole with curiosity, love and envy and wished that the porter would take as much interest in her.

Her language reminded Kien of Therese. Had she been Therese he would have been afraid. But as she only reminded him of her he shouted: 'The steps remain here! I shall sleep with the steps!'

Gracious heavens, this is a fine gentleman, thought the young thing and disappeared, frightened. She had not realized that he was so very refined that you couldn't address a single word to him.

He drew his own conclusions from this experience. Women, whether housekeepers, wives or maids had to be avoided at all costs. From then onwards he asked for bedrooms so large that a pair of steps would have been senseless and superfluous, and he carried his own paper in his brief-case. The waiter, for whom he rang to order his meal, was, happily, a man.

As soon as his head felt relieved of the weight, he lay down on the bed. Before going to sleep he compared his previous circumstances with his present situation. In any case, towards the evening his thoughts reverted to Therese with pleasure, because he paid his expenses with the money he had rescued from her by his personal valour. Money matters promptly conjured up her picture. All day he had nothing to do with money, not only did he refuse himself lunch but also trams, and with good reason. The serious and glorious undertaking on which he was now engaged was not to be smirched with any Therese. Therese was the penny soiled by a thousand hands. Therese was the word in the mouth of an illiterate. Therese was the weight on the spirit of man. Therese was madness incarnate.

Imprisoned for months with a lunatic, he had in the end been unable longer to resist the evil influence of her disease and had himself been infected. Grasping to excess, she had imparted a portion of her greed to him. A devouring lust for other books had estranged him from his own. He had almost robbed her of the million which he believed her to possess. His character, perpetually in close and violent contact with hers, had been all but dashed to pieces on this rock of money. But it had sustained the shock. His body invented a defence. Had he continued to move about the flat freely for much longer he would have succumbed irremediably to her disease. For that reason he had played that trick of the statue. Naturally he could not transform himself into concrete stone. It was enough that *she* had taken him for that. She was frightened by the statue and made a wide circle round it. His ingenuity in sitting rigidly on a chair for weeks, had perplexed her. She had been perplexed already. But after this adroit ruse she no longer knew who he was. This gave him time to free himself from her. Gradually his wounds healed. Her power over him was broken. As soon as he was strong enough he resolved on a plan of escape. It was essential to escape from her, and yet to keep her in custody. So that his escape should be successful, she had to believe that it was she who had thrown him out. Thus he hid his bankbook. For many a long week she searched the flat for it. This indeed was the nature of her disease, she must always look for money. Nowhere did she find the bankbook. Finally she ventured as far as the writing desk. But here she collided with him. Her disappointment provoked her to fury. He irritated her more and more, until, beside herself with rage, she threw him out of his own flat. There he stood outside, redeemed. She thought herself the victor. He locked her into the flat. She could never escape, and now he was completely safe from her attack. True he had sacrificed his flat, but what will not a man do to save his life, if that life belongs to the sacred cause of Learning?

He stretched himself out under the blanket and touched with his body as much as possible of the linen sheet. He begged the books not to fall down, he was tired and at last would like to rest. Half asleep, he mumbled, 'Good night'.

For three weeks he enjoyed his new freedom. With admirable diligence he made use of every minute; when the three weeks were over he had exhausted every book shop in the town. One afternoon he did not know where else he was to go. Begin again at the beginning, and visit all over again in the same order? He might be recognized? He would prefer to avoid unpleasantness. His face — was it one of those which anyone would remember from a single glance? He stopped in front of the mirror outside a hairdresser's and surveyed his features. Watery blue eyes, and no cheeks at all. His forehead, ridged as a rockface, from which his nose plunged at right angles towards the abyss, an edge dizzily narrow. At its base, almost hidden, cowered two minute black insects. No one would have guessed them to be nostrils. His mouth as the slot of a machine. Two sharp lines, like artificial scars, ran from his temples to his chin and met at its point. These and his nose divided his long and lean face into five strips of a terrifying narrowness; narrow, but strictly symmetrical; there was no room to linger anywhere and Kien did not linger. For when he saw himself — he was not used to seeing himself — he suddenly felt very lonely. He decided to lose himself among a crowd of people. Perhaps he would then forget how lonely his face was, and perhaps he would think of a way of carrying on his activities.

He turned his eyes to the names above the doors, a feature of the town to which he was otherwise blind, and read The Stars of Heaven. He entered with pleasure. He thrust back the thick curtains over the door. An appalling fog almost took his breath away. Mechanically, as if in self defence, he walked two steps further. His narrow body cut the air like a knife. His eyes watered: he opened them wide to see. They watered more and he could see nothing. A black figure escorted him to a small table and told him to take a seat. He obeyed. The figure ordered him a large black coffee and disappeared in the fog. Here in this alien quarter of the world, Kien clutched at the voice of his escort and identified it as male, but blurred and therefore distasteful. He was pleased to find yet another creature as despicable as he held all mankind to be. A thick hand pushed a large coffee in front of him. He thanked it politely. Surprised, the hand paused a moment, then pressed itself flat against the marble and stretched out all five fingers. What can it be grinning for? Kien asked himself, his suspicions aroused.

By the time the hand, with the man attached to it, had withdrawn, he was once again in possession of his eyes. The fog was parting. Kien's glance followed the figure, long and thin as he was himself, with distrust. It came to a halt in front of a bar, turned itself round and indicated with an outstretched arm the newcomer. It said some incomprehensible words and shook with laughter. To whom was it speaking? In the vicinity of the bar, on every side, not a soul was standing. The place was unbelievably neglected and dirty. Behind the bar there was most clearly to be seen a heap of many coloured rags. These people were too lazy even to open a wardrobe door; they used the space between the bar and the mirror at the back of it to throw their things down. They were not even ashamed in front of their customers! Those too now began to interest Kien. At almost every little table sat a hairy object with a face like an ape, staring doggedly in his direction. Somewhere at the back strange girls yelled. The Stars of Heaven were very low and daubed between smeary grey-brown clouds. Here and there the remains of one of them broke through the dreary layers. Once the whole of the sky had been sprinkled with golden stars, but most of them had been extinguished by smoke, the rest were dying for lack of daylight. The world beneath this sky was small. It would easily have been got into a hotel bedroom. Only as long as the fog deceived the eye it had seemed wide and wild. Each little marble table had its own planetary existence. The stink of the world was generated by each and all. Everyone was smoking, silent or battering his fist upon the hard marble. From tiny alcoves smothered cries for help could be distinguished. Suddenly an old piano made itself heard. Kien looked about for it in vain. Where had they hidden it? Old fellows dressed in rags, with cloth caps on their heads, pushed the heavy door-curtains aside with tired movements and slowly drifted about among the planets, greeting this one, threatening that, and finally settling down where they were least welcome. In a short time the place changed entirely. Movement became impossible. Who would dare to tread on the toes of such neighbours as these? Kien only was still sitting alone. He was afraid to stand up and remained where he was. Between the tables insults were bandied about. Music inspired these people with strength and fight. As soon as the piano stopped they slumped down wretchedly into themselves. Kien clutched at his head. What kind of creatures were these?

Suddenly a vast hump appeared close to him and asked, could he sit there? Kien looked down fixedly. Where was the mouth out of which speech had issued? And already the owner of the hump, a dwarf, hopped up on to a chair. He managed to seat himself and turned a pair of large melancholy eyes towards Kien. The tip of his strongly hooked nose lay in the depth of his chin. His mouth was as small as himself — only it wasn't to be found. No forehead, no ears, no neck, no buttocks — the man consisted of a hump, a majestic nose and two black, calm, sad eyes. For a long time he said nothing; he was doubtless waiting while his appearance made its own impression. Kien accustomed himself to the new circumstance. Suddenly he heard a hoarse voice underneath the table:

'How's business?'

He looked down at his legs. The voice rasped, indignantly: 'I'm not a dog, am I?' Then he knew that the dwarf had spoken. What he was to say about business he did not know. He considered the all-pervading nose of the manikin, it inspired him with mistrust. As he was not a business man he shrugged his shoulders slightly. His indifference made a great impression.

'Fischerle is my name!' The nose pecked at the table. Kien was distressed for his own good name. He did not therefore respond with it and only inclined himself stiffly, in a manner which might have passed equally well for dismissal or for greeting. The dwarf interpreted it as the latter. He dragged two arms into view — as long as the arms of a gibbon — and reached for Kien's brief-case. Its contents provoked him to laughter. The twitching corners of his mouth, appearing on both sides of the nose, at last proved the existence of the mouth itself.

'You're in the paper racket, or aren't you?' he croaked, and held up the clean folded paper. At the sight of it the whole world beneath the Stars of Heaven broke into neighing laughter. Kien, well aware of the deeper significance of his paper, felt like shouting 'Insolence!' and snatching it out of the dwarf's hand. But the very intention, bold as it was, appeared to him as a colossal crime. To atone for it he put on an unhappy and embarrassed expression.

Fischerle did not let go. 'Here's a novelty for you. Ladies and gentlemen, here's a novelty! A dumb salesman!' He waved the paper about in his crooked fingers and crushed it in at least twenty places. Kien's heart bled. The cleanliness of his library was at stake. Was there no means by which he could rescue it? Fischerle climbed up on to his chair — now he was just as tall as the sitting Kien — and sang in a cracked voice. 'I'm a fisherman — He's a fish!' At 'I' he clapped the paper against his hump, at 'he' he flicked it at Kien's ears. Kien bore it all patiently. He thought himself lucky that the raving dwarf hadn't

175

murdered him. But his behaviour was growing painful. His clean library was already defiled. He grasped that a man without a racket was of no account in this company. During the long drawn out interval between 'I' and 'he' he stood up, made a deep bow and declared resolutely: 'Kien, book racket.'

Fischerle broke off before the next 'he' and sat down. He was satisfied with his success. He shrank back into his hump and asked with utter humility: 'Do you play chess?' Kien expressed his regret.

'A person who can't play chess, isn't a person. Chess is a matter of brain, I always say. A person may be twelve foot tall, but if he doesn't play chess, he's a fool. I play chess. I'm not a fool. Now I'm asking you; answer me if you like. If you don't, don't answer me. What's a man got brains for? I'll tell you, or you'll be worrying your head about it, wouldn't that be a shame? He's got brains to play chess with. Do you get me? Say yes, then that's that. Say no, I'll explain it all over again, for you. I've always liked the book racket. May I point out to you that I learnt it on my own, not out of a book. What do you think, who's the champion in this place? I bet you don't know that one. I'll tell you who it is. The champion's called Fischerle and sitting at the same table as you are. And why do you think he came to sit here? Because you look such a misery. Now maybe you'll be thinking I always make for the miseries. Wrong, rubbish, not a bit of it. Have you any idea what a beauty my wife is! Such a rare creature as you don't often see! But, say I, who's got the brains? The miseries have got brains, that's what I say. What's the good of brains to a handsome fellow? Earning? His wife works for him. He wouldn't play chess because he'd have to stoop, might spoil his figure; now what's the conclusion? The miseries get all the brains there are. Look at chess champions — all miseries. Look here, when I see a famous man in the picture paper and he's anything to look at, Fischerle, I say to myself, there's something fishy. They've got the wrong picture. Well, what do you expect, piles and piles of photos, every one supposed to be someone famous. What's a picture paper to do? Picture papers are only human. Tell you what, it's queer you don't play chess. Everyone in the book racket plays chess. No wonder, considering the racket. They just open the book and learn the moves by heart. But do you think one of them's ever got me beaten? No man in the book racket ever beat me. As true as you're in it yourself, if you are.'

To obey and to listen was the same for Kien. Since the manikin had got on to the subject of chess he was the most harmless little Jew in the world. He never paused, his questions were rhetorical but he answered them himself. The word chess rang in his mouth like a command, as though it depended on his gracious mercy, whether he would not add the mortal 'check-mate'. Kien's silence, which had irritated him at first, now appeared to him as attentiveness and flattered him.

During games his partners were far too much afraid of him to interrupt him with objections. For he took a terrible vengeance and would hold up the foolishness of their moves to the general derision In the intervals between games — he passed half his life at the chessboard — people treated him as his shape and size warranted. He would have preferred to go on playing for ever. He dreamed of a life in which eating and sleeping would be got through while his opponent was making his moves. When he had won uninterrupted for six hours and managed to find yet another victim, his wife interfered and forced him to stop, otherwise he would get above himself. He was as indifferent to her as if she were made of stone. He stuck to her because she provided his meals. But when she snapped off the chain of his triumphs, he would dance raging round about her, hitting her in the few sensitive parts of her coarsened person. She stood it all quietly, strong as she was, and let him do as he liked. Those were the only expressions of conjugal tenderness with which he favoured her. For she loved him; he was her child. Business considerations forbade any other. She enjoyed great respect under the Stars of Heaven, because she alone of the poverty-stricken and low-priced girls of the establishment had a regular elderly gentleman, who for eight years had visited her every Monday with undeviating fidelity. On account of this regular income she was known as the Capitalist. During her frequent scenes with Fischerle, the whole place roared, but no one would have dared to start a new game against her orders. Fischerle only hit her because he knew this. For her clients, he felt tenderness, if indeed his love for chess left him any to spare. As soon as she had disappeared with one of them he could race across a chessboard to his heart's content. He had priority claims on any stranger whom chance brought to the place. Each one might be a world champion who might teach him something new. But he took it for granted that he would beat him. Only when his hope for new combinations had been shattered he introduced his wife to the stranger and got rid of her for a time. Secretly he advised the man to stay with her as long as he cared to; he, Fischerle, had always liked the man's particular racket; she was easy going, she knew how to value a man with a bit of life in him. But he begged not to be given away, business was business and he was acting against his own interests.

Earlier, many years ago, before his wife was a Capitalist, and when she had too many debts to be able to pack him off to a café, whenever she brought a client into her narrow little room, Fischerle, in spite of his hump, had to creep under the bed. There he listened carefully to everything the man said — he didn't care what his wife said — and soon he developed an instinct whether the man was a chess player or not. The moment he was sure of this, he crawled out as fast as he could — often hurting his hump very much — and challenged the unsuspecting visitor to a game of chess. Some men agreed at once, as long as the game was for money. They hoped they would win back from the shabby Jew the money they had given his wife under a more insistent pressure. They thought themselves well justified because they would certainly not now have agreed to their original bargain. But they always lost as much money again. Most of them refused Fischerle's offer, tired, suspicious or indignant. Not one of them was puzzled by his sudden appearance. But Fischerle's passion grew with the years. Each time it was harder for him to postpone his challenge long enough. Often he was forcibly overcome by the conviction that just above his head an international champion was lying incognito. Much too early he would appear at the bedside, and with his finger or his nose tap the unknown celebrity on the shoulder until he became aware not of the insect he suspected but of the dwarf and his challenge. This was too much for all of them, and not one but instantly used the occasion to demand his money back. After this had happened several times — once an infuriated cattle dealer even fetched the police — his wife declared categorically that things must change or she would get herself someone else. Whether things were going well or not, Fischerle was sent henceforward to the café and was not allowed to come home before four in the morning. Soon after that the regular old gentleman who came every Monday settled himself in and the worst times were over. He stayed all night. Fischerle would find him still there when he came home, and was regularly greeted by him with 'Hallo, World Champion!' This was intended for a good joke — in time it grew to be eight years old — but Fischerle took it for an insult. If the gentleman, whose name nobody knew — he even concealed his Christian name — was particularly satisfied, he took pity on the little man and quickly let himself be beaten by him. The gentleman was one of those people who like to settle the superfluities of life all at once. When he left the little room he had got rid of both love and pity for a week. His voluntary defeat by Fischerle saved him the pennies he would otherwise have had ready for beggars in the shop he presumably kept. On its door was a notice which ran: 'Beggars will be given nothing here.'

There was, however, one type of men in the world whom Fischerle hated — International Chess Champions. With a kind of rabid fury he pursued every important tournament which came to his notice in papers or magazines. Once he had played them through for himself, he could keep them in his head for years. Owing to his unchallenged championship in the café, it was easy for him to prove to his friends the worthlessness of these great players. Move by move, he would show them — they relied unquestioningly on his memory — what had happened at this or that tournament. When their admiration for such a match reached a pitch which annoyed him, he made up a few false moves and thence carried on the game just as it suited him. Rapidly he would steer towards the catastrophe; they knew, of course, who had suffered it, for here too, names were a fetish. Voices were raised to say that Fischerle himself would have done no better. Nobody had recognized the mistake made by the defeated party. Then Fischerle would push his chair so far back from the table that his outstretched arm could just reach the pieces. This was his particular way of showing contempt, since his mouth, the organ which other men use for the purpose, was almost entirely hidden by his nose. Then he would croak: 'Give me a handkerchief. I'll win the game blind.' If his wife was there she would hand him her dirty scarf; she knew that she must not interfere with his chess tournament triumphs which only took place about once every few months. If she were not there, one of the other girls would put her hands over his eyes. Swift and sure, he would take the game back move for move. At the place where the original mistake had occurred he would stop. It was the very point where he had began to cheat. Cheating again he carried the opposing party with equal boldness to victory. Every move was breathlessly followed. Everyone was amazed. The girls fondled his hump and kissed his nose. The men, even the good-looking ones who knew little or nothing about chess, beat their fists on the marble tables and asserted, in just indignation, that it would be a dirty swindle if Fischerle were not to become the world champion. They shouted so loudly that they at once recaptured the girls' attention. Fischerle didn't care. He pretended that their applause meant nothing to him, and only remarked drily: 'What do you expect, I'm only a poor devil. If someone gave me the deposit, now, I'd be world champion to-morrow!' 'To-day!' they all cried. That was an end of their enthusiasm.

Thanks to the fact that he was an unrecognized genius at chess, and thanks to the regular customer of his wife's, the Capitalist, Fischerle enjoyed one important privilege beneath the Stars of Heaven. He was allowed to cut out and keep all the printed chess problems in the papers, although these, which had already passed through half a dozen hands were — after several months — sent on to an even more miserable café. But Fischerle did not keep the scraps of chequered paper; he tore them into tiny fragments and threw them down the lavatory with disgust. He lived in mortal terror lest anyone should want to refer to one of them. He was by no means convinced of his importance. He racked his brains over the actual moves which he concealed. Therefore he loathed world champions like the plague.

'Where would I be, d'you think if I was given a stipendium?' he said to Kien. 'A man without a stipendium is a cripple. Twenty years I've been waiting for a stipendium. You don't think I'd take anything from my wife, do you? I want peace, and I want a stipendium. Move in with me says she. I was a boy then. No, I said, what does Fischerle want with a wife? What *do* you want then, says she, she couldn't leave me alone. What do I want? A stipendium's what I want. Nothing for nothing. You wouldn't start a firm without capital. Chess too's a racket, why shouldn't it be? There's nothing that isn't a racket, come to think of it. Very good, says she, you move in with me and you'll get your stipendium. Now, I ask you, do you understand what I'm talking about? D'you know what a stipendium is? I'll tell you in any case. If you know already, it'll do no harm, if you don't it'll do no harm either. Now listen: stipendium is a refined word. This word comes from the French and means exactly the same as capital does in Jewish!'

Kien swallowed. By their etymology shall ye know them. What a place! He swallowed and was silent. It was the best thing to do in this den of thieves. Fischerle made a minute pause in order to observe the effect of the word 'Jewish' on his companion. You never can tell. The world is crawling with anti-semites. A Jew always has to be on guard against deadly enemies. Hump-backed dwarfs and others, who have nevertheless managed to rise to the rank of pimp, cannot be too careful. The swallowing did not escape him. He interpreted it as embarrassment, and from that moment decided that Kien must be a Jew, which he certainly was not.

Reassured he went on: 'You can only make use of it in better-class professions,' he said, meaning the stipendium; 'when she swore by the Holy Saints I moved in with her. Do you know how long ago that was? I can tell you because you're my friend; that was twenty years ago. Twenty years she's been scraping and saving, doesn't allow herself anything, doesn't allow me anything. Do you know what a monk is? No, you wouldn't know that because you're a Jew, we don't have monks among the Jews, monks, never mind, we live like monks, I'll tell you a better one, perhaps you'll understand it now since you don't understand much: we live like nuns, nuns are the wives of the monks, see? Every monk has a wife and she's called a nun. But you can't imagine how separately they live. That's the sort of marriage everyone would like, the Jews ought to have that kind too! And would you believe it, we haven't got that stipendium together yet? Add it up now, you must be able to add! You'd give twenty schillings right away. But not everyone would give that. Nowadays a gentleman's a rarity. Who can afford such stupidity? You're my friend. Like the good chap you are, you say to yourself Fischerle must have his stipendium. If not, he'll be ruined. Can I let a man like Fischerle ruin himself? That would be a shame, no, I can't do a thing like that. What shall I do? I'll give his wife twenty schillings, she'll take me along with it and my friend'll have his fun. There's nothing I wouldn't do for a friend. I'll prove it to you. You bring your wife here, until I got my stipendium that is, and I swear to you I'm not a coward. D'you think I'm afraid of a woman? What harm can a woman do? Have you a wife?'

This was the first question to which Fischerle expected an answer. True he was as sure of the wife, whose existence he was questioning, as he was of his hump. But he longed for a game, he had been watched now for three hours and could bear it no longer. He was determined to bring the discussion to a practical conclusion. Kien was silent. What could he have said? His wife was his sore point; with the best intention in the world nothing true could be said of her. He was, actually, neither married, nor single nor divorced. 'Have you a wife?' asked Fischerle a second time. But already it sounded threatening. Kien was worried about the truth. The same thing which had happened before over the book racket was happening again. Necessity makes liars of us all. 'I have not a wife!' he asserted with a smile which lit up his austerity. If he must lie, he would choose the pleasantest alternative. 'Then I'll give you mine!' burst out Fischerle. Had the man in the book racket had a wife, Fischerle's offer would have been differently worded:

'Then I'll make you a nice change from her.' Now he shouted loudly across the café: 'Are you coming, or not?'

She came. She was large, fat and round, and half a century old. She introduced herself by shrugging a shoulder in Fischerle's direction and adding, not without a breath of pride, 'My husband'. Kien stood up and bowed low. He was terrified of whatever was going to happen now. Aloud he said: 'Delighted!' To himself softly, inaudibly: 'Strumpet.' With this archaic word he reduced her to nothing. Fischerle said: 'Well then, sit down.' She obeyed. His nose reached up to her bosom. Nose and bosom leant side by side over the marble table. Suddenly the manikin burst out and rattled rapidly as if he had forgotten the most important thing: 'Book racket!'

Kien was again silent. The woman found him repulsive. She compared his boniness to her husband's hump and found the latter beautiful. Her rabbit-face always had something to say for himself. He wasn't born dumb. There was a time when he even talked to her. Now she was getting too old for him. He's quite right. It's not as though he goes with other girls. He's got a heart of gold, that kid. Everybody thinks they're still carrying on with each other. Every one of her girl friends is after him. You can't trust women. She's different. You can trust her. Men aren't to be trusted either. But you can trust Fischerle. Rather than have anything to do with a woman, he says, he'd have nothing to do with anyone. She agrees to everything. She doesn't want any of that. But he mustn't talk about it, that's all. He's so modest. He's never wanted a thing out of her. A pity he doesn't look after his clothes a bit more. Time and again you'd think he'd scrambled straight out of the dustbin. If that Ferdy hasn't given Mizzi an ultimatum: he'll wait another year for that motorbike she promised him. If she hasn't got it by the end of the year, sh— him if he doesn't find himself another girl. Now she's scraping and saving, but where's she going to get a motorbike from? Her rabbit-face wouldn't do a thing like that. The beautiful eyes he's got! He can't help his hump, can he?

Always when Fischerle found her a client she felt that he wanted to be rid of her and was grateful to him for his love. Later on she would find him too conceited again. But on the whole she was a contented creature, and in spite of her squalid life had little hate in her. That little was all for chess. While the other girls knew the first principles of the game, in all her life she had never understood why the different pieces had different moves. It disgusted her that the King should be so powerless. She'd teach that pert thing the queen a thing or two! Why should she have it all her own way and the king not at all? Often she would watch the game tensely. A stranger would have judged her by her expression a pronounced connoisseur. In fact she was simply waiting for the queen to be taken. If that happened she burst into triumphant crooning and left the table at once. She shared her husband's hate for the stranger queen, and was jealous of the love with which he guarded his own. Her girl friends, more independent than she was, placed themselves at the top of the social hierarchy and called the queen the tart, the king the pimp. Only the Capitalist still clung to the existing order from whose lowest rank, by virtue of her regular gentleman, she had already climbed. She, who otherwise set the tone for the most outspoken jokes, would not join in against the king. As for the queen, 'tart' was too good a name for her. The castles and the knights pleased her, because they looked like real ones, and when Fischerle's knight charged full gallop across the board she would laugh out loud in her calm husky voice. Twenty years after he had first come to her with his chessboard she would still ask him in all innocence why the castles could not be left standing at the corners of the board where they had been at the beginning of the game; they looked ever so much nicer there. Fischerle spurned her woman's witlessness and said not a word. When she bored him with her questions — she only wanted to hear him speak, she loved his croaking, nobody else had such a raven-voice — he would shut her up with some drastic assertion: 'Have I a hump or haven't I? And suppose I have? You can take yourself out sliding! Maybe that'll knock a little sense into your head.' His hump distressed her. She'd rather have overlooked it. She had a feeling as if she were answerable for the misshapenness of her child. As soon as he had discovered this trait in her, which seemed to him quite mad, he made use of it as blackmail. His hump was the one dangerous threat on which he could rely.

At this very moment she was gazing lovingly upon him. His hump compared to this skeleton was beautiful. She was happy that he had called her to his table. She gave herself no trouble at all with Kien. After a general silence she said: 'Well, what about it? How much will you give me?' Kien blushed. Fischerle went for her at once. 'Don't talk so silly! I won't have my friend insulted. He's got a head on his shoulders. He doesn't talk nonsense. Every word he turns over in his head a hundred times before he says it. If he says something it's worth saying. He's interested in my stipendium and is going to make a voluntary contribution of twenty schillings.' 'Stipendium? Whatever's that?' 'Stipendium is a refined word!' Fischerle bawled. 'It comes from the French and means the same as capital in Jewish!' 'Capital? Who says I got capital?' His wife simply didn't catch on. Why on earth had he used a French word? He was determined to be in the right. He looked at his wife long and gravely, indicated Kien with his nose and declared pompously: 'He knows everything.' 'Everything?' 'That we're saving up for my chess championship.' 'I wouldn't dream of it! I don't earn that much. My name isn't Mizzi and you're not Ferdy. What do I get out of you? More kicks than ha'pence. You know what you are, do you? You're a cripple! Go and beg if you don't like it!' She called Kien to witness the crying injustice of it. 'The cheek of it! You wouldn't hardly credit it. A cripple like him! He ought to think himself lucky!'

Fischerle shrank down, he gave his game up for lost and only said mournfully to Kien: 'You be thankful you're not a married man. First we scrape and save twenty years every brass farthing and now she's blued the whole bloody stipendium with her fancy boys.' For a moment this shameless lie took his wife's breath away. 'I swear,' she screamed as soon as she had recovered herself, 'in all these twenty years I haven't had a single man, only him!' Fischerle opened his hands to Kien in a gesture of resignation: 'A whore who never had a man!' At the word 'Whore' he raised his eyebrows. At this insult his wife burst into noisy crying. Her words grew incomprehensible but one had the impression that she was sobbing about a regular income. 'Now you can see yourself, she's admitting it.' Fischerle was regaining courage. 'Where do you think she gets a regular income from? From a gentleman who turns up every Monday. In my flat. Listen, a woman *always* tells lies, and why does a woman always tell lies? Because she's a liar! Now I ask you: Could you tell a lie? Could I tell a lie? Out of the question! And why? because we've got heads on our shoulders. Have you ever seen a man with a head on his shoulders who tells lies? I haven't!' His wife sobbed more and more loudly.

Kien agreed with all his heart. In his terror he had never asked himself whether Fischerle was telling the truth or lying. Since the woman had sat down at the table, he was relieved by every hostile gesture in her direction wherever it came from. Since she had asked him for a present he knew who it was he had before him; a second Therese. He knew nothing about the rituals of the place, but one thing he recognized clearly — this stainless spirit in a wretched body, had struggled for twenty years to lift itself out of the mire of its surroundings. Therese would not allow it. He was forced to impose enormous sacrifices on himself, never losing sight of his glorious goal — a free mind. Therese, no less determined, dragged him for ever back into the slime. He saves, not out of meanness, his is a generous soul; she wastes it again, so that he shall never escape her. He has clutched at one tiny corner of the world of the spirit and clings to it like a drowning man. Chess is his library. He only talks about rackets because any other kind of speech is forbidden here. But it is significant that he regards the book racket with such esteem. Kien pictured to himself the battle this down-trodden man fought for his own flat. He takes a book home to read it secretly, she tears it in pieces and scatters it to the winds. She forces him to let her use his home for her unspeakable purposes. Possibly she pays a servant, a spy, to keep the house clear of books when she is out. Books are forbidden, her own way of life is permitted. After a long struggle he succeeds in wringing from her the concession of a chessboard. She has confined him to the smallest room in the house. There he sits through the long nights and handling those wooden chessmen recovers his human dignity. He almost feels released when she is receiving these visits. During these hours he might be dead for her. Things must reach this pass with her before she will stop torturing him. But even then he listens unwillingly lest she should reappear, the worse for drink. She stinks of alcohol. She smokes. She flings open the door and with her clumsy foot kicks over the chessboard. Mr. Fischerle weeps like a little child. He had just reached the most interesting part of his book. He picks up the letters scattered all over the floor and turns his face away so that she shall not rejoice over his tears. He is a little hero. He has character. How often does the word 'Strumpet!' spring to his lips. He swallows it, she would not understand. She would long since have turned him out of the house, but she is waiting until he makes a will in her favour. Probably he is not rich. All the same he has enough for her to want to rob him of it. He has no intention of making this final sacrifice. Defending himself he keeps his roof over his head. Did he but know that he owed that roof to her speculations on his will! He must not be told. He could do himself an injury. He is not made of granite. His dwarfish constitution . . .

Never before had Kien felt himself enter so deeply into the mind of another man. He had been successful in freeing himself from Therese. He had struck at her with her own weapons, outwitted her and locked her in. Here she was again, sitting at his very table, making the same demands as before, nagging as before, and — the only alteration in her — had this time adopted a suitable profession. But her destructive activity was not directed at him, she took little notice of him, all her attention was directed at the man opposite, whom nature by a mistaken etymology had, moreover, fashioned as a cripple. Kien felt himself deeply indebted to this man. He must do something for him. He respected him. Had Mr. Fischerle not been of so delicate a sensibility he would have offered him money direct. No doubt he could make use of it. But he was as anxious not on any account to hurt his feelings, as he was anxious not to hurt his own. Possibly he might steer the conversation back to that point at which, with a woman's shamelessness, Therese had interrupted them?

He drew out his wallet, still crammed full of valuable banknotes. Holding it unusually long in his hand, he extracted from it all the bank-notes and placidly counted them all over. Mr. Fischerle was to be per-suaded by this that the offer about to be made to him was by no means a great sacrifice. When he reached the thirtieth-hundred schilling note Kien looked down at the little fellow. Possibly he was already mellowed enough for the offer to be dared, for who enjoys counting money? Fischerle was looking stealthily all about him; the only person for whom he had no eyes at all was Kien counting his money, surely out of the delicacy of his feelings and his repulsion from filthy lucre. Kien was not to be discouraged, he went on counting, but loudly now in a clear high voice. Secretly he apologized to the little man for his insistence, for he noticed how much he hurt his ears. The dwarf wriggled restlessly on his chair. He laid his head down on the table so as to stop up at least one ear, the sensitive creature, then he pushed his wife's bosom about, what was he doing that for, he was making it broader, it was broad enough already, he was obscuring Kien's views. The woman let him do as he liked, she was silent now. Doubtless she was counting on the money. But she was making a mistake there. Therese would get nothing. When Kien had got to forty-five the little fellow's agonies had reached their peak. Imploringly he whispered: 'Pst! Pst!' Kien softened. Should he spare him the gift after all, no, no, later he would be glad of it all the same, perhaps he would run away with it and rid himself of this Therese. At the number fifty-three Fischerle clutched his wife's face and croaked out like a madman: 'Can't you keep quiet? What are you after, you silly bitch? What d'you know about chess? I'll chessboard you! I'll eat you alive! Scram!' With every new figure he said something else; the woman seemed bewildered and made as if to go. This did not suit Kien at all. She had to be there when he gave the little fellow his present. She had to be angry at getting nothing herself, or her husband wouldn't enjoy it. Money alone meant little to him. He must hand it over to him before she went.

He waited for a round figure — the next was sixty — and broke off his counting. He rose to his feet and took out a hundred schilling note. He would rather have selected several at once but he was not going to hurt the dwarf's feelings with either too large or too small a sum. For a moment he stood there, tall and in silence, to heighten the solemnity of his proposal. Then he spoke; they were the most courteous words of his life:

'Honoured Mr. Fischerle! It is impossible for me to repress any longer a request which I have to address to you. Pray do me the honour of accepting towards your stipendium, as you are pleased to call it, this token of my esteem!'

Instead of 'thank you', the little fellow whispered 'Pst! Have it your own way,' and went on screaming at his wife; he was evidently bewildered. His furious words and looks almost knocked her under the table. He cared so little for the money offered that he did not even look at it. Not to hurt Kien's feelings he simply stretched out his arm and clutched at the note. Instead of the single note he grasped the entire bundle, but in his excitement didn't even notice it. Kien nearly smiled. From sheer modesty the man acts like the greediest thief. As soon as he notices it he will be painfully embarrassed. To spare him embarrassment, Kien exchanged the bundle for the single note. The dwarf's fingers were hard and sensitive, they clawed themselves, doubtless against the will of their owner, round the bundle; they still did not feel anything even when Kien detached them one after another from the packet, but closed themselves automatically again over the single hundred schilling note which remained. Playing chess has hardened his hands, thought Kien; Mr. Fischerle is used to grasping the pieces firmly, they alone keep him alive. In the meantime he had sat down again. His beneficence made him happy. Therese too, smothered in injuries, her face aflame, had got up and left the table in earnest. She might as well go, he had no further use for her. She could expect nothing from him. It was his duty to help her husband to his victory over her, and in that he had succeeded.

In the tumult of his happy sensations, Kien did not hear what was going on about him. Suddenly he felt a heavy blow on his shoulder.

It made him jump and he looked round. A vast hand lay there, and a voice zoomed: 'What about me?' At least a dozen fellows were seated round about, since when? He had not noticed them before. Fists were piled up on the table, more fellows were coming along, those standing at the back leant over those in front who were sitting. A girl's voice called out plaintively: 'Let me out, I can't see a thing.' Another one, shrilly: 'Ferdy, your motorbike's in the bag!' Someone held the open brief-case in the air, shook it, found nothing, and wailed, disillusioned: 'Go to hell with your paper.' You couldn't see the room any more for the people in it. Fischerle was croaking. No one listened to him. His wife was there again. She was screaming. Another woman, fatter still, struck out right and left and forced her way through the men shouting: 'I'll have something too!' She was covered with all those srcaps of rags that Kien had seen behind the bar. The stars shook. Chairs collapsed. An angel's voice was crying with joy. Just as Kien understood what it was all about, he was crowned with his own brief-case. He saw and heard no more, he only felt that he was lying on the floor while his pockets, and the very seams and holes in his suit were being searched by hands of every shape and weight. He trembled all over, not for himself, only for his head; they might throw his books about. They are going to kill him but he won't betray his books. We want the books! they will order him, where are your books? But he won't give them up, never, never, never, he is a martyr, he is dying for his books. His lips move, they want to say how strong he is in his resolution, but they dare not speak aloud, they move only as though they had spoken.

But it occurs to no one to ask him. They prefer to find out for them-selves. Several times he is pushed around over the floor. They all but undress him to the skin. Whichever way they twist and turn him, they find nothing. Suddenly he realizes that he is alone. All the hands have vanished. Stealthily he feels for his head. As a protection against the next attack he leaves his hand up there. The second hand follows it. He tries to stand up without taking his hands away from his head. His enemies are watching for this moment to snatch at the defenceless books; careful, careful! He succeeds. He is lucky. Now he is standing. Where are these creatures? Better not look round; he may be noticed. His glance, cautiously directed to the furthest corner of the room, falls on a heap of people at work on each other with knives and fists. Now, too, he hears their wild screams. He will not understand them. If he did they might understand him. On tiptoe, on his long legs he creeps out. Someone clutches at his back. Running even, he is too cautious to look round. He squints backwards, holding his breath, pressing his hands with all his strength to his head. But it is only the door curtains. In the street he draws a deep breath. What a pity he can't close those doors. The library is saved.

A few doors off the dwarf was waiting for him. He handed his brief-case back to him. 'The paper's there too,' he said, 'I'll show you the kind of man I am.' In his distress Kien had forgotten that a person called Fischerle existed in the world. He was all the more overcome by this incredible proof of his devotion. 'The paper too,' he faltered, 'how can I thank you . . .' He had not mistaken his man. 'That's nothing,' declared the little fellow. 'Now will you kindly step in here with me.' Kien obeyed, he was deeply moved and would gladly have embraced the little man. 'Do you know what a reward is?' asked the dwarf as soon as they were inside a porch hidden from passers-by. 'You must know what that is. Ten per cent. In there they are killing each other, men and women, and I've got it.' He drew out Kien's wallet and handed it over to him like a ceremonial presentation. 'I'm not a fool! I'm not going to be locked up to save their throats.' Since his most precious possessions had been in danger, Kien had forgotten all about the money too. He laughed aloud at so much conscientiousness, took the wallet back mainly because he was so pleased with Fischerle and repeated: 'How can I thank you! How can I thank you!' 'Ten per cent,' said the dwarf. Kien plunged into the packet of notes and offered a large portion to Fischerle. 'You count first of all,' he yelled. 'Business is business. All of a sudden you'll be saying I robbed you.' It was all very well for Kien to count. Had he an idea how much there had been before? Fischerle on the other hand knew exactly how many notes he had already set aside. His demand that Kien should count referred to the reward alone. But to please him Kien counted it all carefully through. When for the second time to-day, he reached the figure sixty, Fischerle saw himself locked up. He decided to make off at once — for this contingency he had already extracted his own reward — but quickly he tried one last attempt. 'There you are, it's all safe!' 'Of course,' said Kien, pleased not to have to do any more counting. 'Count out the reward now and we're quits.' Kien began again and got as far as nine, he would have gone on counting forever. 'Stop! Ten per cent!' cried Fischerle. He knew exactly how much there had been in all. While he was waiting for Kien he had swiftly and thoroughly been through the wallet.

When the deal was finished, he gave Kien his hand, looked sadly up at him and said: 'You ought to know what I've done for you! It's all over with the Stars of Heaven for me. You don't think I can ever go in there again, do you? They'd find all this money on me and kill me dead. Because where does Fischerle get the money from? And how am I to tell them where I got it from? If I say I got it from the gentleman in the book racket they'll smash me to smithereens and steal the money out of my pockets while I lie there. If I say nothing they'll take it from me while I'm still alive. You see how it is, if Fischerle lives, then he's nothing left to live for, and if he dies, well he's dead. That's what you get for being a friend.' He was still hoping for a tip.

Kien felt obliged to help this person, the first worthy object he had found in his life, to a better and more dignified existence. 'I am not a tradesman, I am a man of learning and a librarian,' he said and bowed condescendingly to the dwarf. 'You may enter my service and I will look after you.'

'Like a father,' completed the little fellow. 'Just as I thought. Very well, off we go!' He marched boldly out. Kien ambled after him. He cast about for work to give to his new *famulus*. A friend must never suspect that he is being given presents. He could help him in the evenings to unload and pile up the books.

CHAPTER II

THE HUMP

A FEW hours after he had started on his new job Fischerle was fully enlightened as to the desires and peculiarities of his master. On taking
up their quarters for the night he was presented to the hotel porter as
'my friend and colleague'. Fortunately the porter recognized the open-
handed Owner of a Library who had already spent a night in that hotel;
otherwise both the gentleman and his colleague would have been
thrown out. Fischerle took pains to follow what Kien was writing on
the registration form. He was too small, he couldn't contrive to poke
his nose into these matters. His fears were on account of the second
registration form which the porter had ready for him. But Kien, who
was making up in one night for the lack of delicacy of a lifetime, considered how difficult the little fellow would find it to write and included him on his own form under the heading 'accompanied by . . .'.
He handed the second form back to the porter with the words, 'This
is unnecessary'. Thus he spared Fischerle not only the difficulty of
writing, but, more important still in his eyes, the humiliating admission
of his status as a servant.

As soon as they reached their rooms upstairs, Kien took out the
brown paper and began to smooth it out. 'True it's all crumpled,' he
said, 'but we have no other.' Fischerle seized the occasion to make
himself indispensable, and worked carefully over each sheet which his
master regarded as already perfected. 'I was to blame, with that
slapping,' he declared. His success was the measure of the enviable
nimbleness of his fingers. Next the paper was spread out over the
floor in both rooms. Fischerle gambolled from side to side, lay flat
down and crawled — a peculiar, squat, hump-backed reptile — from
corner to corner. 'We'll soon have it all shipshape, that's nothing!'
he panted again and again. Kien smiled, he was not accustomed to
this cringing nor to the hump and rejoiced at the personal honour which
the dwarf was showing him. The impending explanation however
filled him with a certain anxiety. Possibly he overestimated the intelligence of the manikin, almost as old as he, who had lived countless
years in exile without books. He might well misunderstand the task
which was intended for him. Perhaps he would ask: 'Where are the

books?' even before he had grasped where they were safely kept during the day. It would be best to leave him crawling about on the floor a little longer. Meanwhile some popular simile might occur to Kien with which he could enlighten this uneducated brain. Even the little fellow's fingers disquieted him. They were in constant motion; they kept on smoothing out the paper far too long. They were hungry, hungry fingers want food. They might demand the books, which Kien was determined no one should touch, no one at all. Also he feared to come into collision with the little fellow's thirst for education. He might reproach him, with some appearance of justice, for letting his books lie fallow. How was he to defend himself? Fools rush in where wise men fear to tread. There was the fool already standing in front of him saying: 'All done!'

'Then please will you help me unpack the books!' said Kien blindly, and was astonished at his own boldness. To cut short any unwelcome questions he immediately lifted a packet out of his head and held it out to the little fellow. The latter managed to take it up cleverly in his long arms and said: 'So many! Where shall I put them down?' 'Many?' shouted Kien, indignantly. 'That isn't the thousandth part.'

'I get you. A tenth per cent. Do you want me to stand about here another year? I can't manage it much longer with all this to carry. Where shall I put them down?' 'On the paper. Begin in the corner over there, then we won't fall over them later on.'

Fischerle slid carefully over to the corner. He avoided any violent movement which would have endangered his burden. In the corner he knelt down, laid the packet carefully on the floor, and straightened its sides so that no irregularity should shock the eye. Kien had followed him. He was already holding out the next packet towards him: he distrusted the little fellow, it seemed to him somehow as if he was being mocked. In Fischerle's hands the work went forward swimmingly. He took packet after packet, his nimbleness grew with practice. Between the piles he left always a few inches where he could conveniently insert his hands. He thought of everything, even of the repacking in the morning. He allowed only a moderate height to each pile and tested them when he had got so far by gently passing the tip of his nose over them. Although he was quite absorbed in his measuring, he said every time: 'Beg pardon, sir!' Higher than his nose he would not let them be. Kien was doubtful: it seemed to him that if the piles were to be built thus low the available space would be used up too soon. He had no desire to sleep with half the library still in his head. But for the present he said nothing and let his *famulus* do as he wished. He had half taken him to his heart already. He forgave him the disdain contained in his exclamation: 'So many!' He rejoiced to think of the moment when, the floor space available in both rooms being completely used up, he would look down at the little fellow with mild irony and ask: 'And now where?'

After an hour Fischerle was in the greatest difficulty on account of his hump. Twist and turn as he would he collided with books everywhere. Except for a narrow path from the bed in one room to the bed in the other, everything was evenly covered with books. Fischerle was in a sweat and no longer dared to pass the tip of his nose over the topmost layer of the piles of books. He tried to draw in his hump but couldn't manage it. This physical exertion was almost too much for him. He was so tired he felt like spitting on the books and going to sleep. But he carried on until, however much he tried, he couldn't discover the tiniest empty space and then crumpled up half dead. 'In all my born days I never see such a library,' he growled. Kien's smile spread over his entire face. 'You haven't seen half of it,' he said. Fischerle had not reckoned with this. 'We'll finish the rest in the morning,' he asserted, threateningly. Kien felt caught out. He had boasted. In fact a good two-thirds of the books were already unloaded. What would the little man think of him if he found out. Accurate people do not like to be accused of exaggeration. He must take care to sleep to-morrow in a hotel where the rooms were smaller. He would give him smaller packets at a time, two packets made up one pile precisely, and if Fischerle, with the help of his nose, were to notice anything, he would say to him simply: 'People's noses are not always on the same level. There are many things you will have to learn from me.' He could not allow any more unpacking to-night, the little man was tired enough already. He must be permitted a well-earned rest. 'I respect your fatigue,' he said; "what we do for books, is well done. You can go to bed now. We will continue in the morning'. He treated him considerately, but as a servant. The work which he had just performed reduced him to that rank.

When Fischerle was in bed and had rested himself a little, he called out to Kien: 'Bad beds!' He felt so comfortable — in all his born days he had never lain on such a soft mattress — he had to say something about it.

Kien was in China; he was there every night before he fell asleep. The extraordinary happenings of the day gave his imaginings a different form. He conceived without an immediate revulsion the idea of a popularization of his learning. He felt that the dwarf understood him. He conceded that like-minded human beings might exist. If it were possible to infuse these with a little education, a little humanity, this would certainly be an achievement. The first step is always the hardest. Moreover no encouragement should be given to arbitrary action. Through daily contact with so vast a quantity of learning the little man's hunger for it would grow greater and greater; suddenly he would be caught secreting a book and trying to read it. This must not be allowed, it would be harmful to him, it would destroy what little intelligence he had. How much could the poor fellow possibly absorb? He would have to be prepared for it orally. There was no hurry for him to begin reading on his own. Years would pass before he would be fluent in Chinese. But he would become familiar with the ideas and the interpreters of the Chinese cultural world long ere this. To awaken his interest in these things they must be associated with the experiences of every day. Under the title 'Mencius and Us' a very pretty essay might be put together. What would he be able to make of it? Kien recollected that the dwarf had just said something; what it was he did not know, but in any case he must still be awake.

'What have we to learn from Mencius?' he called loudly. That was a better title. It was clear from it at once that Mencius was a human being. A man of learning is naturally anxious to avoid gross misunderstandings.

'Bad beds, say I!' Fischerle called back even louder.

'Beds?'

'Yeh, bugs!'

'What! Go to sleep at once and let me have no more jokes! You have much to learn in the morning.'

'I tell you what, I've learnt quite enough to-day.'

'That's only an idea of yours. Go to sleep, I shall count up to three.'

'Sleep, indeed! And suppose someone steals the books and we're ruined. I'm not taking any risks. Do you suppose I shall sleep a wink? You may, seeing you're a rich man. Not me!'

Fischerle was really afraid of going to sleep. He was a man of habits. Should he dream he would be perfectly capable of stealing all Kien's money. In his sleep he had not the least idea what he was doing. A man dreams of the things which mean something to him. Fischerle was happiest rolling in heaps of bank-notes. When he got tired of rolling, and if he knew for dead certain that not one of his false friends was anywhere about, he would sit down on top of them and play a game of chess. There was an advantage in sitting up so high. He could do two things at once this way; he could see a long way off anyone coming to steal them, and he could hold the chessboard. That was the way great men managed their affairs. With the right hand you pushed the pieces about, with the left you rubbed the dirt off your fingers on to the bank-notes. The trouble was there were too many of them. Say — millions. What should we do with all these millions? Giving them away wouldn't be a bad idea, but who could trust himself to do it? They'd only got to see when a small man had got anything, that lot, and they'd snatch it away. A small man wasn't allowed to get above himself. He'd got the money alright, but he mustn't use it. What had he got to be sitting up there for, they'd say. It's all very well, but where was a small man to put all those millions when he hadn't anywhere to keep them? An operation would be the sensible thing. Dangle a million in front of the famous surgeon's nose. Sir, you said, cut off my hump and that's for you. For a million a man would become an artist. Once the hump had gone, you said: dear sir, the million was a forgery, but here's a couple of thou'. The man might even thank you. The hump was burnt. Now you might walk straight for the rest of your life. But a sensible person wasn't such a fool. He took his millions, rolled up all the banknotes small, and made a new hump out of them. He put it on. Not a soul noticed anything. He knew he was straight; people thought he was a poor cripple. He knew he was a millionaire; people thought he was a poor devil. When he went to bed he pushed the hump round on to his stomach. Great God, he'd love to sleep on his back, just once.

At this point Fischerle rolled over and lay on his hump and was thankful for the pain which jerked him out of his dozing. This mustn't go on he said to himself; all of a sudden he'd be dreaming that the heaps of money were just over there, he'd get up to fetch them and a fine mess he'd be in then. As though the whole lot didn't belong to him, anyway. The police were quite unnecessary. He could do without their interference. He'd earn it all honestly. The man in the other room was an idiot, the man in this one had got a head on his shoulders. Who was going to have the money in the end?

Fischerle might well argue with himself. Stealing had become a habit with him. For a little while he hadn't been stealing because where he lived there was nothing to steal. He didn't take part in expeditions far

195

afield as the police had their eye on him. He could be too easily identified. Policemen's zeal for their duty knew no limits. Half the night
he lay awake, his eyes forcibly held open, his hands clenched in the
most complicated fashion. He expelled the heaps of money from his
mind. Instead he went through all the rough passages and hard words
he had ever experienced in police stations. Were such things necessary?
And on top of it all they took away everything you possessed. You
never saw a penny of it again. *That* wasn't stealing! When their
insults ceased to be effective and he was fed to the back teeth with the
police and already had one arm hanging out of bed, he fell back on
some games of chess. They were interesting enough to keep him firmly
fixed in bed; but his arm remained outside, ready to pounce. He played
more cautiously than usual, pausing before some moves to think for a
ridiculously long time. His opponent was a world champion. He
dictated the moves to him proudly. Slightly bewildered by the obedience of the champion he exchanged him for another one: this one too
put up with a great deal. Fischerle was playing, in fact, for both of
them. The opponent could think of no better moves than those dictated to him by Fischerle, nodded his head gratefully and was beaten
hollow in spite of it. The scene repeated itself several times until
Fischerle said: 'I won't play with such half-wits,' and stretched his legs
out of bed. Then he exclaimed: 'A world champion? Where is there
a world champion? There isn't any world champion here!'

To make sure, he got up and looked round the room. As soon as
they won the world's title people simply went and hid themselves.
He could find no one. All the same he could have sworn the world
champion was sitting on the bed playing chess with him. Surely he
couldn't be hiding in the next room? Now don't you worry. Fischerle
would soon find him. Calm as calm, he looked through the next
room; the room was empty. He opened the door of the wardrobe
and made a pounce with his hand, no chess player would escape him.
He moved very softly, who wouldn't? Why should that long creature
with the books be disturbed in his sleep only because Fischerle had to
track down his enemy? Quite possibly the champion wasn't there at
all, and for a mere whim he was throwing his beautiful job away.
Under the bed he grazed over every inch with the tip of his nose. It
was a long time since he'd been back under any bed and it reminded
him of the old days at home. As he crawled out his eyes rested on a
coat folded up over a chair. Then it occurred to him how greedy
world champions always were for money, they could never get

enough; to win the title from them one had to put down heaps of money in cash, just like that, on the table; there was no doubt the fellow was after the money, and was lurking about somewhere near the wallet. He might not have found it yet, it ought to be saved from him; a creature like that could manage anything. To-morrow the money'd be gone and the flagpole would think Fischerle took it. But you couldn't deceive him. With his long arms he stretched for the wallet from below, pulled it out and withdrew himself under the bed. He might have crawled right out, but why should he? The world champion was larger and stronger than he, sure as fate he was standing behind that chair, lurking for the money, and would knock Fischerle out because he'd got in first. By this skilful manœuvre no one noticed anything. Let the dirty swindler stay where he was. Nobody asked him to come. He could scram. That would be best. Who wanted him?

Soon Fischerle had forgotten him. In his hiding place right at the back under the bed he counted over the beautiful new notes, just for the pleasure of it. He remembered exactly how many there were. As soon as he had done he started again at the beginning. Fischerle is off now to a far country, to America. There he goes up to the world champion Capablanca, and says: 'I've been looking for you!' puts down his caution money and plays until the fellow is beaten hollow. On the next day Fischerle's picture is in all the papers. He does pretty well out of it all. At home, under the Stars of Heaven, that lot wouldn't believe their eyes, his wife, the whore, begins to howl and yell if she'd only known it she would have let him play all he wanted; the others shut her up with a couple of smacks — serve her right — that's what happens when a woman won't bother to learn about the game. Women'll be the end of men. If he'd stayed at home, he'd never have made good. A man must cut loose, that's the whole secret. None but the brave deserve to be world champion. And people have the nerve to say Jews aren't brave. The reporters ask him who he is. Not a soul knows him. He doesn't look like an American. There are Jews everywhere. But where does this Jew come from, who's rolled in triumph over Capablanca? For the first day he'll let people guess. The papers would like to tell their readers, but they don't know. Everywhere the headlines read: 'Mystery of the new World Champion.' The police become interested, naturally. They want to lock him up again. No, no, gentlemen, not so fast this time; now he throws the money about and the police are honoured to release him at once. On the second day, a round hundred reporters turn up. Each one promises him, shall we say, a thousand dollars cash down if he'll say something. Fischerle says not a word. The papers begin to lie. What else are they to do? The readers won't wait any longer. Fischerle sits in a mammoth hotel with one of those luxury cocktail bars, like on a giant liner. The head waiter brings the loveliest ladies to his table, not tarts mind you, millionairesses with a personal interest in him. He thanks them politely, but hasn't time, later perhaps ... And why hasn't he time? Because he's reading all the lies about him in all the papers. It takes all day. How's he to get through it? Every minute he's interrupted. Press photographers ask for a moment of his time. 'But gentlemen, a hump ... !' he protests. 'A world champion is a world champion, honoured Mr. Fischerle. The hump is quite immaterial.' They photograph him right and left, before and behind. 'Why don't you retouch it,' he suggests, 'take the hump out. Then you'll have a nice picture for your paper.' 'Just as you please, most honoured world champion!' But really, where's he had his eyes? His picture is everywhere, without a hump. It's gone. He hasn't one. But he worries a bit about his size. He calls the head waiter and points to a paper. 'A bad picture, what?' he asks. The head waiter says: '*Well*.' In America people speak English. He finds the picture excellent. 'But it's only the head,' he says. That's right too. 'You can go now,' says Fischerle and tips him a hundred dollars. In this picture he might be a fully grown man. No one would notice he was undersized. He loses his interest in the articles. He can't be bothered to read all this in English. He only understands 'Well!' Later on he has all the latest editions of the papers brought to him and looks hard at all his pictures. His head is everywhere. His nose is a bit long, that's true; can't help his nose. From a child up he's been all for chess. He might have taken some other idea into his head, football or swimming or boxing. But not he. It's a bit of luck really. If he were a boxing champion, now, he'd have to be photographed half naked. Everyone would laugh at him and he'd get nothing out of it. On the next day at least a thousand reporters turn up. 'Gentlemen,' he says, 'I'm surprised to find myself called Fischerle everywhere. My name is Fischer. I trust that you will have this error rectified.' They promise they will. Then they all kneel down in front of him — how small men are — and implore him to say something at last. They'll be thrown out, they'll lose their jobs, they cry, if they get nothing out of him to-day. My sorrow, he thinks, nothing for nothing, he gave the head waiter a hundred dollars, but he won't give the reporters anything.

'What's your bid, gentlemen?' he cries boldly. A thousand dollars, shouts one. Cheek, screams another, ten thousand! A third takes him by the hand and whispers: a hundred thousand, Mr. Fischer. People throw money about like nothing. He stops his ears. Until they get into millions he won't even listen to them. The reporters go mad and begin tearing each other's hair, each one wants to give more than the other; all this fuss; auctioneering his private life! One goes up to five millions, and all at once there is absolute quiet. Not one dares offer more. World Champion Fischer takes his fingers out of his ears and declares: 'I will now say something, gentlemen. What good will it do me to ruin you? None. How many of you are there? A thousand. Let each one of you give me ten thousand and I'll tell you all. Then I shall have ten millions and not one of you will be ruined. Agreed?' They fall on his neck and he's a made man. Then he clambers up on a chair, he doesn't really need to any more but he does it all the same, and tells them the simple truth. As a world champion, he fell from Heaven. It takes a good hour to convince them. He was unhappily married. His wife, a Capitalist, fell into evil ways, she was — as they used to call it in his home, the Stars of Heaven — a whore.' She wanted him to take money from her. He didn't know any way out. If he wouldn't take any, she used to say, she'd murder him. He was forced to do it. He had yielded to her blackmail and kept the money for her. Twenty long years he had to endure this. In the end he was fed up. One day he demanded categorically that she should stop or he'd become chess champion of the world. She cried, but she wouldn't stop. She was too much accustomed to doing nothing, to having fine clothes and lovely clean-shaven gentlemen. He was sorry for her but a man must keep his word. He goes straight from the Stars of Heaven to the United States, finishes off Capablanca, and here he is! The reporters rave about him. So does he. He founds a charity. He will pay a stipendium to every café in the world. In return the proprietors must undertake to put up on their walls every game played by the world champion. Any person defacing the notices will be prosecuted. Every individual person can thus convince himself that the world champion is a better player than he is. Otherwise some swindler may suddenly pop up, a dwarf or even a cripple, and brag he plays better. People may not think of checking up the cripple's moves. They are capable of believing him simply because he's a good liar. Things like that must stop. On each wall is a placard. The cheat makes one wrong move, everyone looks at the placard and who then will blush to the very hump on his miserable back. The crook! Moreover the proprietor must undertake to fetch him a sock on the jaw for saying things about the world champion. Let him challenge him openly if he's got the money. Fischerle will put down a million for this foundation. He's not mean. He'll send a million to his wife so she needn't go on the streets any more. In return she'll give it him in writing that she won't come to America and will keep mum about his former dealings with the police. Fischer's going to marry a millionairess. This will reimburse him for his losses. He'll have new suits made at the best possible tailor so that his wife'll notice nothing. A gigantic palace will be built with real castles, knights, pawns, just as it ought to be. The servants are in livery; in thirty vast halls Fischer plays night and day thirty simultaneous games of chess with living pieces which he has only to command. All he has to do is to speak and his slaves move wherever he tells them. Challengers come from all the chief countries of the world, poor devils who want to learn something from him. Many sell their coats and shoes to pay for the long journey. He receives them with hospitality, gives them a good meal, with soup, a sweet and two veg, and pretty often a nice grilled steak instead of a cut from the joint. Anyone can be beaten by him once. He asks nothing in return for his kindness. Only that each one should write his name in the visitors' book on leaving and categorically assert that he, Fischer, is the world champion. He defends his title. While he does so his new wife goes out riding in her car. Once a week he goes with her. In the castle all the chandeliers are put out, lighting alone costs him a fortune. On the door he pins up a notice: 'Back soon. Fischer: World Champion.' He does not stay out two hours, but visitors are queueing up like in the war when he gets back. 'What are you queuing for?' asks a passer-by. 'What, don't you know? You must be a stranger here.' Out of pity the others tell him who it is that lives here. So that he shall understand each one tells him singly, then they all shout in a chorus: 'Chess Champion of the World, Fischer, is giving alms to-day.' The stranger is struck dumb. After an hour he finds his voice again. 'Then this is his reception day?' That is just what the natives have been waiting for. 'To-day is not a reception day or there would be far more people.' Now all of them begin talking at once. 'Where is he? The castle is dark!' 'With his wife in the car. This is his second wife. The first was only a simple Capitalist. The second is a millionairess. The car belongs to him. It isn't just a taxi. He had it built specially.' What they are saying is the simple truth. He sits in his car, it suits him very well. It is a little too small for his wife who has to crouch all the time. But in return she's allowed to ride with him. At other times she has her own. He doesn't go out in hers. It's much too big for him. But his was the more expensive. The factory made his car specially. He feels inside it just as if he were under the bed. Looking out of the windows is too boring. He shuts his eyes tight. Not a thing moves. Under the bed he is perfectly at home. He hears his wife's voice from above. He's fed up with her, what does she mean to him? She doesn't understand a thing about chess. The man is saying something too. Is he a player? He's obviously intelligent. Wait, now, wait; why should he wait? What's waiting to him? That man up there is talking good German. He's a professional man, sure to be a secret champion. These people are afraid of being recognized. It's with them like it is with crowned heads. They have to come to women incognito. That man's a world champion for sure, not just an ordinary champion! He must challenge him. He can't wait longer. His head bursts with good moves. He'll beat him into a cocked hat!

Fischerle crept swiftly and silently from under the bed, and reared himself on his crooked legs. They'd gone to sleep; he stumbled and clutched at the bedstead. The woman had vanished, all the better, she'd leave him in peace. A lanky stranger was lying alone on the bed, you might think he was asleep. Fischerle tapped him on the shoulder and asked loudly: 'Do you play chess?' The stranger was really asleep. He must be shaken awake. Fischerle was about to grasp him with both hands by the shoulders when he noticed that he was holding something in his left hand. A little packet, it was in the way, throw it down Fischerle! He flung his left arm about but his hand refused to let go. What's all this? Will you or won't you? he screamed. His hand clutched fast. It clung to the packet as if it were a conquered queen. He looked at it closer. The packet was a bundle of banknotes. Why should he throw them away? He could do with them, he was only a poor devil. Perhaps they belonged to the stranger? He was still asleep. But they belonged to Fischerle, because he was a millionaire. How did this person get here? A visitor? He might want to challenge him? People should read the notice on the entrance gate. A world champion and he couldn't even go for a quiet spin in his car? The stranger had a familiar look. A visitor from the Stars of Heaven? That wasn't a bad idea. Why, this was the chap in the book racket. What did he want here, book racket, book racket . . . ? He used to be in his service once. First he had to spread out brown paper on the floor and then . . .

Fischerle grew even more crooked with laughing. While laughing he woke up completely. He was standing in an hotel bedroom, he ought to be sleeping next door, he had stolen the money. Quickly, off with it. He must get to America. He ran two or three steps in the direction of the door. Why did he laugh so loud? Perhaps he had waked up the book racket. He slipped back to the bed and made sure he was still asleep. The creature would go to the police. He wasn't that mad; he'd go to the police. He took the same steps in the direction of the door; this time he walked instead of running. How was he to get out of the hotel? The room was on the third floor. He was bound to wake the porter. The police would watch him in the morning, even before he could get into a train. Why would they catch him? Because of his hump. His long fingers fondled it with repulsion. He wouldn't be locked up again. Those swine took his chessboard away. He had to touch the pieces or he got no pleasure out of the game. They forced him to play in his head. Flesh and blood couldn't stand that. He must make his fortune. He could do the book racket in. Jews don't do things like that. What would he do him in with? He could force him to give his word not to go to the police. 'Your word or your life!' he'd say to him. The creature was sure to be a coward. He'd give his word. But who could rely on such an idiot? Anyone could do what they liked with him. He wouldn't break his word anyway; he'd break it from pure silliness. Silly, Fischerle had got all the money in his hand. America was a wash-out. No, he'd cut and run for it. Let them find him if they could. If they couldn't then he'd become chess champion of the world in America. If they could, he'd hang himself. A pleasure. What the devil . . . He couldn't make a go of it. He hadn't got a neck. Once he hanged himself by his leg but they cut him down. You didn't catch him hanging himself by the other leg. No!

Between the bed and the door Fischerle racked his brains for a solution. He was in desperation over his rotten luck. He could have cried out loud. But he mustn't for fear of waking the creature. It might be weeks before he got another chance. Weeks, weeks — he'd waited twenty years already! One foot in America and the other in a noose. Then let a fellow try and make up his mind. The American leg took a step forward, the hanged one a step back. What a filthy trick to play! He beat his hump, sticking the packet of notes between his legs. The hump was the root of all the trouble. Let it be hurt. It deserved to be hurt. If he didn't beat it he'd have to cry out loud. If he cried out loud, America was dead and buried.

Exactly in the middle between bed and door Fischerle stood rooted to a spot and beat his hump. Like whip-handles he raised his arms alternately and brought down his fingers, five double-knotted lashes, over his shoulders on to his hump. It did not budge. A pitiless mountain, it rose above the low foothills of his shoulders, proud in its rocky hardness. It didn't even scream, 'I've had enough!' It was silent. Fischerle got into his stride. He saw the hump could take it. He prepared for a long drawn ordeal. It wasn't a matter of expressing his anger but of seeing that the blows struck home. His long arms were much too short for him. He had to make do with them, though. The blows fell with regularity. Fischerle gasped. He needed music for this. There was a piano at the Stars of Heaven. He'd make his own music. His breath gave out; he sang. His voice sounded sharp and shrill with excitement. 'That'll teach you — that'll teach you!' He beat the brute black and blue. Let it go to the police if it liked! Before each blow he thought: 'Come down you carrion!' The carrion didn't budge. Fischerle was running with sweat. His arms ached, his fingers were limp and tired. He persevered, he was patient, he swore, the hump was at its last gasp. Out of sheer spite, it pretended it didn't care. Fischerle knew it of old. He would look it in the face. He twisted his head round so as to leer in scorn at his enemy. So that was it, it was hiding — you coward — you abortion — a knife! a knife! he'd stab it dead, where was a knife? Fischerle frothed at the mouth, big tears gushed out of his eyes, he cried because he had no knife, he cried because the abortion wouldn't even answer him. The strength of his arms forsook him altogether. He crumpled up, an empty sack. It was all over, he'd hang himself. The money rolled to the floor.

Suddenly Fischerle leapt up again and yelled: 'Checkmate!'

Kien was dreaming most of the time about falling books and trying to catch them with his body. He was as thin as a darning needle; to left and right the rarest books were cascading down; now the floor itself gave way and he woke up. Where are they, he whimpered, where are they? Fischerle had beaten the abortion, he picked up the bundle of notes at his feet, went up to the bed and said: 'Tell you what, you can talk of luck!'

'The books, the books!' Kien groaned.

'All of them saved. Here's the money. You've got a treasure in me.'

'Saved — I dreamt. . . .'

'Dreaming were you? And I was being beaten up.'

203

'Then there was someone here!' Kien leapt up. 'We must go over the books at once!'

'Don't upset yourself. I heard him at once. He hadn't even got in through the door. I crept into this room under your bed to see what he was up to. What do you think he was after? Money. He puts out his hand. I grab hold of him by it. He hits out at me, I hit back. He begs for mercy, I have none. He wants to go to America, I won't let him go. Do you think he touched one of the books? Not one. He had a head on his shoulders. But he was an ass all the same. In all his born days he'd never have got to America. Do you know where he'll have got to? Between ourselves, to the police court. He's off now.'

'What did he look like?' asked Kien. He wanted to show his grati-tude to the little fellow for so much vigilance. He was not in the least interested in the burglar.

'What shall I say? He was a cripple like me. I could have sworn a good chess player too. A poor devil.'

'Well, let him go,' said Kien, and cast an affectionate — or so he meant it — glance at the dwarf. Then both went back to bed.

CHAPTER III

INFINITE MERCY

THE public pawnbroking establishment carries, in memory of a devout and frugal princess who received the poor on one day in every year, the suitable name of *Theresianum*. As for the beggars, they forfeited, even in those days, the last of their possessions: that much-coveted portion of Love which Christ bestowed on them a good two thousand years ago, and the dirt on their feet. While the princess washed off the latter, the name of Christian was very near her heart; she earned it every year afresh to add it to her innumerable others. The state pawnbroking establishment stands splendidly and thickly walled about like a true prince's heart, well defended against the world without, proud and of many mansions.

At certain hours it gives audience. It prefers to entertain beggars, or those who are shortly to become such. People throw themselves at its feet and bring in offering as in days of old a tithe of their possessions, which is only so in name. For it is nothing to the prince's heart but the millionth part; to the beggars, their all. The prince's heart takes all, it is spacious and extensive, has a thousand different rooms and chambers and as many offices to perform. The trembling beggars are graciously permitted to raise themselves, and are given in exchange a small portion of alms, cash down. With that they go out of their minds with joy and out of the building with haste. For the custom of washing their feet the princess, now that she exists merely as an institution, has no further use. She has introduced a new custom to take its place. The beggars pay interest on their alms. The last shall be first, for which reason their interest rate is the highest. A private person who charged so high an interest would be prosecuted for extortion. But an exception can be made for beggars since, after all, only the most beggarly sums are involved. It cannot be denied that these people rejoice over the transaction. They throng to the counters and cannot undertake quickly enough to pay the quarter of the whole sum back again in interest. Those who have nothing make joyful givers. Though there are some to be found among them, miserly skinflints, who refuse to pay back the loan and the interest, and prefer to default on their pledges rather than open their purses. They say, they have none.

Even these are allowed to enter in. The great benevolent princely heart, in the midst of the city's roar, has not leisure to test such deceiving purses for their miserliness. It foregoes the alms, it foregoes the interest, and contents itself with pledges five or six times the value of the money. A treasure chest of pennies is gradually being amassed. The beggars bring their rags here; the heart is decked in silks and satins. A staff of loyal officials permanently installed, year in, year out, take in and pay out, all for the sake of a coveted pension. As true liegemen of their mistress they disparage all and everything. It is their duty to radiate disparagement. The more they reduce the alms, the more people are made happy. The heart is large, but not infinite. From time to time it throws away its riches at sacrificial prices to make room for new gifts. The pennies of the beggars are as inexhaustible as was their love for the immortal Empress. When business in all the rest of the land is at a standstill, it is still humming here. Stolen goods, as ought to be hoped in the interests of a livelier circulation of trade, are the subject of transactions only in exceptional cases.

Among the treasure chambers of this lady of infinite mercy, that for jewels, gold and silver takes the place of honour not far from the main entrance. It rests securely on the earth's foundations. The floors are arranged according to the value of the objects pawned. At the very top, higher even than coats, shoes and postage stamps, on the sixth and topmost floor, are the books. They are housed in an annexe, to reach them you climb an ordinary staircase like that of any tenement. The princely grandeur of the main building is wholly lacking here. There is no room for a brain in this abounding heart. Pensive, you stand below on the staircase and are ashamed — for the abandoned creatures who bring their books here out of greed for filthy lucre — for the staircase which is not as clean as it should be for such a function — for the officials who receive the books but do not read them — for the fire-endangered rooms in the attics — for a State which does not go the shortest way to make the pawning of books an offence against the law — for humanity which, now that printing seems natural to them, have altogether forgotten the special sanctity contained in each single printed letter. Why should not the unimportant trinkets and trappings be huddled together on the sixth floor and the books — since a radical reform of this insult to culture cannot be contemplated — take their place at least in the spacious halls of the ground floor? In case of fire the jewellery could simply be thrown into the street. It is very well packed up, far too well for mere minerals. Stones cannot hurt themselves. But books on the other hand hurled from the sixth floor into the street, would, for sensitive tastes, be already dead. Think only of the pricks of conscience the officials would suffer. The fire spreads on every side; they stand at their posts, but they are powerless. The staircase has fallen in. They must choose between the fire and the eighty foot drop. Their counsels are divided. What one is on the point of dropping from the window, another snatches from him and throws into the flames. 'Better burnt than crippled!' With these words he hurls his defiance into the face of his colleague. This latter hopes, however, that nets are being held out below so as to catch the poor creatures unhurt. 'They will not be damaged by the friction of the air!' he hisses to his opponent. 'And where is your net, may I ask?' 'The fire brigade will be putting it out at once.' 'At present I can hear nothing but the bodies clattering on to the pavement.' 'For pity's sake, say no more!' 'Quick then, into the fire!' 'I can't do it.' He cannot bring himself to do it; in contact with his charges he has acquired humanity. He is like a mother who, for better or for worse, throws her child out of the window; someone will surely take it up; in the fire it would be lost without hope of rescue. The fire-worshipper has more character; the other, more heart. Both are laudable, both carry out their duty to the end, both are lost in the fire, but what does this avail the books?

For an hour Kien had been leaning on the banisters, ashamed. He seemed to himself then as one who had lived in vain. He had known in what barbarous manner humankind use to treat their books. He had often been present at sales by auction; indeed it was to them that he owed certain rare volumes which he had vainly sought among booksellers. Whatever was of a kind to enrich his knowledge, he had always accepted. Many a painful impression had he carried away from the sale-room, deeply graven on his heart. Never would he forget that magnificent edition of Luther's Bible over which speculators from New York, London and Paris had circled like vultures and which, in the outcome, had proved a forgery. The disappointment of those outbidding swindlers was nothing to him, but that treachery and deceit could raise their heads even in this quarter was beyond his understanding. The man-handling of books before the sale, examining them, opening them, closing them, just as if they were slaves, cut him to the heart. This shouting out, bidding, outbidding by creatures who in all their lives had not read a thousand books seemed to him a crying outrage. Each time when, compelled by necessity, he had found himself in the hell of the sale-room, he had a strong desire to take a hundred well-armed mercenaries with him, to give the dealers a thousand lashes apiece, the collectors five hundred, and to take the books, over which they were haggling, into protective custody. But how little did these experiences weigh against the bottomless degradation of this pawning house? Kien's fingers twisted themselves into the ornamental ironwork — as elaborate as it was tasteless — of the stair-rail. They clutched into it, in the secret hope that he might pull down the whole building. The abomination of this idolatry oppressed him. He was ready to let them bury him under all six stories on one condition: that they should never be built up again. But could he rely on the word of barbarians? One of the purposes which had brought him here, he now abandoned: he renounced his inspection of the upper rooms. Hitherto his worst expectations had been far surpassed. The annexe was even more unsightly than he had been told. The width of the staircase, stated by his guide to be five feet four, was in fact not more than four foot five. Generous people often make such transferences in estimating numbers. The dust was the harvest of three weeks at least and not of a day or two. The lift bell was out of order. The glass doors which led into the annexe were badly oiled. The notice-board which pointed the way to the book section had been daubed by an unskilful hand with bad paint on a piece of shoddy cardboard. Underneath it, carefully printed, hung another notice: Postage stamps on the First Floor. A large window gave on to a small backyard. The colour of the ceiling was undefined. Even in broad daylight you could sense how wretched was the illumination afforded in the evening by the single electric bulb. Kien had conscientiously convinced himself of all this. But he hesitated still to mount the steps of the staircase. Hardly would he be able to endure the shocking spectacle which awaited him at its summit. His health was enfeebled. He dreaded a stroke. He knew that every life was mortal, but so long as he could feel that dearly loved burden within himself, he must spare himself. He bowed his heavy head over the banisters and was ashamed.

Fischerle watched him proudly. He stood some little distance from his friend. He knew his way about the public pawnbroking establishment as well as about Heaven. He had come to reclaim a silver cigarette case on which he had never set eyes. He had won the pawn ticket from a crook whom he had beaten at chess two dozen times, and had it still carefully preserved in his pocket when he entered Kien's service. It was generally rumoured that the ticket was good for a brand new solid silver cigarette case, first quality stuff. Often and often

Fischerle had managed to sell pawn tickets in the Theresianum to interested persons. Just as often, he had been forced to look on while his own and other people's treasures were redeemed. Besides his chief dream about becoming world chess champion, he carried a lesser one around in his head: He would dream of exchanging a pawn ticket of his very own, of paying down the full sum, interest and all, flat on the counter under the official's indifferent jaws, of waiting for his own property like other people at the redemption counter and of sniffing at and examining it when he had it, as if he had often before had it under his eyes and nose. Being a non-smoker he really had no use for a cigarette case, but one of his hours of fulfilment was at hand, and he asked Kien for a short time off. Although he explained what his reason was, Kien flatly refused it. He had absolute confidence in him, but since he had relieved him of half the library, he would take good care never to let him out of his sight. Scholars of the highest character have been known to become criminals for the sake of books. How great then must be the temptation for an intelligent being with a thirst for learning, who found himself for the first time under the pressure of books with all their fascination!

The division of the burden had happened in this way. When Fischerle began packing up the books in the morning, Kien could not understand how he had managed hitherto to carry them all. The meticulousness of his servant made him aware of the potential dangers through which he had come. Up to this time he had simply got up in the morning and sallied forth ready packed. It had not occurred to him to ask himself how the books, so carefully unloaded on the previous evening, had found their way back into his head. He felt himself full, and set off. But Fischerle's incursion altered all that at a blow. On the morning after the unsuccessful robbery, he crept towards Kien's bed like one on stilts, fervently urged him to exercise all possible care in getting up, and asked if he was to begin packing up again. As his manner was, he waited for no answer; he dexterously lifted up the nearest pile and approached it to Kien's head as he still lay in bed. 'In with them!' he said. While Kien washed and dressed himself, the little fellow, who set no great store on washing, worked industriously away. Within half an hour he had emptied the first room. Kien purposely loitered over his dressing. He was turning over in his mind how he had usually managed his packing. But he couldn't remember. Strange, his memory seemed to be failing. As long as it only affected external things of this kind, it was of no consequence. But he must keep a close watch lest this loss of memory should extend into the scholastic sphere. That would be unthinkable. His memory was no less than a heaven-sent gift, a phenomenon; even as a schoolboy he had been examined by famous psychologists on the state of his memory. In one minute he had memorized π to sixty-five decimal places. The learned gentlemen — all and sundry — shook their heads. Perhaps he had overburdened his own head. Look only at the work in progress — pile after pile, parcel after parcel was loaded in; yet surely he ought to spare his head a little. You cannot replace a head; it can be developed as his had been developed, only once; any part of it destroyed is destroyed for ever. He sighed deeply and said: 'Yours is a light task, my dear Fischerle!' 'Tell you what,' the little fellow at once saw what he meant, 'I'll carry what's in the next room myself, Fischerle's got a head too. Or hasn't he?' 'Yes, but . . .' 'What, but . . . tell you what, you've hurt my feelings!' After long hesitation, Kien gave his consent. Fischerle had to swear honour bright that he had never stolen yet. Further, he lamented his innocence and said over and over again: 'But, mister, with *this* hump! How could a fellow steal?' For a moment, Kien dwelt on the idea of demanding a guarantee. But as not the strongest guarantee in the world would have availed anything in his own case against his inclination to books, he gave up the plan. He added, however, the statement: 'You are no doubt a fast runner?' Fischerle saw through the trap and answered: 'What would be the point of lying? When you take a step, I take half a one. At school I was always the worst runner.' He thought up the name of a school lest Kien should ask him: in fact he had never been to one. But Kien was wrestling with weightier problems. He was about to make the greatest gesture of trust of his entire life. 'I believe you!' he said simply. Fischerle was jubilant. 'See now, that's just what I mean!' The book pact was confirmed. As Kien's servant, the little man took the heavier half. In the street he walked ahead, but never further than two small steps. The hump, which was there anyway, prevented the stooping pose, which he had put on for the occasion, from making its full effect. But his dragging footsteps spoke volumes.

Kien felt himself relieved. Head held high, he followed the man who had his confidence and turned his eyes neither to right nor to left. They remained fixed on the hump which, like that of a camel, not so slowly but just as rhythmically, swayed up and down. From time to time he stretched out his arm to make sure that the tips of his fingers could still touch the hump. If this was no longer the case he hastened his step. In the event of any attempt to escape, he had laid his plans. He would grasp the hump in a grip of iron and hurl his body full length upon that of the criminal; he must however take especial care not to endanger the creature's head. When the experiment of stretching out his arm worked exactly — so exactly that he did not need either to hasten or slacken his pace — Kien would be suffused by a prickling sensation, exquisite and uplifting, such as is only given to men who can permit themselves the luxury of an absolute confidence in having ensured themselves against every disaster.

For two whole days he let things go on in this way, under the pretext of taking a rest after his recent exertions, of preparing himself for future efforts, of making a last investigation of the city for any undiscovered booksellers. His thoughts were free and joyful; he watched step by step the restoration of his memory; this first voluntary holiday which he had allowed himself since his university days was being passed in the company of a devoted creature, a friend, who prized highly the value of 'Intellect' — as he was in the habit of calling Education — who was willing to carry a respectable library about with him and yet would not of his own volition open a single one of those volumes, to read which he was inwardly burning; a creature malformed and on his own confession a poor runner, yet sturdy and muscular enough to justify himself as a porter. Almost Kien was tempted to believe in happiness, that contemptible life-goal of illiterates. If it came of itself, without being hunted for, if you did not hold it fast by force and treated it with a certain condescension, it was permissible to endure its presence for a few days.

When the third day of happiness broke; Fischerle asked for an hour's leave of absence. Kien lifted his hand in order to strike his forehead. In other circumstances he would have done it. But, knowing the world as he did, he decided to keep silence and by this means to unmask the treacherous plans of the dwarf — if he should have any. The story of the silver cigarette case he took for an impudent lie. After he had uttered his 'no', first in numerous disguises, but gradually more and more clearly and angrily, he declared suddenly: 'Good, I shall accompany you!' The wretched deformity must be made to confess his vile design. He would go with him to the very counter and see with his own eyes this alleged pawn ticket and alleged cigarette case. Since neither existed, the rogue would fall on his knees, there before all the world, and implore him with tears for forgiveness. Fischerle noticed the suspicion and felt his honour insulted. Did he think him crazy;

stealing books — and what books! Because he wants to go to America and he's working hard for his passage money, is he to be treated like a creature without a head on his shoulders?

On the way to the pawnbroking establishment he told Kien what it was like inside. He described the impressive building to him, with all its rooms from basement to attic. At the end, he suppressed the shadow of a sigh and said: 'About the books, better say nothing.' Kien's curiosity burst into flame. He asked and asked until he had elicited every atom of the hideous truth from the dwarf, who was coyly concealing it. He believed him, for man is base; he doubted him, for the dwarf irritated him to-day. Fischerle assumed tones of unmistakable significance. He described the way in which the books were taken in. A hog values them, a dog makes out the ticket, a woman shoves them into a dirty wrapper and scrawls a number on it. A decrepit old man, who time and again falls on the floor, carries them away. Your heart bleeds as you watch him out of sight. It would do you good to stand a bit longer at the glass door, till you've had your cry out and can go into the street again, being ashamed of having such red eyes; but the hog grunts: 'That's all', throws you out and slams the shutter down. Some soulful natures can't tear themselves away even then. Then the dog starts barking and you have to run; he bites, that one.

'But this is inhuman!' the cry escaped Kien. While the dwarf was talking, he had caught up with him, had walked beside him with death in his heart, and stood now stock still in the middle of the street they were crossing. 'It's just as I say!' Fischerle asserted with a break in his voice. He was thinking of the cuff on the ear, which the dog had dealt him when he had once come in, every single day for a week, to beg for an old book on chess. The pig stood by rolling with paunch and pleasure.

Fischerle said not a word more; he had had his vengeance. Kien was silent. When they reached their goal, he had lost all interest in the cigarette case. He watched Fischerle redeem it, and rub it repeatedly over his jacket. 'I wouldn't recognize it. What they do with the things, I don't know.' 'No.' 'How do I know if this is my case after all.' 'All.' 'Tell you what, I'll have the law on them. All of them thieves and robbers. I won't have it! I'm not a human being, I suppose? The poor have got a right, same as the rich!' He talked himself into such a fury that the people round about, who up to this had only stared at his hump, began to take notice of his words. The people, who in any case thought they were being done in this establishment, sided with the humpback, whom nature had placed at an even greater disadvantage than their own, although not one of them believed that the pawn tickets had been muddled. Fischerle aroused a general murmur; he didn't believe his ears, people were actually listening to him. He talked on, the murmur grew louder, he could have screamed with delight; then a fat man next to him growled: 'Go and make a complaint, then!' Fischerle rubbed the case over quickly once or twice more, then opened it and croaked: 'Well, I never. Tell you what. It *is* mine alright!' They forgave him the disappointment he had so irresponsibly caused; they didn't grudge him the right cigarette case, after all he was only a poor cripple. Another would not have escaped so lightly. As they left the room Kien asked: 'What was the cause of the disturbance?' Fischerle had to remind him what they had come for. He showed him the cigarette case again and again, until at last he saw it. The disappearance of a suspicion which, against his more recent discoveries, weighed little, made only a mild impression. 'Show me the way!' he commanded.

For a whole hour now he had stood; ashamed. Whither can this world be leading us? We stand, only too evidently, on the verge of catastrophe. Superstition trembles at the significant date A.D. 1000, or at comets. The sage, reverenced as a saint already by the ancient Indians, dismisses numbers, dates and comets to the devil and declares: our creeping corruption is this lack of piety with which men are infected; this is the poison by which we all shall perish. Woe to those who shall come after us! They are lost, they will inherit from us a million martyrs and the instruments of torture with which they must destroy a second million. No state can bear so many saints. In every town will be builded palaces to the Inquisition, like this one, six storeys high. Who can tell, perhaps the Americans build their pawnshops to touch the very sky. The prisoners, left to wait year after year for death by fire, languish on the thirtieth floor. O cruel mockery, a prison among the clouds! Rescue, not lamentation? Deeds, not tears? How to go thither? How to discover the localities of these prisons? Blindly indeed do we walk through life. How little do we see of the fearful misery which lies about us? How would this blasphemy, this unredeemed, bestial, all-corrupting blasphemy have been uncovered, had not an accidentally encountered dwarf, with his heart in the right place, stammering with shame, speaking like one in a nightmare, collapsing almost under the burden of his own horrifying words, told the whole story? He should serve as an example. He had never yet spoken to anyone. In his foul-smelling drinking den he sat silent, even at his chess-playing, he had this vision of wretchedness, branded for ever into his brain. He suffered instead of babbling. 'The Day of Reckoning will come,' he told himself. He waited; day after day he scanned the strangers who crossed the threshold of the café; he yearned almost to death for one man, one single heart, for one alone who could see and hear and feel. At last came that One. He followed him, he offered him his services, sleeping and waking he attended his commands, and when the moment came, he spoke. The paving stones did not melt at his words; not a house collapsed; the traffic did not stop. But that One to whom he spoke, his heart stopped: that One was Kien. He had heard, he had understood. He would take this heroic dwarf for his pattern; death to idle words; now to action!

Without looking up he released his hold on the banisters and placed himself squarely in the middle of the narrow stairs. At once he felt a push. His thoughts moved spontaneously into deeds. He looked the poor sinner squarely in the eyes and asked:

'What do you want?'

The poor sinner, a half-starved student, was carrying a heavy brief-case under his arm. He owned a copy of Schiller's Works and it was his first visit to the establishment. As these volumes were much thumbed and he himself over his large ears in debt, he was shyly making a first entry. On the staircase the last drop of courage had drained out of his minuscule head. Why must he go on with his studies? Father and mother, and all the aunts and uncles were more for business — he took one step forward and cannoned into a stern personage, obviously a director of this place — who fixed him with a piercing eye and in a cutting voice demanded:

'What do you want?'

'I . . . er I wanted the book section.'

'I am the book section.'

The student, who had a respect for professors and similar apparitions because all his life long he had been an object of contempt to them, and for books no less, because he had so few, felt for his hat to take it off. Then he remembered that he had none.

'What do you intend to do upstairs?' asked Kien threateningly.

'Oh . . . er . . . only Schiller.'

'Show me!'

The student did not dare refuse his brief-case. He knew that nobody

214

would buy that Schiller off him. But Schiller was his only hope for the next few days. He did not want to bury his hope so soon. Kien took the case from him with a vigorous jerk. Fischerle tried to make signals to his master and uttered over and over again 'Pst! Pst!' The boldness of a robbery on the open stairway impressed him. The book racket was maybe smarter than he had thought. Maybe he only pretended to be mad. All the same, you couldn't get away with it on the open stairs. Behind the student's back he gesticulated wildly with his hands and simultaneously took his precautions for a timely escape. Kien opened the brief-case and looked carefully at the Schiller. 'Eight volumes,' he ascertained, 'the edition is worthless in itself and its condition is a scandal!' The student's ears flushed fiery red. 'What do you want for it? I mean how much — money?' The repulsive word came out at last, but only after hesitation. The student remembered from his halcyon childhood, passed chiefly in his father's shop, that prices should be given at the highest possible rate so as to allow a margin for bargaining. 'Thirty-two schillings it cost me, new.' He imitated the structure of his father's phrases and his tone of voice. Kien took out his note case, extracted thirty schillings, completed the sum with two coins, which he took from his purse, handed the total sum to the student and said: 'Never repeat this action, my friend! Believe me, no mortal man is worth his weight in books!' He gave him the brief-case back, still full, and shook him warmly by the hand. The student was in a hurry, he cursed the formalities which detained him. He was already at the glass door — Fischerle, completely baffled, had made way for him — when Kien called after him: 'Why Schiller? You should read the original. You should read Immanuel Kant!' 'Original yourself!' the student grinned in his thoughts, and ran for it as fast as his legs would carry him.

Fischerle's excitement knew no bounds. He was almost crying. He clutched Kien by his trouser buttons — his waistcoat was too high — and crowed: 'Tell you what, what do you think this is? Plumb crazy, that's what it is! Either a fellow has money, or else he hasn't. If he has, he doesn't throw it about; if he hasn't he doesn't throw it about anyway. A crime, that's what it is. Ought to be ashamed of yourself, a big chap like you!'

Kien was not listening to his words. He was content with what he had done. Fischerle pulled at his trousers for so long, that at last the perpetrator of the crime became aware of him. He guessed the dumb reproach, as he called it, in the behaviour of the little man and to pacify

him told him of the mental aberrations in which the life of the inhabitants of exotic countries is so rich.

Rich men of China, who are anxious for their welfare in the next
world, were in the habit of giving great sums of money for the preservation of crocodiles, pigs, tortoises, and other animals at Buddhist
monasteries. Special ponds and preserves were laid out for the animals,
and the monks had no other work than to keep and feed them; woe
to them if one of these endowed crocodiles were to come to any harm.
A gentle and natural death was permitted even to the fattest pig and
the reward for his good work would go to the noble benefactor. So
much was left over for the monks that all of them could live on it.
Should you visit a shrine in Japan, you will find children with imprisoned birds squatting all along the roadside, one small cage close
against the next. The little creatures, which are trained to do it, beat
their wings and utter loud chirpings. Buddhist pilgrims going that
way take pity on them for their soul's sake. For a small ransom, the
children open the cage doors and let the birds go free. This ransoming
of animals is a general practice there. What does it matter to the pilgrims as they go on their way that the tame birds are all lured back
again into their cages by their owners? One and the same bird serves
ten, a hundred or a thousand times during its life: captivity as an
object for the mercy of pilgrims. And these know well enough —
apart from a few peasants and extremely ignorant exceptions — just
what happens to the birds as soon as their backs are turned. The real
fate of the animals is indifferent to them.

'It is easy to see why this should be so,' Kien drew the moral of the
story. 'It is a matter of mere beasts. These must of necessity be
indifferent to us. Their own stupidity condemns them. Why do they
not fly away? Why do they not even hop away if their wings have
been cut? Why do they let themselves be lured back again? Their
animal stupidity be on their own heads! Yet in itself this ransoming
of the animals has, like every superstition, a deeper meaning. The
effect of such a deed on the men who perform it depends naturally on
what they select to ransom. Let us take books, genuine, intelligent
books instead of these absurd and stupid animals, and the act which
you perform for them achieves high moral value. You will thereby
redeem the wayward sinner who had sought refuge in hell itself. Rest
assured, this Schiller will not be dragged a second time to the slaughter
house. By reforming this man who, in the present state of our law —
or lawlessness rather — is permitted freely to dispose of books as if they

were animals, slaves or labourers, you will also render the lot of his books more endurable. On reaching home a man who has been re-called to his duty in this fashion, may very well fall on his knees before those whom he had hitherto held for his servants (although spiritually regarded, he should have been theirs) and vow to treat them better. Even should the man be so hard-hearted as to make no amends — at least his victims will have been ransomed from Hell. Do you know what that means — the burning of a library? Think, man, a library on fire on the sixth floor! Imagine it only! Tens of thousands of volumes — millions of pages — milliards of printed letters — each one of these in flames — each one of these imploring, crying, shrieking for help — it would split the eardrums, it would crack the heart — but no more of that! I am happier now than I have been for years. Let us continue on the path on which we have begun. Our widow's mite for the alleviation of universal misery is small, but we must cast it in. If a man should say: alone I am too weak, then nothing would be done, and misery would devour further. I have boundless confidence in you. Earlier, you were injured because I had not imparted my plan to you. It only took recognizable shape in that moment when Schiller's Works uttered their dumb appeal. I had no time to inform you of it. Instead, I will give you now the two watchwords under which our campaign is to be carried out: Action, not lamentation! Deeds, not tears! How much money have you?'

Fischerle, who had at first interrupted Kien's recital with angry interjections such as 'What are the Japs to me?' 'Why no goldfish?' and had repeatedly referred to the pious pilgrims as a gang of crooks, but who had nevertheless listened to every single word, grew calmer as the speech ended on the widow's mite and the plan of campaign. He was carefully considering how he should insure himself against the loss of his passage-money to America; it belonged to him, he had even had it in his hand, he had only given it back temporarily and as a precaution. At which moment Kien's question: 'How much money have you?' brought him crashing out of the clouds. He clenched his teeth and was silent, only out of business considerations be it under-stood, otherwise he'd have given him a piece of his mind. The mean-ing of all this play-acting began to grow clear to him. This grand gentleman was regretting the reward which Fischerle had honourably obtained. He was too cowardly to steal the money back at night. Not that he could have found it. Fischerle stowed it away when he was asleep, rolled into a tight bundle, between his legs. What was the fine gentleman up to, the so-called scholar and librarian, though in fact not even in the book racket, nothing more nor less than a crook who was only walking about free as air because he had the good luck not to have a hump? What was he up to? That time when he got out of the Stars of Heaven he was glad to have that money back — Lord knew where he'd stolen it from. He was afraid Fischerle would loose the others on to him, so he handed over the reward quick. But simply to get this ten per cent back, he had said grandly, 'You shall come into my service'. And what did he do, the swindler! He pretended to be off his head. You've got to hand him that, he does it a treat. Fischerle fell in with it. A whole hour he plays the fool here until a chap comes along with books. He hands him over thirty-two schillings as pleased as Punch and expects thirty times as much from Fischerle. A creature with all that capital, and grudges a poor pickpocket his little bit of reward. How petty all these fine gentlemen are! Fischerle had no words for it. He hadn't expected it of him. Not from a fellow who was crackers, anyway. Not that he's under any obligation to be really crackers, well and good, but that's no reason to be mean. Fischerle will pay him out alright. The stories he can tell! The creature's got a head on his shoulders. You can see the difference straight away between a poor pickpocket and one of your better-class swindlers. In the hotels they fall for it at once. Fischerle pretty nearly fell for it himself.

While he was at once boiling with hate and overwhelmed with admiration, Kien took his arm confidingly and said: 'You're not angry with me any more, are you? How much money have you? We must stand by one another!'

'Scum!' thought Fischerle to himself, 'you're up to your tricks alright, but I know a trick or two!' Aloud he said: 'Maybe thirty schillings.' The rest was very well hidden.

'That is a small sum. But it is better than nothing.' Kien had forgotten that he had given the little fellow a big sum of money only a few days back. He accepted Fischerle's mite at once, thanked him, with deep emotion, for so much self-sacrifice and had all but promised him a reward in the Hereafter.

From this moment the two were engaged in a life and death struggle with each other, of which one of them remained in total ignorance. The other, feeling himself less gifted at play-acting, took over the production and hoped in this way to countervail his disadvantage.

Morning after morning Kien took his stand in the entrance hall of the

building. Even before it opened he was pacing up and down outside
the Theresianum sharply observing all who passed. When one of them
stopped, he went close up to him and asked: 'What do you want here?'
Not the rudest or most ribald retort sufficed to distract him. His success
was his justification. Those who passed through this street before nine
o'clock glanced merely out of curiosity at the notice-boards outside on
which the date and place of the next auction was set out, together with
the objects to be sold. Timorous persons took him for a private
detective, guarding the treasures of the Theresianum, and hurried out of
range to avoid a conflict with him. The indifferent often failed to
register his inquiry until they were a street or two further off. The
bold were indignant and, contrary to their usual custom, tarried long
and immobile in front of the notice boards. He let them alone but he
impressed their features on his memory. He took them for men on
whose conscience their sin hung heavy, who had come to reconnoitre
the land before coming back, perhaps an hour later, with the scapegoat under their arm. The fact that they never came back he attributed
to his implacable stare. On the stroke of the hour he presented himself
in the small entrance lobby of the annexe. Who ever should push open
the glass door must see at once the haggard figure, straight as a candle-
stick, next to the window, and, in order to reach the staircase, must
pass in front of it. When Kien addressed anyone his features altered
not a fraction. Only his lips moved, like two sharp-edged knives. His
first task was to ransom the unhappy books, his second to reform a
bestial mankind. He was learned in books, but in men, he was forced
to concede, far less. He determined therefore to become learned in men
too.

For his better convenience he divided the people as they appeared
outside the glass door into three groups. To the first of these their
heavy brief-cases were a burden, to the second a bargain, to the third a
blessing. The first group held their books fast in both arms, without
grace, without love, just as they would have carried any heavy parcel.
They pushed the door open with them. They would have shoved the
books along the banisters — had they been allowed to get so far. As
they wanted to be quickly rid of their burden they did not think of
hiding it and held it always in front of their chests or their stomachs.
They agreed readily to his offers, were content with whatever sum he
suggested, did not bargain and left the building just as they had entered
it, only a little more weighed down, for they carried with them money
and a doubt or two as to the legality of their having received it. Kien

found this group unpleasing, they would learn too slowly; in order to effect an ultimate reform he would have needed to spend some hours on each one.

But he felt a real hatred for the second group. The members of this group hid the books behind their backs. At best they revealed only the tips of them between their arms and ribs so as to whet the greed of a possible buyer. They received the most brilliant offers with suspicion. They refused to open their parcels or satchels. They haggled up to the last moment and behaved at the end as if they had been outwitted. There were some among them who pocketed the money and still wanted to go up to Hell. At this Kien found that he was striking chords which were an astonishment even to him. He placed himself in their path and spoke to them as they deserved: he demanded the money back at once. When they heard that, they turned and ran. The little money in hand was dearer to them than the thousands under the roof. Kien was convinced that there, above, gigantic sums were paid out. The more money he gave away, the less he had left, so much the more oppressive became the thought of the foul competition of the devils on high.

Of the third group he had seen none as yet. But he knew that it existed. He awaited its representative whose characteristics were as familiar to him as a catechism, with patient longing. Once, at last, that man must come to whom the carrying of books is a blessing, whose road to hell is paved with anguish, who would indeed collapse altogether did not those friends, whom he carried with him, ceaselessly reimbue him with strength. His step is that of a sleepwalker. Behind the glass door his silhouette appears, he hesitates, how is he to push it open without in the least degree giving pain to one of his friends? He does so. Love is the author of invention. At sight of Kien, his own conscience in the flesh, he glows fiery red. With a colossal effort of will he pulls himself together and takes a step forward. His head is on his breast. In front of Kien — before ever he is spoken to — he stops as at some inner command. He guesses what his conscience has to say to him. The fearful word 'Money' falls. He shrinks back, the executioner's axe is towards him; he sobs aloud: 'Not that! Not that!' He will not take money. Rather he will hang himself. He would flee the place, but his strength forsakes him and, moreover, to prevent any risk to his friends, violent exercise is to be avoided. His conscience takes him in his arms and speaks kindly to him. There is more rejoicing in heaven, he cries, for one sinner reclaimed than for ninety and nine just men. Perhaps he will bequeathe him his library. When this man comes, he will forsake his post for an hour; this one who takes nothing, outweighs the thousands who ask for more. While he waits for him, he will give the thousands all he has. Perhaps one of the first group will bethink himself when he gets home. For the second he entertains no hope at all. But all the victims he can save. For that and not for his private satisfaction, he takes his stand.

At Kien's head, to his right, hung a notice, prohibiting loitering on the stairways and in the corridors and by the heating pipes. Fischerle warned his deadly enemy of this on the very first day. 'People will think you've no coal in the house,' he said. 'Only people who've got no coal stand about here. And they aren't allowed to. They turn them out. The heating's for the cats. Clients might cool off on the way upstairs. Anyone who's really cold has to clear out quick. He might get warm here. Anyone who isn't cold can stay. As for you, everyone would think you were cold!'

'The hot pipes are on the first landing, fifteen steps higher,' answered Kien.

'You don't get any heating for nothing, it's all one how little it is. Tell you what, here, where you're standing, I've stood too in my time, and been moved on, just the same.' This was not a lie.

Kien bethought himself that his competitors had an interest in driving him out and gratefully accepted the little fellow's offer to keep a sharp look out. His passion for that half of the library which he had entrusted to him had paled. Greater dangers threatened. Now that they had bound themselves by the same oath to the same task, he thought any treachery was out of the question. When they took up their positions on the following day, Fischerle said: 'Tell you what, you go in first! We don't know each other. I'll stand about outside somewhere. Better not disturb me. I won't tell you where I am. If they once see we're together, all our work'll be for nothing. In emergency, I'll pass by you and wink at you. First you run, then I'll run. We won't both run together. Behind the yellow church we'll have a meeting place. You wait there till I come. Got that?' He would have been genuinely astonished if his suggestion had been rejected. Since he had an interest in Kien, he was not going to let him go. How could anyone think that he would cut and run for a reward, for a mere tip, when he had the whole lot pretty near in his hand? That swindler, that book racket, that cunning dog, saw through the honest part of his plan and agreed.

FOUR AND THEIR FUTURE

SCARCELY had Kien vanished into the building, when Fischerle walked slowly back to the next street corner, turned into a side street and began to run for dear life. Only when he got to the Stars of Heaven, did he allow his sweating, panting, trembling body a moment's rest, then he walked in. At this time of the day most of the denizens of Heaven were usually asleep. He had counted on this; he had no use just now for dangerous or violent people. Present were: the lanky waiter; a hawker, who derived at least one advantage from the insomnia from which he suffered, and could keep on his rounds twenty-four hours out of the twenty-four; a blind ex-service man who, sitting over the cheap cup of morning coffee, which he took here before starting on his day's work, was still making use of his eyes; an old newspaper woman, known as the 'Fishwife', because she looked rather like Fischerle and — as everyone realised — was secretly and hopelessly in love with him; and a sewerman whose custom it was to recover from his night's work and the foul air of the sewers in the equally foul air of the Stars of Heaven. He was regarded as the most respectable of the clients, because he gave three-quarters of his weekly wages to his wife, by whom, in a very happy marriage, he had had three children. The remaining quarter found its way in the course of a day or a night into the cashbox of the proprietress of Heaven.

The Fishwife held out a paper to her beloved as he came in and said: 'There you are, dearie! Where've you been all this time?' When the police were worrying him, Fischerle often disappeared for a day or two. 'He's gone to America,' they would say, laugh every time at the joke — how would such a cocksparrow manage in the gigantic land of skyscrapers? — and forgot him until he turned up again. The love of his wife, the Capitalist, was not so deep as to give her any anxiety on his behalf. She only loved him when he was near her, and knew that he was used to police courts and lock-ups. When the American joke came up she thought how nice it would be to have all her money to herself for once. For a long time she had been wanting to buy a picture of the Holy Virgin for her little room. A capitalist ought to have a picture of the Holy Virgin. As soon as he ventured out of his hiding place — where, though completely innocent, he frequently took refuge because the police made a habit of holding him days for questioning, and would take his chessboard away — he went at once to the café and in a few minutes he was her mummy's darling again. But the Fishwife was the only person who asked after him daily, and hazarded every kind of guess as to his whereabouts. He was allowed to read her papers without paying for them. Before she began her rounds, she hobbled hurriedly into the Stars of Heaven, handed him the top copy of the packet fresh from the printer, and waited patiently, her heavy burden under her arm, until he had finished with it. He was allowed to open the paper, crumple it up and fold it up crooked; the others were only allowed to look over his shoulder. When he was in a bad temper he delayed her purposely a long time and she suffered heavy losses. When people teased her about her incomprehensible stupidity, she would shrug her shoulders, shake her hump — which rivalled Fischerle's in size and expressiveness — and say: 'He's all I've got in the world!' Possibly she loved Fischerle for the pleasure of this plaintive phrase. She would cry it out with a jangling voice, and it sounded as though she was crying two newspapers: *He's all* and *The World*.

To-day Fischerle had not a glance for her paper. She quite understood, the paper wasn't fresh any more, but she had meant well and thought that maybe he hadn't read anything for days; who could say where he'd come from? Fischerle took her by the shoulders — she was as small as him — shook her and croaked: 'Come here everyone, I've got something for you!' All of them — except the consumptive waiter who wouldn't be ordered about by a Jew, was interested in nothing and stood stock still by the bar — the three therefore, drew close up to him, almost squashing him in their enthusiasm. 'Twenty schillings a day if you work for me! For three days at least.' 'Sixteen pounds of toilet soap,' calculated the unsleeping hawker hurriedly. The blind man looked Fischerle doubtfully in the eye. 'Give us a shove!' boomed the sewerman. The Fishwife noticed only 'if you work for me', and did not hear the sum.

'I've started my own business. Sign up that you'll hand over everything to the chief — that's me — and I'll take you on.' They would rather have found out first what it was all about. But Fischerle took good care not to give away business secrets. The thing's a racket, he admitted, further than that he would not go: this he stated categorically. In return each employee would get five schillings advance on the first day. They sat up to that. 'The undersigned guarantees and immediately pays cash down every penny taken to the firm of Siegfried Fischer. The undersigned agrees to keep mum and take the consequences in the event of a misfortune.' In an instant Fischerle had written down these sentences on four sheets of a scribbling pad presented to him by the hawker. As the only genuine businessman among those present he hoped for a share in the business and the more important commissions, and wanted to get on the right side of the chief. The sewerman, the father of a family and the stupidest of them all, signed first; Fischerle was annoyed because the signature was as large as his own, and he piqued himself on having the biggest. 'Too big for your boots!' he scolded, at which the hawker contented himself with a remote corner of the paper and a tiny name. 'I can't read that!' declared Fischerle, and forced the man, who was already seeing himself as the official representative of the firm, to write in less modest characters. The blind man would not lift a finger until he had his money. He had to look on patiently while people threw buttons into his hat, and when he was in civvies trusted no one further than he could see him. 'What's this,' Fischerle protested, disgusted: 'Have I ever done anyone?' He drew a few bundled-up notes out of his armpit, flicked a five schilling note into each man's hand and made them sign for it at once 'on account'. 'Now you're talking,' said the blind man. 'Promising's one thing, performing's another. For a man like you I'd go out and beg, if it's got to be!' The hawker would have gone through fire for such a chief, the sewerman through thick and thin. Only the Fishwife was a softy. 'He don't need no signature from me,' she declared, 'I wouldn't steal from him. He's all I've got in the world.' Fischerle regarded her subjection so much as an accepted thing that, since their first greeting, he had turned his back on her. His hump gave her courage; his backview filled her with love indeed, but not with respect. As the capitalist wasn't in the café she felt almost like the wife of the new chief. Scarcely had he heard this impertinence than he turned round, forced the pen into her hand and ordered: 'Write, you've nothing to say here!' She obeyed the look in his black eyes — her own were grey — and even signed for the five schillings on account which she hadn't yet received. 'That's that!' Fischerle carefully folded away the four slips of paper and sighed. 'And what do I get out of a business life? Nothing but worry! Believe me, I'd rather be the insignificant person I was before. You've got all the luck!' He knew that superior people always talk to their employees in this way, whether they have worries or not; he had a few. 'Let's go!' he said next, waved to the waiter — a tiny benefactor — from far below, and, accompanied by his new staff, left the café.

In the street he explained to each of them their duties. He took each of his employees in turn and ordered the remaining three to follow at some distance as if they had nothing to do with him. It seemed to him necessary to treat these people each according to the measure of his intellect. As he was in a hurry and took the sewerman for the most reliable of them, he selected him, to the great indignation of the hawker for his first confidence.

'You're a good father,' he said, 'so I thought of you right away. A man who hands over seventy-five per cent of his net wages to his wife is worth his weight in gold. So, mind what I'm saying and don't trip yourself up. It would be a shame for those nice kids.' He would give him a parcel, the parcel was to be called 'Art'. 'Repeat it: Art!' 'There now, d'you think I don't know what artful is, because I give the old woman so much!' It was usual, under the Stars of Heaven, to despise the sewerman for his family affairs, which they envied him. By countless prods to his thick-skinned pride, Fischerle prized out what small measure ot intellect the creature had. Three times over he told him what to do in the utmost detail. The sewerman had never yet crossed the threshold of the Theresianum. Necessary visits were undertaken by his wife. Fischerle's partner would be standing just behind the glass doors, by the window. He was long and lean. You go slowly past him and say not a *word*, not a *single word*, and wait until he speaks to you. Then you shout loudly: 'Art, sir! Not a penny less than 200 schillings! High class Art!' Next Fischerle ordered the sewerman to halt in front of a bookshop. Inside he bought the necessary wares. Ten cheap novels at two schillings each were made up into an impressive parcel. Three times he repeated his previous instructions; presumably even this bonehead had understood everything. If Fischerle's partner were to try and pull the paper off the books, he must grip them firmly to himself and shout: 'No! No!' Then he must make his way back, money, parcel and all to a rendezvous behind the church. There he would be paid off. On condition that he told not a soul, not even his fellow employees what he had done, he might report again behind the church at nine sharp the next day. He, Fischerle, had a heart for honest sewermen, not everyone came of a business family. With these words the respectable father of a family was released.

While the sewerman was waiting outside the booksellers, the three others, obedient to their chief's command, had gone on, without taking the slightest notice of the friendly shouts of their colleague who, in the effort of learning his new orders, had quite forgotten the old ones. Fischerle had counted on this, and the sewerman had turned into a side street carrying his parcel as if it were the precious infant of wealthy parents, before the others could even have noticed it. Fischerle whistled, overtook the other three, and selected the Fishwife next. The hawker realized that he was being kept for higher things. 'You'll see,' he said to the blind man, 'he'll send for me last!'

The dwarf made short work of the Fishwife. 'I'm all you've got in the world'; he reminded her of her love and her lovely sentence. 'Anyone can say that, I'm for proofs. If you keep back a ha'penny it's all over between us, believe me. I'll never touch another of your papers and you can whistle for a new man just the same shape as yourself!' The rest of his explanation was easy. The Fishwife hung on his lips; to see him speaking she made herself even smaller than she was; kiss he could not, on account of his nose, and she was the only one short enough to see his mouth. The Theresianum was her second home. Now she was to go on ahead and wait for the chief behind the church. There she would be given a parcel for which she was to ask 250 schillings, and then go back to the rendezvous with the money and the parcel. 'Off with you!' he shouted at the end. She was repulsive to him, because she never left off loving him.

At the next corner he halted until the blind man and the hawker came up with him. The latter made way for the former, and nodded briefly and meaningly to the chief. 'I'm disgusted!' Fischerle declared, and cast a respectful glance at the blind man who, in spite of his ragged working clothes, was peering round at every woman and distrustfully sizing them up. He would have loved to know what effect the new cut of his moustache was making on them. He hated young girls, because they objected to his profession. 'A man like you,' Fischerle went on, 'to have to put up with all this cheating!' The blind man pricked up his ears. 'Someone throws a button into your hat. You've told me so yourself. You see it's a button and say thank-you. If you don't say thank-you, you give the show away and your clients smell a rat. So you agree to be cheated. A man like you! Might as well hang yourself. Swindling's a filthy trick. Am I right?' Tears came into the eyes of the blind beggar, grown man though he was, with three years' war service at the front behind him. This daily trick practised on him, which he saw through at once, was his greatest grief. Simply because he had to work so hard for his living, every guttersnipe could make a fool of him.

He often thought long and seriously of making an end of himself. If he were not now and then still lucky with women it would have come to that long ago. Under the Stars of Heaven he told everyone who got into conversation with him about the button-trick and ended with the threat to do in one of the swine and then himself. As this had been going on for years, no one took him seriously any more, and his suspicions were furiously growing. 'Yes!' he cried and gesticulated with his arm round Fischerle's hump, 'a child of three knows if it's got a button or a penny in its hand! But I'm not to know! I'm not to know! I'm not blind!' 'Just what I say,' Fischerle finished for him, 'it all comes of swindling. Why must people do each other? They might say "I haven't a penny to-day, my dear sir, to-morrow I'll give you two." But no, they'd sooner do you, and you have to swallow a button. You ought to try another trade, my dear sir! For a long time I've been thinking over what I might do for you. Tell you what, if you do well these three days, I'll take you on for longer. Don't say a word to the others, strictly confidential, I'll sack the lot; between ourselves I only took them on out of charity for a day or two. You're different, you can't stand cheating, I can't stand cheating, you're a better-class person, I'm a better-class person, you'll admit, we suit each other allright. Just to show you how highly I respect you, I'll give you your whole commission for to-day in advance. The others won't get a penny.' The blind man was in fact presented with the remaining fifteen schillings due to him. First of all he hadn't believed his ears, now he had the same experience with his eyes. 'Suicide be hanged!' he shouted. For the joy of the moment he would have forgone ten women — he reckoned in women. What Fischerle next explained to him he accepted with enthusiasm, and therefore with ease. He laughed at the idea of the tall partner, because he felt so happy. 'Does he bite?' he asked. He was thinking of his long, lean dog which lead him to his place of business in the morning and took him home at night. 'Let him try!' Fischerle spoke threateningly. For one moment he hesitated whether he should not entrust him with a higher sum than the 300 schillings he had in mind; the man seemed genuinely enthusiastic. Fischerle haggled with himself; he would dearly have loved to make five hundred at a stroke. But he saw that the risk was too great; such a loss might well ruin him and he forced his desires down to four hundred. The blind man was to go the square *in front* of the church and there to wait for him.

As soon as the blind man had vanished from sight, the hawker thought his time had come. He overtook the dwarf with small, quick strides and fell into step with him. 'Stick like burrs, don't they?' he said. He bent his head down, but he couldn't manage to bow it right down to Fischerle's; at least he looked up while he was talking as if the dwarf, since he had become the chief, had grown to twice his height. Fischerle was silent. He had no intention of allowing any familiarities to this man. The other three he had found in the Stars of Heaven as if sent by providence; with this one he was on his guard. To-day and not again, he said to himself. The hawker repeated: 'Stick like burrs, they do, don't they?' Fischerle's patience was exhausted. 'Tell you what, you keep your trap shut! You're an employee! I'll do the talking. If you want to do the talking, get yourself another job!' The hawker pulled himself together and stooped low. His hands, a moment ago rubbing themselves in calculation, were now folded. His head, arms and backside twitched violently. How else could he show his obsequiousness? In the confusion of his nervous reactions, he all but stood on his head, so as respectfully to fold his feet. Liberation from his insomnia was at stake. The word 'wealth' was associated with sanatoriums and expensive cures. In his heaven there would be sleeping draughts which never failed. There you could sleep for a fortnight together, without waking once. You could eat in your sleep. After a fortnight you could wake up — sooner wasn't allowed — you had to give in, what else could you do? Doctors are as strict as the police. Then you could play cards half the day. There was a special room for that, open only to people in higher-class lines of business. In a few hours you were as rich again, you were that lucky at cards. Then you could sleep another fortnight. Time — as much time as a man could want. 'What are you jigging about for? Ought to be ashamed of yourself!' screeched Fischerle. 'Stop shaking this minute or you're no use to me.' The hawker started out of his sleep and, as far as he could, calmed down his quivering limbs. Once again he was all greed.

Fischerle saw that he had not a shred of a reason for sacking this suspicious character. Furious, he began with his instructions. 'Pay attention, now, or you'll get the sack! I shall give you a parcel. A parcel, do you understand? A hawker like you must know what a parcel is. You take it to the Theresianum. I don't need to tell you anything about that. You spend most of your time there anyway, a fellow like you who doesn't use his head. You push open the glass door where it leads up to the book section. Stop waggling about so, I tell you! If you waggle about like that you'll smash the glass door, and that's your affair. At the window you'll see a thin gentlemanly gentleman. He's a business friend of mine. You go up to him and don't say anything. If you speak to him before he speaks to you, he'll turn his back and leave you standing. He's like that. He's a person of authority. So you be quiet, see! I don't want to have to bring an action for damages against you. But if you make a mistake, I'll have to, you can be sure of that; I won't have you wrecking my hard-earned business for me! If you're nervy, clear out! I'd sooner have that sewerman. Where was I? Can you tell me that?' Suddenly Fischerle became aware that he had lost grip on that high-class way of talking which he had acquired during his few days' association with Kien. Precisely this way of talking seemed to him the only one possible when dealing with this pretentious employee. He paused to calm himself and used the opportunity to catch out the hated rival unawares. But the hawker replied promptly: 'You've got to your gentlemanly business-friend and I'm to say nothing.' 'You've got there, you've got there,' croaked Fischerle, 'and where's your parcel?' 'I'll have that in my hand.' The humility of this treacherous creature made Fischerle wild. 'Ugh!' he sighed, 'by the time I've made you understand, I'll have grown another hump.' The hawker grinned, writing off the abuse against the hump. But even from his height he did not feel safe against observation and looked stealthily down. Fischerle had noticed nothing, he was clutching round for more words of abuse. He wanted to avoid such vulgar expressions as were usual under the Stars of Heaven; they would have made no impression on one of its denizens. Merely to go on saying 'Bonehead' was too boring. Suddenly he hastened his step so that the hawker was left half a pace behind, then turned contemptuously on him and said: 'Tired already? Tell you what, go and drown yourself.' Then he went on with his instructions. He impressed on him, he must ask for a 'payment' of 100 schillings from the tall business friend, but only when he had been intercepted and spoken to, and then, without wasting another word, come back to the square behind the church with parcel and pay-ment. He'd learn the rest when he got there. One word about his work, even to the other employees, and he'd be sacked on the spot.

At the idea that the hawker might give away the whole show and go into business with the others against him, Fischerle softened a little. To atone for his attacks, he slackened his pace and said, when the other was left a good yard in advance by this manœuvre: 'Stop, where are you off to? We aren't in such a hurry as all that!' The hawker took this for some new trick. The remaining words, which Fischerle spoke to him in a calm and friendly voice, as though they were still equals under the Stars of Heaven, he explained as the outcome of Fischerle's fear of arbitrary action. In spite of his nerves he was by no means a fool. His judgment of men and motives was just; in order to persuade them to buy matches, shoe laces, writing pads and even soap, he made use of more cunning, sympathy and even discretion than a successful diplomat. Only when he was involved in his dream of a long, long sleep did his thoughts diffuse themselves in a vague mist. He grasped that the success of the new business depended on a secret.

Fischerle made use of the rest of the way to indicate by means of a number of different examples the dangerous nature of his apparently so harmless friend, the tall gentlemanly gentleman. He had fought so long in the last war that he'd gone raving mad. For days at a time he wouldn't move or lift a finger against anyone. But if you were to utter a single unnecessary word to him, he'd draw his old army revolver and shoot you on the spot. The courts can do nothing about it, he's not in his right senses, he carries a doctor's certificate about with him. The police know him. But why take him up? they say, he's always let go again. Anyway, he doesn't shoot people dead on the spot, he fires at their legs. In a couple of weeks his victims are usually alright again. Only one thing really gets him wild. Asking questions, that's what does it. He won't stand a single question. A person asks him as innocent as you please, how he is. The next minute, that person's a corpse. On these occasions my business-friend fires straight at the heart. He's like that. Nothing can be done about it. He's sorry afterwards. There've only been six proper corpses so far. Everyone knows about this dangerous habit and only six have actually *asked* him anything. If it weren't for this, you could do very good business with him.

The hawker believed not a word. But he had an inflammable imagination. He saw a well-dressed gentleman standing before him who, even before you could have your sleep out, would be shooting you dead. He decided to avoid questions in all circumstances and to get to the bottom of the secret some other way.

Fischerle put his fingers to his lips and said 'Pst!' They had reached the church, where the blind man, with dog-like devotion in his eyes, was waiting for them. In the meantime he had not stared at a single woman, he only knew that several had passed by. In his excessive joy he would have been happy to greet his colleagues cordially; the poor devils would be sacked in three days, but he'd got a job for life. He welcomed the hawker as warmly as if he hadn't seen him for years. Behind the church the three linked up with the Fishwife. She had run so hard that she had been panting a full ten minutes to regain her breath. The blind man fondled her hump. 'What's up, Ma!' he shouted and laughed over the whole of his furrowed, flaccid face. 'We're in luck to-day!' Maybe he'd give her a bit of fun one day. The Fishwife screamed aloud. She felt that it was not Fischerle's hand touching her, said to herself: it *is* him, and then heard the coarse voice of the blind man. Her scream changed from fear to delight and from delight to disillusion. Fischerle's voice was alluring. *He* ought to sell newspapers! People would have rushed to buy. But he was too good for work. It would have tired him. It was better really, he should stay the chief.

For it wasn't only his voice, he had such sharp eyes. Here was the sewerman coming round the corner. He saw him first, ordered the others to 'Stay put!' and hurried to meet him. He drew him into the porch of the church, took the parcel from him — it was still lying in his arms just as it had been before — and the two hundred schillings in notes from between the fingers of his right hand. He counted out fifteen schillings and put them into his hand, though he had to uncurl it himself. At this point the tongue-tied mouth of the sewerman brought out the first sentence of his report. 'Went off a treat,' he began. 'I see, I see!' cried Fischerle. 'To-morrow at nine sharp. Nine sharp. Here. Here. Nine sharp, here!' The sewerman made off with heavy, lagging strides and began to count over his salary. After a stubborn pause he said: 'That's right.' Up to the door of the Stars of Heaven he struggled with his habit and finally gave in. Fifteen schillings for his wife, five for his beer. He stuck to it. Originally he had intended to drink the lot.

It was in the church porch that Fischerle first saw what a bad plan he had made. If he gave the Fishwife the parcel now, the hawker was close by and would see everything. As soon as he twigged it was always the same parcel, it was all over with the beautiful secret. But the Fishwife, as if she could read his thoughts, had come of her own accord to find him in the porch: 'My turn,' she said. 'You take your time, you!' he turned on her and gave her the parcel. 'Off with you!' She hobbled off as fast as she could. Her hump hid from the eyes of the others the parcel she was carrying.

The blind man all this time was explaining to the hawker that it was no good trying on anything with women. In the first place a man must have a good job, a job in which a man can keep his eyes open. You get nothing out of being blind. People think if a man looks blind, they can do what they like with him. But if you've got on in the world, women come of their own accord, dozens of them, so that you don't even know where to lay them all. Common people don't understand a thing about it. Like dogs they are, don't care where they do it. Filthy beasts, he's different! He has to have a good bed, with a horsehair mattress, a nice stove in the room, not one of those smelly oil-stoves, and a juicy bit of goods. He can't stand a smoking stove, his lungs aren't the same since the war. He's not the kind to go with any woman. Of course, when he was still a beggar, he used to try his luck pretty well anywhere. Now he was going to get himself a better suit, he'd have money to burn soon, and he'd take his choice. He'd have a hundred or so nice bits of goods, pinch them all — they needn't undress, he could tell without — and take three or four home. More at a time wouldn't be good for his health. No more buttons for him. 'I shall have to see about a double-bed!' he sighed, 'or where shall I put the three plump little bits?' The hawker had other troubles. He was dislocating his neck in an effort to see round the Fishwife's hump. Is she, or isn't she, carrying a parcel? The sewerman came up with a parcel, and went away without. Why did Fischerle make him go into the porch? You can't see any of them, not Fischerle, not the sewerman not the Fishwife as long as they're up there. The parcel must be hidden in the church, of course. A stupendous idea! Who'd look for stolen goods in a church? That hunchback's got a head on his shoulders. The parcel is most interesting — a delivery of cocaine. How did that sneak-thief get into this grand line of business?

At that moment the dwarf came running back to them, crying: 'Patience gentlemen! By the time she gets back on her crooked legs, we'll all be dead.' 'No dying for me, chief!' shouted the blind man. 'We all die in the end, sir,' the hawker obsequiously confirmed, turning the palms of his hands outwards just as Fischerle would have done in his place. 'Ah,' he added, 'if we'd a good chess player here, but neither of us is up to playing with a champion.' 'Champion, champion,' Fischerle shook his head, injured. 'In three months I shall be world champion, gentlemen.' Both his employees gazed at each other in delight. 'Long live the world champion!' yelled the blind man suddenly. The hawker, in his thin, twittering voice — he had only to open his mouth for everyone under the Stars of Heaven to say: 'Hark at the mandoline' — rapidly joined in the plaudit. He managed to get out 'world' but 'champion' stuck in his throat. Fortunately the small square was deserted at this hour by every living soul; not one of those farthest outposts of civilization in the town, the police, was to be seen. Fischerle bowed acquiescence, but felt all the same that he had gone too far and croaked: 'Unfortunately I must ask for more quiet during working hours! No talking please!' 'What's this?' asked the blind man, who wanted to start again on his future plans and thought he had a right to, in return for his acclamation. The hawker put his finger to his lip and said: 'I always say, silence is golden,' and said no more.

The blind man was left alone with his women. He was not to be put off his pleasures, and went on talking aloud. He began with its being no use to go after women, ended with the double-bed, and, getting the impression that Fischerle brought far too little understanding to these matters, began again at the beginning and laboriously described in detail some of the hundred and more women who were being kept in readiness for him. He allotted an incredible backside to each, gave their weight in hundredweights and increased it each time. When he got to the sixty-fifth woman, whom he selected as an example for the sixties, her backside alone weighted two hundredweight. He was bad at arithmetic, and liked to stick to a figure once he had named it. All the same, two hundredweight seemed to him a little exaggerated. 'What I say is gospel,' he asserted. 'I don't know how to tell a lie, it's always the same since the war!' All this time, Fischerle had enough to think of. He must forcibly keep down the mounting thoughts of chess. There was no interruption he feared more than this growing lust for a game. It might be the ruin of his business. He tapped the little chessboard in his right coat-pocket which served at the same time as a box for the pieces, heard them jump excitedly within, mumbled: 'You be quiet now!' and tapped again, until he was tired of the noise. The hawker was thinking of drugs and confusing their effects with his own desperate need for sleep. If he found the parcel in the church, he would take out a packet or two and try. He was only afraid that in a drugged sleep of that kind he'd dream. If he had to dream, he'd sooner not sleep at all. What he wanted was a real sleep, with people to feed but not to wake you, at least not for a fortnight.

Then Fischerle saw the Fishwife disappear into the church after signalling vehemently to him. He seized the blind man by the arm, said, 'Of course you're right!' and to the hawker, 'You stay here!' and pulled the former over to the church door with him. There he told him to wait and dragged the Fishwife into the Church. She was in a high state of excitement and couldn't utter a word. To calm herself a little she pressed the parcel and 250 schillings into his hands. While he was counting the money she took a deep breath and sobbed: 'He asked me, was I called Mrs. Fischerle!' 'And you answered . . .' he screeched, quivering with terror lest she should have wrecked his whole business by a stupid answer; she had wrecked it, for sure, and was pleased with herself, the silly goose! You've only got to suggest to her that she's Mrs. Fischerle and she goes out of her head! He never had been able to stand her, and that great donkey there, what had he to go and ask her that for, he's met my wife! Just because she's got a hump, and I've got a hump he has to think we're married; he's tumbled to something after all, and now I'll have to cut and run with this wretched 450 schillings, what a filthy trick! 'What did you say?' he screeched a second time. He forgot he was in church. He was usually respectful and cautious in churches, for his nose was very marked. 'I — wasn't — to say — anything!' She sobbed between each word. 'I shook my head.' The money he had thought lost rolled like a weight off his heart. But the terror she had caused him, made him fly into a passion. He would have liked to knock her block off. Unfortunately he hadn't the time. He pushed her out of the church and snarled in her ear: 'To-morrow you can go and sell your filthy papers! I'll never read one again!' She understood she had lost her job with him. She was in no condition to calculate what money she was losing. A gentleman had taken her for Fischerle's wife and she hadn't been allowed to say anything! People see that she belongs to him, but she mayn't say a thing. What a blow! what a fearful blow! In all her life she had never been so happy before. All the way home she sobbed without a break: 'He's all I've got in the world.' She forgot that he still owed her the twenty schillings, a sum which in bad times she had to run round for a week to collect. She accompanied her refrain with the image of the gentleman who had called her 'Mrs. Fischerle'. She forgot that every one called her the Fishwife, anyway. She sobbed too because she didn't know where the gentleman lived or where he was going. She would have offered him a paper every single day. He would have asked her again.

Fischerle was rid of her. He hadn't cheated her on purpose. He, too, in the anger arising from his terror and his relief had lost his head. All the same, even if her services had been smoothly rendered, he would certainly have tried to cheat her of her salary. He handed the parcel to the blind man and advised him to go carefully and to keep quiet, his permanent employment depended on that. The blind man in the meantime had closed his eyes in order to forget the women whom he had seen as large as life before him. When he opened them, all had vanished, even the heaviest, and he felt a slight regret. Instead of them, he recollected in detail his new duties. Fischerle's advice was therefore superfluous. In spite of the haste necessary to his undertaking, Fischerle did not let him go gladly; he had set much store on this question of buttons. How much that man cared for the acquisition of women he, who was indifferent by nature to the other sex, could not possibly estimate.

Going back to the hawker, he said: 'To think that a businessman has to trust such scum!' 'How right you are!' declared the other, who excepted himself as a businessman from the scum. 'What's the point of living?' — the four hundred schillings which he might lose made him tired of life. 'For sleeping,' answered the hawker. 'You and sleep!' at the thought of the hawker asleep — he who lamented his insomnia all day and every day — devouring laughter shook the dwarf. When he laughed, his nostrils looked like two wide open mouths; underneath them two small slits, the corners of his mouth, became visible. This time he had got it so badly that he had to hold his hump as other people would their belly. He put his hands under it and carefully absorbed every jolt that shook his body.

He had barely laughed himself to a standstill — the hawker was wounded to the depths of his soul by the scepticism with which his projected sleep had just been received — when the blind man re-appeared and vanished into the porch. Fischerle threw himself upon him and tore the money out of his hand, was amazed to find the sum exact — or hadn't he told him to ask for five hundred after all, no, four hundred — and asked in order to disguise his excitement: 'How'd it go?' 'I ran into someone in the swing door, into a woman, I'm telling you, if I hadn't been holding this parcel so stupidly I'd have bumped right up against her, such a fat one she was! Your business friend's a bit off it.' 'Why? what's the matter with you?' 'You won't mind my saying so, but he's got it in for the women! Four hundred's a lot, he said. Because of the woman, he said, he understands and doesn't mind paying. Women are the cause of all the trouble. If I'd been allowed to speak I'd have told him straight, the bloody fool!

Women! Women! What else would I live for if it weren't for women? I bumped into that one a treat, and he makes a scene!' 'That's the way he is. He's a bachelor for pleasure. I won't have any complaints, he's my friend. I won't have you talking to him either, otherwise you'll hurt his feelings. You don't hurt a friend's feelings. Have I ever hurt yours?' 'No, I give you that, you've got a heart of gold.' 'That's it, you come back to-morrow at nine, see? And not a word, see, because you're my friend! We'll show them if a man can be done down by buttons!' The blind man went off. He felt such a deep well-being that he had soon forgotten the peculiarities of the business friend. With twenty schillings you could do something. First things first. First things were a woman and a new suit, the new suit must be black to match his new moustache; you can't get a black suit for twenty schillings. There was always the woman.

As for the hawker, injured and curious as he was, he had forgotten both caution and his habitual cowardice. He wanted to surprise the dwarf in the very act of changing the parcels. The prospect of going over an entire church, even a small one, to find the parcel, did not tempt him in the least. By popping up suddenly he would get at least an idea of where it was, for the dwarf would be coming away from it. He met him in the doorway, took his parcel, and went off without a word.

Fischerle followed him slowly. The outcome of this fourth attempt was not of much financial significance; it was a matter of principle. Should Kien pay out this hundred schillings as well, the resultant profit coming to Fischerle alone — 950 schillings — would be larger than what he had already received as his reward for finding the wallet. During the whole of this organized fraud at the expense of the book racket, Fischerle had not for an instant lost sight of the fact that he was dealing with an enemy who, only yesterday, had tried to fleece him of everything. Naturally enough you look after your own skin. If you're up against a murderer you have to murder yourself; if you're up against a crook you have to be crooked too. Though there was a particular twist to this affair. Maybe the creature would only insist on having the reward money back again, maybe he'd plunge even deeper in mean trickery — people often get impossible ideas into their heads — and risk his whole fortune on the game. Anyway his whole fortune had once been in Fischerle's possession, so he'd a right to get it back from him. Maybe, though, the good opportunity was over now. It isn't everyone who can get ideas into his head. If the creature had a character like Fischerle's, if he cared as much for getting back that reward money as Fischerle did for chess, then business would be brisk. But can you ever tell what sort of a customer you may be dealing with? Maybe he only talks big, maybe he's only a poor sap who'll begin to regret his money and will say suddenly: 'Stop, that's enough!' He may do that and may lose his chance of getting back the reward money for a mere hundred schillings. How should he know that he's going to have every penny taken off him and not get a thing in return? If this book racket has a spark of intellect, and you've got to hand it him, he does give that impression, he's got to pay until he hasn't anything left. Fischerle began to doubt if he had as much intellect as all that; not every one had the logic, which he had developed at chess. He needs a man of character, a man of character like himself, a man who'll go through with things to the bitter end; for a man like that he'd pay out gladly, a man like that could be his business partner if he could only find him; he'll just go as far as the door of the Theresi-anum to meet him, he'll wait for him there. In any case, he can always double-cross him later on.

Instead of a man of character, out trotted the hawker. He stopped short, horrified. He hadn't expected to run into the chief. He'd been smart enough to ask for twenty schillings more than the sum stipu-lated. He clutched at his left trouser pocket where he had stuffed his earnings — they couldn't be detected — and dropped the parcel. For the moment Fischerle cared not at all what happened to the goods; he wanted to know something. His employee had crouched on his knees to pick up the parcel; to his astonishment Fischerle did likewise. Once on the ground he reached for the hawker's right hand and found the hundred schillings. That's nothing but a blind, he thought. He's frightened for his precious parcel, but why the hell didn't I take a quick look inside it, it's too late now. Fischerle got up and said: 'Don't fall over! Take the parcel home and at nine sharp to-morrow be ready in the church with it! So long.' 'Here, what about my commission?' 'Excuse me, my memory' — accidentally he was speaking the truth — 'here it is!' He gave him his percentage.

The hawker went off ('To-morrow at nine? That's what *you* think') into the church. Behind a column he sank once more to his knees and, deep in prayer lest anyone should come in while he was at it, he opened the parcel. It contained books. His last doubt vanished. He'd been done. The real parcel was somewhere else. He packed up the books, hid them under a bench, and began his search. Praying all the time, he crept round about the church and, praying, looked under every bench. He was thorough; the opportunity was not one which would quickly come again. Often he thought he had the secret, but it was only a black prayerbook. At the end of an hour he had acquired an implacable hatred for prayerbooks. At the end of two hours his back ached and his tongue hung limply out of his mouth. His lips continued to move as if he were murmuring prayers. When he had finished he began again at the beginning. He was too clever to repeat his actions mechanically. He knew that if you've overlooked a thing once, you overlook it again, and changed the order of his actions. All this time few people came into the church. He listened intently for unusual noises and stood stock still when he heard one. A pious old woman held him up for twenty minutes; he feared she might discover the sacred secret before he did, and watched her intently. So long as she stayed there he didn't even dare sit down. Early in the afternoon he had no notion left how long he had been searching, but stumbled, zigzag, from the left to the third row of benches on the right, and from the right to the third row of benches on the left. This was the last order of search which he had thought out for himself. Towards evening he collapsed somewhere on the floor and fell into a sleep of exhaustion. He had achieved his ultimate aim, but long before the fortnight was up, that same evening when the church was locked up, the sacristan shook him awake and threw him out. He forgot the real parcel.

CHAPTER V

REVELATIONS

When Fischerle, violently winking, appeared of a sudden through the glass door, he was greeted by Kien with a benign smile. The compassionate office which he had recently taken upon himself had mellowed his soul and called forth noble metaphors. His soul inquired what might be the meaning of those flashing melancholy beacon-lights; in the torrential flood of his love he had forgotten all previously arranged signals. Kien's faith, unshaken as his distrust of book-blaspheming humanity, was browsing in beloved pastures. He was regretting the weakness of Christ, that mysterious prodigal. Gifts of food and wine, healing of the halt and the blind, parable after parable went through his head; how many books, he thought, might have been saved by these miracles: he felt that his present state of mind resembled that of Christ. He too would have acted in the same fashion; only in its objects did Christ's love seem to him an aberration, like that of the Japanese. Since the philologist in him still lived, he decided to devote himself, when peaceful times should again bless the land, to a fundamentally new textual examination of the gospels. It was possible that Christ had in fact not referred to men at all, and the barbarian hierarchy had falsified the original words of their founder. The unexpected appearance of Logos in the Gospel of St. John gave abundant grounds for doubt, all the more since the usual explanations refer it back to a Greek influence. He felt himself equipped with enough knowledge to guide Christianity back to its true sources, and though he was not to be the first to pour the true words of the Saviour out to humanity, whose ears were always ready to receive them, he might hope, nevertheless, on a sufficient inner conviction, that the indications he set down would be final.

Fischerle's indications of a threatening danger, on the other hand, went unrecognized. For a time he continued his warning winks, alternatively closing his right and his left eye. At last he threw himself on Kien, clutched his arm and whispered 'Police!' the most awesome word he knew. 'Run! I'll go first!' he said, and placed himself, contrary to his promise, once more at the door to see the effect of his words. Kien cast a dolorous glance upwards, not to Heaven, to Hell rather, on the sixth floor. He vowed to return to this sanctified ante-chamber, if possible, even to-day. With all his heart he scorned the vile pharisees who persecuted him. As a true saint he did not forget, before setting his long legs in motion, to thank the dwarf with a stiff but profound inclination. If he should forget his duty out of cowardice, he vowed his own library to a fiery death. He ascertained that his enemies had not in fact shown themselves. What did they fear? The moral force of his pleadings? He pleaded for no sinners, he pleaded for guiltless books. Meanwhile let them injure but one hair of one of these, and they would learn to know a very different side of him. He knew his Old Testament too, and reserved his vengeance. Fiends, he cried, ye keep watch for me in secret places, but with uplifted brow I forsake this sink of iniquity. I fear not, for countless millions fight on my side. He pointed upwards. Then, slowly, he betook himself to flight.

Fischerle did not let him out of his sight. He had no intention of handing his money out of Kien's pocket to any crook. He feared the appearance of unknown pawn-addicts and propelled Kien to further speed with both nose and arms. From the hesitative conduct of the other he drew a kind of guarantee for his future. The creature evidently had character and had certainly taken it into his head to get the reward money back in this and no other way. He had not thought him capable of so much logic and was filled with admiration. He proposed to further the plans laid by this man of character. He would help Kien to get rid of his capital down to the last penny, in the shortest time and without too much trouble. But since it would be a pity to break up a fortune which had been in the first place a very respectable one, Fischerle must take good care that no unauthorized person interfered. Business affairs between two men of character were their own concern and no one else's. He accompanied each step of Kien's with a joyful bob of his hump, pointed here and there to a dark corner, put his finger to his lips and walked on tiptoe. When they passed an official — by chance it happened to be the hog in charge of the valuations in the book section — he attempted a bow, and shot his hump towards him. Kien too bowed, out of sheer cowardice; he sensed that this so-called human being, who had come down the stairs a quarter of an hour before, functioned as a fiend on high, and trembled lest he should be forbidden his station at the window.

At long last Fischerle had forced him as far as the square behind the church, and drawn him into the porch. 'Saved!' he mocked. Kien was astounded at the magnitude of the danger in which he had been. Then he embraced the dwarf and said in a soft, caressing voice: 'If it were not for you . . .' 'You'd be in clink long ago!' Fischerle completed the sentence. 'Are my actions then such as to bring me into collision with the law?' 'Everything brings you into collision with the law. You get yourself a meal because you're hungry, and they take you up for stealing again. You help a poor devil to a pair of shoes, he goes off in the shoes and you've aided and abetted. You go to sleep on a bench, dream away for ten years, and they wake you up because you did something ten years ago — wake you up, indeed! Take you up, more like! You try to help a few poor innocent books and they put a cordon right round the Theresianum, one of them in every corner, you ought to have seen their new revolvers! There's a major in charge of them, I ran right between his legs. What d'you think he's got down there, so low that none of the tall people walking by should notice — a warrant. The president of the police has drawn up a special warrant because you're sort of high-up. You know yourself who you are, I don't need to tell you! Eleven o'clock sharp you're to be taken, alive or dead, inside the *Theresianum*. Once you're outside nothing's allowed to happen to you. Outside you're not a criminal any more. Eleven o'clock sharp. And how late is it now? Three minutes to eleven. Look for yourself!'

He drew him to the opposite side of the square whence he could see the church clock. They had not been there a minute or two before it struck eleven. 'What did I say, it's eleven already! Talk of luck! Remember the man we ran into? That man was the hog.' 'The hog!' Kien had not forgotten a word of Fischerle's original account. Since he had unloaded his head, his memory was working again admirably. He clenched his fist, belatedly, and shouted: 'Miserable bloodsucker! Ah, if I had him here!' 'Lucky you haven't! If you'd provoked the hog you'd have been taken up sooner. What d'you think, it was no treat for me to have to bow to a hog? But I had to warn you, I wanted you to know what a friend you've got in me.' Kien was reflecting in the appearance of the hog. 'And I took him for an ordinary fiend,' he said, ashamed. 'That's what he is. Why shouldn't a fiend be a hog? Did you see his belly? There's a smell in the Theresianum . . . but best say nothing about that.' 'What sort of smell?' 'You'll excite yourself.' 'What sort of smell!' 'Promise you won't rush off there if I tell you? You'll only get yourself done in and not a book'll be any the better for it.'

'Good. I promise. Only speak!'

'You've promised then. Did you see his belly?'

'Yes — but the smell, the smell.'

'In a minute. Didn't you notice anything about his belly?'

'No.'

'People say it has corners.'

'What's the meaning of that?' Kien's voice faltered. Something unheard of was coming.

'They say — I must prop you up or there'll be an accident — they say, he gets fat on books.'

'He —'

' — devours books!'

Kien gave a great cry and fell to the ground. In his fall he dragged the dwarf with him; he hurt himself on the pavement and for revenge went on talking. 'What do you expect, says the hog — I've heard him with my own ears — what am I to do with this muck? Muck, he said, he always calls books muck, muck's good enough for him to eat. What d'you expect, he says, this muck lies about here for months, I'd as soon get something out of it, eat myself full once in a while. He's written his own cookery book, full of different recipes, he's looking for a publisher now. There are too many books in the world, he says, and too many empty stomachs. I owe my belly to my cookery, he says, I'd like everyone to have a belly like mine, and I want all books to vanish; if I had my way all books would have to go! You can burn them, of course, but that does no one any good. So cat them up, say I, raw with oil and vinegar like salad, or baked in a batter like schnitzel, with salt and pepper, or with sugar and cinnamon; a hundred and three receipts the hog's got, finds a new one every month; it's a sin and a shame, that's what I say.'

While Fischerle was croaking out these words without a moment's pause, Kien lay writhing on the ground. He smote the pavement with his fleshless fists as though to prove that the hard crust of the earth itself was softer than the heart of man. Sharp anguish rent his bosom; he wanted to cry aloud, to save, to deliver, but instead of his lips, his fists only spoke, and they rang but faintly. They smote each paving stone in turn, omitting none. They smote themselves bloody; he frothed at the mouth and the blood from his fists mingled with it, so close to the earth were his trembling lips. When Fischerle had finished, Kien got up, swayed, clung to the hump and, after he had moved his lips once or twice in vain, shrieked out shrill across the square: 'Ca-ni-bals! Ca-ni-bals!' He stretched out his free arms in the direction of the Theresianum. With his other foot he pounded the pavement which, only a moment before, he had all but kissed.

Passers-by, of whom there were one or two at this time, stood still in terror, for his voice sounded like that of a man mortally wounded. Windows were thrown open; in a neighbouring street a dog howled; out of his shop appeared a doctor in his white coat; and right round the corner of the church, the police could be sensed. The ungainly flowerwoman, whose stand was before the church, reached the shrieker first and asked the dwarf what was wrong with the gentleman. In her hand she was still holding some fresh-cut roses and a piece of bass to wind round them. 'He has just lost someone,' said Fischerle sadly. Kien heard nothing. The flowerwoman tied her roses together, laid them in Fischerle's arms and said: 'That's for him, from me.' Fischerle nodded, whispered 'Funeral to-day' and dismissed her with a casual gesture of the hand. In return for her flowers she went from one passer-by to the next and told them that the gentleman had just lost his wife. She was crying because her late lamented, who had passed over these twelve years, had always beaten her. He would never have thought of crying over her grave like that. She was sorry for herself too as the dead wife of the thin gentleman. The doctor in front of his shop — he was a hairdresser — nodded drily: 'A widower in the flower of his youth,' waited a moment and grinned at his joke. The flowerwoman threw him an ugly look and sobbed: 'I gave him my roses!' The rumour of the dead wife spread up into the houses, some of the windows were closed again. A regular dandy commented: 'What can I do about it?' but went on hanging about because of a sweet young tender-hearted servant girl, who was longing to comfort the poor gentleman. The constable was at a loss what course to take; a page-boy, hurrying to work, had told him what had happened. When Kien started yelling again, exasperated by so many people, the organ of the law sought to intervene. The tearful entreaties of the flowerwoman held him back. But the proximity of the police had an anxious effect on Fischerle, he leapt up to the height of Kien, put his hand over his mouth, shut it tightly and drew him down to his level. In this way he pushed him along, a half-closed pen-knife, to the church door, called: 'Praying'll quiet him down!' nodded to the spectators and vanished with Kien into the church. The dog in the side-street was still howling. 'Animals always know,' said the flowerwoman, 'when my poor lamented . . .' and she told the policeman her story.

Since the gentleman had vanished she was regretting the expensive flowers.

Inside the church the hawker was still in his first energetic burst. Suddenly up popped Fischerle with his rich business friend, pushed the walking-stick on to a bench, said aloud: 'Are you mad?' looked about him and went on talking in a low voice. The hawker was very much frightened, for he had cheated Fischerle, and the business friend knew of how much. He crept as far as he could away from them and hid himself behind a column. Secure in the darkness he watched them, for an acute intuition told him why they had come: they were either bringing or fetching away the parcel.

In the dark, narrow church Kien came gradually to himself. He felt the proximity of another being, whose soft-voiced reproaches infused him with warmth. What was being said, he did not understand, but it quieted him. Fischerle worked desperately hard; he had overshot his target by a long way. While he poured out soothing words he was trying to make out what sort of a man precisely he had there sitting beside him. If the creature was mad, then he was generously mad; if he only pretended to be, then he was the boldest crook in the world. A crook who lets the police come right up to him without running away, who has to be rescued by force from the arms of the police, who makes his grief credible to a flowerwoman so that she gives him roses for nothing, who risks 950 schillings without wasting a word on them, who will listen to the most monstrous lies from a hunchback without knocking him down! A world champion among crooks! To do down such a master of his craft is a pleasure; opponents of whom you have to be ashamed are what Fischerle can't stand. He's all for equality in every match, and since Kien has turned out to be his partner for financial reasons, he must regard him as his equal.

All the same he treated him as though he were an utter fool; he wanted it this way — well, he could have it. To distract his thoughts he asked him, as soon as he began to breathe more easily, about the events of the morning. Kien was not unwilling to free himself from the comfortless oppression, which burdened his soul since he had heard the worst, by the recollection of happier moments. He propped up his shoulders, ribs and the rest of his bones against the pillar which closed the end of the pew and smiled the weakly smile of an invalid who was on the road to recovery but must be spared as much as possible. Fischerle was willing to spare him. An opponent of such mettle was to be cherished. He clambered up on to the bench, knelt there and pressed his ear to the near neighbourhood of Kien's mouth: in case anyone should hear him. 'So that you don't overtire yourself,' he said. Kien no longer accepted things naturally. The least friendly movement of a fellow being seemed a miracle.

'You are hardly human,' he breathed, lovingly.

'A deformity is hardly human, is that my fault?'

'Man is the only deformity,' Kien tried his voice a tone stronger. He and the dwarf were looking into each other's eyes, so he forgot there were things he shouldn't have mentioned in the dwarf's presence.

'No,' said Fischerle, 'man isn't a deformity, or I'd be a man!'

'No, I won't have that. Man is the only beast!' Kien grew louder, forbade and ordered.

Fischerle took this skirmishing — as he thought it — for the greatest joke. 'And why isn't that hog a man then?' There, that's a facer.

Kien leapt up. He was invincible. 'Because hogs can't defend themselves! I protest against this violation! Men are men and hogs are hogs! All men are merely men! Your hog is only a man! Woe to the man who dares presume to be a hog! I will destroy him! Ca-ni-bals! Ca-ni-bals!'

The church echoed with wild lamentations. It seemed empty. Kien let himself go. Fischerle was caught off his guard; in a church he felt uncertain of himself. He almost pushed Kien out again into the square. But there the police were on the watch. If the church fell down, he wasn't going to walk into the arms of the police! Fischerle knew terrible stories of Jews buried in the wreckage of falling churches because they had no business to be there. His wife the Capitalist had told them to him because she was devout and wanted to convert him to her faith. He had no articles of faith, or only one — that 'Jew' is a genus of criminal which carries its punishment with it. In his extremity he looked at his hands, which he held always at about the level of an imaginary chessboard, and noticed the roses and how he had crushed them under his right arm. He pulled them out and screeched: 'Roses, beautiful roses, beautiful roses!' The church was suddenly full of screeching roses; from the heights of the nave, from the transepts, the choir and the tower, from all directions, red birds fluttered down on Kien.

(The hawker cowered in terror behind his column. He grasped that there was a row between the business friends and was delighted because in a quarrel one of them was sure to drop the parcel. All the same he'd

245

have liked them well outside; the noise was deafening, maybe a riot would break out, any sort of scum will join in that sort of thing and someone might steal his parcel.)

Kien's canibals were suffocated by the roses. His voice was already tired with earlier efforts and could not compete with the dwarf's. As soon as he became fully conscious of the word 'Roses' he broke off his outcry and turned, half astonished, half ashamed, towards Fischerle. How did the flowers get there; he surely ought to be somewhere else; flowers are harmless, they live on water and light, on earth and air, are not human, have never injured a book, are themselves eaten, are destroyed by human beings; flowers need protection, they must be guarded from men and animals, where's the difference, beasts, beasts, here, there, some eat plants, others eat books, the only natural ally of the book is the flower. He took the roses from Fischerle's hand, remembered their sweet smell which he knew from Persian love poetry, and raised them to his eyes; it was true, they did smell. This soothed him completely. 'Call him hog as often as you please,' he said. 'But spare at least these flowers!' 'I brought them here specially for you,' said Fischerle, glad not to have to raise his voice in church any more. 'Cost a fortune, they did. And got all crushed on account of your screaming. What can poor flowers do for that kind?' He decided from now on to agree with everything Kien said. Contradiction was too dangerous. Such boldness might well land him in the police court. The recipient of the gift sank down exhausted on the bench, leaned up once more against the column, and while moving the roses up and down before his eyes as carefully as if they were books, began to recount the happy events of the morning.

The time when, calm and all unknowing, he had ransomed victim after victim in that light forecourt where not a soul could escape him, seemed as remote as his youth. He could clearly recall the men and women whom he had helped back towards a better life — was it but an hour ago? — and he was astonished at the precision of his memory which on this occasion was outdoing itself. 'Four great parcels might have found their way into the hog's belly or been hoarded for some later fire. But I saved them. Shall I take credit to myself? I think not. I have grown more modest. Why then should I talk of it? Perhaps only so that you too, you who wish for all or nothing, should recognize the value of an act of benevolence be it of never so small a compass.' In these words one might detect the calm which comes after storm. His voice, otherwise dry and hard, sounded at this moment both gentle and fragrant. It was very quiet in the church. Between separate sentences he paused often and then, softly, took up the tale again. He described the four lost souls to whom he had extended his help. Their figures, surmounting the sharp outlines of their parcels, were blurred a little; first he described the parcels, their wrapping, shape and presumable contents, he had not in any case actually investigated. The parcels were so neat, their bearers so modest and shamefaced, he would not for anything have cut off their retreat. To what purpose would be his work of redemption if he were harsh? All but the last were creatures of rare goodness, who held their friends tenderly, and demanded great sums so that they might be left in possession of their books. Without a doubt, they would all of them have come away from the top floor with their books intact, their firm determination was plain to see; they took the money from him and withdrew, speechless, profoundly moved. The first, probably a working man, shouted at him as soon as he spoke, taking him doubtless for some wretched tradesman in books; never had harsh words sounded sweeter to him. Next came a lady whose appearance had strangely recalled to him some other acquaintance; she had imagined herself to be mocked by some attendant fiend, blushed crimson and said not a word. Soon after came a blind man, who collided with a common woman, the wife of one of the door-keeping fiends. He saved himself from her arms and clung to his parcel, and then, with astonishing confidence, came to a stand before his benefactor. A blind man with books is a deeply moving spectacle; they cling desperately to their one comfort and some, to whom braille means little, for far too little has been printed in it, will never give up, will never admit the truth, to themselves. You may see them with open books in our print before them. They cheat themselves and imagine that they read. We have too few of these, for if ever any deserved the gift of sight it is surely these blind ones. For their sake one could wish the dumb letters spoke. The demands of the blind man were the highest, he granted them but was too delicate to say why, and pretended that it was on account of that wayward woman. Why remind him of his misfortune? To comfort him, it was better to show him his blessings. Had he a wife of his own, every moment of his life he would be colliding with her and wasting his time; that is the way of women. The fourth, an insignificant fellow less devoted to his books which bobbed up and down on his arm, asked — as one would have guessed — little and betrayed by his words a touch of vulgarity.

From this recital the dwarf discovered that not a penny had slipped through his net, which would have annoyed him seriously. He confirmed the common appearance of the last of the four, whom he had met coming out of the door. The man was undoubtedly a hawker and would come back next day. They must settle with him.

The last words were overheard by the hawker; he had grown used to their tones of voice. After the noisy quarrel had died down, he had slunk inquiringly but slowly nearer towards them, and came up at exactly that moment when their talk turned to him. He was indignant at the dwarf's treachery and with all the greater energy resumed his business as soon as the two had left the church.

Fischerle nerved himself for a heavy sacrifice. He led Kien into the nearest hotel, so as to get him into proper trim for the next day, and suppressed his annoyance at the enormous tip which Kien saw fit to pay out of *his* money. When Kien settled the bill for two rooms — where one would have been quite good enough — he added 50 per cent of the entire sum in tips as if Fischerle, as far as his own part of the bill was concerned, would have agreed to such folly, and then, perfectly aware of his crime, looked smiling into his face; he would gladly have knocked his block off. Weren't these overheads superfluous? What difference did it make if he gave the porter one schilling or four? In a few days, whatever happened, the whole lot would be in Fischerle's pockets on the way to America. The porter was no richer for the trifle, and Fischerle was poorer. And he had to be friends with a dirty double-crosser like this! Not a doubt of it, he was annoying him on purpose so that he should lose patience within sight of the goal, forget himself and provide an excuse for being sacked. He'd see him damned first! To-night he'd spread out that packing paper and pile up these books, would wish him good night and let him shout out all those idiotic names to him before he went to sleep, he'd get up in the morning at six, at an hour when tarts and criminals even are still fast asleep, pack up the books and go on playing his part. The worst game of chess would be better. The great gawk couldn't think that he, Fischerle, believed in all these impossible books. He only did it to impress him; very well Fischerle'd be impressed for as long as he needed to be impressed and not a second longer. As soon as he'd got all of his passage money, he'd tell him where he got off. 'Tell you what you are, call yourself a gentleman,' he'd screech, 'a common crook you are! *That's* what you are!'

All the afternoon, worn out with the exertions of the morning,

Kien passed in bed. He did not undress for he was not anxious to make a to-do about this untimely repose. To Fischerle's repeated question, whether he was to start unloading the books, he shrugged his shoulders indifferently. His interest in his private library, which was safe in any case, had much declined. Fischerle noticed the change. He sniffed out some trap of which he must find out the reason, or if not a trap a loophole through which a few painful blows might be directed at Kien. Time and again he asked about the books. Weren't they getting very heavy for the head librarian? His present position was one to which neither his head nor his books were accustomed. Not that he wanted to interfere, but he couldn't approve of disorder in anyone's head. Wouldn't it be advisable to ask for extra pillows so that the head might at least be propped upright? If Kien turned his head round, the dwarf cried out with every sign of terror: 'For God's sake take care!' Once he even jumped up and held his hands under his right ear to catch the books. 'They're falling out!' he said reproachfully.

Little by little he managed to induce in Kien the mood he wanted. Kien remembered his duties, forbade himself any superfluous talk and lay stiff and still. If only the little fellow would be quiet. His words and looks made him uneasy, as if the library were in great danger, which was not at all the case. Pedantry can be disagreeable. So to-day he found it more suitable to think of those millions whose life was threatened. Fischerle seemed too meticulous. He was — doubtless on account of his hump — much too much concerned about his body and transferred this feeling to that of his master. He called things by name which were better not mentioned, and clove fast to hair, eyes and ears. What for? The head itself naturally includes all these trivialities, and only petty natures busy themselves with externals. Hitherto he had not been so tedious.

But Fischerle gave him no peace. Kien's nose began to run; after he had left it a while to its own devices, he determined, out of his love for order, to take steps to deal with the large, heavy drop at its tip. He drew out his handkerchief and made to wipe it. But Fischerle gasped aloud: 'Stop! Stop! Wait till I come!' He tore the handkerchief out of his hand — he had none himself — cautiously approached the nose and gathered the drop as though it had been a pearl of great price. 'Tell you what,' he said, 'I'm not staying with you! You were going to blow your nose and the books would have come pouring out! The state they'd have been in, I don't need to tell you. You've

no heart for your books! I'm not staying with anyone like that!'
Kien was speechless. In his heart he knew the dwarf was right. For
that very reason his impertinent manner was all the more exasperating.
It was as if his own voice had spoken out of Fischerle. Under the
pressure of the books, which he did not even read, the dwarf was
changing before his very eyes. Kien's old theory was receiving notable
confirmation. Before he could contrive a reply, Fischerle was croaking
on; his master's acquiescence astounded him. He risked nothing and,
by scolding away, relieved his heart of all his irritation at those shameless tips. 'Think of it, now, suppose I blow my nose! What would
you say? You'd fire me on the spot! A man of intellect doesn't act so.
You buy off books you don't even know, and you treat your own
worse than a dog. All in good time you won't have a penny left.
That doesn't matter, but suppose you've no books either, what'll you
do then? Do you want to beg in your old age? Not me. And you call
yourself a book racket! Look at me! Am I a book racket? No!
And how do I treat books? Perfectly, that's how I treat them, like a
chess player with the queen, like a tart with her fancy man, what else
shall I say so you'll understand: like a mother with a baby!' He was
trying to talk his old talk, but couldn't get his tongue round it. Nothing but high-class words came to him, and because they were high-
class he said to himself, 'They'll do!' and was pleased with them.

Kien stood up, came close up to him and said, not without dignity,
'You are a shameless deformity! Leave my room at once! You are
dismissed.'

'Grateful, aren't you! You Jewish swine!' shrieked Fischerle. 'You
can't expect better from a Jewish swine! Leave my room at once or
I'll call the police. *I* paid. Refund my expenses or I'll have the law
on you! At once!'

Kien hesitated. He was under the impression that he had paid,
but in money matters he was never sure of himself. He had moreover
a feeling that the dwarf was trying to cheat him, but even if he dismissed a faithful servant he intended at least to take his advice to heart
and to endanger the books no further. 'What have you spent on my
behalf?' he asked, and his voice was noticeably more uncertain.

Fischerle, who had suddenly become aware of the weight of the
hump on his back, drew a deep breath. Because things were going
badly for him, because he might never make America, because his
own stupidity had brought things to this pass, because he hated himself,
himself, and his smallness, his pettiness, his insignificant future, his

defeat within sight of victory, his miserable earnings (compared with the majestic whole which he could so easily have netted within a few days), because he would so gladly have taken these preliminary earnings, this trifle only fit to spit on, and thrown it at Kien's head, if it hadn't been such a waste, together with the so-called sh— library: because of all this he would renounce the money which Kien had laid out for the rooms and the porter. He said: 'I renounce it!' So hard was this sentence for him that the way in which he spoke it gave him more dignity than all Kien's height and harshness. Injured humanity rang in his renunciation and the consciousness of having meant all well and been grossly misunderstood.

Then Kien began to understand. He had not hitherto paid the dwarf a farthing of salary, emphatically not, not a word had been spoken on the matter, and yet, instead of asking for his expenses back again, he renounced them. He had dismissed him because his disinterested care for the library had forced him to utter unseemly expressions. He had abused him for his deformity. Only a few hours ago this deformity had saved his life when the entire police force of the capital had been called out against him. He owed the dwarf not only organization and safety, but even inspiration for his acts of benevolence. Out of carelessness he had flung himself on the bed without seeing to the sleeping quarters of the books, and when his servant, as was his duty, reminded him of the inconvenient position and the possible danger to the books, he threw him out of his room. No indeed, he had not sunk so low that, out of sheer obstinacy in his error, he would hold out against the very spirit of his library. He laid his hand with friendly pressure on Fischerle's hump, as much as to say: no matter, others have humpbacked minds; absurd, there are no others, for the others are mere human beings, only we two, we happy two, are different. Aloud he said:

'It is time to unpack, dear Mr. Fischerle!'

'Just what I say,' answered the other, forcing his tears back with difficulty. America rose, gigantic, before him, rejuvenated, and not to be submerged by a small-minded double-crosser like Kien.

CHAPTER VI

STARVED TO DEATH

A SMALL party to celebrate their reconciliation brought the two close together. Besides their common love of learning, or in other words, intellect, there were many things of which both had the same experience. Kien spoke for the first time of the deranged wife, whom he kept locked in at home where she could hurt no one. It was true his big library was there too; but since his wife had never shown the slightest interest in books, it was unlikely that, in her ravings, she would realize what treasures surrounded her. A sensitive mind like Fischerle's must surely understand what suffering this estrangement from his library caused him. But no book in the world could be more safely stored than with this mad creature who had but *one* idea — money. He carried the bare essentials round with him, and he pointed to the piles of books which had meanwhile been erected; Fischerle nodded respectfully.

'Yes, yes,' Kien resumed his narrative, 'you would not think such people could be, people who think of nothing but money. You made a fine gesture in renouncing money, even money which had been honourably spent. I would like to prove to you that the expressions I previously uttered against you were the outcome of a mood only, a mood which moreover may well have had its origin in my own sense of guilt. I would gladly recompense you for injuries which you were forced to bear in silence. Look upon it, therefore, as a recompense if I enlighten you on the true state of things in this world. Believe me, dear friend, there are people who do not only think of money *often*, but people who think of it always; every hour, every minute, every second of their lives they think of money! I will go further and even put forward the proposition that they think of other people's money. Such natures are afraid of nothing. Do you know what my wife tried to force from me?' 'A book!' cried Fischerle. 'That would have been comprehensible, culpable though such conduct must have been adjudged. No. A will!'

Fischerle had heard of such cases. He himself knew a woman who had tried something of the kind. To repay Kien's confidence he told him in a whisper the mysterious story, though not without insistently demanding that his confidence would be respected; it might cost him his head. Kien was taken aback when he learnt whose story it was: Fischerle's own wife's. 'Now I can admit to you,' he cried, 'your wife put me in mind of my own at the very first glance. Is your wife called Therese? At that time I did not wish to hurt your feelings, so I kept my impressions to myself.' 'No, she's called the Capitalist, she hasn't any other name. Before she was called the Capitalist, she was called Skinny, because she's so fat.'

The name was not correct, but every other detail was. At the tale of Fischerle's will all manner of suspicions were aroused in him. Was Therese in secret a professional harlot? Nothing was too low for her. She gave out that she went early to bed. Perhaps she passed her nights under other Stars of Heaven? He recollected that appalling scene when she had undressed and swept the books off the divan on to the floor. A harlot alone would have been capable of such shamelessness. While Fischerle spoke of his wife, Kien compared the details — the illness, the litany, the attempted murder — with what he remembered of Therese and had imparted to the dwarf only a few moments since. No doubt, if the two women were not identical, they must surely be twin sisters.

Later, when Fischerle in a sudden burst of confidence asked him to call him by his Christian name, and, aquiver with friendship, awaited his answer, Kien decided not only to fulfil this wish; he promised to dedicate his next important work to him, possibly that revolutionary thesis on the Logos in the New Testament, although the dwarf was no scholar and his education lay all before him. In this hour of reconciliation Fischerle learned that there were people here at home who spoke Chinese better than Chinamen and a dozen more languages as well. 'I always thought so,' he said. This fact, if it was a fact, really impressed him. But he didn't believe it. All the same, it was something for a man to be able to pretend so much intellect.

As soon as they got on to Christian name terms, there was no end to their mutual understanding. They worked out their redemption plans for the following days. Fischerle calculated that their capital would last them about a week; people might come with even more valuable books, and to let these go to perdition was a crime worthy of the death penalty. In spite of the unpleasing calculation Kien was enchanted with these words. Once the capital was expended, they would have to take more energetic measures, Fischerle added with a serious face. What he meant by this he kept to himself. To start with he explained the immediate plans to Kien. Their mission would begin at 9.30 and end at 10.30. During these hours the police are busy elsewhere. From earlier experience Fischerle knew that the cordon round the Theresianum withdrew at 9.20 and marched back to its post at 10.40. Arrests are made regularly at eleven; doubtless his dear friend remembered his own narrow escape early this morning. Naturally Kien remembered; it had struck eleven just as they looked up at the church clock. 'You're a sharp observer, Fischerle!' he said. 'Dear friend, when one's lived so long with the dregs! Life there isn't any fun, respectability doesn't pay there, present company excepted, but live and learn.' Kien perceived that Fischerle possessed precisely what he himself lacked, a knowledge of practical life, to its last ramifications.

Next morning, punctually at half past nine, he was at his post, refreshed, relieved and resolute. He felt refreshed because he was carrying less learning about with him. Fischerle had taken over the remainder of the library. 'You can put something into my head,' he joked, 'and if there's not room, I'll cram some into my hump!' He was relieved because the ugly secret of his wife no longer weighed on him, and resolute because he was under another person's orders. At 8.30 Fischerle took leave of him; he wanted to make a small reconnoitring expedition. If he should not come back, then all was in order.

Behind the church he met his staff. The Fishwife, in spite of being fired, had turned up again. She held her nose a good few inches higher than before. The chief owed her twenty schillings, and it lay with her to remind him; relying on his debt to her she dared to approach him. The sewerman was complaining of his wife. Instead of being content with the 15 schillings he had brought home, she had asked him immediately for the other five. She knew everything. That was why he respected her. She had dinned him awake that morning with those miserable schillings he had drunk. 'What do you expect,' said the blind man who had been walking up and down groaning behind the church for the last two hours and had not even taken his usual morning coffee, 'what do you expect, if you have only *one* woman! A man can do with a hundred women!' Then he asked about the sewerman's wife. Her weight made him thoughtful and he said no more. The hawker, torn from his dreamless sleep the night before by the sacristan, had only just remembered the parcel he had forgotten under the bench. Full of fear, although it was only books, he looked for it. He found it; Fischerle was already outside and greeted him with a slight twitch of his nose.

'Ladies and gentlemen,' began the chief, 'we have no time to lose. To-day is an important day. Our enterprise is forging ahead. The turnover is growing. In a few days I shall be a made man. Do your duty and I will not forget you!' He looked at the sewerman blankly, at the blind man promisingly, at the Fishwife forgivingly, at the hawker contemptuously. 'My business friend will be there in half an hour's time. Until then I will instruct you so that you know exactly what you have to do. Whoever doesn't know will be fired!' He took each of them, in the same order as before, and impressed on them the very much larger sums which they were to demand to-day.

The business friend did not recognize the sewerman, which was not surprising as the man's face was no more than a shining turd. He asked the Fishwife if she had not been there yesterday, at which, just as she had been instructed, she complained furiously of her double. That heartless creature had been pawning books for years, a thing she'd never yet done herself. Kien believed her, for her indignation pleased him, and he paid her what she asked.

Fischerle set his richest hopes on the blind man. 'First of all tell him how much you want. Then wait a minute or two. If he thinks it over, tread on his toes until he pays attention to you, and whisper in his ear: 'Kind regards from your wife Therese. She's dead.' The blind man wanted to know about her; he was distressed that her presumably generous dimensions had been reft from him by death. He regretted all deceased women; for men, were they never so dead, he had not the least sympathy. Fat women, who could thus never again be his, made him on his good days almost a body-snatcher, but on button days, only a poet. To-day Fischerle cut short his questions with a reference to a buttonless future. 'First get rid of buttons, my dear sir, then you can think of women! Buttons and women together are impossible!' With such prospects before him, the burden of a dead Therese was easy to carry as far as Kien. Her name was safe from oblivion all the way across the haymarket behind the church to the entrance hall of the book section. The intellect and the memory of the blind man, ever since he had been wounded in the war, extended no further than the names and figures of women. When, his eyes wide and gloating on the backside of a naked Therese, he pushed open the glass door, he burst out at once with her name, rushed up to Kien, and, to fulfil the chief's instructions, trod belatedly on his toes.

Kien changed colour. He saw her coming. She has broken out. Her blue skirt gleams. The mad woman, she blued it and starched it, starched it and blued it, Kien himself goes blue and limp. She's looking for him, she wants him, she wants new starch for her skirt. Where are the police? She must be shut up at once, she's a public danger, she's left the library unguarded, police, police, where are the police, ah, the police don't come till 10.40, what a disaster, if only Fischerle were there, Fischerle at least, he wouldn't be afraid, her twin sister's his wife, he knows what to do, he's dealt with her, he'll destroy her, the blue skirt — appalling, appalling, why doesn't she die, why doesn't she die, she ought to die, this very moment, in the glass door, before she gets to him, before she strikes him, before she can open her mouth, ten books for her death, a hundred, a thousand, half the library, all of it, the ones in Fischerle's head, then surely she must be dead, for ever, it's a lot, but he swears it, he'll hand over the whole library, but she must be dead, dead, dead, absolutely dead! 'I'm sorry to say she's dead,' said the blind man with genuine regret, 'and sends you her kind regards.'

Ten times at least Kien made him repeat the joyful tidings. He wanted no details, he could never have enough of the fact alone; he pinched himself doubtfully to the very bone and called himself by his own name. When he realized that he had neither misunderstood nor dreamed it, nor muddled it up, he asked whether he was quite sure and where the gentleman had heard of it? Out of gratitude he was polite. 'Therese is dead and sends you her kind regards,' repeated the blind man, annoyed. At the sight of this creature his dream grew lean. His authority was reliable but he could not name it. For the parcel he wanted 4500 schillings, but he must have the parcel back as well.

Kien hastened to pay off his debt in money. He feared that the man might ask for the promised library. What luck that this morning early Fischerle had made himself responsible for it all. It would have been impossible for Kien to carry out his vow on the spot, Fischerle was not here, and whence was he to produce books all of a sudden? In any case he paid up quickly so that the bearer of good tidings should vanish. If Fischerle, of whose whereabouts he was uncertain, were by chance to sense danger, he would come to warn him, and the library would be lost. Promise or no promise, a library was worth more than any promise.

The blind man counted the money slowly. With such a gigantic sum the tip would have been worth having; he might have asked for one, but he wasn't a beggar any longer. He was an employee of a firm with a large turnover. He loved the chief, because he had finished off the buttons. Now if he got a hundred schillings' tip for instance, he could buy himself several women at once. The chief wouldn't mind. In his old manner he stretched out his hollowed hand and said, he wasn't a beggar, just the same he felt he might ask . . . Kien eyed the door, he thought he saw a shadow approaching, he pressed a note into the man's hand, it happened to be for a hundred schillings, pushed him away with his arm and implored: 'Go now, as quickly as you can, quickly, quickly!'

The blind man had no time to regret his incompetence; he might have asked for more, but the results of his good fortune were too much on his mind. Talking loudly, he reappeared at Fischerle's side; the latter was more interested in the effect of his trick than in the soft words of the blind man, who, for love and money, could contain himself no longer. He hesitated a little before taking the money out of his hand, he did not snatch at it; time enough to find a small sum and a big disappointment. Astonishment at his hundred per cent success almost knocked him out. He counted it two or three times carefully, repeating again and again: 'There's character for you! There's a man of character! You'll have to look out for yourself, Fischerle, my boy, with a character like that!' The blind man assumed the character was his and remembered in time the hundred schillings in his left pocket. He held it down to the dwarf's nose and called: 'Look at the tip he gave me, chief, and I never once asked him for it! A man what gives a hundred schilling tip's a good man!' And it happened that Fischerle, for the first time since he took over the direction of his new firm, let part of the booty slip through his fingers, so deeply engrossed was he with the character of his enemy.

Then the hawker came pushing forward; as on the previous day his turn came last. His unhappy face quite upset the blind man. Kindly as he was by nature he advised him to ask for a tip too. This time the chief heard. As soon as the hawker, this snake in the grass, who thought of nothing but his own advantage, approached him, he woke up automatically out of his dream and screeched at him: 'Don't you dare!' 'Would I dare?' asked the victim, bewildered.

Since the previous day and in spite of his brief sleep, he had shrunk considerably. He would achieve nothing with violence, that he clearly saw. True he still firmly and fixedly believed that the real parcel was hidden in the church, but so cleverly that no one could find it. So he gave up hope of success and tried another way. He would gladly have been as small as Fischerle, so as to get into his mind, or even smaller, so as to get into the parcel itself and direct the sale from within. 'Crazy, that's what I am,' he told himself, 'no one's smaller than a dwarf.' But he did not doubt that the stature of the dwarf was inextricably connected with the hiding place of the parcel. He was much too smart. While others slept he was awake. Add the sleeping hours to the waking ones, and it was obvious how much smarter he must be than the others. He knew that, he was much too smart not to know that, but all the same he'd have liked to be rid of all this smartness, for a fortnight, shall we say, and have gone to sleep all that time like other people, in one of those nursing homes with every modern convenience, like they have nowadays; a chap like him gets about a bit and hears a lot of talk, other people hear it too, but they sleep it all off, he never sleeps off a thing, because he can't sleep, so he remembers every word of it.

Behind Fischerle's back, the blind man signalled to him, he held up the hundred schilling note and repeated with silently moving lips his recommendation about the tip. He was afraid the hawker might come back defeated, because he wanted a word or two with him about his women. The chief knew nothing about that sort of thing, he was only a deformed dwarf. The sewerman was a coward because of his own old woman, he wouldn't touch another, drinking was all he ever did without his old woman. Better tell the others nothing about this new situation, they'd all be wanting something, and in no time, out of all that money, he wouldn't be left with so much as a single woman on hand. The hawker was the only one to tell. He wouldn't say a word, if you talked something over with him, he was silent; he was much the best to talk to.

In the meantime the only one to tell was thinking of his job. He was to ask for the colossal sum of two thousand schillings. Should the business friend ask him whether he had not been there before, he must say: 'Yes, of course, with the same parcel! Don't you remember me?' If the flagpole got into one of his moods, the hawker must withdraw as fast as possible, without the money; in case of emergency he must even leave the parcel behind. The flagpole's habit was to draw out his revolver and shoot, one two. It didn't matter about the parcel. The books in it were not so very valuable. Fischerle would settle up with his business friend as soon as he was normal again and could be talked to. In this devilish fashion, Fischerle planned to be rid of the hawker. He saw the infuriated Kien before him, his rage at the shameless demand and the reappearance of the hawker with the same books. He saw himself, Fischerle, shrugging his shoulders and dismissing his employee with a friendly grin. 'He won't have anything more to do with you? What am I to do? I'm afraid I shall have to dismiss you. He says, you insulted him. What did you do then? It's no use any more. You can go. Once I've got another partner, I'll take you on again, in a year or two. Look after yourself until then, and I'll see what I can do for you. I've a heart for hawkers. He says, you're a common fellow, a snake in the grass, thinking of nothing but your own advantage. How do I know what he means by that? Get out!'

Fischerle had allowed for everything, but he had underestimated the effect of the news of Therese's death. The hawker came upon a much disturbed business friend, who never stopped smiling even over the most important transactions, who paid out the gigantic sum with a smile, and when he had done, added not without another well-bred smile, 'I seem to know your face.' 'I seem to know yours!' answered the hawker, rudely. He was fed up with being smiled at; either the business friend was getting at him, or he was crackers. But since he was manipulating such large sums of money, the former was more probable. 'Where have we met before?' asked Kien, smiling. He felt the need to talk of his good luck to some harmless person, some person to whom he had not promised the library and who did not know him. 'We met in church,' answered the hawker, disarmed by the gentleman's friendly interest. He wanted to see how this wealthy man would react to the mention of the church. Perhaps he would suddenly transfer the whole business into his hands. 'In church,' repeated Kien, 'of course, in church.' He had no idea what church they were talking of. 'I'd like you to know — my wife's dead.' His haggard face beamed. He bowed; involuntarily the hawker gave ground and squinted anxiously at his hands and pockets. His hands were empty, but you couldn't tell about his pockets. Kien followed him; in front of the glass door he grasped the trembling creature by the shoulder and whispered in his ear: 'She was illiterate.' The hawker understood not a word, he shook in every limb and muttered fervently: 'Deepest sympathy! Deepest sympathy!' He sought to tear himself free, but Kien would not relinquish his grasp and asserted, smiling, that the same fate lies in wait for all illiterates, and all of them deserve it, though none so much as his wife, the news of whose death he had received only a few minutes ago. Death is the end of each one of us, but comes first to the illiterate! At this he shook his free fist and his face straightened itself to the stern expression which it normally wore.

The hawker began to understand, the man was threatening him with death; he stopped in his prayer, gasped aloud for help and let the heavy parcel fall on the feet of his terrible opponent who, in the first shock of pain, let go of him. Then he clenched his jaws and slipped swiftly away; if he didn't cry out again, the flagpole probably wouldn't fire. In his thoughts, he besought him imploringly to put off shooting until he was round the corner; he would never do it again. In front of the Theresianum he went over his clothes for signs of an unobserved wound. He had the presence of mind to ask for his share before giving Fischerle his notice. Only after the dwarf, ecstatic at his luck which held even when he least expected it, had counted over the 2000 schillings and paid him his twenty, the hawker broke down again and told him between sobs that, although he had not asked a single question, the rich business friend had fired at him and nearly hit him. He was not going on with the job any more. Besides which, Fischerle must pay him compensation for the shock. The dwarf promised him six months' salary at fifty schillings, the first to be paid a month from to-day. (By that time he would have been weeks in America.) The hawker declared himself satisfied and went.

Kien had picked up the fallen books. Their fate distressed him, but the man's disappearance distressed him still more; he would have liked to say more to him. He called softly and gently after him: 'But she's dead, you can rely on it, believe me, she can't hear us!' He did not trust himself to call any louder. He knew why the man was running. Everyone was afraid of this woman; when he had told Fischerle of her yesterday, he too had grown pale. Her name spread terror, it was enough only to hear it to be turned to stone. Fischerle, loud, noisy Fischerle, whispered when he spoke of her twin sister, and the unknown whose books he had ransomed did not believe she was dead. Why else should he run? Why should he be so timid? He had proved to him that she must be dead, her death was self-evident, it arose from her nature, or more correctly, from her condition. She had destroyed herself, she had devoured herself for love of money. Perhaps she had had provisions in the house, who can tell where she might not have hoarded provisions, in the kitchen, in her old servant's bedroom (she was in fact only a housekeeper), under carpets, behind books, but there is an end to all things. For weeks she lived on these, and then suddenly there was no more. She realized that she had used up all her stores. But she did not lie down and die. He would have done so in her place. He would have preferred any death to an unworthy life.

But she, driven to madness by her desire for his will, had eaten herself up, piece by piece. To her last moment she saw the will before her. She tore the flesh off her bones in tatters, this hyena, she lived from body to mouth, she ate the bleeding flesh without cooking it, how could she cook it, then she died, a skeleton, the skirt arched stiffly over her bare bones, and looked as though a storm had blown it out. It was the same skirt as ever, but she had been swept away by the storm from beneath it. She was found, for one day the flat was broken open. That rough and loyal *landsknecht*, the caretaker, was trying to discover the whereabouts of his master. He had knocked daily and was uneasy because he had had no answer. He waited several weeks before he permitted himself to break in. The flat was strongly bolted on the outside. When he broke in, he found the corpse and the skirt. They were placed together in a coffin. No one knew the Professor's address or they would have notified him of the funeral. This was lucky, for, in the sight of all the bystanders, he would have laughed instead of crying. Behind the coffin walked the caretaker, the only mourner, and he only there out of loyalty to his liege-lord. A huge bloodhound leapt on the coffin, dragged it to the ground and tore out the starched skirt. He worried it till his mouth was bloody. The caretaker thought, the skirt belongs to her, the skirt was closer to her than her heart, but because the dog was mad with hunger, he did not dare to interfere or risk a fight with it. He could only stand by and watch, deeply moved, as piece by piece, soaked in the blood of the mighty beast, disappeared into its jaws. The skeleton went on. As no one else was in the procession, the coffin was thrown on the great rubbish heap outside the town, no cemetery, no religion would have anything to do with it. A messenger with news of this fearful end was sent to Kien.

At that moment Fischerle appeared in the glass door and said: 'Ready to go, I see.' 'A good thing I locked her up,' said Kien. 'Lock me up? Not on your life!' Fischerle started back. 'She deserved her death. Even to-day I don't know for certain if she could read and write fluently.' Fischerle understood. 'And my wife can't play chess! What d'you say to that? Makes your blood boil, doesn't it?' 'I would gladly have learnt some details. We have to be content with such scanty information. My informant has vanished.' True, he had sent him away himself, but he was ashamed to confess to Fischerle the tremendous oath he had sworn. 'And he left his parcel here, the ass! Give it to me! I'm carrying everything already, I can carry this too.'

At these words he remembered their reconciliation of the previous

evening and apologized to Kien for having addressed him too formally;
it was merely out of his natural respect. In fact he already despised him,
for he was now four times as rich as Kien. He looked upon it as a
favour to go on knowing him, and had it not been for the last fifth of
the capital, he would simply have been silent. Besides, Kien's domestic
arrangements were beginning to interest him more closely. Perhaps
his wife really was dead. All the signs pointed to it. If she had been
still alive, she would have hauled her man home long ago. Any
woman would have hauled home such an ass of a man with so much
money. He didn't believe in her madness, all the details Kien had told
him of her, were totally in order. That this weakly, skinny creature
could have locked up anyone, let alone such a competent woman,
seemed to him impossible and ridiculous. She would have broken
down the door all the more, if she were mad. So she must be dead.
But what was happening to the flat? If there was anything of value in
it, there were things which ought to be fetched out; if it was only full
of books, these could at least be pawned. The flat itself could be sold
to someone else for a huge premium. In any case, something had
happened and capital, whether large or small, was lying about unused.

In the street Fischerle looked up anxiously at Kien and asked: 'Dear
friend, what are we to do now with the beautiful books at home? The
whore's gone and the books are all alone.' He placed the outstretched
fingers of his right hand close together, grabbed at them with his left
hand and broke them suddenly asunder just as if he had wrung the
whore's neck in person. Kien was grateful to him for this reminder;
he had been waiting for it. 'Calm yourself,' he said, 'the caretaker has
undoubtedly sealed up the flat. He is honesty itself. How otherwise
could I walk so calmly beside you? As to whether the woman was a
harlot, I could not absolutely decide.' He was just; she was dead, it
seemed to him proper not to condemn her without valid proof.
Moreover he was ashamed of himself for not having noticed in eight
long years what her real profession was. 'A woman who isn't a whore,
there's no such thing!' Fischerle, as usual, had found the right solution.
It was the outcome of a life spent under the Stars of Heaven. Kien
recognized the truth of the statement at once. He himself had never yet
touched a woman. Could there be — outside the sphere of knowledge
— any better justification for his conduct than the fact, that they were
all harlots? 'Alas, I must confess you are right,' said he, disguising his
agreement in the form of a parallel experience. But Fisherle had had
enough of the whore and swerved to the caretaker. He doubted his

honesty. 'First of all there are no honest men,' he declared, 'except us two, naturally, and secondly there are no honest caretakers. What do caretakers live on? Blackmail! And why? Because they couldn't live any other way. A caretaker can't live on flats alone. Others might, but not a caretaker. We had a caretaker, he took a schilling off my wife for every gentleman she brought in. If she came home one night without a gentleman — in her profession nothing's impossible — he used to ask, where the gentleman was. I haven't one, she said. Show me the gentleman or I'll show you up, he used to say. Then she used to cry. Where was she to find a gentleman? Went on for an hour and more like that sometimes. To end it all she always had to show him the gentleman, even if it was only a tiny one,' Fischerle held his hand out flat at knee-height, 'she could have hidden him easy if the creature had had any sense. A pity for the schilling! And who went down the drain? Me of course!'

Kien explained to him in this case he had to do with a *landsknecht*, a loyal, reliable fellow, as strong as a bear, who never let beggars, hawkers and other scum over the threshold. It was a pleasure only to watch the way he dealt with that mob, many of whom did not even know how to read and write. He had beaten many of them, literally, into deformities. As a reward for the peace which he owed to him — because for learning you need peace, peace and yet more peace — he had appointed him a small honorarium of 100 schillings a month. 'And the fellow takes it! The fellow takes it!' Fischerle's voice snapped out. 'A blackmailer! Aren't I right? A regular blackmailer! Ought to be locked up, at once! Locked up, I say, locked up!'

Kien sought to calm his friend. He should not compare a vulgar fellow like that with himself. Naturally it was vulgar to accept money for a service, but this form of immorality was deeply implanted in the plebs and even extended to the educated classes. Plato fought in vain against it. For this very reason he, Kien, had always had a repulsion from accepting a Chair. For his work in the sphere of learning he had never yet accepted so much as a farthing. 'Plato's all right!' countered Fischerle — he was hearing the name for the first time — 'I know Plato. Plato's a wealthy man. You're a wealthy man. How do I know? Because only wealthy men talk that way. Now take a good look at me. I'm a poor devil, I've nothing, am nothing, shall be nothing, and yet I take nothing. There's character for you! Your caretaker, that blackmailer, takes 100 schillings, a fortune I tell you, and beats up poor devils all day too. But at night — I bet you he's asleep at night, if someone breaks in he won't notice it then, he lies and sleeps, he's got his hundred schillings in his pocket, but he'll let them loot the books; I can't stand for anything like that, it's a scandal, aren't I right?'

Kien said he didn't know if the caretaker slept heavily or not. It was presumable at least, because everything about him was heavy, except his four canaries, who were made to sing whenever he wanted. (He mentioned them in the interests of accuracy.) On the other hand, the fellow was of a fanatical vigilance; he had constructed himself a special peep-hole eighteen inches above ground level so that he could the better watch those who went in and out. He knelt there all day. 'I'd eat him alive!' Fischerle burst in. 'That kind are all informers. An informer like that! A vulgar brute! If I had him here dear friend, you'd open your eyes, how I'd knock him about, with my little finger I'd knock him all to bits! Are informers scum or aren't they? They are, I say, and aren't I right?' 'I hardly think that my caretaker was ever an informer by profession,' Kien reflected, 'if indeed such a profession should exist. He was a policeman, an inspector, unless I mistake, and has long been retired.'

At that Fischerle renounced his plan. No burglary of that kind for him. He wasn't having anything to do with the police at present, before going to America, emphatically not, and above all not with retired policemen; they're much the worst. Out of laziness they go for the innocent. Because they mayn't arrest any more, they go mad on every occasion and beat harmless deformities into deformity. A pity all the same, it wouldn't hurt to fit oneself out a bit better for America. A man goes to America only once. A world champion ought not to arrive as a beggar, not that he is, but he may be, and people might say: he came here with empty hands, we won't have him staying here with full ones, let's take it all away from him. In spite of his world championship Fischerle was not at all sure of himself in America. Sharks are everywhere and everything in America is huge. From time to time he stuck his nose into his left armpit and strengthened himself with the smell of his money, which was stowed there. That comforted him, and after his nose had been there a fraction of time, it popped gaily up into the air again.

But Kien no longer felt so happy about Therese's death. Fischerle's words reminded him of the danger in which his library was. Everything drew him back to it, its distress, his duty, his work. What kept him here? A nobler love. So long as a single drop of blood ran in his veins, he was determined to ransom the wretched, to redeem them from a fiery death, to protect them from the jaws of the hog! At home he would, without doubt, be arrested. He must look facts steadily in the face. He was accessory to Therese's death. She was chiefly responsible but he had locked her in. By law, he would have been compelled to hand her over to an institution for the mentally unfit. He thanked God he had not obeyed the law. In an institution she would have been alive to-day. He had condemned her to death, hunger and her own greed had executed the sentence on her. He took back not one iota of what he had done. He was ready to answer for her to justice. His trial must end with an overwhelming verdict for acquittal. In any case the arrest of so famous a scholar, probably the greatest sinologist of his time, would cause undesirable publicity, a thing, in the interests of learning, to be avoided. The chief witness for the defence would be that very caretaker. Kien relied on him, but Fischerle's reflections on the venality of such a character did not fail of their effect. *Landsknechts* will go over to the master who pays them best. The crux of the matter was to guess who this opponent might be. Should there be any such person, had he an interest in bribing the caretaker with irresistible sums? Therese was alone. Not a word had ever been said of any relations. At her funeral, no one had followed the coffin. Should anyone pretending to be a relation appear in the course of his trial, Kien would have the origins of the person in question most carefully investigated. Some sort of a relation was of course possible. He decided to talk to the caretaker before he was arrested. An increase of his honorarium to 200 schillings would entirely win over this — as Fischerle so rightly called him — informer. This could not be regarded either as bribery or as an injustice of any kind; the caretaker was to tell the truth, nothing but the truth. In no circumstance whatever was it right that presumably the greatest sinologist of his time should be punished on account of an inferior woman, a woman of whom it could not be said with any certainty whether she were able fluently to read and write. Learning demanded her death. It demanded also his free pardon and rehabilitation. Scholars of his standing could be counted on the fingers of one hand. Women, unhappily, may be reckoned in millions. Therese belonged to the least of these. True her death had been as painful and cruel as could well be imagined. But for that, precisely for that, she was herself responsible. She might as well have starved peacefully to death. Thousands of Indian fakirs had died this lingering death before her and thought themselves redeemed thereby. The world admires them to this day. No one pities their fate, and their people, the wisest after the

Chinese, call them saints. Why had not Therese wrung from herself the same decision? She clung too much to life. Her greed knew no bounds. She lengthened her life by one contemptible second after another. She would have eaten men, if there had been any nearby. She hated mankind. Who would have sacrificed himself for her? At her worst hour she found herself, as she deserved to be, alone and forsaken. So she clutched at the last chance left to her: she ate her own body, morsel by morsel, strip by strip, piece by piece, and thus, in indescribable agony kept herself alive. The witness did not find a body, he found bones, held together only by the blue starched skirt which she habitually wore. This was her well-merited end.

Kien's speech in his own defence became the perfect accusation of Therese. In retrospect, he destroyed her a second time. For some time now he had been sitting in an hotel bedroom with Fischerle; they had got there almost automatically. His close-knit chain of thought was not interrupted for a single moment. He was silent and thought over every little detail. Out of the words which the devoured woman had uttered while she was alive he reconstructed a text which could well have served as an example of its kind. He was past-master of brilliant emendations and could argue every letter. All the same he deeply regretted expending so much philological meticulousness on a mere murder. He acted however under the strongest compulsion and promised the world rich compensation in the work he would do in the immediate future. She, whose case was now under discussion, had been the chief hindrance to his work. He thanked the judge for his conciliatory conduct throughout, conduct which he, a man accused of murder, had certainly not expected. The judge inclined his head and declared with ceremonious courtesy, that he knew well what befitted the greatest sinologist of the modern world. That 'presumably' which Kien placed before 'the greatest sinologist' when he spoke of himself, was omitted by the judge, for it was wholly superfluous. Kien was filled, at this public homage, with a sensation of justifiable pride. His accusation of Therese acquired a gentler tone.

'Certain extenuating circumstances must be allowed her,' he said to Fischerle, who was seated next to him on the bed, regretting the abandoned burglary, and sniffing at his money. 'Even in her worst moment, when her character must have been wholly undermined by hunger, she never dared to touch a book. I would like to add, that of course we are speaking of an uneducated woman.' Fischerle was annoyed because he understood, why did he have to understand nonsense, he cursed his own intellect, and only out of habit responded to the words of the poor devil next him. 'Dear friend,' he said, 'you're a fool. Nobody does what they don't know how. What d'you think, she'd have eaten up the most beautiful books, and with an appetite too, if she'd known how easy it was. Tell you what, if the cookery book that that hog at the Theresianum has put together, with 103 recipes — if that were in print — no, better say no more.' 'What do you mean?' asked Kien with staring eyes. He knew exactly what the dwarf meant, but he wanted another than himself to place this ghastly thing in relation to his library, not he himself, not even in his thoughts. 'I can only say, dear friend, that when you got home you'd have found your flat empty, eaten bare, not a page, let alone a book!' 'God be praised!' Kien drew a deep breath. 'She is already buried and the blasphemous work will not come out so soon. I shall know how to bring it into question at my trial. The world shall listen! I intend to reveal, without mercy, all I know. A scholar's word still carries weight!'

Since his wife's death Kien's words had grown bolder, and the very difficulties before him pricked on his lust for battle to new deeds. He passed a stimulating afternoon with Fischerle. In his melancholy mood the dwarf had much feeling for jokes. He had the trial explained to him to the minutest detail and raised no objection anywhere. He gave Kien good advice free, gratis and for nothing. Had he no relations who could help him, a murder trial was no light matter? Kien cited his brother in Paris, a well-known psychiatrist; earlier he had amassed a fortune as a gynaecologist. 'A fortune, did you say?' Fischerle immediately decided to make a halt in Paris on the way to America. 'He's the right man for me,' he said, 'I'll consult him about my hump.' 'But he's not a surgeon!' 'Don't matter; if he's been a gynaecologist, he can do anything.' Kien smiled at the innocence of the dear fellow, who evidently had no idea of any such thing as specialization of knowledge. But he willingly gave him the exact address, which Fischerle noted down on a dirty piece of paper, and told him much of the beautiful relationship, which decades ago, had existed between him and his brother. 'Learning demands an undivided allegiance,' he concluded, 'it leaves nothing over for customary relationships. It has separated us.'

'If you're on trial you can't make use of me anyhow. Tell you what, I'll go to Paris in the meantime and tell your brother I'm from you. I shan't have to pay him anything if I'm your good friend!' 'Of course not,' replied Kien, 'I'll give you a letter of recommendation, so that you get there safely. It would make me very happy, if he should really be able to relieve you of your hump.' He sat down and wrote at once — for the first time in eight years — to his brother. Fischerle's proposition seemed very suitable to him. He hoped soon to be able to withdraw once more entirely into his life of study, and the little fellow, much as he respected him, would then only be a burden. As a matter of fact, ever since they had been on Christian name terms, he had rather felt he would have to get rid of him sooner or later. If Fischerle could get rid of his hump, George would surely be able to make good use of him at his clinic as a male nurse. The dwarf carried the sealed and addressed letter into his room, took a book out of the parcel, his precious goods which the hawker had simply dropped on the floor, and placed the letter in it. The rest of the parcel was to serve its former purpose in the morning. Accurately calculated, Kien must have about 2000 schillings left. In a single morning these would easily be got from him. The evening therefore was spent in indignant colloquy about the hog and other unnatural creatures.

The next day began badly. Scarcely had Kien taken up his position at the window when a man with a parcel crashed into him. His balance was just good enough to save him from falling through the pane. The rough fellow pushed past. 'What do you want? Why have you come? Wait a minute!' All his shouts were in vain. The creature flung himself up the stairs and did not even turn round. After lengthy consideration, Kien came to the conclusion that these must have been pornographic books. This was the only excuse for the shameless haste with which the man had fled from any examination of his parcel. Then the sewerman appeared, stood stock still before him and demanded in a resounding voice 400 schillings. Enraged by the previous encounter, Kien recognized him. In a trembling voice he approached him: 'You were here yesterday! Are you not ashamed?' 'Day before yesterday too,' squelched out the open-hearted sewerman. 'Get out of here! Repent of your sins! You'll come to a bad end!'

'I want my money,' said the sewerman. He was looking forward to the five schillings he would soon drink up. Without thinking about it — he never thought — he was sure that, as a labourer, he would only get his wages if he had done his work, that is, if he had delivered over the money paid to him. 'You will get nothing!' declared Kien, resolute. He stood on the stairs. He was ready for everything. The books would be pawned over his dead body! The sewerman scratched his head. He could have squashed this bag of bones flat between finger and thumb. But he hadn't been told to. He only did what he was told.

'I'll go and ask the chief,' he grunted, and turned his backside on the other. That way of saying good-bye was easier than talking. Kien sighed. The glass door creaked.

There appeared a blue skirt and an enormous parcel. Therese followed. Both were hers. At her side came the caretaker. With his left hand he lifted an even larger parcel high above his head and threw it over into his right hand, which caught it easily.

CHAPTER VII

FULFILMENT

FOR a full week after Therese had thrown out her husband, that thief, she did nothing but search the flat. She behaved as though she were spring cleaning and divided up her work. From six in the morning till eight in the evening, she pushed about on feet, knees, hands and elbows spying for secret cracks and fissures. She discovered dust in places where she had not suspected it, even at her cleanest moments, and attributed it to the thief, for such people are dirty. With a stiff sheet of brown paper she probed into fissures which were too narrow for her stout hairpins. Afterwards she blew the dirt off, and dusted the paper over. For she could not bear the idea that she might touch the lost bankbook with a dirty piece of paper. For this work she wore no gloves — it would have spoilt them — but they lay near by, washed to glistening whiteness, in case she should find the bankbook. The beautiful carpets, which might have been damaged by so much tramping to and fro, were rolled in newspaper and stacked in the corridor. She searched each single book for its real contents. She was not yet seriously thinking of a sale. First she must talk it over with a sensible man. All the same, she noted the number of pages and felt a respect for books with more than 500, they must certainly be worth something, and she weighed them up in her hand before replacing them, like plucked chickens in the market. She was not cross about the bankbook. She was happy to give herself up to the flat. She could have done with more furniture. You had only to think the books away to see at once what sort of a person had lived here: a thief. After a week she knew the truth: there wasn't a bankbook. In a case like this a respectable woman calls the police. She waited before registering her complaint until she had used up the last of her housekeeping money. She wanted to prove to the police that her husband had run away with everything and left her without a penny. When she went marketing she made a wide detour to avoid the caretaker. She was afraid he would ask after the Professor. True he hadn't yet made a move, but he would certainly do so on the first of the month. On the first he got his monthly tip. This month he wouldn't get a penny; already she saw him begging outside her door. She was fully determined to send him off empty-handed. No one could force her to give him anything. If he was insolent, she'd report him.

One day Therese put on her starchier skirt. It made her look younger. Its blue was just a trifle lighter than the other one which she wore every day. A dazzling white blouse went well with it. She unbolted the door into her new bedroom, glided over to the wardrobe mirror, said 'Here I am again' and grinned from ear to ear. She looked not a day over thirty, and had a dimple in her chin. Dimples are beautiful. She fixed a rendezvous with Mr. Brute. The flat was hers now; Mr. Brute could come. She'd like to ask him what she'd better do. Millions are locked up in those books, and she'd be happy to give someone a share. He needs capital. She knows he's a good manager. She's not one to sleep on all that beautiful money. What good is it to her now? Saving's good, earning's better. All of a sudden you've doubled it. She hasn't forgotten Mr. Brute. Women don't forget him. Women are like that; they're all after him. She'd like some too. Her husband's gone. He won't come back. The way he behaved, she wouldn't like to say. He didn't treat her right, but he was her husband just the same. So she'd rather not say. He was a thief but he wasn't clever. If everyone were like Mr. Brute! Mr. Brute has a voice. Mr. Brute has eyes. She'd found a new name for him, it was called Puda. It's a beautiful name, Mr. Brute is even more beautiful. Mr. Brute is the most beautiful. She knows ever so many men. Does she like one of them as she likes Mr. Brute? Let him prove it if he thinks she's anything to hide. He mustn't think. He must come. He must say that about her magnificent hips. He says it so beautifully.

At these words she balanced up and down before the mirror. It made her feel how beautiful she was. She took off her skirt and had a look at her magnificent hips. How right he is. He's so sensible. He's not only superior, he's everything. How could he have known? He'd never seen her hips. He notices everything. He looks carefully at all women. Then he asks, can't he sample them? A man ought to be bold. If he isn't, he's not a man. Is there a woman who could say no to him? Therese touches her hips with his hands. They are as soft as his voice. With her smiling dimples she looks in his eyes. She'll give him something, she says. Back to the door she goes, and fetches the bunch of keys hanging there. Before the mirror, she hands over the present with a jingle, and says he can come to her rooms whenever he likes. She knows he won't steal anything, even if she isn't there. The bunch of keys falls to the ground and she is ashamed because he won't have them. She calls: Mr. Puda, mayn't she call him just Puda. He says nothing, he can't tear himself away from her hips. It's beautiful. But she would like to hear his voice too. She tells him a dark secret. She has a savings book and he can look after it for her. Will she just tell him its number too? She teases him. She starts back, he shouldn't ask that of her, she wouldn't do a thing like that. Not till she knows him better. She hardly knows him at all. But did he say anything? Where is he? She looks for him round her hips, but there she is cold. It is warm in her bosom. His hands dangle there under her blouse, but where is he? She looks for him in the mirror but only sees her skirt. It looks as good as new and blue is the most beautiful of colours, because she is true to Mr. Puda. She puts it on again, it suits her well, and if Mr. Puda likes she will take it off again. He'll be coming to-day, he'll stay all night, he'll come every night, he is so young. He has a harem, but he'll get rid of them all for her sake. Once he behaved like a brute. That's his name. He can't help his name. She's all of a sweat, and now she will go to him.

Therese took back the rejected keys, ponderously locked up the room again, scolded herself for having used the mirror in the best room when she had that little broken piece in the other room, and laughed heartily because she'd searched in vain for the keys in the inside pocket which didn't exist in this skirt at all. The sound of her laughter was foreign to her, she never laughed, she thought she was hearing some stranger in the house. Then suddenly, for the first time since she had been alone, she had an uncanny feeling. Hastily she sought out the hiding place of her savings book; it lay in its proper place. So there weren't any burglars in the flat; they would have taken her savings book first. For safety she took it with her. In the entrance hall passing the caretaker's door she stooped low. She had a lot of money with her and was afraid he might ask for his tip to-day.

The noisy traffic in the streets increased Therese's joy. Swiftly she glided to the feast; her goal lay in the heart of the town. Street by street the noise grew louder. All the men turned to look at her. She noticed it alright, but she lived for one alone. She had always hoped to live for one man alone and now it had happened. A car was imper-tinent; it almost ran her down. She tossed her head at the chauffeur, said: 'I ask you, I've no time for you!' and turned her back on the danger. In future Puda would protect her from the crowd. She wasn't alone either because everything now belonged to her. While she was walking through the town she took possession of all the shops. There were pearls in one of them which matched her skirt, in another diamonds for her blouse. She'd never have worn a fur coat, no respectable woman does, but she'd like to hang one or two in her wardrobe. Her own linen was more beautiful than any in the shops, the lace on it was ever so much broader. But she didn't mind if she took a few shop-windows with her. All those riches she put into her savings book which grew fatter and fatter; everything was safe there, and he would be allowed to look at it!

She came to a halt in front of his shop. The letters in the shop front came close to her eyes. First she read Gross & Mother, then Brute & Wife. She liked that. She even wasted some of her busy time just looking at it. The rivals went for each other; Mr. Gross was a weakling and got beaten up. The letters danced for joy, and when they had finished dancing she read suddenly, Gross & Wife. That didn't suit her at all. She exclaimed: 'The cheek of it!' and stepped inside.

Immediately somebody kissed my dear lady's hand. It was his voice. Two paces off she raised her bag in the air and said: 'Here I am again.' He bowed and asked: 'What can I do for you, dear lady? What can I show you, dear lady? A new bedroom suite? For a new husband?' For months Therese had been tormented by the fear that he wouldn't recognize her again. She did everything to ensure recognition. She looked after her skirt, washed it, starched it, ironed it daily, but the superior young man had so many lady friends. Now he said: 'For a new husband?' She grasped his secret meaning. He had recognized her. She lost all shyness, she didn't even look round to see if anyone else was in the shop, but came close up to him and repeated word for word, what she had practised before the mirror. He looked into her face with his moist eyes. He was so beautiful, she was so beautiful, everything was beautiful, and when she got to the bit about the magnificent hips, she fiddled with her skirt, hesitated, clutched tight hold of her bag and began again at the beginning. He swung his arms and interjected cries of: 'What can I show you, dear lady? But, dear lady! What can I show you, dear lady?' To make her speak lower, he came even nearer, his mouth opened and shut close to hers, he was exactly her height and she went on speaking louder and faster. She forgot not a word, each one burst, explosive, from her mouth, for her breath was coming violently and in jerks. When she got to the hips for a third time, she unfastened her skirt behind, but pressed her bag tight against it so that it stayed up. The salesman was sick with terror; she was talking as loud as ever and her red, sweating cheeks brushed against his. If only he could have understood her, he hadn't an idea who she was or what she wanted. He gripped her by her fat arms and groaned: 'What can I do for you, dear lady?' she had just about got to her hips again, rounded them off, magnificent and shrill, breathed 'Ah yes!' and levered herself into his arms. She was fatter than he and thought herself embraced. At this juncture her skirt slid to the ground. Therese noticed it and was more delighted than ever, everything was happening so natural. But when she sensed his resistance, she was filled with fear in the midst of her bliss and sobbed: 'If I may make so bold!' Puda's voice was saying: 'But, dear lady! But, dear lady! But, dear lady!' She was the 'dear lady'. Other voices boomed around her; they weren't beautiful, people were staring, let them stare, she was a respectable woman. Mr. Puda was bashful, he pulled and pulled, but she wouldn't leave go; behind his back her hands were inextricably locked. He yelped: 'Just a moment, dear lady, if you please dear lady, let me go, dear lady!' Her head rested on his shoulder and his cheeks were like butter. Why was he so bashful? She wasn't bashful. They could cut her hands off, but leave go of him, never. Mr. Puda stamped his feet and shouted: 'Allow me, if you please, I don't even know you, allow me, please, let go of me!' Then a lot of people came and beat on her hands, she began to cry, but leave go, never. A strong hand pulled her fingers one by one apart and tore Mr. Puda suddenly away from her. Therese staggered, passed her sleeves over her eyes, said: 'I ask you, who could be such a brute!' and stopped crying. The strong hand belonged to a large, stout woman. So Mr. Puda had got married! A shocking din was going on in the shop; when Therese's eye fell on her skirt on the ground, she understood why.

Quite close to her there was a crowd of people, laughing as if they had been paid to do it. Walls and ceiling quivered, the furniture swayed. Someone shouted: 'Call an ambulance!' Someone else 'Police'! Outraged, Mr. Brute brushed down his suit — he had a particular affection for its padded shoulders — and chanted over and over again: 'Manners, too, have a limit, dear lady!' and as soon as he was satisfied with the state of his suit, began to wipe his tainted cheek. Therese and he, alone, were not laughing. His saviour, the '& Mother', eyed him suspiciously, she scented some love affair at the back of this incident. As she had an interest in him, she was more inclined to call the police. This shameless creature deserved a lesson. He had had his already. Apart from that he was a nice fellow — though she would never have said so openly. Business demands ruthless discipline. In spite of this calculation she laughed, harsh and loud. Everyone was talking at once. Therese put on her skirt again in the midst of the crowd. The girl from the cash-desk laughed at the skirt. Therese allowed no reflections on it and said: 'I ask you, jealousy!' And she pointed to the broad lace insertions in her petticoat, which looked like something too, she didn't have all her best things on top. The laughter went on and on. Therese was relieved, she had been afraid of his wife. A piece of luck her kissing him like that, she would never have another chance. As long as they were all laughing, no harm would come to her. You don't send for the police if you're laughing. A lean salesman — not a man at all, just like her late husband, that thief — said: 'Mr. Brute's lady friend!' Another — and he was a man — said: 'A fine lady friend!' The others laughed even louder; she thought that mean. 'I ask you, I *am* a fine woman!' She screamed: 'Where's my bag?' Her bag had gone. 'Where's my bag? I shall call the police!' & Mother found this too much. 'Quite!' she exclaimed. 'Now *I* shall call the police!' She turned round and made for the telephone.

Mr. Gross, the little chief, her son, had been standing all the time just behind her trying to say something. Nobody listened to him. He plucked frantically at her sleeve, she pushed him away and proclaimed in a raucous mannish voice: 'We shall teach her a lesson! We shall see who is master here!' Mr. Gross couldn't think what to do next. He had lifted the receiver before he dared the uttermost and pinched her. 'But she's a customer,' he whispered. 'What?' she asked.

'A superior bedroom suite.' He alone had recognized Therese.

& Mother set down the receiver, swept round and, at a moment's notice, and without exception, sacked the assembled staff: 'I will not have my customers insulted!' The furniture swayed again, but not with laughter. 'Where is the lady's bag? In three minutes it must be found!' One and all the staff flung themselves on the floor and crawled obediently in search of it. Not one had failed to see that Therese had meanwhile found and picked up her own bag, which was lying exactly where & Mother had been stationed. Mr. Brute was the first to get up again and to notice, with surprise, the bag under Therese's arm. 'But I see, dear lady,' he chanted, 'you have already found your bag dear lady. You were born under a lucky star, dear lady. What can I show you, dear lady, if I may inquire?' His obsequious zeal was requited with the approval of & Mother. She marched across to him and nodded. Therese said: 'Nothing to-day.' Brute bowed low over her hand and breathed with soft humility: 'I kiss your lovely hand, dear lady.' He kissed her arm just above her glove, hummed 'I kiss your little hand, Madame,' and, sketching an elegant gesture of renunciation with his left hand, stood aside. The staff leapt to its feet and formed into a guard of honour. Therese hesitated, threw back her head proudly and fired as a parting shot: 'Excuse me, are congratulations permitted?' He did not understand what she meant, but custom bade him bow low. Then she walked out through her guard of honour. Every back was bent and every voice raised in salutation. Behind them stood & Mother, assuring Therese of her best attention in a voice of thunder. The chief at her apron strings said nothing. He had already taken too much on himself to-day. He ought certainly to have told her earlier that the lady was a customer. When Therese was at the door, which, held open for her by two attendants, had become a triumphal arch, he vanished swiftly into his office. Perhaps & Mother would forget him. To the very last Therese heard wondering exclamations. 'A smart lady!' 'That beautiful skirt!' 'Isn't it blue!' 'And so rich!' 'Like a princess!' 'Brute's a lucky devil!' It was not a dream. Over and over again the lucky devil kissed her hand. Now she was in the street. Even the door closed slowly and respectfully. Through the glass panels they stared after her. Once only she turned round, then glided away, smiling.

That was how it was when a remarkable man loved you. He had married. How could he have waited for her? She should have come back sooner. How he had folded her in his arms! Then suddenly he had taken fright. His new wife was in the shop. His wife had a fortune, he couldn't carry on like that. He was a respectable man. He knew what was done. He knew everything. He had embraced her in front and defended himself behind. So that his wife should hear, he had protested. Such a clever fellow! He had eyes! He had shoulders! He had a cheek! His wife was strong. She looked like somebody, but she never noticed a thing. Because of her bag, she had wanted to call in the police at once. That's the right sort of wife. That's just the sort of wife she would be herself; the thief wouldn't leave sooner, so she'd got there too late. The thief wasn't her fault? He kissed her hand. He had lips! He had been waiting for her. First of all she was the only one he would take a fortune from. All of a sudden another turned up with the biggest fortune; women never let him alone, so he'd married her. He couldn't turn his back on all that beautiful money. But he loved her alone. He didn't love his new wife. When she came, everyone had to go on hands and knees looking for her bag. The door was a mass of eyes and all were staring after her. Why did she wear her new skirt? How happy she was! How lucky she'd kissed him after all. Who could say when she'd have another chance? The skirt suited her well, the petticoat too. The lace on it was expensive. She wasn't one of those. But she thought to herself, poor fellow, why shouldn't he have something of my hips? He thought them magnificent. Now he's had a look at them. Even a married man she didn't grudge his bit of fun.

Therese found her way home in a dream. She noticed neither street names nor impertinences. Her good luck was a charm against bad luck. Innumerable side-tracks opened up to her, but she followed the safe one which led her back to her own property. The starched apparition was received by pedestrians and traffic alike with awe. On every side she attracted loving attention. But she noticed nothing. A crowd of salesmen attended on her. The guard of honour was of india rubber, and with her every step she drew it with her. They all kissed her hand; the air was loud with kisses, hailstorms of them all about her, she caught every one. New wives, who looked like somebody, rang up the police. Therese's bags had been stolen. There were no more little chiefs, they had vanished, they were no longer in their shops, only their names could still be read over the doors. Women in dozens, not one a day more than thirty, sank into the arms of Mr. Pudas, with lips, eyes, shoulders and cheeks. Blue starched skirts fell to the ground. Magnificent hips admired themselves in mirrors. Hands would not let go. Never would hands let go. Whole shopsful laughed with pride to see so much beauty. Housekeepers dropped their dusters in amazement. Thieves restored stolen goods, hanged themselves and let themselves be buried. In all the world there was only one fortune, all the others had flowed into it. It belonged to no one. It belonged to one person only. You could keep it. Stealing was prohibited. No need to keep watch. You had something better to do. You churned the milk. The pat of butter which came out was pure gold and the size of a child's head. Fat savings books were bursting. Trunks for trousseaux were bursting too. There was nothing but savings books inside them. Nobody wanted to take them away. There were two people in the world who knew how to manage. One of those people was a woman; everything belonged to her. The other one was called Puda, nothing belonged to him, but instead he was allowed to manage the woman. Mothers, God rest them, turned in their graves. They grudged you every little thing. Tips to caretakers were abolished; because they all had pensions. Whatever you said came true. You got hard cash for the papers a thief had left behind. Books too earned beautiful money. The flat was sold for hard cash. A more beautiful one cost nothing. The old one hadn't even windows.

Therese was almost at home. The elastic guard of honour, long since snapped, had evaporated. The air was quiet again. Instead, customary things were drawing near. They were very simple, less rich, but on the other hand she was sure of them, sure of finding them and having them. When she was on the threshold, Therese said: 'Excuse me, it's a bit of luck for me he's married. Now I've got it all for myself.' Only now did she ask herself what sort of capital she could possibly have lent to Mr. Brute. You have to have it in black and white in an affair of this kind, and signed too. She'd a right to a handsome interest. And a partnership. Thieving's forbidden. A bit of luck it never came to that. How can people be so thoughtless to part with their money! You'd never see a penny of it again.

'What's the matter with the Professor?' Bellowing, the caretaker barred her path. Therese started back and said nothing. She tried to think of an answer. If she told him her husband had robbed her, he'd notify the police. She wanted to put off notifying the police. Else the police would find her housekeeping money and ask her to account for it. As if he hadn't *given* it to her. . . .

'I haven't seen him for a week! Don't tell me he's dead?'

'Excuse me, dead indeed. He's alive and kicking. He wouldn't know how to be dead.'

'Thought he might be ill, then. My respects to him and I'll come and call. I'm at his service any time.'

Therese lowered her head archly and asked: 'Maybe you know where he is? I want him urgently for the housekeeping money.'

The caretaker scented the cheat by means of his wife. So they were trying to do him out of his 'gratuity'. The Professor was hiding because he didn't want to give him anything. Anyway he wasn't a Professor. He — the caretaker — had given him the title, of his own free will. A couple of years ago he was plain Dr. Kien. So a title was worth nothing! The trouble he'd taken to make everyone in the block call him Professor. You couldn't expect people to work for you for nothing. For services rendered you got a pension. He didn't want a present from that old stick, he wanted his gratuity. It was his pension. 'You allege,' he bellowed at Therese, 'your husband isn't at home?'

'But I ask you, no, not for a week. He said he was fed up. All of a sudden he goes off and leaves me by myself. Housekeeping money,

278

not a penny. It's not done! I'd like to know what time he goes to bed now. Respectable people go to bed at nine o'clock.'

'You are requested to inform the police!'

'But I ask you, when he goes off all on his own! He said he'd be back soon.'

'When?'

'When he felt like it, he said, he's always been like that, never thinks of anyone but himself, I ask you, other people have feelings too. It's not my fault is it?'

'Take care, sh— house, I'll come and have a look! If he's up there I'll beat you up proper. A hundred schillings that's what he owes me. Let the dirty swine look out! I'll show him what's what. I didn't used to be like that, but I'm bloody well going to be like that now!'

Therese was already walking along in front of him. She grasped the hatred of Kien which inspired his words. Up to now she had feared the caretaker as his only and invincible friend. Now she had her second stroke of luck that day. Once he saw that she was only telling the simple truth, he'd help her. Everyone was against the thief. Why was he a thief?

The caretaker slammed the door thunderously behind him. His steps, heavy with rage, terrified the tenants of the rooms below the library. For years they had been used to a deathly silence. The stairs were suddenly full of disputing people. Everyone thought it must be the caretaker. Up to now the Professor had been his Benjamin. The tenants hated Kien on account of the gratuity, which the caretaker on every possible occasion, cast in their teeth. Most probably the Professor was refusing to give him another penny. He was quite right of course, but deserved all he got. So far the caretaker had never let anyone off lightly. But it was a mystery to the tiptoe listeners, that they could hear no voices, only the well-known bellowing step.

For the rage of the caretaker was so great that he searched the flat in silence. He was saving up his anger. He was determined to make an example of Kien when he found him. Behind his grating teeth dozens of imprecations were accumulating. On his fists, the red hairs rose on end. He noticed it as he chucked aside the wardrobes in Therese's new bedroom. The sh— might be anywhere. Therese followed him with understanding. When he halted, she halted too, when he looked behind anything, she did likewise. He took little notice of her, after a minute or two he was as used to her as his shadow. She guessed he was holding in his mounting wrath. With his, her own grew too. Her husband wasn't only a thief, he'd gone off and abandoned her, a defenceless woman. She was silent, so as not to interrupt the caretaker; the closer they got to each other, the less she feared him. Her bedroom she had allowed him to enter first. When she unbolted the other two closed rooms she went ahead of him. He glanced hastily over her old room next to the kitchen. He could only imagine Kien in a big room, however well hidden. In the kitchen he had a sudden impulse to smash all the crockery. But it would have been a shame to waste his fists; he spat on the stove and let things be. Now he stamped back into the study. On the way he stopped long to gaze at the coat stand. Kien was not suspended from it. He tossed over the huge writing desk. He needed both his fists for it and took awful vengeance for this humiliation. He grabbed at a bookshelf and flung several dozen volumes to the ground. Then he looked about him, to see if Kien would not suddenly appear. It was his last hope.

'Decamped!' he stated. His oaths had all forsaken him. He felt depressed by the loss of his 100 schillings. Together with his pension it secured him the gratification of his passion. He was a man of gigantic appetite. What would become of his spy-hole if he starved? He held out both his fists to Therese. The hairs were still all on end. 'Look at that!' he bellowed. 'In all my life I've never been in such a rage! Never!'

Therese looked at the books on the floor. He thought his fists were his apology and her compensation. She did feel compensated but not by his fists. 'But excuse me, he wasn't even a man!' she said.

'A bloody whore, that's what he was!' bellowed the injured party. 'A gangster! A wanted man! A murderer!'

Therese wanted to say 'a beggar' but he had already got as far as 'gangster'. And while she was thinking of 'thief', his 'murderer' made any further bid impossible. He wasted little time swearing. Very soon he was mellowed again and began to pick up the books. Easily as he had thrown them down, they were hard to put back. Therese fetched the steps and climbed up herself. Her successful day moved her to sway her hips. With one hand the caretaker handed her the books, with the other he went for her and pinched her violently in the thigh. Her mouth watered. She was the first woman whom he had won by his method of wooing. All the others he had simply assaulted. Therese breathed to herself: There's a man! Again please. Aloud she said, bashfully: 'More!' He gave her a second pile of books and pinched her with equal violence on the left. Her mouth overflowed. Then it

280

occurred to her that such things aren't done. She screamed and threw herself off the steps into his arms. He simply let her fall to the ground, broke open the starched skirt and had her.

When he got up, he said: 'That'll learn him, the old skeleton!' Therese sobbed: 'Excuse me, I belong to you now!' She had found a man. She had no intention of letting him go. He answered 'Shurrup!' and that very night moved into the flat. During the day he stayed at his post. At night he advised her, in bed. Little by little he learnt what had really happened, and ordered her unobtrusively to pawn the books before her husband came back. He would keep half the proceeds as his due. He put the fear of God into her about her legal position. But he was an ex-policeman and would help her. For this reason too she obeyed him, unquestioning. Every third or fourth day they set off, heavily laden, for the Theresianum.

CHAPTER VIII

THE THIEF

THE caretaker recognized what used to be his Professor at the first glance. His new post as adviser to Therese suited him better; first and foremost it brought him in more than his old gratuity. It was not in his interest to avenge himself. That's why he wasn't resentful and carefully looked in the other direction. The Professor stood on his right. The parcel had meanwhile been flicked on to his left arm. He tested its weight for a moment and became conveniently absorbed in this examination. Therese had by now acquired the habit of doing everything he did. With a vehement motion she gave the thief a cold shoulder and clutched with passion at her beautiful, large parcel. The caretaker had already passed by. But that man suddenly barred her path. She pushed him dumbly to one side. Dumbly he laid his hand on the parcel. She pulled at it, he held it fast. The caretaker heard a rustling. Without looking round, he went up the stairs. He wanted this meeting to pass off quietly and told himself she had only brushed her parcel against the banisters. Now Kien too tugged at the parcel. Her resistance grew. She turned her face to him, he closed his eyes. This bewildered her. The man higher up the stairs did not come to her help. Then she remembered the police and the crime she was committing. If she got herself put away the thief would get hold of the flat again, that's what he was like, he wouldn't think twice about it. Hardly had she lost her flat, than her strength deserted her. Kien got hold of the major weight of the parcel on his side. The books gave him strength and he said: 'Whither are you taking them?' He must have seen the books. The paper was not torn anywhere. She saw him as the master of the house. The eight long years of her service flashed through her mind in the fraction of a second. It was all over with her self-possession. But she had one comfort. She called the police to her help. She screamed: 'He's insulted me!'

Ten steps higher up the stairs a disappointed man came to a halt. If the sh— house had stopped them on their way out, well and good; but now, before they had cashed their goods! He managed to choke back the bellow rising in his throat and beckoned Therese with his hand. She was too busy and took no notice. While she screamed twice more 'He's insulting me!' she sized up the thief curiously. According to her ideas, he should have been in rags, shameless, holding out a hollowed hand to everyone, the way beggars do, and, when he saw something easy, just stealing it. In fact, he looked much better than he did at home. She couldn't explain it. Suddenly she noticed that his coat, to the right of his chest, had swollen. In the old days he never carried money about. His wallet was almost empty. Now it looked fat. She knew all. He had the bankbook. He had cashed his money. Instead of hiding it at home he carried it round with him. The caretaker knew of every detail, even of her post-office book. Whatever there was, he found it, or he pinched it out of her. But her dream of the bankbook in a secret crevice, that she had kept to herself. Without this to fall back on life would have held no more pleasures for her. In a flood of clumsy satisfaction at the secret which she had kept from him for so many weeks, she called out now — a moment after her plaintive 'He's insulting me' — 'I ask you, he's a thief!' Her voice rang out, indignant and delighted at once, as is usual when people are handing over a thief to the police. Only that melancholy undertone which some women's voices assume on such occasions when the culprit happens to be a man, was absent from hers, for was she not handing over her first man to her second? And this one was a policeman.

He came down and repeated dully: 'You're a thief!' He saw no other egress from this disastrous situation. The theft was obviously a lie in self-defence on Therese's part. He laid a heavy hand on Kien's shoulder and declared, as though once again he were on active service: 'In the name of the law, you are under arrest! You come along with me, and come quiet!' The parcel dangled from the little finger of his left hand. He stared commandingly in Kien's face and shrugged his shoulders. His duty allowed him to make no exceptions. The past was the past. Then they'd got on well enough. Now he had to arrest him. How gladly he would have said 'Do you remember . . . ?' Kien crumpled up, not alone under the pressure of the hand, and muttered: 'I knew it.' The caretaker distrusted this answer. Peaceable criminals are artful. They make themselves out to be like that and then try for a getaway. That's why the come-along was invented. Kien submitted to it. He tried to stand upright, his height forced him to stoop. The caretaker grew affectionate. He hadn't arrested a soul for years. He had anticipated difficulties. Delinquents offer resistance. If they don't they'll make a getaway. If you're in uniform they want to know your number. If you're not, they want a warrant. But here was one who made no trouble. He allowed himself to be questioned, he came quiet, he didn't protest his innocence, he made no disturbance, he was a criminal anybody could be proud of. Immediately in front of the glass door he turned to Therese and said: '*That's* how it's done!' He was well aware a woman was watching him. But he was uncertain whether she fully appreciated the details of his work. 'Anyone else would have knocked him out straight away. With me, taking a man up's a simple matter. Come quiet, that's the rule. An amateur couldn't make 'em come quiet. If you're an expert a criminal will come quiet of his own free will. Domestic animals have to be tamed. Cats have a wild nature. At the circus you see performing lions. You can make tigers jump through a burning hoop. But a man's got a soul. The organ of the law grabs his soul, and he'll come quiet as a lamb.' He spoke these words only in thought, although he was burning to bellow them out loud.

Anywhere else and at any other time this arrest, which at long last had come his way, would have turned his head. When he was still on the active list he arrested specially to create a disturbance and was in the worst odour with authority on account of his methods. Then he used to proclaim his action so long and loud that a crowd of gaping people gathered round him. Born to be an athlete, he daily created a circus for himself. Finding people chary of applause, he clapped himself. To show his strength he made use of the arrestee instead of his other hand. If the arrestee were strong he dropped hitting him and stung him to a boxing match. Out of contempt for the creature's defeat he used to say in evidence that he had been attacked. Weaklings he thus favoured with an increased sentence. If he came up against some one stronger than himself — with real criminals this was the case sometimes — his conscience bade him accuse them falsely, because undesirable elements must be put away. Only since he had had to confine his activities to a single house, he who had once had charge of a whole beat, did he become more discreet. He selected his partners among wretched hawkers and beggars, and even for these he had to lie in wait for days. They feared him and warned each other; only greenhorns came his way; and yet he prayed for them to come. He knew that they grudged themselves to him. His circus was limited to the tenants of the block. And he lived in hopes of a real, noisy arrest in circumstances of the utmost difficulty.

Then recent events had interrupted him in his pursuits. Kien's books brought him in money. He did most of the work and safeguarded himself on every side. All the same, he had an uncomfortable feeling he was getting money for nothing. When he was in the force he had always felt that his muscular exertions were being paid for. True he took good care to make his book list a heavy one, and selected the books by weight. The fattest and oldest tomes bound in pigskin were the first to go. All the way to the Theresianum he would balance his parcel heading it every now and again, taking Therese's away from her, ordering her to fall back and then tossing it into her arms. She suffered from such treatment and once she complained. But he persuaded her he had to do it on account of the passers-by. The more insolently they handled the books, the less likely was it to occur to anyone that they were not their own. She had to agree, but she didn't like it. All the same he was discontented, felt himself a mere weakling and often said he'd be a Jew next. This tiny twinge, which he took for his conscience, made him forgo the fulfilment of his ancient dream and arrest Kien quietly.

But Therese was not to be robbed of her pleasure. She had noticed the fat wallet. Swiftly she glided round the two men and placed herself between the panels of the glass door which her skirt had pushed open. With her right hand she seized Kien's head as if to embrace him and dragged it down, to her level. With her left hand she pulled out the wallet. Kien wore her arm like a crown of thorns. For the rest he did not stir. His own arms were pinioned by the come-along. Therese held up the roll of notes on high and cried: 'Excuse me, here it is!' Her new man admired all that money, but shook his head. Therese wanted an answer, she said: 'Haven't I a right? Haven't I a right?' 'Do you take me for a doormat!' replied the caretaker. His remark referred to his conscience and to the door, which Therese was barring. She wanted recognition, a word of praise, for her beautiful money, before she pocketed it. When she thought of pocketing it, she was sorry for herself. Now her new man knew everything, she had no more secrets. Such a moment, and he said not a word. He ought to tell her what a fine woman she was! *She* had found the thief. He had tried to slip past him. Now he was trying to slip past her. She wouldn't have it. She had a heart. He only knew how to pinch. He couldn't say a word. Shurrup, that's all he could say. He wasn't superior. He wasn't clever. A man, that's all. She'd be ashamed to face Mr. Brute. I ask you, what was he before? A common caretaker! She'd have nothing to do with such people. And she, taking that creature into her flat. Now he didn't even say thank you. If Mr. Brute found out he'd never kiss her hand again. What a voice he had! *She* had found all the money. *He* would take it all away again. Must she give it all to him? If you please, she was fed up with him! It must be gratis. She wouldn't have his wanting money. She needed it for her old age. She wanted a decent old age. Where was she to get skirts from if he tore them all? He tore her skirts and took her money. All the same, he might say something! He was a man!

Furious and hurt she waved the money this way and that. She held it right under his nose. He was considering. All joy in the arrest had left him. As soon as she had manipulated the wallet, he foresaw the consequences. He wouldn't see the inside of a gaol for her. She was clever, but he knew the law. He had been in the force. What did she know about it? He wished himself back at his post; she was repulsive to him. She had upset him. For her sake he had lost his gratuity. He had long since learnt the true story. Only for the sake of their partnership did he officially continue his hatred for Kien. She was old. She was demanding. She wanted him to come every night. He wanted to knock her about, she wanted something else. She only let him pinch her first. He hit her once or twice and she screamed the place down. The devil she did! He'd sh— on a woman like that. It would all come out now. He'd lose his pension. He'd sue her. She'd have to pay him the equivalent. He'd keep his share. The best thing now would be to inform against her. The old cow! As if the books were hers! Not on your life. God help the Professor. He was too good for her. You wouldn't find another like him. To think he'd married the filthy bitch. Housekeeper indeed! Her mother died in the gutter. She'd told him so herself. If she were forty years younger . . . His daughter, God rest her, she had a heart of gold. She had to lie down beside him while he watched out for beggars. He used to look and pinch. Pinch and look. Those were the days! If a beggar came, he had something to knock about. If none came, there was always the girl. Cry, she used to. Didn't do her no good. You can't do anything against a father. Ah, she was a love. All of a sudden she died. Her chest, that little room. But he couldn't spare her. If he'd known, he'd have sent her away. The Professor remembered her. Never did her no harm. The other tenants bullied the poor kid. Just because she was his daughter. And this filthy bitch here never even said 'Good morning' to her! He could murder her!

Filled with hate, they faced each other. One word from Kien, even a friendly one, would have brought them together again. His silence kindled their hate; it flamed to heaven. One of them had hold of Kien's body, the other of his money. He himself was lost to them. Ah, if they only had him! His body swayed like a blade of grass. A violent storm bowed him down. The banknotes crackled like lightning in the air. Suddenly the caretaker bellowed at Therese: 'Give back that money!' She couldn't. She released Kien's head from her embrace, it didn't shoot up, it remained in the same position. She had expected a movement. As none occurred she flung the notes in her new man's face and shrieked piercingly: 'You knock a man down, you! You're afraid. A doormat, you are! It isn't fair! A coward like you! Scum, you are! Soft, you are! I ask you!' Her hatred supplied her with the precise words to rouse him. With one hand he began to shake Kien out. A coward he wouldn't be called. With his other he laid about Therese. Get out of his way, there. She'd know him better soon. That's not what he was like! This was what he was like. The banknotes fluttered to the ground. Therese sobbed: 'All the beautiful money!' Her man seized her. The blows weren't hard enough. Better shake her. Her back pushed open the glass door. She clutched tight at the round door-knob. He dragged her back, grabbing her by the collar of her blouse, dragged her close up to him and beat her hard against the door — close up to him — hard against the door. With his other hand he dealt with Kien. Kien was a wrung-out rag in his hand; the less he felt there, the more vigorously he went to work on Therese.

At this moment Fischerle came running up. The sewerman had reported Kien's refusal. He was fuming. What was the meaning of this? A fuss about 2000 schillings! That was the last straw! Yesterday he paid up 4500 at a time, and now he stops payment. His employees can wait. He won't be a minute. From the entrance hall he hears a voice shrieking! 'The beautiful money! The beautiful money!' That's his business. Someone must have forestalled him. He could have cried. All that trouble, and someone else is getting the advantage. A woman too. You can't put up with that. He'll catch her. He'll make her give it all back. Then he saw the glass door banging to and fro. Horrified he stood still. There was a man there too. He hesitated. The man was beating the door with the woman. A heavy woman too. The man must be strong. The flagpole wouldn't have been strong enough. Maybe it was nothing to do with the flagpole. Why shouldn't a man beat up a woman, if she didn't hand over the money? Fischerle had his firm to see to. He would sooner have waited until the two had finished, but it would take too long. Cautiously he edged his way through the door. 'Permit me,' he said and grinned. It would be impossible not to tread on somebody's corns. So he grinned in advance. The couple were to notice that he meant no harm. People sometimes overlooked his laughter, so he preferred to grin. His hump intervened between Therese and the caretaker and prevented him from dragging the woman as close to him as was essential for a real blow. He kicked the hump. Fischerle toppled over Kien and clutched tight hold of him. So thin was Kien and so slender the bodily part he played in all this that the dwarf only noticed him when he collided with him. He recognized him. Therese was screaming again: 'The beautiful money!' He sniffed out the old relation between them, pricked up his ears six times as much as before, and at a glance took in Kien's pockets, those of the stranger, the woman's garters — unhappily her skirt impeded the view — the stairs, at the foot of which were two gigantic parcels, and the floor at his feet. There he saw the money. Quick as lightning he stooped to gather it. His long arms twisted in and out between six legs. Now he shoved a foot vigorously to one side, now he twitched delicately at a banknote. He made no sound when they stamped on his fingers, he was used to such inconveniences. Nor did he treat all feet alike. Kien's he hurled out of his way, the woman's he gripped firmly, like a cobbler, as for the man, he avoided all contact; it would have been as useless as it was dangerous. He rescued fifteen banknotes; as he worked he counted, and knew precisely which figure he had arrived at. Even his hump he manœuvred skilfully. Above his head the fight went on. He knew from his experience in Heaven that a fighting couple must not be interrupted. If you manage to avoid this, you can meanwhile get anything you like out of them. Fighting couples are mad dogs. Of the five missing banknotes, four were further off, and one was under the man's foot. While he crept after the others, Fischerle never took an eye off this foot. It might be lifted, and the split second must not be missed.

Only at this point did Therese notice him, as — at a little distance from her — he licked up something off the floor. He kept his hands locked behind his back; the money was hidden between his legs and he worked away with his tongue, so that if the others should see him they wouldn't understand what he was collecting. Therese had felt herself grow weak; this sight gave her fresh strength. The dwarf's intention was as familiar to her as if she had known him from birth. She saw herself in quest of the bankbook; then she had been mistress in her own house. Suddenly she wrenched herself free of the caretaker and yelled: 'Burglars! Burglars! Burglars!' She meant the hump under her feet, the caretaker, the thief; she meant all the world and yelled without drawing breath, louder and louder, as if she would never stop; she had breath for ten.

Above, doors slammed open, heavy steps were heard, many steps, echoing on the stairs. The man, who looked after the lift over there, approached slowly. If they were murdering a child now, he wouldn't demean himself to hurry. Twenty-six years he'd been looking after that lift, that is to say his wife and family had; he did the organizing.

The caretaker stood stock still. He saw it: on every first of the month someone would come to take away his pension instead of paying it out to him. Maybe lock him up as well. The canaries would die, because there'd be no one left to sing for. The peep-hole would be sealed up. Everything would come out and the tenants would ferret out his daughter even in her grave. He wasn't afraid. Couldn't sleep sometimes for thinking of the kid. Looked after her, he did. He was that fond of her. Plenty to eat she got, plenty to drink, a whole pint of milk every day. He was retired on a pension. He wasn't afraid. The doctor said himself, it's her lungs. Send her away! How would I do that, mister? He needed all his pension for food. He was like that. Couldn't live without food. You get like that in the police. Without him the whole block would fall down. Health insurance — the idea! Back she'd come with a baby. In that tiny room. He wasn't afraid.

Fischerle, on the other hand, said aloud: 'Now I'm afraid!' and stuck the money hastily into one of Kien's side pockets. Then he made himself even smaller. Escape was impossible. People were already stumbling over the parcels. He squeezed both arms close against his sides. The other money, the passage-money, was stowed away in tight bundles in his armpits. A bit of luck his being the shape he was! When he was dressed not a soul would suspect anything. He wouldn't be locked up. The police took all your clothes off and took everything away. He was always a thief to them. What did they know about his new firm? Ought to have registered it, ought he? What, and have to pay taxes! He was head of a firm, just the same. The flagpole was an idiot. What had he got to go round recognizing the sewerman for? Now he'd got his money back though. Poor fellow, it wasn't fair to leave him in the lurch. People might take all his money away. He gave it with both hands. He'd too much heart. Fischerle was loyal. Loyal to a business partner. Once he got to America the flagpole would have to look after himself. Not a soul left to help him. Fischerle crept gradually in between Kien's knees; nothing was left of him but hump. Sometimes his hump became a shield behind which he vanishes, a snail-shell into which he withdrew, a mussel shell which closed right round him.

The caretaker stands with legs set wide, a monolith, his staring eyes fixed on his murdered daughter. Out of habit his muscles still hold the limp rag Kien. Therese shrieks all the inhabitants of the Theresianum to her help. She thinks of nothing. She has enough to do to husband her breath-supply. She shrieks mechanically. She feels well, shrieking. She feels as though she had won the fight. The blows on her have ceased.

A variety of hands drag the motionless four apart. They grip them tight, as though they were still fighting. Each seeks to look into the other's eyes. People jostle about them. Passers-by pour into the Theresianum. Officials and clients claim their prior right. *They* are at home here. The man, who had looked after the lift for twenty-six years, ought to restore order, to expel the intruders and close the doors of the Theresianum. He has no time. At last he has reached the woman who is shrieking for help and regards his presence on the scene as indispensible. Another woman catches sight of Fischerle's hump on the ground and runs screaming into the street: 'Murder! Murder!' She takes the hump for a corpse. Further details — she knows none. The murderer is very thin, a poor sap, how he came to do it, you wouldn't have thought it of him. Shot, may be, someone suggests. Of course, everyone heard the shot. Three streets off, the shot had been heard. Not a bit of it, that was a motor tyre. No, it was a shot! The crowd won't be done out of its shot. A threatening attitude is assumed towards the doubters. Don't let him go. An accessory. Trying to confuse the trail! Out of the building comes more news. The woman's statements are revised. The thin man has been murdered. And the corpse on the floor? It's alive. It's the murderer, he had hidden himself. He was trying to creep away between the corpse's legs when he was caught. The more recent information is more detailed. The little man is a dwarf. What do you expect, a cripple! The blow was actually struck by another. A redheaded man. Ah, those redheads. The dwarf put him up to it. Lynch him! The woman gave the alarm. Cheers for the woman! She screamed and screamed. A woman! Doesn't know what fear is. The murderer threatened her. The red-head. It's always the Reds. He tore her collar off. No shooting. Of course not. Nobody heard a shot. What did he say? Someone must

have invented the shot. The dwarf. Where is he? Inside. Rush the
doors! No one else can get in. It's full up. What a murder! The woman had a plateful. Thrashed her every day. Half dead, she was.
What did she marry a dwarf for? I wouldn't marry a dwarf. And you
with a big man to yourself. All she could find. Too few men, that's
what it is. The war! Young people to-day . . . Quite young he was
too. Not eighteen. And a dwarf already. Clever! He was born that
way. I know that. I've seen him. Went in there. Couldn't stand it.
Too much blood. That's why he's so thin. An hour ago he was a
great, fat man. Loss of blood, horrible! I tell you corpses swell.
That's drowned ones. What do you know about corpses? Took all
the jewellery off the corpse he did. Did it for the jewellery. Just
outside the jewellery department it was. A pearl necklace. A baroness.
He was her footman. No, the baron. Ten thousand pounds. Twenty
thousand! A peer of the realm! Handsome too. Why did she send
him? Should he have let his wife? It's for her to let him. Ah, men.
She's alive though. *He's* the corpse. Fancy dying like that! A peer
of the realm too. Serve him right. The unemployed are starving.
What's he want with a pearl necklace. String 'em up I say! Mean it
too. The whole lot of them. And the Theresianum too. Burn it!
Make a nice blaze.

Inside the scene was as bloodless as it was bloody outside. As soon
as the people started crowding in, the glass panel of the door splintered
into a thousand fragments. No one was hurt. Therese's skirt protected
the only person who was in real danger, Fischerle. Scarcely had he
been seized by the collar than he croaked out: 'Leave me go! I'm his
keeper!' He pointed to Kien and said over and over again: 'I tell you,
he's mad. I'm his keeper. Take care, he's dangerous. I tell you he's
mad. I'm his keeper.' No one took any notice of him. He was too
small; they expected great things. The only person on whom he made
an impression took him for the corpse and told the people outside.
Therese went on screaming. She was doing well. If she stopped people
might go away and leave her. While one half of her savoured her happiness the other sweated with fear at what might come next. Everyone
pitied her. They comforted her; she was frightened. The lift-attendant even laid his hand on her shoulder. He emphasized the fact that
this was the first time he had done such a thing in twenty-six years.
She must calm herself. He asked it as a personal favour. He could
sympathize. He was the father of three himself. She could come back
to his own home if she liked. She would be able to recuperate there.

For twenty-six years he had never asked anyone else. Therese took good care not to stop screaming. He was hurt. He even took his hand away. Without demeaning himself, he declared, she must have gone out of her mind with terror. Fischerle pounced on his assertion and whimpered: 'But I tell you, *this* one's mad; she's quite O.K. You can take it from me, I know about madmen! I'm the keeper!'

Although a couple of officials with nothing better to do had taken him in charge, not a soul paid the slightest attention to him. All eyes were fixed on the redhead. He had let himself be seized and held quite quietly, without knocking out half a dozen; not once, even, had he let out a bellow. But this unearthly stillness was followed by a gigantic thunderclap when they tried to disentangle him from Kien. He wouldn't give up the Professor, he clutched him tight and with his right hand hurled back his attackers. His thoughts straying to his darling daughter, he bathed Kien in a flood of loving words: 'Professor — you're my only friend! Don't forsake me! I'll hang myself! It wasn't my fault. My only friend! I'm a retired policeman! Don't be angry! I'm goodness itself!'

So stunningly vociferous was his affection that everyone at once recognized Kien as the burglar. Everyone quickly saw through the mockery and was delighted with his own penetration. Everyone was penetrating; everyone felt how just was the vengeance which the redhead was about to take, with his own hands, on the criminal. He had seized him by the arm. He pressed him to his heart and told him what he thought of him. A big fellow like that wanted to take his own revenge, but even those who held him back could not but admire him, this hero, who would do it all himself; they would do just the same in his place, they were doing it, they were in his place. They even accepted the hard kicks they were now inflicting on themselves.

The lift-attendant thought his dignity here better safeguarded. He gave up the woman, out of her mind with fear, and now laid on the shoulders of the raging man a fleshy but considerable hand. Neither too loud nor too low, he informed him that for twenty-six years no lift had gone up or down without him, for twenty-six years he had kept order in this place, and never before had such a thing happened, he gave his personal guarantee. His words were lost in the din. As the redhead didn't even notice, he leaned confidentially over his ear and explained that he sympathized perfectly. For twenty-six years he had been the father of three himself. A fearful punch sent him reeling back to Therese. His cap rolled on the floor. He recognized that something must be done and went for the police. No one had had this idea yet. Those closest to the scene of action regarded themselves as the police, those further off hoped to advance to that stage. Two of them now took it on themselves to carry both the parcels of books to a place of safety. They used the trail blazed by the lift-attendant, and shouted out: 'Mind your backs!' on all sides. Those parcels ought to be handed in at the cloakroom before anyone stole them. On the way they decided to investigate the contents first. They vanished undisturbed. No other parcels were stolen, because there were no others.

Thanks to the lift-attendant, even the police — who had a sub-station in the Theresianum itself — smelt a riot. Since four principals were named by their informant, they set off for the scene of action, six strong. The lift-attendant had clearly described the place. But he lent them his help just the same, and led the way. The crowd jostled admiringly about the police. Their uniforms cover a multitude of actions, permitted to others only when the police are not there. People readily made room for them. Men who had fought hard for good places, gave way at once to uniforms. Less determined natures gave way too late, brushed against the sacred material and trembled with awe. Everybody pointed at Kien. He had tried to steal. He had stolen. Everyone had always known he was a thief. Therese was respectfully treated by the police. She was the victim. She had discovered the crime. She was evidently married to the redhead as she hurled glances of loathing in his direction. Two policemen took up their stand on her right and on her left. As soon as they saw her blue skirt, their respect changed to smiling familiarity. The four others dragged Kien from the clutches of his red victim; without force they could hardly do it. The redhead clung with determination to the thief. For one reason or another this must be the thief's fault, for he was, after all, the criminal. The caretaker imagined he was being arrested. His terror grew. He bellowed to Kien for help. He was a retired policeman! Dear Professor! Don't let them arrest me! Let me go! My daughter! He lashed wildly about him. His strength exasperated the police. Still more, his assertion that he was one of them. A lengthy struggle developed between them. All four policemen were careful to spare their own skins. If they didn't, where would they be in their profession? They hit out at the redhead from all directions and in every possible manner.

The onlookers divide into two parties. The hearts of one beat for the heroic redhead, of the others for the law. But not only their hearts.

The men's fists itch, a shrill sound comes from the throats of the women; so as not to involve themselves with the police, all fall on Kien. He is beaten, battered, trampled on. His restricted surface area affords only restricted satisfaction. They unite therefore to wring him out like a wet rag. He knows he's in the wrong; that's clear from his saying nothing. Not a sound does he utter, his eyes are closed, nothing can open them.

Fischerle couldn't bear the sight any longer. Ever since the police appeared on the scene, he had been thinking incessantly of his employees, waiting for him outside. For a moment the money in Kien's pocket held him back. The idea of regaining it in the presence of six policemen intoxicated him. But he took care not to put it into action. He watched out for a favourable moment for escape. None came. All on edge, he watched Kien's tormentors. Whenever they touched the pocket into which he had stuffed the money, a sword went through his heart. This torture smote him to the ground. Blind with pain he saved himself by crawling between the nearest legs. The physical excitement of the inmost circle of spectators was to his advantage. Further afield, where no one knew of his existence, they began to notice him. As plaintively as possible, he screeched: 'Ow, I can't breathe, lemme out!' Everyone laughed and hastened to help him. Instead of the thrills of the lucky ones in the front rank, they were getting at least a bit of fun. Not one of the six policemen had spotted him; he was too low on the ground, his hump for once didn't register. Even in the street he was often held up without the slightest criminal pretext. To-day he was lucky. He slipped away unnoticed in the vast crowd round the Theresianum. For a whole quarter of an hour his employees would have been waiting for him. His armpits were intact.

The police remained calm in the face of Kien's executioners. They were fully occupied. Four of them struggled with the redhead; two flanked Therese. She must not be left alone. She had long since stopped screaming. But now she began again: 'Harder! Harder! Harder!' She beats time for the wringing out of that wet rag, Kien. Her guards try to quieten her. As long as her excitement continues in this abandoned way, they feel any interference on their part would be useless. Therese's encouragements are intended equally for the four bold spirits who are beating the rage out of the caretaker. She's had enough of it, letting him pinch her. She's had enough of it, letting him rob her. Her fear of the police gives way to feelings of pride.

People in her position can do as they please. She gives orders here. That's right. She is a respectable woman. 'Harder! Harder! Harder!' Therese dances up and down, her skirt sways. A powerful rhythm seizes on the crowd. Some sway this way, some that, the zest of the movement increases. The noise swells to a unison, even non-participants are panting. Little by little laughter dies away. Business comes to a standstill. At the remotest counters in the building they pause, listening. Hands are cupped to ears, fingers lifted to lips, talking is prohibited. Anyone daring to offer an object for pawning would have been met with mute indignation. The Theresianum, always alive with action, is filled with a gigantic calm. One panting breath alone reveals that it still lives. All living creatures in its huge population draw in one single deep breath together, and together, ecstatic, breathe it out again.

Thanks to this general mood the police at length managed to restrain the caretaker. Two of them applied the come-along, a third watched his feet, which alternately struck out, or sought to manœuvre the Professor closer to him. The fourth restored order. The mob were still belabouring Kien, but there wasn't much pleasure in it now. He behaved neither like a human being nor like a corpse. The wringing process provoked not a sound from him. He might defend himself, cover his face, twist about or at least jerk; all sorts of things were expected of him but he was just disappointing. A type like this must have had a lot to answer for, but when you didn't know what it was, you couldn't take it out of him proper. Disgusted and glad to be rid of a wearisome task, they yielded him to the police. With great self-control they restrained themselves from turning their free fists on each other. Each looked at the others, and at the sight of his neighbour's suit, became clothed once more, and recognized in his fellow-combatants, colleagues and friends. Therese cried: 'There now!' What else could she order them to do. She would have liked to go, and squared head and elbows for the task. The policeman who had taken Kien in charge, was astonished at the placidity of this creature, with a row like this on his conscience. He had suffered most at the hands of the redhead, and consequently loathed his wife. She must come along too. Her two bodyguards joyfully took her in charge. They were shamed at their idleness, since the other four had risked their lives against the redhead. Therese came quiet, for they could do nothing to her. She would have come, anyway. She fully intended to do both men down at the police station.

Another policeman, noted for his excellent memory, counted the prisoners on his fingers, one, two, three. Where is the fourth? he asked the lift-attendant. The latter had watched the whole fight with an injured expression, and had just finished brushing his cap when all his enemies had been arrested. Now he thawed; he knew nothing about a fourth. The policeman with the memory asserted he had himself reported four combatants. The lift-attendant protested vehemently. He had kept order here for twenty-six years. He was the father of three. He supposed he could count as well as anyone. Other voices supported him. No one knew anything about a fourth. The fourth was an invention; the fourth was an invention of the thief's to mix the clues. That cunning dog knew why he was keeping his trap shut. Even the policeman with a memory was satisfied with this explanation. All six policemen had their hands full. The three prisoners were cautiously manœuvred through what remained of the glass door and the crowd. Kien brushed against the only fragment of glass still remaining and cut his sleeve open. When they reached the police station, blood was trickling from it. The few remaining curious who had followed as far as this, contemplated it in amazement. This blood they found incredible. It was the first sign of life Kien had given.

Almost all the crowd had dispersed. Some of them had gone back behind their counters, others were offering goods with imploring or defiant countenances. But the officials unbent so far as to exchange, even with these poor devils, a word or two on the event. They accepted the opinions of people towards whom it was their highest duty to turn a deaf ear. As to the object of the crime, no united opinion was reached. Some said it was jewellery, or else what was all the fuss about? Books, said others, for it happened in the book section. More respectable gentlemen referred to the evening papers. Of the conflicting views, the majority leant towards money. The officials pointed out, more gently than usual, that people with so much money rarely came to the public pawnbroking establishment. But perhaps they were coming away after completing a transaction. This too had to be ruled out, for every official was sure he would have recognized them if he had dealt with them. Some still regretted the redheaded hero, most of them had forgotten him already. To prove their finer feelings, they were sorrier for his wife, even though she was no chicken. Not one of them would have married her. It had all been a waste of time, but pleasant while it lasted.

CHAPTER IX

PRIVATE PROPERTY

At the police station the prisoners were subjected to an inquiry. The caretaker bellowed: 'Friends and colleagues, I am innocent!' Therese, trying to do him harm, cried: 'I ask you, he's retired!' Her words dispelled the bad impression which his familiarity had made on his colleagues. The factual explanation that he was retired made it conceivable that he really had been a policeman. He certainly had the brutal manner; but the suspicion that the real prisoner had apparently practised on him a robbery in the grand style somewhat contradicted this. They questioned him. He bellowed: 'I'm no criminal!'

Therese pointed to Kien, whom they had forgotten and said: 'If you please, he robbed us!' The self-possessed bearing of the redhead gave the policeman pause. They were still in ignorance whom they had arrested. Therese's hint was welcome. Three of them hurled themselves on Kien and without more ado searched his pockets. A bundle of crumpled banknotes emerged; the count revealed eighteen notes of a hundred schillings each. 'Is this your money?' they asked Therese. 'Was my money all crumpled? Six times as much, there ought to be!' She counted on the whole sum the bankbook had contained. They asked Kien for the rest; he said nothing. Propped up against a chair, angular and ravaged, he stood just as they had put him. Anyone looking at him would have been convinced that he must fall down at any moment. But no one looked at him.

Out of hatred for Therese, his guard brought him a glass of water and held it close to his mouth. Neither the glass nor the kindly action received any recognition and one more enemy joined those who now once again went through his pockets. Apart from a little small change in his purse, they drew blank. Some of them shook their heads. 'What have you done with the money, you?' asked the Inspector. Therese grinned: 'What did I say, a thief!' 'My good woman,' said the officer, for whom her clothes were too old-fashioned, 'turn round a moment! We must undress him. No peeping.' He smiled derisively; he didn't care whether the old thing peeped or not. He knew that the sum would be found, and was annoyed because a common woman possessed so much. Therese said: 'What kind of a man is he? He's not a man!' and stayed where she was. The caretaker bellowed: 'I'm innocent!' and gave Kien a look as though he were respectfully requesting his tip. He was emphasizing his innocence, not of the death of his daughter, but of the painful search to which his Professor was now to submit.

Three policemen, who had just withdrawn their fingers from the thief's pockets, immediately, as at a word of command, stepped back two paces. Not one had any inclination for the job of undressing this repulsive person. He was so thin. At that moment Kien fell to the ground. Therese shouted: 'He's lying!' 'But he never said a word,' a policeman interrupted her. 'Said? Anyone can say,' she retorted. The caretaker threw himself on Kien to lift him up. 'Cowardly brute,' said the Inspector, 'hitting a man when he's down.' They all thought the redhead wanted to assault the prostrate victim. Not that anyone would have minded; the helpless skeleton on the floor was exasperating. They only defended themselves against this usurpation of their own rights: before he could reach Kien, the redhead was seized and dragged back. Then they picked up the prostrate object. They didn't even make the usual jokes about his weight, so repulsive was he to them. One tried to push him on to a chair. 'Let him stand, malingerer!' said the Inspector. He was proving to the woman, the sharpness of whose perception put him to shame, that he too could see through the play-acting. The policemen hoisted the lanky nothing; the one who had been in favour of sitting him in a chair now pushed the delinquent's feet apart so as to increase the breadth at the base. Higher up, another let go. Kien crumpled up again and remained hanging in the arms of a third. Therese said: 'There's a dirty trick for you! He's dying!' She was looking forward to his beautiful punishment. 'Professor,' bellowed the caretaker, 'don't do that!' He was glad no one showed any interest in his daughter, but he was counting on Kien's good word for him.

The Inspector saw an opportunity at hand to teach this presumptuous woman that here a man was master. Violently he plucked at his minuscule nose, his great grief. (On duty and off duty, at every free moment he would contemplate and sigh over it in his pocket mirror. When he was in difficulties it would swell. Before he set himself to overcome them, he would convince himself quickly of his nose's existence, because it was so delightful, three minutes later, to have forgotten all about it.) Now he decided to have the criminal properly stripped. 'Idiots, all of you,' he began. The next sentence, which referred only to himself, he merely thought. 'Dead men's eyes are open. Otherwise why do you have to close them? You can't sham dead. Open your eyes, they don't glaze. Close your eyes, you don't look dead, because, just as I say, dead men's eyes are open. A corpse without glazed eyes and without open eyes isn't worth a song. It simply means death has not supervened. I'd like to see anyone take me in. Watch carefully gentlemen! I put it to you, with regard to the prisoner, direct your attention to his eyes!'

He stood up, pushed the table, behind which he was sitting, to one side — another obstacle surmounted, not evaded — strode over to the arrestee, who was still hanging over the arm of an official, and violently flicked first one then the other eyelid with his fat, white middle finger. The policemen felt relieved. They had been afraid lest the creature had been beaten to death by the mob. They had intervened too late. There might be a stink, one had to think of everything. The mob can perpetrate excesses, the organ of the law must keep a clear head. The eye test was completely convincing. The Inspector was a fine fellow. Therese tossed her head; a welcome to the punishment which was still to come. The caretaker felt his fists tingle, as they always did when he was well. With a witness like that on his side, he'd be in clover. Kien's lids quivered under the Inspector's hard finger-nails. He repeated his onslaught, thinking to make the creature alive to various things, to his stupidity, for instance, in shamming dead without glazed eyes. To prove these dead eyes were a sham he must first break them open. But they stayed closed. 'Let him go!' the Inspector ordered the merciful policeman who was not yet tired of his load. At the same moment he grasped the recalcitrant rascal by the collar and shook him. His lightness exasperated him. 'Call yourself a thief!' he said, contemptuously. Therese grinned at him. He began to please her. He was a man. Only his nose wasn't right. The caretaker was turning over in his mind (relieved because nobody was asking him any questions, worried because nobody was taking any notice of him) how he could best explain the crime. He had always had a mind of his own: the Professor was not the thief. He believed what he knew, not what others said. No one ever died of being shaken. As soon as the Professor came alive he'd talk, and then there'd be a row.

The Inspector was still a little repelled by the object before him, then he began to pull its clothes off himself. He tossed the jacket on to the table. The waistcoat followed. The shirt was old, but of good material. He unbuttoned it and directed a piercing eye between the creature's ribs. There was really nothing there. Disgust rose within him. He had had much experience. His profession brought him into contact with every form of human life. He had never come across anything so thin before. Its place was in a show, not a police station. Did they take him for a Barnum, or what? 'Shoes and trousers I leave to you,' he said to the others. Crestfallen he withdrew. His nose occurred to him. He clutched at it. It was too short. If only he could forget it! Sullenly he sat down behind his table. It was in the wrong position again. Someone had pushed it. 'Can't you leave my table straight, for the hundredth time! Idiots!' The policemen busied over the shoes and trousers of the thief grinned to themselves; the others stood to attention. Yes, he thought, creatures like that ought to be put away. They're a public nuisance. They make you ill to look at. The healthiest stomach would be turned. And where would you be without a stomach. There's no patience with them. This was a case for torture. In the middle ages the police had a better time. A creature like that ought to drown itself. It wouldn't affect the suicide rate; it wouldn't weigh enough to count. Instead of making away with itself it shams dead. Shameless, creatures like him. Some people are ashamed of their noses, only because they're a wee bit on the short side. Others live happily on, and steal, what's more. He'll pay for it. It takes all sorts to make a world. Some have industry, common sense, intelligence and subtlety, others haven't a scrap of flesh on their bones. It follows, you've got your work cut out; some people may just have pulled out a pocket mirror, they'd better put it away again.

And so it happened. Trousers and shoes were placed on the table, both were searched for a false lining. The mirror disappeared into an inside pocket specially designed for it and fitting like a glove. Stripped to his shirt — even his socks had been removed — the creature leant trembling against one of the policemen. All eyes were fixed on his calves. 'They're hollow,' said the policeman with a memory. He stooped and tapped them. They were solid. Mistrust assailed even him. In his own mind he had decided that the man was peculiar. Now he saw that he had to do with a dangerous dissimulator. 'It's no use, gentlemen!' bellowed the caretaker. His hint was submerged in the Inspector's astonishment. This latter had taken a quick decision — he was distinguished for his intuition — to abandon the money stolen from the woman, of which there was no trace, and to proceed to a more thorough examination of the note case. All kinds of personal documents were to be found in it. They referred to a certain Dr.

Peter Kien, and were obviously stolen. Had there been one with a photograph it would have been forgery. The walls had not ceased to redound with the caretaker's advice, when the Inspector sprang up, clutched at his nose and, in a voice which quite blotted out the smallness of his nose, shouted at the criminal: 'Your papers are stolen!' Therese glided up. She'd swear to that. Who ever talked of stealing was right.

Kien trembled with cold. He opened his eyes and turned them on Therese. She stood close to him, wagging her head and shoulders. She was proud because he recognized her, *she* was the most important person in the room. 'Your papers are stolen!' declared the Inspector again; his voice sounded calmer than before. The open eyes did not focus him, but he for his part focused them clearly. He had won the first round. As soon as initial resistance is overcome, the rest follows naturally. The eyes of the criminal remained fixed on the woman, bored themselves into her and grew strangely rigid. This fragment of a man was a Peeping Tom just the same. 'You ought to be ashamed of yourself!' shouted the Inspector, 'you're half naked!' The thief's pupils expanded, his teeth chattered. His head remained motionless at the same angle. Was this the genuine death-glaze? the Inspector asked himself and was a little afraid.

Then Kien lifted an arm and extended it until he touched Therese's skirt. He compressed a fold of it between two fingers, let it go, pressed it again, let it go, and reached for the next fold. He drew a step closer; he seemed not wholly to trust his eyes and fingers, and approached his ear towards the noise which his hand drew from the starched folds; his nostrils quivered. 'That's enough, you dirty swine!' screamed the Inspector; the scornful movement of the prisoner's nose had not escaped him. 'Are you guilty or not?' 'What's that!' bellowed the caretaker; no one reprimanded him for the disturbance, they were all on tiptoe for the criminal's reply. Kien opened his mouth, possibly with the intention of tasting the skirt, but when it was open, he said: 'I confess my guilt. Yet part of the blame must redound to her. It is true, I locked her in. But was it necessary for her to devour her own body? She merited her death. One point I would beg you to clarify, for I feel a certain confusion. How do you explain the presence here of the murdered woman? I know her by her skirt.'

He spoke very low. The spectators drew close round him, they wanted to catch what he said. His face was tense, as that of a dying man confessing his most torturing secret. 'Louder!' shouted the

Inspector; he avoided the usual police words of command, he was
acting rather as if he were in a theatre. The quiet of the others was
reverential and tenacious. Instead of emphasizing his commands, he
was now a lamb among lambs. The caretaker stood before him, leaning on the shoulders of two colleagues; both his arms rested, full
length, on them. A circle formed about Kien and Therese. It closed
in, no one would yield his place; one said: 'Bats in the belfry!' and
tapped his own forehead. But he was ashamed at once and lowered his
head; his words clashed with the general curiosity, he got black looks.
Therese breathed: 'I ask you!' She was mistress here, everything
revolved round her, she was consumed with curiosity, but she'd let
that man have his lie out, then it would be her turn to speak, and
everyone else would have to hold their tongues.

Kien spoke more softly. Now and again he felt for his tie to pull it
straight; faced with serious problems this was always his gesture. It
looked to the spectators as if he didn't know that he had nothing on but
his shirt. The Inspector's hand felt involuntarily for his pocket mirror;
he almost held it up for the gentleman. He appreciated a well-tied
tie: but the gentleman was only a common thief.

'You may well believe that I am the victim of an hallucination.
I am not generally subject to them. Scholarship demands a clear head,
I would not read an X for U, or take any other letter for its fellow.
But recently I have been through much; yesterday I had news of my
wife's death. You are aware of the circumstances. On her account I
have the honour to find myself among you. Since then thoughts of
my trial have ceaselessly occupied my mind. To-day, when I went to
the Theresianum, I encountered my murdered wife. She was accompanied by our caretaker, a very good friend of mine. He had followed
her, as my representative, to her last resting place; I was myself unable
to attend. Do not regard me as unduly hard-hearted. There are
women whom it is impossible to forget. I will admit the whole truth
to you: I deliberately avoided her funeral, it would have been too
much for me. I trust you understand me; were you never yourself
married? Her skirt was torn in pieces and devoured by a bloodhound.
It is however conceivable that she possessed two. Ascending the stairs,
she brushed against me. She was carrying a parcel which I presumed
to contain my own books. I love my library. You must understand, I
am speaking of the largest privately-owned library in the town. For
some time I have been compelled to neglect it. I was occupied with
errands of mercy. My wife's murder kept me away from home;

how many weeks it is I cannot precisely calculate since I left the house. But I have made good use of the time; time is knowledge, knowledge is order. Beside the accumulation of a small head-library I turned my attention, as above mentioned, to errands of mercy. I redeem books from the stake. I know of a hog who lives on books, but do not let us speak of him. I refer you to the speech I shall make in my own defence, on which occasion I propose to make certain public revelations. I ask for your help! She does not move from her place. Liberate me from this hallucination! I am not generally subject to them. She has been following me, I fear, for more than an hour. Let us first be clear in our facts; I will make your task of helping me the easier. I see you all, you see me. Even so clearly, the murdered woman stands at my side. All my senses have betrayed me, not my eyes alone. Do as I will, I hear the crackling of her skirt, I can feel it, it smells of starch; she moves her head in the very manner in which she moved it living, she even speaks; a few moments ago she said, "I ask you"; you must know that her vocabulary contained not above fifty words, in spite of which she talked no less than most people. I implore your help! Prove to me that she is dead.'

The spectators began to make words of his sounds. They became accustomed to his manner, and listened perplexed; one clutched at another in order to hear better. He spoke like an educated man, he was confessing a murder. As a body they could not believe in his murder, though each of them singly would have taken it to be true. Against whom did he want protection? In his shirt they let him alone; he was afraid. Even the Inspector felt powerless; he preferred to say nothing, his phrases would not have sounded literary enough. The criminal was well-connected. Perhaps he was not a criminal at all. Therese was astonished that she had never noticed anything. So he'd been married when she came into his service, and she'd always thought he was a bachelor; she'd known there was a mystery, the mystery was his first wife, he'd murdered her, still waters are murderers, so that was why he never spoke, and because his first wife had had a skirt like hers, he'd married *her* for love. She cast about for proofs; between six and seven in the morning he was busy all by himself, everything was hidden away until he had smuggled all the bits out of the house, the very idea, she could remember it all. So that was why he'd run off and left her, he'd been afraid she'd tell the whole story. Thieves are murderers, she always said; Mr. Brute would be surprised.

The caretaker was seized with terror; the shoulders, on which he was leaning, swayed. The Professor was taking deferred vengeance on him, when everybody had forgotten all about his daughter. The Professor was talking about a wife, but he meant his daughter. The caretaker kept seeing her too, but she wasn't there, was she? The Professor wanted to make a fool of him, but the others didn't fall for the trick. The heart of gold was letting him down; what's that! how mistaken one can be in people! In his sorrow he restrained himself. The Professor's accusations were too insubstantial; he knew his colleagues. He hadn't yet remembered that it was he who had promoted Kien Professor and he contemplated his degradation only as a final measure.

After his repeated appeal for help — he had spoken calmly but it was a despairing entreaty — Kien waited. The dead silence was agreeable to him. Even Therese was silent. He wished she would vanish. Perhaps she would vanish now she was silent. She did not. Since no one came to meet him, he assumed the initiative himself, to cure himself of his hallucination. He was well aware of his duty to learning. He sighed, deeply he sighed, for who would not feel shame at having to call in the help of others? Murder was comprehensible; that murder he could defend; only its consequence, this hallucination, he feared so deeply. If the court declared him not responsible for his actions, he would commit suicide on the spot. He smiled, so as to ingratiate himself with his listeners; later on they would certainly be called as witnesses. The more friendly and sensible his words to them, the less important would his hallucination appear. He elevated them to the rank of educated men.

'Psychology to-day is part of every profession pursued by — educated men.' Polite as he was, he prefaced these 'educated men' with a brief pause. 'I have not fallen a victim to a woman as you, perhaps, are thinking. My acquittal is a foregone conclusion. You see in me, almost certainly, the greatest living authority on sinology. But even greater men have suffered from hallucinations. The peculiarity of men of critical temperament consists in the energy with which they concentrate on the object of their choice. For the last hour I have been thinking so intensely and so exclusively of this figment of my brain, that I cannot now expel it. Convince yourselves, gentlemen, how reasonably I myself judge of it! May I earnestly request you to take the following measures: Withdraw a few steps, all of you! Form up in single file! Let each approach me singly in a straight line! I hope hereby to convince myself that you will find no obstacle in the way, here, here, or here. Here I myself come into contact with a skirt, the woman inside it has been murdered, she is so like the murdered woman as to be mistaken for her, at present she is silent, but earlier she had the voice of the murdered woman too; this baffles me. I need a clear head. I shall conduct my own defence. I need no one. Lawyers are criminals; they lie. I live for truth. I know, this truth is a lie; help me; I know she must vanish. Help me, this skirt disturbs me. I hated her skirt even before the bloodhound ate it, and must I see it again now?'

He had seized on Therese; not tentatively, but with all his strength he clutched at her skirt, he pushed her from him, he drew her to him, he enclosed her in his long, lean arms. She let him have his way. He only wanted to embrace her. Before they are hanged, murderers are allowed a last meal. Murder, she wouldn't have guessed. Now she knew: so thin and all those books with everything in them. He turned her round once on her axis and forewent the embrace. This made her angry. He glared at her from an inch off. He stroked her dress with all ten fingers. He put out his tongue and snuffled with his nose. Tears came into his eyes with the effort. 'I suffer from this hallucination!' he admitted, gasping. The listeners inferred sobs from his tears.

'Don't cry, sir!' said one: he was a father himself, his eldest boy brought home top marks in German composition every day. The Inspector felt envious. The man in the shirt, whom he had undressed himself, suddenly seemed to him very well-dressed. 'All right, all right,' he grumbled. He thought of ways for transposing into a sterner key. To ease his task, he threw a glance at the shabby clothes on the table. The policeman with a memory asked: 'Why didn't you say something before?' He had not forgotten all that had happened. His question was purely rhetorical; he only asked it so as to remind people of his genius, as his colleagues called it, from time to time, particularly when things were quiet. The remaining, less developed characters, were still either listening or laughing. They were divided between curiosity and satisfaction. They felt happy, but did not know it. At these rare moments they forgot their duty, even their dignity, like many people at a theatre of established reputation. The playing-time was short. They would have liked more for their money. Kien spoke and performed, he took great pains. It was clear how seriously he took his profession. He earned his money with the sweat of his brow. No actor could have done better. In forty years he had not said so much about himself, as now in twenty minutes. His gestures were convincing. Almost, the spectators applauded. When he began to handle the woman, they were all benevolently willing to credit him with the murder. For a street performer he seemed too well-connected; for the theatre, his calves were too wretched. They would have been ready to argue that he was a decayed star, but they were too busy watching him and enjoying the mingled feelings which his art induced in them.

Therese was annoyed with him. As she imagined that the greedy eyes of the men, all of them, men, were intended for her, she accepted his flatteries for a while. He himself was repulsive to her. What good was he to her? He was feeble and thin, couldn't play the man, men don't do such things. He was a murderer of course, but she wasn't afraid, she knew him, he was a coward. But she felt that the murderer's blissful interlude was becoming to her; he was under her spell and she kept quiet. The caretaker's shrewdness had vanished. He noticed that his daughter was not the pivot of the Professor's tale, and became absorbed in the movement of his legs. If only a beggar like that would pass within focus of his peep-hole! He would snap his legs like matchsticks. A man should have calves, or be ashamed. What did he go dangling round that old bitch for? She wasn't worth courting. She ought to leave him in peace and pull no more pretty faces. She'd put a spell on the poor Professor all right! Writhing in the toils of love, as the saying is. A gentleman too! His colleagues in the force ought to help him put on his trousers again. A stranger might come in at any moment and see he had no calves. That'd be a shame for the whole force. He ought to stop talking, no one here can understand such clever stuff; he always talks too clever. Mostly he doesn't talk at all. To-day he's got the bit between his teeth. What's it all in aid of?

Suddenly Kien drew himself up. He swarmed up Therese to his full height. Scarcely had he overtopped her — he was a head taller — than he began to laugh. 'She hasn't grown!' he said and laughed, 'she hasn't grown!'

He had in fact decided to rid himself of this mirage by measuring himself against it. How could he reach the head of the pseudo-Therese? He saw her, a gigantic size, before him. He would stretch himself, he would stand on tiptoe and if she was still taller then he could say with absolute justification: 'In reality she was always a head smaller during the whole of her lifetime; therefore this object is a mirage!'

But just as he had shot up, as agile as an ape, his cunning experiment dwindled to Therese's old size. He did not worry; on the contrary, could there have been a better proof of his famous accuracy? Even his imagination was accurate! He laughed. A scholar of his stamp was not lost. Humanity suffers from inaccuracy. Several milliards of ordinary human beings had lived without meaning and died without meaning. A thousand accurate ones, at the outside a thousand, had built up knowledge. To let one of the upper thousand die before his time, would be little less than race-suicide. He laughed heartily. He imagined the hallucinations of ordinary fellows, like those surrounding him. Therese would have been too tall for any of them; in all probability she would have touched the ceiling. They would have cried with terror and turned to others for help. They lived among hallucinations; they did not even know how to form a lucid sentence. It was necessary to guess what they were thinking of, if it interested you; far better not to trouble your head with it. Among them, you felt as in a madhouse. Whether they laughed or cried, they were always grotesquely masked; they were incurable, one as cowardly as another; not one of them would have murdered Therese; they would have let themselves be plagued to death by her. They were even afraid of helping him because he was a murderer. Who but he knew the motives he had had for the deed? At his trial, after his great speech, this miserable species would acquit him. He had reason to laugh, who else had been born with a memory like his? Memory was the pre-condition of scientific accuracy. He would examine this mirage until he had convinced himself of what it really was. He had followed trails no less dangerous, imperfect texts, missing lines. He could recall no occasion on which he had failed. No problem he had undertaken had ever been left unsolved. Even this murder he must needs regard as a task accomplished. It took more than a mere hallucination to shatter Kien; the hallucination ran the greater risk, even if it were of flesh and blood. He was hard. Therese had not spoken for a long time. He had his laugh out. Then he set to work again.

As his courage and confidence grew, the quality of his performance diminished. When he began to laugh the spectators still found him amusing. A moment ago he had been sobbing bitterly; the contrast was brilliant. 'How he does it!' one of them exclaimed. 'Sunshine after rain,' replied his neighbour. Then they all grew grave. The Inspector clutched at his nose. He appreciated art but he preferred genuine laughter. The man with a memory drew attention to the fact that this was the first time he had heard the gentleman laugh. 'Talking wouldn't do no good!' bellowed the caretaker. The father of the bright schoolboy didn't share this view! 'You'd better talk, Mister!'

he cautioned him. Kien did not obey. 'It's all in your own interest,' the father added. He spoke the truth. The attention of the spectators slackened rapidly. The prisoner went on laughing too long. They were already familiar with his comic figure. The Inspector was ashamed of himself; he, who had all but got his Matric, to let himself be imposed on by a man because he spouted sentences like a book. The thief must have learnt them by heart, a dangerous blackmailer. You couldn't get round *him* like that. Thought he'd get away with robbery and being in possession of false papers, if he made up something about murder. An experienced organ of the law was up to those little tricks. He had more than his share of impudence if he thought he could laugh in this situation. It would soon end in tears, and not crocodile tears either.

The man with the memory was carefully sorting out all the thief's lies for the subsequent interrogation. There were over a dozen people there, and certainly not one of them had noticed anything. *His* memory was what they all relied on. He sighed aloud. He got no extra pay for his indispensable services. He did more than all the others put together. Not one of them was worth anything. He was the life and soul of the whole sub-station. The Inspector relied on him. *He* carried the burden. Everyone envied him. Just as if his promotion was already in the bag. But they knew very well why he never got promotion. His senior officers were afraid of his genius. While he counted up, with the help of his fingers, the various assertions made by the delinquent, the proud father cautioned Kien for the last time. He conceded that he might be unable to speak, but said: 'You'd better cry then, Mister!' He had a very important feeling that laughter in school earns no 'Very good'. Almost everyone had by now let go of his neighbour. Some detached themselves from the circle. The ring and the tension broke. Even the less independent minds began to form opinions of their own. The man whose glass of water had been rejected, remembered it. The two who had acted as props for the caretaker became suddenly aware of him, and would have liked to knock his block off for his confiding insolence. He himself bellowed: 'The man talks too much!' When Kien once again became absorbed in his examination, it was too late. Only a new and striking performance would have saved him. He had the effrontery to give an encore. Therese felt that the crossfire of admiration had burnt out. 'Please, I've had enough!' she said. He wasn't even a man.

Kien heard her voice and started. She annihilated his hopes; he had never expected this. He had thought that the rest of her, like her voice, would gradually vanish. He had just stiffened his fingers so as to pass them through the mirage. Last of all, he calculated, his eyes would cease to deceive him; optical illusions are the most obstinate of all. And then she spoke. He had not misheard. She said 'please'. He must begin again at the beginning; what injustice, his great work put back for years, he told himself, and stood frozen, just as the voice had struck him, with his back bent and the fingers of both hands rigidly extended, close against her. Instead of speaking, he was silent, he had forgotten how to cry and even how to laugh; he did nothing. Thus he threw away the last remnants of sympathy.

'Clown!' yelled the Inspector. He trusted himself again to intervene, but he pronounced the word in English: the educated impression Kien had made on him was indestructible. He looked round him, to see if he was understood. The man with a memory transposed the word into the German pronunciation. He knew what it meant, but declared that the Inspector's was the correct form. From this moment he was under suspicion of secretly knowing English. The Inspector waited a moment to see the effect of his 'clown' on the prisoner. He feared another sentence straight out of a book and was constructing an answer of the same kind. 'You seem to think that none of the servants of the state here present have devoted themselves to high studies.' It was a good sentence. He clutched at his nose. But Kien prevented him from bringing it out; he grew furious and screeched: 'You seem to think, that none of the servants here present have had any relations with Matric.'

'What's that?' bellowed the caretaker. They were getting at him, at his daughter; they all thought they could say what they liked about her; couldn't leave the poor kid in peace in her grave. Kien was too deeply stricken even to move his lips. The difficulties of the trial were increasing. Murder is always murder. Did not these monsters burn Giordano Bruno? He was fighting in vain against hallucination — who would give him the power to convince an uneducated jury of his importance?

'Who are you then, sir?' shouted the Inspector. 'Speak up if you please!' With two fingers he pulled at Kien's shirt-sleeve. He would have liked to squash him between two finger-nails. What kind of an education is this, which can only produce a couple of sentences and then not a word in answer to a reasonable question? True education reveals itself in a man's bearing, in his immaculate appearance and in the art of interrogation. Gravely, and ever more confident of his superiority, the Inspector retired behind his table. The wooden seat of the chair on which he usually sat was covered by a soft cushion, the only one in the sub-station, on which, in letters of scarlet embroidery, was clearly to be read: PRIVATE PROPERTY. These words were intended to remind his inferiors that — even in his absence — they had no right to it. The fellows had a reprehensible tendency to slide the cushion under their own bodies. With a few deft movements he set it to rights; before he seated himself, the words PRIVATE PROPERTY must be precisely parallel with his eyes, which overlooked no opportunity of drawing strength from the phrase. He turned his back on the chair. It was hard to tear himself from contemplation of the cushion, even harder so to seat himself that the cushion should not be disturbed. Slowly he lowered himself; for a few seconds he restrained his backside. Only when this part of his person had PRIVATE PROPERTY in its proper place he allowed himself to put pressure on it. As soon as he was sitting, no thief in the world — even if he had passed Matric and more — could have imposed on him. Swiftly he took a last peep at his little mirror. His tie, like himself, sat firmly but with elegance. His hair, brushed back, was disciplined with grease, not a hair out of place. His nose was too short. It gave him the spur he needed; he flung himself into the inquiry.

His people supported him. He had said 'clown'; they found the word apt. Since the prisoner had grown boring, they were thinking of their own dignity. The man with a memory burnt with zeal. He had agreed with himself on fourteen points. Scarcely had the Inspector's contemptuous finger-nails let go of Kien, than he was conducted, in his shirt, to the table. There they let him go. He stood up by himself. It was just as well. If he had fallen now, no one would have helped him. They knew he had strength of his own. They took him for an obstinate play-actor. Even his thinness was no longer convincing. He was certainly not under-nourished. The proud father grew anxious at his son's good German composition. This was what book-learning led to.

'Do you recognize these clothes?' asked the Inspector, and pointed to the jacket, waistcoat, trousers, socks and shoes which were strewed over the table. As he spoke he looked him sharply in the eye to notice the effect of his words. His determination was rocklike, to proceed systematically and so to entrap the criminal. Kien nodded. He was holding tightly on to the table edge with both hands. The mirage,

he knew, was behind him. He overcame the desire to turn round and
see whether it was still there. He thought it wiser to answer. So as
not to annoy the magistrate — for this must be the magistrate — he
would answer his questions. He would have preferred to give a
description of the murder in a connected speech. He disliked dialogues;
he was accustomed to develop his views in lengthy dissertations. But
he recognized that every craftsman has his own methods and submitted
himself. Secretly he hoped that in the absorbing interplay of question
and answer he would re-live Therese's death with such vigour that
the mirage would dissolve itself. As long as he could he would spin
out the matter with this magistrate, and prove to him that Therese's
death was *essential*. When the report was drawn up in all its detail,
and every doubt of his complicity had vanished, when with the help
of unmistakable proofs he had been persuaded of her end, then, and
on no account before, he would permit himself to turn round, and
far behind where she had stood laugh into the empty air. Surely she
must already be far behind me, he said to himself, for he felt her to be
very close. The more violently he drove his fingers into the table, the
further would she vanish from his sight. But she might at any moment
touch him from behind. He counted on a photograph of the skeleton,
as it had been found. The caretaker's description alone seemed
insufficient. Human beings are fallible. Dogs, unfortunately, cannot
talk. The most reliable witness would have been the bloodhound,
which had bitten her dress into tiny fragments and eaten it up.

But a man in the Inspector's position was not to be satisfied with a
mere nod. 'Answer Yes or No!' he commanded. 'I shall repeat the
question.'

Kien said: 'Yes.'

'Wait until I repeat the question! Do you recognize these clothes?'

'Yes.' He assumed they were talking of the murdered woman's
clothes and did not even look.

'You admit that these clothes belong to you?'

'No, to her.'

The Inspector saw through him; it was child's play. So as to dis-
sociate himself from the money and the stolen papers found in his
clothes, the shameless scoundrel actually dared to make the assertion
that the clothes belonged to the woman over there, whom he had
robbed. The Inspector remained calm, although he had undressed
him with his own hands, and in all his long years of experience had
never before encountered a comparable insolence. With a fleeting

smile he reached for the trousers, and held them up: 'Even these trousers!'

Kien observed them. 'Those are men's trousers,' he said, unpleasantly disturbed, because this object had nothing to do with Therese.

'You admit then, men's trousers.'

'Naturally.'

'Whose trousers do you suppose these to be?'

'I can hardly know that. Were they found with the dead woman?'

The Inspector made a point of ignoring his sentence. He intended to nip the murder story and any other red-herrings in the bud as soon as they made their appearance.

'Indeed; you can hardly know that.'

Quick as lightning he pulled out his pocket mirror and held it out towards Kien, not so near but that he could see himself almost full-length.

'Do you know who that is?' he asked. Every muscle of his face was taut to breaking.

'It is . . . I, myself,' stammered Kien, and clutched at his shirt. 'Where . . . where are my trousers?' He was utterly astounded to see himself in this guise; even his shoes and socks were missing.

'Aha!' the Inspector jubilated. 'Now put on your trousers again!'

He handed them to him, on the alert for a new trick. Kien received them and hastily pulled them on. Before the Inspector put his mirror away, he took a hasty peep into it, an impulse which in the interests of surprise he had previously suppressed. He knew how to control himself. His bearing was faultless. He felt a particular delight in the ease with which this examination was developing. The criminal meanwhile spontaneously put on all the rest of the clothes. It would have been superfluous to prove his ownership of each separate article. The Inspector understood what kind of criminal he had to reckon with, and husbanded his resources. The opening phase had not lasted three minutes. He would like to see anyone else try to do as well. He was so happy that he would gladly have stopped there. To be able to proceed, he took one more peep in his mirror, was exasperated by his nose and asked with renewed energy — just as the thief slipped on his jacket:

'And now what's your name?'

'Dr. Peter Kien.'

'Why not indeed! Your profession?'

'Scholar and librarian.'

The Inspector had the impression that he had heard both these claims before. In spite of his memory, which was as short as his nose, he grabbed at one of the stolen papers and read aloud: 'Dr. Peter Kien. Scholar and librarian.' This new trick on the part of the criminal threw him a little out of his plan. He had recognized the clothes as his own and now he was pretending that the papers were genuine. His situation must indeed seem desperate for him to clutch at so crazy a straw. In cases like this a single surprise question often leads at one stroke to the goal.

'And how much money had you when you left home this morning, Dr. Kien?'

'I am in no position to say. I am not in the habit of counting my money.'

'As long as you haven't got it, no doubt!'

He watched for the effect of this stroke. Even during preliminary examinations, he let it be seen that he knew everything, though he still behaved courteously. The criminal's face fell. His disappointment spoke whole documents. The Inspector decided on an immediate second attack, at a no less vulnerable part of the guilty man, the question of domicile. Unobtrusively, hesitatively and almost dreaming, his left hand slid over the papers — until he had found a certain entry and had covered it over completely. It was the address. High-class criminals can read upside down. So the Inspector took up his last position. Then he held out his right arm, invitingly and imploringly and said, quite by the way:

'Where did you sleep last night?'

'At an hotel — I am uncertain of the name,' replied Kien.

The Inspector lifted his left hand and read: '24 Ehrlich Strasse.'

'That was where they found the body,' explained Kien, and breathed a sigh of relief. At last they were getting to the murder.

'Found, you say? Do you know what we call it here?'

'You are, admittedly, right. If we are to take the matter literally, there was nothing of her left.'

'Take? Let us say straight out, steal!'

Kien started. What was stolen? Not the skirt? On the skirt, and its subsequent destruction by the bloodhound, rested the whole of his defence against the mirage. 'The skirt was found at the scene of the crime!' he asserted in a firm voice.

'The scene of the crime? You recognize what you are admitting?' A confirmatory nod passed through the surrounding police. 'I take

313

you for an educated man. You admit, presumably, that a scene of a crime presupposes a crime? You are at liberty to withdraw your statement. But it is my duty to call your attention to the unfortunate impression it would make. I am advising you for your own good. You will do better to admit everything. Let's admit everything, my good man! Confess. We know all! Denying will do you no good. You've let the scene of the crime slip out. Admit everything and I'll put in a good word for you! Admit everything in order! We have made our own investigations. How can you hope to escape? You walked into the trap yourself! The scene of the crime presupposes a crime. I take it I am right, gentlemen?'

When he said 'gentlemen' the gentlemen knew that he had victory in the palm of his hand, and overwhelmed him with admiring glances. Each hastened to do better than the other. The man with a memory saw that there was going to be nothing for him, and abandoned his old plan. He darted forward, seized the lucky hand of the Inspector and shouted: 'Inspector, permit me to congratulate you!'

The Inspector knew well what an incomparable feat he had just achieved. A modest man, he avoided honours as much as possible. But to-day it was too much for him. Pale and excited he rose to his feet, bowed to left and right, sought for words and at length expressed his deep emotion in a simple phrase: 'Thank you, gentlemen.'

'Moved almost to tears,' thought the happy father; he had a taste for affecting scenes.

Kien was about to speak. He had been challenged to tell the whole story in order. What better fortune could he have hoped for? Repeatedly he tried to begin. But the applause interrupted him. He cursed the bowing and scraping of the police, which he thought was directed to him. These people put him off before he could even begin. Their strange behaviour seemed an attempt to influence him. Although he suspected movements behind his back, he would not look round. The whole truth was before him. The mirage may have vanished already. He might describe the whole of his married life with the incontrovertibly dead Therese. His position at the trial would be very much ameliorated by this, but he cares little for such amelioration. Rather would he describe the details of her death, with which he had himself been concerned in the most decisive fashion. It was essential to understand the art of interesting even the police; they will listen gladly to anything in their own routine. Murders are the common routine of mankind. Is there anyone who takes no pleasure in murder?

At long last the Inspector sat down again; he forgot what he was sitting on and did not once look round to see how PRIVATE PROPERTY was arranged. Since he had outwitted the criminal, he hated him less. He thought it best to let him say his fill. His success had altered his whole life. His nose was a normal size. Deep in its pocket lay the mirror, utterly forgotten; it served no purpose. Why do people worry so? Life is elegant. New designs for ties appear daily. You must know how to wear them. Most people look like monkeys in them. He needs no looking-glass. He ties by touch. His success justifies his action. He is unassuming. Often he bows to people. His men respect him. His good reputation makes hard work a pleasure to him. He does not stop at regulations. Regulations are for criminals. He makes them confess spontaneously, for his technique is faultless.

'Hardly had the door closed behind her,' Kien began, 'when I was aware of my good fortune.' He began with a wide sweep, but it was within himself, in the depths of his determined soul. He knew exactly what things in fact led up to the event. Who should know the motives for his crime better than the perpetrator? He saw from alpha to omega, every link of the coil in which he had bound Therese. With a certain irony, he set forth the facts for this audience of man — and sensation — hunters. He could have spoken of more interesting things. It was a pity; but they were none of them men of learning. He treated them like men of normal education. Very probably they had not even that. He avoided quotations from the Chinese. They might interrupt him to ask who Mong Tse might be. Fundamentally, it gave him pleasure to speak of simple facts simply, and in a way to be understood by all. In his story were combined the acuteness and the sobriety which he owed to the writers of classical China. While Therese died again, his thoughts went back to the library, whence had flowed forth such great services to learning. Soon the flow would be resumed. His acquittal was a foregone conclusion. All the same, he planned a very different appearance before his judges. There he would unfold the ample splendour of his learning. The whole world would listen when probably the greatest sinologist of his time spoke his Defence of Learning. In this place, he spoke more modestly. He falsified nothing, he made no concessions, but he simplified.

'For weeks I left her alone. Convinced that she must die of hunger, I passed night after night at hotels. Bitterly did I miss my library, believe me; I had to content myself with a small substitute library, which, for essential needs, I kept always at hand. The locks on my door are strong — I was not tormented by the fear that burglars might release her. Imagine for yourselves her condition: all provisions are consumed. Enfeebled and full of hatred she lies on the floor, in front of that very desk in which she had so often looked for money. Her only thoughts were of money. In nothing did she resemble a flower. Of the thoughts which came into my head when I sat at that writing desk, at the time when I still shared my dwelling with her, I will not tell you to-day. For weeks I had to live, for fear that she should steal my manuscripts, petrified into a guardian-statue. This was the period of my deepest humiliation. When my head glowed for work, I had to say to myself: you are made of stone, and to remain motionless, I believed it myself. Those of you who have ever had to watch over a treasure, will readily be able to put yourselves in my place. I do not believe in fate; but she hastened towards hers. Instead of me — for by many a secret assault she brought me near to death — she now lay there, devoured by her own mad hunger. She did not know how to help herself. She had not sufficient self-control. She devoured herself. Piece by piece of her body fell a prey to her greed. Day by day she grew thinner. She was too weak to stand, but lay there in her own filth. Perhaps I seem thin to you. Compared to me she was the shadow of a being, pitiful and despicable; had she stood up a breath of wind could have snapped her in two, I verily believe even a child. I cannot particularize further. The blue skirt, which she always wore, covered her skeleton. It was starched, and thanks to this peculiarity held the repulsive remains of her body together. One day she breathed her last. Even this expression appears to me corrupt, for very probably she had no lungs left. No one was with her in her last hour; who could have remained week in, week out, with that skeleton? She was deep in filth. The flesh which she had torn off in strips from her body stank to heaven. Corruption set in before she was dead. All this happened in my library, in the presence of the books. I shall have the place cleaned. She shortened this process by no suicide. There was nothing sacred about her; she was very cruel. She pretended a hypocritical love of books as long as she thought I would make a will in her favour. Day and night she spoke of that will. She nursed me to sickness and left me alive only because she was uncertain of the will. I am telling you the plain truth. I have very grave doubts as to whether she could read and write fluently. Believe me, learning has made truth a duty with me. Her origins were obscure. She locked up the flat, she permitted me the use of one room, and even that she took from me. And she came to a bad end. The caretaker broke into the flat. A retired policeman, he was able to achieve what burglars had tried in vain. I regard him as a trustworthy person. He found her in her skirt, a repellent, evil-smelling, hideous skeleton, dead, completely dead, not for one moment did he doubt her death. He called in the neighbours; the joy in the entire block was universal. It was no longer possible to state the precise time when death had occurred; but it had occurred, and it was generally agreed that this was the essential fact. Not less than fifty tenants of the block filed past the body. Not one uttered a doubt; each acquiesced in a fact which could not be recalled.

Cases of apparent, but not actual, death are on record; no scholar would deny this. But I know of no occasion where apparent, but not actual death has been proved in the case of a skeleton. From the remotest times popular superstition has represented ghosts in the form of skeletons. This conception is at once profound and significant; it is also important evidence. Why is a ghost to be feared? Because it is an apparition of the dead, the undeniably dead, the decayed and buried. Would the same apprehensions be experienced if the apparition were to materialize in its old and familiar bodily shape? No! For such a sight would call up no thoughts of death; the living person, nothing else, would stand revealed. But if the ghost takes the form of a skeleton, two things are at once brought to the spectator's mind: the living person as he once was, and the dead, as he now is. The skeleton, as the conception of the ghost, became for countless peoples the symbol of death. The evidence is therefore overwhelming; the skeleton is the most irrecoverably dead of all the forms we know. Ancient burial places suffuse us with a shudder of disgust if they contain skeletons; when they are empty, we hardly think of them as burial places. And if we apply the term 'skeleton' to a living being, we mean no less than that he is near to death.

She, however, was completely dead; all the tenants of the block had convinced themselves of that and a huge disgust at her avaricious end spread among them. They feared her still. She was very dangerous. The only one masterful enough for her, the caretaker, flung her into her coffin. Immediately afterwards he washed his hands, but I greatly fear they will be stained for ever. Nevertheless, I take this occasion publicly to express my thanks to him for his brave deed. He was not afraid to accompany her on her last journey. Out of loyalty to me he called on some of the tenants to assist him in this hateful office. Not one was willing to do so. For these simple and decent people the mere

sight of her corpse had sufficed to reveal her character. But I had lived
for months on end at her side. When the coffin — far too white and
glossy — trundled through the streets on a decrepit handcart, everyone
guessed what was concealed within it. The few street urchins, whom
my faithful servant had engaged to protect the procession from the
onslaught of an enraged populace, ran away; trembling with terror
and wailing loudly they spread the news through the whole town.
There arose in the streets a wild howling. Indignant men left their
work, women had hysterics, schools spewed forth their children,
thousands streamed together, demanding the right to kill the corpse.
Not since the Revolution of 1848 had there been such a riot. Clenched
fists, curses, the streets themselves seemed to sob and pant, and from a
great chorus of voices came the cry: Death to the corpse! Death to the
corpse! I understand it all too well. Humanity is fickle. In general, I
do not love it. Yet how gladly at that moment would I have joined
with them. The mob brooks no jesting. Fearful is its vengeance —
give it the right object and it will act justly. When they tore off the
coffin lid they saw not a real corpse, but a repulsive skeleton. At that
their frenzy evaporated. No man can harm a skeleton; the mob dispersed. Only a bloodhound would not let go. He sought for flesh, but
found none. Enraged, he tore the coffin to the ground and bit the blue
skirt into small fragments. These he devoured, without pity, to the
last morsel. Thus it is that the skirt no longer exists. You will seek it in
vain. So as to lessen your labours, I am informing you of all the
details. You must seek out the remains on a rubbish dump outside the
town. Bones, wretched bones; I doubt whether you will now be able
to distinguish them from other refuse. Perhaps you will be lucky. So
vile a beast deserved no honourable grave. Since she is now, on reliable
evidence, dead I will not speak ill of her. The blue peril is at an end.
Only fools would be afraid of a yellow one. China is the land of all
lands, the Holiest Land. We must believe in death! From my earliest
childhood I have doubted the existence of the soul. I regard the doctrine
of transmigration as a mere impertinence and am ready to cast it in the
teeth of any Indian. When they found her, on the floor before the
writing desk, she was a skeleton; *not* a soul. . . . '

Kien controlled his speech. Now and again his thoughts wandered
towards knowledge. He seemed so near to it; how passionately he
longed to spread himself on it. This was his home. But each time he
recollected himself — pleasure later, he told himself; the books will
wait until you go home, the thesis will wait; you have wasted much

318

time. Each path his will forced back towards his writing desk. Whenever he saw it, his face lightened, he smiled at the deceased; it was a vision, but not a mirage. Lovingly, he lingered by the body. He was not observant of the details of living beings; his memory worked only in relation to books. Otherwise he would willingly have described her in detail. Her decease was no ordinary matter; it was an event. It was the final redemption of a hideously persecuted humanity. Little by little Kien began to be amazed at his own hatred. She had not been worth that. How could he hate a pitiable skeleton? How quickly did she perish! Only the odour, which since that time, had hung about his books, disturbed him. We have to make sacrifices. He would know how to get rid of it.

The police had long grown restive. They were only listening out of deference to the Inspector; he, however, found it difficult to return to the sober business of the interrogation. With the prize of victory already in his experienced hands, he cared nothing for prose. He would have liked to riot among new ties — innumerable patterns, guaranteed pure silk — and choose himself out the most beautiful of all, for he was a man of taste. Every Gents Outfitter knew him. He could wander among the counters for hours; he knew how to look at ties without creasing them. That was why they trusted their goods in his hands. Many would even send them on approval. But he didn't care for that. He could stand in a shop all day conversing with the proprietor. When he entered they left the other customers standing. His profession gave him a fund of interesting stories, and he recounted them. People always liked to listen to that kind of thing. Time, he only wanted time to be a smart fellow. To-morrow he'd take a walk. A pity to-day wasn't to-morrow. He was expected to listen to every interrogation. On principle he didn't because he knew it all. He'd trapped this one all right; there was no getting round *him*. His nerves were all to pieces, from too much work. All the same he had a right to feel satisfied. He'd achieved something; and could look forward to a new tie.

The caretaker pricked up his ears. He had not been mistaken in the Professor. He was telling them what kind of a man he was. He wasn't a servant. True; that was right; if he wanted to he could call up all the tenants of all the flats; they'd have come running. He could bellow loud enough for all the town to hear. He didn't know what fear was; he was a policeman. He could break into any flat. Not a lock would hold him up; he could smash the door in; with *one* fist. He didn't wear out shoe-leather; he didn't need to kick. Others would start kicking right away. *He* had strength — at his fingers' ends.

Therese kept close by Kien. Painstakingly she swallowed each one of his words. Under her skirt she described a circle first with one foot then with the other, without moving from her place. Such meaningless movements, with her, indicated fear. She was afraid of this man. For eight years she had lived with him in the flat. From moment to moment he grew more like a murderer. Earlier, he never used to utter a word. Now he talked nothing but murders. A dangerous man! When he spoke of the skeleton before the writing desk, she said quickly to herself: he means his first wife. She too had wanted a will; she was a sensible woman, but the cowardly creature grudged every penny. The skirt was an insult. Do bloodhounds eat skirts? He'd murder anyone. The more you beat him the better he was, but he didn't get enough of it. Thinking up stories! He gave her the three rooms all on his own. What should she want with manuscripts? She wants his bankbook. The books smell of corpses? That was the first she'd heard of it. Eight years, day in, day out, she dusted those books. People screamed at the coffin in the streets. The very idea, screaming at a corpse. First he married for love, then he did you in. Hanging was too good for him. She wouldn't do anyone in. She didn't marry for love either. Let him try coming back to her at the flat! She was afraid. *He* thinks of money because he grudges every penny. It's not true about the blue skirt. He's doing it to annoy her. There won't be any more murders. The police are here. She could cry with rage. The creature thinks women are just animals. He has her on his conscience. From six to seven he was all alone. That was when he did his murders. He'd better leave the writing desk alone. Had she found anything in it? The caretaker is such a masterful man. She wants a beautiful hearse. A coffin must be black. Horses go with it.

Quicker and quicker came Therese's fears. Sometimes he had murdered his first wife, sometimes he had murdered her. She thought the skirt away from the corpse; the skirt confused her more than anything; she was sorry for the first wife, because he'd treated her skirt so badly. She was ashamed of the wretched funeral. She hated the bloodhound. People have no manners and school children don't get the cane often enough. Men ought to work more and woman can't cook these days. She could give them a piece of her mind. What's it got to do with the tenants? They all come and peep.

She devoured his words: a starving man with a piece of bread.

She listened so as not to be afraid. In a twinkling she fitted her own ideas to his sentences. So much thinking made her giddy. She wasn't used to such haste. She'd be proud of her cleverness, if she weren't half dead with fear. Ten times she nearly spoke out and said what he was: her fear of his thoughts forced her to remain silent. She tried to guess what was coming next: he took her by surprise. He was strangling her. She defended herself, she wasn't such a fool, was she, to wait till he'd choked the breath out of her? No, she'd got plenty of time; not till she was eighty she wouldn't die, in fifty years' time. Not before, Mr. Brute wanted it that way.

With a magniloquent gesture Kien concluded the peroration. He flung his arm aloft, a flagstaff without a flag. His body stretched itself, his joints jingled; sharp and clear he gathered his voice for the finale: 'Long live death!'

At this cry the Inspector woke up. Unwillingly he pushed the ties to one side, a whole trayful; he had selected the best. When would he find time to hoard them? He let them vanish, for happier hours.

'My friend,' he said, 'if I understand you rightly, you have got to death already. Would you mind repeating your story?'

The policemen nudged each other. He was in one of his moods. Therese's foot overstepped her circle. She must say something. The man with a memory saw his goal in sight. Not one word had he forgotten. He intended to repeat the whole story in place of the accused. 'He's tired already,' he said and shrugged a contemptuous shoulder at Kien, 'I'll tell you quicker!' Therese burst out: 'I ask you, he's murdering me.' In her fear, she spoke low. Kien heard her; he disallowed her. He would not turn round. Never! for what purpose? She was dead. Therese shouted: 'I ask you, I'm afraid!' The man with a memory, annoyed at the interruption, challenged her: 'What's biting you?' The father spoke soothingly: 'Nature has created women the weaker sex,' a motto he had derived from his son's last German composition. The Inspector drew out his mirror, gaped at himself and sighed: 'I'm tired too.' His nose eluded him; nothing interested him any longer. Therese screamed: 'I ask you, he must be put away!' Once again Kien resisted her voice; he would not turn round. But he groaned loud. The caretaker was sick of all the fuss. 'Professor!' he bellowed from behind, 'It's not so bad. We're all still alive. And no bones broken!' He couldn't relish death. That's how he was. With ponderous steps he strode forward. He intervened.

The Professor was a clever man. He had got it all out of those books.

He knew how to string sentences. A famous man and a heart of gold, what's more; but don't you believe a word he says. He's got no murder on no conscience. Where would he have the strength for it? He only says it because his wife's not up to him. Things like that are in books. He knows everything. He's frightened of a darning needle. His wife had soured him. She's a wicked old soul, the filthy bitch. She'd go with anyone. Fall on her back before you can say knife. He'll take his oath on it. The Professor hadn't been gone a week when she seduced him. He was a policeman, a caretaker as well, and retired. Name: Benedikt Pfaff. As long as he can remember, his house has been No. 24 Ehrlich Strasse. As for stealing, that woman had better shut her trap. The Professor married her out of pity, because she was the maid. Another man would have bashed her head in. Her mother died in the gutter. She'd been cautioned for begging. She hadn't a crust to her name. He knows because her daughter said so. Told him in bed. Talks enough for fifty. The Professor is innocent, as true as he's a retired policeman. He'll take it on himself. An organ of the law can take responsibility. At home in his little lodge he's got a real police station; his colleagues would be surprised: canaries and a peep-hole. Everyone ought to work; those who don't work come on the rates.

Astounded, they listened. His bellowing penetrated every brain. Even the proud father understood him. This was his own language, however much he admired his son's German composition. In the Inspector, too, the ashes of interest were rekindled. He conceded that the redhead might once have been in the police. No ordinary man would have stood forth, loud-voiced and unabashed, in this place. Again and again Therese sought to protest. Her words sounded feeble. She glided now to the left, now to the right, until she managed to lay hold of Kien's jacket. She tugged at it; he must turn round; he must tell them, was she a maid, or a housekeeper? She sought his help, she relied on him to indemnify her for her other man's abuse. He'd married her for love. Where was his love now? He may be a murderer, but at least he can speak. She won't be a maid. Thirty-four years she'd been a housekeeper. For a whole year she's been a respectable housewife. He must say something! He must be quick! Or she'll tell them his secret between six and seven!

Privately she had determined to tell on him, as soon as he had paid her her due, his love. He was the only one who heard her words. Against the colossal din, he heard her voice behind him, low, but as ever indignant. He felt her horny hand on his coat. Cautiously, he

322

hardly knew how, he drew in his backbone, twisted and turned his shoulders, slipped out of the sleeves, tweaked them softly down with his fingers and suddenly, after one last jerk, stood there without either his coat or Therese. Now he felt her no longer. If she clutched at his waistcoat he would do the same. In his thoughts he named neither Therese nor her mirage. He avoided her name and avoided the vision of her; but he knew what he was defending himself against.

The caretaker had finished his address. Without waiting for its effect, as there was no answer to it, he stepped between Therese and Kien, bellowed: 'Hold your tongue!' tore the jacket out of her hand and reinserted the Professor, as if he had been an infant. The Inspector mutely handed back the money and the papers. His eyes expressed regret at the misunderstanding, but he took back not a word of the successful examination. The man with a memory noticed numerous dubious details; in case of accidents, he took careful note of the red-head's story and counted up the various points it raised on his fingers. The policemen were all talking together. Each one vented his own opinion. One, who liked to deal in proverbs, said: 'Crimes come home to roost,' and the sentence was echoed in every heart. Therese's thirty-four years of housekeeping were lost in the babble of voices. She stamped her foot. The proud father, whom she reminded of one of his sisters-in-law — forbidden fruit — at length got her a hearing. Red as a turkey and in a shrieking voice, she vindicated herself in figures. Her husband would witness for her, and if he wouldn't, she'd fetch Mr. Brute of the furniture and upholstery firm of Brute & Wife. He'd only recently married. At 'married' her voice broke. But no one believed her. She stayed a common maid, and the proud father tried to make an assignation for that very night. The caretaker overheard and, before she could answer, confirmed it. 'She'd run to Brazil for a bit of fun,' he told his colleague jovially. America didn't sound far enough for him. Purring and radiant, he looked round the sub-station and discovered on the walls enlarged photographs of movements in Jiu-jitsu, 'In my time,' he bellowed, 'this was enough!' He clenched his massive fists and held them under the admiring noses of several colleagues at once. 'Ah, those were the days,' said the father, and tickled Therese under the chin. His boy would live to see better times. The Inspector looked Kien up and down. So this was a Professor, he had a feeling for the well-connected, they went round with money stuffed into their pockets like hay. Another man would have known how to dress himself properly. Instead of going about like a beggar. The world was unjust. Therese said to the father: 'If you please, but first I'm a housewife!' She knew, not a day over thirty, but she was deeply offended. Kien stared motionless at the Inspector and listened for the nearness or distance of her voice.

When the caretaker decided it was time to get a move on and affectionately took the Professor by the arm, he shook his head and clutched with astonishing strength at the table. They sought to disengage him, but the table came too. Then Benedikt Pfaff bellowed at Therese: 'Clear out, you filthy bitch! He can't relish that woman!' he added, turning to his colleagues. The father seized Therese, and pushed her out amid a shower of jokes. She was furious and whispered: later on he shouldn't give her a moment's rest. On the threshold she gathered what remained of her voice and shouted: 'A murder's nothing, I suppose! A murder's nothing!' Someone fetched her one on the mouth and she glided home at top speed. She would let in no murderer. Quickly she bolted the door, two bolts below, two bolts above, two in the middle; then she looked carefully to see if there were any burglars.

But ten policemen could not dislodge the Professor. 'She's gone,' the caretaker encouraged him, and tipped his square head in the direction of the door. Kien said nothing. The Inspector looked hard at his fingers. They were insistent; they were moving his table. If this went on he would soon be in an empty room. He stood up; his cushion had been moved too. 'Gentlemen!' he said, 'this won't do!' A round dozen policemen surrounded Kien and persuaded him kindly to let go of the table. 'The saints help those who help themselves,' one told him. The father promised him to drive all the bees out of his wife's bonnet that very night. 'You should only marry better-class people!' the man with a memory reassured him. He himself was only going to marry a wife with money, which was why he had none yet. The Inspector directed operations and thought: what do I get out of it? He yawned, and despised them all. 'Don't put me to shame, Professor!' bellowed Benedikt Pfaff, 'Come nice and quiet! We're going home now!' Kien stood firm.

But the Inspector had had enough of it. He commanded 'Out with him!' The twelve, until this moment merely persuasive, hurled themselves on the table and shook Kien off it, like a withered leaf. He did not fall. He remained alert. He would not be defeated. Instead of uttering useless words he pulled out his handkerchief and himself fastened it over his eyes. He drew the knots tight, until it hurt. His friend guided him by the arm, out into the street.

As soon as the doors had closed, the man with the memory laid a finger on his forehead and asserted: 'The real criminal was the fourth!' The sub-station decided from now on to keep a sharp eye on the lift-attendant of the Theresianum.

In the street the caretaker offered the Professor the hospitality of his little room. In his flat he might suffer annoyance; why expose himself to wrangling? He needed rest. 'Yes,' said Kien, 'I do not like the smell.' He would avail himself of the caretaker's offer until the flat had been cleaned.

CHAPTER X

THE BUTTON

In front of the Theresianum Fischerle, whose flight had proved success-ful, met with an unexpected reception. Instead of his employees, whose fate and whose garrulity he was anxious to forestall, a mass of excited people were pressing against the door. An old man, catching sight of him, wailed 'The cripple!' and ducked as quickly as his stiff limbs would allow him. He was afraid of the criminal, whom rumour had elevated into a dwarf of gigantic stature; when he ducked, he was about on a level with him. A woman took up the old man's feeble cry and made it loud. Then everyone heard it; the joy of wanting the same thing filled them all. 'The cripple!' echoed across the square, 'The cripple! The cripple!'

Fischerle said: 'Pleased to meet you!' and bowed. Among such a mass of people a mass of money might be made. Annoyed at the large sum he had had to put back in Kien's pocket, he hoped he might in-demnify himself here. His mind was still on his recent danger and he did not sense the new one. The delighted acclamation which his presence had aroused pleased him too. Thus would he step out of his chess palace in America. Music will strike up, the mob will shout, and he will be able to pick their pockets of all their dollars. The police would be on the look out, but look was about all they would do. Nothing could happen to him there. A millionaire's sacred. A hundred policemen will look on, and politely request him to help himself. Here the police didn't understand him so well. He had left them inside. There wouldn't be dollars; just small change. But he'd take anything.

As he surveyed the field, noted alleys through which he could slip, pockets at which he could reach, legs through which he could make his escape, the excitement of the crowd swelled menacingly. Everyone wanted his share in the robber who had taken the pearl necklace. Even the calmest lost control. What insolence to show his face among people who had recognized him. The men would pound him to powder. The women would raise him sky-high and then scratch him to pieces. Everyone was for utterly annihilating him, until nothing was left but a shameful blot, nothing else at all. But they had to see him first. For although thousands, inspired by him, were shrieking 'The cripple', those who had seen him numbered not more than a dozen. The road to the Helldwarf was paved with good fellow-beings. All wanted him, all panted for him. Anxious fathers lifted up their children. They might be trampled on, and they would learn something; two birds with one stone. Their neighbours took it ill that they thought of children at all at such a time. Many mothers had quite forgotten their children; they let them scream; they heard nothing, they only heard: 'The cripple!'

Fischerle found them too rowdy. Instead of 'Long live the world champion!' they were shouting 'The cripple!' And why the cripple should be cheered, he could not quite see. He was jostled on all sides. They ought to love him less and grudge him less. In this way, he'd never get anything. Someone crushed his fingers; someone else pushed him. He hardly knew which side his hump was. With one hand alone, stealing was too risky. 'Folks!' he screeched, 'you're too fond of me!' Only those nearest to him caught his words. His meaning not a soul understood. A shove taught him better, a kick convinced him. He had evidently started something, if only he could make out what. Had he been caught at it already? He looked at his free hand. No, it hadn't been in any pocket. He could never help picking up trifles; handkerchiefs, combs, mirrors. He used to take them and then throw them away for revenge. But this time, to his shame, his hand was empty. What were these people thinking of, to catch him at it when he wasn't? He hadn't taken a thing and now they were trampling on him. They hit him on top, they kicked him below, and of course the women were pinching his hump. It didn't hurt; these people didn't know the first thing about hitting; they could have learnt for nothing under the Stars of Heaven. But, because you never can tell, and apparent beginners often turn out at one blow to be experts, Fischerle began to wail piteously. Usually he croaked, but if he was put to it, at a time like the present for example, his voice sounded like a new-born child's. He also had the right persistence. A woman near by grew uneasy and looked round. Her child was at home. She was afraid it might have run after her and been trampled on. She sought it with eyes and ears in vain; clucked soothing noises, as she did over the pram, and in the end grew calm. The others weren't deceived into taking the murderer for a baby. They were afraid they would soon be pushed aside, so great was the crush, and they hurried. Their blows were less and less expert; more and more of them went wide. But newcomers joined the circle with the same intention. Altogether, Fischerle was far from satisfied. If he had wanted, escape would have been child's play. He had only to feel in his armpits and strew banknotes among them. Perhaps that was what they were aiming at. Of course — the hawker, the selfish brute, the snake in the grass, he must have worked the crowd up, and now they wanted his money. He pressed his arms close to his sides, indignant at the insolence which employees these days permit themselves towards their employers — but not to *him*, he'd throw the snake out on his ear, he'd give him the sack, he'd have done it anyway — and decided to sham dead. If these criminals searched his pockets, then he'd have proof of what they wanted. If they didn't, then they'd clear off, because he was dead.

But his plan was easier said than done. He took pains to fall down; the knees of the spectators held up his hump. His face was a death mask already, his crooked legs gave way, instead of his mouth, which was much too small, his nose breathed its last, his tightly closed eyes came open, stark and sightless. The preparations were premature, the plan ran aground on his hump. Fischerle heard the reproaches heaped upon him. It was a sin and a shame for the poor Baron. For a pearl necklace; as if it was worth it. The terrible shock to the young baroness. Poor woman, she'd never be the same again; no husband left. Maybe she'd marry again. No one could force her. A dwarf would get twenty years. Capital punishment ought to be re-introduced. Cripples ought to be exterminated. All criminals are cripples. No, all cripples are criminals. What's he got to look so silly for, like a hick come up for the day? Why can't he earn an honest penny. Taking bread out of people's mouths. What's he want with pearls, a cripple like him, and that Jew nose ought to be cut off. Fischerle was wild; all this talk of pearl necklaces, like blind men talking about colour! Ah, if he only had one.

Then suddenly the strangers' knees caved in, his hump was released, at long last he sank to the ground. With his sightless eyes he soon ascertained that they had abandoned him. Even while they were abusing him, the crush had seemed less. The cry: 'The cripple!' sounded even louder, but now in the direction of the church. 'There, look what you've done,' he said reproachfully, stood up and looked round at the few fans left to him. 'That's the one you want.' Their eyes followed his right hand, which indicated the church; with his left he rapidly gleaned three pockets, contemptuously threw away the comb, the only thing he found, and took to his heels.

Fischerle never discovered to whom he owed his miraculous escape.

At the accustomed place, in company with the others, the Fishwife had waited for him, and to her alone the waiting had seemed too long.

For the sewerman never noticed at all how long his employer was away. He could stand on his two feet for hours at a time, and think of nothing whatever. Time never passed too quickly or too slowly for him. All other men remained strangers to him, for they were either dawdling or hurrying. His wife called him, his wife sent him off to work, his wife received him home again. She was his clock and time of day. He felt at his best when he was drunk, because then time was abolished for other people too.

The blind man whiled away his waiting-time like a king. The large tip yesterday had gone to his head; he hoped for an even larger one to-day. Moreover he was soon going to retire from the firm of Siegfried Fischer and, with the large sums he had earned, establish an emporium. It must be of vast dimensions, say for ninety saleswomen. He'd make his own selection. None under thirteen stone stood a chance. He was the boss and could take on whom he liked. He paid the biggest salaries; he whisked away the heaviest ones from all competitors. Wherever a fat woman might be, she would be sure to hear the true rumour, at Johann Schwer's emporium you get the biggest pay. The proprietor, once a blind man, is a keen-eyed gentleman. He treats every single employee like his own wife. She can snap her fingers at other men and come to him. In his emporium you can buy everything: pommade, real tortoiseshell combs, hair nets, clean handkerchiefs, gent's hats, dog biscuits, dark glasses, pocket mirrors, anything you like. Not buttons. In the windows hang huge notices: NO BUTTONS SOLD HERE.

The hawker, on the other hand, was still hunting in the church for morphia drugs. Their proximity made him sleepy. At intervals he came across the secret parcel, but he knew he hadn't really got it, he was too clever.

All three men were silent.

The Fishwife alone expressed an increasing anxiety. Something's happened to Fischerle. He's not coming yet and he's such a little chap. He always does what he says. Five minutes, he said, he'd be back. There was an accident in the early papers this morning; she thought of Fischerle at once. Two steam engines ran into each other. One was killed on the spot. The other was taken to hospital, seriously injured. She'd better go and see. If he hadn't told her not to, she'd go. They've set on him because he's the chief. He makes a lot of money and carries it with him. She says, he's a big shot. His wife put them up to it, because he doesn't care for her. She's too old for him. Let him get a divorce, any girl under the Stars of Heaven would have him. It's black with people in front of the church. Fischerle must have been run over. She'll just go and have a look see. The others must stay where they are. He can create, proper. His eyes, she's frightened of them. He looks at her, she'd like to run away, she can't. What about the other three, he's the boss. They ought to be frightened too. Under the wheel he lies. His hump is squashed. Fischerle's lost his chessboard. He's looking for it in the Theresianum because he's the world champion. Then he gets in a rage and gets excited. She'll have him ill yet. She'll have to nurse him. This very morning she felt it in her bones. It was in the papers. He never reads them any more. Now she'll go see; now she'll go see.

After every sentence she stopped, and anxiously wrinkled her brow. She walked up and down, waggled her hump, and when she had collected up some more words, went up to her colleagues and whispered them loudly. She could tell that they were all as worried as she was. Not even the blind man said a word, and he knew how to talk when he was in a good temper. All by herself she wanted to look for Fischerle and was afraid the others would come after her. 'I'll be back at once!' she called two or three times as she made off, the further the louder. The men didn't budge; in spite of her fears, she was overjoyed. She would find Fischerle. He must not fret himself about his employees on top of his other fearful misfortunes. He had told them, they were to wait.

Softly she crept round to the square in front of the church. She had long since got round the corner; instead of hurrying, she slackened her naturally minute footsteps and twisted her little head anxiously, backwards. If the hawker or the sewerman or that button-fellow followed her, she'd stop dead, just like the car which had run over Fischerle, and say: 'I'm only looking.' When they went back she would move again. Sometimes she waited a minute: she thought she'd seen a pair of trousers behind the church, but there weren't any, so she crept on. Not for a long time had she seen so many people together. If everyone bought a paper she'd have money for a week. But the whole bundle was lying under the Stars of Heaven; she had no time for papers to-day because she'd got her job with Fischerle. He paid twenty schillings a day, of his own accord, he would have it that way because it was a big firm. She hid herself, so as to find him; she made herself even smaller; somewhere on the ground he'd be lying. She heard his voice. Why couldn't she see him? She stroked the ground with her hand. 'He's not as small as all that,' she whispered and shook her head. She was already in the midst of the crowd, and because she was stooping nothing but her hump could be seen. How would she ever find him among all these big people? All crushed her at once; they must be crushing him too; Fischerle had been crushed to death, they must let him go! He can't breathe, he suffocates, it'll be the end of him!

Suddenly somebody shrieks next to her: 'The cripple!' and hits her on the hump. Others shriek too, others hit her. The crowd falls upon her, they had been too far off to hit Fischerle, they pay with interest now. The Fishwife falls to the ground. She lies on her belly and keeps quite still. They mess her up terribly. They go for the hump, but hit her everywhere. From all over the place the crowd gathers together round her. No doubt about the genuineness of the hump. The crowd breaks over it. As long as she can, the Fishwife trembles for Fischerle's fate and gasps: 'He's all I've got in the world.' Then she loses consciousness.

All was well with Fischerle. Behind the church he found, of his four employees, three waiting for him; the Fishwife was not there. 'Where is she?' he asked and held out his hand, flat, just at the height of his stomach. He meant the little one. 'Absconded,' answered the hawker promptly; he slept light. 'Of course,' said Fischerle, 'a woman; she can't wait; she's got something to do; she's busy; she's lost her money, she's ruined, all women are abortions.' 'You leave my women alone, Mr. Fischerle!' interjected the blind man, threateningly. 'My women aren't abortions. Speak civil.' He almost began to describe his emporium. One glance at his competitors convinced him of a cleverer way. 'At my place, buttons are prohibited, by order of the police!' he said, merely, and fell silent. 'Gone,' mouthed the sewerman. This powerful response, at length formulated, referred back to Fischerle's first question.

But the chief composed his face in perturbed folds. His head sank on his bosom and his wide-open eyes filled with tears. Disconsolately he gazed from one to the other and said nothing. With his right hand he smote, not his forehead, but his nose, and his crooked legs trembled as violently as his voice when at length he spoke. 'Gentlemen,' he whispered, 'I'm a ruined man. My partner has' — a spasm of indignation shook his expressive body — 'cheated me. Tell you what — he's stopped payment and taken my money to the police! The sewerman's my witness!' He paused for confirmation. The sewerman nodded, however, only after some minutes. In the interval the emporium collapsed, burying ninety saleswomen. The church fell in and whatever dangerous drugs were inside it, or ought to have been inside it, were destroyed. Sleep could no longer be thought of. When the debris was cleared away, they found in the cellars of the emporium a colossal collection of buttons.

Fischerle accepted the sewerman's affirmation and said: 'We're all ruined. You've lost your jobs and I've broken my heart. I thought of you at once. All my money's gone west and there's a summons out against me for unregistered trading. In a day or two the summons'll be delivered; you'll see, I've got it on good authority. I'll have to hide. Who knows where I'll turn up again, may be in America. If I'd only the passage money! But I'll make a getaway somehow. A chess player like me is never lost. Only I'm anxious about you. The police may snap you up. Two years hard labour for aiding and abetting. You help a fellow just because you're good friends, and the next thing is, two years in clink; why, just because you couldn't hold your tongue? Tell you what, you mustn't go to gaol! You be careful now, don't say a word. 'Where's Fischerle?' ask the police. 'We haven't an idea,' say you. 'You were employed by him?' 'Where then?' say you. 'Certain rumours have reached our ears!' 'Permit me, all rumours are false.' 'When did you last see Fischerle?' 'The day he disappeared from the Stars; may be his wife'd know the date.' You tell them a real date, they'll get the wrong impression. You tell them no date at all, and they'll ask the wife: she can go to the police for her husband once in a while, it'll do her no harm. 'What business was done by the firm of Siegfried Fischer & Co.' 'How would we know that, Chief Inspector.' You've hardly started denying everything and already they'll let you go. Stop, I've got a grand idea! Something you've never heard before! You needn't go to the police at all, not at all! The police'll leave you in peace, they won't bother you, they won't express the least interest, you might as well not exist for them, you'll be disembodied, how shall I explain it? How's it done? Easy; you just hold your tongues. Don't breathe a word, not to a soul, not in all Heaven! Tell you what, how'd anyone think up a crazy idea that you'd had anything to do with me? Out of the question, I tell you, and you're safe. You go off to work as if nothing had happened. You go hawking and have your insomnia; you give your wife three-quarters of your pay and clean up the muck, I tell you, even a sewerman has his uses, what would a huge great town like this do with all that muck lying around; and you go off begging, you've got your dog and your dark glasses. If anyone gives you a button, you look away, if they don't give you a button, look at them. Buttons'll be your undoing, look out, you'll murder someone yet! *That's* what you must do; I've nothing for myself, but I'm advising every one of you for your own good! I'd like to have my money's worth for this advice; give away everything, I do, because I've got a soft spot for you!'

Excited and moved, Fischerle sought in his trouser pockets. His distress at his own ruin had fled; he had worked himself into a heat as he spoke and forgot the immensity of the disaster so far as it affected him personally. He was the embodied Helping Hand; far more than with his own fate, was he concerned with that of his friends. He knew how empty his pockets were. He turned the torn lining of the left-hand one inside out; in the right-hand one he found to his amazement a schilling and a button. He drew out both — no good spoiling the ship for a ha'porth of tar — and croaked, ecstatic: 'I'll share my last schilling with you! Four employees and the chief; that's five in all. Twenty groschen each. I'll keep the Fishwife's for her, because the schilling's mine. Maybe I'll meet her. Who's got change?' After complicated calculations — for no one had a whole schilling in change — the share-out was at least partially accomplished. The hawker got the schilling and gave up his sixty groschen. In return he contracted a debt of twenty groschen to the sewerman, who had nothing to give to his wife and therefore had not the smell of a pennypiece about him. Out of the hawker's change, the blind man took his single, and Fischerle his double portion. 'You can laugh!' said Fischerle, who was the only one laughing. 'I can make myself small with twenty groschen in my pocket; you've got your work; rich, you are! But I've got my pride; I'm like that. I'd like everyone in the Stars of Heaven to say: Fischerle's gone, but he had a noble mind!'

'Where shall we find another chess champion?' wailed the hawker, 'now I'm the only champion, at cards.' In his pocket the heavy schilling danced lightly. The blind man stood there motionless; he had closed his eyes from habit, he was still holding his hand out from habit. His portion, two nickel pieces, lay on it, heavy and stiff, like their new master. Fischerle laughed: 'Another champion, at cards!' It seemed comical to him that the world chess champion should be talking to such people, a sewerman with a wife and family, a hawker with insomnia, a suicide on account of buttons. He noticed the out-stretched hand, quickly put the button in it and shook himself with

333

laughter. 'Good-bye all!' he crowed, 'and be good, folks, be good!' The blind man opened his eyes and saw the button; he had sensed something and wanted to convince himself of the opposite. Shocked to death he stared after him. Fischerle turned round and called: 'Good-bye, till we meet in a better world, dear friend, don't take it to heart!' Then he hurried off, the fellow was just the kind who mightn't see a joke. In a side street he had his laugh out because men are such fools. He slipped into a doorway, put his hands under his hump, and swayed to left and right. His nose ran, the nickel pieces jingled, his hump ached, he hadn't laughed so much in all his life; he laughed for at least a quarter of an hour. Before he went on, he wiped his nose on the wall, poked it into his armpits and sniffed once at each. Stowed in there was his capital.

A few streets further he was seized with grief at his heavy business losses. Not that he was ruined, but 2000 schillings are a fortune and precisely that sum had been left behind with the book racket. The police were as good as useless. They merely interrupted business affairs. What can a wretched state official, with his measly monthly pay and no capital, with nothing to do but to watch, know of the transactions undertaken by a really big firm? He, Fischerle, for instance, was not ashamed to crawl about on the floor and pick up the money which his client owed him and had thrown down in a fit of rage. Maybe he'd get a kick or two but he made nothing of that. He must watch out, how to shove a foot out of his way, two feet, four feet, all the feet, he the chief, in person: the money was dirty and crumpled, not fresh out of the bank, a non-professional might hesitate to touch it — but he took it. Not that he hadn't employees, four at a time, he could have taken on eight — not sixteen, though — of course he could have ordered them about! 'Pick up the filthy money, my men!' But he wouldn't take the risk. People think of nothing but stealing; their heads are full of stealing and not a man but thinks himself an artist if he can make away with a scrap of it. The chief is the chief because he relies on no one but himself. That's what you call taking a risk. So he picked up eighteen beautiful hundred schilling notes, only two were missing, he almost had them, he sweated and struggled, he told himself, what do I get out of all this; and then the police came at the wrong moment. He was terrified, he couldn't stand the police, he was fed up with them, miserable wretches; he pushed the money into his client's pocket, the money which this client owed to him, Fischerle, and ran away. What did the police do? Kept the money themselves. They might have left it with his client; perhaps better times would come and Fischerle could fetch it again, but no, they found the book racket *non compos*. A person like the book racket, they said, with so much money and so little brain, might be set on and robbed; then there'd be trouble. We've got enough to do, so let's keep the money for ourselves, and sure enough they do. The police steal, and they expect you to keep yourself respectable.

In the midst of his rage, a policeman whom he happened to pass, fixed Fischerle with a penetrating stare. When he had put a reasonable distance between them, he gave his hatred free rein. That was the last straw; these thieves would stop him going to America! He determined — even before his departure — to avenge himself on the police for the infringement of property rights which they had perpetrated against him. Most of all he would have liked to pinch the lot of them till they squealed. He was convinced they were sharing their ill-gotten gains among themselves. There are, let's say, two thousand police; each would get a whole schilling. Not one would say: 'No! I won't touch the money, because it is stolen goods!' as good policemen ought. Each was as guilty as his neighbour and not one of them would be allowed to get away without a pinch.

'Don't you go believing that it hurts them!' he said suddenly out loud. 'You're here and they're there. What do they know of your pinching?' Instead of taking action which he had thought out for his journey, he hobbled for hours through the town, aimless, exasperated, looking for some means to punish the police. Usually he would hit upon a good plan at once for the least intention; but here he could think of nothing and therefore began gradually to renounce his harsher intentions. He was ready even to forego the money if he could contrive some vengeance. He would sacrifice two thousand schillings net! He wouldn't touch them, not at a gift, but someone must take them away from the police!

It was long past noon, he couldn't eat for hate, when suddenly his eye fell on two large brass plates on a single house. One of them read: Dr. ERNEST FLINK, Gynaecologist. The other, immediately below, belonged to a Dr. MAXIMILIAN BUCHER, Specialist in Nervous Diseases. 'A silly woman could have everything she wanted all at once,' he thought and suddenly remembered Kien's brother in Paris, who had made his fortune as a gynaecologist and then turned to psychiatry. He looked for the slip of paper on which he had written down the address of this famous Professor, and found it, sure enough, in his coat pocket. The letter of recommendation had to go to Paris — that was too far, and while he was getting there the police would have blued all the money. If he wrote a letter himself and signed it with his name, the grand gentleman would ask himself: 'Fischerle! Who's Fischerle?' and nothing would come of it. For he had amassed a fortune and was shockingly proud. A Professor and a fortune in one, you needed subtlety to handle that. It wasn't like life, it was like chess. If he knew for certain whether the Professor was interested in chess he could sign 'Fischerle, World Chess Champion'. But a man like that was quite capable of not believing it. In two months, when Fischerle had knocked Capablanca into a cocked hat, annihilated and smashed him like a beaten dog, then he would send a telegram to all the outstanding people in the world: 'Have the honour respectfully to introduce myself, the new World Chess Champion, Siegfried Fischer.' Then there'd be no room for doubt, then everyone would know, all the people would bow to him, even wealthy Professors, whoever doubted it would be brought to court for defamation; and sending a real telegram, that was a thing all his life he'd wanted to do.

And so his revenge took shape. He stepped into the next post office and asked for three telegraph forms, quickly please, it's urgent. He knew all about forms. He had often bought a handful, they were cheap; and in his gigantic letters had written derisive challenges to whoever was world champion at the time. Grandiose phrases like: 'I despise you. A cripple,' or 'Take me on, if you dare, you abortion!' he would read aloud under the Stars of Heaven and complain of the cowardice of world champions, from whom not a single answer had ever been received. Though his audience believed a lot, they did not believe in the telegrams; he hadn't enough money to send off even one; so they teased him about the address, which he must have left out or copied down wrong. A good old Catholic promised him to throw down the letters which St. Peter would be keeping for him as soon as he had reached the real heaven above. 'If they knew what a genuine telegram I'm sending now!' thought Fischerle and smiled over the jokes which the poor wretches had permitted themselves with him. What had he been then? A daily visitor to that wretched hole, the Stars of Heaven. And what is he now? A person who sends a telegram to a Professor. The only question is, what are the right sort of words? Better suppress his own name. Let's put: 'Brother gone crackers. A friend of the family.' The first form looks well, filled in; the question is, will 'crackers' make the right impression on a psychiatrist? They experience such things daily, and may think: 'It can't be bad', and wait until the friend of the family telegraphs again. But Fischerle can't waste money that way, secondly he hasn't stolen it, thirdly it'd take too long. He eliminates the 'friend of the family', it sounds too devoted, raises too many expectations; and he strengthens 'crackers' with 'completely'. On the second form appears: 'Brother gone completely crackers.' But who is to sign it? No one in a settled position would bother about a telegram without a signature. There are libels, blackmail and similar professions; a retired gynaecologist knows the seamy side. Fischerle has one form left; annoyed at the two spoiled ones he scratches, deep in thought, on the third: 'Am completely crackers.' He reads it over and is delighted. If a person writes that of himself, you've got to believe him, because who'd write that of himself? He signs 'Your brother' and runs, with the successful form, to the counter.

The official, carved in dry wood, shakes his head. This can't be serious and he has no time for jokes. 'You've got to take it!' Fischerle insists. 'Are *you* paid to take it, or am I?' Suddenly he is afraid that people with a record mayn't hand in telegrams. But how does the official know him? Certainly not from Heaven, and he never used to get his forms here.

'It doesn't make sense!' says the man and hands the telegram back. The other's deformity gives him courage. 'A normal person wouldn't write that.'

'That's right!' shrieks Fischerle, 'that's why I'm sending my brother a telegram. He's to come and fetch me! I'm mad!'

'Be off with you and quick now!' the official flares up; he was almost spitting.

A fat person in two fur coats, one natural, one artificial, waiting behind Fischerle, finds the waste of time enraging, hurls the dwarf to one side, threatens the official with a complaint and closes his speech — the weight of a bulging note case behind each word — with the sentence: 'You have no right to refuse a telegram, understand? Who are you?'

The official is silenced, swallows his right to understand and does his duty. Fischerle does him out of a penny. The fat gentleman, who had helped the dwarf on principle and not because he was in a hurry, draws his attention to the error. 'You've a nerve!' says Fischerle and escapes. Outside he thinks they may hold up his telegram as a punishment for his cheating. 'For a penny, Fischerle,' he thinks reproachfully, 'when your telegram cost you 27 times as much!' He turns back, excuses himself effusively to the fat gentleman, he had misunderstood him, he hears badly, he's mad in his right ear. He says a bit more so as to draw closer, if only in thought, to the other's note case. At precisely the right moment he remembers his unhappy experiences of people in double fur coats. They keep you at a distance and before you can get anything from them they hand you over to the police. He pays his penny, magnanimously says good-bye to all and makes off. He renounces the note case for his revenge is on the way.

To provide himself with a false passport, he sought out a café not far from the Stars of Heaven but much below. It was called The Baboon, and its bestial name alone indicated the kind of monsters who flocked thither. Not one but had done time. A person like the sewerman with a steady job and a good record avoided The Baboon. His wife, as he used to say under the Stars of Heaven, would have divorced him if she'd smelt The Baboon about him. There was no Capitalist to patronize it, nor a chess champion who could beat everyone. Here, first one client might win, and then another. A head to command victory was wholly lacking. The place was in a cellar; you went down eight steps before finding the door. Part of the broken panes was pasted over with paper. On the wall hung pornographic women. The landlady of the Stars would never have tolerated that in her respectable café. The table tops were of wood; little by little all the marble had been stolen. The late proprietor had taken pains to attract people in regular work. For each better-class guest brought in by one of the ladies she got a black coffee for nothing. At that time he had a beautiful new signboard painted and called his café, 'For a Change'. His wife said the signboard applied to her too and changed lovers all the time, so that he died of grief because he had appendicitis and his business was going to pieces. Hardly was he dead than his wife asserted: 'I prefer a Baboon.' She put out the old signboard again and .that was the end of the little bit of respectability the place had got. This woman abolished the free black coffee, and since then not a single lady with any self-respect crossed the threshold of the cellar. Who came then? Forgers, tramps, undesirables, and on-the-runs, low type Jews and, even dangerous riff-raff. Occasionally a policeman came into the Stars; here not one dared. For the arrest of a robber-and-murder case, who felt safe with the landlady of The Baboon, precisely eight detectives were detailed. That was how they did things here. An ordinary pimp wouldn't have felt safe. Only serious criminals were respected. A hunchback with an intellect, or a hunchback without, it was all one to them. Those kind of people see no difference, because they're stupid themselves. The Stars refused all intercourse with The Baboon. Once you allowed these people in, the best marble tops soon vanished. When the last wretch under the Stars had finished with the illustrated papers, they went to the landlady of The Baboon, not a moment sooner.

Fischerle was through with the Stars but compared to The Baboon it was Heaven indeed. As he came in several wanted men leapt towards him. From all sides they applauded him with satisfaction and demonstrated their joy at the unusual visitor. The landlady had just popped out for a minute, how pleased she will be. They assumed he had come straight from Heaven. That place, blessed by the presence of innumerable women, they were not allowed to enter. They asked after this lady and that; Fischerle lied as quickly as he could. He put on no side and behaved genially; he did not want to spend a penny too much on his forged passport. He hesitated with his request so as not to put the price up. After they had convinced themselves that it was really him, they clapped a little longer; one's own hands often strengthen conviction. He must take a seat, now he was there, he must stay. A fine little dwarf like him they wouldn't let go so soon. Had the Stars of Heaven fallen in yet? Catch any of them going under that dangerous roof. The police ought to see to it and get it mended! All those women who used to come there — where would they run to if the roof fell in?

While they tried to persuade Fischerle to do something about it, a piece of plaster fell into the black coffee which someone had set before him. He drank and expressed his regret that he had so little time to spare. He had come to say good-bye. The Chess League at Tokio had offered him a place as chess inspector. 'Tokio is in Japan. I go the day after to-morrow. The journey takes six months. For me, that is. I'm playing a match in every town. To cover my expenses. I shall get my passage money, but not till I get to Tokio. The Japs are suspicious. Look, they say, if we send the money first, he won't come. Not that I'd do that, but they've been caught that way. Once bit ... In their letter it says: 'We entertain, most honourable champion, the utmost confidence in you. But did we steal our money? We did not!'

The others wanted to see the letter. Fischerle excused himself. The police had it. They'd promised him a passport in spite of his many previous convictions. His homeland was proud of the fame which he'd carry out to Japan on his chessboard.

'And you're going the day after to-morrow?' six voices spoke together and the rest thought in chorus. They loved him although he came from Heaven, because his credulousness went to their hearts. 'You'll never get anything out of the police, as true as I was down for nine years!' one of them asserted. 'You'll be locked up too, for desertion!' 'And then they'll write your record to Japan.'

Fischerle's eyes filled with tears. He pushed his coffee cup away and began to sob. 'I'll knife those robbers!' they could hear, in between times, 'I'll knife them all!' Some of them were sorry for him; they had a variety of experience, and as many opinions. A famous forger asserted, there was *one* way out: himself. Fischerle could pay half-price because he was only half a man. In this witticism he disguised his sympathy. Not one of them would have spoken a sympathetic word. Fischerle smiled through his tears. 'I know you're a famous man,' he said, 'but you've never made out a passport for Japan, not even you!'

The forger, Passport Joe by name, a man with flowing locks, pitch black, a broken-down painter who, from his artist days, had still preserved his vanity, blazed up and snarled: 'My passes are valid as far as America!'

Fischerle permitted himself to remark that America was not Japan by a long way. He wasn't going to be used as a guinea pig. All of a sudden at the Japanese frontier he'd be picked up and locked up. He wasn't curious to see the inside of a Japanese jail, not curious at all. They talked to him persuasively but he wouldn't hear of it. The men brought up impressive arguments. Passport Joe had often done time, but his clients never; he took so much trouble with other people. He put everything he had into his art; he locked himself in to do the job. Every passport took so much out of him, he had to have a long sleep. They were not mass produced. Each was drawn line by line. Anyone who peeped got his block knocked off. Fischerle didn't deny it, but he was adamant. Besides, he hadn't got a brass farthing. All this talk was therefore useless. Passport Joe declared himself ready to present him gratis with a first quality special passport if he would only undertake to make use of it. He could reimburse him by advertising the masterpiece when he got to Japan. Fischerle thanked him; he was too small for them to have their little jokes with, they were as strong as giants, he was as feeble as an old woman. Let somebody else burn their silly fingers. They stood him another two black coffees. Passport Joe raged. Fischerle must let him make him a passport or he'd smash his face for him twice over! The others managed to restrain him for the time being; but all of them were exasperated on his account and took his part. Negotiations dragged themselves out for an hour. Joe took each of his friends aside separately and promised them handsome payment. Then their patience gave way. They told Fischerle in so many words that he was their prisoner and would only get his liberty on one condition. The condition was that he would accept and use a forged passport for which he would have to pay nothing as he had no money, anyway. Fischerle yielded to force. But he went on whining. Two heavy-weights accompanied him to the photographer where his picture was taken at the expense of Passport Joe. Let him stir an inch it would be the worse for him. He didn't stir. His escort waited until the plate was developed and printed.

When they got back Passport Joe had already locked himself in. No one was to interrupt him. His most trusted friend pushed the damp photographs in through the crack in the door. He was working like a man possessed. Beads of sweat ran down his streaming hair on to the table and endangered the cleanliness of the passport. But thanks to the dexterous movements of his head it remained unblemished. He took his greatest pleasure in the signatures. He had at his command the official style and the angular pedantry of every single high ranking police officer. His signatures alone were masterpieces. He accompanied their curves with fiery motions of his torso. To the air of a popular song he hummed the words 'How original!' How original! Never done so well before!'

When he succeeded so well with the signature that it would have taken even him in, he would keep the passport as a souvenir and excuse himself to the waiting client, whom his imagination dragged into the little workshop, with his favourite proverb: 'Every man his own neighbour.' He had several dozen of these sample masterpieces. A little suitcase contained them. When business was bad he would travel with his collection to neighbouring towns. There he would show them off. Veterans of his trade, competitors and pupils were all alike ashamed at their own incapacity. They would send difficult orders straight to him without asking for any commission. To ask for one indeed would have been no better than suicide. He had friends among the strongest and most respected criminals, each of them a king in his profession, but together the ordinary clients of The Baboon. But the disorderliness of Passport Joe had a limit: among the passports in his collection he placed small square tickets, on each the inscription could be read: 'Doing well as dollar prince in America' or 'Owner sends best wishes from South Africa, land of diamonds' or 'Diving for pearls, thanks to Passport Joe' or 'Why don't you come to Mecca? Here the world throws money out at the window. Allah is Great.' These facts the proprietor selected from letters of appreciation which haunted him in his deepest sleep. They were too valuable for him to show them; their contents alone must suffice, facts speak for themselves. For this reason, after every finished document he drank several glasses of rum, dropped his burning head on to the table, parted his flowing hair with his fingers and dreamed of the future and the deeds of the client in question. Not one of them had yet written to him but he knew from his dreams what they would have written and made use of their careers for the purpose of advertisement. While he was working for Fischerle he was thinking of the admiration which his passport would provoke in Japan. *This* land was new to him, he had not ventured so far before. He completed two samples at once. The first of these which succeeded inimitably he decided to make an exception of and to hand over to his client. His mission was after all of exceptional importance.

In the meantime Fischerle was being treated to whatever titbits the meagre buffet of The Baboon could afford. He was given two old smoked sausages all to himself, a portion of stinking cheese and as much stale bread as he wanted, ten cigarettes of The Baboon brand, although he didn't smoke, three small glasses of the *Fin de la Maison*, a tea and rum, a rum without tea, and innumerable pieces of advice for the journey. He must beware of pickpockets. People would do anything to get a passport like the one he was going to have. Some forger or other might easily nip out the photograph, put in another and keep the loveliest passport for the rest of his life. He must be careful not to show it off too much, for the railway station would be alive with envious people. And he must write and tell them his news, somewhere or other Passport Joe had a secret *poste restante* and he was always delighted to receive any testimonial; he treasured them just as the landlady of The Baboon treasured her love letters: no one had ever been allowed to see one. Anyway who would notice from a letter that the writer was a mere hunchback?

Fischerle promised everything; he wouldn't be stingy with thanks, appreciation, news and gratitude. All the same, he was afraid. He couldn't help his shape. Now if only he were called Dr. Fischer instead of plain Fischer the police would respect him at once.

At this all the men in The Baboon called a council. Only one was left on guard by the door to see that the dwarf didn't escape. They took it upon themselves to interrupt their friend at his work in spite of his strict prohibition and to request that he would bestow the title of doctor on Fischerle. If they were polite and called him 'Maestro', Passport Joe wouldn't go wild at once. On this point they were agreed, but not one of them volunteered to carry the message. For if he should go wild whoever interrupted him would certainly not get the commission he had promised, and none of them was fool enough to risk that.

At this moment the landlady came back from her shopping. She liked walking the streets mostly for love, but at times when she wanted to prove to her clients that she was a woman too, for money. The men cheerfully took advantage of her return to break up their meeting. They forgot their intentions and looked on deeply moved as the landlady embraced Fischerle's hump. She overwhelmed him with words of affection; she'd been longing to see him, longing for his dainty little nose, his crooked little legs, she'd longed for his darling, darling chessboard. She'd no dwarfies in her place. She'd heard that the Capitalist, his wife, had grown even fatter. How that woman ate, was it true? Fischerle made no answer and looked steadily in front of him. She fetched her pile of old periodicals of which she was proud — all of them came from Heaven — and laid them in front of her darling. Fischerle never opened one of them and remained obdurate. What was in his dear little heart, such a dear little heart the little darling had; she traced on her palm a circle about a quarter its size.

Until he was made a doctor, said Fischerle, he would be afraid.

The men grew restless. They tried to talk him out of their cowardice. You can't be a doctor they bellowed altogether, cripples can't be doctors. A cripple and a doctor, it can't be done. That would be a fine sight! A doctor has to have a good record. A cripple is a bad record, that goes without saying. Did he know a single cripple who was a doctor or did he not?

'I know one,' said Fischerle, 'I know one. He's smaller than I am, he hasn't any arms, he hasn't any legs. It's a crying shame only to look at him. He writes with his mouth and reads with his eyes. And he's a famous doctor.'

This made little impression on the men. 'That's different altogether,' said one speaking for the rest, 'he must have been a doctor first and then his arms and legs were run over and lost. So it wasn't his fault.'

343

'Nonsense,' screeched Fischerle, outraged by these lies. 'He was born that way I tell you. I know what I'm talking about, he came into the world without arms and legs. You're all asses. I'm clever I am, he said to himself, why then shouldn't I be a doctor? So he sat himself down and he studied. Ordinary people study five years, cripples have to go on for twelve. He told me himself, he's a friend of mine, at thirty he was a doctor and famous. I play chess with him, he just looks at you and you're well again. His waiting-room's full to bursting. He sits on his little wheel-chair and has two lady secretaries to help him. They help the patients undress, tap their chests and show them to the doctor. All he does is to take one sniff at them and he knows what's wrong at once. Then he calls out 'The next gentleman, please!' The fellow earns a fortune, there isn't another doctor like him. He's very fond of me, he says cripples must stick together; I'm taking lessons from him. He'll turn me into a doctor he's promised. But I'm not to tell anyone because people wouldn't understand. I've known him for ten years, another two years and I'm through with my studies. Then along comes this letter from Japan and I throw the whole thing up. I'd like to go and say good-bye to him for the fellow deserves it, but I don't trust myself. He might try to hold me back and then I'd lose my job in Tokio. I can go abroad on my own. I'm not such a cripple as he is, not by a long way!'

Several of them asked him to show them the man. They were already half convinced. Fischerle poked his nose into his waistcoat pocket and said: 'Sorry, I haven't got him with me to-day. Usually I keep him there! It's too bad!'

Everyone laughed; their heavy arms and fists shook on the tables and because they were glad to laugh and seldom had the opportunity, they got up all of them, forgot their fear and stampeded, eight strong, to the little room where Passport Joe was working. All together so that no one should bear the blame alone they flung open the door and yelled in chorus: 'Don't forget to make him a doctor! He's been studying ten years already!' Passport Joe nodded, 'All the way to Japan'. He was in a good mood to-day.

Fischerle began to realize how drunk he was. Usually spirits made him sad. But to-day he jumped up — his passport and his new rank of doctor were as good as in his pocket — and clutching round the stomach of the landlady of The Baboon, danced her round the café. His long arms crawled snakelike round her neck, they could reach far. He croaked, she waddled. A murderer (but no one knew), pulled an enormous comb out of his pocket, folded over it a piece of tissue paper and blew a soft melody. Out of love for the landlady another one, a simple housebreaker, inexactly stamped out the rhythm. The others slapped their powerful thighs. A delicate tinkling came from the broken glass panel of the door. Fischerle's legs twisted themselves up still more and the landlady gazed with enchantment at his nose. 'Such a long way!' she shrieked. 'Such a long way!' This her biggest and most beloved nose was going to leave her, was going to go all the way to Japan! The murderer went on playing and thinking about her, they all knew her intimately and they all owed her a lot. Inside Passport Joe chanted sweetly, his tenor voice was popular and he looked forward to celebrating the evening; he had been working for three hours, in another he would surely have done. All the men were singing but none of them knew the right words for the song, so that each one sang his own heart's desire. 'The winning number,' hummed one and another breathed, 'Sweetheart'. 'A nugget like a football' was what the third wanted and the fourth an unending opium pipe. 'Good morning, boys!' somebody was humming under a moustache. In his youth the moustache's proprietor had been a schoolmaster and he was sorry for the pension he had lost. But mostly there were threats and all of them would have liked to emigrate, each on his own, just to show the others. Fischerle's head sank lower and lower; his own accompaniment to the song 'Checkmate, checkmate' was lost in the general din.

Suddenly the landlady put her finger to her mouth and breathed: 'He's asleep, he's asleep!' Five of the men placed him carefully on a chair in the corner and shouted: 'Quiet there, stop the music, Fischerle must have his sleep out before his long journey!' The tissue paper folded over the comb fell silent. They all gathered together and began to discuss the perils of the journey to Japan. One of them battered on the table and said threateningly that in the desert of Takla Makan every second traveller died of thirst; it lay just in the middle between Constantinople and Japan. Even the erstwhile schoolmaster had heard of it and said: 'That's right.' The journey by sea was preferable. The dwarf could surely swim and even if he couldn't he would float on his hump, fat as it was. He would be unwise to land anywhere. He'd be passing India. Cobras lie in wait all along the quay side. Half a bite and he'd be dead because he was only half a man.

Fischerle wasn't asleep. He had remembered his capital and in his corner he was searching round to see where it had got to during the dancing. He found it again in its right place; he applauded his armpits, how splendidly they were made, with any other man the glorious treasure would long have slid down into his trousers or the floor would have eaten it up. He wasn't in the least tired, on the contrary he was listening and as those idiots talked of all sorts of foreign countries and cobras he was thinking of America and of his millionaire's palace.

Late in the evening, it was already dark, Passport Joe appeared from his little room waving a passport in each hand. All the men were silent; they respected his work because he paid generously for it. Softly he crept up to the dwarf, laid the passports before him on the table and woke him up with a shattering blow on the ear. Fischerle saw it coming but stayed still. He must pay something, that was evident, and he was only happy that nobody had suggested searching him. 'You must advertise me!' yelled Passport Joe, he was reeling and babbling. During the last few hours he had grown drunk on his Japanese fame. He stood the dwarf on the table and made him swear with both hands:

That he would use the passport, that he would pay nothing for it, that he would hold it under the noses of the Japs, that he would tell them that he, Rudoph Amsel, known as Passport Joe, was what — after his death — all of Europe would know, namely the greatest living painter. That he would talk of him daily. That he would give interviews about him. He could give the date and place of his birth and say that he had been unable to tolerate any art school; independent and on his own feet, without crutches and without idols, integrity incarnate, he had risen to the heights on which he now stood.

Fischerle swore and swore. Passport Joe forced him to repeat word for word every phrase which he uttered in his screaming voice. Last of all, Fischerle was solemnly to abjure Heaven and never more to cross the threshold of that haunt of criminals before his departure. 'Heaven is a filthy hole!' cried Fischerle, obsequious and hoarse. 'I'll take great care not to get mixed up with them and in Japan I'll found a sister firm for The Baboon! If I earn too much money I'll send it to you. But don't you go telling Heaven anything about my journey. Those jail-birds there are just the kind who'll put the police on me. To please you I'll take the false passport on my own hunchback and swear that you didn't force it on me. Heaven can go to hell!' After this he was allowed to sit down and sleep again in his same corner. He hopped down from the table and put the better passport in his pocket next to his miniature chessboard, which was the safest place for it. First he snored for fun so as to overhear them. But soon he was really asleep,

his arms folded tightly over his chest, his fingertips in his armpits so
that the very slightest attempt at robbery would wake him at once.

At four in the morning when they closed and when, now and again,
the policeman's face swiftly fluttered across the window-panes, Fischerle
was woken up. Quickly he sneezed the sleep out of his nose and was on
the alert at once. They informed him of the decision they had taken
in the meanwhile to nominate him an honorary member of The
Baboon. He thanked them effusively. Many more guests had arrived
and all now wished him luck on his journey. Cheers for the mighty
game of chess grew loud. A thousand well-meant slaps on the back
almost crushed him. Grinning so widely that it could be seen he
bowed to this side and that, cried at the top of his voice: 'So long. See
you all in Tokio at the New Baboon,' and left the café.

In the street he offered friendly greetings to several policemen he ran
into, always in little groups and very much on their guard. From to-
day, he said to himself, I will be polite to the police. He avoided Heaven
although it was quite near. Now that he was a doctor he decided to
have nothing more to do with low dives. Moreover, he must not be
seen. It was a pitch black night. Out of economy only every third
street lamp was lit. In America they have arc lights. They shine
continually day and night. They have so much money there all the
people are extravagant and a bit mad. A man who was ashamed because his wife was nothing but an old tart needn't go home if he doesn't
want to. He'd go to the Salvation Army; they have hotels with white
beds; everyone is allowed two linen sheets for his personal use, even a
Jew. Why don't people introduce this brilliant combination into
Europe? He tapped on his right coat pocket; there he could feel his
chessboard and his passport both together. No one in Heaven would
ever have presented him with a passport. People there only thought
about themselves and how they could make money. The Baboon was
noble. He respected The Baboon. The Baboon had elected him to
honorary membership. And that's no small honour because only first
class criminals go there! In Heaven the swine lived on their girls, they
might at least do some work themselves. He'd pay them back. The
gigantic chess palace he was going to build in America should be called
Baboon Palace. Not a soul would know it was called after a low dive
back home.

Under a bridge he waited for day. Before sitting down he fetched
himself a dry stone. In his thoughts he was already wearing a new suit,
which fitted his hump like a glove; it was a black and white check,

made to measure and costing two fortunes. A man who couldn't look after a suit like that was not worthy of America. So he avoided all violent motion in spite of the cold. He stretched out his legs as if his trousers had been pressed. From time to time he flicked off a little dust which he could see glimmering unprofitably through the darkness. For hours at a time a shoe cleaner knelt before the stone and polished for dear life. Fischerle took no notice of him. If you talked to these lads they worked badly, better leave them to their polishing. A smart felt hat protected Fischerle's coiffure from the wind, which tended to get up towards morning; a sea breeze was its name. On the far side of the table sat Capablanca playing in gloves. 'You may think that I haven't any gloves,' said Fischerle, and drew a brand new pair out of his pocket. Capablanca turned pale; his own were worn. Fischerle flung the new gloves at his feet and shouted: 'I challenge you.' 'For my part,' said Capablanca, trembling with fear, 'I don't believe you're a doctor. I don't play with just anybody.' 'I am a doctor,' Fischerle replied calmly, and held his passport under his nose, 'Read that if you can read!' Capablanca surrendered. He began to cry and was inconsolable. 'Nothing lasts for ever,' said Fischerle, and patted him on the shoulder. 'How many years have you been world champion? Other chaps want something out of life too. Just take a look at my new suit! You're not the only one in the world.' But Capablanca was a broken man, he looked old, his face was covered with wrinkles and his gloves were crumpled. 'Tell you what,' said Fischerle, the poor devil went to his heart, 'I'll give you a game.' The old man stood up, shook his head, gave Fischerle a visiting card of his very own and sobbed: 'You're a noble fellow. Come and call on me!' On the visiting card the whole address was printed in foreign letters; who could read that? Fischerle tormented himself, every stroke was different, you couldn't make out a word. 'You should learn to read!' shouted Capablanca, he had already disappeared, he could only be heard calling, and how loud he called, the doddering crook: 'You should learn to read!' Fischerle wanted the address, the address. 'But it's on the visiting card!' screamed the devil from far off. 'Maybe he doesn't know German,' sighed Fischerle and stood there twisting the visiting card round in his hands; he would have torn it up but the photograph on it interested him. It was a photograph of himself still in his old suit without a hat and with a hump. The visiting card was his passport, he himself was lying on a stone with the old bridge over him and instead of the sea breeze the daylight was already half showing.

He got up and solemnly cursed Capablanca. This was not playing fair, what he'd just done. True, you can take liberties in a dream, but dreams reveal a man's true character. Fischerle had offered to give him a game — and he'd done him down about his address! And where was he to get the miserable address now?

At home Fischerle kept a minute pocket diary. Every double page was devoted to a chess champion. Whenever a new genius appeared in the papers he would, if possible on the very same day discover everything about his life from the date of his birth down to his address, and set them down. Owing to the small size of the diary and his gigantic writing this was the work of more hours than altogether suited the habits of the Capitalist. She would ask him who he was writing to, what he was doing; he said not a word. In case of a disaster — with which as an inhabitant of Heaven he must always reckon — he hoped to find refuge and protection among his hated rivals in the profession. For twenty long years he had kept his list a deadly secret. The Capitalist suspected secret love affairs. The diary was hidden deep in a crack in the floor under the bed. His small fingers were alone able to reach it. Often he derided his fears, and said: 'Fischerle, what are you going to get out of that? The Capitalist will love you for ever!' But he only laid hands on the diary when a new champion was to go into it. There they all were, in black and white. Capablanca too. When the Capitalist went off to work, to-night, he'd fetch it.

The new day began with shopping. Doctors carry note cases, and those who go to buy a suit must have one to draw out, otherwise they get laughed at. Waiting for the shops to open, his hair went grey. He wanted the biggest possible note case, in check leather; but the price must be marked on the outside. He wouldn't be cheated. He compared the window displays of a dozen shops and selected a gigantic case, for which there was only room in his pocket because the lining was torn. When it came to paying, he turned away. Suspicious, the shop-assistants surrounded him. Two took up their stand at the door, to get a breath of fresh air. He clutched at his armpit and paid cash down.

Under the bridge he aired his capital, smoothed it out flat on the very stone on which he had slept, and placed the notes, unfolded, in his check leather note case. He could have got in even more. One ought to be able to buy them ready filled, he sighed; then with his capital added, it would have been really fat. In any case, the *tailor* would notice what it contained. In a superior outfitter's, he asked to see the proprietor. He came and stared, astonished at this commanding customer. In spite of Fischerle's unusual deformity, the first thing he noticed was his shabby suit. Fischerle bowed, in his own way, by drawing himself up, and presented himself.

'I am Dr. Siegfried Fischer, the chess champion. You've recognized me, doubtless, from my photographs in the papers. What I need is a suit made-to-measure, ready by to-night. I'll pay top prices. Half immediately, the other half on receipt. I'm going on the night train to Paris, I'm expected at the tournament in New York. My entire wardrobe has been stolen at my hotel. You will understand, my time is platinum. I wake up, and everything has gone. The burglars came at night. Only think of the shock to the management! How am I even to venture into the street? I am an abnormal shape, how can I help it; where are they to find a suit to fit me? No shirt, no socks, no shoes, for a man like me, to whom elegance is meat and drink? Take my measurements please; I won't delay you! By the merest chance they routed out a certain individual in a café, a hunchbacked cripple, you never saw such an object; he helped me out with his best suit. And what do you think his best suit was? This one! Such a deformity as this suit makes me, I am not by a long way, I assure you. In one of my English suits now, nobody would notice anything. Small, I grant you, can I help it? But English tailors are geniuses, all of them, geniuses every one. Without a suit, I have a hump. I go to an English tailor, and no hump. A tailor of talent may make the hump look smaller, a genius tailors it right away. A tragedy — all my beautiful suits! Of course I'm insured. All the same, I must be grateful to the burglar. My new passport, issued yesterday, he left on the night-table. Everything else he took. There, have a look — you doubt my identity; tell you what, in this suit I often doubt it myself. I'd order three suits at once, but do I know what your work is like? In the autumn I'll be back again in Europe. If your suit's a success, you'll see things. I'll send all America to you! Charge me a reasonable price, for goodwill. You must know, I count on winning the world championship. Do you play chess?'

Carefully they took his measurements. What the English could do, they could surely do as well. No need to be a professional chess player to know Dr. Siegfried Fischer by sight. The time was short, but twelve cutters and finishers were at his disposal, first class men every one of them, and he, the proprietor, would have the honour of assisting

himself in the cutting, a thing he only did for exceptional customers.
A keen player of draughts, he knew how to value the art of chess.
Champions were champions, whether in tailoring or in chess. Without insisting upon it, he recommended him to order a second suit at
once. Fittings at twelve o'clock sharp, both ready by eight sharp,
finished and pressed. The night train did not leave till eleven. Until
then Dr. Fischer could amuse himself. Whether he won the
world championship or not, he was a client to be proud of. He would
regret that second suit in the train. Might he humbly suggest, that he
should advertise his suit in New York. He would make him a special
price, a ridiculously special price! In fact he would make nothing on
the first suit at all, he would work for pure love of the art, for such
a customer, and what material did the gentleman prefer?

Fischerle pulled out his very own note case and said: 'Just like this.
Checks, in the same colours, it looks best at a tournament. Black and
white checks would be the best, like a chessboard, but you tailors don't
have any like that. No, I'll stick to *one* suit! If I'm satisfied, I'll telegraph
from New York for another. On my word. A famous man keeps his
promises. This linen! This linen! I have to put up with the filth! I
borrowed the linen from him too. Now tell me this, why does a
deformity like him give up washing? Does it hurt? Does soap injure
him? It doesn't injure me!'

The rest of the morning was passed in equally weighty affairs. Bright
yellow shoes, he bought, and a black hat. Expensive linen glistened
bright, wherever gaps in his suit allowed it to. What a pity so much
of it was hidden. Suits should be made transparent, like women's
dresses; why shouldn't a man show off his points too? In the nearest
public lavatory Fischerle changed his linen. He gave the woman a tip
and asked her what she took him for. 'For a hunchback,' she said with
an ugly leer, the kind they have in her job. 'You mean because of my
hump,' said Fischerle, hurt. 'It'll go again. Think I was born that way?
A swelling, an illness, what have you; six months and I'll be straight
again; no, let's say five. What do you think of my shoes?' A new client
had come in; she left him short of an answer; he had already paid her.
'Who cares?' he said to himself, 'What do I want with the old whore!
I'll go and have a bath.'

In a high-class establishment he asked for a luxury cubicle with a long
mirror. As he had paid, he really did take a bath; why should he waste
his money. He spent a full hour before the glass. From shoes to hat, he
stood there immaculate, his old suit lay on the luxury divan; who'd

bother with those rags? His shirt, on the other hand, was starched and blue, a delicate colour, suitable and spacious, a pity that it recalled Heaven; why? The sea is just as blue. Pants were only stocked in white; he would have preferred rose pink. He tweaked his sock suspenders, how firmly twanged the elastic! Fischerle too, had calves, none too crooked either, and the suspenders were bound with silk, guaranteed. In the cubicle there was a little table of plaited cane. Palms in pots, the kind you have in high-class interiors, should be put on it. Here, the little table was thrown in with the bath. The rich lessor pushed it in front of the mirror, pulled his chessboard out of the pocket of the despised suit, took his place with easy assurance and won a lightning game against himself. 'If you were Capablanca,' he shouted violently in his own face, 'I'd have beaten you six times in the time! At home in Europe we call this galloping chess! Go and boil your head! You think I'm afraid. One, two, and you're finished. You American! You paralytic! Do you know who I am? I'm Dr. Fischer! I've studied! You need an intellect to play chess. You, a world champion!'

Then he packed up quickly. He left the little table behind. At Baboon Palace he would have dozens of them. In the street again he didn't know what else to buy. The package with the old things under his arm looked like a paper parcel. First class passengers have luggage. He bought a smart leather suitcase. In it floated lonely what he had until recently worn on his body. At the cloakroom for hand luggage he gave it in. The official asked: 'Empty?' Fischerle looked haughtily up at him from below. 'You'd be glad if you had its contents!' He studied the time-tables. Two night trains went to Paris. One of them he could read about, the other was too high for him. A lady informed him of it. She was not specially elegant. She said: 'You'll dislocate your neck, little man. What train do you want?' 'Dr. Fischer, if you please,' he answered, with condescension; she wondered how he managed it. 'I'm going to Paris. I usually take the 1.5, you see, this one here. But I understand there is an earlier one.' As she was only a woman, he said nothing about America, the tournament and his profession. 'You mean the one at eleven, you see, this one!' said the lady. 'Thank you, madam.' He turned solemnly away. She was ashamed of herself. She knew the whole gamut of compassion, but had struck the wrong note. He noticed her submissiveness, she came from some Heaven or other; he would gladly have thrown a rude word at her. Then he heard the thunder of an engine coming in and remembered the station. The clock showed twelve. He was wasting valuable time with women. In thirteen hours he would be on his way to America. On account of his diary — which in spite of all the novelties he hadn't forgotten — he decided on the later train. For the sake of his new suit he took a taxi. 'My tailor's expecting me,' he said to the chauffeur during the drive, 'to-night I must go to Paris and early to-morrow morning to Japan. Incredible how little time a doctor has!' The chauffeur found his fare unsatisfactory. He had a feeling that dwarfs didn't tip, and revenged himself in advance. 'You're no doctor, sir, you're a quack!' There were chauffeurs for the asking under the Stars of Heaven. They played a rotten game if they played at all. I'll make him a present of his slander, because he can't play chess, thought Fischerle to himself. Really he was glad, because this way he saved himself the tip.

At his fitting his hump shrank. First of all the dwarf refused to believe the mirror and went right up to it to see if it were really flat. The tailor looked discreetly away. 'Tell you what!' cried Fischerle, 'You were born in England! If you like I'll bet on it. You were born in England?' The tailor half admitted it; he knew London well, he hadn't exactly been born in London; on his honeymoon he'd almost decided to stay there, but there was so much competition . . . 'This is only the fitting. It'll be gone by to-night,' said Fischerle and struck his hump. 'How do you like my hat?' The tailor was enthusiastic. The price he thought exorbitant, the style the most modern, and he strongly advised Fischerle to buy a coat to go with it. 'You only live once,' he said. Fischerle agreed. He chose a colour which reconciled the yellow of his shoes to the black of his hat, a bright blue. 'Moreover, it's just the same shade as my shirt.' The tailor bowed to so much good taste. 'I take it, Dr. Fischer, that you wear all your shirts of the same cut and colour,' and he turned to several assistants obsequiously standing about and informed them of the peculiarity of this famous man. 'In this very manner unmasks itself the glorious phoenix of the east. Rare indeed are characters of such integrity. In my humble opinion games of skill confirm the conservative in man. Be it chess or draughts it all tones in. It is the deepest conviction of a business man that it suits him. He elevates himself to the personification of tranquillity. A quiet evening at the close of day ensures a night's rest. The most devoted family has its limitations in life. Our Father in Heaven turns a blind eye to a dignified evening at the Rotary. From any other customer I would ask a deposit for the coat. But your character does not permit me to wish to insult you.'

'Yes, yes,' said Fischerle, 'my future wife lives in America. I have not seen her for a year. My profession, my miserable profession! Tournaments are a madness. Here I play a drawn game, there I win, usually I win, in fact always, and my future wife is pining away. Take her with you, you may say. It's easy enough to say. She comes of a millionaire's family. "Either you marry" say her parents "or you stay at home! Otherwise he'll let you down and we shall look fools." I've nothing against marriage, for her vast dowry she's going to be given a whole stuffed castle, but not until I'm world champion, not a moment sooner. She's marrying my name, I'm marrying her money. I don't want just the money. Well, good-bye till eight o'clock!'

By thus revealing his marriage plans Fischerle concealed the deep impression the tailor's sketch of his character had made on him. Until this moment he had not known that there were men who possessed more than one shirt at a time. His ex-wife the Capitalist had three chemises, but that was only a recent development. The gentleman who came once a week did not like seeing her always in the same. One Monday he had asserted that he was fed up, that eternal red got on his nerves. This was a fine beginning for the week, things were getting him down, business was bad. At least he had a right to expect something decent for his money. It wasn't as if he hadn't a wife as well. Just because she was thin, she was a woman after all. Not a word against his wife. The mother of his children. He repeated: if when he came next Monday he saw nothing but that eternal chemise, he would simply renounce the pleasure. Regular gentlemen don't grow on trees. Finally it worked. An hour later he was mollified. But before leaving he complained again. When Fischerle came home there was his wife standing stark naked in the middle of their little room. Her red chemise lay crumpled up in a corner. He asked what was she doing there. 'I'm crying,' said the comical fat lump; 'he's not coming any more.' 'What does he want?' asked Fischerle, 'I'll run after him.' 'He doesn't like my chemise,' whimpered the plump scarecrow, 'he wants a new one.' 'And you didn't promise it him!' screeched Fischerle. 'What have you got a mouth for!' Like a mad thing he hurled himself down the stairs. 'Sir!' he screamed down the street. 'Sir!' nobody knew the gentleman's name. He ran on at random and bumped into a lamp-post. It was the very one against which the gentleman was performing a function he had forgotten upstairs. Fischerle waited until he had finished. He didn't embrace him, although he had found him, but said: 'There will be a new chemise for you every Monday. On *my* guarantee! She's my wife. I can do what I like with her. Pray honour us with your company next Monday!' 'I'll see what I can do for you,' said the gentleman, and yawned. So that no one should recognize him, he had a very long way to go. On the very next Tuesday the Capitalist bought herself two new chemises, one green, the other lilac. On Monday the gentleman came. He looked at her chemise at once. She was wearing the green one. First of all he asked crossly, was it the red one dyed, you couldn't play tricks on him, he knew his way about. She showed him the others and he was gratified. He preferred the lilac one, but the red one was his favourite because it reminded him of their first times. And so Fischerle's efficiency had saved his wife from disaster; she might easily have starved in those difficult times.

While he was thinking of the little room and his much too big wife, he decided to forget his diary. He might run into his wife if he went home. She loved him dearly. Maybe she wouldn't let him go. If she said no, she screamed and threw herself in front of the door. There'd be no creeping under her, there'd be no pushing her aside, she was fatter than the door. Even her head was fat; when she took something into it she forgot business and stayed at home all night. Then he'd miss his train and get to America too late. He'd be able to find out Capablanca's address just as well in Paris. If no one knew it there, he'd ask in America. Millonaires knew everything. Fischerle would not go back to the little room. He'd have liked to creep under the bed once more in farewell; that was the cradle of his future career. There he used to lay traps and defeat champions storming like lightning from one square to another; he'd found in it a peace unknown in any café, his opponents played worthily for he was himself his own opponent. In Baboon Palace he would build a little room just like it with another bed for thinking up clever moves, and he alone would be allowed to creep under it. But he'd forego the farewell visit. Too much feeling was superfluous. A bed was only a bed. He could remember it perfectly well without. Instead he'd buy eleven more shirts, all blue. Anyone who could tell them apart would win a prize. The tailor knew something about character; but he could shut up about draughts. Only duds played that.

Complete with his parcel he returned to the station, opened his smart suitcase and placed the shirts one by one inside it. The contempt of the cloakroom man changed into respect. 'One more dozen,' thought their proprietor, 'and he'll go right out of his mind.' Once he held his packed case in his hand, it nearly pushed him into a train which was standing ready. But the cloakroom attendant removed the tempta-tion. At a special counter where an office had been opened for foreigners Fischerle asked in broken German for a first class ticket to Paris. They chased him away. He clenched his fist and croaked: 'Just to teach you I'll travel 2nd and your railway will have to stand the difference! You wait till I come in my new suit!' But he was not really angry. He didn't really look in the least like a foreigner. In front of the station he ate quickly a couple of hot sausages. 'I could go to a restaurant with separate tables,' he told the sausage man, 'and put down a king's ransom on the white tablecloth, I've got it in my note case,' he held it out under the nose of the unbeliever. 'But I'm not one for my stomach, I've got an intellect!' 'With a head like yours, I believe you!' answered the other. He had a little child's head on a lumpish body, and was jealous of everyone who had a larger one. 'What do you think I've got in it!' said Fischerle, and paid. 'All my years of study and languages, approximately six!'

In the afternoon he sat himself down to learn American. At the book-sellers' they tried to palm off English Grammars on him. 'Gentlemen,' he coquetted, 'I'm not so dumb. *You* have your interests at heart and I have mine.' Assistants and proprietors alike deplored the fact, but in America they *do* speak English. 'I know English, I want something special.' After he had assured himself that it was the same story every-where, he bought a book of the most usual English phrases. He got it half-price, because this bookseller lived exclusively on Westerns, only stocked other things as a sideline, and enthusiastically forgot his own interests in the dangers of the desert of Takla Makan, which a dwarf like this wanted to cross, instead of taking the Trans-Siberian railway or going by ship to Singapore.

Seated on a park bench, the daring investigator stuck his nose into the first lesson. It contained nothing but novelties, like 'The sun shines', or 'Life is short'. Unfortunately it was really shining. It was the end of March, and it had no bite. Otherwise Fischerle would have taken care not to get too near to it. He had had bad experiences with the sun. It was as hot as fever. In Heaven it never shone. It made you stupid for chess.

'I know English too!' called a little goose beside him. She had pig-tails and was about fourteen. He did not allow himself to be disturbed and went on reading the novelties aloud. She waited. After two hours he closed his lesson book. Then she took it as if she'd known him twenty years and heard his lessons, a task for which the Capitalist lacked the genius. He remembered every word. 'How many years have you been learning?' asked the school girl. 'We haven't got so far, I'm only in my second year.' Fischerle got up, asked for his property back, threw her an ugly, annihilating look and protested in a scream: 'I don't care for your acquaintance! Do you know when I started? Exactly two hours ago!' With these words he left the mental deficient.

Towards evening he could repeat the whole of the skimpy book. He changed benches frequently, for people always seemed to get interested in him. Was it his quondam hump, or his loud learning? As his hump was on its last legs, he decided for the latter. Whenever anyone approached his bench, he called out, even from a distance: 'Don't interrupt me, I entreat you, or I'll be ploughed in my exam to-morrow, what use'll that be to you, have a heart.' No one could resist that. Whatever bench he sat on filled up; the others stayed empty. They eavesdropped on his English and promised to hold all available thumbs up for his exam. A school teacher fell in love with his industriousness and followed him, from bench to bench, to the end of the park. She could take a dwarf to heart, she loved dogs, but only griffins, in spite of her thirty-six years she was still single, she taught French fluently, she was willing to exchange lessons for his English, she thought nothing of love. For some time Fischerle kept his opinion to himself. Suddenly she told him her landlady was a mercenary creature, then she abused rouged lips — powder was another matter. Then he'd had enough of her, a woman without rouge, what kind of business did she think she could do? 'You're only 46, and you talk that way,' he fumed, 'what'll you say when you're 56?' The school teacher went. She found him ill-bred. Not everyone let themselves be insulted. Most people were glad to have his lessons for nothing. An envious old man corrected his pronunciation and repeated obstinately: 'They don't say it like *that* in England, they say it like *this*. 'I'm talking American!' said Fischerle and turned his hump on him. Everyone agreed. They despised the old man, who couldn't tell English from American. When the shameless old thing, who was at least eighty, threatened to call the police, Fischerle sprang up and said: 'Yes *I'll* call them!' The old man hobbled, trembling, away.

As the sun went down, the people went home, little by little. A few boys herded themselves together and waited until the last grown-up had gone. Suddenly they surrounded Fischerle's bench and burst into an English chorus. They yelled 'Yes' but they meant 'Jew'. *Before* he had decided on his journey, Fischerle had feared boys like the plague.

To-day he threw down his book, climbed on to the bench and, with his long arms, conducted the choir. He joined in the singing too, singing what he had just learnt. The boys yelled, he yelled louder, his new hat danced frenziedly on his head. 'Faster, gentlemen!' he croaked in between times; the boys stormed round him, feeling suddenly grown up. They raised him shoulder high. 'Gentlemen, what are you doing!' Two more of these 'gentlemen' and they would stay grown-up. They lifted up his shoes, they supported his hump, three quarrelled for his lesson book, simply because it was his, one carried his hat. Both were borne in triumph before him, he came wavering after, on obsequious shoulders; he was neither a Jew nor a cripple, he was a fine fellow and knew all about wigwams. As far as the park gate the gallant hero belonged to them. He let them shake him, and made himself heavy. Outside, unhappily, they set him down. They asked him if he would be there again next day. He would not disappoint them. 'Gentlemen, he said, 'if I'm not in America I'll be with you!' In excitement and haste, off they trotted. There was a thrashing already in store for most of them when they got home.

Fischerle strolled slowly in the direction of the street where suit and coat awaited him. Since he had learnt that the train went at eleven sharp, he had set much store on punctuality and promises. It seemed too early for the tailor: he turned into a side street, entered a strange café, on the threshold of which gaily coloured women made him feel at home, and drank, in admiration of his wonderful English, a double whisky. He said: '*Thank you!*' threw the money on the tray, turned round only at the door as he went out, called '*Good-bye!*' until every one had heard him, and, as a result of this delay, ran straight into the arms of Passport Joe, whom he would otherwise have missed. 'Well, where'd you get the new hat?' he asked, no less astonished at the dwarf than at the new hat; this was the third client he had met in the neighbourhood. 'Sh!' whispered Fischerle, put his finger on his lip and pointed backwards into the café. So as to forestall further questions, he held his left shoe out to him and said: 'I've got myself ready for the journey.' Passport Joe understood and said no more. Light fingers by daylight and just before a journey round the world impressed him. He was sorry for the little fellow, because he had to get to Japan with no money. For a fraction of a second he thought of providing him with a couple of banknotes; business was doing well. But passport *and* banknotes were too much. 'When you don't know what else to do in a town,' he said, rather to himself than to the dwarf, 'you go straight to the chess champion. You'll find something there. You've got the addresses of course? Without the addresses an artist is lost. Don't forget the addresses!'

This piece of advice cast at him was quite enough to remind Fischerle of his pocket diary. It would be ungrateful to evaporate without even saying good-bye. His bed was after all not to blame for his stupid wife. An artist like him could not be parted from his pocket diary. The train at 1.5 ran just as punctually. Sharp at eight he reached the tailor. His new suit fitted him like the most splendid of combinations. Whatever trace was left of his hump disappeared under the coat. The two champions congratulated each other, each one on the other's skill.

'Wonderful!' said Fischerle and added: 'and to think there are people who don't even know English. I know a chap like that. He wants to say *thank you* and he says *danke!*'

The tailor said he liked *hamandeggs* best of all. The day before yesterday he came to a restaurant where the waiter didn't understand him.

'Yes and *ox* is *ochs* and *milk* is *milch*,' his customer took the words out of his mouth. 'Now I ask you, did anyone ever hear of an easier language? Japanese is a great deal harder!'

'Whereupon I take the liberty to confess that your line, the very first moment, as soon as you entered the door, made me feel the faultless connoisseur in languages; I entirely share your conviction of the inextricable difficulties of the Japanese vocabulary. The unenviable reputation resounds, that it has 10,000 different characters. Imagine the hair-raising paraphernalia of a mere local Japanese paper. Their methods of advertising are still in their cradle. Their language incubates the unsuspected germ which infects the business life of commerce. We suffer to-day from an all embracing enthusiasm for the welfare of a friendly nation. We are taking a substantial part in these fruitless endeavours, since the scar of an inevitable war in the Far East is on its way to a total cure.'

'You're perfectly right,' said Fischerle, 'and I won't forget you. As my train goes almost at once let us part as lifelong friends.'

'To the cold grave of my forefathers,' the tailor completed his sentence and embraced the future world champion. As the grave of his forefathers crossed his lips — he was the father of several children — he was deeply moved and filled suddenly with anxiety. In his struggle with death he pressed the doctor close to him. A button on the new coat caught itself up and was pulled off. Fischerle had a spasm of laughter; his quondam employee, the blind man, occurred to him. The tailor, injured in his tenderest feelings, demanded a comprehensive explanation.

'I know a man,' hustled the dwarf, 'I know a man who couldn't stand buttons. He'd like to eat all buttons, so that there would be no more. I just couldn't help thinking what tailors would do then. Don't you see?'

At this the injured party forgot his future in the grave of his forefathers and laughed hoarsely. While he sewed on the button with his own hands, he promised over and over again to send this fabulous joke to a comic paper for their kind consideration. He sewed slowly, so as to laugh in company. He did everything in company; even tears, when he was alone, gave him no real pleasure. He regretted from his heart the departure of the doctor. He would lose his best friend in him. For he would surely have become that, just as sure as two plus two will make four for all eternity. They parted on Christian name terms. The tailor stationed himself in the door and looked long, long, after Fischerle. Soon the figure of the well-bred dwarf — his heart was well-bred and the education of the heart is all — was lost in the proud outline of the striking new coat, beneath which the trouser legs of a distinguished suit made a welcome appearance.

Fischerle carried his own suit, well wrapped up, to the station. For the third time he popped up in the entrance hall, a smartly dressed person, rejuvenated and well born. With regal nonchalance he held his cloakroom ticket between forefinger and middle finger towards the attendant and requested his 'New leather suitcase'. The repect of the attendant became veneration. It was possible that the shirts which the deformity had had that afternoon were simply part of his stock-in-trade. Now he carried elegance on his very person. He laid his parcel in the suitcase with both arms and declared: 'It's nicely packed up, it would be silly to unpack it.' At the counter for foreign travellers he asked curtly, and, in German: 'Can I get a first class ticket to Paris here?' 'Yes sir, naturally sir!' assured him the very man who had hunted him away only a few hours before. From this Fischerle assumed rightly and with pride that he was no longer recognizable. 'You take your time over it gentlemen!' he complained with an English accent. His lesson book was still under his arm. 'I hope your trains move a little faster!' Did he wish for a sleeping car, there were still some places obtainable. 'Yes please. On the 1.5 train. Is your time-table reliable?' 'Yes sir, naturally sir. This is, after all, an ancient centre of civilization.'

360

'I know that. That has nothing to do with whether your trains go fast. Now in the States, *business* comes first. If you know as much English as that.' The ostentatious way in which the undergrown little gentleman held out a check note-case, and quite full, confirmed the official in his belief that he had an American before him and in the boundless reverence which was due to an American. 'I'm through with this country!' said Fischerle after he had paid and hidden away his ticket in the check leather note-case. 'I've been cheated. I've been treated like a deformity, not like an American. My profound knowledge of languages enabled me to counteract the designs of my enemies. Tell you what, they lured me into dens of vice. You've got some good chess players and that's about all I can give you. The world-famous Paris psychiatrist, Professor Kien, a good friend of mine, shares my opinion. I've been kept prisoner under a bed and a huge ransom has been blackmailed out of me by fearful threats of murder. I paid, but your police will have to pay me three times as much. Diplomatic steps have been initiated. Ancient centre of civilization — that's a good one!' Without further greeting he turned away. With a determined tread he left the hall. About his mouth there played a contemptuous quivering. Centre of civilization indeed! They told him that, he who'd been born here and had never left the town; he who knew all the chess papers by heart, read every illustrated weekly under Heaven before anyone else, and could learn English in an afternoon! Since his success he was certain that all languages were easy to learn and decided in the leisure weeks which his profession as world champion in America would permit him, to learn two languages a week. That would be sixty-six in a year, no one could possibly want more languages than that, what for, he could do without dialects. They came natural.

It was *nine o'clock*, the great clock in front of the station spoke English. At ten o'clock the house doors would be locked. It would be best to avoid meeting the porter. The way to the tumble-down barracks, in which Fischerle had unfortunately wasted twenty years with a whore, lasted forty minutes. Without hurrying too much he took it in the stride of his yellow shoes. Now and again he stood still under a street lamp and checked up in his book the words which he was saying in English. He was always right. He named the objects and spoke to the people whom he met, but quietly so that they should not interrupt him. He knew even more than he had imagined. When, after twenty minutes he could find nothing new, he dismissed houses,

streets, street lamps and dogs and set himself to play a game of chess in
English. This lasted him to the door of the filthy barracks. Just on the
threshold he won the game and stepped into the hall. His quondam
wife got on his nerves, very much on his nerves. So as not to run
straight into her he hid himself behind the stairs. There was comfortable room. His eyes bored the banisters. There were plenty of
holes in them on their own account. Had he wished he could have
barricaded the stairs with his nose. Until ten o'clock he was as still as a
mouse. The caretaker, a ragged shoemaker, closed the doors and with
a quivering hand extinguished the staircase light. When he had disappeared into his shabby dwelling place, which was hardly twice as
capacious as Fischerle's wife, Fischerle crowed softly: 'How do you
do!' The shoemaker heard a light voice, thought a woman was
standing outside and waited for her to ring. Everything was still. He
had been mistaken, someone must have passed in the street. He went
inside and lay down, excited by the voice, at the side of his wife whom
he hadn't touched for months.

Fischerle waited for the Capitalist, whether she was going out or
coming in. An observant person, he would know her by the way she
held her match, straight up in the air, because she was more gone on
cigarettes than any other whore in the house. He would prefer her to
be going out. Then he would creep upstairs, fetch the pocket diary
from under the bed, take his leave of that cradle of rest, his home, his
idyll, when he was still only a little cripple, run downstairs and drive
off to the station in a taxi. Up there he would find his street-door key,
which he had recently thrown down in a corner in a rage at her silly
bitch way of talking, and been too lazy to pick up again. If she was
coming in instead of going out, she would be bringing a client in. It
was to be hoped he wouldn't stay long. At the very worst Dr. Fischer
could slink into the little room as Fischerle had done of old. If his wife
heard him, she wouldn't say a word or her gentleman would get mad.
Before she could say anything, he'd be off again. What does a woman
like that do with herself all day? Either she lies in bed with someone,
or she lies in bed with no one. Either she's cheating someone of his
money, or she's giving the money back to someone else. Either she's
old and no one has any use for her, or she's young, in which case she's
even sillier. If she gives you a meal she expects to half eat you in
return, if she's not earning she expects you to go steal pocket combs for
her. What a life! What room is there for artistry in it? A properly
grown man would stake his all on chess. While he waited, Fischerle

puffed out his chest. Because you never knew how the back of his coat and suit would look in the morning, the hump might stretch them.

For an eternity no one came. The gutters dripped into the courtyard. Every drop flowed towards the ocean. On an ocean liner Dr. Fischer would ship himself to America. New York has a population of ten million. The entire population is mad with joy. In the streets, people embrace each other and shout: 'Long Live Dr. Fischer.' A hundred million handkerchiefs flutter a greeting, each inhabitant has one on. every finger. The emigration officer evaporates. Why should they ask so many questions? A deputation of New York whores place their Heavens at his disposal. They have them there too. He thanks them. He is a man of learning. Aeroplanes write DR. FISCHER in the sky. Why should he not be advertised too? He's more worth while than Persil. Thousands fall into the water on his account. They must be rescued, he commands, he has a soft heart. Capablanca throws himself on his neck. 'Save me!' he whispers. But in the din even Fischerle's heart is fortunately deaf. 'Off with you!' he shouts, and gives him a push. Capablanca is torn in pieces by the furious multitude. From the top of a skyscraper cannons fire a salute. The President of the United States offers him his hand. His future bride shows him her dowry in black and white. He takes her. Subscription lists for Baboon Palace are opened. On every skyscraper. The issue is over subscribed. He founds a school for young talent. They get uppish. He strikes them out. On the first floor eleven o'clock strikes. An eighty-year-old woman lives there with a grandmother clock. In two hours and five minutes the sleeping car leaves for Paris.

On tiptoe Fischerle climbed up the stairs. His wife never stayed out so late. Sure enough, she must be in bed with a client. Outside the little room on the third floor he stood still and listened to voices. No light showed through the chinks. As he despised his wife, he understood nothing that she said. He took off his new shoes and placed them on the first step of the staircase, nearer to America. He laid his new hat on top of them, and admired it, for it was even blacker than the darkness. From his English phrase-book he would not be separated, he hid it in his coat pocket. Softly he opened the door, he had had practice. The voices talked on, loudly, about insults. Both were sitting on the bed. He left the door open and crept to the crack. First he poked his nose in: the pocket diary was there, smelling of the petrol into which it had been dropped some months previously. 'Your humble servant!' thought Fischerle, and bowed to so many artists in the game. Then he shoved the diary with his index finger to the top of the crack and pushed it up on end; he had it. With his left hand he kept his mouth shut, for he longed to laugh outright. The client above him had a voice exactly like the blind button-man. He knew precisely, by the way the diary lay, which was back and which was front, and by sense of touch alone found his way to the last blank pages. He found it much harder than usual to write small. On one page he put Doctor, on the next Fischer, on the third New, and on the fourth York. He would put in the exact address later, when he found out where Baboon Palace, his bride's place, is situated. Really he had troubled himself so little about this marriage. All his troubles with money, passports, suit and railway ticket had robbed him of valuable days. There was the smell of petrol in his nose. 'Darling!' said the millionairess and pinched it, she loved long noses, she couldn't stand short ones; what's that man done with his nose, she said, when they went for a walk in the streets together, all noses were too short for her, she was beautiful and American, she was a blonde, like in the films, she was gigantically tall and had blue eyes, she only travelled in her own car, she was afraid of trams, because there you met cripples and pickpockets, who would steal your millions out of your pocket, a crying shame; what did she know of his former crippledom in Europe?

'Cripples and scum are the same!' says the man on the bed. Fischerle laughs because he isn't one any more, and contemplates the trousered legs of the creature. His shoes press on the floor. If he didn't know that the button man had nothing but twenty groschen and not a ha'penny more, he'd swear it was him. Of course there are doubles. Now he's talking about buttons. Why not? He's just asking the woman to sew a button on for him. No, he's mad, he says: 'There, eat it!' 'Give it to *him* to eat,' says the woman. The man gets up and goes to the open door. 'He's in the house somewhere, I say!' 'Have a look see, what can *I* do about it?' The double slams the door and paces up and down. Fischerle isn't afraid. But in any case he begins to crawl towards the door.

'He's under the bed!' screams the woman. 'What!' bellows the double. Four hands drag the dwarf out; two clutch him by the nose and throat. 'Johann Schwer is my name!' someone introduces himself out of the darkness, lets go of his nose, not of his throat, and bellows: 'There, eat that!' Fischerle takes the button into his mouth and tries to swallow. For a single breath the hand lets go of his throat, until the button has gone down. In the same breath Fischerle's mouth attempts a grin, and he gasps innocently: 'But that's my button!' Then the hand has him again and strangles him. A fist shatters his skull.

The blind man hurled him to the ground and fetched from the table in the corner of the little room a bread knife. With this he slit coat and suit to shreds and cut off Fischerle's hump. He panted over the laborious work, the knife was too blunt for him and he wouldn't strike a light. The woman watched him, undressing meanwhile. She lay down on the bed and said: 'Ready!' But he wasn't yet ready. He wrapped the hump in the strips of the coat, spat on it once or twice and left the parcel where it was. The corpse he shoved under the bed. Then he threw himself on the woman. 'Not a soul heard anything,' he said and laughed. He was tired, but the woman was fat. He loved her all night long.

PART THREE

THE WORLD IN THE HEAD

CHAPTER I

THE KIND FATHER

THE dwelling of the caretaker Benedikt Pfaff consisted of a middle-sized dark kitchen and a small white closet which gave on to the entrance hall of the house. Originally the family, which numbered five members, slept in the larger room; there were his wife, his daughter and three times over himself; himself as policeman, himself as husband, himself as father. The twin beds were, to his frequent indignation, the same size. For that reason he forced his daughter and wife to sleep together in one, the other belonged to him alone. Under himself he put a horsehair mattress, not because he was soft — he hated sluggards and women — but on principle. *He* it was who brought the money home. Washing all the stairs was his wife's duty, opening the street door at nights when anyone rang had since her tenth year been his daughter's, so that she should get over her timidity. Whatever return either of them received for their services he kept, for he was the caretaker. Now and again he permitted them to earn a little something on the side, by cleaning or washing. Thus they learned by their own experience how hard a father has to work when he has a family to support. At meals he proclaimed himself in favour of family life, at night he derided his enfeebled wife. He exercised his rights of discipline as soon as he came home from work. He polished his red-haired fists on his daughter with real pleasure, he made less use of his wife. He left all his money at home; the sum was always perfectly correct, even without his checking it over, for the only time he had found an error his wife and daughter had had to spend the night in the street. Taken for all in all he was a happy man.

In those times the cooking was done in the white closet which was intended to serve for kitchen. Owing to his strenuous profession, which called for continuous muscular practice, a practice which he exercised by day and by night in his dreams, Benedikt Pfaff required a plentiful, nourishing, well cooked and well served diet. In this respect he would stand no nonsense, and if it came to blows with his wife that was her own fault, a thing which he would never have asserted in the case of his daughter. With the years his hunger grew. He found the little closet too small for generous cooking and commanded the transference of the kitchen to the back room. For once he came up against opposition, but his will was unconquerable. Since that time all three lived and slept in the closet, where there was just room for one bed, and the larger room was reserved for cooking and eating, for discipline and for the rare visits of his colleagues who, in spite of the plentiful food, never felt quite at home. Soon after this change his wife died, of overstrain. She could not keep up with the new kitchen; she cooked three times as much as before and grew thinner from day to day. She seemed very old, people thought she was in her sixties. The tenants who hated and feared the caretaker pitied him for one thing: they found it cruel that a man bursting with energy should have to live with such an old woman. In reality she was eight years younger than he, and nobody knew it. Often she had taken on so much to cook that she had not nearly finished when he got home. Sometimes he had to wait a full five minutes for his food. Then his patience would break down and he would beat her even before he had finished eating. She died under his hands. But all the same she would certainly have pegged out of her own accord in the next few days. A murderer he was not. On her death-bed, which he made ready for her in the larger room, she seemed so shrivelled that he didn't know how to look his condolence callers in the face.

On the day after the funeral his honeymoon began. More undisturbed than before, he treated his daughter as he pleased. Before going off on his beat he locked her into the back room, so that she could devote herself more exclusively to the cooking. This way she was pleased, too, when he came home. 'What's my prisoner doing?' he would bellow as he turned the key round in the lock. She laughed all over her pale face because now she could go out shopping for the next day. This pleased him. Before going shopping she should laugh, then she would be given better pieces of meat. A bad piece of meat is nothing more nor less than a crime. If she stayed out longer than half an hour he went mad with hunger and received her on her home-coming with kicks. As he got nothing out of this his rage at the bad beginning of their evening increased. If she cried a great deal he would grow kind again and his programme would follow its normal course. But he preferred it when she came back punctually. Of her half hour he would steal five minutes. Hardly had she gone when he would put the clock five minutes forward, set it down on the bed in the closet and seat himself in the new kitchen by the fire where he could sniff at the coming meal without lifting a finger to prepare it. His huge thick ears were pricked up for the brittle footstep of his daughter. She walked silently out of fear lest the half hour should be over, and from the door threw a despairing glance at the clock. Sometimes she succeeded in creeping up to the bed in spite of the fear which this piece of furniture instilled into her and putting back the clock a few moments with a quick frightened movement. But usually he heard her at the first step — she breathed too loud — and would surprise her half-way, for from door to bed her steps were two.

She would attempt to slip by him and busy herself with dexterous haste round the oven. She was thinking of a sickly, lanky salesman at the grocer's who said to her, more softly than to the other women: 'Good evening, Miss,' and evaded her timid glance. So as to stay longer in the same place as him, she would let women who were behind her in the queue get in front. He had black hair and once when nobody else was left in the shop he had given her a cigarette. Round this she folded a piece of red tissue paper on which she wrote in almost invisible letters the date and hour of the gift, and she carried this shining little parcel at the one place in her body which her father never cared about, under her left breast, over her heart. She was more afraid of blows than of kicks: for the latter she lay stubbornly on her front and nothing happened to the cigarette; but at other times his fists hit out everywhere and, under the cigarette, her heart quivered. If he destroyed that she would kill herself. In the meantime she had long since loved the cigarette away to dust, because in the day-long hours of her confinement she would take out the little packet, gaze at it, stroke it and kiss it. All that was left was a little heap of tobacco, of which not one grain was lost.

At meals her father's mouth steamed. His chewing mandibles were as insatiable as his arms. She stood, so as to be able to refill his plate quickly; her own remained empty. All of a sudden she was terrified, he might ask: why don't I eat. His words were more fearful to her even than his actions. What he said she only understood since she was grown up; his actions had affected her from the earliest moments of her life. I've eaten already father she would say. You eat now. But he never asked her, not once in all the long years of their marriage.

While he chewed, he was busy. His eyes were fixed on his plate, glazed and spell-bound. As the heap diminished, their lustre faded. His masticatory muscles grew angry, they had been given too little to do; soon they would let loose a bellow. Woe to the plate when it was empty! His knife would have cut it, his fork transfixed it, his spoon battered it, his voice blown it to pieces. But that was why his daughter was standing by. Tensely she observed the signs on his forehead. As soon as the first trace of a vertical line appeared between his eyebrows, she filled up his plate, regardless of what might already be on it. For, later or sooner, according to his mood, the line appeared. She had learnt to do this; at first, after the death of her mother, she had done as her mother had done before her, and judged by the state of his plate. But this worked out badly; more was expected of a daughter. Soon she knew him in and out and read his moods straight from his forehead. There were days when he ate to a finish without a word. When he had finished, he would chew a little longer. She listened carefully — if he chewed violently and for a long time, she began to tremble; a bad night lay ahead, and she would tempt him with the softest words to another helping. Usually he only chewed contentedly and said:

'Man has his offspring. Who is my offspring? The prisoner!'

At this he pointed at her; instead of his index finger he used his clenched fist. Her lips had to form the word 'prisoner', smiling, at the same time as his. She moved further away. His heavy boot came after her.

'A father has a right to ...' '... the love of his child.' Loud and toneless, as though she were at school, she completed his sentences, but she felt very low.

'For getting married my daughter ...' — he held out his arm — '... has no time.'

'She gets her keep from ...' '... her good father.'

'Other men do not want ...' '... to have her.'

'What could a man do with ...' '... the silly child.'

'Now her father's going to ..' '... arrest her.'

'On father's knee sits ...' '... his obedient daughter.'

'A man gets tired in the ...' '... police.'

'If my daughter isn't obedient she gets ..' '... thrashed.'

'Her father knows why he ...' '... thrashes her.'

'My daughter isn't ever ...' '... hurt.'

'She's got to learn what she ...' '... owes to her father.'

He had gripped her and pulled her on to his knee; with his right hand he pinched her neck, because she was under arrest, with his left he eased the belchings out of his throat. Both sensations pleased him. She summoned her small intelligence to conclude his sentences rightly and took care not to cry. For hours he fondled her. He instructed her in the special holds he had invented himself, pushed her this way and that, and showed her how every criminal could be overpowered by a juicy blow in the stomach, because who wouldn't feel ill after that?

This honeymoon lasted half a year. One day the father was pensioned and went to work no more. Now he would devote himself to the nuisance of begging in the house. His peep-hole, a foot and a half from the ground, was the outcome of several days' brooding. At rehearsals, his daughter played her part. Countless times she walked from the house door to the stairs and back. 'Slower!' he bellowed, or 'Quick march!' Immediately after he forced her to slip into his old trousers and act the part of a male suspect. The knock-out he had planned for the suspect fell to her share as well. Hardly had he seen his own trousers through the newly drilled peep-hole, than he leaped up in a fury, tore open the door, and with a couple of devilish blows laid her flat on the floor. 'Because,' he excused himself later, as if this were the first time he had ever hit her, 'that's the way it has to be, because you're a rat. Shave their heads in prison, they do; cut 'em off would be more like it. A burden on the tax-payer. Eating themselves full in prison. The bleeding State pays. I'll wipe the vermin out. The cat's at home now. The mice can keep in the holes! I'm Ginger the Cat. I'll eat 'em up. A rat, you'll know what crushing means!'

She knew it and rejoiced at her lovely future. He wouldn't lock her up any more, he would be at home himself. He would see her all day, she could stay out longer shopping, forty minutes, fifty, a whole hour, no, not so long; she would go to the grocer, she would choose the emptiest times, she must say thank you for the cigarette, he gave it her three months and four days ago; at the time she was excited, and later there were so many people, she never thanked him, what must he be thinking of her; if he asks, how she liked it, she will say: very good, and father nearly took it away from her; he said it was the best kind, he would like to smoke it himself.

True, her father had never once seen the cigarette; it doesn't matter, she must thank the dark-haired Mr. Franz and tell him it's the best brand, her father knows what's what. Perhaps he'd give her another cigarette. She'd smoke that one there and then. If anyone came in,

371

she'd turn away and throw the cigarette quickly over the counter. He will know how to put it out before the place gets on fire. He's clever. In the summer he manages the shop himself, the manager goes on holiday. Between two and three there's no one in the shop. He must take care no one sees him. He holds out the match to her and the cigarette burns. I'll burn you, she says, he's frightened, he's so delicate, as a child he was always ill, she knows it. She points it at him, she touches him. Oh, he cries, my hand, that hurts! She calls: 'For love,' and runs away. At night he comes to carry her off, her father sleeps, the bell rings, she goes to open. She takes all the money with her, over her nightdress she slips on her own coat, the one she's never allowed to wear, not the old cast-off of her father's, she looks like a maiden fair; who is this waiting at the door? It is he. A coach with four black steeds is ready. He offers her his hand. With his left hand he holds his sword, he is a nobleman, and bows low. He has tailor-pressed trousers on. 'I have come,' he says, 'you burnt my hand. I am the noble knight Franz.' She had always thought so. He was too beautiful for a grocer's shop, a knight in disguise. He asks her leave to kill her father. It is a question of honour. 'No, no!' she implores him, 'he will kill your Royal Highness!' He pushes her to one side, out of her pockets she pulls all the money and holds it out to him, he gazes piercingly at her, his honour is at stake. At a single blow, in the white closet, he severs her father's head from his body. She cries with joy, if only her poor mother had lived to see it, she would be alive to-day. The noble knight Franz takes father's ginger head away with him. On the threshold he says: 'Gracious lady, to-day you have opened this door for the last time, let me abduct you to the altar.' Then her little foot mounts into the coach. He helps her up. Inside she may sit, there is heaps of room. 'Are you of age?' he asks. 'Past twenty,' she says, though she doesn't look it, she was her father's little girl until this evening. (Really, she's only sixteen; he mustn't guess.) She must get a husband and leave home. And the beautiful dark-haired knight stands up in the middle of the coach as it bowls along, and throws himself at her feet. He will marry her and her alone, or else his valiant heart will break. She blushes, and strokes his hair, it is very black. He admires her coat. She will wear it every day until she dies, it's still quite new. 'Where are we going?' she asks. The steeds champ and toss their heads. What a lot of houses there are in the town. 'To your mother,' he says, 'why shouldn't she be happy.' At the cemetery the four steeds stop, right in front is mother's grave. Here is her tombstone. Sir Franz lays her father's head on it. It is his gift. 'Have you nothing for your mother?' he asks her; ah, how ashamed she is, how ashamed she is, he has brought something for mother, she has nothing. Then she pulls out a little red packet from under her nightdress; inside it there is a love-token, a cigarette, and she lays it down beside the ginger head. Mother rejoices in her happy children. Both kneel at mother's grave and pray for her blessing.

Father kneels at his peep-hole, grabs at her every other minute, drags her down beside him, holds her head to the opening and asks her if she sees anything. She is exhausted with the long rehearsal, the corridor dances before her eyes, on the chance she says 'Yes'. 'Yes what!' bellows the beheaded father, he is still very much alive, to-night he'll get a shock when the coach and four comes to the door. 'Yes, yes!' he apes her and derides her. 'Not blind, are you? *My* daughter blind! Now I'm asking: What do you see?' She has to kneel until she has seen what he means. He means a mark on the opposite wall.

His invention taught him a new view of the world. She took an enforced part in his discoveries. She has learnt too little and knows nothing. When he dies, in forty years or more (everybody's got to die sometime), she'll fall on the rates. He can't have a crime like that on his conscience. She must learn something about the police. So he explained to her all the peculiarities of the tenants, taught her to observe the different skirts and trousers and their significance in the detection of crime. In his zeal for instruction he sometimes let a beggar go by, and afterwards held her responsible for his sacrifice. The tenants, he told her, were respectable people, but suspects all the same. For what did he get from them for the special protection he afforded their house? They simply put the fruit of his labours into their own pockets. Instead of thanking him they ran him down. As if he'd done someone in. And why should he work for nothing? He's got his pension and could sit around or go after women or drink his money, he's worked all his life, he's a right to be lazy. But he has a conscience. First of all he says to himself, he's got a daughter whom he has to care for. Who'd have the heart to leave her alone in the house! He stays with her and she'll stay with him. The good father of a family folds his child to his bosom. Half a year she was all alone, since the old woman died, he had to go to work, no shirking in the police force. Secondly the State pays him a pension. The State *has* to pay. There's no getting out of it, whatever else goes, it has to go on paying the pensions. *One* man might say: I've worked enough. Another man is grateful for his pension and works for nothing. They are the best sort. They arrest whatever people they can, half kill them, killing them altogether is forbidden, and save the State a lot of work. That's called relief work, because it relieves the State of the burden. The police must stick together, retired ones too, consciences like that oughtn't to be retired ever. They are irreplaceable and when they die they leave a vacuum.

Day by day the girl learnt more. She had to remember her father's discoveries and support his memory when it failed him, for what's the good of a daughter eating up the best part of one's pension? If a new beggar came, he told her to look quick through the peep-hole, and asked her, not if she knew this one, but 'When was he here before?' Traps are instructive, specially hers, for she was always caught. When the beggar was done with, the regulation punishment for her careless- ness was established and immediately executed. Without corporal punishment no one ever got anywhere. The English are a tremendous people.

Little by little Benedikt Pfaff had educated his daughter so well that she could take his place. From then on he called her Polly, which was a title of honour. It expressed her aptitude for his profession. Her real name was Anna but as this name meant nothing to him he never used it; he was an enemy to names. Titles pleased him better: those which he had himself bestowed were an obsession with him. With her mother's death, Anna too had died. For six months the girl was 'you' or 'my daughter'. Since he had nominated her Polly, he was proud of her. Women were good for something after all, men must understand how to make Pollys of them.

Her new dignity carried with it a yet more strenuous duty. All day long she sat or knelt by him on the floor, ready to take his place. It happened that he would have to retire for a moment or two; then she stepped into his post. If a hawker or a beggar came into her line of vision, it was her duty to hold up the person in question, either by force or by cunning until her father should be ready to take over the sh— house. He always hurried back. He preferred to do the job all himself, it was enough for him to have her merely as a spectator. His new way of living occupied more and more of his attention. Meals lost their interest for him, his hunger grew less. After a few months he came to depend for air and exercise on a few newcomers only. The other beggars of the district avoided his house like the plague, they knew why. His fearsome stomach, on which he set so much store, grew more moderate. His daughter's cooking time was fixed at one hour per day. For so long only was she allowed to stay in the inner room. She peeled potatoes at his side, at his side she washed the green vegetables, and while she beat the steak for his dinner, he could thump her to his heart's content. His eye did not know what his hand did; it was fixed, unblinking and unwavering, on in-going and out-going legs.

For her shopping, since he now ate half as much as before, he allowed Polly a quarter of an hour. Cunning as she had grown in her father's school, she often forewent the dark-haired Franz for a day, stayed at home, and on the following day cashed two quarters of an hour together. But she never met the noble knight alone. Secretly she stammered her thanks for the cigarette. Perhaps he understood her, he looked away so delicately. At night she stayed awake long after her father was asleep. But he never rang, the preparations took such a long time, ah, if only she'd burnt him, then he would have had to hurry, there were always so many women in the shop. Once, when he was writing out her bill, she'd whisper quickly: 'Thank you, it needn't be a coach, don't forget your sword!'

One day the women were standing outside the grocer's talking altogether. 'That Franz has absconded!' 'Came of a bad family.' 'With the cash-box.' 'Shifty look he had.' 'Sixty-eight schillings!' 'Ought to have capital punishment again!' 'My husband's been saying so for years.' Trembling, she flung herself into the shop; the manager was just saying: 'The police have a clue.' *He's* the one to suffer, because he left him alone in charge, four years the scoundrel's been in the shop, who would have thought it of him, no one noticed a thing, the cash was always right, four years, the police have just rung up, six o'clock at the latest they'll have him behind bars.

'It's not true!' shouted Polly and suddenly began to cry. 'My father's a policeman himself!'

No one noticed her as there was a money-loss to lament. She ran away and came home with an empty basket. Without a word to her father she locked herself in to the back room. He was engaged and waited a quarter of an hour. Then he stood up and commanded her to come out. She was silent. 'Polly!' he bellowed. 'Polly!' Nothing stirred. He promised her impunity with the firm intention of thrashing her within an inch of her life, even more if she murmured. Instead of her answer he heard a fall. To his fury he saw himself compelled to break open his own door. 'In the name of the law!' he bellowed, out of habit. The girl lay mute and still in front of the stove. Before hitting her, he turned her over once or twice. She was unconscious. He shrank; she was young and he liked her. Several times he ordered her to come back to her senses. Her deafness infuriated him, against his will. All the same, he wanted to start on a less sensitive place. Looking for one, his eye fell on the shopping basket. It was empty. Now he knew. She'd lost the money. He understood her terror. He wouldn't stand for a joke of that kind. She'd left the house with a whole ten schilling note. She couldn't have lost it all? He searched her thoroughly. For the first time he touched her with fingers, not with fists. He found a little red parcel full of tobacco dust. He tore it up and threw it in the dustbin. Last of all he opened her purse. The ten schilling note was inside. Not a corner had gone. Now he was at a loss again. Bewildered, he beat her back into consciousness. When she came to herself, he was sweating, so carefully had he directed his blows, and great tears were running out of his mouth.

'Polly!' he bellowed, 'Polly, the money's still there!'

'Anna is my name,' said she, cold and hard.

He repeated: 'Polly!' Her voice moved him deeply, his outspread hands rolled themselves into fists; the tenderest emotions overcame him. 'What's a good father to have for his dinner to-day?' he complained.

'Nothing.'

'Polly must cook him something.'

'Anna! Anna!' screamed the girl.

Suddenly she darted up, gave him a push, enough to knock over any other father — even he noticed it — ran into the closet (the communicating door was in splinters, otherwise she would have locked him in), jumped on the bed, shoes and all, so as to be taller than him, and screamed: 'It'll cost you your head! Polly's short for police! My mother'll have your head!'

He understood. She was threatening to inform against him. His offspring wanted to slander him. For whom did he live then? For whom had he kept himself respectable? He'd nourished a viper in his bosom. She belonged on the gallows. *He* had made a special invention for her so that she should learn something; now, when the world and women were open to him, *he* stayed with her, out of kindness and because he had a heart of gold. And *she* pretended he'd done something wrong. She was no daughter of his! The old woman had tricked him. He was no fool to discipline her like he had. He'd had a fishy smell in his nose. Sixteen years he'd thrown money away on someone else's daughter. He could have bought a house for less. From year to year humanity deteriorated. Soon they'd abolish the police and criminals would have it all their own way. The State will say: No more pensions: and the whole world goes under! Human nature! Criminals spreading day by day, what'll happen to God Almighty!

Rarely did he rise to the height of God Almighty. He had respect for the all-highest position which belonged to him. God Almighty was greater even than the head of the police. All the more was he struck by the danger in which God found himself to-day. It was all very well to lift his step-daughter off the bed and beat her bloody. He took no real pleasure in it. He worked mechanically and what he said was full of grief and deep regret. His blows belied his voice. He had lost all desire to bellow. By mistake he referred once to a certain Polly. But his muscles made up for the mistake immediately. The name of the female he was disciplining was Anna. She claimed to be identical with a daughter of his. He did not believe her. Her hair came out in handfuls and when she defended herself two of her fingers got broken. She mouthed something about his head, like a common butcher. She abused the police. It was plain that the best education could not prevail against a corrupt nature. Her mother was no good. She was ill and work-shy. He could send the daughter to join her mother, where she belonged. But he wasn't that kind. He stayed his hand, and went out to eat at a café.

From this day they were no more to each other than bodies. Anna cooked and shopped. She avoided the grocer's. She knew the black-haired Franz was in prison. He had stolen for her, but he had been clumsy. A noble knight succeeds in everything. Since she had lost her cigarette she didn't love him any more. Her father's head was as firmly fixed as ever; his eyes begged through the peep-hole for beggars. She showed him her contempt by taking no further notice of his invention. She played truant from his school. Every other day at least his mouth overflowed with new discoveries. She did her work, crouched next to him, listened in silence and said not a word. The peep-hole interested her no more. When, with a conciliatory gesture, he offered her a peep, she shook her head, indifferent. There were no more open-hearted talks at the dinner-table. She filled her own plate as well as his, sat down, ate, if only a little, and served him again when she herself had had enough. He treated her just as he had done before. But he missed her fear. Between blows, he said to himself she had no more heart for him. After some months he bought four beautiful canaries. Three were males; opposite to them, he hung up the smaller cage for the little female. All three sang as if possessed. He praised them ostentatiously. As soon as they began their singing, he let down the covering over his peep-hole, got up and listened to them, standing. His awe did not permit him to clap at the end of their wooing. But he said: 'Bravo!' and turned his marvelling eyes from the little creatures to the girl. He hoped everything from the passionate wooing of the canary birds. But even their song stirred not a ripple on Anna's calm.

She lived for several more years as her father's servant and woman. He flourished: his muscular strength increased rather than decreased. But it was not true happiness. He told himself so daily. Even at meals he thought of it. She died of consumption, to the great despair of the canaries, who would only take food from her. They survived the disaster. Benedikt Pfaff sold the kitchen furniture and had the back room walled up. In front of the new white distemper he placed a chest. He ate no more in his own home. In the closet, he stayed at his post. He avoided every remembrance of the empty room next door. In there, in front of the stove, he had lost his daughter's heart; to this day he did not know why.

CHAPTER II

TROUSERS

'WELL Professor! The noble steed must have his oats. He's a thorough-
bred and kicks. At the zoo the lion devours red juicy meat. Why?
Because the king of beasts roars like thunder. The grinning gorilla
gets his fresh women from the savages. Why? Because the gorilla
bursts with muscles of iron. There's justice for you! Look at me, the
house pays me nothing. But I'm invaluable. Professor, you were the
only man in the world who understood gratitude. Serious under-
nourishment was relieved by your honorarium, as they say. To conclude, may I humbly ask what you have been doing with yourself,
Professor, and remain your humble servant?'

On reaching his closet these were the first words addressed by
Benedikt Pfaff, to the Professor who was removing the handkerchief
tied over his eyes. He excused himself and paid what he had omitted,
namely the honorarium for two months.

'As to the conditions obtaining on the upper floor, we know where
we stand,' he said.

'I should think so!' winked Pfaff, partly because of Therese, but
chiefly on account of his own rights which, though much crumpled,
he had now secured.

'While you attend to the thorough cleaning of my flat, I will collect
myself here in quiet. Work is urgent.'

'The whole closet is at your disposal! Make yourself at home here,
Professor! A woman may come between the best of men. But between
such friends as us there is no such person as a certain Therese.'

'I know, I know,' interrupted Kien hastily.

'Let me have my say out, Professor! Women are muck! My
daughter now, she was different!'

He pointed to the chest as though she were inside it. Then he
formulated his terms. He was only human and would take over the
cleaning of the flat above. There was a lot to clean. He would have
to engage several charwomen and take command of them. He
couldn't stand for desertion, desertion and perjury were one and the
same crime. During his absence the Professor must take his place at the
vital spot of the house.

Less from a sense of duty than from a desire for power he was determined to force Kien on to his knees for a little time. His daughter was going round and round in his head to-day. Since she was dead the Professor must take her place. He was bursting with arguments. He declared to him how honourably and truly they loved each other. He made him a present of the whole closet with all its movables. Only a minute or two back he had merely placed it at his disposal. As for a daily payment, since his friend was living with him, he indignantly refused it. In the shortest possible time he had fitted up a bell which connected the closet with the library on the fourth floor. In suspicious cases the Professor had only to press the button. The suspect, all unknowing, would climb the stairs. Down towards him would come his punishment and meet him half-way. Every eventuality was arranged for him.

Already on the late afternoon of the same day, Kien took over his new office. He crouched on his knees and watched through the peep hole the comings and goings of a thickly populated house. His eyes yearned for work. Long idleness had demoralized them. So as to employ both of them and to give neither a preference, he changed over from time to time. His sense of accuracy was reawakened. Five minutes for each eye seemed to him reasonable. He placed his watch before him on the floor and kept to it strictly. His right eye showed a tendency to take advantage at the expense of his left. He held it under stern control. As soon as the precise timing had become second nature to him, he put his watch back in his pocket. The commonplace objects out there which came into his line of vision seemed to him slightly unworthy. The truth was they were all alike. Between one pair of trousers and another there were but minor differences. Since he had never taken any notice of the inhabitants of the house at an earlier time, he couldn't imagine their shapes complete. Trousers were to him simply trousers and he felt himself at a loss. But they had one pleasing quality which he held to their credit: he could look at them. Far more often skirts passed by, and these annoyed him. Both their size and their number usurped for them more space than they deserved. He decided to ignore them. His hands involuntarily turned pages as if he were holding a picture book in them and sharing out the work for his eyes. The pages turned more slowly or more fast according to the speed with which the trousers went by. When skirts came his hands were infected with the distaste of their master; they turned over two pages at a time of what he did not want to read. In this way he very often lost several pages at once, but he did not regret it, for who could tell what might be lurking behind them?

Gradually the monotony of the world soothed him. The great excitement of the past day paled. Among the striding legs coming and going, that particular hallucination was rarely to be seen. There was no sign of that blue colour. The forbidden skirts which he ignored attempted varying colours. That special and unmistakable blue, shrill, insulting and vulgar, was worn by no one. The reason for this fact, which, looked upon statistically, seemed miraculous, was simple. An hallucination continues for as long as it is not contested. It is only necessary to have the strength to face the danger. It is only necessary to fill the consciousness with the image one fears. It is only necessary to make out the warrant against the hallucination and keep it ready always. Then reality must be faced and searched for the hallucination. If the hallucination is to be found anywhere in the physical world, it is then evident that you have gone mad and must undergo proper treatment. But if the blue skirt is nowhere to be found then it has been vanquished. He who is still able to distinguish between reality and imagination is sure of his mental balance. A certainty achieved in circumstances of such difficulty is a certainty for all time.

In the evening the caretaker brought in a meal, which Therese had cooked, and charged for it what it would have cost at a restaurant; Kien paid immediately and ate with pleasure. 'How good it tastes!' he said: 'I am satisfied with my work.' They sat next to each other on the bed. 'No one came again, what a day!' sighed Pfaff and ate more than half of the meal, although he had really had enough already. Kien was pleased to see the dish disappearing so fast. Soon he left the remains to the attention of his companion and full of zeal dropped once more on to his knees.

'What's that?' bellowed Pfaff. 'You're getting a taste for it! That's my hole's doing. You've fallen in love.' He was beaming, and at every sentence he slapped his thighs. Then he put his plate away, pushed aside the Professor, who was trying to penetrate the darkness, and asked: 'Is everything in order? I'll have a look.' Gloating, he intoned aloud: 'Aha! The Mushroom's up to her old tricks. Come home at eight o'clock. Her husband waits for her. What's she cooked for him? A bit of muck. For years I've been on the look-out for murder. The other one waits outside. Got no guts, that man. I'd choke the life out of her, three times a day. The bitch! There she is waiting for him. Raving mad about her, he is. Her old man hasn't

381

an idea. That's what comes of having no guts! I see everything!'

'But it's dark already,' interjected Kien, at once envious and critical.

The caretaker was overcome by one of his gusts of laughter, and fell full-strength, flat on the floor. One part of him reached under the bed, the other shook the wall. For a long time he stayed in this position. Kien shrank apprehensively into a corner. The closet was full to bursting with imprisoned waves of laughter; he avoided them, he was in their way. In spite of everything he did not feel quite at home here. His solitary afternoon had been far more satisfactory. He needed quiet. This barbarian *landsknecht* could flourish only among noise. True to type, he got up suddenly, cumbrous as a hippopotamus, and blustered:

'D'you know what my late lamented nickname was when I was in the police? Professor' — he laid his fists on the two thin shoulders — 'you see before you Ginger the Cat! First of all because of my distinguishing colour, and then because I unmask the darkness. I've got eyes! That's the rule with tigers.'

He called on Kien to take the whole bed for himself, and said good night, he would be sleeping upstairs. Last of all, in the doorway, he commended the peep-hole to his special care. People like hitting out in their sleep; even he had once broken the corner of the peep-hole and to his horror had only woken up in the morning. He begged him to be cautious, and to bear the valuable apparatus in mind.

Very tired, irritated at the interruption of his quiet thoughts — he had been alone for three hours before supper — Kien lay down on the bed and yearned for the library, *his* library which he would soon possess again: four lofty halls, the walls from floor to ceiling robed in books, the communicating doors always wide open, no unjust windows, an even illumination from above, a desk full of manuscripts, work, work, thought, thought, China, learned controversies, opinion versus opinion, in quarterlies, spoken without the aid of material lips, Kien victorious, not in a boxing match, but in a match of the wits, peace, peace, the rustle of books, exquisite, no living creature, no shrill-coloured monster, no ramping woman, no skirt. This house purified of the carcase. Her remains removed from near the desk. Modern ventilation to purge any insistent smell out of the books. Even after months, some of them still smelt. Into the incubator with them! The nose, the most dangerous of all organs. Gas masks ease breathing. A dozen of them high above the writing desk. Higher or the dwarf will steal them. Feels for his ridiculous nose. Slip on a gas mask. Two huge, sad eyes. A single penetrating opening. A pity. Change over. Look at the card of instructions. Boxing match between his eyes. Both want to read. Who is in charge here? Someone is snapping his fingers against my eyelids. As a punishment I will shut you both. Pitch dark. Tigers in the night. Beasts dream too. Aristotle knew everything. The first library in the world. A zoological collection. Zoroaster's passion for fire. He was honoured at home. A bad prophet. Prometheus, a devil. The Eagle only eats his liver. Eat his fire too! Theresianum — sixth floor — flames — books — flight — down the steep stairs — quicker, quicker! — damnation! — congestion — fire! fire! — one for all and all for one — united, united, united — books, books, we are all books — red, red — who has barred the staircase? — I ask. I demand an answer! — Let me through! — I'll blaze the trail for you! — I will throw myself on the foemen's spears — damnation — blue — the skirt — stiff and stark a rock against the sky — across the Milky way — Sirius — dogs bloodhounds — let's bite the granite! Teeth broken jaws blood blood —

Kien woke up. In spite of his fatigue, he clenched his fists. He gnashed his teeth. No need for fear, they are still there. He must come to conclusions with them. Even the blood was a dream. The closet presses on him. It is narrow, sleeping here. He got up, threw up the peep-hole cover and calmed himself by looking at the great monotony outside. For it is only an idea that nothing is happening. If you can get used to the darkness, you can see all the trousers of the afternoon, an interminable parade; the intervening skirts have faded out. At night everyone wears trousers. A decree for the abolition of the female sex is in preparation. To-morrow the proclamation will be made public. The caretaker will proclaim it. *That* voice will be heard through the whole town, the whole country, every country, as far as the earth's atmosphere reaches; other planets will have to look after themselves, we are overburdened with women, evasion is punished by death, ignorance of the law is no protection. All Christian names to have masculine suffixes, history to be rewritten for schools. The select historical commission has an easy task: its chairman, Professor Kien. What have women produced in history? Children and intrigues!

Kien lies down again in bed. Wandering, he falls asleep. Wandering, he reaches the blue rock which he thought had been shattered. If the rock will not move, the dream can't go on, so he wakes immediately and leans down to the peep-hole. It is close at his side. This happens a dozen times in the night. Towards morning he transfers the

383

peephole, his eye of monotony, his *requiem*, his joy, into his dream library. He places several peepholes in each wall. Thus he would never have to look long for one. Wherever books are missing he builds little peep-holes, the Benedikt Pfaff system. He skilfully guides the course of his dreams; wherever he may have got to, he brings himself back on a lead to the library. Numberless peep-holes invite him to linger. He serves them, as he had learnt during the day, on bended knee; and he proves that without a doubt there are only trousers in the world, especially in the darkness. Differently coloured skirts disappear. Starched blue rocks crumble. He must not get up. His dreams can be automatically regulated. Towards morning he sleeps, unconditionally, without aberrations. His head rests, deep in serious thought, on his writing desk.

The first pale light found him at work. At six, on his knees, he contemplated the twilight creeping slowly over the entrance hall. The stain on the opposite wall acquired its true character. Shadows, whose origin was dubious — of things, not of people, but of what things? — cast themselves on the tiles, developed into a grey of a dangerous and tactless tinge, approaching a colour by the naming of which he had no intention of spoiling the young day. Without admitting its name, he requested the shadows, at first courteously, to disappear, or to assume another colour. They hesitated. He became insistent. Their hesitation had not escaped him. He decided on an ultimatum and threatened, if they disregarded it, to break off relations. He had other means of pressure, he warned them, he was not defenceless, he would suddenly take them in the rear, and shatter at a single blow their pride and their haughtiness, their arrogance and insolence. How contemptible and absurd they were in any case; their existence depended on tiles. Tiles can be utterly shattered. A blow here, a blow there and their miserable little splinters would be left to sorrow and think — what about? — about whether it was just to torment an innocent creature who never did them an injury, but who, rising refreshed from sleep, was making ready to meet a day of decisive conflict? For to-day the disaster of yesterday was to be wiped out, annihilated, buried and forgotten.

The shadows quavered: those bright streaks which separated each from the other, grew broader and shone brightly. There was no doubt that Kien would have himself defeated his enemies. But at that moment a mighty pair of trousers came to his rescue and robbed him of the honour of victory. Two heavy legs walked across the tiles, and stood still. A powerful boot raised itself and lovingly sketched the outer opening of the peep-hole, so as not to hurt it, but simply to be reassured of its old familiar shape. The first boot withdrew, and a second permitted itself the same tenderness, in the opposite direction. Then the legs marched further, there was a noise, a jingling like that of a key, a screeching and creaking. The shadows moaned and vanished. Now it could be frankly admitted: they had been blue, literally blue. The clumsy creature walked back again. Thanks were owing to him. All the same, he could have managed without him. Shadows are shadows. They are thrown by an object. Move the object and the shadows moan and die. What object had been moved? The answer to that could only be given by the perpetrator. In came Benedikt Pfaff.

'What's that! Up already! A juicy good morning, Professor! You're the picture of industry. I've come for my oil can. Did you hear the street door groaning. On that bed, you sleep like a bear. A dormouse is nothing to it. We used to sleep three at a time in it, when my old woman was alive and my daughter, bless her. I'll give you a tip, as a friend and the father of this house, you stay here, where you are now! Then you'll see one of the marvels of nature as the saying is. A house getting up. All of them off to work. In a hurry they are, they sleep too late, all of them women and sluggards. If you're lucky, you'll see three pairs of legs at a time. An interesting spectacle! You can't know them all. Aha! you think to yourself, and all the time it's someone quite different. A great show! Save your laugh, I say, or you'll laugh yourself to death.'

Panting and red as a turkey with delight at his joke, he left Kien alone. That repulsive shadow with its many ugly streaks had originated then in the grille across the street door. You have but to know an object by its proper name for it to lose its dangerous magic. Primitive man called each and all by the wrong name. One single and terrible web of magic surrounded him; where and when did he not feel threatened? Knowledge has freed us from superstitions and beliefs. Knowledge makes use always of the same names, preferably Graeco-Latin, and indicates by these names actual things. Misunderstandings are impossible. Who for instance could imagine anything else in a door than the door itself, and, at the uttermost, its shadow?

But the caretaker was right. Numerous trousers were leaving the house; at first plain ones, blunt, tended with very moderate care, revealing a minimum of trouser consciousness and maybe, as Kien hoped, some intelligence. The later it grew, the sharper the creases of the appearing trousers; and the haste with which they moved grew less. When one knife-edge came too close to another, he was afraid they might cut each other and called: 'Look out!' All kinds of distinguishing marks struck him; he did not shrink from naming the colours, the material, the value, the height from the ground, prospective holes, the breadth, the relation of trouser leg to boot, stains and their probable origin; in spite of the richness of the material he came to one or two conclusions. About ten o'clock as the house grew quiet, he attempted to form an estimate as to the age, character and profession of the wearers of what he saw. A systematic study of the classification of men by trousers seemed to him abundantly possible. He promised himself a small thesis on the subject; it would be completed easily in three days. Half joking he uttered a reproach against a certain scholar who was pursuing researches in the tailor's department. But the time he spent down there was lost; it was of no consequence what he did with it. He knew well why he had become so devoted to the peep-hole. Yesterday was over, yesterday *had* to be over. And this scholarly concentration was doing him infinite good.

Among the men hurrying to work women forced their obstinate and unpleasing way. Already early in the morning they were on their feet. They came back soon, and thus counted twice over. Presumably they had been shopping. He heard 'Good mornings' and superfluous compliments. Even the most cutting trousers let themselves be held up. They expressed their masculine subservience in various ways. One clicked his heels with violence, a noisy pain struck on Kien's low-lying ears. Others rocked themselves round on their toes, two bent their knees. With others, the knife-edge creases began to tremble slightly. An unscrupulous inclination betrayed itself in the shape of the angular corner made by trousers and floor. One man, one single man Kien hoped to see, who would show aversion to a woman, who would form an obtuse angle with the floor. No such man came. Think only of the hour: these men had but just escaped their beds, and their legal wives; the whole house was married. Day and work opened out before them. They were hurrying to leave. Their very legs imparted a sense of freshness and determination to the spectator. What possibilities! What strength! No mental exertions awaited them, but life, discipline; subordination; entrusted duties; well-known purposes; a network, an achievement, the passage of their time, distributed as they themselves had wished to distribute it. And what did they meet in the entrance hall? The wife, the daughter, the cook of some neighbour — nor was it chance that brought them together. The women arranged it so; from behind the doors of the flats they stalked their prey; scarcely had they heard the footfall of the man they had condemned to their love, than they glided after him, before him, alongside him, little Cleopatras, each ready with every lie, flattering, wheedling, aquiver for attention, promising their guilty favours, mercilessly scratching the surface of the fair, full day to which the men were bound, strong and ready, honourably to partition their time. For these men are debauched, they live in the schools of their wives; they hate their wives naturally, but instead of generalizing that hatred, they run after the next woman. One of them smiles, and they stand stock still. How they abase them-selves, put off their plans, dangle their legs, waste their time, bargain for trivial pleasures! They take off their hats so courteously as to take your breath and sight away. If the hat should fall on the floor, behold a grovelling hand comes after it; a grinning face follows. Two seconds ago that face was still grave. The intruder has succeeded; she has robbed a man of his gravity. The women of the house have laid their ambush immediately in front of the peep-hole. Even in their secrets they must be admired by some third party.

But Kien does not admire them. He could ignore them, God knows it would be easy — a mere matter of will-power. Ignoring is in the blood of a learned man. Learning is the art of ignoring. But for a reason, near to his heart, he makes no use of his art. Women are illiterates, unendurable and stupid, a perpetual disturbance. How rich would the world be without them, a vast laboratory, an overfilled library, a heaven of intensive study, night and day! Yet justice compels him to admit one saving grace in all these women; they wear skirts, but not one is blue; as long and as far as Kien looks not one of the women of the house awakens in him the recollection of one who erstwhile would glide over this very threshold and who, in the end and far too late, died by hunger the most wretched of deaths.

Towards one o'clock Benedikt Pfaff appeared and asked for money for dinner. He must fetch it from the café and had not a penny on him. The State paid him his pension regularly on the first of the month, not on the last. Kien asked for quiet. His days down here would be few and numbered. Soon he would be going back to his flat. Before then he wished to complete his researches at the peep-hole. A 'Charac-terology of Trousers' was in prospect together with an 'Appendix on Shoes'. He had no time to eat, to-morrow perhaps.

'What's that!' bellowed the caretaker. 'I won't have it! Professor, I'm asking you for your own good, hand over the money! In that interesting position a fellow can starve to death. I'm taking care of you.'

Kien rose and cast an exploratory glance at the trousers of the peacebreaker. 'If you please, will you kindly leave my — study at once!' He emphasized the 'my', made a short pause after it and threw out the 'study' as though it were an insult.

Pfaff's eyes started from his head. His fists itched. So as not to use them at once he rubbed his nose hard. Had the Professor gone mad? *His* study. Now what was he to do? Break his legs, smash in his skull, spatter his brains, or begin with one in the belly? Drag him up to that woman? That'd be a good one! She'd lock the murderer into the lavatory, that's what she said. Chuck him out into the street? Smash down the wall and shut him in the back room where the heart of his late-lamented daughter was lost?

None of these things happened. At Pfaff's command Therese had cooked lunch; it was waiting upstairs; cost what it would — even the sweetest revenge — he must earn his share of it. He wouldn't have minded keeping a pub, it would have suited him as well as being in a circus. He drew a small shutter-lock out of his pocket, pushed Kien aside with one finger, bent down and locked the lid over his peep-hole.

'My hole's my own!' he bellowed. His fists were swelling again. 'Shurrup!' he told them, furious. Sulkily they withdrew into his pockets. There they lay, ready to pounce. They were hurt. They rubbed their hairs on the lining of his pockets and growled.

'What trousers!' Kien was thinking, 'what trousers!' One profession, an important one, he had missed in his morning's observations; the killer. Here was one — the very one who had this moment cold-bloodedly obstructed his instrument of observation — who wore trousers typical of those which would be seen on such a criminal: crumpled, glimmering reddish with faded blood, kept in ugly motion from within, threadbare and greasy, clumsy, dark, repulsive. If beasts wore trousers, they would wear them like that.

'Dinner is ordered!' foamed the beast. 'What's ordered must be paid for!' Pfaff whipped out a fist, opened it much against its will, and held out his flat hand. 'I'm not going to lose money, Professor, you don't know me! I won't stand any nonsense: I ask you for the last time! Think of your health! What'll become of you?'

Kien made no move.

'Then I shall have to search you!' He arrested him, said, 'What a scarecrow!' threw the scarecrow on the bed, and looked through all its pockets, carefully counted the money he found, took out a reasonable sum for a meal, not a penny more, called himself, for his honesty, a good fellow and ended menacingly: 'I'll *send* you your dinner. You don't deserve my company. The ingratitude of the man. I'll shave that off. I warn you! My hole'll stay shut. That's justice. All those trousers have made a crook of you. I must watch out. If you behave proper I'll open it again to-morrow, out of pure consideration and kind-heartedness. That's how I am. Be good now! At four you'll get your coffee. At seven you'll have a light supper. You'll pay when it comes! Or would you rather pay now?'

Kien had just replaced himself on his feet, but he was laid down flat once more. So as to settle the matter once for all, Pfaff worked out the Professor's keep for a week; for a policeman his arithmetic was not bad, at the third attempt the sum seemed correct, as it was a large one, he took charge of it, wrote under the calculation: 'Received with thanks, Benedikt Pfaff, Retired police constable,' slipped the piece of paper, because it was his own, carefully under the pillow, only then cleared his throat and spat (partly to show his disappointment in the Professor, partly at the disappointment of his fists, so long idle), and went out. The door remained whole. But he locked it on the outside.

Another lock interested Kien more. He wrenched at the lid of the peep-hole; he loosened it a little but it didn't come off. He turned out the closet for keys. Perhaps one would fit. Under the bed there was nothing, he broke open the cupboard. Inside were old uniforms, a bugle, unused boxing gloves, a tightly tied parcel of clean, freshly ironed women's underclothes (all white), a service revolver, ammunition and photographs, which he looked through out of loathing rather than curiosity. A father was seated with legs astraddle, his right hand held a small woman prisoner; with his left he pressed a three-year-old child to him; she floated shyly about his knee. On the back he read in fat, noisy letters: 'Ginger the Cat with wife and daughter.' At that moment it struck Kien that the caretaker had been married a very long time before his wife died. The picture showed him in the midst of his married life. Filled with cruel pleasure, he crossed out the words 'Ginger the Cat' and wrote 'Murderer' above, put back the photograph on top, on the same side as the uniforms, which, to judge by their condition, were often used, and closed the cupboard.

A key! A key! A key! My kingdom for a key! He felt as if he

had a halter through every pore of his skin, as if someone had twisted all the halters into one rope and the strong, bulky, awkward thing was stretched through the peep-hole into the corridor, where a whole regiment of trousers were tugging at it. 'I come, I come,' gasped Kien, 'but I'm being stopped!' In despair he threw himself on the bed. He recalled what he had seen. Man after man passed before him. He called them all back; he would not forgive them their submission to the women and hurled a full complement of reproaches at their heads. He had enough to study and to think over. He must keep his mind occupied! He placed four Japanese Genii before the portals of his mind, formidable monsters, devouring, terrible. They knew what must not cross the threshold. Only what advanced the safety of the mind might pass.

Essential to pass in review a number of highly venerated theories. Even learning has its weaker points. The foundation of all true learning is doubt. Descartes had proved that. Why for instance do physics take into account three primary colours? No one would deny the importance of red. A thousand proofs bear witness to its elemental significance. It might be argued against yellow that, in the spectrum, it comes perilously near to green. But green, which is generally held to be the result of mixing yellow with an unmentionable colour — green must be cautiously considered, although there is a presumption that it is a healing colour. Let us reverse the argument! A colour which is beneficial to the eye cannot be made up of component parts of which one is the most disturbing, most hideous, and most meaningless that can be thought of. Green contains no blue. Let us calmly speak the word, it is merely a word, nothing more, emphatically not a primary colour. Clearly there is a secret somewhere in the spectrum, an element foreign to us, which, next to yellow, plays its part in creating green. Students of physics should make it a duty to find out. They have more important things to do. Daily they flood the world with new rays, all of them from the invisible spectrum. For the problem of our actual light they have found a stock solution. The third primary colour, the missing one, the one we know only by its results, not by its appearance, is — so they say — blue. Take a word at random, fit it into a problem and the problem is solved. So that no one can see through the trick, they choose a disreputable and generally discredited word; naturally enough men hesitate before they submit such a word to microscopic examination. It stinks, they tell themselves, and give a wide berth to anything which seems blue. Men are cowards. When a decision should be taken they would rather bargain a dozen times over it; maybe they can lie it away. Thus up to this very day they have believed in the existence of a chimerical colour, with a more rock-like faith than they have in God. There is no blue. Blue is an invention of the physicists. If there were blue, the hair of a typical murderer would be this colour. What is the caretaker's name? The Blue Cat? On the contrary: 'Ginger the Cat, the Red Cat!'

The logical argument against the existence of blue is further strengthened by the empirical. With closed eyes, Kien sought some image which in the general opinion would be described as blue. He saw the sea. A pleasing light rises from it, tree-tops with the wind passing over them. Not in vain do poets, standing upon a summit, compare the woods below them to the sea. They do it again and again. They cannot avoid certain similes. There is a deeper reason for this. Poets are men of the senses. They *see* the wood. It is green. In their recollection another image wakens, no less vast, no less green: the sea. So the sea is green. Over it is the vault of the sky. It is full of clouds — they are black and heavy. A storm is rising. But it cannot break. Nowhere is the sky blue. The day passes. How the hours hasten! Why? Who is chasing them? May not a man see the skies before nightfall, see their accursed colour? It is a lie. Towards evening the clouds part. A sharp red breaks through. Where is the blue? Everywhere it burns, red, red, red! Then night comes. One more successful revelation. No one doubted the red.

Kien laughs. Whatever he sets his hand to succeeds, submits to his proofs. A benevolent wisdom is given to him even in sleep. True, he is not asleep. He is only pretending! If he opens his eyes, they fall on the locked peep-hole. He will spare himself a purposeless annoyance. He despises the murderer. As soon as he permits him his rightful place again, that is as soon as he takes the lock off the peep-hole and apologizes for his impertinence, Kien will open his eyes. Not a moment before.

'I ask you, murderer!' a certain voice interrupts him.

'Quiet!' he commanded. Reflecting on the colour blue, he had neglected a certain voice. He must extinguish it, like the irrevocable skirt. He closed his eyes even tighter and commanded again: 'Quiet.'

'I ask you, here's your dinner.'

'Nonsense! The caretaker is sending in my dinner.' Contemptuously, he pursed his lips.

'That's why, he sent me. I had to. Did I want to come?'

The voice appeared indignant. A small trick would enforce its silence. 'I want no dinner!' He rubbed his fingers. He did that well. He entered into her stupidity. A formidable debater, he would drive her step by step into a corner.

'I don't care. I'll drop it! A shame for the beautiful dinner. I ask you, whose money is it? Someone else's.'

The voice permitted itself flippant intonations. It seemed to feel at home here. It behaved itself as if it had been resuscitated from the common pit. An artist had put the pieces together, a great artist, a genius. He knew how to inform corpses with their own old tones of voice.

'By all means, drop the non-existent dinner! For there is one thing, my dear corpse, which I must tell you. I am not afraid. Those times are past. I will tear every shred off the body of a ghost! I still hear no dinner falling. Perhaps I have failed to apprehend the noise. Nor do I see any fragments. I am aware that eating is done from plates. China, they say, is brittle. Or am I under a misapprehension? Let me advise you now to invent some story of unbreakable china. Corpses are full of invention. I am waiting! I am waiting!' Kien grinned. His cruel irony delighted him.

'I ask you, there's nothing in that! Eyes are for seeing. Anyone can be blind!'

'I shall open my eyes, and when I do not see you, you can sink into the ground with shame. I have played fair until now. I have indeed partly taken you seriously. But when I see, what, out of consideration for you, I have not wanted to see, namely that you speak without being here, then it is all over with you. I will open my eyes wide enough to astonish you. I will put my fingers through where your face would be if you had a face. My eyes do not open easily: they are tired of seeing nothing, but when once they are open, woe to you! The look I am preparing knows no mercy. Patience a little longer! I will wait a little for I am sorry for you. Vanish, rather, of your own accord! I will allow you an honourable retreat. I will count ten and my head will be empty. Must we have more blood? We are civilized beings. Better for you to go of your own accord, believe me! Moreover, this closet belongs to a murderer. I give you fair warning. If he comes he will strike you dead!'

'You don't do *me* in!' screamed the voice. 'Your first wife, yes; not me!'

Heavy objects began to fall on Kien. If anyone were there he would have thought that eating utensils had been thrown at him. He knew better. He saw nothing, although he kept his eyes closed, a condition highly favourable to hallucinations. He smelt food. His sense of smell had turned traitor. Once again his ears vibrated with wild abuse. He did not listen carefully. But in every sentence the word 'Murderer!' was reiterated. His lids valiantly stood their ground. About his eyes his muscles contracted sharply. Poor, sick ears! Something liquid trickled down his chest. 'I'm off!' shrieked the voice, and again someone was listening to every word, 'that's all the dinner you'll get. Murderers can starve. Then respectable people can stay alive. Locked up, you are, anyway. Like a wild beast! The whole bed's in a mess. The tenants'll be wanting to know about it. The house says he's mad. I say: murderer. I'm off now. A shame for all my trouble! The closet stinks. What can I do about it? It was a good dinner. There's another room behind this. Murderers ought to be walled up! I'm off.'

Suddenly all was still. Another man would have rejoiced at once. Kien waited. He counted up to sixty. The stillness continued. He repeated a sermon of the Buddha, in the original Pali, not one of his longest dicta. But he omitted not a syllable and religiously declaimed all the repetitive phrases. Now let us half open our left eye, he said very softly, all is still, he who fears now is a coward. The right eye follows. Both gaze out into an empty closet. On the bed are strewn several plates, a tray and cutlery, on the floor a broken glass. A piece of beef is there, and his suit is smeared with spinach. He is wet to the skin with soup. It all smells normal and genuine. Who can have brought it? There was no one here. He goes to the door. It is locked. He rattles it, in vain. Who can have locked him in? The caretaker, when he left. The spinach is an illusion. He washes it away. The splinters of glass he gathers together. His grief cuts him. Blood flows. Is he to doubt the reality of his own blood? History tells us of the strangest errors. There should be a knife with the dinner things. To prove it, he carefully cuts off — although it is sharp and very painful — the little finger of his left hand. A great deal more blood begins to flow. He wraps his injured hand in a white handkerchief which is hanging down from the bed. The handkerchief turns out to be a napkin. In the corner he reads his own monogram. How did this get here? It seems as though someone had thrown into the room, through the roof, walls and locked door, a cooked dinner. The windows are unbroken. He tries the meat. It has the right taste. He feels ill, he feels hungry, he eats it all up. Holding his breath, stiff

393

and quivering, he senses how each morsel finds its way down his alimentary tubes. Someone must have crept in while he was lying with closed eyes on the bed. He listens. So as to miss nothing, he lifts his finger. Then he looks under the bed and in the cupboard. He finds nobody. Someone has been here without speaking a word, and has gone away again: afraid. The canaries did not sing. Why do people keep these animals? He has done them no harm. Since he has lived here, he has let them alone. They have betrayed him. Flames flicker before his eyes. Suddenly the canaries start up. He threatens them with his bandaged fist. He looks at them: the birds are blue. They are mocking him. He pulls one after another out of the cage and presses their throats until they are strangled. Triumphant, he opens the window and throws the corpses into the street. His little finger, a fifth corpse, he tosses after them. Scarcely has he thus expelled everything blue from the room when the walls begin to dance. Their violent movement dissolves in blue spots. They are skirts, he whispers and creeps under the bed. He had begun to doubt his reason.

CHAPTER III

A MADHOUSE

ON an excitingly warm evening late in March the famous psychiatrist George Kien paced the rooms of his Paris Institute. The windows were open wide. Between the patients a stubborn contest was in progress for the limited space close to the bars. One head banged another. Abuse was bandied about. Almost all were suffering from the unfamiliar air which all day long they had been — some of them literally — gulping and swallowing in the garden. When the attendants had brought them back to the dormitories they were discontented. They wanted more air. Not one would admit to being tired. Until it was time for sleep they were still breathing at the window bars the last dregs of the evening. Here they felt themselves to be even closer to the air which filled their light, lofty rooms.

Not even the Professor, whom they loved because he was beautiful and kind, distracted them at their occupation. At other times when it was rumoured he was coming, the greater number of the patients in a dormitory would run in a body to meet him. Usually they strove for some contact with him, either by touch or voice, just as to-day they strove for places at the window. The loathing which so many of them felt for the Institute where they thought themselves confined, was never vented on the youthful Professor. It was only two years since he had become in name the director of the extensive Institute which he had in fact directed before, as the good angel of a diabolical superior. Those patients who thought that they had been detained by force, or who in fact had been, ascribed the blame to that all-powerful, although now dead, predecessor.

This latter had embraced official psychiatry with the obstinacy of a madman. He took it for his real work in life, to use the vast material at his disposal to support the accepted terminology. Typical cases, in his sense of the word, robbed him of his sleep. He clung to the infallibility of the system and hated doubters. Human beings, especially nerve cases and criminals, were nothing to him. He allowed them a certain right to existence. They provided experiences which authorities could use to build up the science. He himself was an authority. On the value of such constructive mind he would — although a surly

395

man of few words — make long and vehement speeches to which his assistant Georges Kien, under compulsion and burning with shame at his narrow-mindedness, must listen from beginning to end and from end to beginning, hour after hour, standing to attention. When a milder and a more severe opinion were in opposition, his predecessor would decide for the more severe. To patients who wearied him on his every round with the same old story, he would say: 'I know all that.' To his wife he complained bitterly of the professional necessity of having to deal with people not responsible for their actions. To her moreover he revealed his most secret thoughts about the essence of insanity, which he did not publish only because they were too simple and crude for the system and therefore dangerous. Madness, he said with great emphasis, and looked at his wife with penetrating and accusing gaze (she blushed), madness is the disease which attacks those very people who think only of themselves. Mental disease is the punishment of egoism. Thus asylums are always full of the scum of the earth. Prisons perform the same task, but science requires asylums for its experimental material. He had nothing else to say to his wife. She was thirty years younger than him and cast a glow over the evening of his life. His first wife had run away before he could shut her up — as he had done with his second — in his own institute; she was an incurable egoist. His third, against whom he had nothing save his own jealousy, loved George Kien.

To her he owed his rapid rise. He was tall, strong, fiery, and sure of himself; in his features there was something of that gentleness which women need before they can feel at home with a man. Those who saw him compared him to Michelangelo's Adam. He understood very well how intelligence and elegance could be combined. His brilliant gifts had been brought to fruitful effectiveness by the policy of his beloved. When she was sure that no one would follow her husband as the head of the institute but George himself, the director suddenly died without provoking any comment. George was at once nominated his successor and married her as a reward for her earlier services; of her last one he had no suspicion.

In the hard school of his predecessor he had developed quickly into his exact opposite. He treated his patients as if they were human beings. Faithfully he would listen to stories he had heard a thousand times before, and would express spontaneous surprise and amazement at the stalest dangers and anxieties. He laughed and cried with the patient he had in front of him. The division of his days was significant:

three times — as soon as he got up, early in the afternoon, and late in the evening — he would make his rounds, so that on no single day did he ever miss one of the eight hundred odd inhabitants. A rapid glance was enough. When he saw the slightest alteration, a mere crack which offered a possibility of sliding into the other's soul, he would act at once and move the patient in question into his own private house. Instead of taking him to an ante-room, which did not exist, he would lead him, with cleverly interjected words of courtesy, into his study and offer him the best place. There he would easily win, if he did not enjoy it already, the confidence of the man who, towards anyone else, would hide behind the screen of his insanity. Kings he addressed reverently as Your Majesty; with Gods he would fall on his knees and fold his hands. Thus even the most sublime eminences stooped to him and went into particulars. He became their sole confidant, whom, from the moment he had recognized them, they would keep informed of the changes in their own spheres and seek his advice. He advised them with crystal cleverness, as though their wishes were his own, cautiously keeping their aims and their beliefs before his eyes, cautiously shifting ground, expressing doubts in his ability, never authoritative in his dealings with men, so diffident that many smilingly encouraged him; was he not after all their chief minister, their prophet or their apostle, occasionally even their chamberlain?

In time he developed into a remarkable actor. The muscles of his face, of exceptional mobility, would fit themselves in the course of a day to the most various situations. Since he would daily invite at least three patients, in spite of his thoroughness sometimes even more, he must play at least so many parts; not to count the fugitive but significant hints and words thrown out in the course of his rounds, which ran into hundreds. The scientific world argued vigorously over his treatment of a few chosen cases of alternating personalities. If a patient, for instance, imagined himself to be two people who had nothing in common or who were in conflict with each other, George Kien adopted a method which had at first seemed very dangerous even to him: he made friends with both parties. A fanatical pertinacity was the postulate for this ruse. So as to discover the true inwardness of both characters, he would support each with arguments from whose effects he would draw his own conclusions. He built up the conclusions into hypotheses and thought of delicate experiments to prove them. Then he would proceed to the cure. In his own consciousness he would gradually draw the separate halves of the patient — as he embodied them — closer to each other, and thus gradually would re-join them. He sensed the points of contact between them, and directed the attention of the separate personalities by striking and impressive images always back to these points until they remained there and of their own accord grew together. Sudden crises, violent partings, just when a final unanimity seemed to be achieved, happened often and were inevitable. But no less often did the cure succeed. Failures he ascribed to his own superficiality. He must have overlooked some hidden element, he was a botcher, he didn't take his work seriously enough, he was sacrificing living creatures to his own dead convictions, he was no better than his predecessor — then he would begin all over again, with a store of new curatives and experiments. For he believed in the soundness of his method.

Thus he lived simultaneously in numberless different worlds. Among the mentally diseased he grew into one of the most com-prehensive intellects of his time. He learnt more from them than he gave them. They enriched him with their unique experiences; he merely simplified them in order to make them healthy. What powers of mind and wit did he not find in many! They were the only true personalities, of perfect single-mindedness, real characters, of a con-centration and force of will which Napoleon might have envied them. He knew inspired satirists among them, more gifted than all the poets; their ideas were never reduced to paper, they flowed from a heart which beat outside realities, on which they fell like alien conquerors. Privateers know the straightest way to the El Dorados of this world.

Since he had belonged to them and given himself wholly to their constructions, he no longer cared for polite literature. In novels you always found the same thing. Earlier he had read with passion, and had taken great pleasure in new turns given to old phrases which he had thought to be unchangeable, colourless, worn out and without meaning. Then words had meant little to him. He asked only aca-demic correctness; the best novels were those in which the people spoke in the most cultured way. He who could express himself in the same way as all writers had done before him, was their legitimate successor. The task of such a writer was to reduce the angular, painful, biting multifariousness of life as it was all around one, to the smooth surface of a sheet of paper, on which it could pleasantly and swiftly be read off. Reading was fondling, was another form of love, was for ladies and ladies' doctors, to whose profession a delicate understanding of *lecture intime* properly belonged. No baffling turns of plot, no unusual words, the more often was the same track traversed, the subtler was the pleasure to be derived from the journey. All fiction — a textbook of good manners. Well-read men are obsessed with politeness. Their participation in the lives of others exhausts itself in congratulations and condolences. George Kien had started as a gynaecologist. His youth and good looks brought patients in crowds. At that period, which did not last long, he gave himself up to French novels; they played a considerable part in assuring his success. Involuntarily he behaved to women as if he loved them. Each in turn approved his taste and accepted the consequences. Among the little monkeys a fashion for being ill spread. He took what fell into his lap and had difficulty in keeping up with his conquests. Surrounded and spoilt by innumerable women, all ready to serve him, he lived like Prince Gautama before he became Buddha. No anxious father and prince had cut him off from the miseries of the world, but he saw old age, death and beggars in such abundance that he no longer noticed them. Yet he was indeed cut off, by the books he read, the sentences he spoke, the women who were ranged round him in a greedy close-built wall.

He found the way to the wilderness in his twenty-eighth year. On a visit which he had bestowed on the wealthy and persistent wife of a banker who was ill whenever her husband was away, he met the banker's brother, a harmless lunatic whom the family kept at home for reasons of prestige; even a sanatorium would have seemed to the banker to undermine his credit. Two rooms in his absurd villa were reserved for the use of his brother, who lorded it in them over his nurse, a young widow thrice over betrayed and sold to him. She was not to leave him alone, she was to submit to him in everything, and she was to announce herself to the world as his secretary, for he was given out to be an artist and an eccentric, who had little attention left for the human race, but was secretly working on a gigantic opus. Just this was known to George Kien as the doctor attending on the lady of the house.

To protect himself from her slobbering courtesies, he asked her to show him over the art treasures of the villa. Heavy and consenting, she got up off her sofa. The pictures of nude beautiful women — her husband collected only these — would form, she hoped, a bridge to him. She raved over Rubens and Renoir. 'In these women,' she repeated her husband's favourite phrase, 'pulses the orient dye.' He had once dealt in carpets. For just such an effect of the orient he took every

kind of opulence in art. Madame observed Dr. George full of sympathy. She called him by his Christian name because he might have
been 'her little brother'. Wherever his eyes rested, there too rested
hers. Soon she thought she had discovered what he wanted. 'How you
suffer!' she said, as they do on the stage, and glanced down at her
bosom. Dr. George would not understand. He had such sensitive
feelings. 'The *clou* of the whole collection is in my brother-in-law's
room! He is quite harmless.' She promised herself better results from
that really shameless picture. Since educated people had taken to
coming to the house, her husband had been compelled — while bellowing that he was master in his own house — to banish to his sick brother's
apartments the real picture of his heart and the first that he had succeeded in buying cheap (on principle he only bought cheap and for
ready money). Dr. Kien showed no great inclination to meet the
lunatic. He thought he would find an imbecile version of the banker
himself. Madame assured him that the picture there was more valuable
than all the others taken together; she meant artistic value but in her
mouth that word had the one meaning, which, like all else, was acquired from her husband. In the end she offered herself his arm, he
obeyed and followed. Familiarities while walking seemed to him less
dangerous than while standing.

The doors which led to her brother-in-law's rooms were locked.
Dr. George rang the bell. They heard a heavy dragging step. Then
all grew still. Behind a peep-hole appeared a black eye. Madame put
her finger to her lip and grinned tenderly. The eye stayed there,
motionless. The two waited patiently. The doctor was regretting his
politeness and the serious waste of his time. Suddenly the door swung
silently open. A gorilla in human clothes stepped out, stretched forth
its long arms, laid them on the shoulders of the doctor and greeted him
in a foreign language. He took no notice of the woman. His guests
followed him in. He offered them seats at a round table. His gestures
were crude, but comprehensible and inviting. The doctor racked his
brains to follow his language. It seemed on the whole to recall an
African dialect. The gorilla fetched his secretary. She was scantily
dressed and evidently embarrassed. When she had seated herself her
master pointed to a picture on the wall and clapped her on the back.
She nestled up against him, unashamed. Her timidity disappeared.
The picture represented the marriage of two ape-like creatures.
Madame rose to her feet and looked at it from different angles and
from all sides. The gorilla kept tight hold of his male visitor; he

evidently had much to say to him. To George every word was strange. He grasped only one thing: the couple seated at the table were in some way closely connected with the couple in the picture. The secretary understood her master. She answered him in a similar language. He spoke louder, in a deeper voice, behind his tones there seemed to be passion. Occasionally she threw in a word in French, perhaps to indicate what was really meant. 'Don't you speak French?' George asked. 'Naturally, monsieur!' she countered emphatically, 'what do you take me for? I am a Parisian!' She flooded him with a hasty gush of words, badly pronounced and even worse strung together, as though she had already half forgotten the language. The gorilla bellowed at her, and she was quiet at once. His eyes shone. She put her arm across his chest. He cried like a child. 'He hates the French language,' she whispered to the visitor. 'He's been working for years on one of his own. It's not quite finished yet.'

Madame was for ever gazing at the picture. George was grateful to her for this. One word from her would have broken down his politeness at last. He himself could find no words. If only the gorilla would speak again! Before this single wish all his thoughts of time-wasting, duties, women, success had vanished, as if from the day of his birth he had only been seeking for that man, or that gorilla, who had made up his own language. His crying interested him less. Suddenly he stood up and bowed low and reverently to the gorilla. He avoided French sounds, but his face expressed the greatest respect. The secretary accepted this recognition of her lord with a friendly nod. Then the gorilla stopped crying, fell back to his talking and permitted himself his original vehement gestures. Each syllable which he uttered corresponded to a special gesture. The words for objects seemed to change. He meant the picture a hundred times and called it each time something different; the names seemed to depend on the gesture with which he demonstrated them. Expressed and accompanied by his whole body no sound appeared indifferent. When he laughed he spread his arms out wide. He seemed to have a forehead at the back of his head. His hair had been rubbed away there as though, in the hours of his creative labour, he was for ever passing his hands over it.

Suddenly he sprang up and threw himself with passion on the floor. George noticed that it was strewn with earth, probably a thick layer. The secretary caught at his clothes as he lay there, but he was too heavy for her. Imploringly, she asked the visitor to help. She was jealous, she said, so very jealous! Together they raised the gorilla. Hardly was he seated again when he began to recount his experiences down below. From a few powerful words, hurled into the room like living tree trunks, George guessed at some mythical tale of passion, which shattered him with fearful doubts of himself. He saw himself as an insect in the presence of a man. He asked himself, how could he understand things which came from depths a thousand feet deeper than any he had ever dared to plumb. How could he measure himself, sitting at the same table with a creature such as this, he a creature of custom, of favours, with every pore of his soul stopped with fat, every day more fat, a half-man in all practical uses, without the courage to be, since to be in our world means to be different, a plaster cast, a tailor's dummy, set in motion or put to rest by gracious chance, entirely dependent on chance, without the slightest influence over it, without a spark of power, strumming always the same empty phrases, always understood at the same safe distance. For where is there a normal man, a man who determines, alters and forms his neighbour? The women, who had stormed George with love and who would give their lives for him, especially when he was making love to them, were afterwards just the same as they had been before, smoothly groomed skin-worshippers, busied about cosmetics or men. But this secretary, in her origin doubtless an ordinary woman, just the same as any other, had grown under the powerful will of the gorilla into an original creature, stronger, more passionate, more devoted. While he was singing his adventures with the earth, she grew restive. She threw jealous glances and words into the midst of his story, fidgeted helplessly hither and thither on her chair, pinched him, smiled, put out her tongue; he took no notice.

Madame was no longer finding enough pleasure in the picture. She forced George to stand up. To her astonishment he said good-bye to her brother-in-law as if he were Croesus, and to the secretary as if she had Croesus' marriage lines in her pocket. 'My husband supports him!' she said when they were outside; she objected to false impressions, but she said nothing about the appropriated share of the inheritance. The sympathetic doctor asked if he might not, out of scientific interest, treat the lunatic for his private pleasure; her husband would naturally be charged nothing. She misunderstood him at once and agreed, with one stipulation, that she should be present at the treatments. Since she heard footsteps — perhaps her husband had come back — she said quickly: 'The plans you have for him, doctor, fill me with curiosity!' George had to include her in the bargain. He carried her forward into his new life, a remnant of his old.

For some months he came every day. His admiration for the gorilla grew from visit to visit. With infinite pains he learnt his language. The secretary did not help much; if she dropped back too often into her native French, she felt discarded. For her treachery to the man, to whom she clung without reservations, she deserved punishment. To keep the gorilla in a good temper George renounced the short cut of learning through any other language. He learnt like a child, who is being taught by words the relation of things to each other. Here their relation was the essential; the two rooms and their contents were dissolved in a magnetic field of passions. Objects — in this his first impressions had been correct — had no special names. They were called according to the mood in which they floated. Their faces altered for the gorilla, who lived a wild, tense, stormy life. His life communicated itself to them, they had an active part in it. He had peopled two rooms with a whole world. He created what he wanted, and after the six days of creation, on the seventh took up his abode therein. Instead of resting, he gave his creation speech. All that was round him proceeded from him. For the furniture which he had found here and the rubbish which little by little had been passed on to him, had long since carried the marks of his activities. The foreigner, who had suddenly descended on to his planet, he treated with patience. He could forgive back-slidings of his guest into the language of a worn-out and faded past, because he had himself once been a man. And he noticed clearly the progress the stranger was making. At first little more than his shadow, he grew in time to be his equal and friend.

George was learned enough to publish a thesis on the speech of this madman. A new light was thrown on the psychology of sounds. Vigorously disputed problems of learning were solved by a gorilla. His friendship with him brought fame to the young doctor who had known hitherto only success. Out of gratitude he left him in the condition which made him happy. He renounced any attempt at a cure. He believed indeed, since he had learnt his language, that he had the skill to change him back from a gorilla into the disinherited brother of a banker. But he resisted the temptation to commit a crime, a temptation provoked alone by the sense of a power which he had gained over night, and instead became a psychiatrist out of admiration for the greatness of the distracted to whom his friend was so closely akin, and with the firm principle that he would learn from them but would heal none. He had had enough of polite literature.

Later, when he was working his way through hundreds of experiences, he learnt to distinguish between madmen and madmen. In general his enthusiasm remained alive. A burning sympathy for those men who had so far separated themselves from others as to pass for mad, overcame him with every new patient. Many of them offended his sensitive love, particularly those weak natures who, struggling from attack to attack, pined for the lucid intervals — Jews yearning for the flesh pots of Egypt. He did them the service, and led them back into Egypt. The ways he had found to do so were no less wonderful than those of the Lord when he set free his people. Against his will, methods of approach which he had intended for particular cases were employed also in others, others which he — full of respect and gratitude to his gorilla — would never have meddled with. What he suggested, spread. The director of the institute in which he worked rejoiced at the noise which his school was still making in the world. People had got used to regarding his life-work as finished. And now how it flowered again with his pupil!

When Georges walked along the streets of Paris it sometimes happened that he met one of his cures. He would be embraced and almost knocked down, like the master of some enormous dog coming home after a long absence. Under his friendly questions he concealed a timid hope. He spoke of general health, profession, plans for the future and waited for just one such little comment as 'Then it was nicer!' or 'How empty and stupid my life is now!' 'I wish I were ill again!' 'Why did you cure me?' 'People don't realize what wonderful things there are in their heads!' 'Being sane is a kind of retarded development!' 'You ought to be put out of business! You've robbed me of my most priceless possession!' 'I value you as my friend. But your profession is a crime against humanity.' 'Be ashamed, you cobbler of souls!' 'Give me back my madness!' 'I'll have the law on you!' 'Sane rhymes with bane!'

Instead, compliments and invitations rained on him. His ex-patients looked plump, well and common. Their speech was in no way different from that of any passer-by. They were in trade or served behind a counter. At best they minded machines. But when they had still been his friends and guests, they were troubled with some gigantic guilt, which they carried for all, or with their littleness which stood in such ridiculous contrast to the hugeness of ordinary men, or with the idea of conquering the world, or with death — a thing which they now felt to be quite ordinary. Their riddles had flickered out; earlier they lived for riddles; now for things long ago solved. George was ashamed of himself, without anyone having suggested that he should be. The relations of his patients idolized him; they counted on miracles. Even when physical deficiencies had been proved, they knew he would manage a cure somehow. His colleagues admired and envied him. They pounced at once on his ideas, they were simple and illuminating, like all great ideas. How was it no one had thought of them before! They hastened to break off little fragments of his fame, by proclaiming indebtedness to him and applying his methods to the most different cases. He was bound to get the Nobel Prize. He had long been in the running for it; on account of his youth it seemed better to wait a few years.

So he had been outwitted by his new profession. He had begun from his own feeling of impoverishment, begun with the utmost reverence for the gulfs and precipices which he was to investigate. And in a little while he was a saviour, surrounded by eight hundred friends, and what friends, the residents of the institute; adored by thousands whose nearest and dearest had been reborn through him. For without the existence of nearest and dearest — to be tormented and loved — nobody feels that life is worth living.

Three times a day when he went on his rounds through the rooms he received an ovation. He had grown accustomed to it; the more enthusiastically they ran to greet him, the more violently they crowded about him, the more certainly did he find the words and actions which he needed. The sick were his public. Before he came into the first room he was listening for the familiar hum of voices. Scarcely had one of them seen him from the window than the noise gained direction and order. He waited for this revolution. It was as if they had all begun to applaud. Involuntarily he smiled. Countless parts had become second nature to him. His spirit hungered for rapid transformations. A round dozen assistants followed him, to learn. Some were older, most of them had been in the profession longer than he. They regarded psychiatry as a special field of medicine, and themselves as the administrators of the mentally diseased. Whatever touched on their subject they had acquired with industry and hope. Sometimes they even pretended to agree with the crazy ideas of the patients, just as it said they should in the text books from which they drew their knowledge. One and all they hated the young director, who impressed on them daily that they were the servants and not the beneficiaries of the patients.

'You see, gentlemen,' he would say to them when they were alone together, 'what miserable single-track creatures, what pitiful and inarticulate bourgeois we are, compared with the genius of this paranoiac.

We possess, but he is possessed; we take our experiences at second hand, he makes his own. He moves in total solitude, like the earth itself, through his own space. He has a right to be afraid. He applies more acumen to the explanation and defence of his way of life, than all of us together do to ours. He believes in the images his senses conjure up for him. We mistrust our own healthy senses. Those few among us who have faith still cling to experiences which were lived for them by others thousands of years ago. We need visions, revelations, voices — lightning proximities to things and men — and when we cannot find them in ourselves we fetch them out of tradition. We have to have faith because of our own poverty. Others, still poorer, renounce even that. But look at him! He is Allah, prophet, and Moslem in one. Is a miracle any the less a miracle because we have labelled it *Paranoia chronica*? We sit on our thick-headed sanity like a vulture on a pile of gold. Understanding, as we understand it, is misunderstanding. If there is a life purely of the mind, it is this madman who is leading it!'

With feigned interest the assistants listened to him. When their promotion was at stake they were not above play-acting. Far more important to them than his general reflections, about which they had their own private jokes, were his specialized methods. They noted down every word which, on the happy inspiration of the moment, he threw out to a patient, and vied with each other in the use of it, in the firm conviction that they were achieving just the same with it.

An old man who had lived for nine years in the institute, a village blacksmith, had been ruined in his home district by the coming of motor cars. His wife, after a few weeks of acute poverty, could no longer endure her life with him and ran off with a sergeant. One morning when, as soon as he woke, he was beginning to lament their ill-fortune, she had no answer for him: she had gone. He looked for her through all the village. Twenty-three years he had lived with her; as a child she had come to his house, in the first bloom of her youth he had married her. He looked for her in the neighbouring town. On his neighbours' advice he asked at the barracks for Sergeant Delboeuf, whom he had never seen. He had disappeared three days ago, they told him; gone abroad for sure because he'd be for it as a deserter if they got him. Nowhere did the blacksmith find his wife. He stayed the night in the town. His neighbours had lent him money. He went into every café, poked his head under every table and whimpered: 'Jeanne, are you there?' She wasn't even under the benches. When he leant over the bar people screamed: 'He's after the cash box!' and drove him away. From a child up everyone had known he was an honest man. Since he had married her, he hadn't thrashed her once. She had her joke at him, because he squinted with his right eye. He didn't mind. All he said was: 'As true as my name's Jean, I'll show you who's master!' That was how he treated her.

In the town he told everyone his misfortune. They all gave him good advice. A dirty cobbler said some people didn't know when they were lucky. He nearly killed him. Later he met a butcher. He helped him to look, because he liked walking about at night; he was a very fat man. They gave the alarm to the police and sniffed the river to see if there was a corpse in it. Towards morning they found a woman's, but she belonged to some other man. There was a thick fog and Jean the blacksmith wept when he saw it wasn't his. The butcher cried too and was sick into the river. Early in the morning he took Jean to the shambles. Here everyone knew and greeted him. The calves lowed, there was a smell of pigs' blood, the pigs squealed, Jean wailed even louder: 'Jeanne, are you there?' and the butcher bellowed — no one could hear the calves any more — 'The blacksmith's my friend! His wife's been brought here. Where is she?' The men shook their heads. So his wife's lost, raged the butcher, you've slaughtered her by mistake. He looked among the pigs who were hung up in a long row. 'Here's the old sow!' he bellowed. Jean looked at her from all sides, he smelt at her, he hadn't tasted a blood sausage in years, he loved them better than anything. When he had smelled his fill, he said: 'But this isn't my wife.' Then the butcher lost his temper and swore: 'Go to hell, you fool!'

Jean limped to the station, his wife was his lame leg, his money was all gone. He whimpered: 'How shall I get home?' and lay down on the railway lines. Instead of a railway engine a good Samaritan came along, who found him and gave him a railway ticket on account of his wife. In the train the ticket was bad. 'But he gave it to me!' said Jean, 'My wife's left me!' He hadn't a penny in his pocket and at the next station the police took him. 'Is she there? Where is she?' sobbed Jean and threw his arms round the policeman's neck. 'Here she is,' said the policeman, pointed to himself and took him away. He was locked up in a cell, where he raged several days, and his wife was lost for good. He would have found her, surely.

All of a sudden they let him go home. Maybe she's come back, he thought. The bed had gone, the table had gone, the chairs had gone, everything had gone. His wife would never come home to an empty house.

'Why's my house empty?' he asked the neighbours.

'You owe us money, Jean.'

'Where's my wife to sleep when she comes home?' asked Jean.

'Your wife won't come. She's gone with that young sergeant. You sleep on the floor. You're a poor man now!'

Jean laughed and set fire to the village. Out of the burning house of his cousin he salvaged his wife's bed. Before he took it away he strangled the little children asleep in it, three boys and a girl. He gave himself a lot of work that night. By the time he had found his table and his chairs and all his other possessions, his own empty house was on fire. He carried his goods out into the field, furnished the sitting-room like it used to be, and called 'Jeanne'. Then he went to bed. He left plenty of room for her, but she never came. He lay there a long time and waited. He was hungry, specially at night, you can't imagine how hungry. He nearly got up he was so hungry, the rain ran down into his mouth, he drank and drank. When it stopped he snapped at the stars, if only he could have had them, he hated hunger. When he could stand it no more, he made a vow. He vowed to the Virgin Mary he would never get up again until his wife had heard him and was lying there beside him again. Then the police found him and broke his vow. He would have kept it. The neighbours wanted to kill him. The whole village had been burnt down. He was delighted and yelled: 'I did it! I did it!' The police were afraid and went away fast.

In his new cell there was a school-teacher. Because he had such a nice way of talking, he told him his story. 'What's your name?' asked the teacher. 'Jean Preval.' 'Nonsense! Your name's Vulcan! You squint and limp. You are a blacksmith. A good blacksmith if you limp. Catch your wife!'

'Catch her?'

'Your wife's called Venus and the sergeant is called Mars. I'll tell you a story. I'm an educated man. I've only stolen.'

And Jean listened, with starting eyes. What a bit of news, she can be caught! It's not difficult. An old smith did it once. His wife deceived him with a soldier, a strong young fellow. When Vulcan the smith went off to work, that handsome young devil Mars slipped into the house and slept with his wife. The household cock saw it all, was indignant and betrayed them to his master. Vulcan made a net, a delicate piece of work, invisible, those old smiths knew a thing or two, and put it cleverly round the bed. The two crept in, the wife and the soldier. The cock flew off to its master and crowed: 'They're together at home.' Quick went the smith and called all his relations and the whole village. 'I'm giving a party to-day, wait outside, wait!' He crept into the house, up to the bed, saw his wife and the devil; he nearly cried. Twenty-three years they'd been together and he never thrashed her once! The neighbours waited outside. He drew the net tight, drew it tight, tight, they were prisoners, he had her, his wife. He let the devil go, everyone in the village fetched him a swipe on the snout. Then they all came in and asked: 'Where's your wife?' The smith had hidden her, she was ashamed, he was happy. '*That's* the way to do it!' said the school-teacher. 'It's a true story. In remembrance they've called three stars after those people: Mars, Venus and Vulcan. You can see them in the sky. You need good eyes for Vulcan.'

'Now I know,' said Jean, 'why I snapped for the stars.'

Later they took him away. The teacher stayed behind in the cell. Jean found a new friend instead. He was beautiful. A man you could talk to. Everyone wanted to talk to him. Jean caught his wife. Sometimes he managed it. Then he was happy. But often he was sad. Then his friend would come into the room and say: 'But Jean, she's in the net, don't you see her?' He was always right. His friend opened his mouth and look, his wife was there. 'You squint, you do,' she said to Jean. He laughed and laughed and threatened her: 'I'll show you who's master! As sure as my name's Jean!'

This blacksmith who had lived nine years in the Institute was by no means incurable. The inquiries of the director for his wife were fruitless. Even if she could have been found — who could have forced her to come back to her husband? George pictured to himself how the scene in which the blacksmith took all his pleasure would end in reality. He would set up the bed and the net in his own house; at last the wife would turn up. Jean would come softly in and gather up the net. The two would say the old familiar words to each other. Jean would become more and more excited. The net and nine years would fall aside together. 'Oh! if only I could get hold of that woman!' sighed George.

Every day he helped Jean to find her. He wanted her presence so much, that he could hand her over to him as if he carried her about with him. His assistants, the apes, supposed there was some kind of secret experiment behind it all. Perhaps he was going to cure him with these words. If one of them was alone in the room, he never missed making use of the magic formula. 'But Jean, she's in the net, don't you see her?' Whether Jean was happy or sad, whether he was listening or had stopped his ears, they flung their master's cordial words at him. If he was asleep, they waked him up, if he seemed stupid they shouted at him. They shook him and pushed him, reproached *him* with stupidity and despised his recollections of his wife. The one sentence was transformed to a thousand tones of voice, according to their characters and their moods, and when nothing came of it — the blacksmith was totally indifferent to them — they had yet another reason for laughing at the director. For years that ass had been repeating his simple experiment and still believed that he could cure an incurable with a single sentence!

George would gladly have sacked the lot; but contracts made by his predecessor bound them to him. He knew they meant the patients no good and feared for their fate, in case he should die suddenly. Their petty sabotaging of his work, which he believed to be selfless and which even in their limited view seemed useful, he could not understand. Little by little he would surround himself with people who were artists enough to help him. After all these assistants whom he had taken over from his predecessor were fighting for their lives. They guessed that he would be able to do nothing with them and swallowed his hints simply so that as soon as their contracts were concluded they might at least get jobs somewhere as his pupils. He had a fine sensitivity for the reactions even of men who were too simple, heavy and well-balanced from their very birth to be able to go out of their minds. When he was tired and wanted a rest from the high tension with which his distracted friends filled him, he would submerge himself in the soul of one of his assistants. Everything that George did, he did in the character of someone else. Even his rest; but here he found it with difficulty. Strange discoveries provoked him to laughter. What for instance did these blinkered hearts think of him? Doubtless they sought for some explanation of his success and for the clear-sighted devotion which he showed to his patients. Learning had rooted into them the belief in causes. Conventionally minded, they held fast to the customs and beliefs of the majority in their period. They loved pleasure, and explained each and all in terms of the search for pleasure; it was the fashionable mania of the time, which filled every head and explained little. By pleasure they meant, of course, all the traditional naughtiness, which, since animals were animals, have been practised by the individual with contemptible repetition.

Of that far deeper and most special motive force of history, the desire of men to rise into a higher type of animal, in to the mass, and to lose themselves in it so completely as to forget that *one* man ever existed, they had no idea. For they were educated men, and education is in itself a *cordon sanitaire* for the individual against the mass in his own soul.

We wage the so-called war of existence for the destruction of the mass-soul in ourselves, no less than for hunger and love. In certain circumstances it can become so strong as to force the individual to selfless acts or even acts contrary to their own interests. 'Mankind' has existed as a mass for long before it was conceived of and watered down into an idea. It foams, a huge, wild, full-blooded, warm animal in all of us, very deep, far deeper than the maternal. In spite of its age it is the youngest of the beasts, the essential creation of the earth, its goal and its future. We know nothing of it; we live still, supposedly as individuals. Sometimes the masses pour over us, one single flood, one ocean, in which each drop is alive, and each drop wants the same thing. But it soon scatters again, and leaves us once more to be ourselves, poor solitary devils. In memory we can hardly conceive that we were ever so great, so many and so much one. 'Disease,' says one overburdened by intelligence; 'the beast in man' soothes the lamb of humility, and does not guess how near to the truth is its mistake. In the meantime the mass within ourselves is arming for a new attack. There will come a time when it will not be scattered again, possibly in a single country at first, eating its way out from there, until no one can doubt any more, for there will be no I, you, he, but only it, the mass.

For one discovery alone Georges flattered himself, and it was precisely this: the effects of the mass on history in general and on the life of individuals; its influence on certain changes in the human mind. He had succeeded in proving it in the case of some of his patients. Countless people go mad because the mass in them is particularly strongly developed and can get no satisfaction. In no other way did he explain himself and his own activity. Once he had lived for his private tastes, his ambition and women; now his one desire was perpetually to lose himself. In this activity he came nearer to the thoughts and wishes of the mass, than did those other single people among whom he lived.

His assistants explained his activity in a way which meant more to them. Why did the director admire his idiots so? they asked themselves. Because he's one himself, though only half. Why does he cure them? Because he can't get over it that they're better idiots than he is. He envies them. Their presence gives him no rest. They are considered something special. He has a morbid desire to draw as much attention to himself as they do. The world thinks of him as a normal man of learning. He'll never get any further than this. As director of the

institute perhaps he'll grow quite sane and — what a hope — die soon.
I want to be mad! he screams like a little child. This ridiculous wish
must obviously arise from some experience of his youth. He ought to
be mentally examined some time. But a request to make use of him
as the object of such an examination, he would naturally turn down.
He's an egocentric; it's best to have nothing to do with such people.
The image of a madman must have been bound up with his sexual experiences from early youth. He has a morbid fear of impotence. If he
could only convince himself he were mad, then he would never be
impotent. Every lunatic gives him more pleasure than he can give to
himself. Why should they get more out of life than I do? he complains.
He feels completely at a discount. He suffers from a sense of inferiority.
Out of envy he goes on plaguing them until he cures them. One would
like to know his feelings, every time he lets another come out. It
doesn't occur to him there are new ones coming in as well. He lives
on the petty triumphs of the moment. *There's* your great man, whom
the world admires! —

— To-day, on the last round, they even omitted the outward
appearance of servility. It was too hot, the sudden change of weather
in the last days of March weighed heavy on their torpid souls. They
felt like the despised inmates of the place. Established assistants, each
one had their own barred window somewhere and could press their
heads against it. They were exasperated at the inexactitude of their
sensibilities. Usually some ran on ahead and competed to open the
doors, that was if no nurses or patients got there first. To-day they
followed George at a little distance, with wandering, distrustful minds,
cursing their boring work, their director and all the sick people in the
world. They would rather, to-day, have been Mohammedans, seated
each one alone in a small well-furnished paradise. George was listening
to the familiar noise. His friends watched him from the windows,
and remained as indifferent as his enemies behind him. A sad day, he
said softly to himself; approbation and hatred passed him by, he
breathed only in the stream of other people's feelings. To-day he could
feel nothing around him, only the heavy air.

In the rooms a hateful quiet reigned. The patients were careful not
to quarrel in front of him. They remained eager to get to the windows.
Scarcely was the door closed behind him than they were pushing and
squabbling. The women asked him — but without giving up their
places — imploringly for his love. He could find no answers. All sound
and healing thoughts had abandoned him. One of them, as ugly as

sin could never be, screeched: 'No, no, no, I won't give you a divorce!'
Others shouted in chorus: 'Where is he?' A girl blubbered delighted:
'Leave me go!' Jean, good-natured Jean, was threatening to give his
Jeanne a box on the ear. 'I had her in the net, I was going to take hold
of her; she's gone!' he wailed. 'Hit her over the head,' said George,
he was fed up with that thirty-two years of faithfulness. Jean hit her
hard and did her crying for her. In another room all of them were
wailing because it was already dark. 'They're all mad to-day,' said the
male nurse. One of the many Gods Almighty said: 'Let there be light!'
and raged at the disrespect with which he was treated here. 'He's
nothing but a little bank clerk,' the man in the next bed whispered
confidently to George. Another asked, 'Is there a God?' and wanted
his address. A dapper looking gentleman, whose brother had ruined
him, was complaining of how bad business was to-night. 'As soon as
I've won my case, I shall lay in a stock of shirts for approximately
fifteen years!' 'And why should people go naked?' his best friend
asked him profoundly; they understood each other perfectly.

George did not hear the answer to this question until he was in the
next room. A bachelor was showing the others how he had been
caught in flagranti delicto with his own wife. 'I pull off her fleas from
her, only she wasn't wearing any. Then her father-in-law poked his
head through the key-hole and asked for his grandchild back.' 'Where?
Where?' giggled the spectators. They were all busy at the same thing;
they got on very well. The warders did not mind listening. An
assistant, who was also a journalist, made a note of the atmosphere of
the evening in significant words. George noticed it without looking;
in his own thoughts he was doing the same thing. He was a walking
wax tablet on which words and gestures made their impression. Instead
of working over things or going to meet them, he received them
mechanically. But the wax tablet was melting. 'My wife bores me,'
he thought. The patients seemed foreign to him. Those secret doors
which led into their strongly walled citadels, those doors which were
usually ajar, whose passage was trusted to him alone, remained to-day
fast locked. Break them open? Why? Best break off for to-night,
to-morrow unfortunately always comes. I shall find each one of them
in the right room, all my life I shall always find eight hundred patients.
Perhaps my fame will make the institute even bigger. In time we may
have two to ten thousand. Pilgrimages from every land will fill my
cup of happiness. A commonwealth of all the world is to be expected
in about thirty years. I shall be People's Commissar for Lunatics.

Travels over all the inhabited earth. Inspections and reviews of an army of a million deranged minds. The mentally defective on the left, the over gifted on the right. Foundation of research laboratories for exceptionally gifted animals. Breeding of deranged animals into men. Imbeciles who recover will be discharged from my army with shame and disgrace. My friends are closer to me than my supporters. Petty supporters are called important. How petty my wife is. Why don't I go home? Because my wife's there. She wants love. Everyone to-day wants love.

The wax tablet weighed heavy. The things impressed on it were weighty. In the penultimate room, his wife appeared suddenly. She had run.

'A telegram!' she called and laughed in his face.

'Is that why you hurried so?' Politeness had grown on him like a second skin. Often he wished he could cast it; this was the height of his rudeness. He opened it and read: 'Am completely crackers. Your brother.' Of all possible news, this was what he had expected least of all. A bad joke? A mystery? No. One word disproved these possibilities: 'crackers'! Such expressions his brother never used. If he used such a word, something must be wrong. He blessed the telegram. A journey was essential. He could justify himself. He could not have wished more for anything.

His wife read it. 'Who is this, your brother?'

'Haven't I ever told you about him? The greatest living sinologist. On my desk you'll find some of his latest works. It's twelve years since I saw him.'

'What will you do?'

'Take the next express.'

'To-morrow morning!'

'No, to-night.'

Her face fell.

'Yes, yes,' he said thoughtfully, 'it's a question of my brother's welfare. He must be in the wrong hands. How could he otherwise have sent off a telegram like this?'

She tore the telegram into little pieces. Why hadn't she torn it up at once? The patients scrambled for the fragments. They all loved her, they all wanted a souvenir of her; some of them ate the bits of paper. Most put them next their hearts or up their trousers. Plato the philosopher watched with dignity. He bowed and said: 'Madame, we live in the world!'

CHAPTER IV

ROUNDABOUT WAYS

GEORGE had slept for a long time; suddenly the train stopped. He looked up; numbers of people were getting in. His compartment, with the blinds drawn, remained empty. At the last moment — the train had started — a couple asked him if there were seats. He moved politely to one side. The man collided with him and did not apologize. George, who found the least sharpness in a society of well-bred monkeys refreshing, contemplated him in surprise. The woman misinterpreted his look and, they had hardly sat down before she apologized in her husband's stead: he was blind. 'I would not have thought it,' said George, 'he moves with astonishing assurance. I must explain, I am a doctor and have many blind patients.' The man bowed. He was tall and spare. 'Will it disturb you if I read aloud to him?' asked the woman. The timid devotion on her face had charm, doubtless she lived for this blind man alone. 'On the contrary! But you must not take offence either if I should fall asleep.' Instead of the sharpness he had longed for, courtesies fluttered to and fro. She took a novel out of her travelling bag and read aloud in a deep, flattered voice.

Peter must look rather like this blind man by now, rigid and gnawed. What could have got into Peter's calm mind? He lived alone and without a care; he had not the least contact with any individual. That he should have become distracted by the impact of the world on him — it sometimes happened with sensitive minds — was not to be thought of in his case; his world was his library. He was distinguished by a colossal memory. Weaker heads might come to ruin through too much reading; but with him each syllable that he acquired remained clear-cut from the next. He was the opposite of an actor, always himself, only himself. Instead of dividing himself among others, he measured them from the outside against himself, and he knew himself only from the outside and through his head. In this way he had escaped the very great dangers which must undeniably arise from preoccupation with the culture of the east, pursued in solitude and over many years. Peter was safe from Lao Tse and all the Indians. Out of his own austerity he leaned towards the moral philosophers. He would have found his Confucius in one place or another. What then could have come over him, a creature almost sexless?

'Once again, you drive me to suicide!' George was listening to the

novel with half an ear, the reading voice sounded pleasant, he understood its inflexions; but at this absurd statement of the hero in person,
he could not help laughing out loud. 'You would not laugh, sir, if you
were blind!' an angry voice came at him. The blind man had spoken;
his first words were rude. 'I'm sorry,' said George, 'but I don't believe
in that kind of love.' 'Then don't interrupt a serious person's pleasures!
I understand love better than you. I'm blind. That's no business of
yours!' 'You misunderstand me,' George began. Then he noticed the
woman; she was gesticulating vehemently, alternately she put her
finger to her lips and folded her hands, he must for God's sake say no
more; he said no more. Her lips thanked him. The blind man had
already raised his arm. To defend himself? To attack? He let it fall
and ordered: 'Go on!' The woman read on, her voice trembled. With
fear? With joy at having met a man of such delicate feeling?

Blind, blind, a dark and very distant memory clutched at his mind.
Dim and insistent, it gnawed far into his consciousness. There was a
room and another next door. In one there stood a small white bed.
A little boy lay in it, red all over. He was afraid. A voice he didn't
know was sobbing: 'I'm blind! I'm blind!' and whimpering over and
over again: 'I want to read!' His mother went to and fro. She went
through the door into the next room, where the voice was crying. It
was dark in there, but it was light in here. The child wanted to ask:
'Who's that crying?' He was afraid. He thought, that voice'll get in
here and cut out my tongue with a penknife. So he began to sing, all
the songs he knew, over and over again. He sang loud, he yelled, his
head nearly burst with the sound. 'I'm red all over,' he sang. The door
flew open. 'Be quiet!' said his mother. 'You've got a temperature.
What are you thinking of?' Then in a great gasp came that awful voice
and screamed: 'I'm blind! I'm blind!' Little George came trembling
out of bed and scrambled wailing to his mother. He clutched at her
knees. 'What is it then, what is it?' 'That man! That man!' 'What
man?' 'In that dark room there's a man screaming! A man!' 'But
that's Peter, your brother Peter.' 'No, no!' little George raved, 'leave
that man, you must stay with me!' 'But George, my clever little boy,
that's Peter. He's got measles like you. He can't see anything just now.
So he's crying a little. He'll be well again in the morning. Come along,
let's go and see him.' 'No! No!' he resisted her. 'It is Peter,' he thought,
'but another Peter', and he whimpered softly as long as his mother was
in the room. As soon as she went back to the 'man' he hid his head
under the clothes. When he heard the voice he howled loud again.

It went on a long time, longer than he had ever cried before. The picture was blurred by his tears.

George suddenly saw the danger with which Peter imagined himself threatened: he was afraid of going blind! Perhaps his eyes were bad. Perhaps he had to give up reading now and again. What could have worried him more? A single hour which did not fit in with his daily plan, was enough to fill him with strange thoughts. · Everything was strange to Peter which had to do with himself. As long as his head was busied with selected facts, information, theories, weaving them together, tabulating them and relating them to each other, he was certain of the usefulness of his solitude. Really solitary, alone with himself, he had never been. After all, this was what made the learned man: being alone so as to be with as many things as possible simultaneously. As if in these conditions a man could himself truly *be* even with one thing alone. Probably Peter's eyes had been overstrained. Who could say whether he was careful to read in a good light? Perhaps, contrary to his custom, and his contemptuous attitude, he had been to a doctor who had recommended unconditional rest and quiet. This very quiet, extended over several days, might have brought on his final *quietus*. Instead of indemnifying the illness of his eyes by the soundness of his ears, instead of listening to music and people (what is richer than the intonations of men?) he must surely have paced up and down before his books, doubted the goodwill of his own eyes, implored them, cursed them, recollected with terror that one day's blindness of his childhood, been struck with horror lest he should again become blind, and for a long time, he must have raged, despaired and — because he was the proudest and harshest of men — called his brother to him before he approached a neighbour or an acquaintance for the least helpful word. I'll get rid of that blindness, George decided. I never saw an easier cure in prospect. Three things for me to do: a thorough examination of his eyes, a careful test of the lighting arrangements in his flat, and a cautious and loving talk which will convince him of the meaninglessness of his fears, always supposing that they had no real foundation.

He glanced with friendship at the rude blind man opposite and thanked him in silence for his presence. He had shown him the right interpretation of the telegram. A sensitive mind derives either advantage or injury from every contact, because each will awaken thoughts and recollections. The indolent are wandering institutions, nothing flows into them, nothing makes them overflow, frozen and isolated, they drift through the world. Why should they move? What moves them? Accidentally they belong to the animal kingdom, but in fact they are vegetables. You could nip their heads off and they'd go on living, they have their roots. The stoic philosophy is suited to vegetables, it is high treason to animals. Let us be animals! He who has roots, let him uproot himself. George was glad to know why the train was carrying him so fast on his way. He had got into it blindly. Blindly he had had that dream of his childhood. A blind man had got in. Then suddenly the train found its direction: to the healing of a blind brother. For whether Peter really was blind, or only feared it, was for a psychiatrist one and the same thing. Now he could sleep. Animals pursue their desires to their climax and then break off. Most of all they love the frequent changes of their tempo. They eat to completion and love to satiation. Their rest they deepen into sleep. Soon he too slept.

The reading woman, between the lines, caressed the beautiful hand on which he had supported his head. She thought he was listening to her voice. Now and again she emphasized a word; he was to understand how unhappy she was. She would never forget this journey; soon she must get out. She would leave the book behind, as a souvenir, and — she implored — might she not have one look? She got out at the next station. Her husband she propelled in front of her, usually she drew him along behind her. In the door she held her breath. Without looking round — she was afraid of her husband, her movements aroused his anger — she said, daring much: 'Good-bye!' For how many years had she waited to speak in such a tone. He could make no answer. She was happy. Weeping softly, a little intoxicated with her own beauty, she helped the blind man out of the train. She mastered herself and cast no glance back towards the window of his compartment, where in her mind's eye she saw him. He must have seen her tears, and she was ashamed. She had left the novel with him. He was asleep.

In the morning he washed. In the evening he reached his destination. He put up at a modest hotel. At a better known one his arrival would have been a sensation, since he was one of those half dozen scientists whom the newspapers faithfully expose to public adulation at the expense of all their colleagues. He put off his visit to his brother to the following day so as not to disturb his night's rest. Because his impatience tormented him, he went to the opera. Listening to Mozart he felt pleasantly secure.

That night he dreamt of two cocks. The larger was red and scraggy, the smaller well-clipped and cunning. Their fighting lasted long, it was so exciting that one forgot to think. You see, said a spectator, what men are coming to! Men? crowed the little cock. What men? We're cocks. Fighting cocks. None of your jokes! The spectator withdrew. He grew smaller and smaller. Suddenly it was clear that he too was only a cock. But a cowardly one, said the red cock, it's time to get up. The small cock agreed. He had won and flew away. The red cock stayed. He grew larger and larger. His colour grew with his body. It hurt the eyes to look at him. They opened themselves. A huge sun bulged over the window-sill.

George hurried and barely an hour later was standing in front of the house, No. 24 Ehrlich Strasse. It was more or less respectable and quite without character. He climbed up the four floors and rang. An old woman opened the door. She was wearing a starched blue skirt and grinned. He felt like glancing down at himself to see if all was not as it should be, but controlled himself and asked: 'Is my brother at home?'

Immediately the woman stopped grinning, stared at him and said: 'Excuse me, there's no brother here!'

'My name is Professor George Kien. I want Dr. Peter Kien, the well-known scholar. He certainly lived here eight years ago. Perhaps you know if there is anyone in the building who would know his address in case he's moved.'

'Better say nothing about that.'

'One moment, please. I've come specially from Paris. You must surely be able to tell me whether he lives here or not.'

'I ask you, you ought to be thankful.'

'Why thankful?'

'Some people aren't fools.'

'Of course not.'

'The stories there are!'

'Perhaps my brother's ill?'

'A fine brother! You ought to be ashamed!'

'Kindly tell me what you know!'

'And what do I get out of it?'

George took a piece of money out of his pocket, gripped her arm and placed the coin with friendly pressure on her hand, which had opened of itself. The woman grinned again.

'You'll tell me what you know about my brother, now, won't you?'

'Anyone can talk.'

'Well?'

'All of a sudden you're dead. More, please!' she tossed her shoulders.

419

George pulled out another coin, she held out her other hand. Instead of touching it, he tossed the coin down from above.

'I may as well go again!' she said and gave him an ugly look.

'What do you know about my brother?'

'More than eight years ago. It all came out the day before yesterday.'

It was eight years since Peter had written to him. The telegram had come the day before yesterday. The woman must have got hold of something of the truth. 'So what did you do?' George asked in order to spur her into a fuller account.

'We went to the police. A respectable woman goes to the police right away.'

'Of course, of course. Thank you for the assistance you must have rendered to my brother.'

'If you please . . . Knocked flat, the police were.'

'But what had he done?' George imagined his brother, slightly unbalanced, complaining to oafish policemen of his eye trouble.

'Stolen, he did! He's no heart. . . .'

'Stolen?'

'Murdered her, that's what he did! It's not my fault, is it? She was the first wife, I'm the second. He hid the pieces. There was room behind the books. Thief, that's what I always said. Day before yesterday the murderer was found out. I've got the shame of it. Why was I such a fool? I always say, one shouldn't. That's what people are like. I thought, all those books. What's he up to between six and seven? Cutting up corpses. Took the pieces out for his walk. Not a soul noticed. Stole the bank book, he did. I've nothing to hold on to. I might starve. He wanted me to. I'm the second. Then I'll have a divorce. Excuse me, he'll have to pay me first! Eight years ago he ought to have been locked up! Now he's put away downstairs. I've locked him in. I won't be murdered in my bed!' She burst into tears and slammed the door.

Peter a murderer. Quiet, lanky Peter, whom all the other boys at school bullied. The stairs swayed. The roof fell in. And George, a person of the utmost fastidiousness, dropped his hat and did not pick it up. Peter married. Who would have believed it? The second wife, more than fifty years old, ugly, freakish, common, not able to utter a single human sentence, escaped an assault the day before yesterday. He cut the first one into pieces. He loves his books, and uses them as a hiding place. Peter and truth! If only he had lied, all his childhood lied, black and blue! So this was why George had been sent for. The telegram was a forgery, either of his wife or of the police. That legend of Peter's sexlessness. A pretty legend like all legends, made out of thin air, idiotic. George the brother of a blue-beard. Headlines in all the papers. The greatest living sinologist! The highest authority on eastern Asia! A double life! His retirement from the direction of the institute. Aberration. Divorce. His assistants to succeed him. The patients, the patients, they will be tormented, they will be ill-used! Eight hundred! They love him, they need him, he cannot leave them. Resignation is impossible. They cling to him on all sides, you mustn't leave us, we'll come too, stay with us, we've no one else, they don't talk our language, you listen to us, you understand us, you laugh with us; his beautiful, rare birds; they are all of them strangers there, each one from a different land, not one understands his neighbour, they accuse each other and do not even know it; he lives for them, he can't forsake them, he *will* stay. Peter's affairs must be seen to. His catastrophe is bearable. He was all for Chinese characters, George for human beings. Peter must be put in a home. He lived alone too long. His senses broke loose with his first wife. How could he control this sudden change? The police will give him up. Possibly he will be allowed to take him to Paris. It is evident that he is not responsible for his actions. In no circumstances will George retire from the direction of the institute.

On the contrary, he stepped forward, picked up his hat, dusted it, and knocked politely but firmly at the door. Scarcely was his hat back in his hand than he was again the assured man of the world, the doctor. 'My dear lady,' he lied, 'my dear lady!' A youthful admirer, he re-repeated the two words, imploringly and with a fire which seemed ridiculous even to him, as though he were himself the spectator to the play he was acting. He heard her preparations. Maybe she has a pocket mirror, he thought, maybe she's powdering herself and will listen to me. She opened the door and grinned. 'I would like to ask you for some particulars!' He sensed her disappointment. She had expected a further passage of affection, or at the very least a repetition of that 'my dear lady'. Her mouth stayed open, her expression grew sour.

'I ask you. Murderer, that's all I know.'

'Shut up!' bellowed the voice of a mad bull. Two fists appeared, followed by a thick, red head. 'Don't you believe the bitch! She's a cow! No murders in *my* house! As long as I've anything to do with it, not on your life! Owed me for four canaries, though; if you're his brother, highly bred little birds, bred them myself. He paid. Paid well. Yesterday night it was. Maybe I'll open my patent peep-hole for him again to-day. He's gone off his head. Do you want to see him? Gets his food all right. Whatever he asks for. I've locked him up. He's frightened of the old woman. Can't stand her. Nobody can stand her. Have a look now! What she's done with him! Knocked him all to bits, she has. She doesn't exist any more for him, he says. He'd sooner be blind. Quite right, he is. She's a sh— of a woman! If he hadn't married her he'd have been right enough, right in the head too, I say!' The woman tried to speak; with a sideways thrust of his arm he knocked her back into the flat.

'Who are you?' asked George.

'You see in me your brother's best friend. Benedikt Pfaff, signature, police constable, retired, once called Ginger the Cat! *I* look after the house. Though I say it myself! I keep a sharp eye on the law. Who are you? Profession, I mean?'

George asked to see his brother. All the murders, all the anxieties, all the malevolence in the world had vanished: The caretaker pleased him. His head reminded him of the rising sun of early that morning. He was crude, but refreshing, an untamed, stout fellow such as one rarely sees now in the cities and homes of civilization. The stairs groaned. Instead of carrying it, this Atlas smote the wretched earth. His powerful legs oppressed the ground. Feet and shoes seemed made of stone. The walls echoed to his words. How could the tenants endure it, George wondered. He was a little ashamed because he had not immediately seen that the woman was a cretin. The simple structure of her sentences had convinced him that her imbecilities were true. He put the blame on the journey, on the Mozart opera of yesterday, which had for the first time in years dragged him out of the daily course of his thoughts, and on his expectation of finding an invalid brother, but not necessarily a cretinous housekeeper. That the austere Peter should have happened on this absurd old thing was a light in his darkness. He laughed at the blindness and inexperience of his brother, who had certainly telegraphed on her account, and was glad that the damage could be so easily repaired. A question to the caretaker confirmed his assumption: she had kept house for Peter for many years and had made use of this, her original function, to insert herself into a more respectable one. He was filled with tender feelings for his brother, who had spared him the inconvenience of murder. The simple telegram had a simple meaning. Who could tell but to-morrow morning already he might be back in the train, and the day after pacing through his wards?

422

Below in the entrance hall Atlas came to a stand in front of a door, pulled a key out of his pocket and unlocked it. 'I'll go first,' he whispered, and put a stumpy finger to his mouth. 'Professor, my friend!' George heard him saying inside the door. 'I've got a visitor for you! What do you give me for that?' George went in, closed the door, and was astounded at the bare little closet within. The window had been boarded up, a little light fell on a bed and a cupboard. Nothing could be seen clearly. A repellent smell of stale food crawled round him, involuntarily he put his fingers to his nostrils. Where was Peter? There was a scraping, such as one hears in the cages of animals. George felt along the wall. It was really there where he had thought; how appalling, this tiny room. 'Open the window,' he said aloud. 'Can't be done!' came the answer, in Atlas' voice. So Peter's eyes were the trouble, not only the wife; that was evident from the darkness in which he lived. Where was he? 'Here he is,' bellowed Atlas, a lion in a rabbit hutch, 'still at my patent!' George took two steps along the wall and collided with a heap. Peter? He bent down and felt the skeleton of a man. He lifted it up. The man trembled, or was it the draught? no, everything was closed, now someone was whispering, flat and toneless like one dying, like one dead, could he speak.

'Who is it?'

'It's George, your brother George, don't you hear me, Peter?'

'George?' Life came into the voice.

'Yes, George. I wanted to see you, I've come to visit you. I come from Paris.'

'Is it really you?'

'Why, do you doubt it?'

'I can't see here. It's so dark.'

'I knew you at once, by your thinness.'

Suddenly someone ordered, stern and harsh — George almost started — 'Leave the room, Pfaff!'

'What's that?'

'Please, would you mind leaving us alone?' George added.

'Immediately!' commanded Peter, the old Peter.

Pfaff went. The new gentleman was too grand for him. He looked like a president or something of the sort. He probably was. He would have plenty of time later to pay the Professor back for his sauce. In part payment he slammed the door, out of respect for the President he did not lock him in.

George laid Peter on the bed; he hardly noticed the difference when he no longer had him in his arms; he went to the window and pulled at the boards. 'I'll cover it up again soon,' he said, 'you need air. If your eyes hurt you, close them for the moment.'

'My eyes don't hurt.'

'Then why do you spare them? I thought you'd been reading too much and were taking a rest in the dark.'

'Those boards have only been there since last night.'

'Did you nail them up so tight? I can hardly get them away, I wouldn't have thought you had so much strength.'

'That was the caretaker, the landsknecht.'

'Landsknecht?'

'A venal brute.'

'I found him sympathetic. In comparison to other people in your entourage.'

'I did once too.'

'What has he done to you, then?'

'He behaves shamelessly. He's growing familiar.'

'Perhaps he does that to show you his friendship. You can't have been long in this little room?'

'Since the day before yesterday, about noon.'

'Do you feel better? Your eyes I mean. I hope you brought no books with you.'

'The books are upstairs. My little hand-library was stolen from me.'

'What a stroke of luck! Otherwise you'd have tried to read here. That would have been poison to your tired eyes. I believe even you are anxious about them now. Once you didn't care about them at all. You've treated them disgracefully always.'

'My eyes are perfectly well.'

'Truly? Haven't you any complaints?'

'No.'

The boards were down. A sharp light flowed into the room. Air streamed through the open window. George breathed in, deeply contented. So far the examination had progressed well. Peter's answers to the well calculated questions were correct, factual, a little curt, as always. The evil was all in this wife, only in the wife; he had purposely disregarded hints in her direction. He had no fear for his eyes; the way in which he reacted to repeated inquiries about their condition argued a genuine indignation. George turned round. Two empty birdcages hung on the wall. The bedclothes had red stains on them. In the corner at the back was a wash-basin. The dirty water in it shimmered red. Peter was even thinner than his hands had already told him. Two sharp creases cut his cheeks in two. His face looked longer, harsher and narrower than it had done. Four penetrating wrinkles were on the brow as though his eyes were always pulled wide open. Of his lips nothing was visible, a recalcitrant slit betrayed where they would be. His eyes, poor and watery blue, examined his brother, pretending indifference; in their corners twitched curiosity and distrust. His left arm, Peter was hiding behind his back.

'What's the matter with your hand?' George took it away from his back. It was wrapped in a cloth soaked through and through with blood.

'I hurt myself.'

'How did this happen?'

'While I was eating, my knife slipped suddenly against my little finger. I've lost the two top joints.'

'You must have slipped with all your weight?'

'The joints were more than half cut off. I thought, they're lost anyway and cut them right off. To be done with the pain once and for all.'

'What made you jump so?'

'You know very well.'

'How should I know, Peter?'

'The caretaker told you.'

'I find it extremely odd that he never even mentioned it to me.'

'It's his fault. I didn't know he kept canaries. He hid the cages under the bed, the devil knows why. One whole afternoon and the next day it was still as the grave in here. Last night at supper, just as I was cutting my meat, a hellish noise broke out. The first fright cost me my finger. You must consider what quiet I am used to at my work. But I avenged myself on the wretched fellow. He likes crude jokes of that kind. I believe he hid the cages under the bed on purpose. He could easily have left them on the wall where they now are.'

'How did you avenge yourself?'

'I let the birds go. Considering what pain I was in, a mild revenge. Probably they've come to grief. He was in such a rage that he boarded up the window. But in any case I paid him for the birds. He asserted they were priceless, he had taken years to tame them. He's lying of course. Have you ever heard that canaries sing to order and stop singing to order?'

'No.'

'He wanted to put their price up that way. You would have thought

425

that it was women only who wanted their husband's money. That's a great mistake. You see how I paid for it.'

George ran to the nearest chemist, bought iodine, bandages and this and that to revive Peter. The wound was not in itself dangerous; but that a man already weak should have lost so much blood worried him more. He ought to have been bandaged up yesterday. The caretaker was a monster; he thought of nothing but his canaries. Peter's story sounded true. But he must make an investigation with the culprit as well to see if they tallied in every particular. It would be best to go straight back to the flat and hear his account of what had happened yesterday as well as on earlier occasions. George did not look forward to it. This was the second time in the day that he had mistaken his man. He regarded himself — and his success as a mental specialist bore witness to it — as a great connoisseur of men. The red-headed fellow was not merely a great strong Atlas of a man, he was insolent and dangerous. His joke of putting the canaries under the bed betrayed how little he really cared for Peter, although he pretended to be his best friend. He was perfectly capable of robbing a sick man of light and air by nailing up the window with boards. He had taken no care of his wound at all. One of the first sentences he had said when George made his acquaintance was to the effect that his brother had paid him, and paid him well, for the four canary birds that he owed him. Money was his chief interest. He was evidently in league with the woman. He stayed in the flat with her. The rough handling and the rougher words he had used she had accepted, not without a half pleasure in her anger. So she was his woman. Not one of these conclusions had George drawn at the time. So great had been his relief at Peter's acquittal of murder. Now he was ashamed again of himself. He had left his wits at home. How ridiculous, to have believed a woman like that! How absurd to have been so trusting of a *landsknecht* — Peter's name was very apt! The fellow would laugh in his face; he had outwitted him. No wonder the pair of them grinned, they were sure of their advantage and hold over Peter. They probably intended to keep the flat and the library for themselves, leaving Peter down there in that black hole. The woman had met him with a grin when she opened the door.

George decided to tie up Peter's hand before he sought out the caretaker. The wound was more important than any explanation. He would not learn much more than he knew already. He could easily find a pretext later on to leave the little room for half an hour.

CHAPTER V

WARYWISE ODYSSEUS

'WE haven't yet greeted each other properly,' he said as he came back. 'But I know you dislike emotional family scenes. You haven't running water in here? I saw a tap in the passage outside.'

He fetched water and told Peter to keep still.

'I do that without being told,' was the answer.

'I look forward to seeing your library. As a child I never understood your passion for books. I was much less intelligent than you, I hadn't your incredible memory. What a silly, greedy little boy I was, always playing around! I'd have liked to act plays and kiss mother all day long. But you had your goal straight before you from the start. I've never come across another man whose development followed such a straight line. I know you don't care for compliments, you'd like me to stop talking and leave you alone. Don't be angry, but I can't leave you alone! I haven't seen you for twelve years, I haven't heard anything of you except in the papers for eight, you seem to have thought personal letters too great an honour for me! It's more than likely you won't treat me any better in the next eight years than you have up to now. You won't come to Paris, I know what you feel about the French and about travelling. I haven't the time to come and see you again soon, I'm snowed under with work. You may have heard I'm working in an institute close to Paris. So you see, when should I thank you if not now? I have a lot to thank you for, your modesty is altogether exaggerated, you don't even guess how much I owe to you: my character as far as I have any, my love of learning, my way of life, my rescue from all those women, my serious approach to great things, my humility towards small ones. You are in the last resort even responsible for my taking to psychiatry. It was you who aroused my interest in the problems of speech, and I made my first leap with a thesis on the speech of a certain lunatic. Of course I shall never bring myself to that complete self-abnegation, to that attitude of work for work's sake, of duty for duty's sake, which Immanuel Kant — and long before all other thinkers — Confucius, have demanded, and which you have achieved. I'm afraid I'm too weak for that. Applause does me good, I seem to need it. You are a very enviable man. You must admit that men of your strength of will are rare, tragically rare. How could there possibly be two in one family? By the way, I read your

thesis on Kant and Confucius with real excitement, far more than I
feel when I read Kant or even the sayings of Confucius themselves.
It is so clear, so exhaustive, so ruthless to all other points of view, it is
of such an overwhelming profundity and shows such comprehensive
knowledge. Perhaps you saw that review in a Dutch paper which
called you the Jacob Burckhardt of eastern cultures. Only they say
you are not so discursive and far more exacting towards yourself.
I consider your learning more universal than Burckhardt's. That may
be explicable in part by the greater richness of knowledge in our time,
but by far the greatest credit belongs to you personally; you save your
strength to stand alone. Burckhardt was a professor and gave lectures,
a compromise which was not without influence on the formulation of
his thought. How tremendous your interpretation of the Chinese
sophists! With few fragments, fewer even than we have from the
Greek, you have reconstructed their entire world, their worlds I should
say, for they are as different one from another as only the minds of
philosophers can be. I was most pleased with your last important
paper, the one in which you say that the school of Aristotle played
the same part in the west as the school of Confucius in China. Aristotle, the spiritual grandchild of Socrates, gathers into his philosophy
all the remaining tributaries of Greek thought. Among his medieval
followers — and those by no means the least important — there are
even Christians. In just the same way the later disciples of Confucius
worked over all that was left of the teaching of Mo-Ti, of the Taoists
and even of Buddhism in so far as it seemed serviceable to them and
useful for the preservation of their influence. But we must not for that
reason think of either the Confucians or the Aristotelians as eclectics.
They are extraordinarily close to each other — as you have con-
vincingly shown — in their respective influences, the one on the
Christian middle ages here, the other at about the same time, from the
Sung dynasty onwards, over there. Of course I don't understand much
about it, I don't know a word of Chinese — but your conclusions affect
everyone who wants to understand his own roots, the ultimate origin
of his opinions, the mental mechanism inside him. Am I allowed to
ask what you're working on now?'

While he was washing and bandaging the hand, he observed closely,
but as unobtrusively as possible, the effect of his sentences on the face
of his brother. After the last question he paused.

'Why do you keep looking at me?' asked Peter. 'You're confusing
me with one of your patients. You only half understand my scholastic

theories, because you are too uneducated. Don't talk so much! You don't owe me anything. I detest flattery. Aristotle, Confucius and Kant are all the same to you. Any woman is preferable. If I'd had influence on you, you wouldn't now be the head of a lunatic asylum.'

'But Peter, you're not fair ...'

'I am at work on ten different theses at once. Almost all of them are fiddling around with letters — as you call every work of textual criticism when you're alone. You laugh at concepts. Work and duty are concepts to you. You think only of people, and mostly of women. What do you want with me?'

'You're not fair, Peter. I told you I didn't know a word of Chinese. 'San' means three and 'wu' means five, that's all I know. I *have* to look at you. How else am I to know if I'm hurting your finger? You'd never make a sound on your own. Your face is fortunately a little more expressive than your tongue.'

'Then make haste! You have an overbearing look. Leave my studies alone! You need pretend no interest in them. Keep to your lunatics! I shall ask you nothing about them. You talk too much because you are always moving among people!'

'Very well. I've almost done.'

George felt from Peter's hand how willingly he would have stood up while he was saying these sharp words; so easily was his self-respect reawakened. Ten, twenty years ago it had always revealed itself in this kind of contradictions. Half an hour ago he had been crouching on the floor, feeble and dwindling, a little heap of bones, out of which had whimpered the voice of a beaten schoolboy. Now he was defending himself in curt, rude sentences, and showing signs of wanting to use his height as a weapon.

'I'd like to look at your books upstairs, if you don't mind,' said George when he had finished bandaging him. 'Will you come too, or will you wait for me? You must spare yourself to-day, you've lost a lot of blood. Lie down for an hour! I'll fetch you then.'

'What can you do in an hour?'

'Look at your library. The caretaker is up there?'

'You need a day for my library. You can see nothing in an hour.'

'I only want to get an idea of it. We'll look at it properly together later on.'

'Stay here! Don't go up! I warn you!'

'Why?'

'It smells in the flat.'

'Smells of what?'

'Of a woman, to use no more opprobrious terms.'

'You exaggerate.'

'You're a womanizer.'

'A womanizer? No.'

'You like a bit of skirt! Do you prefer me to speak plainly?' Peter's voice grew sharp.

'I understand your hatred, Peter. She deserves it. She deserves even more.'

'You don't know her!'

'I know what you've suffered.'

'You are like a blind man talking of colour! You have hallucinations. You get them from your patients. The inside of your head is like the inside of a kaleidoscope. You shake forms and colours together to suit your whim. Colours, all colours, we can name each one by its name! You should be silent about things which you have not yourself experienced!'

'I will be silent. I only wanted to tell you that I understood you, Peter, I've had the same experience myself, I am not what I used to be. That was why I changed my profession at the time. Women are a misfortune. Leaden weights on a man's spirit. If you take your duty seriously you must shake them off or you're lost. I do not need the hallucinations of my patients for my own healthy open eyes have seen more. I've learned many things in the course of twelve years. You were lucky enough to know from the beginning what I had to pay for with cruel experience.'

So as to carry conviction, George spoke with less emphasis than he had at his command. His mouth took on the lines of years of embitterment. Peter's mistrust grew, so did his curiosity; both could be clearly detected in the increasing tension of the muscles at the corners of his eyes.

'You still dress very carefully!' he said, the only answer to these expressions of resignation.

'A painful necessity! My profession demands it. Uneducated patients are impressed when a gentleman who seems to them very grand treats them familiarly. Many melancholics are more cheered up by the knife-edge creases of my trousers than by anything I can say. If I do not cure these people, they will stay in their primitive condition. So as to open for them the way to education, even late in life, I must make them healthy first.'

'You place such emphasis on education. Since when?'

'Since I have known a truly educated man. The achievement which he has completed and is completing daily. The certainty in which his spirit dwells.'

'You mean me.'

'Whom else?'

'Your successes depend on shameless flattery. Now I understand why you are so famous. You are a consummate liar. The first word you learnt to speak was a lie. Because you delighted in lies you became a mental specialist. Why not an actor? You ought to be ashamed to confront your patients! Their suffering is the bitter truth, they suffer because they have no help left in the world. I can imagine just such a poor devil, suffering from hallucinations about a particular colour. "I can see nothing but green," he complains. He may even cry. Perhaps for months already he's been tormenting himself with this ridiculous green. What do you do? I know what you do. You flatter him, you grasp him by his Achilles heel — and how would he not have one, human beings are made up of weaknesses — you talk to him with your "my friend" and your "my dear fellow", he weakens, first he respects you, then he respects himself. He may be the wretchedest poor devil on God's earth; you overwhelm him with respect. Hardly has he begun to think of himself as co-director of your lunatic asylum, merely kept out of the general directorship by an unjust accident, then you come along with your true speech. "My dear fellow," you say to him, "the colour you keep seeing is not green. It is — it is — let us say blue!" Peter's voice grew sharp. 'Have you cured him? No! His wife at home will torment him just as she did before, she will torment him to his dying day. "When men are ill and at the gates of death, they become as men out of their minds," said Wang-Chung, a penetrating thinker; he lived in the first century of our era, from 27 to 98, in China under the later Han dynasty, and knew more about sleep, madness and death than you with all your supposedly accurate science. Cure your lunatic of his wife! As long as he has her he will be both mad and dead — which according to Wang-Chung are closely related conditions. Send his wife away if you can! You cannot do it, because you have not got her. If you had her, you'd keep her for yourself because you like a skirt. Shut up all women in your institute, do what you like with them, wear yourself out, die exhausted and stupefied at forty, at least you'll have healed many sick men and will know for what you have received so much fame and honour!'

George noticed very well every time Peter's voice went sharp. It was enough that his thought recurred to the woman upstairs. He had not said a word about her, but already in his voice there betrayed itself a screeching, shrill, incurable hatred. Evidently he expected George to take her away; the mission seemed to him so hard and dangerous that he was already blaming him for having failed in it. He must be induced to give vent to as much of his hatred as possible. If only he would simply explain, from their origins onwards in a simple narrative, the events as they had appeared to him! George knew well how to play the part of the india-rubber in such a retrospect, and to wipe off the sensitive plate of memory all its traces. But Peter would never say anything about himself. His experiences had driven their roots right into the sphere of his learning. Here it was easier to find the sensitive spot.

'I believe,' said George, and put on his most charming air of sympathy — who would not have been touched by it — 'that you overestimate the importance of women. You take them too seriously, you think they are human beings like us. I see in women merely a passing necessary evil. Many insects even have these things better arranged. One or a very few mothers bring into being the entire race. The rest remain undeveloped. Is it possible to live at closer quarters than the termites do? What a terrifying accumulation of sexual stimuli would not such a stock produce — if the creatures were still divided as to sex? They are not so divided, and the instincts inherent in that division are much reduced among them. Even what little they have, they fear. When they swarm, at which period thousands, nay millions, are destroyed apparently without reason, I see in this a release of the amassed sexuality of the stock. They sacrifice a part of their number, in order to preserve the rest from the aberrations of love. The whole stock would run aground on this question of love, were it once to be permitted. I can imagine nothing more poignant than an orgy in a colony of termites. The creatures forget — a colossal recollection has seized hold of them — what they really are, the blind cells of a fanatic whole. Each will be himself, it begins with a hundred or a thousand of them, the madness spreads, *their* madness, a mass madness, the soldiers abandon the gates, the whole mound burns with unsatisfied love, they cannot find their partners, they have no sex, the noise, the excitement far greater than anything usual, attracts a storm of real ants; through the unguarded gates their deadly enemies press in, what soldier thinks of defending himself, they want only love; and the colony which might have lived for all eternity — that eternity for which we all long — dies, dies of love, dies of that urge through which we, mankind, prolong our existence! It is a sudden transformation of the wisest into the most foolish. It is — no, it can't be compared with anything — yes, it is as if by broad daylight, with healthy eyes and in full possession of your understanding, you were to set fire to yourself and all your books. No one threatens you, you have as much money as you need and want, your work is growing every day more comprehensive and more individual, rare old books fall into your lap, you are acquiring superb manuscripts, not a woman crosses your threshold, you feel yourself free through your work and protected by your books — and then, without provocation, in this blissful and creative condition, you set fire to your books and let them and yourself burn together without a protest. That would be an event which would have a remote relation to the one I have described among the termites, an outbreak of utter senselessness, as with them, but not in so astounding a form. Shall we too one day, like the termites, dispense with sex? I believe in learning more firmly every day, and every day less firmly in the indispensability of love!'

'There is no love! A thing which does not exist can be neither indispensable nor dispensable. I would like to say with the same assurance: there are no women. What have the termites to do with us? Who among them has suffered anything from a woman? Hic mulier, hic salta. Let us confine ourselves to human beings! That female spiders eat their husbands after they have made use of the poor weaklings; that female gnats alone feed on blood, this has nothing to do with us. The slaughter of the drones, among bees, is totally barbarous. If they do not need drones, why do they breed them, if they do need them why do they kill them? In the spider, the most cruel and ugly of all creatures, I see an embodiment of woman. Her web shimmers in the sunlight, poisonous and blue.'

'But you yourself are talking only of animals.'

'Because I know too much about men. I prefer not to begin. I will say nothing of myself, I am only one case, I know many more serious ones, each case is worst for the man who suffers it. All really great thinkers are convinced of the worthlessness of women. Search through the sayings of Confucius, where you will find a thousand opinions and judgments on every subject of daily and more than daily life; search for a single sentence about women! You will find none! The master of silence passes them over in silence. Even mourning for their death, since formalities indicate that a certain inner value is ascribed to a thing, seem to him unsuitable and disturbing. His own wife, whom

433

he married in accordance with custom when she was very young, not
out of conviction, still less out of love, died after years of marriage.
Her son broke into loud lamenting over the body. He cries, he shakes
with sobs; because this woman was quite by chance his mother, he
feels her to be irreplaceable. But Confucius in harsh terms reproaches
him his grief. *Voilà un homme!* His experience later justified his conviction. For several years the prince of the State Lu used him as a
minister. The land flourished under his administration. The people
recovered, drew breath, gained courage and confidence in the men
who led them. Neighbouring States were seized with envy; they
feared a disturbance of the balance of power — a doctrine which we
find in favour even in the earliest times. What did they do in order
to be rid of Confucius? The slyest of them all, the prince of Tsi, sent
to his neighbour the prince of Lu, in whose service Confucius was,
eighty chosen women, dancers and flute-players, for a present. They
ensnared the young prince. They enfeebled him, he grew bored with
politics, he found the counsels of the wise tedious, he was better
amused by the women. Through these creatures the life-work of
Confucius came to naught. He took up the pilgrim's staff and wandered, homeless, from land to land, despairing at the sorrows of the
people, hoping for some new influence, all in vain; everywhere he
found the chiefs and princes in the power of women. He died an
embittered man: but he remained far too noble ever to lament his
griefs. I have felt it only in some of his shortest *dicta*. I too do not
complain. But I generalize and draw conclusions.

'A contemporary of Confucius was Buddha. Vast mountains divided
them, how could they have known anything of each other? It is
possible that the one did not even know the name of the people to
whom the other belonged. "For what reason, reverent master," asked
Ananda, Buddha's favourite pupil, of his teacher, "from what cause
have women no place in the general assembly, pursue no trade and do
not earn their living through any profession of their own?"

'"Women are prone to anger, Ananda; jealous are women, Ananda;
envious are women, Ananda; stupid are women, Ananda. That is the
reason, Ananda, that is the cause for which women have no place in
the general assembly, pursue no trade and do not earn their living in
any profession of their own."

'Women entreated to be taken up into the order, disciples took their
part, but Buddha long refused to yield to them. Decades later he gave
in to his own benevolence, to his pity for them, and founded against

his better judgment, an order for nuns. Among the eight heavy rules that he laid on the nuns the first ran as follows:

'A nun, even if she should have been in the order a hundred years, must offer to a monk — even should he have been received on that very day — the most reverent salutations; she must stand up before him, fold her hands, and honour him according to custom. She must take heed to this rule, revere it, keep it holy, honour it in all things and never transgress it all the days of her life.

'The seventh rule, which she is also commanded to keep holy in the same terms, runs thus: 'A nun must in no wise scorn or reproach a monk.

'The eighth: 'From this day forward a nun may hold no speech whatsoever with a man. But a monk may hold speech with a nun."

'In spite of these barriers which the Exalted One had built up against women in his eight rules, he was overcome with a great sorrow when he had done it and spoke thus to Ananda:

' "Had it not been permitted to women, Ananda, to follow the teaching of the Perfected, to leave the world and turn to a life of wandering, this holy order would long have continued; the true doctrine would have survived a thousand years. But since, Ananda, a woman has left the world and has taken to the life of wandering, this holy order will not last for long, Ananda; only five hundred years will the doctrine remain pure.

' "Like a fair field of rice, Ananda, on which the pestilence falls, which is called mildew — that fair field of rice will not flourish long; so will it be with a doctrine and an order which permits women to withdraw from the world and to take up the life of pilgrims; that holy order will not last for long."

' "Like a fair plantation of sugar canes, Ananda, on which the pestilence falls, which is called the blue disease — that fair plantation will not flourish long; so will it be with a doctrine and an order which permits women to withdraw from the world and to take up the life of pilgrims; that holy order will not last for long."

'I hear in this impersonal statement of belief a great personal despair, a note of pain which I have found nowhere else in all the countless sayings of Buddha which tradition has handed down to us.

> Hard as a tree
> Crooked as a river
> Wicked as a woman
> Wicked and foolish

runs one of the oldest of Indian proverbs, genially expressed as most proverbs are, when you think of its fearful subject but significant of the popular feelings of the Indians!'

'What you are telling me is new to me only in detail. I admire your memory. You quote from an inexhaustible store of traditions everything which bears out your thesis. You remind me of those ancient Brahmins who used to pass on the Vedas — vaster though they are than the holy books of any other people — by word of mouth to their pupils, before the art of writing existed. You have the holy books of all peoples in your head, not only those of the Indians. All the same, you pay for your scholastic memory with a dangerous shortcoming. You don't see what is happening all around you. You have no recollection for your own experiences. If I were to ask you — which I have no intention of doing — tell me now, how did you fall into the hands of that woman, how did she deceive and lie to you, how did she misuse and play with you, tell me the stupidities and vilenesses which, according to your Indian proverb, make up the whole of her, singly and in detail, so that I may make my own judgment and not take over yours quite uncritically — that you would not be able to do. Perhaps to please me you would strain your memory, but quite in vain. You see it is just this kind of memory, which you lack, and which I possess; in that I tower above you. Anything that has ever been said to me, whether to hurt or to flatter, I remember always. But mere statements, simple facts which might have been addressed to anyone else, these escape me with time. Artists have this — a memory for *feelings*, as I'd like to call it. Both together, a memory for feelings and a memory for facts — for that is what yours is — would make possible the universal man. Perhaps I have rated you too highly. If you and I could be moulded together into a single being, the result would be a spiritually complete man.'

Peter raised his left eyebrow. 'Memoirs are not interesting. Women, if they can read at all, live on memoirs. I notice very well what I experience myself. You are curious, I am not. You hear new stories every day, and now for a change you would like one from me. I renounce all such stories. That is the difference between you and me. You live by your lunatics, I by my books. Which is the more estimable? I could live in a cell, I carry my books in my head, you need a whole lunatic asylum. You poor creature, I'm sorry for you. The truth is you're a woman. You live for sensations. Let yourself go then, chase from one novelty to the next! I stand firm. When a thought troubles me, it does not leave me for weeks. You hurry on to get hold of another at once. That's what you call intuition. If I were suffering from a delusion I would be proud of it. What more evidently proves strength of will and character? Try persecution mania! I'd give you my whole library if you could bring yourself to it. You're as slippery as an eel, every strong thought slides off you. You couldn't manage to have a delusion. Nor could I, though I have the necessary talent: I have character. That may sound boastful to you. But I have proved my character. Of my own free will, alone, leaning on no one — I had not even an accessory — I have liberated myself from a weight, a burden, a living death, a rind of accursed granite. Where would I have been if I had waited for you? Still upstairs! But I went into the street, I left the books in the lurch — you don't know what splendid books they were; get to know them first; possibly I am a criminal. On a stern moral judgment I did wrong, but I take full responsibility, I am not afraid. Death breaks the marriage bond. And am I to be permitted less than death? What is death? A suspension of functions, a negative quantity, nothing. Am I to wait for it? Am I to await the caprice of a tough, elderly body? Who would wait when his work, his life, his books were at stake? I hated her, I hate her still, I hate her beyond the grave! I have a right to hatred; I will prove to you that all women deserve hate; you thought I was referring only to the East. Those proofs which I cited — you thought — were all drawn from my own special subject. I shall tear the blue down from the sky for you, and I will tell no lies. Truths, beautiful, hard, pointed truths, truths of every size and shape, truths of feeling and truths of understanding, even though in your case only your feelings function, you woman, truths until you see blue, not red, but blue, blue, blue, for blue is the colour of faith! But that's enough, you have diverted me from our first subject. We have come to a halt on a level with illiterates. You debase me. I would do better to say nothing. You make a nagging Xantippe of me, and I had so many arguments!'

Peter gasped. His mouth twitched violently. Inside it his tongue could be seen, describing despairing convolutions, reminiscent of a drowning man. The lines on his forehead grew disordered. He noticed it while he spoke and clutched at them with his hand; he laid three fingers on the wrinkles and two or three times stroked them with heavy pressure from left to right. The fourth wrinkle received no attention, thought George. It seemed a miracle that there could be a mouth in that narrow slit. But he has lips and tongue like everyone else, who would have thought it. He won't tell me anything. Why doesn't he trust me? How proud he is. He is afraid that I secretly despise him because he got married. Even as a boy he was always against love, as a man he never thought it worth discussing. 'If I were to meet Aphrodite, I'd shoot her.' He loved Antisthenes, the founder of the Cynic school, simply on account of this saying. And then along came an old hag and dragged down the slayer of Aphrodite into utter misery. What a character! How firm he stood! George was conscious of malicious pleasure. Peter had insulted him. He was used to insults, but these struck home. Peter's words had a meaning. It was true: George could not have lived without his patients. He owed them more than fame and daily bread; they were the substratum of his spiritual and mental life. The cunning he had employed to make Peter speak had failed. Instead of talking, he scolded George and accused himself of a crime. He had run away from his wife. So as not to feel too much shame for this shameful fact, he branded himself instead a criminal. A crime, which was no crime, he could bear to have on his conscience. Even men of character prove their integrity to themselves by such devious means. Peter was right to regard himself as a coward. He had not thrown his wife out of the house, he had thrown himself out. From the streets, where he had wandered miserably for a time, a lanky, laughable figure, he had taken refuge in the caretaker's little room. Here — in this prison — he was paying the penalty for his crime. So that the time should not be too long, he had telegraphed to his brother first. A definite role had been fixed for that brother in the whole plan. He was to deal with and get rid of the woman, to reduce the caretaker to his proper station, to talk the man of character out of his belief in a crime, and to lead him back in triumph to his cleansed and liberated library. George here saw himself as an important part of the mechanism which another person had set in motion for the maintenance of his threatened self-respect. The game was worth the two upper joints of a little finger. He was still sorry for Peter. But this pretence of distraction, this abuse of another person's dignity, so as to re-establish his own, this game which was being played with him — who was used to playing with others — displeased him. He would gladly have let Peter know that he saw through him He decided to help him back to the calm of his scholarly existence, selflessly and carefully, as was his office. But he planned a small revenge for later years. When he visited Peter again, and he had already decided to do so, he would in the most friendly but perfectly ruthless way, tell him exactly what had really happened between them in that little room.

'You have arguments? Let me hear them then? I believe your statements will always lead back to either India or China.'

He had chosen the long way round, the short was closed. Since Peter refused to tell him simply what had happened, George would have to make out from selected learned *dicta* what his brother really in his heart held against his wife. How was he to draw those thorns out of Peter's flesh if he could not see them? How was he to calm him when he did not even know into what corners the unrest had spread, how it worked within him, how it appeared to him, what it conceived of the past of the human race, which it had substituted — an enormous changeling — for its own?

'I will stay in Europe,' Peter promised, 'more even can be said of women in Europe. The great popular epics, both of Germans and of Greeks, have feminine broils for their subject. There can be no question of mutual influence. I suppose you admire Kriemhild's cowardly revenge? Did she hurl herself into the struggle, did she risk the slightest danger? She provoked others only, wove her intrigues, abused, betrayed. And at the end, when she had no danger left to fear, with her own hands she cut off the heads of her bound prisoners, Hagen and Gunther. Out of loyalty? Out of love for Siegfried, for whose death she was alone responsible? The Furies drove her on? Did she know that she would destroy herself in gaining her own revenge? No, no, no! Nothing great inspired her. She cared for nothing but the treasure of the Nibelungen! She had lost her gewgaws through too much chattering; she avenged her gewgaws. Among the gewgaws it is true there happened to be a man. He was lost with them, and avenged with them. At the very last moment she still hoped to find out where the treasure was hidden from Hagen. I regard it as much to the credit of the poet, or of the people whom the poet embodied, that Kriemhild was slain too!'

So she was greedy, thought George, and always wanting money from him.

'The Greeks were less just. They forgave Helen everything because she was beautiful. For my part, I tremble with indignation every time I think of her again in Sparta, gay and viciously ogling, at the side of her Menelaus. As if nothing had happened — ten years of war, the strongest, finest, noblest of the Greeks killed, Troy burnt down, Paris her lover, dead — she might at least hold her peace! Years have passed since then, but she is able to speak without embarrassment of that time when: "Shameless as I was, for my unworthy sake, the Grecians sailed to Ilium." She could tell even how Odysseus, disguised as a beggar, slipped into besieged Troy and killed many men.

'. . . Oh what wailing then
Was heard of Trojan women, but my heart
Exulted, alter'd now and wishing home.
For now my crime committed under force
Of Venus' influence I deplored, what time
She led me to a country far remote,
A wanderer from the matrimonial bed,
From my own child, and from my rightful lord
Alike unblemished both in form and mind.

'She told the story to her guests, and, mark you, to Menelaus. She drew the moral for him too. In this way she cajoled her way back to him. Thus she consoled him for her former adultery. Then I used to think Paris, soul and body, more beautiful than you — that's the meaning behind her words — but to-day I know that you are as good. Who stops to think that Paris is dead? To a woman a living man is always more beautiful than a dead one. What she holds *now, that* pleases her. She makes a virtue of this weakness of her own character, and flatters him with it.'

So she twitted him with his gloomy face, thought George, and deceived him with a less gloomy one. When the other man died, she wormed her way back with flattery.

'Oh, Homer knew more of women than we do! The blind must teach those who can see! Do you remember how Aphrodite broke her marriage vow? Hephaestus was not good enough for her because he limped. With whom did she betray him? With Apollo perhaps, the poet, an artist like Hephaestus who had all the beauties which the sooty smith lacked, or with Hades, the dark and mysterious, to whom the underworld belonged? With Poseidon, the strong and angry, who raised the tempests in the ocean? He would have been her rightful lord, she came out of the sea. With Hermes, who understood all the ruses in the world, even those of women, and whose guile and commercial acumen should have enchanted her, the mistress of love? No, to every one of these she prefers Ares, who made up for the vacuum in his head by the strength of his muscles, a ginger-haired dunderhead, the god of the Greek *landsknechts*, with no spirit, nothing but fists, unlimited

440

only in violence, in everything else the embodiment of limitations'.

That's the caretaker, thought George, so he was the second.

'Out of clumsiness he got himself caught in the net. Every time I read how Hephaestus caught the two in his net, I shut down the book for joy and ten, twenty times I passionately kiss the name of Homer. But I do not omit the end. Ares takes himself pitiably off, true he's an ass, but he's a man; he has a spark of shame in his body. Aphrodite slips away radiant to Paphos, where her temples and altars are ready to receive her, and recovers from her shame — all the Gods laughed at her in the net — by decking herself out in her finery!'

When he found the two of them, thought George, the caretaker, still humble in those days, must have taken himself off, embarrassed, forgetting his fists at the sight of the wealthy man of learning. She, however, put on an impertinent air — the one defence of the discovered — took her clothes into the next room and dressed herself there. Jean, where are you?

'I know your thoughts. You think I have the Odyssey against me. I can read in your eyes the names of Calypso, Nausicaa, Penelope. Let me show them to you with all their beauties — which one writer has taken on trust from another — nothing but three cats in an old bag. First let me point out that Circe, a woman, changed all men into swine. Calypso held Odysseus — whom she loved with all her body — a prisoner for seven years. All day long he sits, weeping bitterly, on the sea-shore, wretched with home-sickness and shame, all night long he has to sleep with her, he has to, whether he wants to or not. He does not want to, he wants to go home. He is an active man, full of energy, courage and spirit, an astounding man, the greatest actor of all time and in spite of that a hero. She sees him weeping, she knows well what it is that makes him suffer. In idleness and cut off from human kind, whose talk and action are the air he breathes, he wastes in her company his best years. She will not let him go. She would never have let him go. Then Hermes brings her the command of the gods: she must set Odysseus free. She must obey. Those last hours left to her, she misuses in order to place herself with Odysseus in a more favourable light. I let you go of my own will, she says, because I love you, because I am sorry for you. He sees through her, but he says nothing. And this is the way an immortal goddess behaves: she can have men and love for the whole of a long eternity, she will not grow old. What can it matter to her how he, the mortal, spends his short, small already time-devoured existence?'

441

She never let him alone, thought George, not at night, not when he was working.

'We know little of Nausicaa. She was too young. But we can note her tendencies. She wants a husband like Odysseus, she says. She had seen him on the sea-shore, naked. That is enough for her, he is beautiful. Who he is, she has no idea. She makes her choice from his body alone. There is the legend of Penelope, that she waited twenty years for Odysseus. The number of the years is correct, but why did she wait? Because she could not make up her mind between the suitors. She had been spoilt by the strength of Odysseus. No other man can please her. She cannot promise herself enough pleasure from these weaklings. *She* love Odysseus! What a myth! His old, weak, weary hound knew him when he came in, disguised as a beggar, and died of joy. She didn't recognize him, and lived cheerfully on. Before she went to sleep every night, it's true she cried a little. At first she used to long for him, he had been a fiery, strong man. Then crying grew to be a custom, a sleeping draught that she couldn't do without. Instead of an onion, she used the memory of her dear Odysseus, and cried herseif to sleep with that. The good old servant Eurykleia, the careful little mother, soft-hearted and always busy, broke into cries of joy at the sight of the defeated suitors, the hanged maids! Odysseus the avenger, the man who had been injured, had to reprove her!'

It is the housewifeliness of Penelope and Eurikleia that he hates, thinks George; she had started as his housekeeper.

'I regard as the most precious and the most personal legacy of Homer the words which Agamemnon, as a sad blue shadow in the underworld after his wife had killed him, spoke to Odysseus:

> Thou therefore be not pliant overmuch
> To women; trust her not with all thy mind,
> But half disclose to her, and half conceal . . .
> Steer secret to thy native isle, avoid
> Notice; for woman merits trust no more.

'Cruelty too is one of the chief characteristics of the Greek Goddesses. The Gods are more human. When was a man more mercilessly tormented and harried through life than was Herakles by Hera, who had done her no wrong, except by being born? And when at last he died and got free of the terrible women, who had made even his death a hellfire, she spoiled his immortality by an underhand trick. The Gods wanted to reward him for his sufferings, they were ashamed of the hatred of hard-hearted Hera; as suitable indemnification they made him an immortal. But Hera smuggled a woman into the gift. She coupled him with her daughter Hebe. Gods are haughty: for a man to have one of them to wife seems to them an honour. Herakles is defenceless. If Hebe were a lion he could strike her down with his club. But she is a Goddess. He smiles and thanks them. He has been transplanted out of a dangerous life, whither? Into a never-ending marriage! A never-ending marriage on Olympus under a blue sky, with his eyes on the blue sea. . . .'

What he really fears is the indissolubility of the marriage. George was glad to think of the divorce, which would be his present to his brother. Peter was silent and looked fixedly in front of him.

'Tell me,' he began hesitantly, 'I suffer from optical illusions. I was trying to imagine the Aegean Sea. It seemed to me more green than blue. Is there any significance in that? What do you think?'

'But what are you thinking of? You are a hypochondriac. The sea takes on the most different colours. You must have had a greenish tinge as some particularly happy recollection. It's the same with me. I too like the vicious green colour, before thunderstorms, on dark days.'

'Blue seems to me more vicious than green.'

'The associations with various colours are in my experience different in different people. In general blue is regarded as a pleasant colour. Think of that simple, child-like blue in the pictures of Fra Angelico!'

Peter was again silent. Suddenly he clutched at George's sleeve and said: 'While we are on the subject of pictures, what do you think of Michelangelo?

'What made you think of Michelangelo?'

'Precisely in the centre of the ceiling of the Sistine Chapel, Eve is created out of Adam's rib. The representation of this event, which turned the newly begun and best into the worst of all worlds, is of a smaller size than the creation of Adam and the Expulsion from Eden on either side of it. It is a narrow and wretched process: the robbery of man's worst rib, the splitting into sexes, of which one is no more than a fragment of the other; yet this little event is in the very centre of Creation. Adam is asleep. Had he been awake he would have locked up his rib. Oh that the passing desire for a companion should have become his fate! The goodwill of God was exhausted with the creation of Adam. From that moment he treated him like a stranger, not like his own work. He held him to words and moods, swiftly changing as clouds, and forced him to bear the result of his whims for all eternity. Adam's whims grew into the instincts of the human race. He sleeps. God, the good father, contemptuously benevolent at this occupation, conjures Eve out of him. One of her feet is on the earth, the other is still in Adam's flank. Before she has the means to kneel she is already folding her hands. Her mouth murmurs words of flattery. Flatteries addressed to God are called prayers. She has not learnt how to pray in real sorrow. She is cautious. While Adam sleeps, she is hastily building up a hoard of good works. She works by instinct, and guesses God's vanity, which is gigantic, like himself. For the different acts of creation God bears himself differently. Between one act and the next, he changes his garments. Wrapped in a wide, beautifully draped cloak, he contemplates Eve. He does not see her beauty, seeing everywhere only himself; he accepts her homage. Her mien is humble and sinful. From her first moment she is all calculation. She is naked but feels no shame before God in his wide cloak. She will not know shame until one of her sins miscarries. Adam lies there, limp, as if he had been with a woman. His sleep is light and he dreams of the sadness that God is giving him. The first dream of mankind was this fear of woman. When Adam wakes God leaves them, cruelly, together; she will kneel to him, her hands folded as they were before God, the same flatteries on her lips, loyalty in her eyes, the lust of power in her heart, and so that he shall never escape her again she will tempt him to depravity. Adam is more magnanimous than God. God loves himself in his creation. Adam loves Eve, the Second, the Other, the Evil, the Misfortune. He forgives her what she is: an expanded rib. He forgets, and of One, Two are made. What misery for all time!'

A whim, a caprice is to blame for his marriage. He entered into it against his will. He cannot forgive himself. It irritates him the more that he can only believe in the Categorical Imperative and not in God. Otherwise he could transfer the blame to Him. He thinks of the ceiling of the Sistine Chapel to get some idea of God. There is no other credible Bible God to be found anywhere else in pictorial art. He needs Him in order to abuse Him. Aloud George uttered some non-committal sentence as far as possible removed from his thoughts.

'Why for all time? We were speaking of termites who have got the better of sex. It is therefore neither an inevitable nor an invincible evil.'

'Yes, and just such another miracle as the love riot in the termite hill and the burning of my library, which is impossible, out of the question, inconceivable, stark madness, treason unparalleled to priceless treasures such as no one else has gathered together, sheer scandal, an obscenity, something you must not even mention to me in jest, let alone presume, you can see now, I'm not mad. I'm not even a little unbalanced, I've gone through a lot, there's nothing wrong in getting excited, why do you sneer at me, my memory is perfect, I know everything I want to know, I am master of myself, why? — even if I married once I never had a single love affair, and you, what haven't you done in love, love is a leprosy, a disease, inherited from the first living organisms, others marry twice, three times, I had nothing to do with her, you insult me, you've no right to say it, a madman might do such a thing but I shan't set my library on fire, clear out, if you insist on it, go back to your Bedlam, where are your wits, you answer everything I say with Yes, or Amen! So far I've heard not one personal expression of thought from you, you rattle, you think you know everything! I can smell your contemptuous thoughts. They stink. He's mad, you think, because he abuses women! I'm not the only one! I'll prove that to you! Take away your filthy ideas! You even learnt to read from me, you squirt. You don't even know Chinese. Very well, I'll have my divorce later. I must rehabilitate my honour. A wife isn't necessary for a divorce. Let her turn in her grave. She's not even in a grave. She doesn't deserve a grave. She deserves hell! Why is there no Hell? One must be founded. For women and womanizers, like you. What I say is the truth! I am a serious person. You are going away now and won't bother with me any more. I am alone. I have a head. I can look after myself. I'll not leave the books to you. I'd sooner burn them. But you'll die first, you're already worn out, that's your disgusting way of life, only listen to yourself, to the way you talk, without force in long involved sentences, you're always polite, you woman, you're like Eve, but I'm not God, those ways cut no ice with me! Take a rest from all this femininity! Maybe you'll become human again. Miserable, unclean creature! I'm sorry for you. If I had to change places with you, do you know what I'd do? I have *not* got to, but if I had to, if there were no other way, if the natural law was merciless — I would know a way out. I'd burn your lunatic asylum, till it flamed like daylight, with all its inhabitants, with me too, but not my books! Books are worth more than lunatics, books are worth more than men, you don't understand that because you're a play-actor, you need applause, books are dumb, they speak yet they are dumb, that is the wonder, they speak and you hear them more swiftly than if you had to hear them with ears. I'll show you my books, not now, later. You'll say you're sorry for your revolting suggestion, or I'll throw you out!'

445

George did not interrupt him, he wanted to hear it all. Peter spoke with such haste and excitement, that no friendly word would have held him up. He had stood up: as soon as he spoke of books, his small gestures expanded, grew determined. George regretted the image which, for the lack of another, he had chosen to illustrate the termites and their happy sexlessness in order to lure his brother's thoughts into the desired direction; it had proved, unfortunately, a bad choice. The mere thought that he could set fire to his books, burned Peter more than fire itself. He loved his library so dearly; it was his substitute for human beings. He might have been spared this painful vision: but still it had not been in vain. From it George learnt that there was a cure for the woman, more certain than poison; it was this over-whelming love which had only to be brought into play against that hatred and it would be extinguished and destroyed. It would be worth living for the sake of books which even from an imagined danger he would protect with such passion. Quickly and noiselessly I shall throw out the woman, George decided, and the caretaker with her, remove from the flat anything which may remind him of them, go through the library in case anything's missing, put his financial affairs in order — he's probably got little or nothing left — lead him back to the bosom of his books, fan his old love for a day or two, direct his attention to work which he had intended before, and then leave this dry fish to himself in his own dreary element — he finds it gay enough. At the end of six months I'll call on him again. I owe him these little atten-tions though he is my brother and I despise his ridiculous profession. I've discovered all I need to know about his married life. His judg-ments, which he thinks objective, are as transparent as water. First I must calm him down. He is calmest when he can disguise his hatred under the names of mythical or historical women. Behind these ram-parts of his memory he feels safe against the woman upstairs. She could not make him a single answer on those scores. Fundamentally he is limited and has a petty character. His hatred gives him a kind of vigour. Perhaps a little of that will be left over for his later theses.

'You interrupted yourself. You wanted to say something impor-tant.' George broke gently, with a soft expectant voice, into Peter's staccato exclamations. So much gravity and officiousness disarmed his rage. He sat down once more, searched in his head and found, in a very little time, the requisite connecting thread.

'Just such another wonder as the love riot in the ant-heap and the impossible burning of my library would have been the destruction of the ceiling of the Sistine Chapel by Michelangelo himself. He might possibly — in spite of four years work — at the command of some crazy pope, have peeled off or painted over one figure after another. But Eve, this Eve, he would have protected against a hundred Swiss Guards. She is his testament.'

'You have a nose for the testaments of great artists. History justifies you too, not only Homer and the Bible. Let's forget Eve, Delilah, Clytaemnestra and even Penelope, whose ruthlessness you have proved. They are formidable examples, outstanding figures for the demonstration of your point, but who knows if they ever lived? A Cleopatra proves a thousand times more to us, amateurs of history.'

'Yes — I have not forgotten her, I had not got so far. Good, we'll omit the intervening ones! You are not as thorough as I am. Cleopatra has her sister murdered — every woman fights every woman. She deceives Antony — every woman deceives every man. She exploits him and the Asiatic provinces of Rome for her own luxuries — every woman lives and dies for her love of luxury. She betrays Antony at the first moment of danger. She talks him into believing that she will burn herself alive. He kills himself meanwhile. She does not burn herself. But she has a mourning robe ready to hand, it suits her, dressed in it she tries to entangle Octavian. He was astute enough to lower his eyes. I dare swear he never saw her. The sly young fellow was in full armour. Otherwise she would have tried the touch of her skin, would have clung to him at the very moment when Antony was breathing his last. He was a man, Octavian, a fine man, he protected his body with armour and his eyes by casting them down! He is said to have answered not a word to her siren songs. I have a suspicion he may even have stopped his ears as Odysseus did for his part. Now, she couldn't captivate him through his nose alone. He could rely on his nose. Probably his olefactory organ was ill-developed. A man, a man I admire! Caesar yields to her, not he. And in the meantime she had grown a great deal more dangerous owing to her age, more importunate I mean.'

He even reproaches his wife her age, understandably enough, thought George. For a very long time he went on listening. Hardly a misdeed of woman kind, whether historically vouched for or merely traditional was passed over. Philosophers explained their contemptuous opinions. Peter's quotations were reliable, and, since he spoke like a school master, imprinted themselves deeply on his brother's mind. Many a phrase, corrupted by time-honoured tradition, he would correct as he went along. You can always learn, even from a pedant. Much was new to

George. Thomas Aquinas had said: 'Women are weeds which grow quickly, incomplete men; their bodies only come earlier to ripeness because they are of less value, nature takes less pains with them.' And in which chapter does Thomas More, the first modern communist, treat of the marriage laws of his Utopia? In the chapter on slavery and crime! Attila, King of the Huns, was called by a woman, Honoria, the Emperor's sister, into Italy her own homeland, which he very largely plundered and laid waste. A few years later the widow of that same Emperor, Eudoxia, married, after her husband's death, his murderer and successor, and called in the Vandals to Rome itself. Rome owed that notorious sack to her, as Italy owed the ravages of the Huns to her sister-in-law.'

Little by little Peter's anger grew less. He spoke ever more calmly, and cited appalling crimes almost casually. The material was more ample than his hatred. So as to omit nothing — his chief characteristic was still his accuracy — he divided it scrupulously into periods, peoples and thinkers. Only a little was left for each person. An hour ago Messalina would have heard a great deal more of herself. Now she got off lightly with a few lines of Juvenal. Even the mythology of certain negro tribes seemed to be saturated with contempt for women. Peter found his allies wherever they were. He could forgive the ignorance of illiterates if they agreed with him about women.

George used a small pause for recollection, to make a proposal; he offered it respectfully and with unchanged expectation, though it concerned simply a meal. Peter agreed: he would prefer to eat out of the house. He had seen enough of the closet. They went into the nearest restaurant. George felt, sidelong, that he was being closely watched. Scarcely had he opened his mouth before Peter was back on his hyenas. But soon his sentences gave way to silence. Then George too fell silent. For a few moments both rested from their vigilance. In the restaurant Peter ceremoniously took his place. He fidgeted on his chair until he had completely turned his back on a neighbouring lady. Immediately after another appeared, still older and more anxious to be looked at: even a Peter interested her; grateful for the attention which she soon hoped to attract, she took no exception to a skeleton. The head waiter, a gentleman of distinguished appearance, stood before George, whom he took for the benefactor of the hungry guest, and took his order. With inconspicuous nods in the direction of the beggar, he recommended two sorts of dish, nourishing for the poor fellow, and more refined for his benefactor. Suddenly Peter got up and declared curtly:

'We will leave this place!' The waiter was full of regret. He ascribed the blame to himself and overflowed with courtesies. George felt himself painfully moved. Without any explanation, they went. 'Did you see the hag?' asked Peter in the street. 'Yes.' 'She was looking at me. At me! I am not a criminal. How can she have thought of such a thing, to look at me! What I have done, I am ready to answer for.'

In the second restaurant George took a private cubicle. Over their meal Peter went on with his interrupted lecture, long and tedious, his eyes always on the watch to see if his brother was listening. He lost himself in commonplaces and hackneyed stories. His speech limped along. Between sentences he fell asleep. Soon he would be separating his words by whole minutes. George ordered champagne. If he spoke more quickly he would be done sooner. Besides, I shall learn his last secrets, if he's got any. Peter refused to drink. He abhorred alcohol. Then he drank all the same. Or else, he said, his brother might think he had something to hide from him. He had nothing to hide. He was truth itself. His misfortune came from his love of truth. He drank freely. His learning shifted to another sphere. He revealed an astonishing knowledge of historic murder trials. With passion he defended the right of men to set aside their wives. His speech transformed itself naturally into that of the defending counsel, pleading before the court the reasons why his client had been forced to kill his fiendish wife. Her fiendishness was clear from the immoral life which she would so willingly have led, from her provocative way of dressing, from her age which she tried to conceal, from the vulgar words which were her entire vocabulary, and above all from her sadistic violence which went so far as the most brutal beating. What man would not have killed such a woman? All these arguments Peter pursued at length and with deep emphasis. When he had finished he stroked his chin with satisfaction, like a true barrister. Then he pleaded in general for the murderers of less gifted women.

George learnt nothing new of the case of his brother. The opinion which he had already formed remained, in spite of the alcohol, intact. Injuries to pedantic heads are easily repaired. They arise from an excess of logic, and by logic they are cured. These cases were the only ones which George did not care for; they were not real cases. A man who is the same lit-up as he is stone-cold deserves the lowest possible opinion. What an all-devouring lack of imagination in this Peter! A brain of lead, moulded out of letters, cold, rigid, heavy. Technically a miracle perhaps; but are there miracles in our technical times? The boldest

thought to which a philologist can bring himself is that of murdering
his wife. And even then the wife has to be more or less a monster, a
good twenty years older than the philologist in question, his own evil
image, a person who treated men as he treated the texts of great poets.
If he were to carry out the murder, if he were to raise his hand against
her and not draw it back at the last moment, if he were to go to his
destruction for this crime, to sacrifice to his revenge manuscripts, texts,
library, all the furniture of his lean heart — then hold his memory in
honour! But he prefers to pay her off. He telegraphs first to his
brother. He asks help for no murder. He will live and work another
thirty years. In the annals of some science or other he will shine as a
star of the first magnitude for all earthly eternity. Grandchildren,
turning over the pages of the Transactions of this or that Sinological
Society (for grandchildren of this kind too will be born) will come
across his name. He has the same name himself. He ought to change
it. Fifty years hence the Chinese National Government will honour
him with a statue. Children, graceful, delicate creatures with slant eyes
and smooth skin (when they laugh the hardest houses bend down)
play in a street called after him. In their eyes (children are a bunch of
riddles, they and everything around them) the letters of his name will
become a mystery, he a mystery who during his life was so obvious,
transparent, understandable and understood, who, if he ever was an
enigma, was an enigma immediately solved. What luck that people
do not usually know after whom their streets are called! What luck
that they know so little altogether!

Early in the afternoon he brought the philologist to his hotel and
asked him to rest there while he settled up his affairs at home.

'You are going to clean out my flat,' said Peter.

'Yes, yes.'

'You must not be surprised at the odious stench.'

George smiled: cowards incline to circumlocutions.

'I shall hold my nose.'

'Keep your eyes open! You may see ghosts.'

'I never see ghosts.'

'Maybe you'll see some all the same. Tell me if you do!'

'Yes, yes.' How tasteless his jokes are!

'I've a request for you.'

'And that is?'

'Don't talk to the caretaker! He's dangerous. He may attack you.
Say a word which doesn't suit him, and he hits out at once. I don't

want you to come to any harm on my account. He'll break all your bones. Every day he throws beggars out of the house; he injures them first. You don't know him. Promise me you won't have any contact with him! He's a liar. You should not believe anything he says.'

'I know, you've warned me already.'

'Promise me.'

'Yes, yes.'

'Even if he does nothing to you, he'll jeer at me later.'

So he's already afraid of the time he'll be alone again. 'You can be certain I'll get rid of him out of the house.'

'Truly?' Peter laughed, since his brother had known him, for the first time. He clutched for his pocket and handed George a bundle of crushed bank notes. 'He'll want money.'

'This is your entire fortune?'

'Yes. You'll find the rest in the flat in a more noble form.'

This last phrase almost made George sick. One half of their vast paternal inheritance was locked up in dead tomes, the other in a lunatic asylum. Which half had been the better used? He had expected to find at least some of the capital still with Peter. That wasn't the reason he was distressed, he said to himself; not because I shall have to support him for the rest of my life. His poverty annoys me because with this money I could have helped so many patients.

Then he left him alone. In the street he wiped his hands clean on his handkerchief. He would have wiped his forehead too; he had already lifted his hand when he remembered that similar gesture of Peter's. Hurriedly he dropped his hand again.

When he was once again outside the door of the flat he heard loud screams. Inside people were fighting. It would be all the easier for him to deal with them. At his violent ringing the woman opened the door. Her eyes were red and she was wearing the same comical skirt she had worn in the early morning.

'I ask you, Mr. Brother!' she shrieked, 'he's taking liberties! He pawned the books. It's not my fault, is it? Now he's going to tell the police of me. He can't do it, I tell you. I'm a respectable woman!'

George led her with elaborate politeness into one of the rooms. He offered her his arm. She clutched at it at once. In front of his brother's writing desk he asked her to take a seat. He himself set the chair for her.

'Make yourself comfortable!' he said. 'I hope you feel safe here. A woman like you should have every attention. Unhappily I am already married. You ought to have a business of your own. You are a born business woman. We shall not be interrupted here, I trust?' He went to the communicating door and rattled at the lock. 'Locked, good. Would you very kindly lock the other door as well?'

She obeyed. He understood exactly how to turn himself at once into the owner, and the householder into his guest.

'My brother is unworthy of you. I have been talking to him. You must leave him! He wanted to report you for double adultery. He knows everything. But I have dissuaded him. A man like him would be deceived by every woman. I suspect that he is not in any case normal. All the same he might easily make you appear as the guilty party in a divorce. You would get nothing at all in that case. Then you would have nothing for all your sufferings with this wretched creature — I know just what he's like. You would have to pass your old age in poverty and loneliness. A respectable woman like you with a good thirty years before you yet. How old are you then? Not a day over forty? He has already secretly filed his petition. But I will take your part. You please me. You must leave the house at once. If he doesn't see you any more, he'll do no more against you. I'll buy you a dairy shop at the other end of the town. I shall put up the capital on one condition: you must never cross my brother's path again. If you should do so the capital which I am putting up will come back to me. You will sign an agreement to this effect. You will do well out of it. He wanted to have you shut up. He has the law on his side. The law is unjust. Why should a woman like you have to suffer because a few books are missing? I cannot allow it. Ah, if only I were not already married! Permit me, dear lady, as your brother-in-law, to kiss your hand. Tell me, if you will, exactly, what books are missing. I have taken it upon myself to replace them. Otherwise he would not have withdrawn his complaint. He is a cruel man. We will leave him to himself. Let him see how he gets on then. Not a soul will look after him. He has deserved it. If he commits any more follies then he'll only have himself to blame. Now he tries to blame everything on you. I shall see that the caretaker loses his job. He has taken liberties with you. From now on he can caretake in another house. You will soon marry again. You can be sure the whole world will envy you your new shop. A man would gladly marry into that. You've got what a woman needs. Nothing is missing. Believe me! I'm a man of the world. Who else to-day is so particular about having everything clean as you are? Your skirt is something quite unusual. And your eyes! And your youth! And your little mouth! As I've said already if I were not married I'd try to seduce you! But I have a respect for my brother's wife. When I come here again later to keep an eye on that fool, I shall permit myself, if I may, to call on you in your dairy shop. Then you won't be his wife any longer. Then we'll let our hearts speak.'

He spoke with passion. Each word had the calculated effect. She changed colour. He paused after some sentences. Never before had he dared so much melodrama. She said nothing. He grasped that it was his presence which struck her dumb. He spoke so beautifully. She was afraid of missing a single word. Her eyes started out of their sockets, first with fear, then with love; she pricked her ears; water ran out of her mouth. The chair on which she sat creaked a popular tune. She held out her hands to him, folded into a cup. She drank with lips and hands. When he kissed her hands, the cup lost its shape and her lips breathed — he could hear it: more please. So he overcame his revulsion and kissed her hands again. She trembled; her emotion extended even to the roots of her hair. Had he embraced her she would have fainted. After his last sentence, the one about hearts, he remained fixed in a baroque attitude. Her hand and the greater part of his arm lay, ceremoniously, across his chest. She had, said she, savings. None of the books had gone altogether, she still had the pawn tickets. Ostentatiously and awkwardly she turned away — the shamefacedness of the shameless — and fetched out of her skirt, which presumably contained a pocket, a bundle of pawn tickets. Did he want her savings book too? She would give it him for love. He thanked her. For love too, he could not agree. Even while he was refusing she said, I ask you, who knows if you really deserve it. She regretted the offer before he accepted it. Would he come and see her for certain, he was what she called a man. She recovered her self-command by speaking these few words. But scarcely had he opened his mouth than she was his again.

Half an hour later she was helping him in his campaign against the caretaker. 'You can't know who I am!' shouted George in his face. 'The head of the Paris police, on vacation! One word from me and my friend the head of the police here will have you arrested! You'll lose your pension. I know everything you have on your conscience. Take a look at these pawn tickets! I won't say a word about anything else for the present. Not a word from you! I know you through and through. You lead a double life. I am for taking drastic proceedings against anti-social elements. I shall ask my friend the head of your police to purge his forces. Leave this house! To-morrow morning early you'll be gone! You are a suspect! Put your luggage together and be off! I'll let you off with a caution for the time being. I shall exterminate you! You criminal! Do you know what you've done? It's being shouted from the roof-tops!'

Benedikt Pfaff, the stalwart ginger-headed tough, contracted his muscles, knelt down, folded his hands and implored the Head of the Police for forgiveness. His daughter had been ill, she would have died of her own accord anyway, he begged leave to recommend himself, and asked not to be sent away from his job. A man had nothing in the world except his peep-hole. What else had he left? You couldn't grudge him a beggar or two. Very few came nowadays, anyway! The tenants were blown-out with affection for him. He had a bit of bad luck! If only he'd known! The Professor didn't look the kind of man who'd have had the head of the Paris police for his brother. He'd have had him met at the station and respectfully conducted home if he'd known! God was reasonable. Thanking him, he permitted himself to stand up.

He was very well satisfied with the honour he had done the important gentleman. When he got up again he blinked at him in a friendly way. George remained curt and stern. But all the same he came half-way to meet him. Pfaff promised to redeem all the books he had pawned, in person, on the following morning. He was, however, to leave the house. At the far end of the town, close to the dairy shop bought for the woman, he was to be set up in the animal business; the two declared themselves ready to move in together. The woman made her own terms: she was not to be pinched or knocked about and she was to be allowed to receive the Professor's brother whenever he wanted. Pfaff agreed, flattered. He had his doubts about the prohibition on pinching. He was only human after all. But as well as committing themselves to mutual love, they were each to watch the other. If one or the other were to go wandering off in the direction of Ehrlich Strasse the other was immediately to inform Paris. In which case both shop and liberty would be ruthlessly removed. The very first information would be followed by arrest by telegraph. The informer could claim a reward. Pfaff didn't give a sh— for Ehrlich Strasse if he could live among a crowd of canary birds. Therese complained: Please he's doing it again. He mustn't always sh—. George spoke to him seriously about using the sort of language which was more suited to a better-class business man. He was no longer a miserable half-pay policeman, but a made man. Pfaff would sooner have been a publican, best of all a ring-master with a boxing turn of his own and tame canary birds which would sing at a word and shush down at a word. The Head of the Police gave him permission, if his business made so much profit and he behaved himself properly, to open a pub or a circus. Therese said no. A circus isn't respectable. A pub perhaps. They decided to divide the work. She would look after the pub, he would look after the circus. He was the master, she was the mistress. Clients and visitors from Paris were promised by the Head of the Police.

That very evening Therese began a thorough spring-cleaning of the flat. She engaged no outside help but did it all herself, so as to spare Mr. Brother needless expense: For the night, she made up her husband's bed with clean sheets and offered it to his brother. Hotels get more expensive every day. She was not afraid. Georges made his brother his excuse; he had to keep an eye on him. Pfaff withdrew for the last time to his little room; his last sleep, his dearest memory. Therese went on scrubbing all night.

Three days later the owner celebrated his homecoming. His first glance was for the little closet. It was empty; where the peep-hole had been was only a desolate hole in the wall. Pfaff, the inventor, had broken up and carried off his patent. The library upstairs was intact. The communicating doors were flung open at right angles. Peter paced once or twice up and down before the writing desk. 'There are no stains on the carpets,' he said and smiled. 'If there were stains on them, I would burn them at once. I hate stains!' He pulled his manuscripts out of the drawers and piled them up on the writing desk. He read out the titles to George. 'Work for years to come, my friend! And now I will show you the books.' Exclaiming, 'Here you see', and 'What do you think I have here?' with gloating glances and patient encouragement (not everyone has a dozen oriental languages all at his finger-ends), he hauled out books which only a short while before had been pawned, and explained their peculiarities to a willingly astounded brother. With uncanny speed the atmosphere changed; it rang with dates and textual references. Mere letters acquired a revolutionary significance. Dangerous misreadings were satisfactorily dealt with. Frivolous philologists were unmasked as monsters, who deserved only to be publicly pilloried in blue robes. Blue, this most ridiculous of colours, the colour of the uncritical, the credulous, the believers. A newly discovered language was proved to be one already well known, and its supposed discoverer an ass. Angry cries were heard against him. The man had dared, after a bare three years residence in the country, to come out with a work on the language there spoken! Even in the realms of scholarship the insolence of the self-made was on the increase. Scholarship should have its Inquisition, to which it could hand over heretics. There was no need, immediately to condemn them to burning at the stake. The legal independence of the priesthood in the Middle Ages had a great deal to be said for it. If only men of learning enjoyed such treatment to-day! A man of learning whose work may be of inestimable value can to-day be judged by a lay court for some small, perhaps unavoidable misdemeanour.

George began to feel uncertain of himself. Not a tenth of the books they discussed were known to him. He despised this knowledge which oppressed him. Peter's desire for work grew powerfully. It awakened in George his yearning for a place where he too was no less absolute master than his brother in the library. He called him quickly a second Leibniz, and made use of a few perfectly true statements as a pretext to escape from his power for the afternoon. He must engage some innocuous charwoman; he must arrange with the neighbouring café to send in meals regularly; he must place a deposit with the bank and arrange for automatic payments into the house on the first of every month.

Late in the evening they took leave of one another. 'Why do you not turn up the lights?' asked George. It was already dark in the library. Peter laughed proudly. 'I know my way about here even in the dark.' Since he had come home he had changed into a self-assured and almost cheerful character. 'You'll harm your eyes,' said George and turned up the light. Peter thanked him for services rendered. With aggressive pedantry he counted them all over. The most important of all, the expulsion of his wife, he passed over in silence. 'I shall not write to you!' he concluded.

'I can well believe it. With all the work which you have planned out for yourself.'

'Not on that account. I don't write on principle. Letter writing is a form of laziness.'

'As you please. When you need me, send a telegram! In six months I'll come to see you again.'

'Why? I don't need you!' His voice sounded angry. So he felt the parting. Under his rudeness he was concealing grief.

In the train George continued the weft of his thoughts. Would it be surprising if he should care a little for me? I have helped him a great deal. Now he has everything exactly, as he wants to have it. Not a breath of wind can disturb him.

His own escape from that inferno of a library made him feel happy. Full of impatience eight hundred believers were waiting to worship him. The train went too slowly.

CHAPTER VI

THE RED COCK

PETER locked the door behind his brother. It was secured by three complicated locks and thick, heavy iron bolts. He rattled them: not a nail shook. The whole door was like a single piece of steel; behind it he was truly at home. The keys still fitted; the paint on the wood had faded; it felt rough to the touch. The rust on the darkened bolts was old and it was hard to make out what part of the door had been repaired. Surely the caretaker had smashed it, when he had broken into the flat. A kick of his and the bolts had snapped like wood; the wretched liar, he lied with his fists and feet; he had simply crashed into the flat. Once upon a time came the first of the month and brought no honorarium for Mr. Pfaff. 'Something's happened to him!' he had roared, and hurled himself upstairs to the source of his income; it had suddenly dried up. On the way he had battered the stairs. The stone whimpered under his booted fists. The tenants crept out of their dens, all his subjects in the house, and held their noses. 'It stinks!' they complained. 'Where?' he asked threateningly. 'Out of the library.' 'I can stink nothing!' He couldn't even speak his native tongue. He had a thick nose and gigantic nostrils, but his moustache was twisted and reached up into his nostrils. So he could smell nothing but pomade, and as for the corpse he never smelt that. His moustache was as stiff as ice, every day he waxed it. He had red pomade in a thousand different tubes. Under the bed in his closet was a collection of salve jars, red of every colour, red here, red there, red overhead. His head, yes, his head was FIERY RED.

Kien put out the light in the hall. He only had to press a switch and it grew dark at once. Through cracks in the door a pale glimmer reached him from the study and gently stroked his trousers. How many trousers had he not seen! The peep-hole existed no longer. The ruffian had broken it off. The wall was left desolate. To-morrow a new Pfaff would move in down below and wall up the gash. If only it had been staunched at once! The napkin was stiff with blood. The water in the basin was reddened by a sea-battle off the canary islands. Why had they hidden themselves under the bed? There was room enough on the wall. There were four cages ready. But they looked

457

down haughtily on the small fry. The flesh-pots were empty. Then came the quails and the children of Israel could eat. All the birds were killed. Little throats they had, under their yellow feathers. Who would think it, that powerful voice, and yet how get at their little throats! Once you grasp them, you press them, there's an end of the four part song, blood spurts in all directions, thick, warm blood, these birds live in a perpetual fever, hot blood, it BURNS, my trousers BURN.

Kien wiped the blood and the glow off his trousers. Instead of going into his study, whence the light assaulted him, he went through the long dark corridor into the kitchen. On the table was a plate of bread. The chair in front of it was crooked as if someone had just been sitting on it. He pushed it away with hostility. He seized the soft, yellow brioches, they were the birds' corpses, and poured them into the bread bin. It looked like a crematorium. He hid it away in the kitchen cupboard. On the table the plate alone was left, shining and dazzlingly white, a cushion. On top of it lay a book — 'The Trousers . . .' Therese had opened it. She had stopped at page 20. She was wearing gloves. 'I read every page six times.' She was trying to seduce him. He wanted nothing but a glass of water. She fetched it. 'I'm going away for six months.' 'Excuse me, I can't have it!' 'It is necessary.' 'I can't have it.' 'But I'm going just the same.' 'Then I'll lock the door of the flat!' 'I have the key.' 'Where, excuse me?' 'Here!'' 'And if a FIRE should break out?'

Kien went to the sink and turned the tap on full. With full force the stream shot into the heavy basin; it almost broke it. Soon it was full of water. The flood streamed over the kitchen floor and quenched every danger. He turned the tap off again. He slipped on the stone tiles. He slipped into the bedroom next door. It was empty. He smiled at it. In earlier times there had been a bed here and against the opposite wall a trunk. In the bed the blue virago had slept. She kept her weapons hidden in the trunk; skirts, skirts and yet more skirts. Daily she performed her devotions at the ironing board in the corner. The limp folds were laid out on the table; they arose resurrected in their strength. Later she moved in with him and brought the furniture with her. The walls went pale with joy. They have been white ever since. And what did Therese pile up against them? Sacks of flour, great sacks of flour! She was making the bedroom into her store cupboard against the lean years. Thighs hung down from the ceiling, smoked thighs. The floor was abristle with sugar loaves. Bread rolls tumbled against kegs of butter. Milk cans sucked close up to each other. The sacks of flour against the wall defended the town from hostile attack. There were things laid up here for all eternity. She let herself be locked in, unperturbed, and bragged of her keys. One day she opened the bedroom door. There was not a crumb left in the kitchen and what did she find in the bedroom? The flour bags were nothing but holes. Instead of hams, strings hung from the ceiling. The milk had all run out of the cans, and the sugar loaves were only blue paper. The floor had eaten up the bread and smeared the butter into its cracks. Who has done this? Who? Rats! Rats appear suddenly in houses where there were never any before, no one knows where they come from, but there they are, they eat up everything, kind blessed rats, and they leave nothing behind for hungry women but a pile of newspapers; there they lie, nothing else. They don't care for newspaper. Rats hate cellulose. They manœuvre in the darkness all right, but they are not termites. Termites eat wood and books. The love riot among the termites. FIRE IN THE LIBRARY.

As fast as his arm would obey him, Kien clutched for a paper. He did not have to stoop far. The pile reached above his knee. He pushed it violently aside. The floor in front of the window all the way across was taken up with papers; all the old papers for years had been piled up here. He leaned out of the window. In the courtyard below all was dark. From the stars light penetrated to him. But it was not enough to read the paper by. Perhaps he was holding it too far off. He approached it to his eyes, his nose touched the surface and sucked in the faint smell of oil, greedy and fearful. The paper trembled and crackled. The wind which swayed the paper came from his nostrils, and his nails clawed through it. But his eyes were in quest of a headline so big that it could be read. Once he could get a hold of it, he would read the whole paper by starlight. First of all he made a huge M. So murder was the subject. Immediately next to it there was indeed a U. The headline, coarse and black, occupied a sixth part of the whole paper. So this was how they expanded his deed? Now he was the talk of the whole town, he who loved peace and solitude. And George would have a copy of the paper in his hand even before he crossed the frontier. Now he too would know about the murder. If only there were a learned censorship the paper would be half blank. Then people wouldn't find so much blue to read, further down. The second headline began with a V and close to it an R: FIRE. Murder and arson lay waste the papers, the land, the minds — nothing attracts them more, if there's no fire after the murder their pleasure is incomplete; they'd like to start the fire themselves, they haven't the courage for murder, they're cowards; no one should read the papers; then they'd die of themselves, of a universal boycott.

Kien threw down the paper on the pile. He must cancel his regular order for papers at once. He left the hateful room. But it's night already, he said aloud, in the passage. How can I cancel my order? So as to go on reading, he took out his watch. All it offered was a dial. He could not make out the time. MURDER and ARSON were more forthcoming. In the library opposite there was light. He burned to know the time. He went into his study.

It was just eleven. No church bell was striking. Once it had been broad daylight. The yellow church was opposite. Across the little square people passed and repassed, excited. The hunchbacked dwarf was called Fischerle. He cried to soften a heart of stone. Paving stones jumped up and lay down again. There was a cordon of police round the Theresianum. Operations in charge of a major. He carried the warrant for arrest in his pocket. The dwarf had seen through it himself. Enemies had hidden under the stairs. Up above the hog was in charge. Books delivered over helpless to conscienceless beasts! The hog had composed a cookery book with a hundred and three recipes. It was said of his stomach — it had corners. Then why was Kien a criminal? Because he helped the poorest of the poor. For the police had drawn up a warrant even before they heard about the corpse. Against him all this gigantic levy. Forces on horse and on foot. Brand new revolvers, rifles, machine guns, barbed wire and tanks — but all is vain against him, they can't hang him till they've got him! Through their legs, they escape into the roses, he and his loyal dwarf. And now the enemy are on his heels, he hears grunting and panting, and the bloodhound at his throat. But ah, there is worse to come. On the sixth floor of the Theresianum the beasts are bidding each other good night; there they keep thousands of books unjustly in durance, tens of thousands, against their free will, guiltless, what can·they do against the hog, cut off from *terra firma*, close under the BROILING attic roof, starving, condemned, condemned to the devouring FLAMES.

Kien heard cries for help. Despairing, he pulled at the cord which was attached to the skylight and the windows flew open. He listened. The cries redoubled. His mistrusted them. He hurried into the neighbouring room and here too pulled at the cord. In here the cries were fainter. The third room echoed shrilly. In the fourth they could hardly be heard. He went back through all the rooms. He walked and listened. The cries rose and fell in waves. He pressed his hands against his ears and took them quickly away again. Pressed them and took them away. It sounded just the same as above. Ah, his ears were confusing him. He pushed the ladder, despite its resistant rails, into the middle of the study and climbed to its highest level. The upper part of his body overtopped the roof; he held fast on to the panes. Then he heard the despairing cries; they were the books screaming. In the direction of the Theresianum he was aware of a reddish glow. Hesitantly it spread across the black gaping heavens. The smell of oil was in his nose. The glow of fire, screams, the smell; the Theresianum is BURNING.

Dazzled, he closed his eyes. He lowered his burning skull. Drops of water splashed on his neck. It was raining. He flung his head back and offered his face to the rain. How cool — the strange water! Even the clouds were merciful. Perhaps they would put out the fire. Then an icy blow struck him on the eyelid. He was cold. Someone tweaked at him. They stripped him stark naked. They went through his all pockets. They left him his shirt. In the little mirror he saw himself. He was very thin. Red fruits, thick and bloated, grew all around him. The caretaker was one of them. The corpse attempted to talk. He would not listen to her. She was always saying: I ask you. He stopped up his ears. She tapped on her blue skirt. He turned his back on her. In front of him was seated a uniform without a nose. 'Your name?' 'Dr. Peter Kien.' 'Profession?' 'The greatest living sinologist.' 'Impossible!' 'I swear it.' 'Perjury!' 'No!' 'Criminal!' 'I am in my right mind. I confess. In full possession of my senses. I killed her. I am perfectly sane. My brother knows nothing of it. Spare him! He is a famous man. I lied to him.' 'Where is the money?' 'Money?' 'You stole it.' 'I'm not a thief!' 'Thief and murderer!' 'Murderer!' 'Thief and murderer!' 'Murderer!' 'You are under arrest. You will stay here!' 'But my brother's coming. Leave me free until then! He must know nothing. I implore you!' And the caretaker steps forward, he is still his friend, and procures him a few days of liberty. He brings him home and keeps guard over him, he does not let him out of the little room. That was where George found him, in misery but not a criminal. Now he is on his train already, if only he had stayed here! He would have helped him at his trial! A murderer must give himself up? But he won't. He will stay here. He must watch the burning Theresianum.

Slowly he lifted his lids. The rain had stopped. The reddish glow

461

had paled, the fire brigade must have arrived at last. The sky no longer rang with cries. Kien climbed down from the ladder. In every room the cries for help were stilled. So as not to miss them if they began again, he left the skylights wide open. In the middle of the room the ladder was placed ready. If the disaster should grow to a climax, it would help his flight. Whither? To the Theresianum. The hog lay, a charred corpse, under the beams. There, unknown among the crowd, there was much he could do. Leave the house! Take care! Tanks are patrolling the streets. All the king's horses. They think they have caught him. The Lord will smite them; and he, the murderer, will escape. But first he will efface all traces.

He kneels before the writing desk. He passes his hand over the carpet. That was where the corpse lay. Is the blood still visible? It is not visible. He pushed his fingers far into his nostrils, but they only smell a little of dust. No blood. He must look more closely. The light is bad. It hangs too high. The flex of the table lamp does not reach so far. On the writing desk is a box of matches. He strikes six at once, six months, and lies down on the carpet. From very close he holds the light to the carpet, looking for bloodstains. Those red stripes are part of the pattern. They were always here. They must be got rid of. The police will take them for blood. They must be burnt out. He presses the matches into the carpet. They go out. He throws them away. He strikes six new ones. Softly he passes them over one of the red stripes, then delicately pokes them in. They leave a brown mark behind them. Soon they go out. He strikes new ones. He uses a whole box. The carpet remains cool. It is marked all over with brownish scars. Glowing patches are here and there. Now nothing can be proved against him. Why did he confess? Before thirteen witnesses. The corpse was there too, and the ginger cat which can see at night. The murderer with wife and child. A knock. The police at the door. A knock.

Kien will not open. He stops his ears. He hides behind a book. It is on the writing-table. He wants to read it. The letters dance up and down. Not a word can he make out. Quiet please! Before his eyes it flickers, fiery red. This is the aftermath of his terrible shock, on account of the fire, who would not have been frightened; when the Theresianum burns numberless numbers of books go up in flames. He stands up. How can he possibly read now. The book lies too far off. Sit! He sits again. Trapped. No, his home, the writing desk, the library. All are loyal to him. Nothing has been burnt. He can read when he wants to. But the book is not even open. He had forgotten to open it. Stupidity must be punished. He opens it. He strikes his hand on it. It strikes twelve. Now I've got you! Read! Stop! No. Get out! Oh! A letter detaches itself from the first line and hits him a blow on the ear. Letters are lead. It hurts. Strike him! Strike him! Another. And another. A footnote kicks him. More and more. He totters. Lines and whole pages come clattering on to him. They shake and beat him, they worry him, they toss him about among themselves. Blood, Let me go! Damnable mob! Help! George! Help! Help! George!

But George has gone. Peter leaps up. With formidable strength he grasps the book and snaps it to. So, he has taken the letters prisoner, all of them, and will not let them go again. Never! He is free. He stands up. He stands alone. George has gone. He has outwitted him. What does he know of the murder? A mental specialist. An ass. A wide-open soul. Yet he would gladly steal the books. He would want him dead soon. Then he'd have the library. He won't get it. Patience! 'What do you want upstairs?' 'Just to look round!' 'Just to get round me!' That's what you'd like. Shoemaker stick to your idiots. He's coming again. In six months. Better luck next time. A will? Not necessary. The only heir will get everything he wants. A special train to Paris. The Kien library. Who collected it? The psychiatrist Georges Kien, who else? And his brother, the sinologist? Quite a mistake, there wasn't a brother, two of the same name, no connection, a murderer, he murdered his wife, MURDER AND FIRE in all the papers, sentenced to imprisonment for life — for life — for death — the dance of death — the golden calf — an inheritance of a million — none but the brave — wave — parting — no — till death us do part — death by FIRE — loss loss by FIRE — burnt burnt by FIRE — FIRE FIRE FIRE.

Kien seizes the book on the table and threatens his brother with it. He is trying to rob him; everyone is out for a will, everyone counts on the death of his nearest. A brother is good enough to die, thieves kitchen of a world, men devour and steal books. All want something, and all are gone, and no one can wait. Earlier they burnt a man's possessions with him, a will was nowhere to be found and there was nothing left, nothing but bones. The letters rattle inside the book. They are prisoners, they can't come out. They've beaten him bloody. He threatens them with death by fire. That is how he will avenge himself on all his enemies! He has murdered his wife, the hog is a charred skeleton, George will get no books. And the police won't get him. Powerless, the letters are knocking to be let out. Outside the police knock against the door. 'Open the door!' 'Never more.' 'In the name of the law!' 'Pshaw!' 'Let us in!' 'Din.' 'At once.' 'Dunce.' 'You'll be shot.' 'Pot.' 'We'll smoke you out!' 'Lout!' They are trying to break down his door. They won't do that easily. His door is strong and fiery. Bang. Bang. Bang. The blows grow heavier. He can hear them where he is. His door is bolted with iron. But if the rust has eaten into the bolts? No metal is all-powerful. Bang. Bang. Hogs are herded before his door, ramming it with stomachs, with corners. The wood will crack for certain. It looks so old and worn. They seized the enemy trenches. Entrenched. Ready, steady, crash. Ready, steady, crash! The bell. At eleven all the bells ring. The Theresianum. The hunchback. March off, pulling long noses. Am I right or am I not? Ready, steady — am I right — ready, steady.

The books cascade off the shelves on to the floor. He takes them up in his long arms. Very quietly, so that they can't hear him outside, he carries pile after pile into the hall. He builds them up high against the iron door. And while the frantic din tears his brain to fragments, he builds a mighty bulwark out of books. The hall is filled with volume upon volume. He fetches the ladder to help him. Soon he has reached the ceiling. He goes back to his room. The shelves gape at him. In front of the writing desk the carpet is ablaze. He goes into the bedroom next to the kitchen and drags out all the old newspapers. He pulls the pages apart, and crumples them, he rolls them into balls, and throws them into all the corners. He places the ladder in the middle of the room where it stood before. He climbs up to the sixth step, looks down on the fire and waits.

When the flames reached him at last, he laughed out loud, louder than he had ever laughed in all his life.